A
Gentleman's

Romance Collection

9 Modern Romances with an
Old-Fashioned Quality

A
Gentleman's

Romance Collection

Ginny Aiken, Kristin Billerbeck, Lynn A.Coleman,
Peggy Darty, Rebecca Germany, Bev Huston,
Yvonne Lehman, Gail Sattler, Pamela Kaye Tracy

BARBOUR BOOKS
An Imprint of Barbour Publishing, Inc.

Print ISBN 978-1-63058-711-6

eBook Editions:
Adobe Digital Edition (.epub) 978-1-63409-411-5
Kindle and MobiPocket Edition (.prc) 978-1-63409-412-2

Published by Barbour Books, an imprint of Barbour Publishing, Inc., P.O. Box 719, Uhrichsville, Ohio 44683, www.barbourbooks.com

Our mission is to publish and distribute inspirational products offering exceptional value and biblical encouragement to the masses.

 Member of the
Evangelical Christian
Publishers Association

Printed in Canada.

Contents

The Great Expectation by Ginny Aiken 7

Mattie Meets Her Match by Kristin Billerbeck 51

Harmonized Hearts by Lynn A. Coleman 95

Spring in Paris by Peggy Darty 147

The Garden Plot by Rebecca Germany 197

Mix and Match by Bev Huston 241

Name That Tune by Yvonne Lehman 293

Sudden Showers by Gail Sattler 347

Test of Time by Pamela Kaye Tracy 393

The Great Expectation

by Ginny Aiken

Dedication

To the best support system:
Elizabeth, Karl, and Natalie, critiquers extraordinaire;
Ivan and Shiloh, Greg, Geoff, and Grant,
the best kids in the universe;
Goldie and Buffy, my creative canine contributors;
and as always, to George, who didn't realize
that first computer was a Pandora's box in disguise.

*They sing to the music of tambourine and
harp; they make merry to the
sound of the flute.*
JOB 21:12

Chapter 1

Honestly, Rissa," Ty said with a grunt. "Are you packing rocks in Bertha the Beast?" Marissa Ortíz glanced at her fellow musician. "Quit griping, Tyrone Carver. We're a *string* quartet, and I play a bass. Bertha's no heavier today than she was yesterday."

"Easy for you to say," Ty countered, as his six-foot frame handily maneuvered the unwieldy instrument. "You have me to haul the Beast around."

Rissa gave her best friend—well, one of her three best friends—a knowing look. "Want to trade jobs? I can give you the schedule roster anytime, anywhere."

Fear widened Ty's hazel eyes. "Don't you dare. You know how much time it's taking me to compose—"

"Don't try to pull that one on me. I know what your secret project means to you and how much time you've committed to it, but the truth is, you just can't be bothered with schedules, keeping track of dates, times, or locations. As long as you lock info in your head, you're fine, but where would that leave the rest of us?"

Clattering footsteps prevented Ty's response. "In the dark," chirped Eva Alono, hugging her violin case. "We'd never know where or when we were expected to perform."

The lights in the dim Sunday school classroom suddenly went on. "The Lord did say, 'Let there be light.'" Viola player Tristan Reuben acknowledged the others' groans with a profound bow, then turned to Rissa. "Is this lug complaining about dear Bertha again?"

Rissa arched a brow.

As the others laughed, she winked and grinned. "I still love him—even though he's a nut bar."

Eva chuckled. "You should know. Me? I just want to know where you pack your candy calories—you're wispier than fog."

With another wink, Rissa tossed her hair over her shoulder and struck a dramatic pose. "I'm blessed."

As she said the words, she wondered if she would ever feel that blessing deep inside her heart. She recognized the gifts the Lord had given her, and she'd developed them so she could use them to His glory, but was she truly blessed?

She thought of her family, her world-renowned harpist mother and late grandmother, her Nobel Prize nominee physicist father. A father who hid in his office at East Central University of Florida and a mother whose physical disabilities and uncertain mental state kept her, if not hidden, then certainly unavailable.

Pushing back the imminent self-pity as she always did, Rissa reminded herself that God loved her, that she and her fellow quartet members made up a loving family since they'd met in college, and that she'd recently found herself the perfect companion.

Soraya.

What joy the lovely Afghan hound brought her each and every day, how loyal she was, how unconditional her love. The dog's innate goodness made Rissa's decision about pet care during the quartet's upcoming twenty-one-day South American tour even tougher.

"Earth to Rissa," Ty called. "Is there intelligent life under those beautiful curls?"

She ducked away from his approaching hand and strove for a scrap of dignity. "Enough, already. The Altamonte wedding's this Saturday, and today's my only chance to rehearse— I'm giving ten hours of back-to-back lessons over the next three days. Let's get to work."

Eva's perusal intensified. "What's wrong?"

A rueful smile curved Rissa's lips. "I can't hide anything from you, can I?"

Hurt flickered in and out of Eva's eyes. "Do you really want to?"

"No, Silly," Rissa said, patting her friend's shoulder. "It's just that—well, it's kind of dumb for me to worry, but. . ."

"Okay, kid," Ty ordered, "tell Big Brother what's wrong. And don't give us any more of that 'it's dumb' stuff. I've been wondering what put the flagpole in your spine and the tight smile on your mouth."

Rissa gusted a sigh, then grabbed her nearly waist-length hair, twisted it, and drew it into a knot at the base of her neck. "I can't believe you guys. The FBI could use you—"

"Quit stalling," Tristan said, concern on his face.

"That's right, Ris," Eva concurred. "You don't have to carry the world on your shoulders. We're here—you know, 'A friend loves at all times, and a brother'—or a sister—'is born for adversity,'" she quoted from Proverbs 17:17.

"Okay, okay." Taking a deep breath, Rissa forced her shoulders to relax. "You guys are right. I am stressing about this next tour. Mom. . .well, she's not doing well these days. Her pain meds are failing her, and you guys know what that does to her state of mind. And Dad. . ."

A murmur of sympathy rippled through the friends. Rissa held up her hand to ward off further pity. "That's just part of it. You guys remember Soraya's breeder, right?"

All three nodded. "Mrs. Gooden decided to retire a few months ago and sold her entire operation. That wouldn't have been half bad, but you guys won't believe who she sold to."

Expectant silence followed.

"Well?" Ty asked. "Who has enough cash to buy all that property and those luxe kennels?"

Rissa worried her lower lip, shook her head, and finally shrugged. "None other than the infamous, unethical, and slimy Jason Easton, attorney-at-law."

Eva frowned. "The shark? The one from that millionaires' firm? What's he doing with pampered pooches?"

"You know as much as I do," Rissa said, "but not as much as I intend to learn."

"Uh-oh," said Tristan. "The guy doesn't stand a chance. The hypermeticulous Marissa Ortíz is on the case. She'll sniff out even the most minute vestige of slime, clean it up, and have the place running by the book in less time than it takes to sneeze."

"Hey!" Rissa jabbed her pal on his solid shoulder. "If I weren't careful, we'd never make any of our bookings. You guys don't pay much attention to details."

"Yep," he countered, "none of us is particularly neurotic about minutes, dates, and stuff like that. That's why we love you so much."

"That's beside the point," Ty said. "I want to know what Rissa's planning in that over-zealous little mind of hers."

"I'm just checking it out," she said with a nonchalance she didn't feel. "I know how Mrs. Gooden ran the place, and if anything's not as it should be, I'll make sure the ASPCA and the police learn all about it. Less than one minute after I do."

"How'll you know if he's really running a decent show or not?" Tristan asked.

"That's why I'm going there," she said. "I bet he's the kind of absentee owner who buys an operation as a tax write-off, hires out the dirty work for peanuts, and then rakes in as much as clients will shell out. After all, he's the one who got that. . .that Elliott-what's-his-face—the SEC crook—off a year ago."

She thought back to the splashy trial of the man who'd cooked the books at a snooty investment firm. "Southwycke!" she exclaimed. "Elliott Southwycke, who's now living in a mansion in the Bahamas. Jason Easton's the one who got him off on some shady loop-hole or technicality or some other slimy lawyer thing."

Ty gave her a narrow-eyed stare. "So you're going out there loaded for bear."

"Yes, and that's why we have to finish the gabfest. The Altamontes are paying us a nice chunk of change to waft their daughter up to the altar and then triumphantly march her down the aisle a high-society matron." She rummaged through her black leather portfo-lio and withdrew a well-thumbed Vivaldi score. "Thankfully, they chose 'Spring' for the processional, Pachelbel's 'Canon' as background, 'Amazing Grace' for communion and the lighting of the unity candle, and finally, 'Lohengrin' for the recessional. We know all that and only need a run-through. Once we do the sound check in the sanctuary, we're done."

They then plied their craft, the art that soothed and brought them joy and comfort in times of turmoil. Rissa reveled in the sparkling notes of "Spring," put her whole heart into praising the Father with her music, and thanked Him for this, the one blessing she had no trouble identifying.

If only she could as easily identify anything questionable in the kennel at the mercy of the shady man now at its helm. . .

❧

Two hours later, Rissa turned her geriatric yet still strong European station wagon into the palm-lined drive of SilkWood Kennels. The place looked no different than it had four months ago when she'd retrieved Soraya after the quartet's last trip. Then again, looks could be, and often were, deceiving.

As she pulled up to the yellow-stucco office building, however, dismay swam in her stomach. She counted three teens—one walking a gorgeous brindle Affie on a leash, while another danced to the rhythm in his earphones as he hosed the chain-link-fenced run closest to the parking lot. The last one stood not ten feet from the faded gold hood of her car, a quizzical look on his face.

"D'you bring it?" he asked as Rissa opened her door. "I thought it'd been sent overnight."

She stood. "Bring what?"

"You know. The. . ." He blushed under his deep Florida tan. "The. . .*stuff.*"

Oh, no. Matters were worse than she had imagined. Drug dealing was the order of the day. Well. Not only had SilkWood lost a regular customer, but they'd also gained themselves an imminent visit from the authorities—as soon as she called them.

Hoping to extract more incriminating info from the shaggy-haired kid, she played along. "No. Was I supposed to?"

Overlong wiry arms swung upward. "I don't know. All's I know is that Jase's all bent out of shape about the delay, and you don't even have—" Again, his flushed golden-olive skin highlighted his chiseled features. "You don't have the *stuff* with you."

In the interest of gaining the unsuspecting canary's confidence and subsequently getting him to sing, she went for the basics. "So. What's your name?"

He narrowed dark, lushly lashed eyes. "Why?"

She strove for nonchalance. "Just being polite."

Evidently she hid her ulterior motives well. "I'm Paul," he said. "Who're you?"

In the further interest of her budding investigation, she opted for veracity and held out her hand. "Pleased to meet you, Paul. I'm Marissa. Are you new around here?"

"Yeah. Jase needs help, and I would do just about anything for him."

No doubt. Most addicts were under their dealers' total control. Poor child. She wondered how she might help him leave his destructive lifestyle. "You must know and love dogs a great deal."

Paul gave her a wry grin. "Nope. Never had one, but I sure am learning fast."

Inexperienced and ignorant, to boot. Poor dogs. "Afghans are wonderful, aren't they?"

"At least they're not rat-sized yapping dust bunnies."

Rissa laughed at his patent disgust. Loud rumbling on the gravel drive then caught their attention. A parcel delivery truck stopped behind her station wagon and a sandy-haired man leaped out, holding a package embellished with FRAGILE stickers.

Paul grinned. "Finally."

"Are you the new owner?" the driver asked Rissa, staring at her as though she'd oozed out from some disgusting mire.

She read his name tag. "No, Sean. I've been a kennel customer for some years now, and I came today to meet the shys—Mr. Easton."

Sean studied her, then reached into the truck's cab for a clipboard. "If you're not the owner, then who's signing for this?"

Paul stepped forward. "They gave you the. . .stuff? Freeze-dried and all?"

Sean shrugged. Then the teen's words seemed to register. "Freeze-dried?"

Paul blushed even more. "They'd have to, otherwise it wouldn't be any good by the time it got here."

Marissa frowned. What kind of drug were they dealing? She'd never heard of any that required freeze-drying. Before she thought of a clever way to ask, Sean glared at the box.

"If I'd known what it was," he grumbled, "I might have. . .uh, dropped it—accidentally, of course."

Huh?

Paul reached for the unprepossessing box. "Gimme that. If Jase heard what you just said, he'd call and report you."

"Some of us have principles."

Paul rolled his eyes. "Shoulda known you're one of *them.*"

"And proud of it. What you guys do here is unethical."

"You're nuts."

Rissa's gaze ping-ponged between the two. What was going on?

"Really?" asked Sean. "I bet this is twenty- maybe thirty-year-old sperm—"

Her eyes popped wide open.

"And I bet the donor was the bitch's late great-great-granddaddy," Sean added. "Inbreeding leads to nasty mutations. Besides, aren't there enough dogs around already? Why do you guys have to make more?"

Relief left Rissa lightheaded. "You mean. . .that's just a specimen for breeding?"

Both turned and glared.

"What'd you think it was, lady?" Paul asked in disgust. "I sure haven't spent the last three hours out here to work on my tan. Jase runs a breeding kennel, you know."

She waved a hand before her face, needing every drop of humid Florida air she could dredge up. She shrugged. And waved some more.

Finally, when she found the starch to firm her voice, she said, "If it's so important, then sign and take it to Mr. Easton. I'll go with you, since I did come all the way out here to meet him."

Paul graced her with a head-to-toe-and-back-again scrutiny. "Jase's going to be busy for awhile yet. Why don't you come back day after tomorrow—better yet, Saturday afternoon."

His attempt at a brush-off wasn't about to dislodge her. "I'm busy from now until Sunday after church. As I said, I'll follow you."

Forehead furrowed, Paul signed the paper on Sean's clipboard and held out his hand. The delivery truck driver glared at the controversial box yet again, then relinquished it. Without another word, he hopped into the truck and sped away, tires spewing gravel. Marissa winced as a couple of pieces dinged her car.

"Shall we?" she said to Paul, marveling at Sean's intensity. Animal rights' activists were, if nothing else, committed to their cause. She supported many of their efforts, but extremism didn't appeal to her. Besides, SilkWood Kennels' breeding program had produced Soraya. There couldn't be too much wrong with that.

As Paul led Rissa into the long building of runs, she took the opportunity to check out their condition. She didn't see food spilled on the cement floors or nastier stuff, either, and the water pails were full. Most of the dogs had come inside to enjoy an air-conditioned reprieve from the fiery Florida sun, and they looked well if excited by the stranger in their home away from home.

Way at the back, however, in a dim run to the right, Rissa finally found what she'd expected. A wadded pile of rags, damp-looking at that, surrounded a man in a ratty T-shirt and jeans that had seen better days. A pair of bowls had rolled into the central aisle and lay overturned, soggy kibble scattered all around.

The silver Affie in the run let out a pain-filled wail. Rissa's hackles went straight up, and she marched right to the abuser's side.

"That's it," he murmured as she reached him. "Good girl!"

The Affie moaned, relaxed somewhat, and then dropped shoulders and head onto her portion of the rags.

"Just what do you think you're doing to that poor, suffering animal?" she demanded.

The man turned.

Rissa gasped. "Jason Easton?"

Those clean-cut good looks had stared out from the *Miami Herald*'s front page too many times for her not to recognize him. What shocked her was the unadulterated emotion on his features. . .and the tears in his deep blue eyes.

"Helping God with a miracle, ma'am," he said, his voice rough.

Then she noticed his outstretched hands. A tiny creature snuffled and wriggled in the well of his big palms, seeking its mama where only a scrap of towel could be found. Pale wet fuzz on its body suggested a future coat to match that of its mother.

A lump filled Rissa's throat. She dropped to her knees at Jason Easton's side and reached a careful finger to the newborn. It rubbed against her, full of promise.

Her eyes welled. "The miracle of life."

Their gazes met, and, to Rissa's astonishment, his reflected the reverence and awe she felt for the Master's power. This couldn't be the real Jason Easton. Not the one who'd let crooks get away with ill-gotten gains.

Yet it was. As she cupped her hand over the pup in his, she found herself unable to look away. A shimmer ran through her, the acknowledgment of a precious, shared moment.

She drew in a ragged breath. Somehow her life had just changed.

Irrevocably.

But had it changed for good?

Or had it changed for ill?

Only the Lord knew.

Chapter 2

Rissa shook free of the spell around them. She felt disoriented, as though one of Florida's hurricanes had tossed and turned and dropped her upside down. Nothing was as it should have been, as she'd imagined.

Well, that wasn't true either. Since arriving at SilkWood, she'd seen only kids—just what she'd expected. To find Jason Easton wearing ragged clothes, kneeling in a run on a pile of wet, bloody towels, and moved to tears by the miracle of birth. . .she hadn't expected that.

Oh, sure, he was a hunk. That build, chiseled features, and blue eyes impressed whether he wore his usual three-piece suit or these garment industry relics. His almost palpable genuine emotion, however, moved her. It didn't match her expectations. It was too real, too similar to her reaction, too easy to share.

She didn't know how to handle it. Or her response to it. . .to him.

That frightened her.

"Sorry you had to see this mess," he said, breaking into her thoughts.

Rissa blinked, then looked where he indicated. Ah, yes, the rags, the littered kibble, his disheveled appearance. She brought her gaze back to his face and took note of the self-deprecating smile. Before she could say she understood, he spoke again.

"Mahadi and her puppies come first, then the mess." He ran a gentle finger over the chubby newborn. "Now that this last one is out, Mama and brood can become acquainted while I clean up."

He rose, wiping his hands on a relatively clean towel, then held a hand to Rissa.

She took it and stood at his side. "I would have done the same."

His sincere grin made something tickle from her throat to her middle. Whoa! This guy's smile was potent. As was that down-home honesty he presented. Was any of it real?

It looked real. But he was a killer-shark lawyer, too.

He hung up the towel on a hook in the metal support beam and faced her again. "I'm Jason Easton, the new owner, and you're. . . ?"

Still off guard, she said, "Oh, yes. . .ah. . .Marissa—*Rissa* Ortíz."

"I won't shake your hand again until I've washed mine," he added, smiling yet another time. "What brings you out here?"

Yes, Marissa, why did *you come out here?* "Well, you see. . .I. . ." *Get a grip, woman!*

Firming her posture, she went on. "Mrs. Gooden sold me one of her pups, and I've kenneled Soraya here every time I've traveled. I'm preparing for another trip, and I wanted to see you—meet the new owner. . . ."

She fought to gather her scattered thoughts. "I wanted to make arrangements for her stay while I'm gone."

I can always cancel if things go sour out here.

"In that case," Easton answered, "let's go to the office and take care of business."

Rissa nodded and followed him from the kennel to the yellow-stucco offices. Would she come to regret this? She was too shaken to make a sound decision, and she knew she'd second-guess herself until she dropped off Soraya, then every day of the tour and right up to the minute she returned to SilkWood to pick up her pet.

Father, help me do the right thing. I can't tell what's up or down anymore, but I know You know what's best.

Sign for the reservation and get out of Dodge seemed like the best course right then.

As Jase opened the door for the breathtaking woodland nymph who'd floated into his kennel, he shook his head. *Lord, couldn't You have kept her away a few minutes longer? Just until I had time to wash up and put on something besides rags?*

Nothing like making a rotten impression on the most beautiful redhead he'd ever seen. Marissa Ortíz looked like something out of an illustrated fairy tale, tall, whisper slender, fair skinned, and blessed with the greenest eyes this side of heaven. She had to be a model or maybe an actress, one of those who'd bought land around Miami since a prominent Cuban band had helped popularize Key Biscayne, SoBe, and the mansions dotting the waterfront.

He'd never seen her at any event, and he'd suffered enough of the artificial parties and benefits to know who was who in Miami. Then he realized she stood expectantly at the counter. He grinned again, amazed by his unusual lapse of attention. "When do you leave?"

Rissa pulled a black-leather planner from her caramel-colored bag and flipped through scribbled-on pages. Slender fingers with short, well-kept nails danced over the writing to stop almost at the bottom edge.

"Our flight leaves at 6:51 p.m. on Tuesday, the seventeenth of June," she answered, "so I'll drop off Soraya at. . .hmm. . . I'll have to leave her at 3:25 p.m. if I'm to have any hope of clearing the security at the airport on time."

"Okay," Jase drawled, amused by her extreme precision, "and you'll be back for her. . .?"

More page-flipping and finger-dancing. "Our flight gets in at 11:23 a.m. Sunday, July thirteenth. By the time I clear the baggage claim. . .and you're seventeen and one-quarter miles west of the airport. . ."

As Rissa microcalculated times and distances, Jase watched a length of wavy strawberry-blond hair slip from behind her ear and slide across her cheek. Gold strands and red strands blended in the same exotic richness found only in old-fashioned rose-colored gold.

"I'll factor in three minutes for what little traffic I might find on a Sunday morning. . . . I should be here between 11:53 and 11:58."

What a tortured way to say she'd arrive around noon. "Okeydokey," he said with humor, marveling at her eccentric ultraprecision. "Noon on the thirteenth it is."

The hint of a frown brought her light auburn brows close, but she didn't comment on his rounded-up estimate. Thankfully.

"We're all set then," he added when she made no move to leave.

She nodded. She zipped her hobo-style handbag open, and the maw swallowed her planner as she ran her free hand through miles of red-gold waves. Still, she stood at the counter.

"Is there something else I can do for you?" he asked, feeling somewhat stupid.

Rissa looked right through him—more accurately, past his left ear to the wall at the back of the office. She squared her shoulders and took a deep breath. "Yes," she then said. "You can tell me who will care for Soraya while she's here."

Now that was a new one for him. "Uh. . .I will, and my kids. . ." He paused and gestured toward the front window through which he could see Paul, Alida, Jamal, Dale, Matt, and Tiffany. "We'll do some of everything here."

Her dainty nose tipped up. "I was afraid of that."

Great. "Why?"

The green eyes narrowed. "You expect me to trust my baby to an inexperienced kennel owner who's at home with the crème de la crème of white-collar criminals and a bunch of goofy kids."

Jase steamed. His instincts told him to kick her snooty attitude, preconceived expectations, and pretty self off his property and back to Miami, but he knew she wasn't the only one who saw him that way. And he wouldn't alienate a customer with the kind of behavior expected of a shark.

Help me, Lord. "I don't intend to defend myself to you. You have two choices. You can leave Soraya here and assess her care after your trip, or you can take your business elsewhere. I'd rather you didn't, since I know what I'm doing and I love dogs—"

"I'm not questioning your feelings. I saw your response to the pup's birth and I know how much it moved you. My concern stems from your inexperience running a kennel—not to mention the lack of experience of the juveniles out there."

He could have told her they were actually repentant juvenile delinquents in the process of rehabilitation, but that wouldn't help.

"Again," he said, "it's your choice. Look, you have time to think about it. I hope you choose to leave Soraya with us, but I won't beg for your business. As far as my kids go, I'd trust them with my life. I don't say it as a cliché—I know them and know what they can and will do."

Rissa turned to leave, then stopped and stared out the window. Jase groaned. Paul and Jamal were on the ground locked in an esoteric wrestling move while the other four cut up the figurative rug in a wild salsa. They sure knew how to choose their moments.

"What do you want from them?" he asked, taking in the tight white edge of her lips. "Everyone needs a break, especially those who work as hard as they do."

Glancing over her sundress-bared shoulder, Rissa's eyebrow arched up above her right eye. "Do you know where your specimen is?"

"Huh?"

"Do check with your hard-working Paul. Who knows where the prized sperm you received awhile ago wound up."

She left in a swirl of green-and-white foliage-print crinkle cotton and the hint of jasmine he'd failed to notice before.

As Rissa opened the car's door, Handel's "Hallelujah Chorus" tinned out from her handbag. "Hello," she said into her cell phone.

"*Buenas tardes,* Marissa," her mother responded in her most polite and fear-inducing, querulous tone.

Alarm stole her breath. First Jason Easton, now her mother. *Oh, Lord Jesus, help me. I'm not prepared to deal with her, not now!*

"*Buenas, Mamá.*"

"How are you?" Then, as usual and without waiting for an answer, Adela Ortíz went on. "I am terrible. I'm sure the end is near. A person cannot bear such pain—*if* she wants to keep living. *If* she has something for to live. . ."

Rissa sat down hard in the driver's seat. With her free hand, she clutched the steering wheel as she would a lifeline. *Please, Lord, please.*

"Did you take your medicine?" she asked.

"What you say, *niña?* That I'm addict? Or that I'm crazy and need drugs?"

Rissa took another deep breath. "No, *Mamá.* Nothing of the sort. I just know how hard it is to tolerate the pain, and the doctors have urged you to make sure you take the prescriptions round the clock."

Adela huffed. "Of course, I have take all the pills. *Y nada.*"

This wasn't the first time her mother's painkillers stopped helping. "Have you called the doctor?"

"Hah! *¿Para qué?* For what?" Then, again without waiting for Rissa's answer, she went on. "I'm think all those doctors is the problem. They too happy taking your *papá's* money. Maybe they giving me drugs to make me hurt more for to keep the dollars coming."

"*Mamá,* that's outrageous, and you know it. The doctors wouldn't do such a thing. They're experts on spinal injuries." A thought occurred to her. "Have you said that to them?" Dreadful silence confirmed her worst fears. "You should be ashamed of yourself, Adela Ortíz. You owe them an apology."

"I do *not!* They owe me a new body for all we pay these years."

They'd reached today's impasse. "Look," Rissa said, "I'm on the way to my condo. What if I call Dr. Kaszekian from there? I'm sure he can find something to help you."

A high-pitched wail came from the other end of the call. "You just want be rid of me. See? I have nothing for to live. I cannot play my beloved harp, your father. . .bah! He's always play with numbers, and you? My flesh and blood? You don't take time for to talk to me. I have nothing for to live. . . ."

A knot twisted Rissa's innards and searing tears welled up in her eyes. "I love you,

Mother, but I'm ninety minutes away from you and can only do so much. I'll call Dr. Kaszekian when I get home, then I'll check on you after he's had time to prescribe something new. I do need to go now."

She cut off yet another stream of misery. She wondered where Mrs. Janssen was. Her mother's nurse-companion rarely left her unattended. Then again, the poor woman did occasionally need to use the bathroom or prepare Adela's meals.

Rissa turned the key in the ignition, then left SilkWood.

"Why, Lord? Why is she like that?" she asked in the silence of the car. "And why me? I don't know what to do with her. . .for her." She swallowed hard and blinked even harder, to no avail. The lump in her throat didn't budge, and the tears spilled down her cheeks, followed by many, many others.

Doubting she'd sleep that night, she slipped in a CD and forced herself to focus on the lyrics. Rissa knew that if she took her mind off God's glory and power and might, even for a scant moment, she'd never make it home in one piece. The tears would return, and who knew what she'd fail to see in the road ahead. Joining her voice to the singer's, she sang the Lord's praises, wondering how the day could have gone so wrong.

In His Word, God promised to be with her during the bad as well as the good days. Today was one of the bad. Yet He remained the best of the best. King of all kings. Jehovah, Messiah, Almighty God. In Him she would place her trust. . . relinquish her fears. . .confide her heartache. In Him she would find peace. Only in Him.

❧

The Altamonte wedding went off without a hitch. The quartet's music, even if Rissa did say so herself, was the perfect accompaniment to the exchange of vows at the altar. The bride, with her olive skin, exotic brown eyes, and masses of black hair piled under coronet and veil, looked lovely, excited but solemn. Her voice trembled when she pledged herself to her groom before God and man.

Even though Rissa was in no hurry to marry, she hoped she would someday reflect the same emotions and commitment she'd witnessed.

Now, at the reception, the quartet would play until the multicourse dinner. At that time, a pianist and harpist would take over, and the foursome would eat with the other guests.

As Ty huffed and griped about Bertha's imaginary, ever-increasing weight problem, Rissa scanned the vast ballroom in one of Miami's most venerable hotels. She recognized many of the guests from their appearances in the *Herald*'s society pages. A smattering of politicians, local and state level, was also in attendance.

Then she spotted a familiar snow-white mane. Dread filled her. It couldn't be.

The crowd shifted, and Rissa caught a glimpse of what she'd feared she'd see. *Papá*, elegant in his dinner jacket, wore the vague expression that indicated the presence of convoluted computations. At his side, Adela's wheelchair reflected the sparkle of the crystal chandeliers overhead. Not a single hair strayed from Mother's dyed-to-perfection auburn French twist.

Rissa wished she'd realized ahead of time that her parents knew the Altamontes, even though she shouldn't be surprised they did. Her father had been prominent in certain pre-Castro Havana circles, and now, as a result of his Nobel Prize nomination, he was highly sought after as a guest at numerous society gatherings.

Praying for strength, she tuned her bass as the others joined in. Then she saw Ty glance up.

He turned to her, frowning. "Isn't that. . . ?"

Rissa swallowed hard. "The one and only. I had no idea she—*they'd* be here."

"Would you've backed out if you'd known?"

She worried her bottom lip. Would she have run out on her friends? "I'd never do that, no matter how difficult my parents are."

Ty reached out and squeezed her shoulder. "Even if you had, you're not alone, you know."

Rissa felt her friend's love as a special gift, the Father's warm blessing. "Thanks. I know you guys are here for me, and I know the Lord will see me through tonight."

"Amen," he said.

As she rosined her bow, she heard a hiss to her left.

"*Pssst!*" her mother called again. "*Marisita*, over here."

When she turned and made herself smile, her mother pressed one of the wheelchair controls and propelled herself near. Rissa saw Eva's eyes narrow and Tristan's jaw jut forth. Ty took a protective step forward.

Love bubbled up for her three friends. "It's okay, guys," she murmured. Then, turning to Adela, she said, "*Hola, Mamá*. I had no idea you'd be here tonight."

"Of course we're here. We know Rodrigo and Estersita Altamonte since university in Havana. We couldn't miss Sarita's wedding."

Adela seemed calmer than she had earlier in the week. Perhaps her new prescription was helping. Rissa hoped so. She knew the toll the unrelenting pain had taken on her mother—and the family—over the years.

She smiled tentatively. "I hope you enjoy the pieces we've chosen. We're doing some of the mellow old *danzones* you like so much."

"Ah, *sí*. The music your father and I loved so much when we were *novios*, before we married." A dreamy expression softened Adela's features. Rissa breathed a prayer of thanksgiving and felt her friends' tension ease.

Then *Papá* approached. "Come, Adela, we must take our place at the table. It takes some doing to arrange your wheelchair so that no one jostles you."

Mamá's features hardened. "*Sí*, Francisco. *Vamos ya*. Marissa, I wish you'd open your eyes. Why you must to play that great masculine thing, I no understand. The harp, *niña*, the harp you should play. You're my daughter and the great Brigitte Cardoza's granddaughter."

Rissa winced. She hadn't escaped this encounter unscathed. She lowered her head to keep her feelings to herself and watched her father propel the wheelchair to the opposite side of the room. As she blinked to keep the tears from melting her mascara, she saw Eva put her treasured violin on the floor.

"I'm so sorry," her friend whispered, wrapping her arm around Rissa's shoulders. "I'm sorry for her suffering and for the misery she spreads as a result. The Lord knows your heart, Ris. He knows you want to praise Him with your music and you do. A quartet— *we*—couldn't perform without a bass. Besides, you can always play your marimba instead. Not that I want you to abandon us for some percussion ensemble or anything, but you do have that, too."

A cross between a sob and a giggle escaped Rissa's lips. "Don't even mention the marimba in the same room where *Mamá* might overhear. You should hear what she says about 'cacophonous percussion *things*.'"

Eva came around and gripped Rissa's forearms. "Just answer one question: Are you doing God's will?"

The two friends had hashed out this point frequently since college-roommate days. Rissa shrugged. "I believe with all my heart that I am, but it's just. . .well, she's my mother."

"And He's your Father in heaven. With God beside you, no one can stand against you, remember?"

She nodded and donned a weak little smile. "I'm okay." At Eva's roll of the eyes and Tristan's snort, she added, "No, really, I am. Let's do what the Altamontes hired us to do. Let's play."

As Eva retrieved her violin, Rissa squared her shoulders and settled Bertha in the curve of her shoulder. She drew her bow, poised to glide it over the thick strings that enriched the sound of the other instruments, and looked at the glad-handers in the receiving line.

She gasped. "Great, just what I needed."

"What's that?" Ty asked.

"Look who just arrived."

"Uh-oh."

"Mm-hmm. The slimy shark-*cum*-kennel-owner himself."

And dressed to the nines. This was the Jason Easton she pictured as she drove to SilkWood the other day. Polished, impeccably groomed, his evening whites in gleaming contrast to his tanned face, his blue eyes shining with intelligence and shrewdness. This was the man who worked for the wealthiest and most unsavory present here tonight.

The man to whom she'd contracted to entrust Soraya for three weeks—in a moment of utter discombobulation, of course. The man who, just by his mere presence, made her heart beat a little faster, her cheeks burn a little warmer, and her senses perk a little livelier.

The man she expected would prove himself unequal to caring for a kennel full of dogs, but thanks to his legal knowledge, would get away unscathed by his incompetence.

Chapter 3

Upon entering the ballroom for the Altamonte– Echeverría wedding reception, Jase spied the gleam of rose gold in an unforgettable waterfall of hair. He'd never expected to see Rissa Ortíz at this Miami society wedding, but after one glimpse of those almost waist-long waves, no one could mistake her for anyone else.

Then he noticed the massive instrument in her embrace. Hmm. . .so she wasn't a model or an actress after all. He'd heard of the Classical Strings Quartet, and he'd attended events where they'd performed, but he'd never taken note of the musicians. Now he wished he had. He might have met her when he could have made a better impression on the ethereally beautiful woman.

Rissa displayed a mixture of dramatic contrasts. Her exquisite delicacy belied her strength—it took an abundance to handle a full-size upright bass. And while she looked as though she belonged in an illustration of woodland beings with her willowy frame and old-master coloring, she grounded herself in precision, as her exacting focus on time and schedules testified.

She'd caught him off guard at the kennels, and after she left, his senses reeled hours later with her jasmine scent and feminine loveliness. Now, witnessing yet another of her facets, he found himself flat-out intrigued.

And attracted.

To his dismay, the kind of woman who'd make him a logical partner never appealed to him, yet the much-prejudiced Rissa Ortíz drew at him more than any of the earlier inappropriate candidates.

Lord, help. Show me a suitable woman so that I can set aside this attraction to one who hates me because of my former job.

Jase donned a smile and congratulated the Altamontes and the Echeverrías, both families longtime clients of his father and friends of his parents. Then he spotted his law-school mentor, the frail and gray Dr. Pierpont, holding court near a floor-to-ceiling window, and joined the debate on the more esoteric points of habeas corpus. He snagged scrumptious seafood and Cuban delicacies the wait service offered on silver trays. He drank geranium-scented iced tea seemingly by the bucketful. He smiled, nodded, shook hands, and chatted.

But he couldn't evict the musician from his thoughts.

Conceding the futility of his efforts, Jase leaned on a fluted column and watched Rissa and her fellow performers. He noted the camaraderie between the foursome, their obvious love and respect.

He envied them. He had nothing similar in his life.

Then Rissa's posture changed. The fluidity of her movements and the poise she displayed, even while kneeling at Mahadi's birthing, vanished. With jerky spurts of motion, she tuned her instrument, head lowered close to the bass's bridge. When she looked back up at the gathered guests, a chill grimace replaced her smile.

He followed her gaze. "So that's who you are, lovely Rissa."

The still-famous former harpist, Adela Ortíz, whirred her motorized wheelchair to Rissa's side. Mother and daughter shared a resemblance, but Rissa looked most like her legendary grandmother, Brigitte Cardoza, the height by which all harpists were measured since the 1940s. Even Adela never reached Brigitte's level of mastery, and many said that failure still fueled her burning bitterness. Her career, cut short by a fall down the marble steps of a European opera house, never fulfilled its promise.

Whatever mother and daughter, now joined by Nobel Prize nominee Dr. Francisco Ortíz, were discussing couldn't be pleasant—at least not for Rissa. She grew pale, drew in sharp breaths, winced, and then finally, when the professor wheeled his wife away, lowered her head again, letting the spectacular cascade of curls hide her face.

Jase had the distinct impression she wept.

Something impelled him toward her, the urgency significant. Despite the three concerned musicians converging upon her, he kept on. As he approached, she smiled weakly at her friends, squared her shoulders, leaned her head back, and shook the wealth of hair away from the bass. She then drew her bow, poised to perform.

Admiration filled him.

The music began. Rissa's rigidity disappeared, and she shuttered her eyes, the softest, most reverent expression illuminating her features. As the lush notes of Corelli's "Sarabande" underscored the murmur of the gathering, she gave in to her art.

The attraction deepened. His need to know her better grew, and Jase knew that, regardless of how she felt about him at the moment, he was going to try to change her opinion.

He wanted her to look at him with the emotion and trust she showed her friends. And, if God so willed it, he would become a part of the circle Rissa showered with love.

❧

After cajoling the bewildered Estér Altamonte into squeezing his place card between Rissa's and that of some other guest relegated to the musicians' table, Jase soaked in the quartet's music.

When the maître d' announced dinner, he took his new seat and watched the quartet store the instruments. All displayed a profound respect for the magnificent tools of their trade, even Rissa, despite her struggle with the unwieldy bass. As Jase pushed his chair back to go help her, the African-American cellist assumed the onerous task. The familiarity between the two sent a foreign pang through Jase, and, to his amazement, he recognized. . .jealousy?

Moments later, his tablemates approached.

"I'm telling you, Ris, you overfeed the Beast," her good-looking and overly helpful friend said. "My poor back suffers more each day."

Rissa tossed her glorious hair over her left shoulder. "And I keep telling you, Ty, you're just a big baby."

The other two musicians pulled out their chairs and sat, chuckling. Ty struck a pose, one hand on Rissa's chair back and the back of the other at his forehead. "You wound me, oh, carrottop!"

Rissa narrowed her gaze. "Them's fighting words, brother mine."

"Nah, nah, nah," Ty chided and slipped into his chair. "We're too mature for sibling rivalry."

Then Rissa noticed Jase. *"You're* sitting *here?"*

Her dismay rubbed him the wrong way, but he controlled his response. "That's what the card says," he answered. "I must congratulate you—all of you. You've extraordinary talent."

The praise pleased Rissa's partners, but it brought a skeptical gleam to her eyes. Thank-yous rang out, hers the most muted. Turning to the other woman in the group, she made it plain she would not be furthering their acquaintance. Jase bided his time.

Moments later, a starched and ironed waiter delivered a lobster first course. As Jase lowered his head to pray, he noticed subtle movement among the others and glanced sideways. He caught his breath. Rissa and her partners, holding hands, were about to ask a blessing over their food.

He said, "May I join you in prayer?"

Shocked green eyes met his. While Rissa seemed unable to speak, the viola player raised a brow. "You're a Christian?"

"Nearly twelve years now."

"Then welcome, brother. I'm Tristan Reuben. And you're. . . ?"

"He's Jason Easton, Tris," Rissa said, rousing herself from her stupor. "The new owner of SilkWood Kennels."

"Aren't you a lawyer?" Ty asked.

"Passed the bar many years ago."

The other woman's eyes darted from Rissa to Jase and back again. "I'm Eva Alono," she said, "and Tyrone Carver's the last of our group. Let's pray, shall we?"

The lobster chunks in lime butter were delicious, as the hotel's reputation led one to expect, and the conversation remained polite. Then the last guest at the table arrived.

Resplendent in gray swallowtails, pink shirt with white collar, sunset-orange tie, top hat in hand, and spats over shiny black shoes, the diminutive elderly dandy took the seat to Jase's left, cresting a wave of liniment and aftershave over the lobster and lime.

He plopped his chapeau in the center of the table in front of his plate. To Eva, he said, "Evenin', chickadoodledee. My name's Horatio Davenport Jones, but all my friends moniker me Wem—don't ask me why, 'cause after eighty-three years, I still haven't clairivisioned the whyfore to that. Still, I'd be mighty honorized if you'd call me Wem." He glanced at the others. "All of you, too."

Jase suppressed a chuckle and held out a hand. "Pleased to meet you, Wem. I'm Jason Easton."

Bushy white brows beetled together. "The advocate, eh?"

Jase nodded.

"Well, rattle my rafters, sonny-boyo! I've got me a question for a legal beagle like yourself." Plunking both elbows on the table in a sidesaddle sort of way, Wem fixed Jase with his beaming brown eyes. "D'ja think I got me a case against the ambulance chaser that refused to sue city hall for me when I stubbed my toe and tripped on one of them too-tall nuisance curbs over on Hialeah Boulevard? At night, and under one of those dim-bulbed streetlights?"

To Jase's relief, the well-pressed waiter arrived right then and slid before him a fragrant, golden-skinned Rock Cornish hen accompanied by asparagus soufflé and three-peppered baby corn. Wem received his lobster as well as his hen and, from his glee, would not soon return to his imagined matter of jurisprudence.

Jase suspected that, despite the sartorial excess and advanced age, a laser dwelt in Wem's mind. But Jase no longer practiced law.

For the rest of the meal, Wem entertained his neighbors with tales of a long career as a jockey and greyhound breeder. Nowadays he ran a race-dog retirement home and dabbled in the market—he took a bath in the dot-com crash. Racing ran in his blood, he said, and Jase saw the man's need to replenish his caloric output in the speed with which he inhaled vast quantities of food.

"Now," Wem said, "after all those years, I've got PETA nuts marching at my front gate, accusing me of treating my dogs like dogs. I take good care of my old-folk-dogs. Where'd they get the impresception that canines are people, too? I've never hurt a soul—not even a dog's—yet."

The lights went out with those words. A line of waiters marched flaming Baked Alaskas through the ballroom, eliciting the guests' appreciative oohs and aahs.

Wem raised an interesting issue, but a wedding reception wasn't the place to debate the topic. Jase decided to hunt down the free-spirited philosopher some other time and continue the discussion.

As he forked up a bite of ice cream and cake dessert, Rissa asked, "Why can't one hate animal cruelty and support good breeding practices?"

Jase, noting that Wem, busy with his Alaska, seemed impervious to Rissa's question, answered. "I don't think the two are mutually exclusive but there are those who believe breeding interferes with the flow of nature and produces too many unwanted animals."

"Hmm. . . ," she said, "sounds like what the delivery guy told Paul."

"Paul? The delivery guy?"

Rissa nodded. "The day I visited SilkWood, Paul was waiting for your breeding specimen. It arrived via a parcel service, and the driver made a negative comment when he realized what he'd delivered."

The pianist and harpist who took the quartet's place during the meal packed up their instruments as a small orchestra set up. Throughout the ballroom, chairs scraped against the polished terrazzo, indicating the end of the banquet.

Jase stood and held a hand to Rissa. "May I?"

To his surprise, she accepted. The warmth of those talented fingers imprinted his palm with evidence to her vibrancy.

"Thank you," she said with a smile.

They turned from the table and, through the room's enormous windows, Jase caught sight of the blazing sunset. Shards of light shone the same shade as her hair.

"It's beautiful," he said, tilting his head toward the west. "I'd like to enjoy it from the balcony. Care to join me?"

Rissa hesitated. Jase tugged on her hand. After a shrug and a glance at her scattering friends, she nodded. "Miami's sunsets are gorgeous."

No more than you are. The words nearly slipped from Jase's mouth, but he managed to exert his considerable control over his tongue. This wasn't the right moment.

When he opened the glass door, humid evening warmth met them.

She shivered. "I didn't realize how chilly they keep the ballroom until right now."

"It is cool inside," he commented, then grinned. "Well, as long as Horatio 'Wem' Davenport Jones isn't in the vicinity, the room feels cool. He certainly spices things up."

An indulgent smile lit her face. "He's an original, isn't he?"

"I don't think God's in the copy business."

She turned, stared at the setting sun. "You surprised me," she said. "I wouldn't have thought you knew the Lord."

"Why?" he asked, not sure he wanted to hear her answer.

With a deep breath and that squaring of the shoulders he recognized as a bracing, courage-giving gesture, she leaned sideways on the stucco banister and met his gaze square on.

"Your legal triumphs don't strike me as particularly Christian."

He *hadn't* wanted to hear her answer. "You mean my defense of clients to the best of my ability, as required by law?"

Green eyes blazed. "How can you defend criminals? You know they're guilty, and you set them free to rob and steal again."

"I couldn't choose between defending them or not—it was my *job.*"

"It may be your job, but is it what God expects from His own? Does it rise to the level of integrity Jesus exemplified?"

Jase clenched his jaw. He'd argued that point with himself—and his late father—many times, but he now chose to reiterate reality. "The law requires equal representation and due process for all."

"Then that law should be changed."

"How would you change it? And how would you decide who deserves legal representation? Only the innocent? Then perhaps you should remember Jesus' admonition about casting stones."

She bit her lower lip. "I can't judge," she answered, a troubled expression on her face. "But you, as a Christian, can choose another career or to practice another branch of the law. You don't have to help criminals escape the consequences of their crimes—their sins. You don't need to betray the cause of Christ."

The memory of heated arguments with his father, of endless nights on his knees in prayer, of interminable wrangling with himself flooded Jase and brought the anguish back. "You're right," he said. "I betrayed the cause of Christ. But then I walked away."

He walked away again, difficult though it was.

⁂

You're right.

Two simple words, yet they bore an impact Rissa didn't expect. They followed her through the remainder of the reception as she sought but failed to find Jason Easton.

Evidently, her questions chased him from the event.

She avoided thinking about it as long as she could. But by the time she stood in her bathroom removing the remnants of mascara from her lashes, she could no longer dodge the queasy feeling that started when he left her.

Water dripping from her chin, she met her gaze in the mirror. Jase mentioned casting stones. Was she without flaw? Without sin?

No.

Her conscience forced her to avert her gaze. She wasn't sinless, especially in view of her judgmental attitude toward Jase. The Father alone had the right to judge His children.

She'd put herself in His place.

If that wasn't the height of pride, she didn't know what was. Pride was sin, the log in her eye. No wonder her stomach lurched all evening long. Faith in Christ honed one's conscience to a fine point.

She sopped up the mess on the vanity top, finished her ablutions with a light coat of moisturizer, then turned off the light and picked up her Bible on the way to her prize piece of furniture.

The soft sage green chaise by the window was her one and only brand-new purchase. Its chenille upholstery felt like pure indulgence against her skin, and the down filling molded itself to her body in a comforting embrace. Although new, it didn't look out of place in a shabby chic room full of antiques and flea market treasures.

She prayed for guidance from tonight's passage and opened God's Word. She found she couldn't concentrate at all.

She had to confess her sin, not just acknowledge it to herself. She also had to ask forgiveness, of God, and of Jase. Sliding to her knees by the chaise, she figuratively crawled into her Father's lap and let her troubles flow from within. She confessed, sought absolution, praised, and worshipped her Master and King.

And, eventually, acknowledged she had to swallow her pride and seek Jase. The sooner, the better.

Feeling more at peace, she devoured the Bible passage and spent time meditating on its teaching. Then she went to bed.

Taking her cue from her mistress, Soraya approached the padded dog bed Rissa kept next to the nightstand, spun tonight's requisite turns, nosed the rim in various spots, and finally plopped down with a heartfelt sigh.

Turning off her bedside lamp, Rissa knew how she would approach Jase. Soraya and the newborn pups gave her the reasons she needed—and another chance to see him again. Despite their argument, he appealed to her. Honesty made her admit she wanted to know him better, even though she'd rather deny the fact.

With a clearer conscience, she dropped off to sleep, her dreams filled with beautiful sleek baby Affies, rolling and tumbling under their mama's watchful eye.

Chapter 4

After church the next day, Rissa retrieved her pet from her condo. Butterflies churned her stomach as she drove to SilkWood, while Soraya, as usual, simply enjoyed the drive.

"You lucky dog," Rissa said to the Affie strapped in the front passenger seat of the car with a canine safety harness. "You don't have a bellyful of trepidation about this visit."

Soraya turned loving eyes toward her. At a red light, Rissa reached out and rubbed the silky head. The dog closed her eyes and leaned into her owner's caress.

"Yep," she said, "you're innocent, Soraya, but I'm not. I have to apologize. Apologies never come easy, but this one promises to be harder than most."

The need for honesty made Rissa acknowledge that today's difficulty came from the height of the fall for which her pride had set her up. "Oh, yes, the bigger we are, the harder we fall."

Soraya then yipped her response—she would remain noncommittal.

Rissa added, "Funny how when one's at the receiving end of a cliché, it becomes an unfunny truism."

The Affie tipped her head, shot her a quizzical look, and added a soft yap.

"Hey, that's why you're lucky. You don't have to worry about sticking your foot in your mouth. For you, that's fun. Me? I made a very dumb move."

Then Rissa faced the moment of truth. She'd reached SilkWood. As she turned onto the long gravel drive, her pulse raced and the butterflies became dive-bombing buzzards. She stopped at the parking area in front of the office building and opened her door.

The heavy throb of hip-hop's bass line buffeted her ears. Soraya's excited if outraged yowls at her restrained condition set Rissa's already rattled nerves on edge. She hurried to the passenger-side door and released her hound. With the ease of familiarity, Soraya ran to the kennel run closest to the car. She sniffed up and down its length, stuck her long, slender muzzle in and out of various links in the fence, and barked in exuberant joy.

The hip-hop beat mercifully stopped at the end of the song.

Rissa approached the office, a prayer for courage and humility on her lips. She pushed the door inward, shivered at the blast of arctic-conditioned air, and called, "Anyone here?"

"I am," Jase answered, "but why are you?"

Oh, great. He wasn't going to make this easy. "Umm. .I—well, I felt. . ." She cut short her stammered efforts when she failed to see him. Rissa needed a face by which to gauge the effect of her apology. "Where exactly are you?"

He sighed. Something scraped across the floor. Then, with obvious reluctance, he rose on the opposite side of the laminate-covered divide. His chiseled jaw jutted and a muscle in one lean cheek twitched. "So you're the kind who likes to lob attacks eye-to-eye."

Rissa winced. "That's a fair jab, considering my actions last night, but it's not why I came."

He stared, arms crossed over his ratty T-shirt.

She didn't blink. "I came because I had to." A deep breath and another quick prayer gave her courage. "After you left—at least, I assume you did, since I didn't see you again—I couldn't forget what I'd said, and believe me, I tried."

He arched a brow.

"By bedtime, my conscience burned hotter than the sun"—Rissa gestured toward the window—"and the Holy Spirit's convicting worked."

The jaw eased by a hint—*just* a hint.

She leaned on the counter. "I owe you an apology. I was wrong. I had no right to set myself up as your judge and jury, never mind convicting you. I know only God can do that, but I let pride take over. I put myself in the Father's place, and. . .well, we both know that's sin, plain and simple."

His shoulders relaxed a fraction.

She'd hoped for more, the uncrossing of those arms or a gentler light in his blue eyes. He offered nothing more.

"Last night I asked the Lord's forgiveness," she continued, "and now I ask yours. I know I don't deserve it, but I hope you can forgive me at some point. I'm sorry for what I said and for hanging onto an opinion without even hearing your side."

Then his demeanor changed. He exploded out of his internal constraints. He flung his arms to his sides. He looked away. He ran a hand through his dark blond hair. He turned and walked to the desk at the right rear corner of the office. He didn't say a word.

Still, Rissa sensed that she'd reached him. "What's worse," she added, her voice soft, "I did to you what my family has done to me for years. I boxed you in by my preconceived notion. I expected you to be a sleazy lawyer out to make a buck, and then you sent me and my expectations on a roller coaster ride when you said you were a—"

"Christians can't be lawyers?" he asked, spinning to face her again. "Or are they only supposed to follow the law when it's convenient? God called us to respect the earthly rule under which we live, and last time I looked, in America we live by the rule of law."

Rissa bowed her head. "Yes, He did, and if I'd listened to what you tried to say instead of only my judgmental thoughts, I would have heard you. I didn't want to hear it, just as my family doesn't want to hear what I have to say about my life and my choices. As wrong as it is for them, it's equally wrong for me."

A shudder racked her. "You said you walked away from the law—"

"I *did* walk away. That's why I'm—"

"Give me a chance, please." She dropped her purse on the counter and reached out as though to touch him, but he was too far on the other side of the chasm. "If only I'd given some thought to your actions—which I only did later on—I probably would have seen the truth. You haven't represented anyone in nearly a year, have you?"

"No, I've—"

"Wait! Let me finish. You spent a fortune buying out Mrs. Gooden, right?"

At his nod, she continued. "You can't litigate while mucking out runs, and I've never heard of a lawyer who wears torn jeans and T-shirts to court."

He glanced down at himself, groaned, and to her amazement, blushed. "I suppose I could wear my three-piece suit to feed and walk the dogs, but that wouldn't make much sense. I changed when I got home from church."

Rissa gave a tentative chuckle. "I'd judge you a raving lunatic if you hadn't."

He smiled back. "You'd have every reason to."

As he rounded the counter and came to her side, Rissa allowed herself a measure of relief. Then she noticed the unusual sparkle in his blue eyes.

"You weren't exactly dressed for labor and delivery the other day," he said. "You reminded me of illustrations of fairylike beauties in old, Victorian storybooks."

His words stole her ability to respond. She stared at him, stunned by what he'd said. He'd called her a beauty.

Her silence seemed to make him bolder. "You look like that again today. This lacy dress you're wearing looks very old-timey, and your hair. . ."

His words died as he reached, paused, then caught the lock of hair resting on her arm. Twirling it around a finger, he reeled himself right up to her, a look of wonder on his face. Rissa's breath caught in her throat, and his intense eyes snagged her gaze.

"Beautiful. . . ."

Somewhere in the back of her mind, the thought of panicking wafted in and out—mostly out, since right then she felt more than thought. The frigid air in the office suddenly turned sultry, weighty. Time paused. Seconds drifted rather than passed. All the while, Jase continued to stare, his face approaching.

She suspected he hovered just a breath away from kissing her, and she didn't know how she felt about it. She merely felt the warmth of his nearness, the excitement of his interest, the pull of their attraction, the beginnings of—

"Hey, Jase—Oops!" Paul careened to a stop in the open doorway.

Jase and Rissa turned, virtually cheek to cheek.

"Bummer," the blushing teen said. "I'm sorry. I just—umm, well, I'll be seein' ya! Later, *much* later."

As Paul turned, Jase tore himself from Rissa's side. "Hold it. What's up?"

The teen stopped, but kept his face averted. "Nothing much. We were just with Mahadi and the babies, and her pooch"—he pointed at Rissa—"flipped for the pups. She's crazy for them. You should see it. But it's not important, you know." He sidled along the door he still clutched in one hand. "I'll be getting back now. You're cool. Just go back. . . . *Never mind.*"

He ran out as though the Hound of the Baskervilles had set its sights upon him and licked its chops.

Rissa smiled. Then she chuckled.

Jase turned and sent her a questioning look.

She laughed. "It's—*he's* just too funny!"

A lopsided grin widened Jase's lips. He ran his hand through his hair, then shook his head. "Kinda killed the mood, didn't he?"

Rissa only laughed harder.

He joined in.

Moments later, when they both caught their breath, Jase opened the door and gestured for Rissa to precede him outside. "We may as well join them, don't you think?"

Stepping into the late afternoon heat, she said, "I'm a dog lover and Affie crazy in particular. I'd love to take a look at that cutie I met the other day."

They went to the building of runs, hurried down the center aisle, and met up with four teens, a curious Soraya horning in on the action, an anxious, defensive Mahadi, and her litter of sweet pups.

"Oh!" Rissa exclaimed, looking at the wriggling infants. "They're beautiful." She turned to Jase. "Do you think she'd let me come close? Pick one up?"

Jase tipped his head, studied the canine family. "I don't think she'll mind if you come into her kennel and go right up to them, but you may have trouble touching. She's a fantastic mother, and she might take a snap since she doesn't know you."

"I was afraid of that," Rissa said. "It's disappointing, but I should know better. Soraya's mother went crazy when I came to visit her and her litter."

"Affies are very protective of their pups," Paul stated with surprising certainty.

Stepping around him, Rissa placed a hand on his shoulder. "Looks like you've learned a thing or two about dogs."

The shoulder rose in a shrug as she dropped down to his side. "They're pretty cool," he said. "Just watch them play. They roll all over each other, and they don't even have their eyes open. Yeah, they're cool."

Rissa turned her attention to the "cool" dogs. A soft rumble rolled from the new mother's throat, warning Rissa away from the infants. Remembering her experience with Soraya's mother, she sat quietly, not moving, letting the dam get used to her scent. In the meantime, she watched the puppies romp.

The plump little wigglers wore soft fuzz quite unlike the long, silky hair they would later grow. Mahadi's litter promised a variety of traditional Affie colors. One sported silvery fuzz, very much like its mother's. Two were dark, and their coats would probably grow in glossy black or rich brown. Another looked like it would be red, and two had blond fuzz, similar to Soraya's coloring.

Rissa heard a sniffle behind her. She glanced over her shoulder and saw tears on the stocky brown-haired girl's face. Jase placed a hand on the teen's shoulder.

"You okay, Tiff?" he asked.

Tiffany drew a shuddery breath. "Yeah. It's just that. . .well, it's kind of hard. I can't forget, you know?"

Jase placed an arm across her shoulders, and with the ease of familiarity, Tiff turned into his chest. He held the girl as she sobbed, patting her back with a fatherly tenderness that brought a lump to Rissa's throat. There was just something about Jase. . . .

When Tiff's anguish lessened, he said, "You were so sure you were doing the right thing. Do you regret it now?"

"Yes—no. . . ." She met his gaze. "No, I don't regret giving my son away. The O'Malleys really wanted a baby, and they have what mine needs. I don't, not now."

Rissa's throat burned and tears filled her eyes.

"But you will someday," Jase stated.

"You bet. The next baby I have will have a mother *and* a father who want it and are ready to really take care of it." She lifted a shoulder and rubbed her wet cheek. "It's just that a baby is a baby, dog or human, and a mother *feels*. I'm really glad you helped me find the O'Malleys. I don't know if I could have done the right thing if I'd just had to hand him to just any old couple."

So Jase *had* done more than represent crooked rich guys. She was glad she'd apologized—God didn't convict without reason.

The slam of the kennel door put an end to the emotional moment. "Well, howdy-dowdy-do there, counselor," crowed a familiar voice.

Rissa stood. Wem? Here? She glanced at Jase.

He said, "I'm surprised to see you, Wem. I meant to call, since I hope to debate some points you made last night, but I never expected to see you so soon."

"Ah-ha ha *ha!*" Wem said. "Even the pretty, red-topped chickadoodledee is here, too."

Rissa voiced a weak "Hi."

Wem removed his snappy tartan golf tam, grabbed her hand, enveloped her in the aroma of liniment and aftershave, then kissed her fingers. "You're a better sight and scent and sound than even my dear, sainted great-aunt Gertie's lively Sunday chicken dinners."

Rissa didn't know whether to run for her life or laugh. She glanced at Jase and recognized the error in *that*. The mirth in his eyes made chuckles bubble up from her middle. She clamped her lips tight.

Wem noticed nothing. "I reconfiggered that, having nothing better to do today, I could come and pick your jurisprudicious brain, sonny-boyo."

Jase groaned.

Tiffany giggled.

The boy named Matt snorted.

Paul sidled behind Rissa, making for the great outdoors.

The movement caught Wem's attention. He looked at Paul, narrowed his gaze, and lost his amiable expression. "You!"

Paul stepped lively.

Wem snagged Paul's arm in the curve of his carved ebony cane. "Hold it there. I thought you were locked up tight."

Paul's eyes flashed. "I did my time."

Rissa gasped.

"Not nearly enough," bellowed Wem.

"I didn't take it," argued Paul.

"You and your pals did."

"So what?" Paul shot back. "That junky old Studebaker wasn't worth my two years. It only had scraps of metal around the rust."

"You hoodlum, you—"

Jase stepped between them as Wem's free hand shot out for the boy's neck. "Now listen here, you two. Paul was in the wrong place at the wrong time, and he paid for his poor choices. Last night you looked familiar, Wem, but I'd forgotten the case."

Wem sputtered, as though Jase had spouted heresy.

Jase added, "I believe insurance paid for your loss."

Wem dithered. He hemmed and hawed. Finally, he glared at Jase. "It's the memories, counselor. You can't go putting dollar signs on a man's recollections, and this. . .this hooligan stole a passel-load of mine. From the best years of my life, I might add."

Jase narrowed his gaze. "I thought you'd recently bought the car."

Wem blushed so bright that even the dim light in the kennel couldn't hide the red. "It's the memories it joggered loose in my mind that he stole from me."

With an indignant "Harrumph!" Wem marched down the kennel hall, opened the door, then slammed it in his wake.

A pregnant teen. An auto thief.

A tinge of suspicion colored Rissa's thoughts. "Mr. Easton?"

Jase blinked, shook himself. "Huh?"

"Might I ask you a question?"

He nodded.

"In private," she added.

The jaw clenched and the muscle leapt in his cheek. "Follow me."

As soon as they left the building, she turned. "How many of your employees have juvenile records?"

He fisted his hands, and the expression on his face hardened further. "They all do."

Lead landed in Rissa's stomach. "You expect me to trust my valuable pet to a class of junior thugs?"

He took a step closer, and Rissa gulped.

"As I told you before," he said, "the choice is yours. Tell you what. Leave your animal with us, as a test of sorts, overnight if not for a couple of days—free, of course—and judge us then."

With great obvious effort, he opened his hands and stepped toward the office building. "Just keep in mind that God will forgive your sins as you forgive those of others."

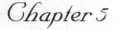

Chapter 5

The next day, Rissa puttered around the condo as she usually did on her rare free days. She saved Sundays for the Lord and Mondays for herself, and today she'd finished the boring necessities before noon. But nothing felt normal. She missed Soraya and couldn't relax. She wouldn't until she picked up her pet later that evening.

She regretted accepting Jase's challenge, but he'd left her little choice.

She turned to her favorite hobby, despite the lousy outdoor light, and set up her easel in front of the patio doors. The lofty palm visible through the slider's frame looked disheartened and reflected her mood—not to mention that of the day.

As she squeezed generous blobs of black, phthalo blue and green, alizarin crimson, and a dab of titanium white onto her palette, she mentally composed the painting. But as her thoughts ran images of an intriguing lawyer and a mental recording of their parting words, she found she couldn't concentrate. She hated admitting—even to herself—how much Jase appealed to her. They shared a common faith, a love of dogs, and she couldn't deny the sizzle between them. Still, that wasn't enough—he thought her as judgmental as her parents, and she had serious doubts about his connection to former criminals.

The doorbell rang, and Rissa responded, glad for the reprieve from her thoughts.

"Surprise!" chorused Eva, Tristan, and Ty.

"Huh?"

Ty reached around and tugged the long braid running down Rissa's back. "What is *wrong* with you? You never forget the year, the month, date, day of the week, hour, minute, or even the millisecond. You really forgot your birthday?"

Rissa frowned, then realized she hadn't checked her planner. "You're right. This is unusual for me. And it is my birthday."

Tristan pushed past Ty. "Phew! I balanced this frosting extravaganza for three whole blocks while Eva drove. I'd hate to think it was for nothing."

"Hey!" Eva closed the door behind her bouquet of helium balloons. "I'm an excellent driver. You're just doing a guy thing because you hate to have someone else behind the wheel."

"Maybe," Tristan said with a grin, "but you have to admit a car ride is scary with this sugar-and-butter football field on your lap."

Ty feinted a jab to Tristan's shoulder. "Get over it."

"Watch it, funny guy," the cake-bearer warned as he dodged and landed the dessert on the kitchen counter. "I bet you'd rather eat it than have the birthday girl's pooch slurp it from the floor."

Rissa gulped. "Soraya's not here."

Three shocked faces turned her way.

"Jase challenged me to trust her to him for one night to see how she does before I leave her there during our tour."

Her friends changed the subject, and Rissa appreciated the ongoing, good-natured banter. It let her mask her dismay. She prided herself on her attention to detail, and forgetting the date—her birthday, no less—was not at all like her.

Last night's heated argument still troubled her. Missing her dog didn't help.

"Earth to Rissa," called Ty.

"I'm here, I'm here," she answered. "You guys are too sweet. You didn't have to do this. No one celebrates birthdays once they turn twenty-one. At least, no woman does."

"Those are the ones who fork over fortunes for so-called miracle wrinkle cures," Eva countered. "They prefer to eliminate the beauty God created for every age."

Ty howled. "How old are you, Miss Wise *Old* Sage? The same twenty-eight as Rissa, only five months sooner, last time I checked."

Tristan waved Rissa's message pad and pen. "I'm recording Eva's statement for posterity. I'll reread it on her fiftieth b-day."

"I'm so glad you guys came," Rissa said, laughing. "It's gross and gray, and I can sure use your nuttiness."

The impromptu party went off with great success. Gag gifts balanced true tokens of affection, and the hot dogs, chips, veggies and dip, and cake soon vanished. They played excellent recordings throughout the afternoon, enjoying the new Aaron Copeland CD Tristan gave Rissa. She loved the twentieth-century American composer's music, and as his adaptation of the Shaker hymn, "Simple Gifts," soared around her, Rissa finally began to feel more like her normal self.

Then her mother called, ostensibly to wish her well on her birthday, but in truth to relate her latest tiff with Mrs. Janssen, her nurse-companion.

"Are you okay?" Eva asked as Rissa hung up the phone.

She nodded. "Mom seems better. I hope it lasts."

"We all do," Tristan added. "She's not a happy woman. We know how trying she can be, but her situation would be tough for anyone."

Rissa's eyes welled. "Thanks for understanding. Even though she has no feeling from the hips down, she suffers a lot. Her middle back and neck are in bad shape, too. I pray—"

Another phone call let her escape without voicing a specific prayer. She offered many for her mother. "Hello?"

"Rissa?" Jase said.

Oh, no. She wasn't ready for him. "Yes."

"I regret bothering, but you must come to SilkWood right away."

His formal tone disturbed her even more. "Why?"

"I wouldn't ask if it weren't important." He fell silent for a moment, then went on. "Mahadi's only girl pup is missing. No one's seen her since yesterday afternoon in the kennel."

"That's awful," Rissa said, "her eyes aren't even open. She couldn't have gone far. Have *you* looked for her or did you have the kids do the searching?"

His silence grew ominous. Then, "No, I didn't dump the search for a valuable, already-sold dog on the kids. They helped. We all looked for her, even the police."

That put matters in a different light. "I don't understand. If everyone's already looked for her, why do you need me?"

"Because *they* need to question everyone who's been here since noon yesterday. You were, remember?"

The memory of everything—their near kiss; Wem's kennel invasion; the revelations about Tiffany, Paul, the other kids; Jase's parting words—hadn't left her, no matter how hard she tried to shake them. She didn't want to think through the implications, but she didn't seem to have a choice.

"Have the police questioned Paul?" she asked.

"Just get out here," Jase said, his voice curt. "It's theft—she's valuable—and the cops want to talk to you."

He hung up.

Rissa stood, staring at the palm she'd wanted to paint, holding the phone partway between its cradle and her ear. Why was Jase so insistent on her presence? He couldn't possibly think she had anything to do with the pup's disappearance. Not with that crew of criminals running his place.

What a pity. She'd grown to like Paul. But he was a thief, tried and convicted. What could you expect?

And Jase? That moment, the shared intimacy that led to the near kiss. . .she'd foolishly thought it might lead to something. He was a poor judge of character, however, putting any chance in doubt.

Ty took the phone, and Tristan took her by the shoulders. "What's going on?" he asked.

She shuddered. "One of Mahadi's babies is missing."

Eva erupted from the rose velvet settee. "Who's Mahadi? Is she divorced? Could it be drug related? Did they call in the FBI?"

Rissa patted Tristan's hands, then removed them from her shoulders. She went to Eva as though slogging through the heavy steam that replaced the earlier rain and pulled the two of them down onto the settee.

"Mahadi's one of Jase's Afghans," she said. Eva rolled her eyes. Rissa continued. "He'd sold the pups before she gave birth last Wednesday, and one's missing. He thinks someone took her for the money. The police are there, and he says they want to question me—I don't know why. I know he knows I had nothing to do with the theft."

Ty joined the women in the seating area. "Didn't you say you left Soraya there yesterday? It's police procedure to talk to anyone who has contact with a crime scene."

"But I haven't even touched the babies. Besides. . ."

"Besides what?" Tristan asked. "You can't just leave us hanging. What else do you know?"

Rissa glared. "You don't have to grill me like some TV cop. I'm going to face the real ones soon enough."

He stared on, unrepentant.

She stood. "It turns out the teens that work for Jase have juvenile records. One of them stole Wem's Studebaker."

Ty frowned, also rising and heading for the door. "The old jockey from the wedding? One of Easton's employees stole his antique car? Anyway, wouldn't the kids know the pup's too young to survive without the mother?"

Rissa sighed. "The junior car thief knows nothing about dogs."

"If he's no longer in custody," Eva said thoughtfully, "then he must have paid his debt and been rehabilitated."

"Who knows how rehabilitated he really is," Rissa said.

Ty led Eva and Tristan outside. "God knows, Ris. Please pray before you say anything. Only the Lord knows the kid's heart."

Rissa closed the door and headed for her room. She'd need sturdy shoes, as the rain must have made a mess of SilkWood's grounds. She glanced at her computer and realized she hadn't checked her e-mail yet. Mondays usually brought potential business for the quartet.

Moments later, she was glad she'd paused to check. The sponsor for their upcoming tour had written to request an earlier departure and the Ramos gallery about performing at an exhibition.

Rissa didn't like the tour change. She had to retrieve Soraya. SilkWood was no longer safe; she needed safer accommodations, the sooner the better.

Mulling over the pros and cons of various other kennels, she logged off, donned socks and running shoes, slung her bag over her shoulder, and left for SilkWood, dreading the upcoming ordeal.

❧

Rissa stormed from the police interview, hot tears scalding her face, rage burning her stomach, pounding her temples. No wonder Jase had been nowhere in sight when she arrived.

"There you are." She ran toward him. "How dare you not tell me Soraya's missing? She's mine, and someone took her from *your* property. I demand you find her—"

"I'm doing all I can to do just that," he said, his voice revealing exhaustion. Worry plowed furrows on his brow. His blue eyes looked irritated, and the circles under them were deep and dark. "I wanted you to drive safely. If you'd known, who knows?"

"You assured me I could trust you." Another sob ripped through her. "But you let someone take her."

The crunch of gravel muffled his response. Rissa turned and saw the parcel delivery truck followed by a well-preserved, copper-colored Pacer, circa 1978. As the truck stopped in the parking area, the car darted around it and pulled up mere inches from where Rissa and Jase stood near the office door.

Wem, in blazing white pants, neon green-and-purple plaid shirt, and Stewart tartan tam-o'-shanter extricated himself from the car. "Hey, there, chickadoodledee," he said, bowing over Rissa's hand in a cloud of liniment and aftershave. "Fancy seeing you here again. Of course, it's a pure-dee-pleasurement, you know."

"They took my dog, too," she said bitterly, "and I just spoke with the police—not much pleasure there."

Wem's shaggy brows shot up. "Surely they don't suspect you."

She scoffed. "I didn't steal my dog. They questioned me as her owner and because I was here yesterday afternoon—just as you were."

The aged man spun his walnut cane in the air. "And just like you, *I* know nothing of the missing pups." He pointed at Jase with the prop. "I bet your thieving pup of the human variation does, though."

"I'll vouch for Paul any day," he said, sparks in his eyes. "And I'm sure you want your interview over as soon as possible. The police are waiting in my office."

Hearing Wem voice her fears, Rissa's anger flared again. Jase hadn't represented many innocents. "I don't know how you can trust delinquents," she said. "Especially Paul. He stole Wem's Studebaker."

Jase stepped forward, standing toe-to-toe with her. "Paul was with his brother and two friends when the older boys stole the car. And yes, he did share in the profits from the sale of the parts. At the time, he had a drug habit."

Rissa reared back and pointed at the boy, now cleaning a fenced run. "There you are. He probably wanted another hit."

Jase took her accusing hand, using it to reel her in. "There, Rissa," he said once she faced him, "is a repentant sinner. Like Saul, our Paul had an epiphany. He kicked his habit and accepted Christ during one of my Bible studies at his halfway house. He loves the Lord and wouldn't betray Him."

"But—"

"Do you question that Bible conversion?"

"No, but—"

"Then consider this one real, too. If God can turn a man like Saul into an apostle, then He can change a drug-addicted boy. I trust Jesus' redeeming power. Do you?"

As though he'd landed a physical blow, Rissa couldn't catch her breath. As Jase's words whirled in her head, she noticed Sean, the delivery truck driver, hold out a stack of parcels. She gestured to Jase.

He took it, forcing a smile despite his obvious anger. "Thanks."

Sean grunted, then stomped back to the truck. He peeled away, scattering gravel, just as he had the other time.

"That's one strange guy," Jase said.

Wem strolled from the office, a grin spanning ear to ear. Despite their serious situation, Rissa couldn't stop a smile. "There's another one," she murmured.

Jase's steely stare softened enough to acknowledge her effort at levity. "No argument there."

Cane hooked on his right arm, Wem approached, his left hand picking imaginary lint from his fluorescent shirt. "Cleared of any imprevarication, sonny-boyo! I knew I would be. Not like some others I won't mention."

He didn't need to mention anyone. His gaze flew straight to Paul. Rissa shared the gent's certainty, but couldn't discount Jase's words. If Paul had sincerely accepted Christ, then he now lived by different standards than before. Had he really chosen God? Or had he just chosen the easy way to con a powerful champion?

From what she knew about addicts, recidivism was nearly a given. Had Paul fooled Jase? Was he using again? Had he ever stopped?

A purebred Affie sold for a good bit of change—times two, in this case. And Paul might not know that separating the pup from her mother would lead to death without sophisticated supplementation.

"I'll be moseydrifting along, now," Wem said, hastening to his car. Something in the way he admired the kennel buildings set off Rissa's mental alarms. He'd mentioned investment losses at the wedding reception, and although his sense of style was. . .oh, one could call it unique, the outdated garments looked expensive. The compact car wasn't, but it dovetailed with recently reduced financial means.

"Jase," she said, her gaze following the copper-colored ovoid car down the drive, "could Wem have taken the dogs?"

"Why would you think that?"

She drew a bracing breath. "Well, he said he lost a bundle in the dot-com crash, and he takes in old greyhounds. I expect it's expensive to care for them, and his coffers are probably pretty empty by now, since he retired from racing years ago. Besides, he'd know how to keep a newborn alive."

"It's possible. Anything is. But you know? Something else troubles me even more."

"Really?" she asked, desperate for any nugget of information.

"Yes, really." His eyes narrowed, not in suspicion or anger. He looked puzzled, yes, questioning, bewildered. "I'm concerned about your expectations of everyone you meet. They're pretty negative."

She gasped.

"If people don't fit your assumption, then you try to shoehorn them into that mental mold. You said you're the victim of your family's expectations. I think you're twice a victim."

Anger filled her. "What do you mean, twice a victim?"

"Yes, twice."

As she went to speak, he placed a finger on her lips. "Hear me out," he urged. "Yes, you're a victim of their expectations, but it strikes me that you're also a victim of the expectations you put on others. I don't think you can see those around you for who they really are. You seem to see only what you expect to see."

His indictment left her speechless.

He went on. "I fought to break free from my father's expectations, and because of my clumsiness, we parted on bad terms. He died before I had a chance to mend our relationship. I have no intention of letting anyone else's opinion cage me again. I decided at my father's funeral that I would concern myself only with God's greater expectations and trust Him to deal with what others expect of me. You should examine your heart. Maybe you're letting your expectations bind you in ways far worse than the family ones you say you've fought to break."

Rissa severed the connection between them. She ran to her car and drove home through a blinding flood of tears.

How could Jase say such hurtful, untrue things? She of all people knew how expectations hurt. She didn't put expectations on anyone. People were people, temptations were tough, and change harder, even with God's help. She certainly wasn't bound by any bizarre backlash of the expectations he thought she imposed. She didn't force expectations on others, she simply saw people as God's flawed, sin-prone children—just like her.

Didn't she?

Chapter 6

It was the worst week of Jase's life—other than the one after his father's death. Then, the failure to bridge the breach he carved when he told his father he could no longer in good conscience practice law as he had deepened his sense of loss. The elder Easton saw Jase's departure from the firm as a personal insult, a betrayal. Jase saw it as part of his commitment to Christ. Father hadn't understood. He'd never recognized his own need for the Savior.

This time, in addition to the loss of two lovely, valuable animals, Jase also felt the loss of what might have been. He'd sensed something special growing between him and Rissa. Now, in her view, he'd been negligent with her dog.

He also had to deal with the buyer who'd paid for the pup in advance. Jase had used that money and his savings as down payment for the future King's Kids Downtown Ministries building—his secret dream. He couldn't return the money. He couldn't replace Soraya.

Both weighed heavily on him, each important in its unique way.

His heart said Rissa was special, that if somehow they overcame this crisis, they might have a future together. But he couldn't see how, not unless he found the missing Affies. The police had no leads.

As he turned off the lamp on his nightstand, he couldn't stop a grimace. What a way to spend a Saturday night. The cops had grilled him for hours again, then he'd seen to all the dogs' needs, locked the kennel building, and finally returned to his lonely home.

In spite of the day's busyness, Rissa hadn't been far from his thoughts. "Lord," he whispered as he drew the cotton sheet over his shoulders, "will she ever be?"

❧

"There's no question," Rissa said into the phone, "this was the worst week of my life."

Eva didn't answer right away. Then, "Worse than the time after your mother's accident?"

"Maybe not worse, but pretty close. I was little when *Mamá* fell. Grown-ups took care of things then. Now—"

"Yes," Eva said, chuckling, "now you have to fix what you goof up as well as deal with the problem."

"Oh, spare me. I apologized to you guys about a zillion times."

"And we forgave you. You're just lucky we didn't have anything else scheduled for tonight besides playing at my parents' restaurant. They understood when I told them we'd had a glitch in our schedule."

Rissa sighed. "I'll say we had a glitch—me. I can't believe I didn't write down the info when Robert Ramos called on Tuesday."

"I think you had a few things on your mind. Like your missing dog and a very intriguing kennel owner."

"Intriguing nothing," she countered. "He's negligent. A lawyer should know better."

Again, silence reigned. As Rissa went to ask Eva to share her thoughts, her friend said, "I think you protest a bit much."

"*What?* The guy challenged me to leave Soraya at SilkWood so he could show me I could trust him with her during the tour. Less than twenty-four hours later, he let some-one steal her."

"As I said, you're protesting too much. You know that little deters a determined thief. I think you're just a teeny-tiny wee bit scared of the *guy* in question."

Rissa's cheeks began to burn. "I'm not scared of Jason Easton."

"Sure, you might not be scared of *him,* but I think you're scared of the sparks be-tween you."

Thankfully, Eva couldn't see her blazing skin—and hadn't witnessed the near kiss. "You're crazy, you know?"

"Mmm. . .maybe," her friend said. "Time will tell."

"Umm. . .well, yes. Speaking of time, it's late and I do teach third-grade Sunday school. I'd better turn in, otherwise wild-man Tommy Young will run circles around me in the morning."

Eva laughed. "You think Tommy's pretty special, and you know it. But it is late, and performing tonight with only a mini run-through wasn't easy on the old nerves."

"Okay, okay," Rissa conceded. "I'm sorry, *so* sorry I forgot to tell you guys about the gig at the Ramos Gallery. Thankfully, Robert called this morning to request some Mozart. Otherwise"—she shuddered—"we would have been a no-show. And then—"

"And then you'd spend even longer beating yourself up for not keeping track of every last second that goes by. You're forgiven. Now go to sleep."

After a quick good-bye, Rissa perched on the edge of the bed and faced facts. She'd changed since meeting Jase. First, she forgot her birthday. Then she forgot to write down the gallery engagement for the quartet—not to mention forgetting to tell the other mem-bers their services were needed. What else did she forget?

Jase scared her. Not personally, but the way he made her feel. Especially since, despite her anger over Soraya's loss, she still wanted to see him.

He wasn't responsible for the dogs' theft.

Somewhere in the back of her mind, she wondered. . .what if that kiss *had* happened? What would it have meant? To her.

To Jase.

To them.

❧

Tommy Young behaved like an angel, as did all the third-graders. The sermon inspired Rissa to listen more closely for God's voice, and, after lunching on a Cuban sandwich bought on the way home, she curled up on her chaise and mulled over the pastor's words.

Honesty was a virtue, one she valued, and as an honest woman, she had things to confess. For one, she cared about Jase. The worry she'd seen etched on his face, the lines on his forehead, the circles under his eyes, all testified to his concern for the missing animals. It moved her.

For another, since Jase remained adamant about Paul's faith, she couldn't blind herself to the possibility of the boy's innocence.

And last, she did put rigid expectations on others—expectations that colored her response to them. She expected unconditional love and nurturing from her parents, and since their personal frailties kept them from giving it, she stayed at arm's length and withheld forgiveness. She'd expected Jase to be a pricey if rank ambulance chaser, but his love for Mahadi had surprised her. She hadn't known how to respond, even though his true nature proved him admirable.

She could love Jason Easton.

And Paul. . .dare she trust Jase's opinion of the boy? Or would her expectations of a former drug addict and thief color her actions?

She thought about what Jase had said, and in view of the morning's sermon, she admitted he was right. She'd tried to take God's place. What's worse, she'd failed to trust in Him. He had the situation in control. He knew everyone's heart. She had to trust and obey, since He remained sovereign regardless of what she did, said, or, for that matter, expected.

She had to ask Jase's forgiveness. Not the easiest thing to do, but the honest one, and so she soon left for SilkWood, feeling lighter than she had in ages, despite her pain over Soraya's loss.

"I'm surprised to see you," he said, rising from his chair as she walked into the frigid kennel office.

Although flustered, Rissa refused to let nerves keep her from doing what she had to do. "You shouldn't be. You were right—about the cage I've built for myself with the expectations I place on others."

Jase rounded the counter. "I was right because I used to do it, too. I desperately wanted—expected—my father to see the error of his ways. I expected him to face his need for Christ, and instead of emulating the Savior, I hung on to my judgmental attitude."

The crease on his forehead deepened. "I never had the chance to ask forgiveness for trying to be his Holy Spirit, for judging and convicting him instead of loving him as God called me to do."

"Oh, Jase, I'm sorry for your loss and for being so blind. I did that to you, and you were still kind when you pointed out where I'd gone wrong." She gave him a crooked smile. "I don't think I'd have been as kind. I'd have put on my pride and self-righteousness, and demanded—expected—you to see the error of your ways."

She touched his arm. "Will you forgive me? For being blind? Self-righteous? Prideful? Obnoxious?"

He covered her fingers with his, smiling back. "I wouldn't go so far as to call you obnoxious. In fact, I . . ." Blue eyes sought hers, asking the question that hovered between them.

Rissa took a step closer, laced her fingers through his.

He cupped her chin in his free hand. "As I was saying, I . . . I've come to . . . care for you. A lot."

She placed her other hand on his cheek. "Me, too." She chuckled and blushed. "I mean, I care for you, too—*you* know."

"Yes," he said, "I think I do." He brought his lips to hers, and she closed her eyes, relishing his tender, warm caress. Her senses sang, joy filled her, and she soared in a crescendo of hope, happiness, and the promise of more. Love.

When the kiss ended, she whispered, "Please forgive me. I know you had nothing to do with Soraya's disappearance, not even through negligence. I was angry and scared, and I dumped my anger on you."

"What were you scared of?" he asked.

She squirmed. "You're not going to let me off easy, are you?"

"What do you mean?"

She lowered her gaze. "Ever since we met, you had a strong effect on me, and I'd never felt that before. I'd always controlled my emotions, so I didn't know how to react. That scared me."

"More than your fear for Soraya's well-being?"

She shot him a hard look. "Just as much, I'll have you know."

"Then, Rissa," he answered, a smile on his lips, in his eyes, "there's only one thing to do. We need to pray."

Holding hands, they asked the Lord to bless their budding feelings, to forgive them for their occasional trespasses on His authority, to bless them with courage and strength as they grew closer and in their search for the missing dogs.

After hushed amens, they went outside, Jase's arm around Rissa's shoulders. She marveled at the thrilling newness of the contact, the unaccustomed intimacy, and smiled, knowing something wonderful was happening between them. For a moment, she let herself forget about Soraya and basked in the glow of romance.

Movement in the saw grass to the left rear of the SilkWood property caught her attention. "Look! There's Paul, sneaking away. I bet he knows where the dogs are. I'm going after him."

"Rissa!" Jase yelled as she ran across the parking area, past the kennel building, into the overgrown area where Paul had gone.

As she waded through the grasses and wove around the malaleuca trees, she prayed, asking the Lord for guidance, for wisdom in dealing with the teen, whatever she uncovered.

She came to a halt when she found him. In the shade of a huge malaleuca, he knelt, eyes closed, hands fisted at his hips.

"Father, please," he prayed, his urgency stunning Rissa. "Help us find the dogs. I can't go back to court, especially since this time I wasn't even there when someone else did the stealing."

Rissa heard a whimper in the distance, a familiar sound. Evidently, Paul recognized it, too. He stood, rustling the grass.

"Shh!" Rissa hissed.

He spun. "Where'd you come from?"

"I followed you, but that doesn't matter right now. Let's go find them, and quietly, so that we don't scare away the thief."

She took the lead, her ears keen on the faint cries of the newborn. Was she all right?

"If anything's happened to that baby," Paul muttered, his expression grim, "I'm gonna kill whoever took her."

"No," Rissa whispered, "you won't. You're going to trust the Lord to deal with those responsible."

"*You're* a Christian?"

Her cheeks flamed. "Yes, even though I haven't acted like one toward you. I'm sorry, Paul. I judged you by your past, a very unfair thing to do. Please forgive me."

He shrugged, never looking up from the ground. " 'S okay. Everybody does it. Except Jase, but he's different."

"Yes, he is. I promise to be more Christlike, too."

They fell silent as they approached an abandoned cement-block building that might once have been a garage.

"Do you think they're here?" Paul asked.

"I don't know," Rissa answered, her heart beating like tympani at the hand of a demented drummer. "Let's listen. We can't just barge in without knowing what we're getting into."

He bristled. "I'm not scared. The Lord knows what I'm doing. He'll protect me and see us through this."

"You know what?" Rissa said. "I've got a lot to learn from you."

He measured her mettle. "You just might be cool, you know?"

She grinned. "I hope so."

Just then, Jase ran up. "What do you two think you're doing?"

"Looking for the dogs," Paul answered. "We heard the puppy."

Jase looked at the decrepit building. "You think they're here?"

Before Rissa or Paul could answer, the puppy whimpered again. Then Soraya sailed into sight from behind a half-wild red-blooming bougainvillea at the far corner of the garage, baby in her mouth. She trotted to an old wooden door on that side of the structure, and Rissa noted the splintered bottom panel. The canines vanished.

"There you girls are," a man said. "Look what I brought."

Jase's jaw squared. "You two stay here. I'm going after him."

"Not alone, you're not," Paul countered.

The older male frowned at the younger, who glowered right back. Rissa slipped past them. Let them posture. She was going after her pet—and the tiny infant who should still be with her mother.

She walked in through the gaping hole left by another, long-gone door. When her eyes adjusted to the dark, she watched a familiar figure in a corner pour a white liquid into a baby bottle. On the floor beside him, she noted a sack of Soraya's favorite kibble, two metal bowls, a can of specialized dry puppy formula, and a clean but torn flowered bedspread.

"Glad I spotted you the other day," he told Soraya, who lay curled on the blanket, the puppy suckling at her belly. "I'd never thought you'd take off with a baby, but you did, and I'm glad. Now they won't turn either one of you into puppy-incubating machines."

"It's called grand theft, Sean," Rissa said.

The deliveryman dropped the bottle. He paled, shot a glance at the door as if to make a run for freedom, but Jase walked in. "And I intend to press charges," he said.

Soraya gently pushed the baby aside, trotted to Rissa, rubbed up against her thigh, and licked her mistress's hand. She yipped, then ran back to the pup.

Sean faced his accusers. "I didn't steal the dogs. When I brought last Monday's delivery, I saw her running through the saw grass. I drove around your property, parked by this old place, and found her nursing the puppy in here. Even though she can produce milk, that amount's limited, and I was afraid the little one might starve, so I brought formula from the ASPCA hospital where I volunteer. I've taken good care of them."

"You're telling us *her dog* stole the puppy?" Paul asked, eyes big as saucers.

"That's what happened. I just didn't return them." Sean stared at Jase. "What breeders like you do to dams is abusive and cruel. All you want is litter after litter to sell pups for all you can get. The world doesn't need more dogs. We have too many at the shelter."

Whereas Rissa's anger simmered and threatened to boil over, Jase's steely expression showed signs of softening. "You didn't take the dogs?"

"No," Sean answered. "I found them and took care of them. I made sure they had water, food, and even comfortable bedding." He pointed to the blanket. "It's not my fault the older one insists on carting the little one around. She thinks she's the puppy's mother."

"Oh, Soraya," Rissa chided. Hearing her name, the gorgeous golden Affie gave a happy bark, nudged the pup into a mound of blanket, and pranced to Rissa. She danced before her mistress, barked again, then returned to the pup and studied the gathered humans.

When the Affie barked again, Rissa glanced at Jase, shrugged, then joined her. "You goofy dog, this baby's not yours." Wrapping her arms around the lovely animal's neck, she pressed her face against the warm silky fur. "You needed more than just my love, didn't you?"

Jase knelt behind her, reached around Soraya, and cupped the baby in his hand. "God is love," he murmured, "and love is essential. Even though dogs don't have the capacity to know Him, they know how to love—unconditionally, generously, and without expectations."

Rissa nodded. "But she needs to return the pup she stole."

"Do you think she might enjoy the company of my dogs? On a regular basis?"

"What do you mean?"

"Well, I can't deny that I'd like to have you here, with me all the time, but it's too soon to ask you something like that."

Rissa's breath caught in her throat. Was he saying. . . ?

He continued. "We can start by kenneling her here during your trip. That way she can visit her little pal and maybe make other friends or find a mate. Dogs are pack animals, and they can do weird things because of their need for company, for a partner with whom to share their lives."

"Like people," she whispered.

"Yes," he answered, hugging her back against him with his free arm. "Like us."

GINNY AIKEN

Ginny Aiken, a former newspaper reporter, lives in Pennsylvania with her engineer husband and their three younger sons—their oldest son got married and flew the coop. Born in Havana, Cuba, raised in Valencia and Caracas, Venezuela, she discovered books early and wrote her first novel at age fifteen while she trained with the Ballets de Caracas, later known as the Venezuelan National Ballet. She burned that tome when she turned a "mature" sixteen. Stints as a reporter, a paralegal, a choreographer, a language teacher, and even a retail salesperson followed. Her life as a wife, a mother of four boys, and the herder of their numerous and assorted friends, brought her back to books and writing in search of her sanity. She's now the author of twenty-five published works and a frequent speaker at Christian women's and writer's workshops, but Ginny has yet to catch up with that elusive sanity.

MATTIE MEETS HER MATCH

by Kristin Billerbeck

Chapter 1

J eff Weatherly is back in town." Gram's voice was the epitome of casual, but Mattie knew what the simple sentence conveyed. *The man you let slip away, the one you were meant to marry—he's back in town. Let the church bells ring!*

"Gram, if Jeff is back in town, he's probably brought his new wife with him." Mattie took out a glass vase from its cardboard home, unwrapped the newspaper, and placed it on the mantel. She smiled to herself, knowing Jeff wasn't married and that her grandmother harbored the same information. But Gram, being the social butterfly she was, undoubtedly knew something more. Against Mattie's better judgment she longed to hear the latest. Her stomach twisted waiting for the story.

Luckily, Gram practically burst out, "Jeff's *not* married! Had his grandmother tell me so herself." Gram winked, while Mattie's eyes narrowed. "He says he'd love to see you again."

Mattie wagged a finger at her grandmother. "Aha! I knew it, Gram. That innocent act doesn't play here anymore." Mattie smoothed the emotion from her voice. "Jeff is a very nice man, but he's not the man for me." The infamous "they" always said you never got over your first love. Sadly it was true for Mattie. She'd nursed her broken heart for ten years now, waiting for a new Mr. Right to steal the memories away. She was still waiting.

"If you'll remember correctly, Gram, Jeff dumped me for more time with the chess club. If I wasn't more important than a pawn then, why would you think ten years would make any difference?"

"Oh, that was ages ago. Have you no forgiveness in your heart? He was just a boy then, interested in boyish things. Who says he's not the man for you?"

"Perhaps it's the fact that he packed up and left town after high school, and I haven't heard from him since. Could be me, but I think that pretty much sends a message. Besides, I heard Mel had a date with him first." She heard the accusatory note in her tone that she'd meant to keep to herself. "Did you really think you could set him up with Mel and I wouldn't hear about it?"

Gram went about unpacking the boxes from the attic, humming as she did so.

"Mel said he was a geek, Gram."

More humming.

"If you're so certain he's the man for me, why did you set Mel up with him first?" Mattie crossed her arms before picking up another knickknack to display. The very idea of booted Mel with choir boy Jeff Weatherly made Mattie giggle. What could Gram have been thinking?

"Oh, you girls, you're always scheming against your poor old Gram. I should have had grandsons. If you must know, I didn't think you'd be interested unless someone else was."

Mattie grimaced. "But someone else wasn't interested." She forced a laugh. "Someone else thinks he's a nerd!" *A nerd who would regret the day he said good-bye to Mattie Stevens.* She tossed her hair subconsciously. Hadn't she become a successful artist? Renowned among Scottsdale's elite? Her ego gave way to real emotion. The truth was she longed to see Jeff again. Just to prove to herself she was over him.

"Mel was just more interested in another young man, Mattie. There's no crime in that. Jeff Weatherly will find someone to marry. You might as well see if anything's there, you know, any of that spark left before it's too late."

"Gram, Jeff dumped me for chess. What on earth do you think has changed?" Mattie swallowed hard, hoping for an answer. If Gram knew something Jeff had said, Mattie longed to hear about it.

"Pshaw!" her grandmother said, complete with the Victorian hand motion. "He's all grown up now. You can't hold his childishness against the man. He probably wasn't ready to get married after high school. Men mature slower than women, and he's twenty-eight now. It's time. I only thought of Mel first because I thought it might pique your interest. You can be such a stubborn thing."

"Should I pick out the ring now? Or after I set the date?" Mattie raised her eyebrows, but her sarcasm belied the lift she felt inside.

She watched her grandmother closely. Although Gram was seventy-five now, that fact hadn't slowed her in the least. She'd moved into the equivalent of a senior Club Med and had a social calendar that made Mattie's look pathetic. Gram's complexion had grayed with her hair, but her blue eyes never lost their sparkle. Her personality never lost its magnetism.

"Now you're just being a smart aleck. Hand me that vase. I'm tired of looking at that old thing. I'm going to put it in the box with the other ancient artifacts. Maybe they'll get something for it at the sale." With a spry motion she put the vase out of sight. "Forget about Jeff. I suppose if he wasn't right for Melissa, he's probably wrong for you, too. On another subject, I need help at the church flea market. Will you work in a booth on Saturday morning?"

Mattie's pulse slowed. That was it? That was all her grandmother had on Jeff? Even Melissa shared more than that! Mattie's mood lilted as she realized the day wouldn't be spent thwarting Gram's matchmaking tendencies. She'd been looking forward to feigning lack of interest and hearing more about what Jeff had been up to since returning to town. "Sure, Gram—I can help at the sale, whatever you need."

"Be in the church parking lot at eight a.m. Josephine will set you to work."

The doorbell rang. "I'll get it." Mattie surveyed the new, cleaned-out apartment. "It looks great, Gram—don't you think? We should have done this before you moved."

Her grandmother smiled. Opening the door, Mattie lost her breath. Jeff Weatherly stood much taller than she remembered him, at least six foot, and bigger. Much broader in the shoulders. Gone was the lanky teen with feathered bangs, replaced by a self-assured and traditional gentleman.

Jeff's hand laced the doorway, and Mattie found herself without words. She swallowed, multiple times, but still a simple sentence wouldn't form. Suddenly his shoulders bent toward her, and he embraced her. She felt her heart pounding, and she prayed he wouldn't hear the persistent drumming that filled her own eardrums. His arms around her made her silence more pervasive. *Geek? Where was the geek, Mel?*

He pulled away, planting a simple kiss on her cheek. "Well, if it isn't little Mattie Stevens. What a surprise! All grown up and prettier than ever."

Mattie simply nodded, her limbs unable to listen to the message her mind sent them. Feeling the complete idiot, she nodded and forced a smile.

"Hi, Mrs. Stoddard." Jeff waved. "That furniture ready to go to the sale?"

"All set. Right there by the door. Mattie can help you get it to the car." Gram winked at Mattie.

"Where are your glasses?" Mattie finally said.

"Glasses?"

"Mel said you wore glasses." *Big, ugly, doofy glasses were her exact words.*

"No, I wear contacts." He paused for a moment, putting an end table down. "Oh." He chuckled. "The night with Mel. Well, I guess I should say *almost the night* with your cousin. She stood me up. I'd lost a contact, and my good glasses were at work, so I had my old pair." He laughed again. "I made an impression on Melissa, huh?"

"Not one you'd want to brag about." Mattie's heart stirred in confusion. She loved the way he looked: tall, handsome, conservative, and yet she was so angry that he seemed so put together, not the helpless nerd Mel described at all.

"Do you really think the president of the Sequoia High School chess club is worried about impressions?" Jeff smiled at her and raised his eyebrows.

The mention of her former rival for attention infuriated Mattie. "You still wear that title like the badge of honor it is." Mattie rolled her eyes. "Gram, I'll take these things out."

"Be my guest," Gram said.

Mattie took a box full of trinkets toward Jeff's waiting Cherokee. The dark blue color sparkled in the hot Arizona sun, and she waited for Jeff to open the door rather than sizzle her own hand against the dark paint. Jeff lifted the hatchback, and all the anger Mattie had felt for ten years flooded into her. With her whole being she wanted to kick the smug Jeff in the shins just to make him feel something. She swallowed the bitter pill of resentment.

"Thank you for helping my grandmother. It was nice to see you again."

He reached for her hand. "That's it? That's all you have to say to me?"

She searched his presence, letting her eyes drink in his serious good looks. Although he still made her heart pound, there was so much pain built around it. Scar tissue that hadn't ceased since the day he'd called her on the phone and put an end to their innocent, blossoming romance.

She pulled her hand away. "What is it you expect me to say?"

"Come on, Mattie—you can't possibly be angry with me." His innocence enraged her.

"I had to take my prom dress back to the store. The only more humiliating thing would be returning a wedding gown. All my friends went, and I missed out on one of the highlights of high school because *you* had a chess match. I know it sounds childish to you now, but it was important to me. I thought I was important to you. Important enough to forego a chess game."

"It was the state championship, Mattie! I couldn't help it if we had to travel to Phoenix."

Mattie laughed aloud. "I cannot believe I am standing here at twenty-eight years old, debating the importance of a high-school chess match. As I said, it was nice to see you again, Jeff. I hope life treats you well." She turned to walk away and heard his deep voice follow her.

"I didn't know what to do with a girlfriend, Mattie. You probably expected me to kiss you. I didn't know how to kiss you."

Mattie turned and saw the blue of his eyes masked under his downcast eyebrows. Her pulse quickened, and she saw briefly that hidden place in Jeff. The corner of his secret world that called out to her, beckoning her.

Her eyes teared up. "Why didn't you tell me that then? You might have saved me a lot of heartache."

His hands became animated. "Mattie, I was a nerd. You were a cheerleader. All the boys wanted you to be their girlfriend. I was the president of the chess club. All the girls wanted me to set up the AV equipment. I used to hear what the guys said about how fine you were."

They both laughed at the dated expression before resuming their conversation. "I wasn't a cheerleader in my heart, Jeff. I was a geek, and I thought the sun rose and set on one boy, and one boy only. I'm sad if you thought I cared about appearances. I thought you knew me better than that." She hesitated. "The boy I was attracted to was the smartest kid in school. He was quietly handsome and studying calculus while the rest of the class did simple math. But there was a catch. That boy just wanted to play chess. He didn't want to have a girlfriend." She smiled and started for the door, but again his voice stopped her.

"I don't just want to play chess now." His voice was deep and full of a strength she wouldn't have known he possessed. "Have dinner with me."

Her eyes closed. She'd waited for this moment for ten years: the chance to hurt him as she'd been hurt; but the barbed words she'd planned, the ones she'd rehearsed in the mirror, didn't come. Looking into the depths of his blue eyes and into the soul that had just opened to her, she couldn't do it. She had to fight saying yes with all her being.

"No. . . ." Her voice trailed off. "No, thank you. I appreciate the offer, though." She smiled faintly. "More than you'll ever know." But she wasn't about to let him hurt her again. Jeff took everything seriously except romance, and she'd do well to remember that.

She walked into her grandmother's apartment and wiped the moisture from her forehead. "I'm going to head down to the pool for a break, Gram. Do you need anything?"

Her grandmother glanced toward her; then, in Gram's knowing way, she kept quiet about Jeff. "You go ahead. You look as if you could use the break."

Mattie spoke her thoughts aloud. "I thought there would be magic. Fireworks. There's only reserved politeness, and my heart is breaking all over again."

Gram smiled gently and nodded.

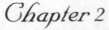

Chapter 2

Even in her air-conditioned condominium, the heat of the blossoming day swelled around Mattie. Had she really volunteered for an outside yard sale? In Heaven, Arizona? In the summer? She groaned at the thought. Gram could talk the saguaro out of water. Mattie dressed in a modest pair of cuffed shorts with a T-shirt and slipped into a light pair of flip-flops. She crinkled her nose at her freshly washed face in the mirror. *Good enough.*

After loading the last few items from Gram's things into her compact car, Mattie drove the familiar road to church. The hustle and bustle of preparation filled the entire parking lot, and Mattie found Josephine Wessex ordering everyone about and maintaining calm amidst chaos. Mattie grinned. Maybe someday she would be organized like that with age, too, but somehow she doubted it. The artist in her was never far away.

"Hi, Mrs. Wessex!" Mattie called with a wave.

Josephine turned and broke into a wide grin. "Well, Mattie, what a treasure you are. Always here to help when you can." She pinched Mattie's cheek so firmly a rosy blush must have appeared. "You are so much like your grandmother, unselfishly giving your free time. Did you see all the beautiful Depression glass your grandmother donated? That will bring a pretty penny for the church."

"Gram never did care much about trinkets, Mrs. Wessex."

"No, she's what they call a people person." Suddenly the shattering of glass broke their conversation. "I had better get over there. You're with Jeff Weatherly in booth seventeen." Josephine pointed to a booth.

Seeing Jeff's tall frame bent over a folding table full of junk, Mattie suddenly wished she'd taken more care with her appearance. She hadn't even bothered with lip gloss. She drew in a deep breath and walked forward with the last box. She cleared her throat, and Jeff looked up.

"Mattie!"

"Hi, I guess my grandmother arranged for you to help here, huh?" Her toe twisted inward, as though she were a small girl in a calico dress. *Gram's magic touch has run dry,* Mattie reminded herself. Mel had found her own husband, and Chelsea and

Callie were just dumb luck.

Jeff's sapphire gaze disappeared behind a wink. "Actually I offered to help with the sale, and your grandmother said she'd find me a partner. I think she did well by me, wouldn't you say?"

Mattie nearly laughed aloud. *And will she ever find you a partner, if you let her.* "I guess she figured we're old friends. It would be nice to reconnect."

"Really? I thought she might be trying to set us up." He raised his eyebrows, and Mattie thought she'd faint from humiliation. At the same time, she wished she understood what was behind his emotion. Was the idea ridiculous to him, or was he just nervous?

"She has been known for her set-ups, but I'll be sure to let her know we're just friends." She tried to giggle, but it came out most unnaturally. Jeff's warmth unnerved her to no end. "You're safe with me. I promise you Gram's matchmaking days are over."

"Really? That's too bad. I was hoping we could do lunch afterward." He leaned over and whispered. "Too forward, huh?"

"No!" she blurted out louder than she intended. "No, not at all." She shook her head. Hadn't she promised herself willpower? Mattie groaned inwardly. She was useless to her quickening heart. "Lunch between old friends is just that. A simple meal to reacquaint. There's certainly no harm in that."

She smiled, and when he returned it, the steeled blue of his eyes forced her to think about breathing. After all these years she was still a hopeless schoolgirl beside Jeff's weathered intelligence. In high school, the attraction had been his maturity beyond his years. She supposed it still was. Jeff always remained a step ahead of the average. Something about the way he knew so much made Mattie feel safe, as though her flaky artist's mind could wander in creativity while he stayed grounded.

"I hear you're an artist now. A pretty popular one." He placed a price sticker on a dish. "Just like in high school, as sought after as ever."

"I paint murals in children's rooms or in dining rooms usually. I don't know if I'm an *arteest*, as I imagined I'd be. Especially if you consider my work eventually gets covered over by boy band posters and bubble gum."

"My grandmother told me about your success as soon as I got back into town. I'd love you to paint one of your works in my new house. The walls are so plain."

"What?" Perhaps the hot sun was making her hear things. Jeff Weatherly wasn't interested in art on his walls—it couldn't be. "What did you have in mind? A chess board in your kitchen?"

"No, nothing like that. My sister's going through an ugly time right now. Her son has been staying with me on and off for the last year. I thought it would be nice to personalize his room a bit. Kenny's the reason I moved back to Heaven. The traveling would be too hard on him now that he's going to school next year."

Mattie's stomach lurched. Of course she'd heard the rumors about Jeff's sister and the continuous battle with drug addiction. She hadn't paid them any mind other than as idle gossip. Judging by the clouded gray in Jeff's eyes, there must have been a spark of truth to them. Mattie mentally calculated her six-month waiting list and wondered how she could push them all back without harming her carefully built reputation.

"What did you have in mind for a mural?" she asked.

"He's four, and he really likes trains." Jeff's expression softened. "He'll build tracks all day long, and he sits in there and names them all. They're his friends." All hint of a smile faded. "With as many struggles as he's had, they're his only friends sometimes."

Mattie felt her own eyes tearing. She was ready to drop the flea market altogether and go to buy the supplies. "I can paint at night for you. I have a full schedule with a new house in Scottsdale during the day right now, and with the commute. . . . The woman wants a Roman theme in her bathroom—which is bigger than my condo, I might add—and her daughter wants pink ponies on her ceiling. I'm almost finished with that job, but it's been a bear working for this woman, so I don't want to do anything to ruin my shot at getting out of there as soon as possible."

"No, I don't want you to go through any trouble, Mattie. I'm sorry I brought it up. I just thought—"

"Jeff, I want to do this. I want your nephew to have a place that feels like it was made especially for him. A place where he can know God loves him and so do you."

Jeff still shook his head, and Mattie grasped his hand. "I want to do this. It's important to me because it's important to you." Had she really said that? Her fingertips flew to her lips. As hard as she was trying to keep her emotions at bay, she still cared about Jeff. More than she wanted to admit to him or to herself.

Jeff turned and faced her, his intense gaze meeting hers until she thought she'd melt from the heat. "Mattie, would you paint the spare bedroom for my nephew? I wouldn't normally ask. I want you to charge me whatever the going rate is for your work." His chin tilted toward the radiating cement. "I can't put it into words, but I need to do more for this little boy. To give him some semblance of a home, even if it's a place he just visits. I feel as if he's my own. Who knows? If things keep going the same way, he may be at some point."

Mattie smiled at their first customer of the day before turning again toward Jeff. "I'll sketch my ideas, and we'll buy the paint early next week, okay?" She inhaled dreamily. To think such a softhearted person lurked behind that stoic facade unnerved her. To see a man love a child the way Jeff loved Kenny was everything Mattie wished for in a lifetime. If only she knew what to do to grasp such a love for herself.

After helping a few customers, one approached looking familiar. Mattie couldn't place the face, but she knew it had an unpleasant memory associated with it. Once the woman spoke in her gravelly, straightforward way without thought to standard conversational practices, Mattie instantly remembered. Jeff's sister, Joan.

"If it isn't the high school princess." Joan laughed, a low throaty cackle that brought an underlying fear bubbling to Mattie's surface. "Still wearing your cheerleading skirt for kicks? Still leading my brother on?"

"Joan!" Jeff chastised before grabbing his sister by the arm and walking her away a bit. His loud, angry whisper wasn't hard to overhear. "Do you mind? This is my friend. Do I ask your friends about their freaky tattoos? Or why they feel the need to pierce every orifice?"

Mattie looked away but suddenly felt her hand grabbed, and a tiny hand curled into her own. She looked down to see a little boy with sandy brown hair, styled easily into a well-coifed bowl cut. His large blue eyes were unmistakably Jeff's. This had to be the nephew, and Mattie kneeled to speak.

"Hi, there, little guy. What's your name?"

"Kenny." The big blue eyes blinked, and little pudgy lips spoke with a lisp. "I get to go with Uncle Jeff today. Mommy says she has stuff to do, and little kids can't come."

"Well, we need lots of help selling all these good things today. Do you think you could help us?"

His head bobbed excitedly. "Uncle Jeff says I'm a great helper."

Jeff's voice increased in volume. "Did you even feed him today, Joan?" As Jeff saw Mattie's widened eyes, he lowered his voice.

"Are you hungry, Kenny?" Mattie asked.

He rubbed his tummy. "I'm weally ungry. Mommy said all the cereal was gone, and I ate it too fast. She's got no money for more and has to get some, but if I keep eating it too fast, I'm outta luck."

"Come on, then. Let's get a donut over here. Krispy Kremes."

"Ooh, those are my favorite! Mommy likes them, too."

"Let go of my kid! You got that, princess?" Joan's wild black tresses fell over her face as she yelled.

Kenny's blue eyes widened, and he looked first to his mother then to the stranger holding his hand. Mattie only clung tighter to Kenny's hand and took him to the refreshment table. "It's all right, Kenny. Your uncle Jeff is right there, and so is Mommy. We'll be able to see them the whole time, okay?"

Kenny nodded. Jeff looked adept at handling his sister, and Mattie would gladly let him. With all these church folk gathered around, Joan wasn't likely to get away with too much.

"Mrs. Wessex." Mattie smiled at the older woman. "This is Kenny, and he is so famished, he says. He simply must have a donut."

Josephine pinched the little one's cheeks, and Mattie noticed it was with less force than she'd endured. "I think he might need two. He looks like a big boy."

After downing three donuts and two glasses of milk, Kenny had more than a bit of energy to run off. Josephine noticed and eagerly offered to take him to the church playground for a time. Mattie agreed and went to find Jeff, to see if there was anything she could do to help.

Jeff's face was drained of color, as Mattie found him sitting in a folding chair behind table seventeen. He looked up and blinked slowly then stood frantically. "Where's Kenny?"

"Relax—he's with Josephine Wessex. They went to play off some of the sugar high from the donuts. They're right over there." Mattie pointed, and Jeff exhaled.

"I guess you remember my sister now, huh?" Jeff's defeated expression gave way to a resolve. His shoulders straightened. "I have to get that boy, Mattie. I can't let him grow up like this. Look—I hope you don't mind, but I'm going to have to cancel lunch. As long as

I have Kenny, I don't want to do anything to destroy that or cause my sister not to trust me." He looked away for a moment. "Joan thinks our goody-two-shoes ways will harm her son, that we'll fill his head with religious notions if we take him out together." He held his forefinger and thumb up. "She's this close to signing over custody."

Mattie swallowed hard. Joan had always hated what Mattie represented, and it was no different ten years later. Jeff wasn't willing to sacrifice his nephew for the chance at a relationship that had already failed once. That made perfect sense to her, but logic wasn't on her mind.

"Of course, I understand," Mattie said over the lump in her throat.

"I'll make it up to you. I promise." Jeff's head shook back and forth. "Don't give up on me, just yet. Your Gram has a lot of wisdom, and I think there's something here we have yet to discover."

"Can I still help you with the mural? No strings attached. We'll do it when Kenny isn't around so Joan will have no qualms."

He paused momentarily. "I'll see you Monday night." He took out a business card and wrote his home address and phone number on the back. His eyes were filled with sadness, and Mattie fought the urge to touch his face and try to take some of his stress away. But she would pray, oh, how she would pray.

Chapter 3

"What did you think of your sale partner yesterday?" Gram lifted the corner of her mouth. "Pretty handsome?"

"I thought it looked quite obvious, as if I were using my grandmother to get a date. It was a little humiliating actually." Although they'd enjoyed a nice, homemade meal her grandmother had prepared, the subject of Jeff was saved until now. All part of her grandmother's well-executed plan, she supposed.

Gram shrugged. "All that matters is that he didn't mind you as his partner. He enjoyed seeing you, so I see no harm done. We tested the waters, and we're ready to move forward." Gram rubbed her hands together.

"No harm done? He probably thinks I'm an old maid. That no one wants to date me, and my grandmother has to force innocent single men into working flea markets with me." Mattie's eyebrows rose. "Your plan might be dead in those waters, Gram. Jeff has far more important things on his mind right now."

A giggle rumbled from her grandmother. "Mattie, you always were the dramatic one. You see so much that isn't there."

"I'm an artist. Being colorful is part of my charm."

"It is," Gram agreed. She put a Corelle dish into the cabinet, ignoring the new dishwasher like an abandoned shopping cart.

"Gram, are you ever going to use that dishwasher? Your kitchen looks like a showroom."

"A dishwasher. Whatever for? I can wash a dish without wasting electricity. You young people are wasteful. If you had to go through the Depression, you'd be more careful with resources. Especially with water in Arizona. This may be Heaven, but I don't take that name literally."

Mattie sighed. "Time is valuable today, Gram. That's why we have modern-day conveniences, so that we can do more important things than wash dishes."

"What's more valuable than spending time with the ones you love while cleaning the kitchen? A dishwasher doesn't enable you to do that." Gram dried the last dish and changed the subject back to her matchmaking ideas. "When you were young, we called you the princess, Mattie. Whenever anyone came to dinner you would dance in wearing

63

some wild sparkly outfit you'd taken from my closet. Back from my younger days when your grandfather and I would cut a rug."

"What does this have to do with the price of rice in China?" Mattie said, quoting one of her grandmother's famous sayings.

"I'm saying you're a princess in your mind. The reason you haven't married is because you're waiting for Prince Charming to return, and no one else will do. I can't imagine you settling for a man who doesn't make your heart whirl like that smoothie blender you bought me. My opinion is that no one else will ever take Jeff's place in your heart, so what choice do you have?"

Mattie's chest deflated in defeat. What choice did she have indeed? Seeing Jeff look after his nephew would send the normal, rational woman running for cover. A situation that involved addiction, custody hearings, and ugly court battles did not exactly inspire romance. The idea sent a shiver up Mattie's spine, and yet the red flag wasn't hoisted. Mattie only thought more of Jeff for his endearing care of little Kenny.

"Jeff's sister doesn't appear to be doing well, Gram. I think little Kenny will be his priority."

"As it should be, Mattie. That little boy hasn't had an easy time of it. I know his great-grandmother tries to do what she can, but she's getting older. Preschoolers have a lot of energy."

"It would never be just Jeff and I. Even if he were interested in me that way."

"Can you ever settle for coming in third? Behind God? Behind Kenny? You dreamed of being a princess. That life doesn't sound like the one you've dreamed of."

"Gram, you're baiting me. You don't really think I'm still a princess in my mind."

"The only thing that's missing is the tiara, sweetheart."

"You're trying to get me to admit I like Jeff, that his issues are not big enough to squelch my love. But I don't love Jeff, Gram. I don't even know him anymore. It was a child-hood crush that lives on for the moment after seeing he's grown more handsome with age. It's just physical attraction. Certainly not something to build a commitment on." Mattie straightened her shoulders, trying to convince herself she felt nothing. "I don't need a man to complete me, Gram. I am a big girl, a successful artist. How many people make their living doing exactly what they dreamed of? Jeff would be lucky to have me."

"Mattie, who are you trying to convince? I'm convinced, or I wouldn't have set the two of you up."

"Aha! So you admit you set me up."

Gram smiled her secret smile.

"Don't they have shuffleboard or something here to do so you can give up these matchmaking dreams?"

Gram laughed. "If they do, you won't find me there. I have too much interest in great-grandchildren. I figure I'm well on the way with Callie, but my prayer is to leave for heaven with a good number of little hearts for Jesus. I've prayed for their salvation, and I want to meet them before I leave."

"Gram, please. You're going to outlive us all."

"I doubt that, but I am going to live to see my great-grandchildren. I know you think your Gram is just a funny old lady, but I have three successful matches under my belt, sweetheart, and I don't plan to stop until I'm finished. Do you remember *Pride and Prejudice*? Mary and Kitty were left with no marriage prospects. I might have rewritten that book had I been around." Gram shook her head. "To me matchmaking is like the quilting Lorraine Henke does. She cuts all those special shapes and patches them together until the pattern is such that it will be cherished for an heirloom. I think of marriage that way. Those two separate shapes must come together by some careful sewing."

Mattie sighed loudly. "Gram, enough with the romantic analogies. I'm painting Jeff's wall. Let's not read too much into that. He has enough to think about, so leave him be, all right? And I'll try to do the same."

"I hear your tone, Mattie. You're worried I'll scare him off. I'm much more subtle than you give me credit for. Ask your cousins."

Mattie bubbled over with laughter. "Gram, you're about as subtle as a city bus in a backyard!"

"Watch your tongue, little lady." Gram settled into her favorite easy chair and clicked on the television news. "Don't you have a date, Mattie?"

"Don't you?"

"No, I've kept my entire weekend free. I'm having a prayer-a-thon for myself."

"I don't even want to know what you're praying for, so don't tell me. You'll be fasting for the love potion number nine if I'm not careful."

"Mattie, sarcasm is your problem. Sarcasm shows a prideful heart. You can go home and use some prayer yourself."

"You're probably right, Gram." Mattie bent over the easy chair and kissed her grandmother. "Thanks for dinner, Gram. That's something else you might pray for, a man who can cook for me." Mattie made her way toward the door and puckered up to blow her grandmother a good-bye kiss. "Love you, Gram."

"Love you, too, sweetheart. Call me and let me know how Monday goes. I'll be praying."

Mattie knelt in prayer and climbed into bed exhausted and uneasy. Jeff's furrowed brow kept coming to mind. Mattie wondered how much of his high school years had been spent pulling Joan from dangerous situations. Visions of Joan taunting Mattie in the hallway came flooding back.

"Little cheerleader wants to slum with my geek brother. Little cheerleader wants to be worshipped."

The raspy manly voice would never leave Mattie, not for as long as she lived. Guilt rose within her. She'd never shared Christ with Joan, not in all their horrible encounters. Mattie thought about Jeff's abandoning her on prom night and wondered how she'd left him alone to deal with his sister's issues. Mattie had been so oblivious to the burden and instead focused on a lace dress. No wonder he'd lost interest. Mattie's faith had been shallow and merely words.

Nightmares besieged her, and she tossed and turned all night. The memories woke

Mattie with a start. It was then she realized the phone was ringing.

"Hello?" she croaked, her morning voice raw and dry.

"Mattie, it's Jeff. Listen—I'm sorry to call so early, but I'm at the hospital with Joan. She got some bad stuff yesterday and was rushed here. My grandmother has Kenny. She's pretty energetic, but I don't know how long she can keep up with a four-year-old. Can you go by and check on them after church? She's staying home this morning in case anything else happens. I'm sorry. I didn't know of anyone else to call."

Mattie sprang from bed. "Of course. Of course I'll be right over there."

"No need to hurry, Mattie. You know my grandmother—she and yours could outrun any cart on the golf course, if they had to." Jeff forced a laugh, but Mattie could hear the strained nature of his tone. "She lives on Agave Circle, 448."

"Jeff, take down my cell phone in case you need anything. Do you need anything in the hospital?"

"No, thank you. I have my Bible, and I think that's all I'll need for awhile."

The melancholy in Jeff's voice seemed familiar, and Mattie wondered how long he'd been dealing with these issues. Perhaps he wasn't as interested in chess or secondary things in high school as she'd thought. Maybe there was a reason Jeff seemed like an old man, wise beyond his years, in school. Her own obliviousness to the matter and her callousness in chastising him for a high school dance ten years later struck her as the height of selfishness.

"I'm sorry you're dealing with all this, Jeff."

"It's nothing new," he said, his voice absent of feeling. "Joan's been leading this family on a path to the depths since I can remember. The only difference is now she's involving Kenny, and I'm not willing to support that. I've paid for Joan's sins since I can remember; I'm not letting Kenny do the same thing." He paused for a moment. "The doctor's here. Tell my grandmother I'll call her as soon as I have word."

"Jeff!" she rushed before he hung up.

"Yeah?"

"My cell phone number is 555-4488."

"Mattie, look—I appreciate what you're trying to do, but we can handle this. We've been dealing with this longer than you and I have even known each other."

"I know, but something tells me you're tired of dealing with it alone."

He grew quiet, and they both hung up without another word.

Chapter 4

Church was uplifting, but Mattie's mind was elsewhere. She wondered about Jeff and how he was at the hospital and worried about the little ball of energy wearing out his great-grandmother. After the service Mattie quickly drove to Jeff's grandmother's house. She maneuvered through the labyrinth of pink adobes, taking a few wrong turns until she found Agave Circle. She parked alongside the house and ran toward the door.

Helen Weatherly's home looked as if a flash flood had rushed through a toy store and left a wake of toys strewn in chaotic disarray. Helen's face was drawn and anxious, her gray hair still in curlers. "I must look a fright, but I'm so glad to see you, Mattie."

"Where's our little bolt of lightning?" Mattie asked, as she instinctively picked up the maze of toys that led to the boy asleep in a ball on the couch.

"He finally fell asleep watching his train video. He's been up since five a.m., but that didn't seem to deter him. I'm sorry the house looks so bad, but after chasing him I didn't have the strength to bend over and pick all that up. I wanted to."

Mattie smiled and patted Helen's shoulder. "Helen, I don't think I could keep up with his energy. I can't imagine how you did it this long. Why don't you sit down and take a rest? I'll look after him now."

"You always did have the heart of an angel, Mattie. It's too bad Jeff had too much on his plate when it was time to gather you up."

I'm still gatherable, Mattie thought.

As though reading her mind, Helen kept speaking. "I hope there's a chance for Jeff to settle down. He's always taken on too much responsibility, always been an adult. I wish the man would have some fun. I always thought you were the one to bring it to him, Mattie. Maybe I still do."

Mattie laughed. "That's something you have in common with my grandmother."

"Well, you know us old goats. We have too much time on our hands, and we hate to see our loved ones unhappy. Your grandmother and I married too well not to want the same things for you kids."

The door opened, and Jeff filled the doorway. His blue eyes looked tired but animated. When he saw Mattie she thought she saw excitement in those worn eyes. "Mattie, you're still here."

"I just got here, Jeff. It's only noon."

Jeff looked at the sleeping Kenny on the couch. The little boy's knees were tucked under him, and his backside pointed toward the ceiling. "That doesn't look too comfortable, but I might settle for that myself."

"How's Joan?" Helen asked.

Jeff shrugged. "She's fine. That woman is a cat, and she's well past her nine lives." He collapsed into an easy chair. "So, Miss Mattie, what do you say to that lunch I promised you? I missed out on cafeteria food especially for the chance."

Mattie looked toward Kenny. "I was about to give your grandmother a break. She hasn't had one yet."

"Oh, go ahead," Helen insisted. "He'll sleep until at least three now. When Kenny crashes, he crashes but good. Besides, it will do my heart good to see Jeff enjoy himself for a change." Helen crossed her arms, tapping her foot. "He's been an old man too long." She nudged Jeff in the stomach.

Jeff grasped Mattie's hand. He stopped for a moment, staring into her eyes, and she fell silent. What did he hide in that look? What did he possess that hypnotized her so?

"I intend to forget all about my sister for the afternoon. I intend to focus on the beauty of life, of God's gifts for the day." Jeff pulled Mattie forward a bit and led her to his Cherokee with its fancy leather seats and electronic dashboard. She'd seen only the back when they loaded her grandmother's items for the sale.

"Nice car."

"It's my daddy-mobile. I needed something practical for Kenny. I traded in my jeep with the ragtop for something safer."

"You've done a lot for that boy." Mattie slipped into the front seat, and Jeff shut the door behind her and came around to the driver's side.

"That boy has done a lot for me, but I don't want to talk about him. I want to know what you've been doing, Mattie. Are you dating anyone?"

Mattie's ear suddenly itched. "No, I've been a bit consumed with painting. My business is going gangbusters." She saw Jeff look at her questioningly. "And there's no one that's interested me enough to take me away from the palette."

"Do I interest you enough?"

Mattie swallowed over the lump that rose in her throat. Jeff hadn't started the car yet; he still looked at her. His forwardness was completely out of character for the Jeff she remembered. The intensity of his gaze caused confusion, and she didn't know how to answer, but for some reason the truth bubbled out of her.

"Yes," she said. *You interest me enough to make me forget the color wheel altogether,* she added silently.

Jeff started up the car. "Good. That's all I needed to hear. You still like Mexican?"

Mattie grinned. "I love Mexican. What kind of self-respecting Arizonan doesn't?"

"Still like it as hot as it comes?"

"You bet."

"*Muy caliente.* Very hot. I'm glad to know some things never change."

"Me, too," Mattie said, the intent in her voice clear. "Too many things have changed."

"Not the important things, Mattie. You are still beautiful and full of life. God is still sovereign."

"Amen to that last."

"You know, I plan to be there for Kenny as long as I'm able, but if I weren't there, God would raise up somebody else. God doesn't need me. I have to remember that when I'm in such turmoil. He can fix things without Jeff Weatherly."

"What are you saying, Jeff?"

"I'm saying that I have put off courting you for ten years. I'm sorry if that expression sounds dated, but that's exactly what my plans are, Mattie Stevens. To court you until you can't resist me."

"Well, if that includes caliente Mexican food, I fear I'm putty in your hands."

The sound of their laughter mingled together brought tears of joy to Mattie's eyes. She was the princess, and this was her Prince Charming, just as Gram said. Nothing else mattered at the moment.

Once at Pedro's, Mattie felt the lightheartedness she'd felt in high school. She felt proud to be on the arm of Jeff Weatherly and wished he'd understood her fascination with him had been more than a high school crush. His spiritual maturity magnetized her, and she felt his pull stronger than ever. It wasn't her imagination the restaurant patrons stopped eating to watch them walk to their table, and she knew that whatever it was between them other people felt it, too.

Jeff pulled out her chair for her and placed the napkin in her lap. "Mademoiselle."

Mattie giggled. "I believe the word you're looking for is *señorita*."

Jeff cleared his throat. "I'm trying to be classy here—do you mind?" His eyebrows rose in mock annoyance, and the blue of his eyes gleamed, like the brilliant turquoise of the local Indian jewelry.

"I fear it's going to be futile to put on airs while eating chile relleno served muy caliente."

"You remember my order. Well, get a load of this." He lifted his hand for the waitress to come. "Watch the gringo at work." He winked toward Mattie. "*Yo quiero un chile relleno, muy caliente, y un pollo enchilada, muy caliente tambien, y dos Pepsi.*"

Mattie couldn't hold back her smile. "You remembered."

"You know, I never have been able to take another woman out for Mexican food. To watch a woman pick at her meal daintily, eat the tame stuff and complain. It was more than I could bear." He shook his head in apparent disgust. "I lost respect for them. I like a woman who can handle her jalapeños and serranos. Is that too much to ask?"

"Not in Arizona." Mattie winked. "It was all those fancy girls you probably dated back East during college. Fancy girls can't appreciate good Mexican."

"Well, there is no good Mexican food back East." He mumbled under his breath. "I won't comment on the women. I dated very little in college. I don't think I was cut out for the casual relationship. I'm too intense by nature. I've seen too much to make light of dating."

"Is dating something you want? Or something you think our grandmothers want?"

"Both." The waitress brought their sodas and a basket of chips and salsa. "I almost forgot. Can you bring us an extra cup of salsa?" Jeff asked the waitress, picking up a water glass to insinuate size. "My girlfriend here, she kinda hogs it," Jeff whispered aloud. He turned to Mattie and laughed uproariously. The sound was like a pleasant jingle in her ear.

"So now I'm your girlfriend?"

"Hey, it wasn't nice to call my date a piggy. I made myself look good there—don't you think?"

"You are terrible."

"And you love me anyway." Jeff grinned from the side of his mouth, and Mattie had to agree. Who wouldn't love Jeff's easy candor and selfless style? If the woman was out there who could resist him, she'd like to meet her. It was then that Mattie started to giggle aloud. The woman was out there, and she came in the form of her cousin Melissa. The thought struck her as overwhelmingly humorous.

"What's so funny?"

"The idea of you and Mel on a date."

"We never got that far, but I knew I'd get the information I wanted through that date. I'd hear what Mattie Stevens was up to through Mel. That's the only reason I agreed in the first place."

Mattie's eyes thinned. "You're a convincing liar."

Jeff slapped his chest. "I do not lie, Mattie. I would think my AV classes from high school might convince you I never took the date seriously."

"You *are* terrible."

"I'm simply a man who knows what he wants."

Jeff's cell phone rang, and he paused, looking at the number before he answered it. "It's the hospital."

"You have to answer it," Mattie said.

"My life is on hold for my sister. Always. I don't want her to ruin this."

"Jeff, you won't ruin anything with me. It's me, Mattie."

Jeff answered his phone, and his lighthearted countenance changed instantly. "Thank you." He hung up and stared at Mattie. "My sister has run away from the hospital. They don't know if she's strong enough to make it without the IVs they had her on." He shook his head, his teeth clenched.

"Well, we have to go look for her."

Jeff sighed. "I know. Can you ever forgive me?"

"There's nothing to forgive. You go ahead. I'll get our food to go and meet you at your grandmother's."

Jeff dropped a twenty-dollar bill on the table. "I'm sorry, Mattie." He then kissed her on the lips. "Hang in there with me, Mattie. This can't go on forever."

But Mattie thought it could, and yet she hardly cared. A little of Jeff was better than none at all. She'd had ten years to come to that conclusion.

Chapter 5

Monday came, and no sign of Jeff's sister was reported. Mattie loaded her paints into the car and headed out for the long, traffic-laden drive to Scottsdale. Most of her supplies were still in the magnificent hacienda where she'd been working. Mrs. Cox, the home's owner, had allowed Mattie to keep things in the pool house so that transport wouldn't be as difficult. But this Monday morning the drive away from Jeff and Kenny, who needed her support, burdened her heart. Her task of finishing an elaborate mural almost embarrassed her while Jeff searched for his sister, tried to care for his nephew, and held down his job.

The drive went unusually fast, as Mattie's mind flittered in and out of conscious driving. It appeared the car knew the way, regardless. Mrs. Cox was directing some furniture movers as Mattie appeared. She parked her car around back, lest anyone see her tacky economy car in the neighborhood. Mrs. Cox met her at the back door.

"Mattie, darling, you won't believe what's happened."

Try me, Mattie thought sarcastically but smiled instead. "What has happened, Mrs. Cox?"

"Alexa says the ponies on her ceiling scare her. She can't sleep. I've had workmen paint over them, but she still wants the ponies on her wall, so you can get started on that today." Mrs. Cox's thin smile was genuine. The woman had no idea she'd set Mattie's schedule back a week, and Mattie thought she would burst into tears right there. She felt her own lip quiver. A week might cost her the next job or, worse yet, Jeff's extra room for Kenny.

With uncharacteristic boldness Mattie spoke. "Mrs. Cox, I will have to come back to do the ponies again. I have other clients waiting for my services." Mattie flipped open her ragged paper calendar while Mrs. Cox put her hands on her hips.

"This is ridiculous. Your other clients will have to wait. I have you now, and that's the way it works. You finish your job for me first."

Mattie tried quickly to calculate if she could afford to drop the job and take only the advance she'd received. Figures of her car payment floated through her head then her reputation. Would Mrs. Cox tell her friends Mattie was unreliable? Or would her waiting clients be more of a problem?

"Mrs. Cox, I'm sorry, but I was scheduled to finish up today, and my murals are highly sought after during the summer when schedules are easier to manage." Mattie squared her shoulders. "Alexa can wait for me to paint her ponies, or I can give you the names of some other artists I could recommend."

Mrs. Cox inhaled like some kind of zoo animal, with depth and snarl. "Mattie, I told my husband this house would be done by a certain date. I've given you every allowance—even let you keep the paints in my pool house. Surely you owe me something akin to finishing the job I paid you to do."

Mattie wavered. She hated to let anyone down. Yet the employer had technically only paid for the supplies, not the work. And Mattie had done the work.

Mrs. Cox's phone rang inside the house, and the waif-like woman walked away in her black capris, looking very much like the long limbs of a spider easing across a sparse desert.

"Hello?" Mrs. Cox paused. "Yes, she's here, but she's here to work, Mr. Weatherly. I suggest you find another time to arrange a date. Humph." The click of the phone resonated in Mattie's head, and Mrs. Cox came back to the door. "I'd appreciate it if you would tell your friends this is a private number, and you are working here. I am not your secretary."

Mattie's cheeks heated. "I need to use your phone, Mrs. Cox. I gave that number to my grandmother in case of an emergency only."

"Anything you have to say to Mr. Weatherly can wait until you're off my clock."

Mattie could barely breathe she was so nervous. And angry. Jeff would never interrupt her work for something trivial. "If you won't let me use your phone, Mrs. Cox, I have no choice but to find a payphone. My cell phone doesn't work out here."

"Mattie, my daughter wants her ponies. I hate to be an ogre, but you're leaving me little choice. You were contracted to do a job."

"A job which I did."

"Not to my satisfaction." Mrs. Cox opened a drawer and pulled out her contract. A contract Mattie wrote and felt confident about.

"I have to go." Mattie threw what supplies were hers into the car and rushed toward town to find a payphone. Mrs. Cox screamed something at Mattie while the car left the driveway. Mattie considered herself fortunate she hadn't heard the barb.

She wound around the desert roads and pulled into a mall parking lot. She ran toward the payphone, beads of sweat building quickly. She dialed her calling card into the phone and punched Jeff's cell phone number.

Jeff answered on the first ring. "Hello?"

"Jeff, it's Mattie. You called me?"

A long sigh erupted. "Oh, Mattie, I had to tell someone. My sister called the authorities. She's left custody to me. She's abandoned Kenny. I'll have to go through all the channels to make it final, but I need you here to pray with me. To help me with God's will."

"I don't understand, Jeff. I thought you wanted custody."

"Not this way, Mattie. How do I tell Kenny his mother isn't coming home?" Jeff paused for a moment. "I can't even fathom what this will do to him. He's so much older in his mind than a four year old."

"But he is a four year old, Jeff, and you need to let him rest in his childhood. Is your sister all right?"

"She's okay," Jeff practically spat out. "She met up with some of her biker buddies, in some bar nearby, and took off for California. Says she wants to be free again and that her new man doesn't want Kenny around."

"Her new man? Jeff, she's been gone two days."

"It's the drugs talking, Mattie. Don't try to make sense of it. I want to be with you, to pray with you, and just have your support. Can you take the day off?"

"I think I'll have a little time, Jeff. Mrs. Cox probably won't want me back."

"I'll pay you whatever she was paying you to paint Kenny's room. Then we're together, and you're not out a job."

"I appreciate the offer, but I couldn't take your money. Especially not in a situation like this. I'm a Christian. I did what I vowed to do for Mrs. Cox, and I tried to please her, but it's over now."

"Meet me at my grandmother's, will you? I'm going over there to tell Kenny now that his mother is gone for awhile."

"I'm praying, Jeff."

Jeff explained everything to Kenny, and with adult awareness the child nodded and complied. The ease at which he took the news only reiterated that Jeff was doing the right thing. He'd come back to Heaven with two goals: to help Kenny grow up and to court the only woman he'd ever loved. Now that he was ready to start a family, not as he'd once planned, but a family just the same, he needed to let Mattie understand his love.

The last thing he wanted was for Mattie to think he needed a mom for Kenny and she would do. He questioned God's timing on his family's chaos and prayed with his whole heart that his sister would get help. Jeff's grandmother prepared hot dogs for their lunch, and it wasn't long before Mattie's car pulled up in the driveway. He walked to her car and opened the door. Mattie's fresh complexion and sage green eyes glistened under the hot Arizona sun. Her freshness was so inviting; she was like the morning dew on a summer peach.

Jeff clutched her in an embrace. "Mattie, thank you for coming."

Mattie talked into Jeff's shoulder, muffling her voice yet bringing him an intimacy with her he'd dreamed of countless nights. "I know you wouldn't have called if it wasn't bad."

He pulled away; his heart was caught in his throat. How could he be so happy and yet so miserable at once?

"It's hard to imagine Joanie will ever turn away from drugs now. If Kenny wasn't enough to make her want to change, what else is there?"

"There's God. And you're underestimating Him. Joan's only been away from Kenny for a weekend. Things could change overnight."

"Let's go grab breakfast. Kenny is at the pool with my grandmother and a group of her friends. They'll be gone until lunch, and we have yet to finish our date."

Mattie looked down at her paint-laden shorts and T-shirt. She brushed her hair from her face, and the motion moved Jeff to his core. "Do you think I'm dressed okay to go out? Should I go home and change first?"

"No!" Jeff said too abruptly. "We have tried this date twice before, and today I'm going to finish it. You would look beautiful in a garbage bag, and we're going out." He grabbed her arm and his keys, and they were soon headed toward town.

Jeff pulled into a small pink shopping center and parked near a natural-type breakfast spot. He mentally thought about the meetings he was missing today and which clients would have to be rearranged. But he needed this. Mattie was one of the main reasons he'd come back to Heaven, and for one day he intended to show her his seriousness.

"Do you like Angel's?" Jeff asked, pointing toward the restaurant where he could already smell the strong cinnamon from the signature tea.

"I love it. Breakfast out is such an indulgence. I can't remember the last time I did it." Mattie licked her upper lip. "Here I thought I'd be spending my day painting a ceiling for a spoiled child, and instead I'm eating breakfast out with an incredibly gorgeous man. Life holds so many wonderful surprises."

The smile on her face appeared angelic, and he was reminded of how Mattie enjoyed the simple pleasures in life. How her freshness and enthusiasm permeated everything she did. The energy within her filled him with a joy he couldn't describe. It made him thank God for the privilege of being beside her. He forgot about work and all the bullet points on his to-do calendar. He sucked in a deep breath and focused on what the Lord had given him today.

"I'm sorry, Jeff. I'm rambling. I suppose things aren't looking so cheery for you."

"On the contrary. For once, things are looking grand."

"What do you do now for fun? Do you still play chess?"

"Not too often. Sometimes I'll find a willing partner at Grandma's social club, but I play rugby on Saturdays. I learned in college, and it just stuck."

"Rugby? Isn't that a little violent?"

Jeff thought about all the nicks and scratches he'd endured. Not to mention the broken wrist in college. "Not all that violent. Active, and it certainly gets my mind off the numbers. I find that with accounting I don't have the mind to enjoy chess as I once did. What about you? What do you do for fun?"

"My job is fun. I get to paint every day, which is pure joy for me. In my spare time I enjoy changing my apartment around quite a bit, depending on which color I'm in the mood for. But mostly I read voraciously. My library card looks like my cousin Callie's credit card. It's worn out."

His eyes focused on her beautiful, full lips as they spoke. How was it he'd never realized how intelligent Mattie was? That she was capable of doing anything—yet she wanted to do something creative like painting? He chastised himself for always thinking he was so brilliant and for seeing Mattie as the beautiful cheerleader, instead of the multifaceted mind and pure heart that she was. What Mattie possessed, Jeff wanted to take hold of for himself. To look at life with the glass half full for a change. He wondered who indeed the smartest kid in school was. He wasn't it, or he wouldn't be living the same life he'd lived for twenty years. He'd be playing more rugby, enjoying more time with Mattie.

"What do you like to read, Mattie?"

"Oh, everything! I love Greek literature, and I love the latest murder mysteries and the biographies on the bestseller lists. For me, reading isn't about a style; it's about grasping as much information as I can and trying to see how other people see the world. Why they don't have Christ in their lives and what types of things stop them."

"It all sounds fascinating. Do you have anything you'd recommend?"

"I couldn't begin to give you one title, but I'm happy to share my personal library with you. That's another hobby, by the way. I've learned to install my own bookcases."

"Mattie, is there anything you don't do?"

"I don't really like to cook. I can—Gram taught me—but it's not my favorite thing in the world. I love to see what other people cook, though." Mattie held up her menu. "Did you see this omelet with Brie in it? Doesn't that sound heavenly?"

"I'm more of a pancake man, myself." He winked at her, and the grin she returned poured over his heart like the freshest, thickest maple syrup in his college state of Vermont.

"I'm sure those are wonderful, too." She nodded.

"Thank you for taking the day off for me. You don't know how I needed this."

"I believe I do. You can't do everything for everyone else without refreshing at church and being around friends who support you. It's the way God made us. He wants us in fellowship."

"Why do you make me feel like a lightweight spiritually?"

Her smile faltered, and she shook her head. "I didn't mean to do that, Jeff. I'm no spiritual giant. I'm weak myself—that's how I know these things."

"Mattie Stevens, I never stopped loving you. And I never will."

Mattie dropped her spoon in her tea with a clank. She blinked rapidly but said nothing in return, and Jeff hoped he hadn't ruined their future together by scaring her away. She grasped Jeff's hand but said nothing. She only blinked her wide blue eyes at him until he thought he might steal her away to Las Vegas and get the wedding over with at once. No one would ever touch his heart like this. If only Mattie felt the same way, but her thoughts remained hidden throughout breakfast.

Kenny's angry gait marched out the front door. His arms swung straight out to the side. Without warning he hauled off and punched Mattie in the thigh. "You're the reason my mom left. She didn't like you." Kenny's brows were furrowed in an angry V-shape.

"Kenny!" Jeff was in shock. "Mattie? Are you all right?"

"Yes, I'm all right." She knelt beside Kenny and tried to speak with him at his level, but rage engulfed the little boy, and Jeff had to stop Kenny from hitting Mattie again.

"Kenny! What are you doing? Mattie is my friend, and we don't treat anyone that way."

"She stole my mommy!" The venom with which he said the words flustered Jeff. He didn't know much about parenting, but he knew this was not normal behavior for a four-year-old. Yet he felt powerless about what to do.

"Mattie did no such thing. Now you apologize to my friend," Jeff finally said.

"No!" Kenny crossed his arms defiantly across his chest.

"Kenny."

"No!"

Mattie shifted uncomfortably, and her wide eyes blinked in obvious confusion. "Jeff, this is going to take some time. Why don't you call me when things calm down?"

Jeff looked to Mattie and then to Kenny. He closed his eyes and sighed before facing the two people he loved. One much too young to understand, and the other not believing his heart.

"No, we're going to settle this. Kenny, this is my girlfriend. I love her, and you will, too, once you get to know her."

"I hate her!" Kenny stamped his foot vehemently.

Mattie put her hand on Jeff's shoulder, and it took all his willpower not to embrace her again. The pain in her eyes forced him back. "Mattie, please don't leave. We have to discuss this. We have to discuss our future."

"Not today we don't. Thank you for breakfast." She placed a kiss on his cheek, near his lips. "Kenny needs you right now."

"Stop talking about me! Don't say my name! I hate you!" Kenny spat out.

If Jeff had said such things as a child, his father would have reminded him painfully not to do so again. But Kenny needed unconditional love right now. "Kenny! That's enough. You are hurting. We know that, but it does not excuse rudeness. Now go in the house and see Great-Grandma for awhile. We'll talk about this later."

Kenny stomped away but turned before reaching the door and stuck his tongue out toward Mattie.

"Well, that went well." Mattie smiled slightly.

Jeff threw up his hands. "Mattie, I'm sorry. I'm a terrible parent. I don't know why I was thinking I could take this on." He rubbed his forehead to stop the throbbing.

"Jeff, this isn't ideal, but Kenny will adjust. You have to let him know he comes first."

"But he doesn't come first. My wife comes first. That's how I was raised."

Mattie stepped back, her face as pale as the jimsonweed. "I'm not your wife, Jeff. We had a great time, but you obviously have bigger priorities, and I don't want to get in the way of those."

"Mattie, you don't understand. I planned this before Kenny and I were an option. I came home for two reasons, and you were one of them." Jeff hated the desperation he felt, and he could have kicked himself for not being forthright with Mattie. Now he sounded like some hopeless loser in search of anyone for a mate.

"But I wasn't the only one, Jeff. And one of those reasons needs you more than the other." She stood on her tiptoes and kissed his cheek again. "I love you, too, if it's any consolation."

"Consolation? No, it isn't a consolation. Mattie, what can I do? That boy needs me, but there's only one woman for me. I knew that ten years ago."

"I knew it ten years ago as well, but now I'm not so sure. Love shouldn't be this complicated. This much of a game. I loved you, Jeff, and you left town without a word."

"Mattie, I explained all that. Why must we go back to that again and again?"

"Then let me explain something to you. You're a great man, Jeff, but my life was so peaceful until you came. I don't think love should be this much turmoil." Mattie grabbed his hand then climbed into her hatchback. "I have to get back to Scottsdale and apologize to Mrs. Cox."

"Mattie, wait—"

But she closed the door. Jeff saw the tears in her eyes as she backed down the driveway, and he kicked the grass in frustration. He closed his eyes in prayer, asking the Lord to show him the way. He listened to silence for a moment before calling out to Mattie's taillights. "This isn't what you want, Mattie! I'll do whatever it takes this time."

Chapter 6

Mattie couldn't see the road through her veil of tears, so she pulled to the side. Staring out at the expanse of Sonoran desert, Mattie wondered if such a barren life lay before her. Would she ever find a man who wanted her? Not to be the mother of an adopted child or selected because of proximity and familiarity, but because someone sought her out to love her truly?

She knew better than to hope. Hope pulled everything you had within you and lifted you up, not to have you drop back in a deep pit of despair. She laughed through her tears. Gram always said she was the dramatic one. Yet her mood couldn't be helped today. Everyone else managed to find love. Callie, Mel, and Chelsea had no problems with Gram's arrangements.

While life rushed at her like a monsoon thunderstorm or a drowning flash flood, Mattie watched idly as her loved ones gripped all life had to offer. They were the desert flowers on the levee, the spot of rain in the midst of drought, while she waited for a small refreshing drop.

She could turn the car around, she reasoned. She could tell Jeff she loved him solely and that she didn't want to think about a future without him. But what kind of Christian stole the only parent a child would have? Kenny's behavior told Mattie how much he needed security. To know Kenny was first would haunt Mattie like the night when her prom came and went. Second to chess. Second to Kenny. Always second to something.

Mattie had no business messing with that arrangement. Kenny needed Jeff. Mattie did fine on her own, and she guessed that's how God wanted it. She wiped the tears from her eyes and headed to Gram's.

Gram would know what to do, and if she didn't, Mattie could drown herself in chocolate chip cookies and avoid thinking of the subject. Revert to her childhood and be happy with a tall glass of milk and Tollhouse joy.

Mrs. Cox and her "unfinished" job fell to a distant memory. Mattie wouldn't go groveling for the job she didn't need nor agree to do. God had ordered the day differently, and Mattie tried to find peace in that.

Gram's pink apartment shone brightly in the hot afternoon sun. The apartment looked sparse and abandoned, and Mattie guessed Gram was off to internet class or the like. She knocked on the door and was surprised when Gram answered, a look of shock covering the weathered face.

"Mattie, what on earth? Why aren't you at work?"

"Mrs. Cox—" Mattie started her explanation but quickly resorted to tears. "Oh, Gram." She clutched her grandmother and felt the older woman's comforting arms around her. A cave of shelter underneath a late summer storm.

"What's the matter, sweetie? Is it something with Jeff?"

Mattie sniffled and nodded her head through her violent inhaling of jagged, little breaths. "I'm never going to get married. I'm an old maid!" Mattie wailed. "I won't even be a bridesmaid anymore, because everyone I know is married."

Gram pulled away and smiled. She shook her head, "Mattie, Mattie. Come and sit in the kitchen. I'll get you some cookies."

"I know what you're thinking. I'm the dramatic one."

"You should have gone to Hollywood." Gram lifted her eyebrows and led Mattie to the kitchen. "Now tell your Gram what could be so bad. Is Jeff marrying someone else?"

"Worse. He has custody of Kenny now. His sister ran off to California and left that poor boy with no one but Jeff and his grandmother. What kind of Christian would I be if I stood in the way of that? The boy needs a home."

"Mattie, did Jeff say he didn't want to pursue a relationship with you because of Kenny?"

"Well, no, but—"

"Mattie, aren't most parents married?"

"Yes, but this situation is different. Kenny hates me. He told me so himself." Mattie crossed her arms.

"And how old is this child?"

"He's four." Mattie sat up straighter, to make her argument more effective. Gram had that way of making something so real to Mattie seem ridiculous. "But you don't understand, Gram. Jeff came back to Heaven to care for Kenny. Kenny's the priority. I'll never be a priority. I'll always come third. After God and after Kenny."

"Honey, Jeff is not willing to sacrifice everything for the boy. Besides, the boy will need a mother. Have you thought of that?"

"A mother he likes, maybe. But not me."

Gram set a glass of milk on the table. "I'm going to tell you this once. It may sound harsh, but I think you need to hear it, Princess. You, unlike the rest of us, are a princess. You've always had people bow down before your beauty. You've had whatever you wanted to be disposed of as you felt led. But Jeff's the one thing you've wanted that you couldn't control. Go ahead—tell me it's not true. I dare you."

Mattie pondered the thought for awhile, unwilling to admit it might be true.

"You're afraid if you admit how deeply you love Jeff, and if he doesn't love you back in the same way, you'll be made a fool of. Am I right?"

Mattie's jaw twitched. How she hated that her grandmother saw right through her. How she hated that it was truly pride that held her back from Jeff. Not her sacrificial love for a child. That's what she wanted it to be, but it wasn't that. She was afraid of coming in second.

"You lost him once to pride, Mattie. Will you let it happen again?"

Mattie steeled herself, pushing away the plate of cookies her grandmother had set down. "How can you say that, Gram? Jeff left me all those years ago. I didn't control anything."

"You know, you've been telling that story so long that you actually believe it, don't you?"

"It can hardly be disputed. I'm still in Heaven, aren't I? I went to junior college here. I've made my living locally, painting rich people's houses. I didn't go off to some fancy school and grow away from this place."

Gram sat on the couch and smirked.

"No, no, Gram. You are not right about this. Jeff did leave me, and he'll do it again."

"Jeff didn't leave you, Mattie. You never gave that boy an inch. If he wasn't at your beck and call, like the night of the prom, you decided he wasn't worthy. This woe-is-me stuff might work on some of your friends, or even your cousins, but I know better. I know that man's heart, Mattie, and I know yours. Now swallow your pride and go tell that man how you really feel. The boy will get over it, and he will love you as his mother."

Mattie shook her head. "No, I don't think so. He's had an earful from his real mother. She probably told him what to think of me."

"You're a smart girl, Mattie. You'll figure it out. He's four. I have no doubt that you're brighter than he is. You probably have more up your sleeve to win his heart. Now quit being a spoiled brat and go find Jeff. He needs your support, not your games."

"Gram!"

"You won't get any sympathy from me, Mattie. You've been single long enough so that I know it's your choice to remain that way. You rarely accept dates, and if you do, you've never accepted a second date that I know of. I've lived a long time, and I'm no fool. If I'd played this many games with your grandpa, he'd have married someone else. And that's the truth. Now the only thing you have to lose is that pride of yours. Go tell Mr. Weatherly how you feel before he decides you're too high maintenance." Gram shoved a cookie into her mouth.

Visions of Mrs. Cox floated through Mattie's mind. The desperately flawed, rich woman who never had enough, who thought the sun rose and set against the red rocks for her alone. Was that how Mattie appeared to her cousins? Was she waiting for someone who didn't exist to ride off into the pink romantic sunset? The possibility tore Mattie's heart to shreds. Jeff deserved better. All the people in Mattie's life deserved better.

"Thank you, Gram. It's been an enlightening afternoon. I don't like it, but I suppose I have it coming."

"I love you, sweetie, and I'm praying for you. Now go."

Mattie grabbed a cookie and started for the door. "You have a funny way of showing love, Gram. But all I can say is I'm happy you like me, or I don't think I could take what you've said."

Jeff cleared the lunch dishes from the table and set Kenny in front of a TV cartoon for an afternoon break. Jeff had a major presentation for a client due, and yet his mind was full of racing, more pressing thoughts. Where was Mattie? Would he see her again? Or had his profession of love scared her away for good? How did he let Kenny know the boy was loved, without giving up everything he'd worked so hard for? Without giving up Mattie? He felt so powerless, and it drove him crazy. With work he just took what he wanted: promotions, clients—it all came easy to him. But Mattie was another story. She confounded him like nothing else.

His grandmother came up behind him at the sink and stroked his back.

"Kenny will adjust. He's adjusted to far worse."

"I scared Mattie off for good this time."

"I don't think so, honey. Mattie's a good girl. Give her some time, and she'll realize this may be the life God planned for her."

"What if it isn't?"

"It has to be hard for someone to accept an instant family. You'll find the right girl to share your life if it's not Mattie. Kenny can't take over every part of you, Jeff. Don't let him. He's a hurting little boy, and if I had the vigor, I'd take him myself. But I don't. He's blessed to have you and that you chose a different path from his mother."

"I'll need to find a day care center for him."

Grandma nodded. "He's been in day care for some time now. It might be a little out of your way, but I think it's best to keep him in familiar surroundings. It might not be the best situation, but being born into an illegitimate family, with a drug-addict mother, has its consequences, unfortunately."

"I wanted to provide the best for him," Jeff said. "I wanted Mattie to be his mother. I wanted to give him a little brother or sister."

"Did you ask the Lord about any of that? Or Mattie for that matter?"

The doorbell rang, interrupting a conversation Jeff didn't want to have anyway. He dried his dishpan hands and lamented how his life had become distinctly not his own.

He opened the door to Mattie's wide blue eyes. He watched her swallow then search for the right words. He couldn't hide his own smile.

"You—"

"No, I'm going to say what I came to say, Jeff." Mattie's chin locked, and she looked the epitome of seriousness, but Jeff had to say something.

"I was just going to tell you that you have cookie crumbs on your face. Have you been to your Gram's?" He brushed the crumbs from her lip and kept his hand there to feel the current between them. She closed her eyes and kissed his fingers as softly as a pink cloud in the magnificent Arizona sky.

She giggled and brushed self-consciously at her face. The sweeping tendrils that surrounded her face moved easily from around her chin to behind her neck. Jeff took in the sight as though he'd never seen it before.

"How about another date, Mattie? Just you and me out on the town like normal people."

"Normal people? What are those?"

"Maybe I assumed too much, and maybe you don't want to be part of my very messed-up life. But if you do—if you're willing—I'll make it worth your while."

"But Kenny—"

"Kenny is a child, and we're not talking about him. This is about you and me. We deserve the chance, Mattie. I'll be everything I can to Kenny, but I've saved the best for you, if you're willing."

Mattie's cheeks were flushed. "I—" she stammered. "I would be first?"

"Yes, you'll be first. Come to dinner with me and let me prove it. I have so many things I want to tell you. Go home and put on your best dress. You and I are going to be the talk of the restaurant."

Mattie didn't speak, but her wide eyes did so for her.

"Can you do that for me?" Jeff asked, unsure if he'd been understood.

Mattie nodded. "Yes, I'll be ready by—"

"Six. I'll keep Kenny up all day, and my grandmother can put him down at seven. That's only one hour, and they can watch a video tonight. I'll run him ragged on the soccer field after his quiet time."

"Jeff, really?"

"I want nothing more than to court you as I intended to court you, Mattie Stevens. You deserve nothing less. You've had a whole lot less." He bent down and placed a light kiss on her nose. "See you at six, at your house."

She nodded then turned on one toe and skipped to her car. Jeff's heart followed at a rapid pace.

Chapter 7

Mattie's shower felt cleansing and more refreshing than normal. She emerged from the steamy stall ready for anything. The emotional strain of the day had been far more stifling than the Arizona summer heat.

In a single day Mattie had managed to lose a job, lose a boyfriend, and get a four-year-old to hate her with the venom of a heat-seeking rattlesnake. Now, as if all the bad events had simply evaporated, she dressed for the man she loved. She had a new determination not to play childish games, but to speak her heart and take the consequences, whatever they might be. With a light step she slid into some strappy heels she'd been saving for the next wedding. Which, undoubtedly, would be someone else's.

Mattie dried her hair with a brush and a hair dryer, which was a rarity in dry Arizona. Usually before she could get the dryer out, her hair hung limp and set in its ways. With a complete lack of humidity her full dark hair barely made it past ten minutes of being wet. She patted a little powder on her face and a dab of blush and applied a sheer lip gloss. She smiled to herself in the mirror feeling that tonight she and Jeff could overcome anything.

Mattie went to the closet and looked for something to wear to match her great new sandals. Being a casual person and most of her clothing being strewn with dried paint of various colors, Mattie looked in her church clothes for something appropriate. She decided on a gray linen sheath that brought out the blue of her eyes and added a Navajo silver bangle bracelet with touches of turquoise. She spent the final minutes straightening up the living room and fluffing her pillows. When the doorbell rang, Mattie was ripe with anticipation, and she was not disappointed.

Jeff's appearance at her door made her stomach flip like those early days in high school. He wore a pair of khaki linen pants and a white dress shirt, and he looked as casual as he looked good.

He shook his head, letting his gaze fall to the ground and land on her new shoes. "You look incredible, Mattie."

"I was about to say the same thing to you."

"I like the shoes." He raised and lowered his eyebrows.

Mattie smiled to herself, lifting one foot off the ground. "I'm glad I finally had a place to wear them."

"We've established we look good." Jeff laughed. "Now we need a place to go that's worthy of our dressing up."

"I agree." Mattie playfully stuck her chin toward the sky. She sighed. "But what place is worthy of such glamour? Does Heaven have such a place?"

"Of course. Les Saisons. We'll see what the country-club set enjoys."

"Les Saisons? Do you know—I've never been."

"Then you've obviously never been courted properly here. It's a good thing I came home. These men are oafs here in Heaven." Jeff feigned disgust. "It's a travesty, I tell you. Such beauty wasting away."

"It is a good thing you came home, Jeff. The women of Heaven don't know what they've been missing."

Jeff shook his head. "Oh, this deal isn't good for anyone. There's only one woman who can redeem such a courting coupon." Jeff winked, and Mattie's stomach tumbled in her exhilaration.

Mattie closed the door behind them, and Jeff took her hand. He opened the door of his Cherokee and waited for her to be seated before shutting it behind her. An inner grin spread throughout Mattie's frame. She was with Jeff Weatherly, and things felt right. Troubles with Kenny and Joan seemed to slip away. Tonight was theirs alone, and she would do everything in her power to forget all the outside people who threatened to take away the only man she ever loved. She would enjoy what she had of him, however long it lasted.

Jeff drove slowly to the restaurant, as if he were trying to take in every moment. He looked over to her often, smiling as though he knew some secret. The restaurant was tucked away on a long drive near one of Heaven's most prestigious golf clubs. Everything reeked of money. From the bright splash of green against the taupe color of the desert to the expensive foreign cars in the parking lot, this was where Heaven's richest came to play. Mattie suddenly panicked, thinking about the college girls Jeff had probably dated in college. Would they know how to act in such a place?

Mattie fretted she might use the wrong fork or, worse, appear to be the Arizona native she was. She pressed her lips together before getting the courage to ask about the restaurant. "Will I be dressed okay?"

Jeff pulled the vehicle into a slot and put his hand over hers. "I'm sorry, Mattie. Does this place make you feel uncomfortable? I can cancel the reservation, and we can go somewhere else." He turned off the car and looked straight at her. "Where would you like to go?"

Mattie rubbed the back of her neck. "Jeff, I'm not like those college girls you've dated. I don't know about French food or the difference between grape juice and an expensive bottle of wine."

Jeff laughed. "Mattie, I don't drink. Nothing's changed there. I brought you out here to impress you, and all I've done is make you a nervous wreck. Look at you—you're shaking."

Mattie slouched down in the seat. "Oh, no, there's Mrs. Cox! What is she doing way out here?"

"Who's Mrs. Cox?"

"She's the woman I painted the ponies for. They scared her daughter, and so she had a painter cover everything on the ceiling, and now she wants me to do the walls again."

"Well, I'm not going to cover for you if you're scaring small children." Jeff winked. "Seriously, Mattie, I'd take you anywhere you wanted to go, but you need to stop separating yourself from the wealthy. God didn't give you a spirit of fear."

"Oh, sure—quote Scripture at me. Make me feel guilty for not wanting to indulge in an expensive meal."

"We're going in," Jeff said with authority, as if they were talking about fighting some sort of battle. Mattie could almost hear the marching music. Jeff came around and opened her door and held out his hand. She forced herself to remember this was Jeff, and he was the same person she'd always known. Even with his fancy education and advanced degrees.

Once they entered the restaurant, she heard the quiet tinkling of silverware and hushed conversation. It was almost like entering a cathedral. The maitre d' gave them a quiet corner table with a view of the extensive golf links and called Jeff "Dr. Weatherly."

Mattie laughed at the table. "Did you tell him you were a doctor for a better table?"

"I am a doctor, Mattie. I have my doctorate in economics. I just don't use the title very often."

Mattie felt faint. Jeff was nothing as she remembered. Everything in his life was complicated and beyond her, and she felt like a country bumpkin beside him. She fanned herself with the leather menu and took a quick sip of water. She got caught up in the lemon, which had a tiny net wrapped around it to keep the seeds from falling in the water.

"I think we should go," Mattie said.

"Mattie." Jeff's low tone was that of a stern parent. "You belong here. You belong anywhere you want to be. I brought you here to try the lobster bisque, which I know you will love. I'm not asking you to live this way. I like Mexican food, too, but this night is special. Let me make it special for us."

Mrs. Cox suddenly appeared at the side of their table. "Mattie, is that you?"

"Yes, Mrs. Cox. How are you?"

"I'm so glad you're here. I want my husband to talk some sense into you. There are no other artists. I'm sure you know that, which is the reason for your attitude, but I want you to finish that room. You don't make your murals kitschy or something that will be out of style in a year. We want that for our home. Something classic."

"Very well, Mrs. Cox. I'll check my calendar on Monday and get back to you. We'll work something out."

Mrs. Cox exhaled audibly. "Wonderful. I'm sorry for the way I treated you, Mattie. I was worried what my husband would say about more workmen in the house. He so likes his privacy." Mrs. Cox said "pri-vi-cee," and Mattie had to contemplate what she meant for a moment.

"That's understandable, Mrs. Cox. Privacy is a very important state. Now if you'll excuse us, this is my date, Dr. Weatherly, and I'm on his clock now." Mattie suppressed a grin as the woman walked away, and she noticed that Jeff shook his head ever so slightly.

Jeff leaned in toward her, and she could feel the warmth of his breath. "You are incorrigible."

Mattie giggled and covered her lips with her fingers. "I didn't think that doctor bit would come in so handy so quickly. This is fun."

"So I guess it doesn't make you uncomfortable anymore."

"Gracious, no, Dr. Weatherly. I'm quite enjoying it." Mattie stuck her chin toward the sky. "I'm seeing a doctor."

"Mattie Stevens, you are trouble, and the worst of it is, you know it. And enjoy it. Do you want me to order for you?"

"Nothing weird. I want to know everything I'm eating. No snails or anything like that." The tension in her shoulders eased, and she relaxed against the high-back chair. She might actually start to enjoy this good life.

"I'll find you the French equivalent of the chicken enchilada. Deal?"

"Deal."

The courses for dinner kept coming, and Mattie thought she'd explode until she saw dessert. Then she had a whole new outlook on hunger. Scanning the tray the waiter brought, she had a terrible time deciding.

"What is this?" she asked, pointing to one.

"Crème Caramel," the waiter said.

Mattie leaned into Jeff and whispered, "It looks just like flan."

"That's basically what it is. That's how I knew you'd like it. I didn't think you'd like the soufflé as much, and it cost twice as much."

Mattie thinned her eyes. "Ever the economist."

Jeff leaned in on his elbow and watched her eat the luscious dessert. "You are so beautiful, Mattie. I can't believe I'm sitting here with you now."

She lost all interest in dessert. The sweetness of Jeff's words was far superior to anything with calories in it. She placed the fork on the plate and took his hand across the table. "I feel the same, Jeff. That I'm so fortunate to be here, that I waited so long for this moment."

"Do you remember in the Bible when the servant is sent out to find a wife for Isaac—and the man prays that the woman for his master will bring water? And Rebekah is there?"

"Yes." Mattie nodded.

"I prayed that, if I came back and you were still available, I would take it as a sign from God." Jeff knelt on the floor beside her and took both of her hands. Two violinists came behind him and quietly played romantic music on their stringed instruments. Jeff took a small blue velvet case from his pocket, and Mattie's fingers flew to her mouth.

She shook her head, unable to believe what was happening.

"Mattie Stevens, you make the world turn for me. You make me excited to be back in Heaven. You make me remember all I lost when I left this town. You are the woman God created for me. I know it in my heart." Jeff opened the little box, and a sparkling diamond the size of a small marble glistened toward her. "Will you do me the honor of becoming my wife?"

Chapter 8

Mattie looked at the ring then into Jeff's aqua-blue eyes. Her first thought was how she wanted her future children to have those eyes, but then she thought of the ring and its enormous size. She would be a wealthy wife. She would have a four-year-old right away. Everything in her life would change for Jeff Weatherly. Yet her mouth betrayed all these objections.

"Yes, Jeff. Yes, I will marry you."

A spattering of applause followed, and she looked around to see the patrons smiling at them. He lifted her chin and kissed her lightly. "When?"

She looked self-consciously at the violinists and wondered if she heard right over their romantic squealing. "When?"

"When."

"I guess when the church will marry us." *Let your yes be yes.* Those words haunted her at the moment. Was she ready to make such a big commitment? Such a change in her life? Yes, she loved Jeff, but Kenny still despised her. Mattie knew nothing of parenting, and trading in her paintbrush for baking cookies scared her feverishly.

Jeff took her arm and led her from the restaurant. Once in the car she felt herself exhale. *Oh, Lord, help me. What am I doing? Is it enough to love this man?* Although she'd been in love with Jeff since she was sixteen, how much of that was real? And how much was the imaginary hero she'd created for herself in her mind? She'd known he had his doctorate for less than two hours. What else didn't she know? She needed to pray.

"Jeff, I am so flattered. I am so incredibly happy and the idea of being your wife sends shivers down my spine—"

"But?"

Mattie took a deep breath. "But this is all happening so fast. I'm worried we don't know the new Mattie and Jeff well enough yet."

Jeff nodded, pursing his lips together in obvious thought. "I completely understand. But, Mattie, one question."

"Yes?"

"Have you ever known me to do anything lightly? Anything by the seat of my pants?"

"Only play in a certain chess match that changed your plans for our senior prom."

Immediately she wished she could take her accusatory words back.

"I prayed long and hard about that night, Mattie. And I've prayed even harder about this. I bought this ring before I came home to Arizona. I knew in my heart we were meant to be together, and when I found out you were still free, I knew God thought so too."

His certainty scared her. Mattie couldn't remember being certain about anything except salvation. Even now she wondered if she should have become more educated. Would her painting business have been more successful if she were a better manager? These thoughts and doubts plagued Mattie. She tried to focus, to think what else might come along that was better than this offer. An offer from the man she loved. That old saying haunted her: *Marry in haste, repent at leisure.*

"May I remind you, Mattie—you said yes."

"I did, didn't I?"

Jeff laughed. "Relax, Mattie. I'm teasing. This ring belongs to you. If you don't feel you're ready to wear it yet, I'll keep it for you until such a time comes." Jeff reached for the ring, and Mattie felt a surge of anger.

"Don't you touch that ring!" She raked her hands through her hair. "Oh, Jeff, I'm so sorry. I don't know what I'm thinking. You must think I'm absolutely crazy. I'm just so taken off guard, so surprised. Everything is too good, too right. Something has to be wrong."

Jeff leaned in and kissed her forehead. "Why does something have to be wrong because you're happy?"

"What if I'm a terrible mother to Kenny?"

"What if I'm a terrible father?"

Mattie shook her head. "That's ridiculous. You're wonderful at anything you choose to do."

Jeff's eyebrows went up. "As are you, Mattie. Now is this a yes or a very slow no?"

For the first time since leaving the restaurant, Mattie looked into his eyes. The pale light of the evening pink sky provided a soft light, and Mattie knew. In those eyes was a soul she loved more than anything on earth. Nothing had changed about Jeff. Only their circumstances.

"I can do all things through Christ who strengthens me."

"Pardon me?"

"Do not be anxious for anything, but by prayer and petition, with thanksgiving, present your requests to God."

Jeff's eyebrows furrowed. "Is the Scripture for me or for you?"

"It's for both of us. Come on." Mattie opened the door and slipped out of the Cherokee. Jeff met her at the back, and she walked alongside him to a perfectly groomed piece of grass on the golf course. The Arizona sky lit up in a million sparkling lights, and Mattie reflected on the greatness of God. She wondered if she would ever be this happy again. All her joy culminated in this one moment in time. The creation of God called to her from the stars. The realization of the love she had sought for so many years stood beside her, beckoning her, and she would not be the only cousin unmarried. Was it possible?

Jeff and Mattie prayed together until they didn't have enough light to see. In the desert without the moon shining, the darkness surrounded them. Mattie laughed out loud as she and Jeff tried to find their way to the Cherokee by Braille. She felt perfectly at ease now. Ready to take on the world. And a certain four-year-old. Her heart was light and her whole being never happier.

Once inside the vehicle, Mattie breathed in Jeff's delicious scent. He smelled masculine and attractive. And dangerous. Being married was obviously the only safe course of action.

"I'm ready to go home now, Dr. Weatherly. And when you pick me up the next time, I shall be sporting this rather gaudy rock to show all my friends I am to be married." She fluttered her hand in the air, but it was far too dark to see her movements.

"Mattie, if you don't like the ring, we can get something simpler."

She shook her head vigorously. "Bite your tongue. It's grown on me. We'll get you a simple one to make me feel better—how's that?" Mattie enjoyed teasing her straight-laced love almost as much as she loved looking into his eyes.

"Is tomorrow okay to get the supplies for Kenny's room?" Jeff asked, abruptly changing the conversation.

"Absolutely. I have a portfolio of ideas I'll drop off before work tomorrow. He can dream about the perfect mural all day. Maybe that will get him excited about shopping with us."

"Work is going to be harried for me in the next couple of days. I'm afraid I've let some things go to care for Kenny lately. I also need to make sure I approve of his preschool. If it's not okay, it's better to pull him out now."

All the severity of their relationship rushed into Mattie with the vengeance of a hungry coyote. Jeff seemed to sense in her quietness that something was bothering her.

"I'm sorry. This is our night, and I'm rambling about parental duties. I guess if you haven't figured it out by now, I'm not very romantic."

Mattie found his lips in the dark. "Then I can't imagine what romantic is. I've been whirlwind-romanced, and I get to marry my Prince Charming. All I'm missing is the glass slipper."

"Well, those expensive sandals you bought should make a nice substitute."

"Jeff, you made a joke!"

"Come on—let's get somewhere into the light. I miss looking into your beautiful face." Jeff opened the sunroof, and a shadow of light danced across his jaw. "There's the woman I fell in love with. Stars or no stars, I want to see my beauty in the light."

Mattie practically danced on air when she arrived home. Once inside, she studied the ring again and again, wondering how she'd ever thought it was too big. It seemed perfect now.

Thank You, Jesus.

She fell into a dreamy sleep with her jeweled hand resting on her heart.

The next morning Mattie made a special trip to see Kenny before he started back to preschool. She brought her portfolio and a big smile, hoping the little boy would forget his last reaction toward her. As she knocked at Jeff's grandmother's door, hope filled her.

"Hi, Helen. Did Jeff tell you I would be stopping by before I went to work?"

Helen nearly squeezed Mattie with an embrace. "Did my grandson tell me about my future granddaughter-in-law coming by, you say?"

After returning the warm greeting, Mattie felt as though she'd stepped into a new family. A family she would love as much as her own.

"Did you see the ring?" Mattie lifted her ring finger, wishing she'd taken the time to buff her nails or use nail polish. Something worthy of the ring that now graced her usually paint-covered hand.

Helen winked. "I saw it when Jeff announced his first date with you, Mattie. I've never known my grandson to set his mind toward something he didn't follow through on. With him and his prayers I don't think you ever stood a chance." Helen backed away from the door and allowed Mattie to step over the threshold. Kenny sat watching a train video but was wholly interested in Mattie's entrance.

"Hi, Kenny."

Kenny sent her a glowering glance then turned his head away without speaking.

"Uncle Jeff told me you liked trains so I brought you some of my paintings. We're going to paint your new room with trains."

"No, thanks." Kenny sunk his elbows into the carpet and turned back toward the television.

Helen stepped forward and turned off the set. "That's enough, young man. You apologize to Miss Stevens."

"Oh, please, Helen—I want him to call me Mattie."

"Apologize to Mattie, Kenny, or there'll be no macaroni and cheese for lunch. You'll eat a liver sandwich."

Kenny's eyes widened. He apparently wasn't sure if he believed his grandmother or not. But clearly he wasn't willing to risk it. "Sorry," he answered, but the curl of his lip and defiant tone told Mattie the apology was in word only.

Mattie knelt down on the carpet and opened her oversized book. Her children's fantasy creations quickly captured Kenny's attention. "Is that Thomas?"

Mattie nodded. "It is."

"I like James the best. James is the red engine."

She turned the page, and Kenny's eyes grew round. But they quickly reverted to normal size. "I don't want nothin'."

"Your uncle and I are going to take you to pick out the paint tonight. You just need to choose one of these pictures."

"No! I don't want any dumb picture. My mom hates you." Kenny's eyes thinned to slivers, with a look so angry that Mattie feared what lurked inside the child. She quickly banished such thoughts, knowing this little boy needed her. Whether he knew it or not.

"Kenny, your mom knew me a long time ago. We didn't get along so well then, but I'll tell you what: I'm going to marry your uncle Jeff, and I want to love you because he loves you. And because Jesus loves you. I don't care if you love me. That's not your job, honey." Mattie resisted squeezing the little boy's shoulders affectionately.

"My mom's coming home, and she still won't like you."

"But your uncle Jeff likes me. Can't you try to put up with me because he likes me?"

"No!" Kenny crossed his pudgy arms, and Mattie knew it was going to take time. Nothing else would help the situation. She would start James the red engine tonight and be there for Kenny. She would pray and look to God for comfort. She said her good-byes and focused on all that was right in her world.

Now it was time to tell Gram she was batting one thousand in the matchmaking department. Gram took the news with all the grace of a professional quarterback, whooping and hollering and talking about prayer's outcome like Mattie didn't have a thing to do with Jeff's affections. Mattie smiled to herself. All was right with the world for the time being.

Epilogue

Six months passed as if they were mere seconds. Of course, Gram still took all the accolades for scoring a perfect ten for her four granddaughters. Gram welcomed everyone at the church doors as though she herself were marrying today. If Mattie had any doubts left, they had quickly passed with her family's happiness. Jeff was an admired man, and it was impossible not to feel everything for him that everyone around her felt. She was fortunate to be marrying such a kind-hearted, successful, intelligent man, and she never wanted to forget it.

As she stared down the church aisle at Jeff's tall build, with his gentle hands upon Kenny's shoulder, she knew there would never be another for her. There never had been. Mattie almost turned to see if Jeff was looking toward her. Her heart was swelled with joy like a ripe, red strawberry.

Callie, Cassie, and Mel looked elegant in their bridesmaids' gowns, and Mattie closed her eyes for a moment. She wanted to capture everything inside her mind and never forget this moment when love and family collided into one precious mold.

She reached the end of the aisle, and Jeff took her hand. Together they faced the preacher. She promised to follow Jeff anywhere, to be his helpmate, come what may.

Jeff pulled out a letter, and Mattie's heartbeat became rapid as he cleared his throat to speak.

"I thought I might be too nervous to speak, so I wrote some things down. For those of you who don't know our history, Mattie and I met in our high school youth group and fell in love. We might have married right out of school were it not for a very important chess match."

The congregation laughed, and Jeff cleared his throat again.

"If you're not familiar with this woman, all I can say is that it is a privilege to know her. All through my college career, both undergraduate and post-graduate, she never left my mind. I knew someday I would return for her as my bride. My mind never contemplated anyone else. I only prayed that she would still be here for me when I returned. In my heart I knew God meant for us to be together, though, and that prayer was answered. We've had an interesting voyage. I almost dated her cousin Melissa, hoping to spur some interest and announce that I was back in Heaven."

Mattie felt her cheeks flame red, and the congregation gave a spattering of applause.

"Besides being incredibly beautiful, Mattie has a heart wholly for God. She has readily agreed to help me parent Kenny until Joan returns, which for those of you who have been praying, should be soon. Joan met a wonderful biker, who led her back to the God of her youth. She has been in rehabilitation for three months now, and we will soon have to part with Kenny."

Jeff rubbed Kenny's hair lovingly.

Mattie recalled all the miracles God had performed in their lives in the last six months. Joan's phone call had been a desert bloom. Once Kenny heard from his mother that it was okay to love Mattie, the little boy's allegiance was no longer divided. Raindrops of joy fell into their lives one by one.

Jeff continued. "So thank you to all of you who are here to celebrate the happiest day of my life. I have a feeling it only gets better from here." He folded the paper and slipped it into his pocket.

"You may kiss the bride," the preacher said.

Jeff kissed her for the first time as her husband, and Mattie thought she might burst from emotion. Jeff had come home again, and they would live in Heaven together.

KRISTIN BILLERBECK

Kristin Billerbeck makes her home in the Silicon Valley with her engineering director husband and their four children. In addition to writing, Kristin enjoys painting, reading, and conversing online.

HARMONIZED HEARTS

by Lynn A. Coleman

Dedication

This story is dedicated to my granddaughter,
Serenity Paige, who loves to sing
and has a smile that lights up the room.
May your heart always be in harmony
with our Lord Jesus.
Love, Grandma

Chapter 1

"Marissa, did you put lead inside Bertha the Beast tonight?" Tyrone teased as he hoisted the stand-up bass into the van.

Marissa giggled and looped her arm around Jason's. "Possibly. 'Night, all; I'll see you tomorrow at the studio." They headed out of the reception hall of the Miami Country Club. They'd been dating for awhile now, and the idea of the group growing with the addition of spouses increased Tyrone's longing to find just the right woman.

Tristan handed over his viola. "Guess we can't quite call ourselves 'the quartet who always plays at weddings but never participates in them' any longer."

Eva placed her arm around Tristan's waist. "True, but we're still a quartet, plus one now."

"Don't get me wrong, I'm happy for them." Tyrone straightened his back. The staging seemed to be getting heavier. "Seriously, I know my parents wouldn't mind me settling down. Mom's been giving me more and more hints."

Eva groaned. "Mine reminds me of my biological clock."

Tristan chuckled. "That's one advantage we have over you gals. Me, I don't have a clock. I live in Miami. Can you say, Miami time?"

"Ticktock, ticktock. You'd better remember to wind your clock. Tomorrow at the studio will cost us if you come on Miami time," Tyrone quipped. Getting used to Miami time had been a problem, but after spending summers here for three years and having lived here for five, he understood it. He didn't agree with it, but he'd become more relaxed about the late concert starts. They'd show up on time to do a wedding reception only to discover they'd have to wait an additional two hours before the guests arrived.

"You don't have to remind me. I know exactly what that studio is charging."

"Well, I'm off. I'll see you two tomorrow." Tristan jogged toward his car.

"I better get going, too. I'll see you at the studio." Eva handed Tyrone her violin.

"Let me walk you to your car, Eva. I'm sure it's safe but—"

"Thanks," she interrupted, giving him a wink. "I love having a big brother."

"You're welcome."

Tyrone loved his partners. They'd become their own musical family since college. Strolling across the parking lot, he took the keys from her hand and unlocked the car door.

"You're the perfect gentleman, Ty. You'll make a great husband someday."

"Thanks, sis. Isn't it strange how weddings compel us to talk about marriage? It's not like I'm unsatisfied with my life."

A quirk of a grin rose on her dimly lit face. "Yeah, maybe we should stop playing for them."

"Nah, it's good money." Ty winked.

"Oh, right, money, food, survival. . .I forgot about that."

Tyrone chuckled with her. "At least you've got a side job." Eva was becoming a fantastic violinmaker. His spare time, on the other hand, was spent working on a special project. He'd kept the details secret from the others, wanting to see how it developed before asking them to contribute.

She closed the door. " 'Night. See you tomorrow."

He waved her off and watched as she left the parking lot. *Always the last to leave,* he mused.

Tyrone headed over to his van. A real "grocery getter," as he would have called it in high school. Somehow, vans and station wagons were always identified in his mind with parents' cars. But someone had to be responsible for lugging the equipment back and forth. Generally, everyone would go back to their studio and help unload the equipment. Tonight was different. The van would stay loaded, and he'd drive it to the recording studio early and set up for their session.

He slipped into the driver's seat and headed for home. A new neighbor had moved into his complex, but he hadn't seen her yet. The local gossip down by the pool said she was a nurse. No one he'd spoken with knew her name. However, she worked the graveyard shift. Tyrone rolled his head from side to side, working the stiffness out of his neck and shoulders.

At his condo, he noticed a fancy sports coupe with a convertible top glistening in the moonlight in the new tenant's parking spot. "Not bad," he admired. *Must pay to be a nurse these days.* Most of the gals he'd known who'd studied nursing were headed for the mission field. Obviously, this gal wasn't. *Now that's not fair,* he corrected himself. He didn't know this woman, and what she drove was her business, not his. Not to mention, it wasn't his responsibility to judge anyone.

He took the steps two at a time and hustled to his own place.

Cassandra held the door open to her apartment. "Good night, Harold." She motioned for him to leave. "Why does every guy think a woman is a plaything?" she muttered under her breath.

"Come on, sweetheart," he purred. Her stomach felt like it was about to hurl.

"Good night," she said a bit firmer.

"Hey, I can dig it. You want to take it slow. That's fine with me, baby."

Cassy was beginning to think not one decent, single man existed in Miami. "Please don't call, Harold. I'm not interested." He stepped through the open doorway, then started to turn around. "Ever." Cassandra slammed the door shut.

Never again would she go out on a blind date. They couldn't pay her enough. Harold thought he was God's gift to women, and then some. "That man's ego is bigger than his car. No wonder he owns a convertible."

"Vanessa, you're dead." She stomped over to the wall phone and tapped in Vanessa's phone number.

"Hello?"

"Vanessa, this is Cassy."

"So soon. Isn't he marvelous?"

"Girlfriend, did someone turn off your brain? His ego—"

"Cassy, you didn't? What did you do to the poor guy?"

"Nothing he'll ever notice. He's an octopus, all hands. No more dates, Vanessa. I've had it. I'm not interested." She had to stop Vanessa from trying to set her up in these unbearable situations.

"Come on, Cassy. They're just for fun. It's not like we're planning on marrying them."

Cassy collapsed in her circular rattan chair. "Try to understand me, Vanessa. I don't consider sex before marriage fun. I'm a Christian."

"No way. You're not one of those. You're too much fun."

Cassy thought of all the times at the hospital when she'd joked around with Vanessa. She'd never proclaimed her faith, but she hadn't hidden from it, either. "I believe in fun. But I also believe in the sanctity of marriage."

"Whatever." Vanessa snapped her gum. It was an annoying habit to Cassy, but much more tolerable than cigarette smoking, which Vanessa had given up six months ago.

"Promise me, Vanessa, no more blind dates."

"Yeah, yeah, all right. But I think you're crazy. It's not like we live in the Stone Age anymore."

Cassy wasn't in the mood to get into a deep theological discussion. She fired up a quick prayer, asking the Lord to make the right opportunity in the near future to share the gospel with her friend. "I'm beat. Moving is a pain."

"I hear ya, girlfriend. Good night, and sorry about Harold. I thought the two of you would hit it off, him being a doctor and all."

"I'll survive; see you at work." They each hung up and Cassy headed for the shower. A late-night dip in the pool would be wonderful, but the complex had rules about no swimming past ten p.m. She supposed it had to do with the way the complex wrapped itself around the pool. She liked the quaintness of the place, but it did have more rules than most. So far, she appeared to be the only Afro-American in the place. But, then again, she hadn't met many of her neighbors yet.

Rinsing off in a quick shower, she felt the unpleasant evening wash away. She dried off, dressed in her robe, and sat down on her darkened deck. Biscayne Bay shimmered in the moonlight. The high-rise condos lining the beaches across the bay lit up the Miami skyline. And a faint, mournful sound played in the night air. Cassy looked around. No other lights appeared on, on this side of the complex. She squinted across the bay, looking for the source of the low cries from some stringed instrument. Then, as mysteriously as the somber tones had captured her attention, a lively beat took its place.

She leaned back and closed her eyes. Classical music always soothed her. In fact, as happy as she was for her friend, Diane, getting married on Saturday, the only reason she had agreed to spend time at the reception was because they had hired a classical string quartet. One that Diane went on and on about. Not that she didn't want to be supportive of Diane's marriage. . .

The beat shifted yet again. Was someone playing an instrument, or was this some bad recording? Classical music should be something to savor. Didn't the person playing the music understand that? Probably not. It was probably some kid studying for a crash course on music to pass a class. She listened again. A cool breeze slipped behind her bare legs. *Definitely amateur.*

Who was she kidding? She hadn't picked up her flute in ages. She slid her eyelids closed and concentrated on the once again mournful sounds coming from the. . .the what? It was too low for a viola and too high for a bass. *Cello, it has to be.*

Her mind drifted to the music. The faint hint of a harmony line in flute took flight in her mind. Lost in the music, she drifted off to sleep.

Tyrone moaned as he pushed himself out of bed. He'd stayed up too late, playing and replaying the piece he'd been working on. The psalms were difficult to set to music. He'd begun dreaming of doing this since first realizing they were originally sung in the Jewish temple. Perhaps it wasn't his place to put these originally stringed psalms back into music. Perhaps that wasn't what God intended. Many of the psalms meant for stringed instruments were songs of mournful pleas to God. And every time he lost himself in the compositions and the words of the psalms, he had to fight off the same depression the psalmist had written from.

He opened his refrigerator, pulled out a carton of orange juice, a couple hard-boiled eggs, and a bagel. Not the type of breakfast his mother would make, but it had the protein and the carbs he needed to start the day.

A thirty-minute period of laps in the pool came next. Every day he started with breakfast and followed it up with his morning exercise. If the quartet finished early this afternoon, perhaps he could get in a sail. He glanced at his sailboard lying on the dock. *You'd think living on the water and in a city of perpetual sun, you'd get to windsurf more often.*

Tyrone let out a deep sigh. Perhaps twelve years was too long to work on one concept. In reality, only the past year had he been working on it every free moment. Tyrone sat down on the white vinyl lawn chairs under the tiki hut. He glanced up at the thatched ceiling and marveled that the management had hired an Indian from the Miccosukee tribe to thatch it. For months, the other tenants had him convinced they'd hired Englishmen to come over and do the job.

The tropical blue water of Biscayne Bay worked its magic, allowing his mind to drift away from the various psalms to the majesty of God the Creator. *Lord, if I could create a fraction of what You can do, it would testify to You. I feel the words of the psalms, but they are so depressing, they even depress me. What am I missing, Lord?*

A pelican swooped down in the water and scooped up a fish. Tyrone stretched his neck and worked out the morning kinks. A deep sigh escaped. "Get back to work." He pushed himself from the chair and headed back to his condo.

Dry and changed, he sat down with the cello between his legs. It was a familiar feeling, a calming one. The cello seemed to be a part of him now. He remembered when he was eight and first trying to wrap his legs around the instrument. At the time, being short for his age, he ended up playing the cello standing up for the first year. As he grew, the instruments became smaller, more manageable. Now the cello embodied a lot of who he was. He looked at the beautifully carved wood and reflected on its hollow body. "Am I like the cello, Lord? Hollow on the inside?"

Tyrone stared at the cello in a way he never had before. "I have to stop this project. It's draining the life right out of me." He set the cello back in place and began to play a piece he hadn't played in years. He closed his eyes and allowed the music, the praise, to come from his fingers, from beyond his fingers, from deep in his soul. The place only God could unlock.

Away his spirit soared. The music grew louder; the intensity of the rhythm increased. Joy warmed him deep within.

A loud banging noise jerked him from his thoughts. A female voice shrilled, "Don't you ever stop?"

Chapter 2

Cassandra rolled over in her bed and covered her head with a pillow. "How inconsiderate," she muttered and pounded on the apartments' adjoining wall. As her mind cleared, she peaked beneath her right eyelid and looked at the clock. She groaned. It was eight thirty, and not a totally unreasonable hour for one to practice an instrument. "Lord, You knew I needed a condo with quiet neighbors. I visited this place three times during the day before I signed, and every time it was quiet, real quiet. Why? I'm not trying to complain here. I mean, I know I am, but You know I need my sleep if I'm going to work the graveyard shift."

The music stopped. She felt a little guilty for being rude and just banging on the wall. But she needed to go back to sleep. And getting up, changing, going over to the neighbor's, knocking, waiting for him to answer, and reversing the process would have awakened her too much. Arguing with herself and God produced the same results. She tossed the pillow to the foot of the bed and stumbled out from under the covers. *Maybe I can get a nap in later,* she hoped.

Feeling convicted enough to apologize and explain her situation, Cassy dressed to meet her new neighbor. With determined steps, she marched over to the next unit and rapped on the door.

No answer.

She took in a deep breath and knocked again.

Again, no answer.

Who is this guy? First he wakes up the entire complex with his playing, now he doesn't have the nerve to face his neighbors? Cassandra stomped back.

Betty Ann waved. " 'Morning, Cassy, how's the moving in coming?" Betty Ann's silver-gray hair glistened in the morning light. She worked at the same hospital and had been her lead on this prime location. Which this morning seemed a little less than prime.

"Good, I'm just about done." They met halfway down the exterior hallway toward Betty's condo. There were several units between them. Betty Ann owned the corner condo on the second floor that faced the bay on two sides.

"I thought you and Tyrone would hit it off. You just missed him. He left just a couple minutes ago."

"Tyrone?"

Betty Ann wrinkled her forehead. "Your neighbor. You were at his door. I just assumed…"

"No, I haven't met him. I was going over there to ask him not to play in the morning."

"Uh. He always plays in the morning. I am a bit surprised he didn't play for the full hour."

Cassandra felt the heat rise on her cheeks. "I might have been the cause of that. I'm not a morning person. I banged the wall and yelled at him."

"Oh, no. He's quite an accomplished musician, Cassy," Betty Ann said in Tyrone's defense.

"I could hear that. I went to apologize for banging the wall. But does he have to play so early every morning?"

"Well, I don't know. You'll have to ask him. It's his occupation as well as his passion. He and his quartet gave a free mini-concert last Fourth of July. You must have heard me mention it. The residence had more visitors than usual that fourth. When the fireworks grand finale was going on, they played the 'Star Spangled Banner.'" Betty Ann sighed. "It was truly breathtaking."

"I wish you'd have told me about—what did you say his name was?"

"Tyrone."

"Tyrone and his playing. I probably wouldn't have moved here. I need to sleep during the days and…"

Betty Ann reached out and patted the top of her hand. "I'm sorry, Dear. I wasn't thinking. I guess I'm so used to hearing him, it's almost reassuring. Although lately he's been playing some mighty depressing music. Never would have thought a cello could sound like it was in agony." She shook her head as if shaking off the memories of those songs.

"He must have been playing some of that last night." *I wonder if the tone of his music caused me to wake up in such a sour mood this morning?* "Well, I'll see how it goes, but I might just have to sell this place and move somewhere else."

"Or stop working the graveyard shift." Betty Ann winked.

Cassy grinned. "Someone has to do it, and it pays well." They chatted for a few minutes, then Cassy returned to her apartment. Two boxes remained in the bedroom to unpack. Since she was up, she might as well work.

Sorting through the mail on the kitchen counter, Cassy found the wedding invitation from her former patient and friend, Diane Kelly. She reopened the ivory envelope and pulled out the misty-rose invitation. The wedding ceremony was private, but the reception was open to friends and family. Cassy sighed. Diane's fiancé, Ken, had not wavered from his love and support of Diane, even while she recovered from the accident.

She'd scheduled the evening off in order to attend. Cassy glanced up at the calendar. This Saturday. "Oh, no!" She ran to her room and retrieved her purse. "What should I get them for a wedding present, Lord?"

❧

"Tristan, I need your help, man. My new neighbor hates music," Tyrone droned into the cell phone. "I just came from the supply store and purchased some acoustic tiles to put up on the wall."

"When do you want to put them up?"

"After rehearsal today would be good. I can't imagine not playing every day, can you?"

Tristan laughed. "Occasionally, I take a day off. Sure, I'll call my brothers and let them know I'm busy. Hey, why don't I convince them to help? You spring for the steaks, and I'll bring the laborers."

"You're on. Thanks, I really appreciate this."

"No problem. So, have you met her yet?"

Tyrone turned toward the local grocery store. He didn't have enough meat in his freezer to feed Tristan and his brothers. *This new neighbor is costing me.* "Nope, just heard her shrieking through the walls. With a temper like that, she must be ugly as sin."

"Or as tempting." Tristan chuckled.

Tyrone groaned. "I'll see you later. Thanks again."

"You're welcome. See you at two."

Tyrone clicked his mobile phone off and headed into the grocery store. He'd worked with Tristan's brothers before. They all had healthy appetites. Quickly, he made his purchases and unloaded them at his apartment, along with the tiles to soundproof the wall. He glanced at the mirror panels. They'd have to come down.

The elaborate wall clock, a miniature cello, played a single note. *One o'clock. I better get going.* Hustling out the door, he just missed a collision with a lady carrying a large bundle. "Do you need a hand?" he asked.

"No, thank you. I have it," she replied.

Not seeing the woman's face, he didn't want to press his luck. If it was his new neighbor, he wasn't certain she'd appreciate his gentlemanly offer.

He arrived at the studio half an hour before the rest, unloaded the equipment, and set it up before the quartet arrived. He tuned the cello. Tyrone moved on to Marissa's "beast," his affectionate term for her stand-up bass. With him and Tristan each being six feet or more, it still struck him as strange that a gal as short as Marissa was the bass player.

Next, he took the viola and found it still in tune. Finally, he reached for Eva's violin and marveled at the workmanship. Eva's talents with the violin didn't end with her playing of the instrument. She was rapidly becoming a fine maker of the instrument herself. He didn't know how long she could keep up her pace, working as she did in her family's restaurant as well as her hobby.

By five of two, all of the members had arrived. The studio engineer wasn't in the control booth yet to do a sound check. "Shall we warm up while we wait?" Eva asked.

"Sounds like a plan." Tyrone sat in the chair and set the cello in place.

Everyone took their spots. Today they were recording some additional songs to go with their second wedding CD. They had recorded one years ago, but this would be full of additional selections, most having been requested over the years.

They'd made it through the first song when the engineer came into his booth. "Sorry," the voice came over the speakers. "Let's do a sound check. The boss says you have an additional fifteen minutes if you want it."

Tyrone looked over at Tristan and winked. He'd appreciate the financial savings for the group.

The session went great, plans were made for the next—and hopefully final one—for this album. The young engineer gave them a freshly burned CD for them to go over. Tyrone slipped the CD in the cello case. He had the responsibility of checking the recording and making the decisions for the final mix of each album they cut.

&

Back at the condo, the men went to work, first moving the furniture, removing the mirror panels, then scraping the wall, making it ready for the tiles. Soon the hammers, music, and laborers were in full swing.

"Tyrone, you have a visitor," Aaron, Tristan's brother hollered over the noise.

Tyrone jumped up and banged his head on the tray of the stepladder. "Ouch," he yelled. "Who is it? Can it wait?"

"Ahh, I don't think so. It's your neighbor," Aaron offered.

&

Cassy sucked in a deep breath. The man was beyond handsome, from the top of his bronzed head to the richness of his deep plum lips. "I'm sorry," she apologized. "I was wondering if you could stop the noise. I'm a nurse, and I have to work tonight. I didn't get enough sleep this morning."

"I'm sorry I woke you this morning. I'm putting up a soundproof wall so I won't bother you again." He pulled his hand from his head. Blood.

"Sit down, let me look at it."

"No, thanks, I'm fine. I just nicked it on the corner of the ladder. I'm sorry about the noise, but after tonight it shouldn't be a problem."

"Fine." She wasn't going to stand and argue with the man. He obviously was in pain, and she'd dealt with too many patients with no patience when they were in pain.

She retreated to her condo, knowing sleep would elude her once again. "Lord, please make it an easy evening tonight."

He's building a soundproof wall just because I knocked on it? He's either very concerned about his neighbors or he absolutely hates to be interrupted. Given his state of mind when she came to the door, she assumed the latter.

Cassy put on her swimsuit and went to the pool. *Maybe I can get some sleep there,* she mused. Slathered with sunblock, she lay down. The sun and surf lulled her to sleep.

&

A shiver woke Cassy. The sky had darkened. She pushed herself up. *How long have I slept?* she wondered. She sat up. "Ouch!" *A sunburn, great. Just great.* Her naturally dark complexion meant she'd suffered far less than some of her fairer skinned friends, but she obviously had spent too much time in the sun even with sunblock on.

The best solution was a cold shower. Aloe would help, too. She searched the bathroom cabinet. The bottle held less than a handful of the precious lotion. She chided herself and went into the shower. "Four days, Lord. Only four days and I'm not liking this new home." She lay back against the ceramic tiles under the refreshing pulse of the shower. At first her body wanted to protest. But soon the raw nerve endings allowed the cool water to stop the burning.

In the mirror, she caught a glimpse of her burned body. "Girl, you've got to be the only black woman in America to look like black forest cake." Thankfully, she knew if she treated the burn properly, she'd heal quickly.

The burn helped her stay awake Monday night. Tuesday through Friday, she calmed. Her new neighbor had been quiet as a mouse. She couldn't imagine how soundproofing the wall could have such a positive effect. It then occurred to her, it had been rather nice last Saturday to listen to him play as she relaxed from her date.

"Admit it, girl; you don't know what you want." She grinned at her reflection. Tomorrow was Diane's wedding. The gift was bought, her dress back from the cleaners, and the night off after seven nights on would be a welcomed relief. Oddly, she'd barely seen Tyrone Carver. His handsome face played through her mind more times than she cared to recall. No man should affect a woman like that. Especially not a man who had paid no attention to her. Dressed for work, she headed out the door.

"Good evening." A voice like rich caramel worked its way down to her toes.

She grasped the rail tightly. It was him, with his cello case in hand. "Hello, are you just getting in?" It was a dumb question to ask, but it slipped out anyway.

"Yes, we played at a dinner party tonight."

"A dinner party?"

"Yes. Once in awhile we're asked to do a private concert for some folks."

"I see." *So, he's one of those. Socially elite. Of course, he could afford a waterfront condo.* She had to sell everything she owned in order to get the down payment.

He stepped past her. "Have a good night, tonight."

"Thanks, you, too."

Tyrone nodded. His keys jingled as he sorted through them with one hand, finding the door key.

She continued down the stairs, whispering a prayer, "Be still, my heart. Lord, what kind of temptation have You put in my path?"

Coming in early at work to relieve Vanessa, she found Betty Ann and got a rundown on the patients and their various needs. "So, have you and Tyrone made up yet?" she eventually asked.

"What are you talking about? We're just neighbors."

"Uh-huh. I've seen how you look at him when you think no one is watching. There are advantages to being in the corner unit on the second floor."

"Really, woman, there's no harm in looking. But he's barely even spoken to me."

"Well, that's a start. What's he said?"

" 'Good evening,' 'have a nice night.' Nothing major. Besides, I don't have time for a relationship."

Betty Ann sat on the corner of the desk and braced the metal clipboard between her thigh and hands. "I'm not one to tell anyone their business."

Cassy laughed out loud. "Right."

"Well, maybe a little," Betty Ann acknowledged. "A good man is hard to find. And if you find one, you have to get their attention. Banging on his door and complaining about his playing isn't the way to do that."

"Look, I didn't know he was a musician. Besides, he woke me up. I do need to sleep, you know."

"And so does the entire complex. They're all afraid to breathe if they see your car in the parking lot."

Cassy swallowed hard. "I'm sorry. I'm looking for a new place. But it will take me awhile to find one and to sell this."

"Oh, fiddlesticks. People will get used to you and be their old selves soon enough. Tyrone would be good for you. And if I was twenty years younger, you'd be in stiff competition with me. The man is the perfect gentleman."

Cassy wagged her head. "I'm not interested."

"You do have a screw loose up there, don't you? First, you like this horrible shift, and now you pass up one of the finest specimens of Homo sapiens this side of heaven." Betty Ann leaned over and checked Cassy's forehead with her wrist.

The phone buzzed. Cassy picked it up. "Station four?"

"Cassy, this is Rita from ER. Is Betty Ann still there?"

"Yeah, just a minute." Cassy cupped the phone. "It's Rita from ER. She needs to speak with you."

Betty Ann took the phone. "Hi, Rita; what's up?"

Betty Ann paled. "Oh, no, I'll be right there. Yes, yes, he's my neighbor, I can vouch for him. Just treat the man; I'll be right there."

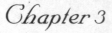

Chapter 3

T y moaned. His body ached from head to foot. He felt like he'd been hit by a large truck. Then again, a good-sized motorboat was probably more comparable. Thank the Lord they brought him to Aventura Hospital where his neighbor, Betty, worked. One didn't bring their wallets and personal identification sailboarding.

"Tyrone, what happened?" Betty Ann stood beside his bed, reaching for his wrist.

"I tried to get in a short sail this evening, and some kids weren't watching where they were going."

"You're lucky to be alive."

"It's only by God's grace."

"Well, we can thank Him for that." She placed his hand beside him on the bed after checking his pulse and carefully examined his head wound. "Concussion?" she asked.

Ty fought to focus. Her soft image blurred. "Yeah, I believe so."

She grabbed his chart. "Are they keeping you for observation?"

Ty attempted to speak. He closed his eyes and drifted off to sleep. Then he was aware of voices around his bed. He forced his eyes open. "Hey, man, what were you thinking?" Tristan stepped a bit closer to his bed.

"It wasn't me."

"Yeah, I heard. Thank God, you're still alive."

"Amen." Tyrone couldn't have been more pleased to see his best friends and business partners beside him. The girls huddled up closer. "How'd you guys hear?"

"Your neighbor called," Eva offered.

"Ah. Thanks for coming."

Marissa held his hand. "We're calling around for another cellist for the wedding tomorrow. You rest."

"Nah, I'll be fine." Ty tried to sit up. The room spun. "Maybe not."

"I went to your place and retrieved the keys for the van, your wallet, and some clothes," Tristan said. "I've settled up with the accounting office. They have all your insurance information. The police need a statement. Although the kids on the boat admitted they weren't paying attention. It's a good thing, too. From what I hear, they're the ones who pulled you out of the water and rushed you to shore."

Ty nodded his head slowly.

Tristan continued. "The doctor says you've got a mild concussion and you'll be fine. No broken bones or internal injuries."

"I tried to dive away from the boat."

Tears rimmed Marissa's eyes. "Don't scare us like that again."

Ty swallowed down his own. His mouth dry, he asked, "Is there any water?"

Eva quickly poured him a glass and helped him hold it. When his hand steadied, she backed away. "Thanks."

A male nurse walked in with a small basin. "Excuse me, folks. You'll need to leave. It's time for the patient's bath."

Ty sat up. "I'll take a shower."

"Are you up for it? Any dizziness?" the nurse asked.

"I'll stay with him while he showers," Tristan offered.

The girls left along with the male nurse. "Thanks."

"No problem. Come on, let me help you to the showers. It'll remind us of college years."

"I am dizzy," Ty admitted.

"I could tell."

The next hour Ty spent getting showered and settling down for an evening's rest in the hospital. Every muscle in his body ached. He and Tristan talked about tomorrow's wedding. So far, the girls hadn't managed a replacement. Saturdays were hard to find a fill-in. And Tyrone only once had to bow out of a concert because of family needs back home.

"I'm feeling better," said Ty. "I might be able to play tomorrow."

"We can play without you. We'll just pick some other pieces."

"Seriously, I think I'll be all right."

"Okay, why don't we just wait until tomorrow to decide. If," he emphasized, "we don't find a replacement."

"Sure." Ty wasn't going to argue.

"Well, do you need me for anything further?"

"No, thanks. I'd like to get some sleep."

Tristan looked at his watch. "Well, I've kept you up long enough, so I guess you can sleep now."

Ty raised his eyebrows.

"Doctor's orders."

"Ah. Thanks again."

"No problem, brother. That's what we do for one another."

Ty's chest swelled with healthy pride. It was so good to be a part of this family. God's family. Within minutes from Tristan's departure, Ty found himself falling asleep.

❧

Cassy stopped by her neighbor's room to check on him before she returned home. She tapped on his doorway. "Hi."

He pulled the covers up to his chest. She held back a chuckle. "Hi," he replied.

She took a step into his room. The bed beside him was empty. His hazel eyes and hazelnut skin tone set the man apart. "Betty Ann said you came in last night, so I thought I'd check on you before I went home. Need anything?"

"No, thanks."

"Hey, Ty."

Cassy turned to see a man with olive skin and black hair walk into the room. He turned to her and extended his hand. "I'm Tristan, Ty's partner."

Cassy took the proffered hand and shook it. "I'm Cassandra Jones. I just moved into the same apartment complex."

"Ah, the neighbor we built the sound wall for."

Cassy looked down at her feet.

"I'd been meaning to build one anyway," Tyrone offered.

Cassandra nodded and headed for the door. "I'll see you around. Bye."

She marched to the elevator and pushed the button. Why had she bothered to visit the man? Naturally, his only memory of her was her rude thumping on the wall and then complaining when he put up a sound wall she hadn't even asked for. And Betty had said everyone in the apartment complex was nervous around her for that. *I'll just move again,* she reasoned. *Maybe I ought to just buy a house and not worry about neighbors.*

At the apartment, she took a warm shower and readied herself for bed. She'd need a good rest before the wedding tonight.

Later that day, Cassandra slipped into a layered dress. The lower layer was a nice blend of satin in a rich plum color, the upper layer of fine, handmade, antique lace. A replica, of course, but nonetheless exquisite in its ivory design. She placed a teardrop pearl necklace around her neck and added the matching earrings. She let her hair down for the evening. Normally, she wore it in a tight bun or braid. It was easier that way when she was working. Tonight she was bound and determined to have a good time, giving no thought to neighbors or the problems she had with them, self-made or otherwise.

She should have gotten a date. The wedding invitation allowed for her to bring a guest but. . .who would she have asked? The only man that got her attention of late was her neighbor, but the first impression she'd made on him had been—well, less than perfect.

Cassy took one final glance in the car mirror and willed herself to enjoy the evening. In the hotel lobby, she followed the signs for Diane and Ken's wedding reception. The hall was lavishly decorated with white fences covered with ivy and small white roses. Strings of miniature white lights draped around each section of fencing. Each table was elegantly set with fine white china and silver, with a centerpiece of off-white candles on a mirrored surface. Cassy sighed. *It's beautiful.*

She heard the stringed quartet playing softly in the background and took her assigned seat. Others seated at the table made their introductions. Soon, she found herself engaged in light conversation and no longer felt out of place. When the bride and groom entered, Cassy stood and scanned the room. The quartet was dressed in black tuxedos and played the wedding march. Cassandra's eyes stopped on the cellist, along with her heart. Tyrone, her neighbor. She scanned the other members and discovered Tristan was playing the viola. Her palms began to sweat. *Oh, this is foolishness. You knew he was a musician. Tristan introduced himself as Ty's partner. So why are you so shocked?* she chided herself.

Reseated, she tried to get back into the table's discussion, but her mind and her eyes kept returning toward the quartet. "They're marvelous, aren't they?" Mildred, an older woman who sat to her right, commented.

"Yes. They are."

"I've purchased a couple of their CDs. I've been waiting for their newest."

Cassandra focused on her tablemate. "CDs?"

"Oh, yes. I've been listening to Classical Strings Quartet for the past eight years." She straightened in her chair. "I hope I played some small part in their staying in Miami after they finished their European tour."

Cassy blinked. Hadn't he sounded like an amateur the first time she'd heard him?

Mildred rambled on for a bit about Classical Strings Quartet, and Cassy found herself caught up in the woman's enthusiasm.

Suddenly there was a crash from the direction of the musicians, and the room let out a collective gasp. Cassandra ran over and discovered Ty lying on the floor. "What happened?" she asked.

"He passed out. I knew he shouldn't have been playing."

Cassandra took charge. She asked for a private room, and Tristan escorted the semi-lucid man to the secluded area. Cassy examined him as best she could. A doctor attending the reception came in and gave him a more thorough exam. "You say he was released from the hospital this morning for a concussion?"

"Yes," Cassandra and Tristan answered in unison.

"He appears fine, but you'll want to take him to his physician if he passes out again."

"Thank you." Tristan turned to her. "I hate to ask this, but could you stay with him? I'll need to go back to the reception and let everyone know he's all right. We should probably play a few numbers, also."

"No problem. I'd be happy to." Cassandra glanced over to her patient.

Embarrassed, Ty tried to sit up.

"Stay down," Cassy ordered.

"I'm fine," Tyrone weakly defended himself.

"I'm sure." Her voice softened. "Rest a bit longer. I'll take you home, if you like."

He liked the way "home" rolled off her lips. The woman was drop-dead gorgeous. Perhaps having a pretty nurse wasn't all that bad. He lay back down on the sofa.

"What?"

"Nothing."

Cassy chuckled. "I've seen that look more than once," she said, blushing. "I'm sorry we got off on the wrong foot. I love your quartet and how you play your cello. I miss not hearing it."

Tyrone smiled. "I'll open the slider when I play."

"Thanks. Although there were some awfully depressing sounds coming out of that cello. What were you playing?"

Ty closed his eyes. "Something I'm working on."

"It shows." She covered her mouth. "Sorry. I'm always doing that, speaking before I think."

"You're forgiven. And you're right, they are mournful sounds. It's hard to reflect the words and not reflect their meaning in the piece."

"Are you putting something to music?"

"Yes. But it's a secret. I haven't even told the others what I'm working on, not until I'm content with its structure. Then, they can give me additional input."

"Ah. Well, I'm no musician. I played a little flute while I was in high school and less while I was in college. But I certainly never tried to compose."

Ty found himself liking this beautiful woman, even with her no-nonsense straightforwardness. After several minutes of conversation, he asked, "Can I sit up now?"

"You sound more alert. Let me check your eyes."

He found himself looking into her auburn brown eyes and caught a spark of passion. "Cassy. . ."

"How's my patient?" The doctor came back into the room. Tyrone didn't know if he was grateful or angry—maybe a mixture of both. Cassandra popped up and took a step back.

"Fine," Tyrone answered.

"His eyes are clear and his conversation has become quite lucid."

"Good, go home and rest, young man. You overdid it," the doctor commented and exited the room.

An awkward silence fell between the two.

Cassy cleared her throat. "Would you like me to take you home?"

"I need to pack up the equipment."

"I think Tristan can take care of that. You, Sir, need to rest. Doctor's orders."

What he wanted to do and what he should do were two different things. They had chemistry. Should he pursue her? "I'll let the others know I'm going home."

"You sit; I'll take care of it. I need to grab my purse anyway."

Ty sat with his head back on the sofa. He had to admit his entire body still ached from the impact. He'd been sweating just before he passed out. No doubt the exertion to stay focused on his playing and not on his body caused the overload. *Father, I hope the wedding party isn't upset by this.*

Classical Strings Quartet had a good reputation in the area. Always on time. Always professional. He should have let them go on with only the three of them and given the wedding a rebate.

Cassy returned and strolled up beside him, extending her arm. He latched on. Her strength startled him. Of course, she was a nurse, and helping patients up and down was part of her job.

They started home in relative silence. Her car was not the same one he'd seen in her parking space the first night. "I'm sorry to take you away from the reception."

"Diane was a former patient. But I didn't know anyone there. . . ." She halted her words. "It's not a problem."

"You worked seven days straight this week. Is that normal?"

"No, normally. . ." She paused. He caught a glimpse of her staring at him. "Normally, I work five days on, two off."

"Oh."

"I had to adjust my schedule this week to get Saturday off for the wedding."

He felt like a heel. She should be back at the reception. "Perhaps you can return after you drop me off."

"I'm fine. I wouldn't have offered if I didn't mean to."

"All right, thanks."

"You're welcome. Now tell me how you're feeling."

"Sore. I think trying to sit up straight to give the impression I was fine while playing exerted more energy than I expected."

"You're probably right. Betty said a boat rammed you when you were sailboarding in the bay."

"Yeah. A couple of kids going too fast and not paying attention. Tristan said they pulled me out and brought me to shore. Not only that, but they called the paramedics."

"You're fortunate."

"Very. God was looking out for me."

"You're a Christian?"

"Yes, the entire quartet is. We met at college."

"That's great. One of the women at my table was raving about your quartet, said she had a hand in getting you established in Miami."

Ty chuckled. "Mildred. She's a sweetheart." The woman told all her friends and insisted if they wanted the best, they should hire Classical Strings Quartet. With her connections in the upper class on the beach and in Aventura, she had helped them move forward quickly.

Cassy pulled into her assigned parking space. "We're here. I'll help you up to your place."

"Thanks, but I think I can handle it."

"Nonsense. I live next door. I'm going the same way anyway," she argued.

"You've made your point." Besides, wrapping his arm around this beautiful woman comforted him.

At his doorway, an awkward moment passed. He pulled out his keys and said, "Good night."

" 'Night."

Inside his apartment, he opened the slider and allowed the gentle breeze from the bay to wash over him. The moonlight shimmered on the water "She's nice, Lord."

Crash. Something broke on the patio floor next door.

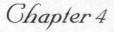

Chapter 4

Okay. Cassy leaned back from the bathroom sink. "He's a Christian. He's handsome. And he's everyone's dream musician, according to Betty Ann and others." She wagged the hairbrush at her mirrored image. She had to admit his quartet was superb. If Vanessa had anything to do with her getting this new condo, she'd be certain she was headed for another blind date. But Vanessa didn't know anything about Tyrone or this condo, so she hadn't been set up.

Cassy closed her eyes and pictured her handsome neighbor. Hazel eyes on a sea of mocha coffee with rich cream had invaded her dreams all night. She moaned, opened her eyes once again, and worked the brush through her hair. Noticing the kinky new growth, she decided she'd have to get a perm.

With will and sheer determination, she dressed for church. Letting her mind run through frivolous thoughts was a useless exercise and only ended in disappointment.

She grabbed her keys and headed out the door.

"Good morning." Tyrone grinned. His bronzed skin shimmered with droplets of water.

"Hi," she fumbled.

He scanned her from head to toe in one swift gaze. "Church?"

"Yes."

"I'm running late, myself. I overslept this morning."

"Are you feeling okay?"

"Fine. My head still has a dull ache. I worked most of the stiffness from my body with a swim this morning."

"You need to be careful. Don't overdo it."

"Yes, Doctor," he said and saluted.

She thought of giving him a lecture, but what would it matter? He was obviously noncompliant. Thankfully, he wouldn't be assigned to her floor. Well, her floor at the hospital. "I need to get going. Our church is hosting a special concert this morning."

"Really, which church?" he asked.

"Christ Community, near I-95."

Ty gave her a quirk of a smile.

He couldn't be, could he? Did she dare ask? Nah, he couldn't. He wasn't even dressed or ready for church.

"Yo, Tyrone, what's taking you so long?" Tristan yelled from the lower level entryway.
"Sorry, I'll be right down."

Unsure of how to depart, Cassy gave a slight wave and bounced down the stairway.

All through the church service, Cassy kept hoping to see Tyrone and his quartet appear on the chancel. But he didn't, and while the concert had included a wonderful testimony of what God was doing in the performers' lives, the music lacked the classical flare, which Cassandra adored.

Before leaving, the pastor came up beside her and asked if she'd be ready to share in music in two weeks. She'd been putting off polishing up her flute for ages. But having heard Tyrone play the other night, the long hidden pleasure of playing her flute had resurfaced. "Yes, Pastor Paul, I'd love to."

"Great. I'll put you on the schedule."

She mingled for a bit longer, talking with old and new friends, then returned to her condo.

Over the next couple of days, she'd bounce into Tyrone and wave. They'd share light chitchat. Finally, after a week, she no longer felt weak in the knees when she saw him. Toward the end of the week, she found him sitting under the tiki hut. Boldly, she came up beside him. "Hi."

"Hi. Isn't this gorgeous?" He indicated the moonlit, peaceful bay with a sweep of his hands.

"Yes." She hadn't taken her eyes off of him.

He glanced up at her. "Do you have a night off?"

Cassandra pulled up a chair and sat down beside him. "As a matter of fact, I do."

"Me, too. I was planning on working on my project. But sometimes it's far too depressing."

"What are you working on? If you don't mind me asking."

He took in a deep breath and sighed. "I've been praying over the matter. I haven't liked how the music has made me feel. I was trying to put the psalms that are specifically mentioned as having been written for string instruments to music."

Cassandra thought it a wonderful idea, but hesitated telling him so. She could see the frustration etched on his forehead. "What's wrong?"

"They're depressing psalms."

"How so?"

"Most are written in anguish, grasping for the Lord as the world hits the writer. Usually there is a verse that reminds the reader that God is there and He cares, but it's generally a single verse and often followed with more cries of anguish."

Cassandra reached over and touched his forearm. "Why do you want to put these particular psalms to music?"

Tyrone leaned back in the chair. "I was a kid when the thought struck me. I was still in high school. It's never left me. But now that I've decided to buckle down and write it, it's been depressing me, and I don't like it."

"I'm no expert, but I do love classical music. If you'd like to play them for me, I'd be happy to give you my input. If you think it would help."

Tyrone's smile was like liquid gold and sent shivers slipping down her spine. *Lord, help me, I could fall in love with this man far too easily.*

"I have a better idea. Why don't I take you out to dinner? I mean, if you're free. I'm sorry. . .I don't know if you're involved with anyone or. . . ," he fumbled.

"I'm unattached, and I'd love to go."

"Great." He looked down at his swimming trunks. "I'll need to change."

"How shall I dress?"

"Comfortably casual," he said.

Cassy took Tyrone's hand as he helped her out of the chair.

"Shall I pick you up in fifteen, thirty minutes?"

"How about forty-five?"

His smile sent a shiver of excitement through her veins. *Lord, protect my heart from falling too hard and fast for this man.*

❧

"Tell me about yourself," Tyrone asked as he opened the door to the van for Cassandra.

"Not much to tell. I'm a nurse, work nights, and that's about it."

Ty shut the door and jogged around to the driver's side. "Come on," he said as he slid behind the wheel. "There's got to be something more. What's your favorite food?"

"Anything. Well, almost anything. I'm not a fan of sardines, anchovies, or any other slimy, crittery thing."

Tyrone chuckled. "Okay, no anchovies. Are you in a beef mood? Chinese? Cuban? Thai? We have it all down here."

"A simple steak dinner would be nice."

"Steak it is." He headed north on Biscayne Boulevard toward Aventura. "What excites you about nursing?"

"I like helping folks."

He looked into the side-view mirror and pulled into the middle lane. "Why the night shift?"

"It pays well, and I'm single. Few nurses want to give up their family time for that shift."

"Makes sense." They drove to the restaurant and continued their light chatter.

During dinner their conversation turned from friendly "I'm your neighbor conversation" to more pointed topics about their pasts, goals, and relationship with the Lord. Tyrone found himself wanting to know more and more about her. Their meals finished, desserts ordered and eaten, Tyrone searched for another reason to keep their conversation going.

"What made you decide on our complex?" he asked.

"The quiet. I'm sorry about the time I banged on your wall."

He raised his hands. "You've already apologized."

"I know, but I felt terrible. My girlfriend, Vanessa, had set me up on one of the worst blind dates the previous night and, well, I just wasn't in a very good mood."

"I should have checked with the new neighbor before playing."

"For what it's worth, I do enjoy your playing."

"Except for the psalms written for stringed instruments," he added.

"Right. Why are they so depressing?"

"They're moments of anguish where people are calling out to God."

Cassandra moved the empty dishes from in front of her and placed her elbows on the table. "You know, that first night, I had this melody come into my head. It was really strange. It had an unusual tempo, even, and was meant for a flute."

"Tell me more." Tyrone shifted closer.

Cassandra went on to explain how in her mind the flute's melody line was soft, but peacefully woven in between the mournful strains of his melody.

"Interesting, a contrasting melody line. Would you be willing to play a bit for me so I can get a sense of what you were hearing?"

"I'm not very good, and I don't know the first thing about writing music. I'm not sure—but I'm willing to try."

"Great." Ty jumped up from the table, laid a few bills down, and reached for Cassandra's hand. "Let's get started."

"Now?" She glanced at her watch. "It's nearly eleven."

"Oh. I suppose it could wait 'til morning. I just thought. . . since you're used to being up in the wee hours. . ."

Cassandra chuckled. "Lead the way. I can see you won't sleep tonight if I don't give you something to work with."

"Woman, I like your style." He winked.

"I can honestly say, I've never been asked to come to a guy's apartment to play my flute before."

Tyrone chuckled. "I'll spring for the coffee."

"You're on. But won't we keep the others up in the complex?"

"True. Okay, tell you what. I'll play the last recording I made of the Fifty-fifth Psalm and we can wear the headsets." She looked at him quizzically. "It's wireless, I can have as many headsets as I can afford."

"Oh."

They were back in the van and headed toward their condo in no time. Cassandra went to her apartment and picked up her flute. Ty set up and had everything in place by the time Cassy came back.

"I really appreciate this." He took the light box from her hand and escorted her into his condo.

She scanned the room. "I like what you've done with your space."

"Thanks."

"I think I might like to take down the wall in my kitchen. I like the effect of the island between the two rooms."

"Come over here." He led her into the living room. "I've set up the computer."

Cassy chuckled. "You really do seem to get into this stuff, don't you?"

"Afraid so." Tyrone found himself captivated by her smile. Was he really interested in hearing her idea or simply interested in spending more time with her? *Both,* he mused.

After a few minutes, Cassandra picked up her flute and tentatively played a few notes. Tyrone watched as her hands shook while playing for him. He'd seen it before when teaching music lessons. Lately, he'd been too busy to take on students. He closed his eyes and tried to picture the melody line she was trying to play.

"I'm sorry, I'm horrible at this. I can't believe I let my pastor talk me into doing special music in two weeks."

"No, you're doing fine. I'm catching a glimpse of the music."

"Seriously? I was thinking—with your psalms, if you added a gentle, secondary melody that eventually took over the piece when you met up with the positive verses of reassurance of God's love and grace, you might have a powerful piece."

"That's it." Ty jumped up and went over to his desk, riffling through the sheets of music scores. He sat down and went to work. At some point, he mumbled good-bye to Cassandra. At least, he thought he had. He hoped he had.

≈

Cassandra huffed as she made up her bed. She didn't know whether to be upset or excited about her time with Tyrone last night. Memories of their conversation flooded her with joy. Memories of working on his music with him also brought some satisfaction. However, the way in which he plummeted into his work was downright obsessive. *I doubt he even heard me leave, Lord.*

Not that she'd gotten her hopes up that they could possibly begin a relationship. "Friends, that's all I want in my life, right now, Lord. Just friends."

The doorbell rang.

Tyrone stood tall and dangerously handsome, offering a single yellow rose. "Peace offering," he volunteered.

"You didn't have to." She took the proffered rose. "But it's gorgeous. Thanks."

"My mom tells me yellow is the sign of friendship." He shuffled his feet. "In roses, that is."

"Your mother is right. Not that I'm an expert, but I've learned a little from all the bouquets that come into the hospital. Personally, I love orange lilies. But I've been told they are a sign of extreme hatred."

"If I ever buy orange lilies for you, please note it's because you like the flower and there's no hidden message."

"Noted." She took a step back into the apartment. "Would you like to come in?"

"I'd love to, but I stayed up most of the night. I need some rest before our concert this afternoon."

"Another wedding?"

" 'Tis the season." Tyrone stepped back. "I'll let you go. Thanks, and thanks again for the input last night. I think we might be on to something. By the way, you should practice your flute more often."

Cassy stiffened.

"No, no, I'm sorry. I was going to say because you've got the touch."

"Oh." Cassy relaxed her shoulders. *Why should I be so concerned about what he thinks of my playing?* She waved him off and leaned back against the counter as he shut the door. "Father, slow this thing down, and fast. I'm not good with sudden and quick decisions."

She looked down at the yellow rose and inhaled. "Hmm, yellow, friendship. Who's really speeding up this relationship?" she asked herself, looking straight into the reflection on the toaster oven. She didn't like the answer.

For the next couple of days, she hardly saw Tyrone. He seemed to be locked day and night in his condo working on his project. "Definitely obsessive," she mused. She wanted to spend time with him. She wanted to get to know him. But wasn't it her own fault that he wasn't coming around? Wasn't it her own prayer? "Girlfriend, you don't know what you want."

Cassy poured herself a tall glass of iced tea and sat outside on the back deck that overlooked the bay. She loved this view and, admittedly, loved this apartment complex. It was quieter than any other place she'd lived. Taking in a long, cool sip, she leaned back on the chaise lounge and closed her eyes.

"Woman, you're too beautiful."

"Ty?"

Chapter 5

Hang on, Mom, my neighbor just called me." Tyrone cupped the phone with his hand. "What do you need, Cassy?" He leaned out over the side wall so he could peak into her patio. She reclined there, intoxicating to the eyes.

"I'm sorry, I thought you said something to me. I didn't realize you were on the phone." She lowered her glance and avoided his eyes.

Ty held up a finger. "Hi, Mom, sorry about that."

"Was that the new neighbor?"

Ty slipped behind the wall and back into his apartment. "Yes, and I've been praying about her. It's too soon to tell if anything will develop."

"I'm glad to hear it. You know how much I'm looking forward to being a grandmother again."

Ty chuckled. "Not this week. Unless Denise is having another."

"Don't you be fussing with me. Back to what you were asking—I'll ship the box labeled 'high school scores.'"

"Thanks, Mom. I appreciate it. I'll let you know when I'm finished."

They said their good-byes and Ty went back out to the patio. "Cassy?" he called.

"I'm still here."

"May I come over?" Ty asked. He'd been fighting the urge to pester her. He liked Cassandra and wanted to spend more time with her, but he also picked up on the vibes from their one evening together that she wanted to keep men at a distance.

"Sure. I'll unlock the door."

Ty watched as she placed her glass of iced tea on the small table beside the chaise lounge. She had lots of plants on her patio. He glanced back at his own. A couple chairs and a table. Functional, not homey.

"Are you going to stand there all day, or are you coming over?"

"Sorry." How was it possible to have so many feelings for a woman he barely knew? *And how will she react when she knows? If she reacts, then she's not the right person for me,* he resolved. During high school and college it never seemed to matter until he brought Shawna home to meet the folks. Tyrone shook off the old memory and went to his neighbor's door.

Cassy opened the door for him. A sweet smile brightened her face.

"Do you know how beautiful you are?" Ty asked.

"Were you saying that to me or to your mother, earlier?"

Ty chuckled. "My mom. But you're beautiful, too."

"Come in, before the entire complex hears our business." Cassy stepped back and opened the door for him.

"Go out with me again, please."

She glanced into his eyes.

"You're as addictive as semisweet chocolate." He opened his arms, and she took a tentative step closer. "Please, tell me you're feeling some of the same chemistry between us. You are, aren't you?"

She nodded.

He wrapped his arms around her and gently pulled her into his embrace. She felt wonderful. They felt wonderful together. *Lord, help me say the right things,* he silently prayed. "Cassy, I'm a Christian, and I take my Christianity seriously."

She gently made some distance between them. "Ty, what's happening here? I'm thinking of you night and day, and I barely know you. You've hardly spoken a word to me since we went out. I'm not sure where this is going or if I can deal with this intensity so fast."

Ty took in a deep breath. "You're right. I'm impulsive, and then shy away when I think I've been too forward. And I haven't managed to get you out of my thoughts, either. So where does this leave us?"

"How about we start as friends and see if we can get a handle on our intense attraction."

Ty stepped away and leaned against the kitchen counter. Cassy's apartment didn't have the open wall like his. The kitchen was a glorified hallway at best. "Okay, no touching."

Cassy wagged her head. "I didn't say that. After all, I rather liked being in your embrace."

Ty chuckled. "You're a breath of fresh air. I've never known a woman to be so honest. Please, don't stop. I like it. It lets a fella know right from the start where he is and where he shouldn't go."

"That quality has cost me more relationships and friendships over the years. 'I tell it like it is, child,' my mama would always say. I guess I picked the trait up from her." Cassy opened the refrigerator. "Would you like some iced tea?"

"Thanks, I would. We'll need to figure out some times we can set aside for each other. Our schedules are so different."

"True, but I think we can work that out." Cassy poured and handed him a tall glass of iced tea. "So, do you always tell your mother she's beautiful?"

"Only when I'm flattering her. She's sending me some of my old scores. I've kept them in storage in my parents' attic. As you've learned, storage in Miami is the pits."

Cassy led them back out to her deck. Ty sat down in a chair across from her.

"So, you use flattery to get what you want," she teased. "I'll make a note of that."

"Only if it works." He took a sip. "Nice tea."

"Thanks. I added mango juice to it."

They talked about each other's families, where they were located, and how close they were with them.

"Mom's really pushing me to settle down," Ty said. "She doesn't realize how difficult it is to meet someone who's not... how do I say this? A groupie, I guess. It's not like rock and roll groupies, but there's a definite pattern. And, of course, many of the places we play we're surrounded by the older folks. They have the money and they have the time to appreciate the music."

"My mother drummed it into my head, 'Get your education, girl. Don't get serious with a man. Be a self-sufficient woman before you settle down.'"

"My folks were big on education, too, but being a musician—well, we just don't make money the same way other folks do. Classical Strings Quartet has been fortunate. We were able to get a couple of European tours in during our summer vacations before settling down in Miami after college. Thankfully, South Florida has quite a few regular European visitors throughout the year. With Marissa wanting to get married, I'm thinking we'll be doing fewer concerts during the week, and I'll probably start private lessons again."

"Speaking of lessons, I'm supposed to be practicing that number for my church."

"How's that coming?"

"Lousy," she mumbled. "I never should have agreed to it."

"Show me, if you don't mind."

"Do you know how hard it was to play in front of you the other night?"

"A little. Come on, you can trust me. I didn't say anything critical the other night, did I?"

Cassy consented and got out her flute. She sat down, went through the number, and waited. "Well?"

Ty chuckled. *You're as impatient as I am.* "Okay, you've got the technical part down. What you're missing is the feel of the music. And that's normal, because you're so nervous playing in front of me. Can I touch you?"

"Uh, sure, I guess."

Ty came up behind her and massaged her shoulders. At first she tightened, then slowly began to relax.

She closed her eyes and sighed. "You ought to work in a hospital. The patients would love you."

"My mother taught me. Dad loved good back rubs. Desiree and I were just toddlers when we began to learn how to give a good massage."

"Remind me to thank your mother," she moaned.

He whispered into her ear, "Now think about the song, the words, and its message. Now, play it again."

Cassy picked up the flute and played. The music wafted into the open air, fluid and light as the breeze. "That's wonderful. How'd you do that?"

"I didn't. You did. I simply helped you relax enough to let it come out of you."

She glanced up at him, then closed her eyes. "We have a problem."

"What?"

She opened her eyes and he saw the fires of desire. It ignited his own. He closed his eyes and stepped back. "I see what you mean."

"This is ridiculous. We're two grown adults, strong in our Christian faith and convictions. We shouldn't be having a problem with this. I mean if we had been together for awhile I could understand it. But this is so sudden and. . ."

Tyrone placed his hands back on her shoulders. "With God's grace, we'll work this out, Cassy." He massaged her shoulders again. "My folks always told me that when I met the right woman, my passionate personality would be hard to control. I thought I'd met the right woman once before. Our passions were high for each other. I believed so strongly in what I thought was our love for one another that I even brought her home. That brief visit was the end of our relationship."

Cassandra turned around in her chair and faced him. "What happened?"

Chapter 6

Cassandra had no trouble staying awake last night at work. Ty's pained confession about his old girlfriend, Shawna, and how horribly she reacted to his mother being white, was ridiculous. How many African-Americans have no white blood in them? By the same token, she'd seen prejudice on both sides, and the sin was just as evil whether it came from a white man or a black man. It was sin and destructive to God's plan of all men being created in His image. Few things got her dander up more than hearing something like this.

Tyrone's fairer black skin color made it obvious he had some parent or grandparent who was white. She remembered a friend whose mother used to put her on the fire escape when she was a baby in order to help her darken. Both parents were black, but their daughter was fairer than either of them. People often do foolish things, she knew, but to just dump Tyrone like that. . . Unfortunately, she'd had to dress for work after learning about Shawna. All night she had wanted to call Ty and reassure him that it wasn't a problem for her. But he also had an evening engagement, and she didn't know when he'd return.

She parked her car in the assigned slot and headed up to her condo.

"Morning."

Cassy jumped.

Ty handed her a cup of hot chocolate.

"You startled me."

"Sorry. I've been waiting for you. I wanted to apologize for telling you everything about Shawna and my folks."

"Not a problem. I can't believe she refused to walk into a white woman's home. What was she afraid of?"

Ty chuckled. "I don't know. I never thought to tell her because I always thought in terms of everyone knowing. I forgot that my parents weren't able to come to the campus very often, and even if they had, it was a large enough school that most wouldn't have met them. I grew up in a small town, and all my life people always knew about my heritage. It never occurred to me it might be a real problem. I'd been called names—but my real friends never seemed to be phased. So, it didn't phase me."

"Would you like some breakfast?" Ty asked.

"What are you cooking?"

"Simple feast of poached eggs on toast and a couple of microwaved strips of turkey bacon."

"Sounds wonderful. Let me change out of my uniform and I'll join you." Cassy handed him back the mug of cocoa and went to her apartment. *Lord, he's so incredible. How can we continue to spend time with each other and not let our carnal desires run amok?*

She slipped into a casual top and pair of shorts, removed her knee highs, and slipped on a pair of sandals. A finishing touch of a breath mint, and she was out the door and knocking on his in minutes.

"Come in, it's open," Ty called out.

"Hi." Tristan stood on the other side of the half wall that doubled as a breakfast nook.

"Hi." She blinked. His presence would certainly help with desires running wild, she figured.

"Tristan generally joins me for breakfast on Saturdays so we can go over the business's schedule and finances."

"I'm sorry, I can take a rain check."

"Nonsense. I invited you, and we're more than happy to have a pretty face to look at." Ty winked.

"Hmm, I'm not sure how I should respond to that."

"Trust me, it was a compliment," Tristan offered.

Cassy found she liked Tristan, and she enjoyed the friendship of the two men. Before long, the weariness of the hour was getting to her and she began to yawn. "I need to go, guys. I've got a shift tonight and church in the morning."

"I understand, and thanks for joining us." Ty walked her to the door.

Cassy went home and dressed for bed. She closed the drapes and darkened the room. She had probably eaten too much to go to sleep on, but if she stayed up to do some sit-ups, she'd wake herself up for another couple hours. No, she'd deal with the extra pounds another day. Sleep. . .she needed to sleep.

Tristan whistled. "You've got it bad."

"Tell me about it. I barely know the woman, and yet I can't spend enough time with her. It's scary. I've never fallen this hard for anyone, not even Shawna."

"Talk about a disastrous relationship. I still can't believe she went ballistic on you and your mother."

Ty shook his head. "I still can't believe I didn't see it in her. I mean, she hung out with the quartet, and there was never a sign of a problem."

"She was a peculiar one, for sure. But let's get back to the present. We've done all right meeting expenses and salaries this quarter, but the cost of the album production cut into the profits. I don't see a problem making up the revenues within the year."

Tyrone lifted the dirty dishes from the table and brought them to the sink. "By the end of the year we should have more than covered the expenses. Look how well the first wedding album continues to sell."

"I agree. Marissa asked me to mention the staging under her. She thinks a few boards might need replacing."

Tyrone filled the sink with warm soapy water. "I'll check it out. With Marissa getting married, I've been thinking about taking on students. I can't imagine us keeping this schedule and her having time for her husband."

"Agreed. I was thinking along the same lines. Perhaps we should consider a different shop. Perhaps a storefront. Something where we could give lessons."

"It should have good lighting and security for parents transporting kids to and from."

"Agreed. Should we ask the girls to start praying about this?"

"Yeah, I think it's something all of us should be praying about. I know we've talked about the quartet staying together even after Marissa marries, but what happens when she starts having kids?"

"Let's cross that bridge when we come to it. I can't imagine it not being the four of us. We've been together so long." Tristan finished off his coffee, then glanced at his watch. "I need to be going. I promised my brothers I'd hang out with them today."

"No problem. Oh, by the way, my mom's hinting about how long it's been since she's seen me."

Tristan raised his hand. "Say no more. A few days off would be wonderful. Mention it to Marissa and let her know I think a few days off would be good, too."

"Will do. Take it easy."

Tristan headed out the door, and Tyrone finished picking up from their breakfast meeting. His apartment cleaned up, he headed to the pool to put in some laps. He hadn't replaced his sailboard and still wasn't sure he would. *A larger vessel might be in order, but who has the time for the maintenance?* On the other hand, windsurfing had a definite downside.

Later that evening he heard Cassandra playing her flute and could hear the nervousness in her playing. Ty left his deck and went through his apartment to knock on Cassy's front door. "Hi."

"Hi. Am I disturbing you?"

"No. But if you don't mind me saying so, I could hear your fear."

Cassy closed her eyes. "I'm about ready to call Pastor Paul and let him know I just can't do it."

"Can I help?"

"Are you busy tomorrow morning?"

"No, but I wasn't offering to take your place." Ty grinned.

Cassy stepped back, allowing him to enter her apartment. "Oh, come on, you'd be wonderful. The church would be so blessed."

"Play the piece again for me."

"Only if you work your magic fingers on my neck and shoulders," she teased.

"Not a problem."

Cassy sat down and positioned herself with the music. Ty worked her stiff muscles. "Why are you so afraid?"

"Stage fright, I guess. It's probably why I never went further with music. I love it, but

I'm terrified playing in front of people."

"I'm obsessive in getting a piece just right. Ask the quartet. They'll all agree. I've held back on playing pieces for events if I didn't feel we were at a certain level. Of course, all of us have that in us to some extent."

"The four of you are really close, aren't you?"

"Yeah, kinda like an extended family."

"Ty, would you please play with me tomorrow?"

"But we haven't practiced together."

"Please. I know I'll be more confident playing with someone than by myself."

Tyrone gazed into her auburn eyes and saw her sincere pleading. "All right. Let me get my cello and see if we can work it out well enough to perform together."

"Thanks."

What had he agreed to? Hadn't he just told her he was a perfectionist when it came to performances? Was it possible to play together with only one rehearsal? He stopped himself at the door. "On second thought, bring your flute to my place. A flute is a lot less to lug around."

Cassy chuckled and grabbed her music. An incredible urge to pull her into his arms and kiss those sweet lips rushed over him. *Lord, give me strength.*

They played "Amazing Grace" over and over for an hour. "I need a break," Cassy said.

"No problem. I think we've got it down pretty well."

"You weren't kidding when you said you were a perfectionist."

Ty placed the cello in its stand. "Sorry."

Cassandra rubbed her cheeks. "No, it's okay. I'm obviously not a professional. Thanks for being so patient with me. So often I just wanted to put my flute down and listen to you."

Tyrone chuckled. "You did."

"Oh, sorry."

He loved the playful banter that played out when they were together. She was so comfortable to be around. "As you can tell, I've played the piece many times before. But I do like the difference of the string and the wind instruments together. It's a nice sound."

"I was noticing that, too."

He wondered how well the rest of their lives would blend together. "Cassandra, I'm not sure how to ask this. I like you. I'm attracted to you. But I don't really like the dating scene. And I'm a man who, well, once I've made a commitment to go out with someone, it's exclusive. I guess what I'm trying to ask is if you'd like to go out with me on a regular basis."

"Go steady?"

Ty hadn't heard that term in years and chuckled. "For lack of a better term, yes."

"When you obsess you obsess," she quirked a grin. "Wasn't it just yesterday we decided to take it slow and begin as friends?"

Ty inhaled and let out a slow sigh. "You're right. I'm sorry. It's hard to believe that was only yesterday. It seems like weeks have passed. Well, maybe not weeks but. . ."

She stepped up to him and placed her finger to his lips. "It's all right. I feel the same things, too. I think we were right yesterday about our friendship, but I also think we have to be honest about our growing attractions."

He wrapped his arms around her and held her close. Cassy wanted to protest because she wanted him too much. She closed her eyes and prayed for strength. "Ty," she whispered.

"Yes," he purred.

That was all it took. She pushed herself away from his embrace.

"Sorry," he mumbled.

"Let's talk on the patio," she suggested. It was dangerous to be alone in a secluded place with him.

"Wise woman." Ty escorted her outside.

She loved being in his arms. She ached to be there right now. "How do we control this?"

"You've got me." Ty sat down on a patio chair. "Maybe we should talk about some neutral subjects, say, like baseball or something."

Cassy giggled. "Have you been to a Marlins game?"

"A couple times. It's so hard with the team struggling so. You?"

"Same. What about the Dolphins?"

"Now football's another matter. I've gone as often as I could reasonably afford it."

"How does the quartet survive financially?"

"Right now, we're doing well. We don't need second jobs. But with Marissa getting married, I foresee the day when our schedules will have to lessen and we'll be faced with a need to earn some money apart from the quartet."

"Ah." *I wonder if he can afford a wife and kids.*

Wife? Kids? And I think he's *obsessive.* She groaned.

"What?" he asked.

"Nothing."

"Cassy, be honest; what went through your mind?"

Honesty, something she prided herself on. "I wondered how you could provide for a wife and children."

Ty blushed. "I'm doing all right. I've tried to make wise investments. But, admittedly, the first two years out of school, I spent far more than I should have. Now I'm saving for the rainy day and preparing for my future. If I find the right house, I could provide well for a family at my current income."

"I'm sorry, I didn't mean. . ."

He cut her off. "It's okay, your thoughts haven't gone anywhere that mine haven't. Isn't it odd that we barely know each other, but when we sit down to talk it's as if we've known each other for years? And we've both admitted to our mutual attraction.

"I've been praying about us, Cassy. I know that's rather bold, especially since we've just begun to get to know each other. But I do want the Lord in our relationship right from the start."

Cassy smiled. "You don't know how long I've waited to hear that from a man. I've basically given up on dating also, especially after that blind date my girlfriend set me up with the night before I pounded on your wall—he was a real winner. She'd been trying to set me up for ages. Somehow, I agreed to that blind date. But I refuse to go on another one again."

"I don't have much free time for traditional dating. I'm generally the guy playing in the background for the romantic events."

"Well, if I can be so bold, I think it's time to come to the foreground and pick up a romance."

Ty got up and crossed the patio to her. "Are you serious?"

"Yes."

He pulled her up from her chair and into his arms. "Oh, Cassy." He covered her lips with his own. A wave of warmth flooded her body. She tightened her grasp of him and lost herself in the kiss.

Cool air flowed between them when he pulled back. Moments passed before she opened her eyes. Ty's beautiful hazel eyes gleamed back at her. "Wow," she managed to say.

Ty wiggled his eyebrows. "Wow back." He took her by the hand and led her into the apartment. Fear washed over her.

"Cassy, let's pray and ask the Lord for guidance."

Peace washed over her. "I'd like that."

He led them in a prayer. When it was over, she glanced up and noticed the clock on the wall. "Oh, no." She jumped up and grabbed her flute.

Chapter 7

What's the matter?"

"I'm late for work. I should have left a half hour ago."

"When are you due in?"

"Five minutes ago."

"Oh. Can I call work for you while you get dressed?"

Cassy gave him the numbers. She ran out, and he heard her banging drawers in her apartment. *Her slider must be open, too,* he thought. He'd have to remind her to close it. He called the hospital and let them know. He waited for her and caught her as she left. "Good night, Cassy."

" 'Night. I'll come by in the morning when I get home."

"Great." He hesitated. Should he kiss her?

She leaned over and gave him a quick kiss on the cheek. "I'll call you later from work."

"Thanks." He waved good-bye and felt like a seven-year-old. He shoved his hand in his pocket. Tonight was a rare Saturday off. If he hadn't been home, he wouldn't have heard her playing. And if he hadn't heard her playing, he wouldn't have agreed to rehearse with her. And if he hadn't agreed to play with her, they wouldn't have shared that awesome kiss. His pulse quickened just recalling it. Tristan's words came back to mind: "You've got it bad." Tristan had no idea how bad.

Over the next few weeks, Cassandra became a regular part of his life. He couldn't spend enough time with her. And she had admitted to him that she felt the same way. They worked their schedules out together. Cassy would come to any event that wasn't private, as her schedule allowed, in much the same way that Jason had when he and Marissa started dating. The quartet loved and accepted Cassy. Ty began to think in terms of marriage. *It's happened all so fast. Would she even consider it at this time?* he wondered.

His trip home to visit with his parents had been disastrous. He couldn't get his mind off Cassandra. He'd rung up more time on his cell phone than one should and knew he had gone over the allotted minutes. He'd behaved so distractedly, his mother sent him home a day early.

Ty smiled after the thirteen-hour drive. He was finally home. The blue sedan sitting in Cassandra's spot heightened his excitement. Taking the steps two at a time, he passed his apartment and knocked on Cassy's door. Having driven all night, he tried telling himself he should be in bed, not waking up the one person he loved most.

Cassy opened the door, her hair mussed from sleep. "Ty?" Shock widened her eyes. She stepped back and closed the door.

"Cassy?"

"Ty, you should have told me you were coming home," she protested through the closed door.

"I wanted to surprise you. Cassy, let me in."

"No," she screeched. "I'm a mess."

Ty chuckled. "You're beautiful. Come on, let me in."

"No," she protested.

"How about a quick kiss? Then I'll leave you to your beauty sleep."

"No." He couldn't believe his ears. Hadn't she missed him just as much as he missed her?

"Cassy, open up," he pleaded.

A deep male voice answered. "She said no. Now beat it."

Anger burned like an ignited fuse throughout his body. What was a man doing in her apartment?

He heard some arguing going on behind the door. Ty shuffled back to his apartment, unlocked the door, and tossed the keys on the counter. "What just happened, Lord? Who is that man? And what's he doing in her apartment?" Ty held up his hands toward heaven. "Don't tell me; I don't want to know."

Thirteen hours on the road to surprise Cassy, and this. He pulled his grandmother's ring out of his pocket and tossed the velvet box onto his bureau. "So much for thinking she was the right one," he mumbled.

He set the headset over his ears and put on ten hours of classical music. Whenever stressed, he'd retreat to the music he loved. After an hour of pacing, he collapsed in his recliner and fell into an uneasy sleep.

Ty woke to find the sun setting. An orange hue blanketed the patio. Thoughts of Cassy emerged, and anger stirred once again in his body. How could he have been so wrong about her?

He dialed Tristan.

"Hey, Man, when did you get back?" he heard from the other end.

"This morning. I need to talk. Can you meet me at the shop?"

"Sure, what's up?" Tristan asked.

"I'll tell you at the shop."

"All right. See you in a few."

Tyrone hung up, packed an overnight bag, and headed to the shop. Once there, he paced the length of the room. At last, he heard Tristan's car pull in.

Tyrone met him at the door.

"What's up? You look horrible."

"Cassy." Tyrone sucked in a deep breath. "She had a man in her apartment this morning."

"What? No way."

"I heard him. She wouldn't let me in. And then he spoke up and told me to beat it."

"Sorry, man, that's terrible. What happened?"

"What do you mean, what happened? I went to my place, put on my headset, and fell asleep. I called you when I woke up. I drove straight through the night to get home a day early, and this is what I find."

"There's got to be some mistake."

"There's no mistaking a deep male voice. I thought she was the one, Tristan. I really did. I'm wondering if I can bunk with you for a couple days."

"Couch is all yours. But shouldn't you talk with Cassy, find out what happened?"

"Maybe, but not now. I'll say something I'll regret."

"All right. But why stay at my place?"

"Because Cassy has the next two days off. We timed my return with her days off."

"Ah, I see." They made their way back to Tristan's place, each in his own car. Could he handle seeing Cassy again? Could he handle seeing her daily? No, he didn't think so. At least not yet.

❧

Cassy couldn't believe Ty's immaturity, not answering his door the entire day of his return. The van had been parked in his slot, so she knew he was home, avoiding her, like a spoiled child. It wasn't often her brother came for a visit, but when he did, he'd stay at her place. What bothered her more was that Ty had jumped to the wrong conclusion. Of course, she should have told him C. J. was her brother. But if he truly loved her, why hadn't he given her a chance to explain?

On the other hand, he'd never once said "I love you." In all their time together, those words never tumbled from his lips. And she, too, had held back claiming her love for him. How was it possible for an educated woman to fall head over heels for a man she barely knew?

She called his cell phone one more time and got his voicemail. She hung up, not bothering to leave another.

"Come on, sis, the guy's not worth it. How about I take you out to dinner tonight, someplace special?" C. J. gave her an encouraging smile.

"I don't know."

"Come on, it'll be good for you. Besides, absence makes the heart grow fonder." C. J. wiggled his eyebrows.

Cassy chuckled. "Since when have you become an expert on love?" Her brother was more of the "love 'em and leave 'em" kind of guy. His relationship with the Lord, if he ever had one, ended when he was ten.

"Where would you like to have dinner?" C. J. changed the subject with little finesse.

"Houstons?" The restaurant sat on the water, not too far up the road from where she lived, and did not have classical music playing in the foreground. Though, to be honest, she knew Tyrone wouldn't be playing tonight since they had planned her days off to end with his trip home from seeing his parents. Perhaps she should have gone with him? It wouldn't have been too difficult to arrange for a few days off. Why had she resisted? Was she as afraid of commitment as her brother?

⤡

Dinner and her visit with C. J. had gone well the night before. But her mind kept going back to Tyrone. Where was he? He hadn't come home. She thought of tracking down Tristan Reuben, since he and Ty seemed to be fairly close. But her stubborn pride would not allow her to track the man down. If he loved her, he'd come to her and apologize.

Cassandra chewed her inner cheek. Her body was filled with tension. *And how do you eliminate tension if you don't have the opportunity to speak with the person you're upset with?* she asked herself. *God?* an inner voice whispered.

"Father, please bring Tyrone home so we can talk," Cassy prayed.

She dressed in her swimsuit and placed a white-laced beach cover on and headed for the pool. She'd been thinking about, praying about, and worrying over Tyrone since he'd knocked on her door. Grabbing her towel and slipping on her sandals, she made her way out to the farthest edge of the concrete dock that extended into the bay and sat on the bench. The sounds and sight of Biscayne Bay always helped soothe her frayed nerves. White-hulled boats glistened in the sunlight. The gentle waves rolled up against the concrete dock. Tropical fish swam below. "I can't imagine what the crystal sea is going to look like if this is a mere faded reflection of heaven," she said into the onshore breeze.

"It will be awesome," Ty responded.

"Tyrone, where have you been? I've been worried sick about you!" She clamped her mouth shut. It wasn't wise to tell the man how greatly he affected her, she reasoned on second thought.

"I'm sorry I didn't return your calls. I didn't trust myself. It hurt to hear a man was in your apartment."

Cassy fought down her anger. "That man was my brother."

"Your brother?"

"Yes, my brother, C. J. And if you'd bothered to answer the door when I knocked on it ten minutes later, I would have told you."

Ty sat down beside her on the bench, clasped his hands together, and looked down at his feet. "I didn't hear you knock. I put my headset on and listened to music. It calms me. I'd just driven all night to come home a day early and, well... I'm sorry."

Cassy placed her hand on his forearm. "I'm sorry, too. I should have opened the door. But I was a mess, and I didn't want you to see me when I wasn't my best. I know it's silly but..."

Ty smiled. "Honey, you always look good." His gaze locked with hers. "I love you," he confessed.

Tears filled her eyes. "I love you, too."

He took her into his arms and kissed her softly on the lips.

Lost in his kiss, she leaned farther into his arms. She wanted to kiss him forever, or so it seemed. *Wait a minute; what about his assumption?* She realized she was falling for that old trick men use of persuading women by distracting them from the real issues. She pushed herself back from his embrace. "It won't work," she stammered.

Ty blinked open his hazel eyes. "Huh?"

"Kissing me is not going to distract me from my original anger with you."

Ty crossed his arms across his chest. "Oh?"

"Seriously, Ty, we've got a problem here. How can we develop a relationship if there isn't mutual trust?"

"You're right," he sighed. "I couldn't stop thinking or talking about you when I was with my folks. But as soon as you didn't respond the way I had been expecting, I jumped to the wrong conclusion."

"And you acted like a child, stomping off and not giving me a chance to explain. Why did you do that?"

Shrugging his shoulders, he got up and walked to the edge of the dock. "I don't know. I've never been this jealous before."

Jealous? Cassandra grinned.

Chapter 8

Tyrone watched the fish playing in the water, swimming in and out of the various seaweed-lined rocks. Cassandra had a point. They were easily upset with one another, and that wasn't healthy. Perhaps his desires to ask her to marry him had been too impulsive. He turned back to her. "You're right. We do have a problem. What do you suggest we do about it?"

She tapped the bench seat. He followed her lead and sat back down beside her. "I think we need to spend more time with each other and more time discussing our inner thoughts and desires. Not just our physical attraction."

"All right, where do we begin?" he asked.

Shaking her head, she asked, "Tell me about your trip?"

Ty went on to tell her about the past few days, how much he enjoyed being home but couldn't wait to get back to Miami. He'd missed her so much.

"I missed you, too," she whispered. "I know it was my vanity that wouldn't open the door. I'm sorry."

He placed his arm across her shoulders. "It's all right. I shouldn't have overreacted. By the way, don't be surprised if you get a call from my mother. She's quite curious about you."

"Oh?"

"Yeah. She's protective of her son and interested in the woman who's caught his eye."

"So, I've caught your eye, huh?"

"Woman, you have no idea." He laughed and kissed her again.

"Well, aren't you two giving the complex something to talk about." Betty Ann stood with her hands on her hips and winked.

Tyrone and Cassandra released each other at once. He'd forgotten the favorite pastime in the complex was gossip, and he and Cassy must have given them a week's worth with their kisses. Almost every condo in the place could see this spot of the dock.

"Nice to see you two getting along," Betty Ann said and chuckled. "Seriously, I didn't come here to embarrass you. The hospital called and was wondering if you could come in tonight."

Cassandra's glance caught his. He didn't want her to go to work, but understood they must be desperate to track Cassy down via Betty Ann. Ty released her hand and nodded his understanding.

Taking in a deep breath, Cassandra asked, "What's the problem?"

"Amy's got the flu and Vanessa's out of town for the week."

"Ah, I guess I have little choice."

"Oh, you have a choice, and I'm sure they'll find someone from some other floor, but you did mention wanting some overtime." Betty Ann cocked her head to the right. "Of course, I can think of another reason that might have a more desirable reward than extra money." Betty Ann flashed a smile at Tyrone. Heat blushed his cheeks.

Cassy turned toward him. "Should I?"

"Honey, I'd love to spend the rest of the day and evening with you, but if you need the income, I certainly understand."

She'd have to go to bed soon if she was going to work the graveyard shift, he reasoned. "We need to talk. . . ."

"I'll let you two discuss this in private." Betty Ann waved and retreated toward the condo.

Tyrone brushed the windblown hair from her face. "We have plenty of time to talk. And I promise I won't let my tiredness or foolish thoughts get the best of me next time."

Cassy chuckled. "Walk me back to my place?"

"With pleasure. Would you like to borrow my headset and CDs? You'll never hear a thing."

They slowly made their way down the dock holding each other around the waist. "Including my alarm. I don't think so."

"I'd be happy to wake you up. Let's see, I could take down the sound wall and bang on it with a hammer," Ty teased.

Cassy playfully swatted him on the shoulder. "No, thanks, I like my peace and quiet. Let's have breakfast together."

"I'll have it ready." He stopped outside her door. "I'm sorry, Cassy. I should have trusted you. I shouldn't have overreacted."

"You're forgiven." She leaned into him and gave him a quick kiss on the cheek. "I'll see you in the morning."

"Good night," he said, wanting to say more. Wanting to spend more time with her. But she needed her rest, and standing here, keeping her from entering her apartment, wouldn't let her rest.

" 'Night." She slipped her key in the lock and turned it to the right. He waved, and felt like a child waving good-bye on the bus for the first time. Sucking in a deep breath, he marched over to his place. What would he do now? He ached to speak with Cassy. So much had been left unsaid. So many things yet to discuss. If he were to ask her to marry him, how could they merge their schedules?

Ty sat down with his cello and began to play. The words of Psalm 108:1 suddenly came to mind. "My heart is steadfast, O God; I will sing and make music with all my soul." He let the bow drop from its rightful position on the strings. He ached to spend more time with her and yet at the same time felt overjoyed in her proclamation of love. They had taken the next step in their relationship. Why was he nervous about the things not yet said?

Cassandra tossed and turned all evening. She wanted to be with Tyrone. She didn't want to go to work. But she did need the extra cash the hours would bring in. She'd set her mind on a special gift for Ty, and extra hours would help the dream become a reality.

Work dragged. By breakfast, she was ready to go home and crash for the morning. Tyrone had set a wonderfully romantic table, and she barely had the energy to thank him for it. Fortunately, she had remembered.

The next few days blurred into a series of a moment here and a moment there. As much as they tried to mesh their schedules, there always seemed to be a conflict. Cassy longed to find a way to make this work. *But how?* she wondered.

Cassandra looked down at her appointment book. She'd blocked in all of Tyrone's concerts and practice times. There were a couple of ways to arrange her sleep time if she worked from eleven p.m. to seven a.m. One was to sleep as soon as she got home until midafternoon. The other was to stay awake until midafternoon and sleep the rest of the afternoon and evening. Cassy had always found the morning sleep suited her better. But with Ty's schedule, the afternoon and evening might be best. Would altering her schedule help? Or should they continue to try to line up days off? But that wouldn't work, since her schedule rotated between five days on and two days off.

Ty knocked on her door. "Come in," she called out.

"Hi. What ya doing?"

"Trying to figure out how we can spend more time together. It's been a horrible week."

"True, but it shouldn't be this bad all the time. I've just been putting in extra hours to set up the private lessons."

Cassy drummed her fingers on the countertop. "Even still, our schedules conflict most of the time. I'm sleeping when you're free. You're working when I'm sleeping."

Ty leaned back against the counter. "True," he sighed.

"I've been thinking of rearranging my sleep time. It'll take a week or so for my body to adjust, but it might be better in the long run."

"How so?" he asked.

She went on to explain the advantages and disadvantages of what she'd been trying to hammer out.

"I could schedule lessons in the afternoons while you're sleeping. That would leave the mornings free for us. How does that sound?"

"Worth trying." Cassy gave him an appreciative smile as she turned to meet him in her narrow kitchen. She really did like the way Tyrone had opened his wall up in his kitchen, making it feel less blocked in. "If you don't mind me asking, how much did it cost to open up your kitchen?"

"A couple thousand, because I replaced all the countertops and cabinets. Gradually, I've replaced all the appliances. These are great condos, but they are over thirty years old and minor adjustments are needed."

"I'd like to open up my kitchen, but I'm afraid it will have to wait for a while."

"Let me know when you decide. I'll get Tristan and his brothers to help. We can knock it out in no time."

Cassy chuckled. "I imagine you can."

Ty stepped closer. "Are you free for a bit?"

"I can spare an hour. What's up?"

"We've found a new location for the quartet. I'd like your opinion. It's important to me."

"Sure. I'd love to."

Ty brought her to the possible new location. The place needed some work, but it had enough square footage, and parking space was more than adequate.

"What do you think? I know it needs paint and some remodeling but. . ." He left the sentence unfinished.

"I think you've picked a good location." Cassy looked up at the ceiling. "Will you need to put in some acoustic tiles?"

"Definitely. Here's what we're picturing." Ty went through the entire building and described some of the changes he saw taking place. "In the end, I think it will take us a good month, possibly six weeks to have it finished."

"You might want to work on a temporary front for possible passerby. You'll never know who might be going to the music store down the block and notice your new construction," Cassy suggested.

"Good point. We've already thought about giving the music stores some flyers. At the moment, Tristan and I will be the only ones giving music lessons. But Marissa is looking forward to it after her wedding and honeymoon."

"I don't know much about business, and I certainly know little about yours, but I think you guys are making a wise decision."

"We've prayed about this. We really want to continue to play as a quartet, but we'll each have different needs." Ty looked down at his feet and coughed. "Well, you did say you only had an hour."

Cassy looked at her watch, "Right, thanks. And thank you for the tour. I can't wait to see it finished."

"Huh, you're going to help with the renovations." Ty smiled.

"Oh, really?"

His voice softened. "If you don't mind."

❧

Tyrone felt a little bad for being so forward in assuming Cassy would help. On the other hand, he needed to work on the studio and he didn't want to be apart from her more than he had to. Working together at the studio, playing together in his apartment, and working on his psalms compositions took up most of their free time.

He needed to do something special with her.

The doorbell rang and his door opened immediately. "Hey, got a minute?"

"Sure, I was just thinking about you."

Cassandra smiled. "Great." Her smile slipped. "Unless you're planning on working today," she quipped.

"No, but that is in part what I was thinking about." Ty walked up to her and grasped her hand. "I want to take you somewhere, anywhere. I was thinking we've had precious little time when we weren't working."

Cassy took in a deep breath. "Great minds think alike."

"What would you like to do?"

"Anything."

"How about a trip to the zoo?" he asked.

"I've never been."

"Good. It's been several years since I have. Date?"

"Date."

"Can you be ready in fifteen?" He asked. She did tend to spend a lot of time before going out on dates, he mused.

"For the animals, I can dress down and be ready. . ." She looked over her shoulder and whispered in his ear dramatically, "In five."

Ty laughed. He loved this woman. With each passing day, his love was growing. Their mutual respect and trust for each other was growing, too.

"Let me grab my purse and I'll be ready."

"Great."

Cassy left, and Ty pulled a couple of bottled waters, apples, and grapes from his refrigerator. He pulled a small blue-and-white cooler from under the sink and loaded it. He then selected some cheese and crackers to round off his impromptu picnic at the zoo.

The rest of their day was spent not discussing work or schedules or remodeling or even the psalms. Instead, they focused on each other, on memories from childhood. They admired the animals and simply enjoyed each other's company.

They stopped and sat down on a bench at a play area right after the elephant exhibit. "Thirsty?" he asked.

"A little," she replied.

"I've got some bottled water, but I'd be happy to buy you a soft drink or juice."

"Water's fine, thanks."

He pulled out a bottled water and handed it to her, then placed the small cutting board on the bench between them. "How about some cheese and crackers?"

Cassy's eyes sparkled. "You're a romantic."

"Sometimes. Most of the time I get too focused on the present and, well, my music."

"I've noticed."

"Sorry." He glanced away. "I know I'm a bit obsessive."

She laughed and placed her hand upon his. "Honey, it's all right. Just as long as you agree to my interrupting you from time to time."

"Please do." He placed some cheese on the cracker and handed it to her. "I love you."

"I love you, too."

He felt happy they had decided to take some free time with each other. Their schedules would definitely cause them problems. She seemed to like her shift at the hospital. But what if they were to marry? Would she still want to work those hours? Would they find themselves sleeping at separate times? Tyrone didn't care for that thought. Would she be willing to make that adjustment to her work schedule? His was set by the customers. There was little he could do. But if he had a wife, he certainly wouldn't want to keep the schedules they'd been keeping.

Wife? Jumping ahead, aren't you, buddy? he silently quipped.

Chapter 9

Switching her sleeping hours had produced a little more time with Tyrone, but it didn't satisfy her desires to spend more time with him. They were quickly becoming the best of friends, seeking each other's advice, and working together on his project to bring music back to the psalms created for string instruments. The flute wasn't exactly a stringed instrument, but Ty easily converted the harmony for a violin.

Cassandra wiped the sweat off her palms. Today she and Tyrone would be playing his pieces for the quartet. This would allow the others to help fill out the musical structure of the various accompaniments. It was hard enough playing for Tyrone, but to be playing in front of the other three accomplished musicians seemed overwhelming.

She felt Tyrone's presence behind her before she felt his wonder-working hands on her shoulders. She closed her eyes and relaxed under his soothing ministrations. "Thanks," she mumbled.

"You're welcome," he whispered in her ear.

A pulse of electricity coursed through her spine. "I love you."

"I love you, too." He kissed the tip of her ear. "Come on, it's time."

The newly renovated storefront reflected the classical yet contemporary appearance of Classical Strings Quartet. Tyrone had picked up several students, and even the bookings for various functions seemed to be coming in more easily.

Tyrone cleared his throat. "Cassy's a little nervous and, admittedly, I am, too," he told the other members of the quartet who sat down in a semicircle, awaiting their private concert.

"I've had a dream since I was in high school," Tyrone continued, "and that was to score the psalms written for string instruments. It's been difficult, to say the least. Most of these psalms are referring to very hard, often mournful times.

"Cassy's helped me create a harmony to counter the mournfulness and use it as the answer that Christ gives us in our lives."

Cassandra gave a weak smile as all three turned their heads and looked directly at her.

"I'm figuring from what I've scored, the four of us can come up with some amazing pieces." Tyrone sat down. Cassandra stiffened and raised the flute to her lips. *Lord, help me.*

Before they began, Ty winked at her in his usual way and she relaxed. They made their way through the first number. Cassy only missed three notes. Not too bad, she mused. The others picked up their instruments and worked through the same piece, playing the scores Tyrone had written for them. Cassy sat back and enjoyed the concert, marveling at hearing the others never miss a beat.

Pleased with how well the others dove into Tyrone's creation, Cassy excused herself. After all, she needed to go home and go to bed. Maybe it was time to consider working another shift?

At home, she slept restlessly. She and Tyrone had been dating for awhile. Their relationship had developed, and yet she wanted more. She wanted to marry the man, have his children, and grow old together. She couldn't think of a more satisfying life. "Lord, is he the one I've been waiting for? I think he is. It feels like he is. From the first moment we connected, there's been an incredible bond between us. But Ty seems content with life the way it is. I don't want to push him, Lord. And, admittedly, we haven't known each other all that long but. . ." But what? What did she really want? A miscreant smile crept up her face. "To marry him," she sighed.

She looked over at a bow she had purchased for Tyrone. She prayed it was as good as she'd been told it was. A good bow was as important as a well-made cello. She'd looked long and hard to find one that would meet Tyrone's approval. She'd even gone into research, learning who made the best ones and why. She prayed she'd made the right choice. She couldn't afford the eighteen-thousand-dollar ones she'd come across and knew Tyrone would love, but settled for one slightly over four thousand dollars, a replica of a historical bow.

They'd made special plans for breakfast the next morning. In fact, they'd planned the entire day together. *That will be the perfect time. . . .*

Dressed for work, she made her way north on Biscayne Boulevard toward the hospital. She didn't know if she should pray for a calm night or a busy one. Both had their own advantages. A busy one would go fast. A calm one wouldn't wear her out for their special date. She decided not to worry about it and checked in at the nurse's station.

Everything went well until three a.m., when the quiet floor erupted in turmoil. The patient in 5B had awakened suddenly, disoriented and violent. She restrained him with the help of an orderly, then injected some medication to help him sleep. His stitches had torn, which required she report the event to the doctor on call. Fashioning some quick butterfly stitches over the aggravated area, Cassandra reported the incident to the doctor on call, not surprised he didn't come up to check on the patient. From that point on, Cassy watched the gentleman like a hawk. She wasn't going to allow a lawsuit to be levied against the hospital on her shift.

Ty took the velvet box from the top of the dresser and opened it. His grandmother's ring sat cradled inside the dark velvet. The pink diamond had a unique Royal Asscher cut. If he remembered correctly, it was around two-thirds of a carat. "Lord, I love her with all my heart, and I know I want to spend my life with her. So why am I afraid?"

Tyrone closed the velvet box and placed it lovingly back on his dresser.

The phone rang and broke into his thoughts. "Hello."

"Hey, Ty, it's me." Cassy's voice warmed his heart.

He glanced back at the ring box. "It's good to hear your voice."

"I've got bad news. I need to work a double shift."

Tyrone's heart sank. "There's no one else?"

"I'm afraid not. I've personally called a couple of the nurses. I don't like my schedule, Ty. It's frustrating. We need more nurses, but budget restraints hold back on the hiring, and private duty nurses aren't always an option."

He closed his eyes. "I'm sorry. I know you tried to get off work."

"I don't give up our special days together easily. If it's any consolation, I'll have the next two days off. I already told them my phone will be disconnected. I'm working far too many hours. It's not healthy."

He had to agree there. "I wish there was something I could do."

Cassy chuckled. "Come to the hospital and join me for breakfast. I miss you."

"I'm on my way. I miss you, too." Making adjustments to his schedule, and her making adjustments to hers, was the only way they would be able to spend time together. *Cassandra is definitely worth the sacrifice, Lord.*

The highlight of Tyrone's day had been their breakfast together. Once Cassy returned home from work, she went straight to bed. He prepared a breakfast of fresh fruit and bagels. Today he would brave it and ask her the question. In a box on the counter sat fresh-cut exotic flowers, ones he believed would blend well with her natural color.

Next, he put on some classical music and lit the candles lining his apartment for the occasion.

The doorbell rang. He glanced over at the clock. Right on time. *Gotta love that,* he thought with a smile. He opened the door and she returned his smile. "Good morning, sunshine."

" 'Morning. I'm sorry about yesterday."

"Shh, no problem. Work is work, and sick people need their nurses."

She looked down at her feet. "I almost quit. I told the hospital administrator he had to hire someone soon or I would quit. I also pointed out how much they were paying me and others in overtime by not hiring another nurse."

"Did it help?"

Cassy chuckled. "The bottom line with them is the money, not the patients. So, yeah, I think it worked." She looked to her left and to her right. "Do you think I might be able to come in?"

"Oh, sorry." Ty stepped back and let her pass before him.

"What's all this?" She gazed around the open room.

"I missed you."

"I missed you, too, but I didn't. . ." Her eyes fixed on the long white box on the kitchen counter.

"Do you have a tall vase?" he asked.

She hesitated. "Yes."

"I thought so. These are for you." He handed her the box.

She opened it. "They're gorgeous."

He liked pleasing this woman. And giving her simple gifts brought a deep, resounding pleasure and satisfaction.

"Since this is a day of gift giving, I have one for you. I'll be right back." Cassy fled to her apartment.

Tyrone paced, fingering the velvet box in his pants pocket.

Cassandra bustled back in through the front door. She held a long, thin, gift-wrapped box in her hand. "I hope you like it. If not, I can return it."

What had she purchased? He received the box in tentative hands. It was as light as a feather. His mind raced. Only one thing he knew came in a box of this size. "What did you do?"

Cassy smiled. "Open it."

Ty sat down. She shouldn't have. He ripped the wrapping off the package. The name of a well-known bow maker was on the outer box. "Cassandra, I can't accept this."

"You haven't opened it yet. How do you know?" she teased.

"I know the company, and they aren't cheap." His hands caressed the long box. "How did you come across them?"

"Well, open it before I explode," she demanded.

Ty chuckled.

"Trust me; it's paid in full."

"But, honey. . ."

"Tyrone David Carver, open it and accept the gift as it's been given, with all my heart and love," she chastised.

"Yes, Ma'am." Inside he found what he'd expected. "It's beautiful. Thank you. But how can you. . .?"

"Honey, I love you. I researched bows, and I felt I knew a little about your preferences, so I took a risk and purchased this replica."

"It's wonderful."

"Try it out. If it doesn't feel right or if it doesn't bring complete satisfaction, the company will replace it."

"I'm sure it's fine. I've been looking at this same bow for awhile now. It's perfect." Tyrone placed the bow on the coffee table. "I have another gift for you. Actually, it's more than a gift." He cleared his throat. "Come here. Sit beside me."

She took his hand and sat down.

"Thank you." He kissed her gently on the lips. "I love you, Cassandra."

"I love you, too."

He did not have a doubt of her love. Not because she'd spent far too much money on the beautiful bow, but because he could feel the honesty in her kiss. He could hear it in her voice, in the way she walked and in the way she moved. He loved her, and he knew she was the one for him. "Cassandra." He caressed her fingers. "I know our schedules will be a problem. But I want to spend every free moment I have with you. I want to rise with you in the morning and experience everything the Lord would have us experience together. I know we've spent few days together, but I know my heart, and I think I know yours. Please do me the honor of becoming my wife."

Gentle tears filled her eyes. Ty fought down the lump in his throat.

"Yes," she whispered. "I love you."

"I love you, too." He kissed her warmly on the lips. He pulled away and fumbled for the ring box in his pocket. "Honey, if you'd like to pick out a new ring, I understand. But my grandmother gave me this awhile ago. She didn't wear it any longer, with Grandpa gone, and she didn't feel safe keeping it with her in the assisted living facility." He popped open the box.

"Oh, Ty. It's beautiful. I've never seen a diamond like that."

"It's a Royal Asscher cut. Grandmother said it was first designed in 1902. It's also a pink diamond, which is very rare. My grandpa used to say it was 'a special ring for a special lady,' and I think I know how Grandpa felt."

Cassy's hand shook as she reached out for the ring.

Tyrone took her hand into his and kissed her ring finger. "I love you, Cassandra." He placed the ring on her finger.

"Oh, Ty, I love you, too." She tipped her head to the side. "Just how many kids did you say you wanted?"

Tyrone roared with laughter. "All in good time, my dear. All in good time."

Peace washed over them both. Ty clasped both of her hands with his and prayed. "Father, bless us and watch over us. May we remain true to you and true to each other." Then he quoted from Psalm 108, verses 1 and 2. " 'My heart is steadfast, O God; I will sing and make music with all my soul. Awake, harp and lyre! I will awaken the dawn.'"

"Amen." Cassy smiled. "I look forward to a lifetime of making music with you."

"We do harmonize well." Ty clicked off the stereo and picked up the bow. He sat down with his cello and played.

LYNN A. COLEMAN

Lynn A. Coleman is an award-winning and bestselling author of Key West and other books. She began her writing and speaking career with how to utilize the Internet. Since October 1998, when her first fiction novel sold she's sold thirty books and novellas.

Lynn is also the founder of American Christian Fiction Writers Inc., and served as the group's first president for two years and two years on the Advisory Board. One of her primary reasons for starting ACFW was to help writers to develop their writing skills and to encourage others to go deeper in their relationship with God. "God has given me a gift," says Lynn, "but it is my responsibility to develop that gift."

Lynn has spoken at writers groups, women's groups, homeschooling organizations, church groups, conferences, workshops and retreats. "Lynn is informative, humorous, and approachable—what more can you ask for?" said one attendee.

She makes her home in Keystone Heights, Florida, where her husband of thirty-six years serves as pastor of Friendship Bible Church. Together they are blessed with three children and eight grandchildren.

Spring in Paris

by Peggy Darty

Chapter 1

It was five a.m. in Paris when Melanie Roberts' plane touched down at Charles de Gaulle airport. Melanie felt every mile of the journey. Her clothes were rumpled, and she had reverted back to her thick lenses because she was still adjusting to her new contacts. Her shoulder-length, glossy hair had now been whisked back from her face and secured with a rubber band.

Her shoulder bag tugged hard on her shoulder and she gave over to the slump. Despite aspirin, soothing music, and earphones, she hadn't slept more than an hour. She kept thinking about all that water underneath the plane.

Glancing around her, she noted the other passengers looked as bedraggled as she did. They were businessmen, or women who were probably visiting family, and a few stray singles like her.

She sighed and took a firmer grip on her bulging shoulder bag, but not before it had slammed into the passenger behind her.

"Sorry," she called over her shoulder to the man who looked far too crisp at this hour in his expensive suit.

"No problem," he answered in a slurred voice, but she could tell from his expression that he considered the jab of her shoulder bag a big problem.

She turned back around, shuffling with the line, realizing why the Ivy League types never appealed to her. Too arrogant.

She was herded into the long customs line, proof that at last she was in Paris.

"Business or holiday?" the customs officer asked.

"Holiday."

His eyes lingered on her passport then returned to her. She looked down at the passport picture, recalling it was made before she got a different hairstyle, but at least she was wearing the same glasses. His eyes swept her five-foot-seven-inch frame, all one hundred thirty-five pounds of it; then he stamped the passport and handed it back.

She fought her way to the luggage carousel where she spotted the Ivy Leaguer again. There was the usual wait for the luggage to arrive, so she sank into a hard chair and closed her eyes. Her second-graders flashed through her mind, and she wondered how they were spending their spring break. Then she thought of her wonderful grandmother, who had passed away in January. The money she had left Melanie had been earmarked in a special note. "Go see Paris for me. . . ."

Paris was a long way from little Milton, Ohio. *Thank You, God.*

A flurry around her jolted her back to her senses and she struggled to her feet as a jumble of luggage rolled around the carousel. She spotted Ivy League again. Watching him hassle his sleek luggage gave her a bit of satisfaction so that she almost missed her maroon canvas bags.

After another tussle, she ended up out on the street, her mind suddenly blank. She reached into her jeans pocket, fumbling around for the engraved card with the address of the Ritz. She had told herself she was going first class, especially with the hotel, and by the price, she knew she had.

The limos were disappearing, along with the taxis as the crowd elbowed ahead. She hesitated, wondering what to do. Then suddenly a taxi screeched to the curb before her. A little Frenchman hopped out and tossed off some words that didn't seem to match anything in her French-English dictionary.

"Want to share a taxi?" Ivy League suddenly appeared. "Where are you headed?"

"The Ritz," she informed him with pride.

He nodded. "I'm staying near there."

He related all of this to the driver who was loading their luggage into the trunk. Ivy League opened the back door and glanced over his shoulder at her. "Well, do you or don't you want a ride?" The slur was actually a southern accent, because the lazy drawl had been sharpened with crisp consonants. He was clearly irritated.

"I do," she snapped back, piling into the backseat and staring pointedly out the window. As she gazed, she quickly forgot about her grouchy traveling companion. It was still early morning in Paris, and the taxi zipped right along. Melanie watched with delight as they approached the famous landmarks she had studied about in the travel books. She knew exactly where she was. She didn't need to speak French!

They had passed the Champs-Elysées and were heading toward the Arc de Triomphe. Melanie pressed her face closer to the window, pushed her glasses securely in place, and peered at the French flag from inside the Arc. Soon the taxi was pulling into the Place Vendome.

She bit her tongue to keep from saying, *There it is.* She glanced quickly at Ivy League who was fast asleep, even snoring! How could one sleep when the statue of Napoleon crowned the middle of the square?

She turned in her seat as they swept past it, and now the driver was pulling to the curb where a green canopy overhung the entrance to a hotel. It took a moment for her to realize this was the Ritz. It was obviously understated elegance, so typical of Paris class.

The driver had announced their arrival as he swung to the curb, and Melanie gripped her shoulder bag and glanced again at her sleeping traveling companion. *So long, Ivy League.*

She stepped out onto the curb and discovered her driver knew English for his fares; he briskly told her exactly what she owed him. She added a generous tip, and then he led the way through the revolving doors where a smartly dressed concierge took charge, escorting her up to the reception desk.

There was no line here, and the concierge at the desk spoke English. She listened carefully as he handed her a registration form while explaining the amenities of the hotel. She went through the process, nodding gratefully while handing over her passport and credit card. She had preregistered by mail weeks ago, so the paperwork went swiftly, and soon he was handing back her passport and credit card, motioning for one of many fast-paced bellboys.

She was ushered down a couple of steps and across the lobby, where several distinguished-looking men wearing business clothes and reading newspapers glanced disinterestedly at her.

Melanie ran a hand self-consciously over her hair, realizing she hadn't put on any lip gloss in hours or even brushed her hair. It was no wonder she was not attracting any attention. On they went, down a long hall flanked by impressive little boutiques.

"Is this your first trip to Paris?" the concierge asked as they reached the elevator. She wondered if it was that obvious.

"Yes, it is," she replied as the elevator door slid open and they stepped inside.

He glanced at her once again as he led the way down the hall and unlocked a door. He seemed to sense how tired she was and didn't attempt to continue polite conversation. She reached for her billfold to tip him as he opened the door and placed her luggage inside.

"If you need anything—"

"I'll be fine," she smiled as he walked out, softly closing the door.

Her eyes widened as she surveyed her new home for the next six days. The room was filled with antiques, which would bring a rare gulp of enthusiasm from her mother, but which held little fascination for her. What she did like was the gorgeous soft pink brocades and marble fireplace. Her bedroom was a gracious blend of more pale pink in the satin coverlet of the bed with its matching pink chair. She peered into the bathroom and spotted the same marble elegance there.

She quickly opened her canvas bags, shook out the new clothes, and proudly hung each treasured garment on a padded hanger. Then after she had luxuriated in the beaded-oil bath water of the huge tub, she pulled on a loose gown and sank into the pink satin bed. She felt as though she had just melted into a pink cloud.

When she awoke and glanced at the ornate clock on her bedside table, she had slept until noon! She stirred lazily, enjoying the comfort and luxury.

"Oh, Granny," she said, hugging the companion pillow, "thank you for making a dream come true!"

Melanie had dressed in her least-wrinkled outfit, a floral silk skirt that swirled about her ankles and a yellow silk blouse that matched the delicate buttercups in her skirt. She had found some comfortable yet attractive sandals.

She took more care with her hair and makeup today, then sauntered down to the lobby. There were people everywhere and she quickly hurried out to the sidewalk. A warm sun greeted her, and just ahead, the aroma of coffee and freshly baked bread lured passersby to a cozy sidewalk café.

Since she was not a coffee drinker, she bypassed the espresso in favor of a morning tea. She watched with delight as the tea was delivered to her in a beautiful little floral teapot and a proper-looking English china cup. She poured the steaming tea and added honey. Ah, this was living!

Sipping her tea, she studied the entertaining array of people passing the café. Men in lightweight suits, stepping quickly along. Women of all ages and sizes wore flowing dresses or skirts, looking chic, fashionable, and *thin*.

But she took a deep breath and reminded herself that she was no longer overweight with mousy brown hair and simple clothes. To reaffirm her thoughts, she ran her slender, manicured fingers over her silk skirt and enjoyed the idea of feeling pretty and moving at her own pace, for a change. She had chosen not to sign up for any tours, preferring instead to roam around at her own leisure.

The man from last night—Ivy League—had just come in and was looking for a seat. Suddenly, his eyes landed on her and widened in recognition. She stared back. He looked so different today. Khakis and a green golf shirt had replaced the well-tailored business suit and flashy tie. Somehow seeing him more relaxed made her take notice of him in a way she hadn't during their first meeting. For example, she hadn't noticed what a nice tan he had.

He had smooth dark brown hair, worn short with a side part on the left, a rather long jawline, offset by a nose that just missed being too short, and wide-set blue eyes. Actually, he was quite handsome until she remembered his attitude.

Then she dropped her eyes to her cup, not acknowledging him; after all, he had been downright rude. Almost. But then so had she. As she concentrated on placing her cup on the table and looking out at the crowd, she saw from the corner of her eye that he was slowly approaching her.

"I almost didn't recognize you," he said, standing uninvited at her table. The southern drawl floated smoothly on the balmy spring morning, sounding both interesting and appealing. "You. . .look so different from last night."

Since she had recently checked her image in the mirror of her compact, she knew what he was seeing. Gray eyes with the contacts in place and the caramel highlights in her brown hair gleaming in the sun.

"You look different, too," she said with that edge to her voice that had emerged during her adolescence. For her, it had been a wall of defense against being fat, but her father termed her defense an "attitude."

She smiled to soften any trace of sarcasm as she looked into the blue—very blue—eyes.

An awkward moment of silence followed, and she realized he was lingering because he wanted her to invite him to sit down, so she did.

"I'm Dave Browning," he said, settling into the seat.

"Melanie Roberts," she said, not offering her hand.

"Bonjour." Her waiter had returned and was looking interestedly at Dave.

He ordered one of the strong espressos like everyone else was drinking then turned back to her. "So did you sleep well at the Ritz?" he asked politely.

"Very well," she replied, touching a linen napkin to her mouth. "And you?"

He leaned back in the chair and stretched, showing off nice shoulders and muscled tan biceps. He either was a sportsman or he pumped iron.

"Everything was fine," he replied as the waiter delivered coffee. "I was so tired I think I could have slept on a park bench." He paused and frowned. "In fact, you were already out of the taxi and the driver was shaking me awake before I knew what had happened."

"You fell asleep; in fact, you were snoring when I got out."

He chuckled, a nice rich sound that the southern drawl somehow complemented. "The perfect traveling companion, right?"

She smiled, and he was staring into her eyes and smiling back. She hoped he liked what he saw. "I was envious because I was so exhausted I could hardly think," she replied honestly. "But I've never been able to sleep in a moving vehicle."

"Didn't you sleep on the plane?"

"Not really."

He shook his head, taking a sip of the strong coffee. "I guess I snored all the way to Paris."

"I wish I could have! We've been busy at school and there's never any time to rest before a vacation."

"School? Grad school?"

She smiled. "No, I teach second grade."

"My mom's a teacher," he said, taking another deep sip of his espresso.

"What grade?"

"Ninth and tenth. Mostly English."

"Mine too! Her field is history. Thank God she's at the high school or she'd be strolling down to my second grade class to observe my method of teaching."

"Or reminding you about your passport?"

She had to laugh. "How did you know?"

"Well," he said, giving her a long look, "we have more in common than I thought."

She picked up a spoon to stir the honey from the bottom of her cup. It was merely an action to cover a moment of embarrassment. He must have thought of her in much the same way she had judged him: *not my type.*

"Where are you from, Melanie?"

"Milton, Ohio. Small town you've probably never heard of. And where in Dixie do you call home?" she asked, suddenly very interested in him. Her mind seemed to produce questions and supply answers more easily now. Perhaps it was because she was in Paris and had left the old Melanie Roberts back in Milton.

His lips spread over even white teeth into an amused little smile. "Atlanta. Deep in the heart of Dixie."

She didn't have to ask which state, for there was only one Atlanta that people talked about.

"I've never been to Atlanta," she admitted. "We took a family vacation in Florida when I was in high school. The area was pretty and I liked it, but that's the only part of the South I've visited."

"Really?" He seemed amazed. "Then you should come in the spring. If you like beautiful flowers and the flavor of the Old South, there are lots of tours of historical homes and beautiful gardens."

"Oh? Then I'd either have to come south soon or wait until next spring." Her words flowed easily, because it seemed so natural to be sitting here in Paris, France, on a weekday morning, talking to a complete stranger yet feeling incredibly comfortable with. . .*Dave Browning*. She even liked the name as she repeated it again in her mind.

"Well, you could come in the fall. We have lots of hardwoods that turn beautiful colors—and there are always tours then," he added, grinning.

"Maybe I will," she said lightly, as the waiter stopped to lift her pitcher and pour more tea. "*Merci beaucoup*." There, the phrase from her book sounded okay after listening to Dave.

"What are you doing in Paris?" he asked as he sipped his coffee.

"I'm on spring break. What about you?"

"Not on holiday," he said, and for the first time a slight frown rumpled his tanned forehead. His dark hair gleamed in the sunlight as though he had just shampooed it.

"I'm here on business. My company is having one of its international meetings." When he named the company, she recognized it immediately as one of the top dogs in the computer industry.

"And what precisely do you do for your company?" she asked, trying not to sound too impressed, although she was.

"I work with a development team designing software programs." His blue eyes grew serious as he spoke of his job. "We're trying to work the kinks out of a new program that will be a major breakthrough in the world of computer programming."

"That sounds exciting," she said, trying to imagine him behind a desk, staring at a computer screen, his mind conjuring up new techniques to keep abreast of the expanding world of technology.

He tilted his head slightly and looked at her. "Well, my job interests me but—"

"But what?" she leaned forward, placing her elbows on the table and cupping her hands under her chin. She was aware that her French manicure complimented her long slender fingers, and she was glad that she had added a few rings to her fingers, other than the usual birthstone.

"But. . .I guess it sounds dull to other people," he continued. "At least, most women I talk with frown and change the subject when I mention computers. Or they launch into something negative about their experiences with computers."

"My second-graders are already learning the basics." She thought about that for a moment and decided to voice her feelings. "It's remarkable how quickly their young minds pick up on computer knowledge, and I'm always amazed at how their little hands handle the mouse. . . ." She stopped herself before adding *better than I do.*

She was by no means computer illiterate, but she had never bothered to get e-mail or browse the internet, as most of her friends had. She spent her spare time curled up on the sofa, reading a new book. Taylor, on the other hand, was constantly zipping out e-mails from Cincinnati to her mom and all of her friends.

Dave was saying nothing, sipping his coffee and she realized her mind had dashed off again. "How long will you be here?" she asked quickly, noticing that his coffee was almost gone and he was refusing another serving from the waiter.

"Just until Friday," he replied. "And you?"

"Until Saturday."

"So what are you planning to do and see?" he asked.

"As much as I can," she admitted honestly, glancing toward the busy boulevard and wondering where to start.

"You were alone on the plane," he recalled suddenly. "Do you have friends here?"

"No. But then I'm a bit of a loner."

He nodded. "So am I." He looked at his watch but he didn't stand as she had expected. She knew the noon hour was over, and he was probably due somewhere.

"Do you have plans for tonight?" he asked suddenly.

"I. . .well, no. Not yet."

"Would you like to go to dinner? One of the advantages of my job is that I do get to come here twice a year. I know a few places to dine, and I've seen the major landmarks."

"Then maybe you can give me some advice. I have certain places in mind, but I'm not sure about the best times to visit." It was something she had been worrying about as she left the hotel this morning.

"My pleasure," he said, the southern accent dripping with charm. And she really liked the smile. It all fit together just right. She was aware that her heart was beating a bit faster, as though she had just climbed a flight of steps.

"In fact, I'd like to skip out of the afternoon meetings and go with you today," he said, his soft voice holding a tone of regret, "but I have to be at this particular meeting."

"Oh, I wouldn't want you to miss it," she replied, a bit too quickly, and she wondered if her "attitude" had surfaced. *Dinner*, she remembered. "I'd love to have dinner with you," she smiled up at him, hoping, if there had been any sarcasm in her tone, she had just erased it.

"Great! How about if I pick you up in the lobby of the Ritz at eight? Nightlife starts late here. But then it does in Atlanta, as well."

Nightlife never starts in Milton, she could have added. Instead, she replied casually, "Eight will be fine."

"Okay." The waiter had magically appeared with both checks and Dave took hers as well.

"You don't have to do that," she said, but then shut her mouth. She realized he was doing something nice for her, and she had to learn how to accept compliments, another failing of hers. "But thanks," she added sweetly. Not saccharine sweet, like Taylor, but the kind of sweet she used when her students brought her little gifts.

"You're very welcome. Thanks for perking up my day. And I'll see you this evening," he said, glancing again at his watch then shaking his head. "I'm already late, which is out of character for me."

"Then you'd better hurry," she said, keeping her seat. She intended to have another cup of tea and absorb the flavor of a spring day in Paris.

"Bye," he called over his shoulder as he quickly paid and hurried onto the sidewalk. He walked in the opposite direction, so she could stare after him, sizing him up. He might be only a couple of inches taller than she, but his build suited him well. He was not too muscled, not too thin or heavy, and he walked straight and purposefully, as though he knew where he was going and exactly how he was getting there.

She gave the waiter a big smile as he poured more tea for her. She was having the time of her life.

Chapter 2

At precisely eight that evening, Melanie stepped off the elevator into the lobby and saw Dave seated on a sofa, dressed in a nice suit with a more conservative tie. As she walked toward him, she thought the blue eyes lit up as he came quickly to his feet.

"Hi. I hope you haven't been waiting long." She wondered if she had misjudged her timing.

"Just got here," he said with a smile. "You look great."

"Thanks."

His gaze swept down her new dress. The dress was a jade-green linen with a mandarin collar that hugged her neck. As the salesgirl pointed out, this shade of green accented her gray eyes and pink skin and picked up the highlights in her hair. It was a long dress featuring the popular slit on the side of the skirt. She had worn delicate gold sandals with flat heels so she wouldn't be taller than Dave.

She glanced through the hotel window. "I didn't bring a jacket," she said absently. She had picked a fine time to worry about that, but she hadn't the right jacket for the dress, anyway.

"You'll be fine. It's a wonderful evening, warm with balmy breezes. Not as warm as Atlanta, but that's a blessing."

"It's already warm in Atlanta in May?"

"It's warm in Atlanta as early as March, but March is usually windy and undependable. April brings the showers and flowers and all that. The summers are hot and humid." His hand cupped her elbow as they crossed the lobby to the revolving front doors.

"It's still cool and windy in Milton," she said as they stepped onto the sidewalk, and he hailed a taxi and gave the driver an address that meant nothing to her.

"You really know your French," she said with a smile.

"There are certain phrases that I do well because I use them often. But as far as carrying on a lengthy conversation with the locals, I'd be at a loss."

She felt he was deliberately being modest because he had already witnessed how little she knew.

He put his arm up on the leather seat above her head, and they both gazed out at the beauty before them as they sped past the Place de la Concorde.

"How beautiful," she said, looking out at the fountains and the Eiffel Tower in the distance.

"Yes, it is. How did you spend the day?" he asked.

She told him about the souvenirs she had purchased, and the cards, and admitted it was a relief to get that behind her.

"You too? I really hate that sort of thing. Mom and my sister Alison love it."

"So do my mom and Taylor; that's my sister."

"Older or younger?" he asked interestedly.

"A year older."

"Alison is two years younger than me. There are only the two of us. No other siblings. And your family?"

"Just Taylor and me," and they both laughed.

She enjoyed the full, rich sound of his laughter as she tossed her head back and looked at him a bit closer.

He reached over to brush a tendril from her cheek, and for a moment he stared at the strand of the rich brown hair, a color chosen by an expert hairdresser to relieve the mousy brown of before. "You have nice hair," he said, smoothing it back. "My sister would be envious. She's always fussing about her hair. Too thin, too curly, or too straight. Every day is a bad hair day for Alison."

She could relate to that but she didn't say so. She merely smiled. "How old is she?" It was a sly way of learning his age after he had told her Alison was two years his junior.

"Twenty-three. She's a registered nurse engaged to be married just before Christmas."

"Oh really? Do you like the guy?"

He chuckled. "He was my roommate at the University of Georgia. Yeah, I like him. Actually, I used to bring him home on weekends. We were sophomores and Alison was a big-eyed, high school senior. For her, it was love at first sight. Trey is more cautious, but I could see that he liked her right away. So could Mom and Dad. They got engaged the next Christmas when Alison was a freshman at Georgia. My parents insisted on her finishing college before getting married; that's the reason they waited."

She liked everything he had told her. He seemed to come from a good family, and she wondered about his faith but was unsure how to ask.

They had reached their destination, for the driver had pulled to the curb and Dave was paying the fare. Then they were out of the taxi, entering a restaurant that she recognized from a picture in the guidebook. She was impressed that he had taken her to such an exclusive place for dinner.

"I've been going on about my family. What about yours?" he asked, as they entered the candlelit dining room, which reeked of elegance and gourmet food.

"Taylor is married and has two children. She married her high school sweetheart, and she was *not* one to get her college degree. She went a couple of years and that was it. Said she always knew what she wanted to be: a wife and mother."

Dave nodded agreeably, as he held the chair for her while men in white uniforms rushed forward to attend to their every need. Never in her life had she eaten in such an elegant restaurant, even though Springfield and Cleveland had some fine ones. This one was different, and she remembered under the picture she had seen in the guidebook that this one was highlighted as a four-star with excellent French cuisine. There had even been something about the chefs, but she had forgotten.

Huge menus were spread before them. Water was delicately poured into fine crystal goblets; wine was offered, but Dave refused. "Unless you would like some?" he asked quickly.

"No, thank you. If you've dined here before, I'm going to depend on you to choose for me."

Somehow it didn't embarrass her to say that to him, for he seemed so accepting of her and she had really begun to feel comfortable with him.

He ordered a French dish that she interpreted as some kind of chicken. He handed the waiter the menu, smiled, then turned back to her.

"Tell me more about your family." He looked genuinely interested and so she tried to capsule their varied natures. "My mother teaches in high school, as you already know, and my father is an accountant. Both are very sensible, down-to-earth people. I guess Taylor is more sensible than I want to admit," she added slowly, speaking honestly to him.

"She's been a great mom to her girls, not spoiling them too much or giving in to their every whim. And yet she is kind and patient with them. I admire that," she added, hoping to assure him that she wasn't jealous of Taylor. But of course she was. In fact, she had always been jealous of Taylor, for whom life seemed to come so easy during their teens.

"Your parents are still together," he said, proving he had been listening. "So are mine. Most of my friends have stepparents and an assortment of family—you know, his, hers, ours. My parents will celebrate their thirtieth anniversary in July, and Alison wants to give them a party."

She had to laugh. "Mom and Dad celebrated their thirtieth last February, and Taylor did give them a party. Well, I did too. This is amazing."

"What?"

"I wouldn't have thought that first night. . ." Her voice trailed, as she dropped her eyes to the gleaming silverware.

"I know what you mean. I wouldn't have thought that first night we had so much in common. That *is* what you were going to say, right?"

She looked back at him, relieved to see that he wasn't making fun. He was admitting he had been just as turned off by her as she was by him. She smiled. "I was tired and grumpy."

"I was tired and rude," he said, taking the brunt of their unpleasant first meeting.

"No, you weren't," she laughed. "You were tired; I was tired."

They were both laughing as the waiter rolled up the salad cart and skillfully tossed their salad from a huge crystal bowl then expertly wielded his silver tongs, serving each of them a mixture of greens on a small crystal plate.

"Hey, it's interesting that we picked up the same flight in New York," he said, as his eyes roamed over her hair and settled on her gray eyes.

"Funny I didn't see you," she said, looking across at him.

"That's because I was buried down into the seat, half asleep when most of the passengers boarded. Our paths might not have crossed if—"

"If I hadn't jabbed you in the stomach with my bulky shoulder bag," she finished for him.

"And I wasn't planning to go out of the hotel for coffee this morning, but it was such a pretty day, I decided to take a quick stroll before the afternoon meeting."

"Quite a coincidence," she said, and then an important question moved to the forefront of her mind. Whether it was coincidence or romance, she already knew quite a bit about him, yet she didn't know the most important thing.

"What do you do on weekends?" she asked, after she swallowed a bite of the tasty salad, enjoying the sweet delicate flavor of the dressing.

"If I told you I work most Saturdays, you'd probably think I was a workaholic."

"Are you?" she asked honestly.

"In a way. But it's been a tough year, and I try to do the best I can at whatever I undertake. I really like this company and want to stay with them."

She nodded. That still didn't answer her question.

"I manage to get in a little golf on Sunday, or go to the lake fishing with Dad."

She dipped into her salad again, feeling her spirits sink. "So that's how you spend Sundays?"

"Sunday afternoon, or I fish with Dad on Saturdays. We usually go to church on Sunday, then I go to my parents' house and pig out on Mom's Sunday dinners."

She leaned back in her chair and breathed a deep sigh of relief.

"What?" He apparently sensed there was something meaningful in what he had told her, but he had not yet figured it out.

"I go to church too. We're. . .a Christian family."

"So are we," he said, as though it were as natural as eating or breathing. "Oh, I get it." His eyes lit up again. "You were wondering if I was a party guy?"

"I was wondering if you were a Christian," she said seriously. "That's very important to me. My. . .former boyfriend wasn't, and we. . .well, it presented problems that we couldn't resolve. You see, he didn't believe in God. Neither did his family. It made a drastic difference in our values. I mean, he was a decent person, but—"

"I know what you're saying. Of course, I live in what is sometimes referred to as the Bible Belt, and yet we have nonbelievers there, just like everywhere else. I dated a girl in college who flaunted her atheism on our third date. Our last date," he added, shaking his head. "She was one of the prettiest girls in school, and I couldn't see past the huge green eyes and outgoing personality. Then I learned the true meaning of that old phrase Mom had worn out when I was growing up."

"Beauty is only skin deep?"

He laughed. "You're amazing. You know what I'm going to say before I say it, Melanie."

"My grandmother said the same thing to me, about beauty being only skin deep."

"But you are beautiful," he said quietly, his blue eyes sincere as he studied her face.

For a moment, the agony of sitting in the bleachers during the high school football games with Tracy, her best friend and mirror image, flashed into her mind. They would stare grudgingly at the long-legged majorette and bouncy cheerleaders and wish with all their hearts that they could trade places.

She hesitated for a moment then decided to tell him her true feelings. He was such a good listener that he seemed to pull the truth from her. "The truth is, when I was growing up, I was overweight, wore braces, and was quite plain compared to Taylor."

"See, that's the problem."

"Excuse me?"

" 'Compared to Taylor,' you said. No doubt you heard too many people make that comparison and drew the wrong conclusion."

"I was compared to Taylor openly and often," she admitted. "I always wondered why people didn't realize how much it hurt when guys looked at me and said, '*You* are Taylor's sister?' in the tone of voice you would use if you were trying to figure out why someone had two heads. Or even worse, when Mom kept suggesting that I run track or play soccer or even basketball, which she knew I hated. What she wanted to ask me was why I didn't try for size six clothes like Taylor and compete in beauty contests."

"That must have been terrible," he said, the blue eyes sad, his face serious as he focused on her completely.

Her eyes met his. "It was. And you know what I never told Mom and Dad? I didn't *want* to be like Taylor. I preferred to work in Bible school with the little kids or take up a craft I could teach to the handicapped, something useful that made sense to me."

He looked at her in amazement. "You were remarkably mature for a teenager."

She shrugged. "Aside from that, I preferred to read stacks of books or see a play or a movie that really touched my heart. I didn't care about being popular or going to all the parties. I guess it should have been more important to me," she said, breathing a heavy sigh. "But I did what made me happy. And that didn't always make my parents happy. Oh, they were happy about my grades, which were always better than my sister's. But I was a loner and didn't really mind it. They just never understood."

"You were being Melanie Roberts," he said, looking at her with admiration. She loved the sound of her name on his lips; she even liked the southern drawl, which was beginning to do strange things to her senses. She could almost smell the magnolias, and for a moment her romantic nature created a mental image of standing in a flower garden beneath a full moon with him.

And then he added the final words that truly stole her heart. "I admire your honesty and your courage."

"Well, I can thank my grandmother for that. She and I were very much alike. In fact, I was named for her," she continued, since he was so attentive. "She was Melinda Virginia. Kids started calling me Mel and I hated that, so Tracy, my best friend, and I had one of those very serious conversations over colas and chips."

"One of those late-night girl chats?" he teased.

"Right. I decided I liked the name Melanie after I had read *Gone With the Wind* for the fourth time."

"Melanie," he nodded slowly. "It suits you."

Then their attention was diverted by a flurry of silver-domed platters and a display of beautifully prepared chicken drizzled with an almond and mushroom sauce, complimented by a wonderful brown rice and lean spears of fresh asparagus and a skillfully designed fruit medley.

"You mentioned feeling that you were always being compared to your sister and that you always felt your mother wanted to change you," Dave said. "It took courage to grow up in those circumstances. Some people get bitter and ugly about it, but you seem like such a sweet, nice person."

"Thank you," she responded. Her eyes lingered on him for a moment, still amazed by the way Dave really listened to what she had to say. He was not one of those guys who had to constantly talk about himself.

He had turned his attention to the meal, and she did the same, appreciating the opportunity of dining on such an elegant meal.

"How did your meeting go today?" she asked, wanting to be equally interested in subjects he enjoyed.

"It was long and boring, giving me an idea of what the week holds. Lengthy debates between one of the leading executives from our company and one from another company here, who has unlimited questions about our programs."

Their server appeared refilling their water goblets as they worked their way through the meal.

"However," he added slowly, "I'm afraid I'll be forced to cancel a meeting or two."

She looked startled. "Why?" She had no idea.

"Because I have met a wonderful woman that I want to get to know better, and I'll be attending a hundred other meetings. But I won't get to see Melanie Roberts and I won't be in Paris with her."

There was a touch of romance to his voice, and she was pleased and relieved that she would be seeing him again. She had not allowed her mind to stray beyond tonight, for she didn't want to feel the ache of disappointment that she would surely feel when the time came to say good-bye to Dave Browning.

"And you don't want to miss hearing all about my dysfunctional childhood!" she teased, arching an eyebrow and deliberately making light of the situation.

"I don't want to miss hearing you talk about your life— whatever, however—and I don't want to miss walking along the Seine in the moonlight. Which is exactly what I suggest we do now."

She smiled. "Sounds like a good plan."

They had waved aside the dessert menu and coffee, and the server had appeared with a thick leather case containing their bill, which she didn't want to see. She knew their meal was very expensive, but Dave was generous and kind, and she didn't know how to express her appreciation other than to say, "Thank you for dinner. I enjoyed every bite and I have thoroughly enjoyed your company."

Her gaze took in the well-dressed people talking in quiet tones over the crisp linen tablecloths. Even the servers managed to deliver and retrieve silver in a way that muted the sound. One heard only the pleasant strands of classical music from somewhere in the background.

Chapter 3

Melanie and Dave had taken a taxi to a favorite spot for tourists to stroll over the Seine. Dave had removed the coat to his suit and placed it around her shoulders, as they walked hand in hand, staring at the glow of streetlights reflected in the Seine.

"It is so beautiful here," she said dreamily, studying the way the lights sparkled on the water. "I see why it's called the City of Lights."

"I'm still amazed that we met," Dave said, looking at her, rather than at the scene before them.

Melanie rolled her head lazily and looked at him. He was standing close to her, his arm around her shoulder. "So am I," she replied gently.

He was looking into her eyes, as though trying to see to the depths of her soul. He wouldn't have to. Melanie felt that her emotions were flashing in neon all over her face.

"Why did you choose this spring break to come to Paris?" he asked curiously.

"Because of my grandmother," she answered. "I'm seeing the Seine by moonlight for her." She took a deep breath and looked back at Dave, who hadn't questioned her. It was as though he understood.

She began to talk about her grandmother, how special she had been in her life, and that led to the wish money, and the reason she was here.

"I hope you have the most wonderful vacation ever," he said, squeezing her shoulder and smiling into her eyes. "I hope you will allow me to help make that possible. If I can," he added gently.

Gripping the front of his coat with both hands, to keep it snug and warm around her, she thought about their meeting and how romantic and wonderful everything had been. "You can make it possible," she said, admiring his modesty and a dozen other characteristics about him. "You know, you are a very thoughtful person, Dave. Are all southern gentlemen as kind and polite as you? I keep waiting for you to say 'ma'am' to me."

He laughed. "No, they're not all gentleman. They can be as disagreeable as men everywhere."

"Then you have been raised well," she said. Suddenly, she was beginning to feel like a teacher again, speaking to one of her students. "I noticed right off that you didn't just come plop down at my table today. You waited for permission."

"Well, that isn't being a southern gentleman," he said, tweaking her nose. "Most guys with half a brain would have waited in case you hated the sight of me."

She laughed, daring not to comment for fear of how much she would reveal. "It goes back to being a southern gentlemen," she insisted.

"Then I'll take that as encouragement to ask you to go sightseeing with me tomorrow."

Her heart jumped. It was as though she were spinning her own perfect dream. "What about your meetings?" she finally managed to ask though her tone was weak. Why was she reminding him? Now she was afraid he would start thinking more seriously and she didn't want that.

"I know the topic that's being covered. In fact, we've already been over it half a dozen times at the conference table in Atlanta. The competition is going to present their side, and we already know where they stand. I'll just say I have a more important appointment."

"Great. I'll have my own tour guide since you've been here before." She couldn't resist the smile that spread over her face. She fought the impulse to reach up and plant a kiss on his cheek, which would be quite a departure from the old Melanie Roberts. But she really wanted to touch his cheek, trace the outline of his broad jaw with her finger.

He glanced at his watch and took her arm. "Did you know it's ten o'clock in the evening in Atlanta?"

"What time does that make it here?"

He grinned. "Three o'clock in the morning."

"You're kidding!"

She couldn't believe they had spent so much time together and that, for the first time in her life, she was out at this hour of the night—no, morning, she corrected herself. There were still couples out strolling together, and one was actually clenched in a tight embrace, kissing as though they were the only couple in the world. This truly was a city of romance. Snuggling into Dave's coat and against his side, as he gently wrapped his arm around her, she thought how wonderful and *natural* this felt.

Their footsteps echoed over the sidewalk as they walked underneath a streetlight, enveloping them in a soft golden halo. She simply could not believe this was happening to her. Then she remembered the Bible verses Granny had taught her about patience and the importance of understanding that God works things out by His calendar, not hers.

She wished the evening could go on and on, even though they were already getting into a taxi and all too soon they were back at her hotel. He paid the fare, and automatically their steps slowed as they approached the door of the hotel. It was as though he regretted leaving her as much as she did him. But she was beginning to feel the weariness of a very long day. "You must be exhausted," she looked up at him.

"On the contrary," he said, nodding at the doorman as they entered the brightly lit lobby. "I'm wide awake."

He stopped in the lobby, and she realized that again he was being a gentleman. "Do you want me to walk you up to your room?"

She shook her head. "No, you need to get back to your hotel and get some rest." Reluctantly, she removed the coat from her shoulders and handed it to him. "I'll remember to bring a sweater the next time."

"Tomorrow will be a pleasant spring day," he said with only a trace of weariness in his voice. "Dress for comfort. And be sure to wear comfortable shoes."

She nodded. Her comfortable thick-soled leather loafers were already laid out.

They hesitated for a moment longer, as though unable to tear their gazes from each other. Then she did what she had wanted to do earlier. She reached up and kissed him on the cheek, not caring what the concierge thought. They had probably seen much more passionate embraces at this hour in the hotel lobby.

Her quick gesture pleased him, she could tell, for his blue eyes were glowing as he squeezed her hand. "Will ten o'clock be too early to get started? I only require about seven hours' sleep, but you may want to sleep in later than that."

She shook her head. "I have all summer to sleep in. I don't want to miss a thing while I'm here."

"See you then," he said, but he made no move to leave.

Melanie decided to take the initiative. She squeezed his hand back. "I had a wonderful time," she said, taking a step back from him.

"So did I." His eyes followed her as she took another step back, then she forced herself to turn around and walk to the elevator. But in her heart she had taken flight and was drifting through thin air like an angel. Or at least tonight she had become Cinderella, the enchanted heroine of the fable she often read to her little girls in school while the boys wiggled in their seats and pretended to be bored.

Chapter 4

When she looked out of the hotel window, she saw to her great pleasure that it was a gorgeous spring day. The chestnut trees were in full bloom and there was a slow, lazy beauty to everything. She took a deep long breath, feeling totally relaxed after a good night's rest.

Pink. This was definitely the day for the pink linen dress with the square neck, cap sleeves, and long skirt with its deep side slit. Too bad her skin wasn't yet tanned enough to do the dress justice. But she had her own opinion about tanning beds. She preferred the natural vitamin D. She hurried to the shower, deciding to shampoo her hair for the second day in a row, just to be sure it really gleamed in the sunlight. *Have I ever shampooed my hair two days in a row?* she asked herself absently as she gathered up her toiletries.

She was making progress toward being the desirable woman she had always dreamed of becoming. Humming an old song Granny used to sing about April in Paris, she smiled to herself when she got to the part about not feeling a lover's warm embrace until April in Paris. As she turned the shower on, she wondered if Dave had ever heard the song.

❧

It was exactly ten when she stepped into the lobby, but Dave was already there, wearing khaki chinos, a white knit polo shirt, and a pair of loafers that looked as though they were made for comfortable walks around Paris. Clean and nice, but the leather was obviously a bit worn. Stretched to fit his feet, her father would say when he wanted to pay a compliment to his favorite shoes.

A smile quickly appeared when Dave spotted her and walked over to meet her. His eyes swept down her dress then returned to her face. He was looking at the short curly tendrils she had spent some time styling about her face before braiding the length of her hair in a French braid. It felt right, and she thought he must like it though he didn't say so. He merely smiled, as though she was exactly what he had expected.

"So do you have our itinerary?" she asked, initiating a conversation.

He whipped a pocket-size notebook from his pocket and flipped open the pages. "I studied the map last night and decided we should begin with the farthest point first, if that suits you."

"It suits me fine." She looked down at the notepad and saw the neat handwriting.

Each line was numbered as though he had carefully outlined the plan. "You did all that after three this morning?" she asked, staring at the pad, completely amazed.

"Actually, I wake up every morning at six. Doesn't seem to matter if I went to bed at ten in Atlanta or at three in Paris," he said, placing the notebook back in his pocket. "I'm afraid I'm a slave to routine," he said. "When you get to know me better, you may not see that as an asset."

She had to smile at that. It had always been something she strove to accomplish. "Everyone needs a plan," she said, having told herself that each morning as she woke up and faced a stack of haphazardly folded papers that she had not graded. "Since I'm trying to set a better routine for my work habits, you'll be a good example for me."

They had crossed the lobby, taking turns through the revolving door, and were out on the sidewalk, where everyone around them seemed to be smiling and happy. Not one dour face like she often glimpsed in the adjoining cars at the corner red light on her way to school every morning.

He waved over a taxi and she looked at him questioning. "Thought we were walking."

"That's how we'll end up," he said, opening the door for her. "If it's okay with you," he added quickly. "I hope you're ready for brunch."

She hadn't even thought of food, which surprised her, when once she lived for meals. "I will be. I had a cup of tea in my room and that was all I wanted."

"And I had my usual pot of coffee," he said, laughing, as they settled into the backseat.

"I would have the shakes by now if I had drunk a pot of coffee," she said, glancing at him. She found it so easy to smile at him whenever they talked. She was not in the habit of smiling so much, except of course with her students, and they made it easy.

"And I would have a throbbing headache if I hadn't, addicted as I am to caffeine."

She shrugged and laughed softly. "Oh well, we all have our favorite things, I guess."

"Thank you."

"For what?"

"For not lecturing me like one anorexic friend who thinks caffeine is only half a step away from an illegal drug. Sorry that was an unkind thing to say about my last girlfriend."

She tilted her head and looked at him honestly. "It's your choice and your life. My parents don't even speak to anyone until they've had at least two cups of coffee, and we learned early to respect that."

He chuckled. "My brain doesn't truly function until it has been stroked by the presence of coffee." He had given the driver their destination and now the taxi was flying past all the landmarks she wanted to photograph. But then it occurred to her that she had forgotten her camera. What had happened to her common sense?

Dave had reached for her hand, and it seemed a natural gesture as they both took note of the passing scenery.

It would be a day she would treasure for the rest of her life. Dave solved her problem by picking up a disposable camera at a quaint little tourist shop.

"The pictures probably won't be the quality of the ones your camera would have taken."

"It doesn't matter. I can always buy postcards if I blur the pictures or get them off center, which usually happens."

He laughed as they entered the Louvre and strolled leisurely to admire the statues. Out in the courtyard, she took a few pictures, and then they moved on to the Eiffel Tower, the statue of Napoleon, a museum that she found interesting, and finally ended up back at the hotel, their feet dragging. Dave was unable to suppress another yawn.

"What you need is a nap," she teased him.

"And miss dinner with you?"

She paused before the revolving door, since he had kept the taxi waiting. "Why can't you do both?" she suggested helpfully. It was something that she had already plotted sometime during the afternoon when she realized she enjoyed being with him so much that she dreaded saying good-bye. That would come on Friday; why not make the most of the few days together?

"Hey, great idea. So, a later dinner suits you?"

"Perfectly." She winked at him, pleased that he smiled at the gesture. It was amazing the way another person seemed to have emerged from the presence of Melanie Roberts, as though the fairy godmother had touched her with a wand and turned her into the woman she had always longed to be. She had never winked at a guy; it seemed so silly. But since meeting Dave, everything she said and did were honest reactions to his charm.

"Let's see. . ." He studied his wristwatch, which she noted was a frequent habit. He had admitted to routine, and she saw now how he stayed on schedule. He kept up with time, which always seemed to elude her. "It is now six o'clock. We could rest a couple of hours and meet up again at nine," he glanced at her, "or even ten."

She recalled he had admitted he only needed seven hours of sleep. She was an eight-hour sleeper, and a vague weariness clung to her body and dimmed her eyes. Yet in her heart, she was so exuberant that she wondered if she could even nap. But she must, her healthy nature reminded her. And she must have a cup of herb tea for energy when she awoke. She had come prepared with tea bags and vitamins.

"Nine is okay with me if you want to be here by then. If you don't make it until nine thirty, or even ten, just look for me on one of the sofas." She nodded in the direction of the comfortable areas within the lobby.

"See you tonight," she said softly, and this time it was he who reached down and touched his lips to hers in a sweet, brief kiss. He leaned back and stared down into her eyes and for a moment, neither said anything. Then she was conscious of the elevator opening behind her, at the same time she realized they were still holding hands. "See you later," he said, watching her as she got on the elevator and the door closed between them, closing off her view of him. She breathed a long, deep sigh of pure bliss. Was she dreaming? If so, she never wanted to wake up.

Chapter 5

He had selected another perfect restaurant for them. The one he had chosen last night had been exclusive and rather formal, and yet she was happy to have eaten there. It was one of those "must go" restaurants according to her guidebook—and even Nan Harper, who had gone once in her fifty-five years. After learning Melanie was going to Paris, Nan had tossed out names and places as though she hung out in Paris every summer. Melanie knew Nan's strategy: She had been studying the same tour book from their library. As usual, Nan always had to be one up on everyone else.

"We had authentic French last night; I thought you might like to sample a true Italian restaurant."

"How did you know it's my favorite food?"

He held the chair for her and she settled in, casting a glance over the wonderful ambiance of Old Italy recreated. "That's easy, because I always try to get one meal here whenever I come. Maybe I should just fly on over to Rome one of these days. I think there has to be Italian blood in my genes, the way I go after pasta."

Her eyes widened as he went around the table and took a seat while an eager waitress rushed to their side. "Which do you like best—lasagna or spaghetti?" Melanie asked, wondering if he really was that much like her.

"Pizza," he grinned, opening the menu. "But tonight I want something a little fancier. Do you like veal?" he asked.

She shook her head. "Not really. Just pasta of any flavor, any variation, as long as the chef uses pure olive oil and only a mild dash of garlic."

"Absolutely," he agreed, studying the selections.

She forced herself to do the same. The prices were less staggering than last night's famous French restaurant. Still, the food was expensive. She knew it would be, having done her research. But, thank God, he was buying. She had felt wealthy when she boarded the airplane, but already those funds were vanishing like magic, and she couldn't even remember what she had purchased. Souvenirs, naturally, and postcards, still unwritten, and the clothes, of course. *All a wise investment,* she told herself, as Dave ordered a veal dish and a spinach salad.

Melanie asked for the dish that seemed to offer the most tomato paste and pasta, which to her were twin components. It was authentic spaghetti, and when it was placed before her and she dipped a fork into it, a tiny mouthful thrilled her taste buds and she savored its delicate flavor.

They had both ordered coffee, an unusual departure for her, but she wanted to stay awake. Even though the French made their coffee strong, the rich cream made it pleasant. She discovered that it was possible for her to like coffee.

"Thought you didn't drink that stuff," he said, glancing at her half-empty cup, looking slightly amused.

"I don't. Often, I mean. But after watching you enjoy yours so much, I was tempted to give it a fair try. And I'm glad I did," she lifted the demitasse to her lips, taking another little sip.

"I've had a great time, Melanie," he said as they finished their meal and again refused dessert.

"So have I," she admitted, looking squarely into the blue eyes that she had come to adore. And as for the southern accent, it now lulled her senses; in fact, she was going to miss it. Somehow his drawl softened the harsh realities of the world and drew her into a special world that included only the two of them.

"I have to put in an appearance at tomorrow's meeting," he said, almost in apology.

"Oh, I understand. After all, you're here on business, not holiday, like me."

He looked across at her, and she saw genuine regret in his eyes. "I wish I were on holiday. There are so many things to do, so many places. . . ." His voice trailed, and she could see that he hated missing out.

She decided to make him feel better. "Actually, I need to write those postcards, so I don't beat them home, and I want to return to that little bookstore on the corner and browse. So I won't be doing anything significant for you to miss."

"It isn't that," he said, then hesitated.

"It isn't what?" she echoed, watching him carefully, wondering if it were possible that he had the same feelings for her that she had for him.

"I'd just like to spend the day with you," he added simply.

She smiled deeply. He was so honest and open and sincere about everything that she was deeply touched.

"Maybe it's my turn to do something nice," she said, wondering if she should offer to buy dinner.

"Like getting together a picnic lunch for us tomorrow?"

"What a wonderful idea," she beamed. "And go to a beautiful park someplace?"

He nodded. "Tomorrow I can sneak out about eleven and take a very long lunch hour. There's a beautiful park right across the street from my hotel." He repeated the address, although she had already memorized it. "Since it's so near my hotel, would you mind just meeting me in the park?"

"Not at all. In fact, I had hoped to stroll through one of the parks here before I left." Why did she feel she had to make excuses to justify every action?

He looked disappointed. "I don't have to be present for you to enjoy the park."

"Yes, you do," she said, tossing the old inhibited Melanie into the night. She believed in honesty and used it as a basic tool for her students. Why be different with adults? For the first time, the things she said and did seemed to make sense. She wondered why she had to come all the way to Paris, France, to resurrect the person who had been hiding underneath the layers of self-consciousness. She was shedding her defensive attitude much faster than she had shed the surplus twenty pounds. This pleased her.

Was it because of Dave Browning? Was it true that the right person complemented your strengths and softened your weaknesses? Yes, she decided; Granny was right. That was true! Or at least that was what was happening to her.

What else was happening? Melanie wondered as their gaze locked and neither spoke. It was one of those special moments when words are unnecessary, when eye contact is more important, when thoughtful silence allows one to slowly process what is taking place inside. It was something she had never been able to explain to Taylor, who talked incessantly. But Dave understood this, she could tell that he did.

He blinked and shook his head slightly, like one just coming out of a dream, and for a moment she felt it would be a necessary gesture for her too, but she refrained.

"Tell me more about your grandmother. She seems to have had a major impact on your life."

"She did." Melanie hesitated for a moment, studying his expression. He wasn't just being a polite southern gentleman. He was interested in her grandmother because he was interested in *her*. And when she realized that, she felt the same satisfaction that came to her from watching a beautiful sunrise or sunset, or hearing the church choir singing Christmas hymns.

Where did she begin in describing the woman who had been so important in her life? "She came to live with us after having a mild stroke that left her right side paralyzed so that she could longer be the independent woman she once was. She said her mind wasn't as sharp, but I never agreed. She had a remarkable mind, and she could captivate me with stories, which she often did. She even did a funny little shuffle of feet when she came into my room once and my radio was playing hits from the fifties," she laughed softly as she lifted her gaze over Dave's face and stared into space.

She raised a napkin to her mouth, aware she could no longer hold another bite. "My grandfather, Solomon Brown, was a salt-of-the-earth kind of guy, which Granny said was exactly the type she needed to keep her on balance. But she didn't like the name Solomon so she simply called him Brown. From their first meeting, I suppose."

Dave laughed. "I'm sorry I never met her. She sounds like so much fun."

Melanie felt the threat of tears. "Yes, she was many things. In fact, she's the reason I'm with you tonight."

Dave was suddenly serious. "How? What do you mean?"

She told him about the "wish" money she had inherited upon her grandmother's death in January and her grandmother's little note to see Paris for her. She had been determined to follow Granny's instructions, although her parents both argued she should pay off her car, or her college loan, or something typically sensible and responsible.

She was still talking about Granny when the waiter appeared rather discreetly at their table, inquiring again about more coffee.

Dave finally got the hint and looked at his watch. "It must be near closing time."

The waiter merely smiled, too polite to admit that it was. When Melanie looked around the cozy restaurant, however, she realized they were the only couple left.

"I'm sorry...," Dave began as his eyes followed hers. "I didn't realize it was so late." He got up tucking an impressive wad of bills within the folder that held their ticket.

"Merci beaucoup," the waiter acknowledged.

They hurried out, both feeling a bit embarrassed as Dave hailed a taxi. "I can't believe the time went by so fast," he was saying as they hopped into a taxi and the driver roared off as though he was trying to set a record on speed. All too quickly, they were back at the Ritz and out on the sidewalk. Dave pushed the revolving door for her, and she stepped into the glass enclosure, glancing over her shoulder at him, directly behind.

Should she invite him up to her room? No, that wasn't quite right. It wasn't as though she were back at the apartment where she could invite him to take a seat on the sofa while she grabbed the fruit bowl from the eating bar and joined him with a handful of grapes.

She was vaguely aware that he was walking her to the elevator, pushing the button, and she felt nervous and awkward about what to do. But just as quickly, he settled the matter.

"Thanks for another wonderful evening," he said, lowering his lips to lightly brush hers just as the door of the elevator slid open. "See you tomorrow at eleven in the park," he called to her as she stepped inside the elevator. The door closed on his smiling face, and she stood very still, staring at the closed door as the elevator lifted upward.

It was absurd but she already missed him. She could spend hours with him and never tire of hearing him talk about his work, and he was equally interested in the funny little antics of her students. She had even told him about nosy Nan at some time during their hours together.

When the elevator doors parted, she stepped into the carpeted hall and sauntered down to her pink satin nest. Leaving Paris, and Dave, was going to be very difficult. But she refused to allow that thought to linger in her mind.

She inserted her card into the lock and held tight to the memory of his warm smile and the way his blue eyes took on a special light when he was amused. And she liked the aftershave and whatever he used on his hair that kept it soft and gleaming. The lock clicked, she opened the door, and floated off to her bedroom.

Chapter 6

Another beautiful day awaited them as she stopped at a market nearby, carefully choosing bread, fresh fruit, and cheese, and adding bottled water. That looked French and healthy, but she wondered if she should order an espresso for Dave and impulsively decided to do so, adding extra cream the way she had noticed him doing.

As usual he was right on time and found her easily under a large tree, their food tucked away in the picnic basket she had splurged on at the market.

"Hey, this is a real picnic," he said, looking around the grass.

She hadn't considered that he would be in his business suit and quickly suggested they move to a nearby table. When she laid all the treats out on the table he smiled with approval. Then, deliberately, she placed the espresso before him. "Hope it's okay."

"Thanks, Melanie. You really are a thoughtful person."

They began to eat heartily for it was a warm spring day in Paris and the pleasant breeze seemed to encourage their appetites. . .and romance. She was conscious of his gaze on her almost constantly, and once or twice she darted a glance in his direction. Once, she caught his blue eyes looking sad and regretful.

"What's wrong?" she asked, sensing something was spoiling the picnic lunch.

He sighed heavily. "I can't get out of the meeting today, and my boss has issued an ultimatum that we all get together in his suite until we iron out some complications that have come up in the meetings."

"You look worried," she said gently.

"We'll work out the kinks. It's just going to take a lot more work than I had thought. Which means," he had been staring into his cup but now his gaze rose to hers, "I may not get to see you again. Our plane flies out at seven in the morning."

Melanie's heart sank, but then she tried to gather her courage and be grateful for the time they had spent together. "Well, you have to do what you have to do," she said. She couldn't believe tomorrow was already Friday. Where had the week gone?

"I wish I could change my plans and stay over another day, but I can't," he said on a sigh. "My boss is great except for a few quirks. And one quirk is that no one gets special treatment in veering from the routine he sets."

She nodded. "Then I guess you've been pushing your luck, sneaking out of the meetings to sightsee with me."

He hesitated and shrugged, giving her time to wonder if maybe he had been scolded already.

"Melanie, I don't know how you feel, but I don't want this to be the end of our...friendship."

She looked into his eyes, suddenly feeling all the emotion in her heart well up in her throat. "I don't either," she replied softly.

"Do you have e-mail?" he asked, glancing at his watch.

She sighed, hating to admit she didn't. "Actually, I'm getting it when I return," she said, instantly making up her mind.

"Great. We can e-mail back and forth and then... maybe make some plans to see each other again," he said, getting up from the picnic table, glancing back toward the hotel.

Her heart was beating faster and she again wondered if this had all been a dream. But as he reached out and squeezed her hand, she realized this was real; it had actually happened. Finally. To her.

She squeezed his hand back, and then he took a step closer and gently touched her shoulders, then lowered his head and gave her a deep, warm kiss that literally took her breath away.

"I do hate to go," he said.

She abruptly opened her eyes, realizing she was still locked in the sweet moment they had shared. She nodded, unable to say anything.

He reached into the pocket of his coat and withdrew a business card. "There's my address and telephone number, office and home, and on the back I've written my e-mail address at home."

She turned the card over and read the address. "I'll e-mail you as soon as I get hooked up," she promised.

He looked at his watch again, and she wished with all of her heart that she could make time stand still. But she couldn't. He kissed her again, more briefly this time, but the gentle brush of his lips still thrilled her.

"Good-bye," he whispered softly and quickly walked away.

She felt as though he was taking her heart with him. Her gaze sadly followed him. He purposefully crossed the street to the front of the hotel. Then he turned and looked at her again.

"Dave, I had a great time," she called to him.

He smiled. "Me too." Then he walked into the hotel and disappeared from her vision. She stood staring at the door for the next five minutes, aware that tears were gathering in her eyes. She wandered over and slumped down on the picnic bench, staring at their plastic plates and the leftovers that she would take back to her room. She reached over for his empty coffee cup and, remembering his kiss, put the rim of the cup to her lips.

"Dave Browning," she whispered, "you made my dreams come true."

Chapter 7

Melanie slept late the next morning and awoke feeling tired and something more. She rolled her head and glanced at the parted drapes. Outside, it was a gray day, and for the first time since she had been in Paris it was raining. She glanced at the ornate bedside clock. Nine thirty.

She took a deep breath and hugged her pillow, as a deep sadness grew stronger. She frowned. *What?* And then she came fully awake and reality loomed to the front of her mind. Dave was already on a jet heading back to Atlanta. Just that knowledge brought a terrible emptiness to her heart. She tried to think of something fun to do today, but nothing appealed to her. She decided to order room service of croissants and a pot of tea and lounge around for a while.

The rain thickened beyond her window, and she forced herself to go down to explore some of the unique little boutiques inside the Ritz, but soon she was back in her room, slumped in the satin chair. Maybe she should call home. She calculated the time back in Milton. It was Friday morning, and with Mom off from school, Dad had taken a week from his office as well. They had planned several projects for the home and flower garden, all of which sounded so boring compared to the week she had spent, a week she would never, ever forget.

Methodically, she checked her flight schedule and noted that she was scheduled to fly out early, as well. She really should force herself to go out and do something on her last day in Paris, and she wandered to the window trying to think of something that would appeal to her. But the truth was, without Dave, Paris had lost its charm. And her time would be better spent getting her clothes together, resting up for the long flight back, and mentally preparing herself to return to work on Monday. And first on her list, when she returned, was getting e-mail set up on her computer. The most sophisticated thing she had done on her computer was type up simple little tests or words on colored paper. She hadn't even bothered with the Internet. But now the computer held endless possibilities. Communicating with Dave was foremost.

Chapter 8

Melanie continued to marvel that it had only been two days since her return to Milton. To her parents, she had blamed her melancholy on jet lag and even skipped church on Sunday. She couldn't seem to get out of her bed for any reason other than to call Taylor with the pretense of a sisterly chat, but what she really wanted to know more about was e-mail.

And so, on Monday morning, as she greeted her second graders and proceeded with the difficult job of trying to establish a routine for them, and for herself, she hailed down the school's computer whiz over lunch. He agreed to come to her apartment that afternoon to show her the basics of e-mail and get her hooked up.

That idea lifted her spirits and she was actually humming "Somewhere over the Rainbow" by the end of the day, despite a barrage of questions over lunch from all the teachers; they wanted to hear every detail of her trip to Paris. She had always been a private person, and true to form, she did not mention Dave. The closest she came was to admit she'd met some interesting people.

But when nosy Nan Harper began to prod, she excused herself to get back to her room to work on a project.

That evening, the excitement of being "online" thrilled her as she shyly typed in Dave's e-mail address and sent her first message: a friendly hello to him and a thank-you for the wonderful time in Paris. Carefully she read and re-read her message and checked half a dozen times to be sure her e-mail address was correct. Then she placed a check mark in the box to indicate she wanted to be notified when her e-mail was opened.

She managed to get through the morning, and with the excuse that she forgot her lunch, she dashed home to check her e-mail. Nothing. She rushed back to school, puzzled.

That night, she sent Dave another e-mail to inquire if he got her first one. She showered and dressed for bed, although in the next hour, she could not approach the computer without checking her message box, but there was nothing except a two-pager from Taylor with news of the kids and, predictably, only a few general questions about Melanie's trip to Paris. Taylor was basically selfish, and Melanie knew it. She dashed back a quick e-mail, then checked her message box again and saw with pleasure that her e-mail to Dave had been opened. Tomorrow she would hear from him, and with that hope, she hopped into bed and turned out the light.

Did I give Dave my phone number?

The thought struck her seconds before the bolt of thunder that crashed outside her window, preceding the heavy rain that drummed on her roof. She loved the sound and usually it lulled her into a deep sleep. Not tonight.

She kept racking her brain to see if she had mentioned a telephone or address in Milton. He hadn't asked, a voice reminded her. She didn't want to hear that voice, so she turned the light back on and read the entire book of Psalms, got up at midnight, and checked her e-mail again. Nothing.

Sighing, she got back in bed and reminded herself that tomorrow was a school day. She forced herself to close her eyes and say her prayers.

The next afternoon, Melanie went to the video shop and picked up *You've Got Mail*, one of her favorite romantic comedies. She watched it as soon as she got home and then again after a light meal of soup and fruit. Every fifteen minutes she checked her computer, only to find to her dismay, and growing disappointment, that there were no messages. And that her e-mails had been opened.

Her hopes grew dimmer as the week progressed, during which time she resorted to checking her message box several times a day. She even went into the principal's office and informed the secretary that she might be getting a call from a friend in Atlanta, and if so, to please come to her room and get her.

"You want me to take the number?" Mrs. Winters looked at her curiously, for she had been instructed not to pull teachers out of class for a phone call unless it was an emergency.

"Yes. It's very important," she added matter-of-factly and hurried out, vaguely aware that Brent Warren, the principal, had been watching her curiously the past two days. Her best plan was to simply avoid him, just as she had tried to avoid her parents; but there was no getting past the Wednesday night supper at the church before prayer meeting. She had decided she must attend; after all, she had missed church on Sunday, and she knew it would be easier to have a conversation with her parents with a group of church members eating beside them. This way her mother couldn't get too personal, although she doubted that her mother would ever envision her daughter having a romantic interlude in Paris.

Her father, on the other hand, was enough like Granny to glance at her occasionally and winked at her once when she was obviously out of the zone of conversation; her mind locked on Dave.

She simply smiled at her father, wondering if she could talk with him sometime, appealing to his softer nature, which occasionally surfaced when he was not immersed in tax figures or engaged in one of Mom's yard projects.

At prayer meeting, when prayer requests were taken, her throat suddenly felt tight and she wished with all of her heart that she could lift her hand and say, "Please pray that Dave Browning responds to my e-mail." Or more honestly, "Please pray that I don't get my heart broken."

The thought had crossed her mind more than once in the five days since she had been home. For as she gravitated toward Cinderella and all the romantic little fairy tales which appealed only to the girls, she realized that it had happened to her, despite everything.

She had fallen in love for the first time. She actually understood now the "burning heartache" and the "incessant longing" she had read about could now be applied to her. All she thought about from the time she awoke until she crawled back in bed was the Dave she had met in Paris. But now that they were each back in their old environment, it was as if they'd never met. She missed him so much it was like a physical ache that could only be compared to the flu. Only the heartache seared into her soul in a way nothing ever had.

Each night when she checked her message box, her heart sank when there was no reply. . .except for the acknowledgment that her e-mail had been opened.

She was renting romantic videos every night now, huddled on the sofa, picking at a light dinner on a TV tray. She had gone through the old classic *April in Paris*, and on this Thursday night, as she watched Cary Grant and Deborah Kerr in *An Affair to Remember*, she sobbed deeply and unashamedly. With only her cup of tea and the rapidly disappearing tissue in her box, she made a decision when at last the movie ended and she was weak from crying. As she pushed the rewind button on the VCR, she squared her shoulders and marched resolutely to her computer. This was her last attempt to contact him. But maybe, for some strange reason, her e-mails were not getting through. She took a deep breath and began the words that choked her as she typed them. For this could be good-bye.

Dave,

This is my last attempt to contact you. I've gone past being offended to being concerned. Are you all right? I checked, there were no plane crashes, and in case you're interested, I arrived back in Milton on Saturday. I hope you will at least let me know that you arrived home safely.

Melanie.

After she finished the carefully worded e-mail, she checked her e-mail address again to be sure it was correct, then she glanced again at the check mark indicating that she wanted to be notified when the message was opened. By ten thirty, the message still had not been opened.

As she crawled into bed and turned out the light she felt more than hurt, she felt confused and disillusioned. She just couldn't believe that Dave was the kind of person to be insincere in a relationship. He had cared about her; surely she hadn't just imagined it. Each day when she didn't hear from him, she reminded herself of how busy he was, the meetings, his rigid boss. . . But this was now Thursday and she had sent her first e-mail on Monday. And she knew how painfully quick it was to zip one off. No matter how busy he was, he could have found a few seconds to at least say, "Hi, Paris was fun, wasn't it?" Never mind, "I've missed you" or "I think about you" or any of the dozens of things that flooded her mind when she thought of him. Just a simple "Hi" would at least keep her hopes up, even though the idea of a continuing romance with him was fading fast.

The next morning, as soon as she awoke, she flew to her computer and waited impatiently for the message box to appear. No messages. . .except for the fact that her e-mail had been opened. Again.

Tears filled her eyes as she slowly closed down the program and turned off her computer. *Maybe Paris and Dave were a dream after all,* she thought, feeling utterly miserable as she headed for the shower. Or if it were not a dream, it was painfully apparent that a week had gone by and now the dream was only a memory.

Chapter 9

She awoke on Saturday morning, wishing she hadn't committed herself to go along with the second-and third-graders to the museum. How would she dredge up the energy for such a trip? Not to mention the pretense she now kept of being happy, wearing a stiff smile, and trying not to remember Paris or Dave.

She forced herself to get up and shower, dress, and get ready to meet the bus at the school at twelve. Passing her computer as she gathered up her purse and lunch, she stared at the blank screen. Still no e-mail. She promised herself she was going to quit looking in that direction. The telephone rang, and she glanced at her watch, debating on whether to answer it. She hadn't the energy for another grilling from Mom. She walked past the phone, but then the possibility of the trip being canceled stopped her. On the fourth ring, she walked over and murmured a very unenthusiastic hello.

There was nothing but an odd croaking on the other side. She frowned, wondering if this was a crank call. But then through the muttered garble she recognized a name that struck magic and made her grip the phone tighter.

Dave? Had he said "Dave"?

"Who is this?" she asked pointedly.

There was a pause on the other end, and she could hear a snuffle. What was going on? Then a distinctly southern accent came on the line and her eyes widened.

"Melanie, this is Tom Barker. You don't know me but I'm Dave Browning's room-mate. He's been in the hospital with pneumonia and bronchitis the past week, and though he's totally incoherent, he insisted on trying to call you. I've been delivering your e-mails to him, by the way."

"In the hospital?" she repeated, trying to take in everything he had told her, but it was quite a shock.

"Yep. He got sick the day he came home. Apparently, he picked up a flu bug in Paris and by the time he got to the doctor, he was so feverish and dehydrated that he was admitted to the hospital. He's been pretty much out of it until yesterday, but I've heard your name mumbled so many times, I think I can speak for him."

She smiled, sinking into the nearest chair, winding the phone cord around her slim fingers and feeling as though she had just been turned into Cinderella again. "I'm sorry he's so ill. Could I speak with him? I'll do the talking."

181

"Great!"

Another shuffle followed, and then a choked sound, and Melanie began to tell him how concerned she had been, that she was sorry he was sick, but that she hoped he would be out of the hospital soon. And she was glad to hear from him.

A garble followed but she made out the words "will call again."

"Okay, hope you feel better," she said, wishing she could be there at the hospital with him now.

It was the glance at her watch that forced her into action. She had exactly three minutes to get to school. But she felt she could fly, if necessary. Dave had not forgotten her! He had called her name often, or so his roommate said. She believed Tom. She believed Dave. And she believed that life was clouds and rainbows once again, just like the pictures she painted for her second-graders.

Melanie approached her school day in an entirely different manner. Will's constant excuses to go to the bathroom did not ruffle her feathers, nor did Harry's antics on the back row, which usually required a stern voice. All the little girls were beautiful to her, and in a burst of appreciation for the spring day, she got permission from Mr. Warren, who was still watching her curiously, to take the children outside to examine the new rock garden the fifth-graders had designed.

As they sat out in the warm sunshine with the kids playing happily, Mary Beth sidled up to her. It was hard not to favor blond little Mary Beth who was always bringing her gifts. They were in the midst of a discussion about Mary Beth's spring break to visit her grandmother in Springfield, when she noticed that Harry and Will were engaged in competition over who could throw one of the smaller rocks the farthest.

She jumped up from her comfortable spot on the lawn and rushed to their side, scolding them more gently than usual and telling them they must pick up the rocks they had thrown, and now everyone was going back inside.

She hadn't even minded her mother's routine phone call every afternoon. This time she decided to favor her with a tiny bit of her news. She told her about meeting Dave from Atlanta, and one thing led to another, until Melanie stopped just short of saying she had fallen in love. Instead, she ended the conversation with a mellow admission: "He is the nicest guy I've ever met."

"But why haven't you told us about him? Why...," and on and on.

"Er, Mom," she interrupted, "something is boiling over on the kitchen stove." Actually, her teakettle was. She had already had two cups of tea, but she couldn't seem to control herself; a wonderful sense of abandon had overtaken her. She loved the world, even Nan and her mother.

That night she rushed home and found her computer filled with messages—all from Dave. He had gone home from the hospital today, armed with antibiotics and fruit baskets. There were four e-mails written within an hour of each other. All began with an apology for not having contacted her sooner, then he was quickly into their trip to Paris, reminding her of places they had seen and things they had done.

"It's all I thought about when I lay in the hospital bed being poked with shots and fighting the frustration of losing my voice."

Each e-mail got more personal, and after she had read each one twice, she changed into her jeans and T-shirt, made herself tea, and bypassed food since her stomach had knotted up again. But it was a wonderful feeling. She had put on a CD and Harry Connick, Jr. was now crooning one of her favorite Cole Porter songs, and she felt her heart soar toward the heavens.

In the midst of her reverie she rushed to her bedroom, knelt by her bed, and said, "God, thank You. Thank You so much. Please don't let me lose Dave. I haven't asked for much in a long time, but I am asking You to bless my life with this wonderful Christian man. And I will be grateful forever," she added.

She had just returned to the computer when the telephone rang. During the conversation that followed, she could hardly believe that God seemed to be answering her prayer so quickly.

It was Tom again, Dave's roommate, and he was calling from his office.

"Melanie, Dave has had such a rough time the past week. Had to spend his birthday plugged into IVs and feeling miserable. His friends want to do something special for him. We're planning a surprise birthday party soon and. . ." He seemed to have difficulty going on with his plan.

"And?" she prompted. "What? I think it's great that you're doing that for him."

"Well, I realize you don't know me, but I've known Dave for years, and I can honestly tell you he is the greatest guy I've ever known."

A smile slipped over her lips, and she closed her eyes dreamily, recalling Dave's face when they sat talking that first day at the sidewalk café. But she was drifting again, so she yanked her mind back to the subject.

"So. . .I gather I can help in some way or you would not be calling?"

"I know it's asking a lot, and believe me, I will understand if you say no. In fact, he'd kill me—well, not really —just strangle me with one of his wild ties. . ."

She smiled recalling the one on the plane.

"But I'm going to be frank and invite you to fly down. We'll plan the party around whenever you can make it. We had a weekend in mind."

"Which weekend?"

He took an eternity before answering and then in a weak voice ventured the date. "This weekend. It's a surprise, and what I had in mind was paying for your plane ticket— our little present to him—and Julie, that's my girlfriend, can pick you up at the airport and you are more than welcome to stay with her. Her condo is only two blocks from ours." His rapid flow of words came to a thoughtful silence. "You probably think I'm being too forward. We Southerners tend to seem too friendly to a lot of people."

"Not to me," she said tenderly. "I think that is a wonderful gesture of friendship on your part, Tom. And I know Dave will be pleased. But. . ." She frowned.

The weekend! What would she wear? Could she possibly be packed and into Cleveland to catch a plane in three days? And could she even get a flight at this late date?

"I would really like to come, Tom. But it's such short notice. . . ."

"I understand completely. To make your decision easier, I took the liberty of making two plane reservations for you Friday night out of Cleveland. Whichever time is most convenient. There's a flight at seven and another at nine and—you must think I'm insane," he finished lamely. "But for as long as I've known Dave, I've never seen him so in love."

In love! The words jolted Melanie back in her chair, and she bit her lip as tears rushed to her eyes. Her heart felt as though it would leap from her chest and fly away like the little doves she loved so much. She swallowed hard. This was a big decision, and yet it wasn't. She had never met anyone like Dave; it might never happen again. And the sweetest miracle of all was that he was in love with her.

Tossing all of her mother's careful caution to the wind and conjuring up an image of Granny smiling down at her, she cleared her throat. "I'll come," she announced, and as she said the words, she knew she was making the right decision. In fact, she couldn't wait to see Dave again.

A huge sigh of relief filled the air. "You're just as great as he said you were. Most women wouldn't be as understanding or as nice. Which flight would be better for you?"

Melanie made a quick calculation, and since she had pondered plane schedules and fares for a month before scheduling her trip to Paris, she already knew the answer. "Seven."

"I hope you don't think I'm being too presumptuous but I'm a salesman and I tend to get aggressive. About the flights, I mean. Sorry."

She laughed. "Don't apologize. Someone has to think fast in this situation." She debated the amount of time it would take her and immediately realized she would have to leave school early, but she would not be deterred. She rarely asked for time off, and Mr. Warren would just have to understand.

"What time does it arrive in Atlanta?"

"Well," he hesitated, "you're going to lose some time because that particular flight makes a stop. But we won't expect more from you than a good night's sleep at Julie's and then we'll plan the party for Saturday. Actually, we'll start early, and that will surprise Dave even more."

She was laughing like one of her second-graders. She loved the idea, and with Tom and Julie so accommodating, how could she refuse? In the split second she was having those thoughts, Tom rushed in with one more appealing plea to cinch the decision. "Dave hasn't had a real birthday party in years. Says he prefers his birthdays low-key. He's so good to everybody else it will be our pleasure to do something special for him."

"And mine too," she added, feeling the warm fuzzies inside.

"How will I recognize Julie at the airport?"

"She'll be the little blond with the big smile, probably wearing jeans and a University of Georgia sweatshirt. Dave has described you enough for her to easily spot you."

Melanie lifted an eyebrow. "Really?"

"Just teasing. You won't have any trouble finding each other. Meanwhile, I'll have Dave occupied with something so he won't suspect anything. Actually, I'll probably have to go drag him away from his desk at the office. He's practically holed up there day and night, until he drags in and puts Harry Connick, Jr. on to play with the same CD over and over until I have to put in earplugs. He's kind of eccentric at times." He stopped talking, which seemed abrupt. She had already learned that Tom was the kind who liked to talk, and she wondered how well he and Dave got along because she had an idea that Dave might need more silence.

"I hope you don't play hard to get," he said, sounding more southern now as his words slowed down.

"Why?" she asked curiously, staring across at her CD as it lulled out a soothing Harry Connick, Jr. tune.

"Because I've really ruined it for him if you do. I mean some women think the chase is half the fun."

"Not me." Melanie smiled again, thinking how blessed she was. "No, actually Dave and I are very much alike. That's why we got along so well in Paris." *And that's why we both like the same music,* she could have added. But Tom already knew enough to be dangerous; he didn't need any more ammunition. Dave would probably want to strangle Tom at all the private things he had revealed to her, but she was glad that he had. During her week of torment the old insecurities had toyed with her mind. Staring into the mirror, she felt fat and ugly again, though she knew she was not. And she felt scattered and dumb and overemotional. But now one phone call had restored her self-confidence. And her simple, humble prayer had been answered.

"Okay, Tom. I'll come. And let's keep it a surprise. I think that's a great idea."

"Fabulous. Your ticket will be waiting at the airport." He gave her the airline's gate and flight numbers and she wrote them down, astonished at all he had accomplished. "Sorry if I've assumed too much, but I just wanted to make it as easy as possible for you. And I really did not want you to say no. Thanks, Melanie. I understand why he said you were such a terrific person."

"Thanks, Tom. Oh, by the way, what should I bring? I've never been to Atlanta."

"It's already hot and humid. Dress for comfort because we're very casual. Well, we will probably go out for dinner Saturday night, but just something a bit dressy will be fine. Not too dressy. I mean, the kind of outfit you'd wear for dinner there."

"Okay." Dinner at the best restaurant in Milton wouldn't be dressy enough for Atlanta, she decided. But her new Paris wardrobe presented her a wide array of choices, and as soon as she hung up she flew to her closet and started mulling over her options.

Chapter 10

There was definitely an air of "what's going on?" among the teachers' buzz during their coffee break and lunch. After she had answered the anticipated questions of why she was going to Atlanta so soon after her return, she gave a simple, honest answer. She had looked everyone directly in the eye and said, "I've met someone, and he's being given a surprise birthday party. I'd like to be there."

Everyone simply stared, totally at a loss for more questions. It was unlike Melanie to share her private life; it was even more unlike Melanie to "meet someone" and then go dashing off to. . .Atlanta, Georgia!

Her mother, on the contrary, had insisted on knowing every detail, but for once Taylor, thank God, had come to her rescue. "Mom, for heaven's sake, let her have a life," Taylor had scolded more than once. "We want to see her happy, and I've never heard her voice so soft and dreamy."

Even her dad seemed to understand, and she noticed he had been staring more at his mother's portrait, deep in thought.

She left school early and arrived at the airport in plenty of time to board. True to his word, Tom had seen to it that a round-trip ticket was paid for and waiting for her at check-in. She boarded the plane in comfortable slacks, a knit top, a lightweight jacket, and loafers and did her best to nap on the flight to Atlanta.

As the plane approached Atlanta she stared out the window in awe at the millions of lights spread out underneath the canvas of black sky. Melanie found herself wondering precisely which part of this huge city Dave lived and worked in and whether Julie would have to drive far to get to the airport. When the plane touched down, she could feel the humidity seeping into the jet at about the time the pilot informed the passengers it was a pleasant seventy-eight degrees.

She was struck by a pang of nerves as she deplaned and walked up the concourse. As Tom had predicted, Julie was easy to spot. She was the first person in the reception line. A wide smile flew over her face when she spotted Melanie. It was obvious that Julie was a bundle of nervous energy, fidgeting as she waited, shuffling from one foot to the other, and tossing her short blond hair back from her face.

"Melanie," she called out in a thick southern drawl.

"Julie?" she asked, smiling, although there was little doubt.

As soon as she reached Julie, who was no more than five foot two, Melanie felt herself being enveloped in an affectionate hug. "I'm *so* glad you came," she said, her blue eyes twinkling.

"Thank you. Me too," Melanie added, returning her smile as Julie quickly ushered her down the escalator to the baggage area. "How was your trip? Long and boring of course. I just hate plane rides, don't you?"

Melanie opened her mouth to respond but quickly realized a reply was unnecessary because Julie plunged right on. "Last December Tom and I flew up to New York to see a Broadway show and do some Christmas shopping. . . ."

"How fun," Melanie interjected, not wanting to seem void of personality, but Julie wasn't worried about that.

"Have you ever been to New York at Christmastime? Well, don't bother. It's a mad scramble, although I guess it's worth it. The shopping was the best part, but we were disappointed in the play that had been so highly recommended to us."

Melanie merely smiled down at Julie, aware that it was unnecessary to try to answer every question. Julie usually answered them herself. In an amazingly short time they had retrieved her canvas bag, but then Julie turned to her with a frown of concern. "Just one?"

"I decided to keep it simple."

Julie nodded, apparently seeing the logic to that. "And you had very little time to get ready, right? Well, you've really been a good sport about this," she said, motioning for a skycap to pluck the bag from Melanie's hand, although she could have managed. However, she had decided it was easier to let Julie take the lead, since she seemed to take her job seriously. Clearly, she was in charge of getting Melanie safely to. . .wherever they were going.

"I'm parked right out front," Julie said, slipping a bill to the porter then offering a blazing smile to the security guard patrolling the parked cars. Melanie watched with fascination as Julie charmed her way past all obstacles, and soon they were settled safely into her little convertible.

"I put the top up," Julie glanced at Melanie with a smile, as she turned the key in the ignition and they plunged into the traffic. Another blazing smile toward the man she had cut in front of, and they were off. "I know we can all be fussy about our hair. That's why I keep mine short and simple."

"It looks nice," Melanie said, observing the very short, casual cut that allowed her hair to be easily maintained.

"You have a Southern name," Julie said, whipping onto the interstate, even though traffic was heavy. "I love it, though."

"Actually, I was named after my grandmother," Melanie said, leaning back against the thick leather seat and relaxing a bit. "She was Melinda, and Dad was insistent about my being her namesake."

"It fits." Julie shot her a quick glance before careening into another lane, barely missing an SUV roaring up just behind them and responding with an ugly screech of brakes. "Guess you've read *Gone with the Wind?*"

"Half a dozen times," Melanie laughed. She found it so easy to talk with Julie whose chatter and laughter was infectious.

"I always think of myself as Scarlet," she whipped her head toward Melanie, sending her short waves toppling about her face. Above the faint glow of the dashboard, Melanie could see the twinkle in the wide blue eyes and could only imagine how crazy Tom was about her. She decided to get to the point, since Julie was an easy conversationalist.

"So tell me about Dave's friends. I already like you and Tom and—"

"You do?" She giggled. "Tom said I would talk your ear off but he knows I'll just be me and can't help it. Tom and I are probably the most liberal of Dave's friends. As you must know, he's a bit conservative, works too hard, never plays, all that. Tom and I barely get through the week until Friday and then its nonstop playing until the weekend's over. He's usually at my place or I'm at his, but it seems to be no problem for Dave because he works all the time. Too much," she said, frowning for the first time since Melanie had met her. "We've been relieved to see a more relaxed, happy Dave since he returned from Paris. Actually, since he got out of the hospital. In fact," she stopped at the light and took the opportunity to give Melanie an appraising eye, "we all think you've been very good for him. That's why it was so important for us to get you down here for his birthday party. We wanted it to be perfect."

Melanie liked the sound of that. "What do you have planned?"

"I'm going to get you settled in, and then let you shower and get comfortable, then I'm dashing back out to meet Tom at the Party Place. We're buying some stuff for tomorrow. As usual, Dave is working tonight and probably plans to go into the office in the morning. Because he was out sick for a week, he feels he'll be letting his coworkers down if he doesn't catch up on his part of the project by yesterday." She paused and shook her head as if she found him hopeless. "But that's Dave. Dedicated and conscientious. I used to complain to Tom that Dave was boring, but I've seen a different side of him lately. I hope we can be good friends," she said, tossing a glance at Melanie as Julie steered her little car into the driveway of a huge apartment complex.

"I'm sure we will be," Melanie said, turning to survey the nice surroundings. "I'll grab a luggage cart from the garage closet and we'll dash on up to my place."

Melanie had already figured out that Julie did nothing in slow motion, so she hurriedly got out of the car, hooked her shoulder bag on her arm, and ran a hand over her hair.

"You look great," Julie said, not missing a single gesture as she managed to find the cart, roll it to the trunk of her car, and pop the lid. "Love your hair. The length is right, and those highlights compliment your facial features and those fabulous gray eyes." She stopped suddenly in the midst of her fast-forward movements and peered closer at Melanie. "Do you wear contacts?"

Melanie laughed. "Yes, I do."

Julie nodded, turning back to her task of pulling out Melanie's bag, though Melanie tried to assist her. "That's why your eyes look so clear and gray. Thank God, I've never had to bother with glasses. I'm too scatterbrained to keep up with them."

They were practically racing toward the elevator, and Melanie grabbed a breath, aware that the humidity was causing her to move slower. Her clothes suddenly felt slightly damp, as did her skin.

"What's your part of Ohio like?" Julie asked, as they stepped onto the elevator and she pushed a button as she rearranged her ring of keys.

Melanie was fascinated at how Julie always managed two things at once. "It's a small town, but we're not too far from Cleveland."

"I've never been to Cleveland," Julie glanced again at her.

"Then I'd love for you to come visit."

Julie smiled at her. "I like you, Melanie."

Her honesty almost startled Melanie, but then she remembered Dave explaining that some of the people he knew were outspoken and frank, but everyone was friendly and to some people almost seemed insincere because of their responses. Melanie realized Julie was being honest, and she smiled and accepted the compliment.

"Thank you. I like you too. Bet you wondered what kind of person Dave had met?"

Her thin blond-brown brows shot up and down. "I wondered that any woman could steal his heart so fast. I've fixed him up so many times that I finally gave up. He was too hard to please." The elevator door slid open and they stepped out onto the soft, plush beige carpet. "But I see why now. The right person is worth waiting for, don't you think?"

Melanie looked at her carefully, wondering if she should commit herself to that. "When you're sure it's the right person."

Julie was unlocking the door but just before she pushed it open, she shot a questioning glance at Melanie. "Haven't made up your mind yet, huh?"

"Well, we've only known each other a week," Melanie tried to be rational, though Julie obviously believed in love at first sight.

She hurried on ahead, switching on lights, and Melanie looked around, impressed with the nice furnishings and the good taste of the decor. "This is your room," she said over her shoulder, leading the way into a comfortable room done in soft blue with an adjoining bath. "If there's anything you can't find, just prowl through my room across the hall." She waved a little hand in that direction. "The fridge is stocked, so help yourself." She paused to draw a breath.

"Thanks, Julie. You've been most gracious. I'll be fine. You go on and meet Tom and do whatever you need to do about tomorrow. I'd like a hot bath—about half an hour in that tub." She glanced toward the bath.

"We knew you'd be tired after working all day, driving into Cleveland, and then the long flight. It's after eleven," Julie glanced at her watch, "so I have to hurry. The party supply store closes at midnight, and I have to call Tom on my cell phone to say I'm on the way."

"Go ahead. I'll be fine."

"See you in the morning," Julie called over her shoulder, grabbing her purse from the hall table and rushing out the door. The latch clicked loudly, assuring Melanie that she was safely secured.

She found the kitchen and grabbed a bottle of milk and located the cereal, dishes, and flatware. She had a bowl of cereal with a banana from Julie's fruit bowl, feeling the weariness of the strenuous week and the long trip settling into every bone of her body. And yet her mind was wide awake and spinning with everything Julie had told her and the awesome realization that she was in Atlanta, near Dave, and that she would see him tomorrow. After a relaxing bath and a couple of aspirin, she crawled between the smooth, crisp sheets, turned off the light, and dissolved into the softness of the bed.

The distant bounce of music reached her slowly. She noticed her door had been closed sometime during the night, a thoughtful gesture on Julie's part. As she lay there luxuriating in the soft bed and wondering what the day held, she recognized the music as a popular group whose songs were not particularly to her taste, but she realized that Julie's quick personality would respond to that type of beat. The bath had eased her sore muscles, and now her eyes moved toward the closet and the clothes she had brought—those she had worn in Paris. She remembered exactly the ones Dave had complimented.

She had already planned to wear the skirt and blouse she had worn when they met. And if they went out for dinner, she would wear the dressy jade number. She hadn't brought heels, because Dave was only a couple of inches taller and she wisely chose dressy flats and gold sandals.

Tossing the covers back, she rushed to the bathroom to wash up, pulling on her new terry cloth robe as she went. After quickly freshening up, she wandered out into the living room where she spotted Julie perched at the eating bar, the wall phone cord stretched to accommodate her as her hand sped over the notepad.

The smell of fresh coffee filled the air. Since meeting Dave, Melanie had developed a taste for coffee, so she quietly crossed to the kitchen with a brief wave at Julie, not wanting to interrupt her conversation.

"She's up now," Julie said, looking fresh and bright-eyed in a short white sleep shirt that showed off her deep tan. "So we can get right on with it. This is Tom," she explained to Melanie. "Yep, we can be there in an hour."

An hour? Melanie hastened her movements around the kitchen, wondering what time it was. She spotted a kitchen clock and noted that it was only eight, which meant this was the earliest Saturday morning she had seen in awhile. But she'd had plenty of sleep, and she didn't want to waste another second of her short weekend.

"Okay. Love you," Julie said sweetly and hung up. "Glad you found what you needed," she said, as Melanie poured cereal into a bowl. "I never eat breakfast. Well, maybe a banana on the run."

"That's how you keep your nice figure." Melanie glanced at her, amazed at her perfect size.

"Now, here's the plan. Dave just left for the office, so we'll get dressed and Ginny and Chad, that's our two other mutual friends, will meet us at the apartment, and we'll string up the decorations we got last night. Tom is blowing up balloons already."

Melanie smiled at her. "Dave is going to be so pleased."

"And so surprised, I hope. The pleased part will take place when he sees you. I'm so glad you came," she said on a slow romantic sigh. "Well, I'm going to shower and dress. Is forty-five minutes too soon?" she asked suddenly, as though aware she might have acted hastily.

"No, that's fine. I'm accustomed to hurrying to get to school."

"That's right!" Julie suddenly looked amazed. "Second -graders, right?"

Melanie nodded, amazed that Julie and Tom knew so much about her.

"I work over in Buckhead. Assistant manager of a little boutique in the mall. It's fun." With that explanation, she hopped off the barstool, and her bare feet with their bright red toenails padded quickly toward her room.

"I'll be ready," Melanie called after her. It seemed the appropriate thing to say. They had all gone to so much trouble for Dave's party. She only hoped he would be surprised and pleased at their efforts. *What will Dave really think about my coming?* she wondered as she finished her breakfast and put away the cereal and milk. Would he think she was being too presumptuous? Julie and Tom didn't seem to think so, but knowing them, he would understand that maybe they had pressed her to come. The truth was, it had taken very little persuasion.

After washing her bowl and drying her hands, she hurried back to her room to make her bed and begin dressing.

Chapter 11

Between Julie and Tom and Ginny and Chad, whom she also liked, they seemed to have thought of everything. Melanie relaxed and began to enjoy stringing up the Happy Birthday signs, then joined Ginny in putting out a lunch buffet they had picked up at a local delicatessen.

Ginny was easier to be with than Julie was, because, like Melanie, she ran at a slower speed. She was a physical therapist at one of the hospitals where Chad worked as a medical technologist. Their tie to Dave was first high school and then Georgia where they had all gone to school.

"We've been friends for years," Ginny said, arranging the finger sandwiches on a platter and then glancing up at Melanie, who was about the same height and size. "Dave is a great guy. We just want him to meet a girl deserving of him."

Melanie didn't know how to respond to that, because she didn't know if she was that girl, so she merely smiled at Ginny and spread dip on crackers.

"And you seem deserving," Ginny added thoughtfully.

"Thank you. But we really haven't known each other very long."

"I know. But it doesn't take long to know, does it?"

Their eyes met and Melanie knew exactly what she meant. She decided to be honest with her. "No, it doesn't."

"Hurry up, you guys!" Tom called from his perch on the ladder where he was adding one last cartoon sign to the chandelier. Melanie had thought him the perfect match for Julie; he was tall and lanky, calm when she was in high gear, yet aggressive when she couldn't make a decision. They looked at each other with adoring eyes, and that fascinated Melanie. To have been blessed with a good relationship for so many years seemed strange to her. When she considered her short time with Dave, the first twinge of doubt crept in.

Were they rushing into this? They didn't really know one another, she hadn't met his family, nor had he met hers.

And then Julie was motioning wildly toward the kitchen. "Everyone in there quick. He just drove up."

Tom cast one last satisfied glance around the room, and Melanie had to admit it was perfectly decorated and was sure to surprise and please Dave. It was twelve o'clock, and Dave had told Tom he would be in to relax for a quick lunch before going golfing with

Chad. But Chad was hiding in the kitchen with the rest of the conspirators, and they had something quite different planned. Melanie found herself extremely nervous. Her hands were cold and her throat dry, as they grouped together in a quiet little circle in the kitchen, awaiting the key in the lock.

All was silent, the music had been turned off, along with all the lights, and the cassette Tom had made of deep snoring was propped just behind the door so that would be the first sound that greeted Dave. When the door opened and Melanie glimpsed his crisp white business shirt and perfectly groomed hair, her heart jumped to her throat and her hands turned to ice. He had already heard the snoring and was quietly closing the door and gently opening the closet door to hang up his jacket.

At that moment all the lights went on, and everyone yelled "SURPRISE!"

He whirled, turning pale as his eyes widened on all the decorations and the sudden blare of a CD playing an old-fashioned "Happy Birthday." One by one they moved into the living room, though Julie motioned for Melanie to stay in the kitchen.

Melanie waited, holding her breath, as he hugged Ginny and Julie and shook hands with Tom and Chad, thanking them for the party. "We're on a budget and couldn't afford a nice gift," Chad began to explain.

Dave put up his hand, and now she caught a side profile of him, for he still had not turned toward the kitchen. She felt a surge of tenderness well up within her just at the sight of him.

"So we decided to try to get you something you really needed," Tom said matter-of-factly, and Julie gave her the eye signal to come forward.

Slowly, Melanie came out of the kitchen, and Dave, following everyone's gaze, turned around. For a moment, he could only stare as though unable to believe his eyes. Then he covered the distance between them in a few short steps and pulled her quickly to him, smiling into her face.

"Melanie. You came down for my birthday."

She could only nod as she looked up at him and realized that nothing had changed. He was still just as she imagined him, except a bit thinner from his illness and a bit peaked. But the blue eyes that blazed into hers told her everything she needed to know. And then his lips were brushing hers, and she couldn't keep her arms from sliding up his arms to his shoulders. The kiss deepened until someone cleared his or her throat and Melanie jerked back, startled.

What was happening to the self-conscious girl who never made a move without thinking it over at least half a dozen times?

"Okay, time to eat," Tom broke the moment.

Dave's eyes still held hers, as though there were only the two of them in the room and the mood of Paris was still very much with them. The crowd was putting out the food, gathering around the counter, while Dave kept holding Melanie's hand and thanking her for coming.

"You've lost weight," she said, hoping to bring them both back to the moment.

"Yeah, but I'm fine now."

"Come on, you two," Chad nudged him. "Fill your plates. You're too thin, Dave. See, Melanie has already noticed."

"Oh, I didn't mean. . . ," she began then stopped. Those days of apologizing for everything were behind her now, and standing next to Dave she felt herself being led toward a bright new and very different future. She took a deep breath and forced her eyes away from Dave toward the crowded buffet.

"We should at least be sociable," she said gently. "They've really worked hard."

Dave blinked and turned around, surveying the food, the decorations, everything as though for the first time. "You are the greatest friends a guy could ever have," he said, and to everyone's surprise it looked like businessman Dave was about to cry.

She slid her hand into his. "Come on, I'm hungry."

They joined in then, filling their plates and joining in the conversation as Chad related news of the new golf course that was being built, knowing this would capture Dave's attention. The meal went pleasantly and then they moved to the sofa, talking easily, the way friends who had known each other for a very long time often did. Strangely, Melanie felt as though she fit right in, because she could relate to some of the things they were saying. She was delighted to learn that Ginny enjoyed reading, knew where the best bookshops were located, and that they shared a fondness for the same authors.

A knock on the door startled all of them for a moment, then Tom leapt to his feet and rushed to the door. A cart of sweets was pushed into the room by a pleased-looking caterer. A giant chocolate cake was the centerpiece, flanked by an assortment of other little goodies. And there were special decorative candles, already on the cake.

"Hey, this is too much."

The caterer was generously tipped in the background by Chad and disappeared back through the door.

"No. . .actually, we had planned to have Melanie jump out of the cake," Tom said, with mock seriousness, "but we couldn't find the right size cake."

Everyone laughed uproariously while Julie reminded Dave that he *had* to make a wish and blow out the candles. All of them. Tom was dutifully lighting each candle, as though there were hundreds, instead of twenty-six.

"Okay, you've made your point," Dave laughed. "But this is the happiest birthday of my life," he said and looked at Melanie.

"Make your wish," she reminded him.

"That's easy," he said, his eyes lingering on her before he turned and with a great whoosh of breath blew out each candle. Ginny and Julie then set about serving the rich cake with a colorful mint and a fortune cookie tucked on each side of the delicate china plate.

Everyone had fun reading their fortunes and debating whether there was anything to them or not. Julie staunchly believed in fortune cookies. Chad did not. Meanwhile, Ginny was busy in the kitchen.

"Hey, knock it off," she called. "I'm making Dave his special espresso."

With that Julie joined her in the kitchen and they began to load the dishwasher.

"We've made reservations at The Globe for dinner at nine. But that gives you two a few hours together before dinner," Tom began.

"In privacy," Julie called from the kitchen.

Melanie glanced toward the kitchen and then said to Dave, "I really would like to help them clean up."

"Okay."

A couple of gifts had appeared out of nowhere for him: golf balls with engraved hand towels and a new desk set. Melanie decided to wait on hers.

When the party began to wind down and the others had gathered up all the debris, thrown it away, and pushed the caterer's cart into the kitchen, they made their excuses.

"See you at The Globe," Ginny smiled first at Melanie then Dave.

"And don't be *too* late," Chad teased.

At that precise moment, the bedroom door opened and the sound of accordion music, mostly out of sync, reverberated across the room, drawing everyone's attention to Tom who was wearing a French beret and had an accordion strapped to his chest. He was doing his best to give an imitation of a French song, but everyone erupted in laughter, quickly offending him.

"Thank you, Tom," Melanie called out. "That was very thoughtful of you."

He shrugged as Julie tugged at his sleeve while he removed the beret and placed the accordion on a chair. He started to go then turned back and looked at Melanie and Dave.

"You were right," he said to Dave. And they both understood the meaning, and strangely, Melanie did too.

After the door had closed and the voices had died away down the hall, Melanie realized that someone had put on a romantic sound track from a favorite movie, which seemed perfect for the occasion.

"You know what?" Dave said, lifting her hand to his lips and kissing each finger.

"What?" she asked softly, staring up into his eyes and feeling as though they were drifting on a cloud again.

"We're not in Paris," he said slowly, "and I'm more in love with you than before."

Tears glowed in her eyes for a moment as the romantic words about two people falling in love forever echoed to her. "Me too."

They reached for one another and at last Melanie knew the meaning of being a complete woman, of knowing the wonder of romance.

And she knew Granny was probably smiling down from her own special cloud.

PEGGY DARTY

Peggy Darty authored more than thirty novels before she passed away in 2011. She worked in film, researched for CBS, and taught in writing workshops around the country. She was a wife, mother, and grandmother who most recently made her home in Alabama.

THE GARDEN PLOT

by Rebecca Germany

Dedicated

. . .to my wonderful family—
the families of
Germany, Betts, Acheson, and Royer—
a network of parents, grandparents,
siblings, aunts, uncles, cousins, and more
who have made my life complete.
Thank you for carrying
the torch of Christianity,
demonstrating the walk to me
and the generations to come.

"Arise, my darling, my beautiful one,
and come with me.
See! The winter is past; the rains are over and gone.
Flowers appear on the earth;
the season of singing has come,
the cooing of doves is heard in our land.
The fig tree forms its early fruit;
the blossoming vines spread their fragrance.
Arise, come, my darling;
my beautiful one, come with me."
Song of Solomon 2:10–13

Chapter 1

F ew things have disturbed me more than watching my children and grandchildren move away from this town. It's good to have you home, Dandy."

Debra Julian giggled like a young girl. It had been years since she had heard her grandmother use that nickname for her oldest grandchild. Debbie, as a toddler with arms full of the flowering dandelion weed, had earned the nickname in this very backyard and on just such a warm spring day.

"Well, Gran, it is good to be home. I'm sorry I haven't been able to unpack and get organized much the last couple of weeks while I've been learning my job," Debbie said as she gently propelled the wicker porch swing for the two of them. "Walking the halls of Dover High School again sure makes me realize that I'm not a kid anymore. So many of the students are taller than me and only a few of my old teachers are still around after ten years, but the whole attitude is different. Each new class of teens is in such a hurry to grow up."

"Maybe your counseling will help them slow down. Have you been able to figure out the system?"

"The school secretaries have been very helpful, but it is obvious they still grieve the loss of Mr. Knight. He was a well-liked middle-aged man and no one was prepared for such a sudden death. He had requested two weeks leave for his surgery, so some things were in good order."

"Just goes to show that no one knows when the Good Lord will call them home," Grandma said with a soft, reverent tone.

"Why does it seem that his loss was my gain just when I needed to find new work and make the major decision about moving back and buying your home?"

"God's timing is perfect timing," Grandma almost sang. "He knows what each of us needs. Now, if your parents would only stay home for more than a week at a time they could enjoy having you back, too. But they—" Grandma suddenly stopped. She jumped to her skinny legs, waving her handkerchief at two dogs that were very interested in her flowering lilac bush. "Now scoot!" Soon the dogs ran into a neighboring yard. "Some of my best perennials have been ruined by those pesky strays," Grandma huffed as she settled back onto the swing.

"I'm surprised you never fenced in your yard, Gran. This corner lot is tempting for cross-through traffic."

"It's just not the neighborly thing to do," she crooned. "Besides, I don't want to cut off the little view I have. If I had a fence, I wouldn't be able to see Mr. Kelly's pink crab apples in bloom or Myrna Yoder's birdbath. . .and I may not have met my new neighbor."

"You could always use a see-through chain link or a low picket." Debbie sighed and rose to go inside. "Don't you think you ought to put your sweater on, Gran? The wind is picking up."

"Don't you want to know who he is?"

"Who?" Debbie paused with the back door open.

"Oh, never mind, dear." Grandma shook her gray head.

Debbie soon returned with a soft white sweater and helped Grandma slip her frail arms inside.

"Do you remember the Robillards?" Grandma asked.

"Of course. They lived in this neighborhood as long as you and Grandpa."

"I sure hated to see them pass on. . .and so close together," Grandma spoke softly as she picked at the balled wool on her sweater. "The house sold back in September."

"I've noticed the yard is looking very nice again." Debbie looked across the backyard. The Robillards' large Victorian home faced Sixth Street while Grandma's house—now hers, too—sat on the corner of Sixth facing Maple Street with her backyard bordering the south side of the Robillard lot. She remembered that the Robillards were always good neighbors and friends to her grandparents. Good neighbors could be hard to find. Debbie only hoped that the property had sold to a friendly family. *That house was made for a large, happy family*, Debbie mused.

"Debbie, girl, why don't we put in a garden this year?" Grandma asked, bringing Debbie back to their conversation.

"A garden, Gran?"

"I always had a garden until about four years ago. It got to the point that I hurt too much to bend down and tend my plants."

"A vegetable garden?"

"Why, yes. You'll have the whole summer free to work on it." Grandma paused. "Or, don't guidance counselors get summers off like teachers do?"

"Yes, Gran, I'll have a few weeks free, until August, when I will be helping the cheerleaders train."

"Who needs to train to know how to jump around and shout?" Grandma muttered.

Debbie just laughed and volunteered to fix them some lunch.

⌗

The very next Saturday morning, the first in May, Grandma called from the bottom of the stairs and woke Debbie from her slumber, insisting that Debbie start breaking ground for the garden that day. After spending all but one evening of the past week helping her grandmother with various projects at home and at church, Debbie had anticipated Saturday as her catch-up day. She was beginning to understand one of the reasons why her parents enjoyed spending most of their retirement in Arizona. Grandma could be quite demanding, but Debbie loved being near family again, and she was happy to be in the position to buy Gran's Cape Cod style home. Gran needed to be relieved of the responsibility and have someone around part of the time to avoid going into a retirement home. And Debbie loved this old house, full of sweet memories. It would at least make a good starter home for her while she waited for the right man to come knocking on the door of her heart.

Debbie peaked out the dormer window to check the weather. Many yards in this small Ohio town showed signs of new life in the landscaping as well as the people who had come out to enjoy the warm spring day that promised even sweeter days to come. She left her laundry in sorted stacks around her bedroom and school files strewn across her tiny desk and headed downstairs.

Debbie found Grandma in the living room, wrapped up in an afghan as she quilted.

"Gran, don't you feel like coming out and helping me plan the garden plot?" Debbie asked, suddenly concerned about her grandmother's health. Grandma had just hit seventy-nine without having had any major health complications, unlike her long-deceased husband, but her family worried that arthritis and age were wearing Grandma down.

"Oh, I better stay in out of the breeze today," Grandma spoke slowly. "I know you will do fine without my direction."

Debbie didn't know what to make of Grandma's mood. She didn't look ill, but Grandma usually didn't miss a chance to be near the action. Still, Debbie decided it would be best to start the work.

"Now, I don't need to tell you how to operate a rotary tiller, but the old one in the shed will need a bit of oil and could take a few cranks to get going," Gran instructed.

"That's all right, Gran."

"And. . .the garden is your project, but I would suggest that you go to the back of the lot, past the grape trellis, to start your digging. My other gardens were always right along the west side of the shed, and I'm afraid there wasn't sufficient morning light there."

"Fine, Gran." Debbie tried to head for the back door.

"Now, I like rows that are no longer than about twelve feet, and there should be plenty of room between each, especially when it comes to cucumbers. I just hate it when those vines twine through my other plants. But you build it how you like it."

Debbie smiled and nodded.

"About fertilizer. Did you buy the natural kind?" Grandma smiled sweetly. "You know. . .the kind from farms?"

Debbie prayed silently for patience. "No, Gran."

"Well. . .it is your choice, but natural is always the best."

After a trip to a nursery for bags of natural fertilizer and a couple of tools, Debbie was finally ready to step off her garden plot. She would make it twelve feet wide and twenty-four feet in length, starting the length at Grandma's grape arbor and working back toward a grove of evergreens near the neighbor's yard, where the Robillards had always lived until they passed away and the house had gone up for sale. Debbie knew a bunch of rabbits were just waiting among those pines to eat her plants as soon as they sprouted, but there was no other spot big enough for the garden—except along the shed.

Inside, the shed smelled like damp earth, the floor covered only by a thin layer of gravel. One whole wall was lined with shelves of flowerpots in every imaginable shape and size, while the opposite wall housed a collection of Ohio license plates that dated back to the late 1930s. Once, the building housed Debbie's grandparents' car before her grandfather had had a new garage built that connected to the house.

She pulled an old rug off the tiller and tugged the machine out into the yard. It took more than a couple cranks, and a lot of tinkering on Debbie's part, to get the old relic running, but eventually she directed the bouncing dirt digger to her garden spot.

It required every ounce of her strength to keep the tiller moving in a straight line, but by noon she had dug up the whole garden. It would need to be gone over again to work out the clumps, but she stopped for a much-deserved rest, her hands numb from the strain and vibrations.

Debbie slipped her dirty tennis shoes off on the porch and paused inside the kitchen door to watch as Grandma bustled around preparing tomato soup and sandwiches. She looked as happy and healthy as ever.

"Are you feeling better, Gran?" Debbie asked as the porch door slammed behind her.

Grandma jumped and gripped the counter. "Mercy, girl, you scared me. I was just getting ready to call you in. From what I can see from the window, you are making real progress out there."

Debbie washed up before joining Grandma at the old Formica table.

"Let's pray that God gives you a very successful afternoon," Grandma insisted. And before long, she was shooing Debbie back outside to her project.

Debbie went over half of the freshly turned garden again with the tiller before she had to stop and rest. The sun was shining directly down, and she wiped away a stream of perspiration as she tucked her long chestnut curls behind her ears. It would have been a good day to wear a ponytail. Her hands and arms ached from the tiller's vibrations. She rolled her shoulders.

"Hey!"

Debbie spun around with a gasp, startled by the angry male voice.

"It's about time you turned off that antique and listened to me."

Debbie stared at a man of about thirty who wore old jeans and a polo shirt that were tailored to his athletic frame as if they had been a classic business suit.

"I came out here to clean leaves from my flower beds," he gestured widely with lean arms, "only to find you digging up my seed grass."

"I...uh," Debbie had a hard time finding her voice as her cheeks flushed hot with her embarrassment. "There is no clearly marked property line. Did I get into your yard?" was all she could think to say.

"I'd guess that at least half of your mess is in my yard," he grumbled. "Who gave you permission to dig here anyway?"

"My grandmother assured me that this was the best spot for our garden," Debbie said lamely, feeling like one of her scolded students. This handsome man stood at least a head taller than her and could have every right to be upset. Debbie detested her sudden lack of communication skills, and anger at herself and the situation began to rise. "Perhaps we should speak with her about the matter," she gritted through clenched teeth.

Without a word, the man followed Debbie across the backyard and up the porch steps, then waited as Debbie shed her dirt-caked shoes and went inside to find her grandma. She searched the whole house, upstairs and down, calling for Grandma. Debbie couldn't find her anywhere and had to assume she walked to visit a neighbor, as she was often known to do. Debbie dreaded facing the grim neighbor again, but she straightened her shoulders and returned to the back porch.

His back was to her as he leaned against a post. She had to admit that he was nice to look at but wondered how she would ever make a friend after such a poor start.

Chapter 2

A much relaxed face turned to greet Debbie. "You wouldn't be little Dandy that Maxie speaks so fondly of, would you?"

"Maxie?" Debbie's mouth dropped open in surprise. "My grandmother is Maxine Julian. I've never heard anyone call her Maxie."

The man chuckled, transforming his whole face into a wide grin, and though it didn't seem possible, he became even more handsome. "Mrs. Julian and I have become good friends since I moved in last September. You know, she makes the best apple crisp I have ever eaten. By the way, I'm Scott Robillard, the town's newest optometrist. I bought my grandparents' house. You may not remember, but I spent a few summers here."

Debbie looked closer at his masculine features and her face flamed. How could she not have recognized him? She was just fifteen and he was a "mature" seventeen-year-old who, along with a couple of his cousins, spent most of a summer with his grandparents. Debbie clearly recalled having spent her whole summer trying to gain his attention.

Oh, how foolishly she had behaved. It all came rushing back to her like it had been a month ago instead of thirteen years full of growth and change into adulthood.

Debbie was confused by this revelation and his sudden friendly change in attitude toward her. "Uh. . . Scott. . .my grandmother appears to have gone to a neighbor's." She pointed a thumb over her shoulder toward the open back door.

"Yes, feel free to call me Scott, if I may call you Debbie?" he said, seeming to ignore the issue at hand while his gaze roved her face.

She nodded and hurried on. "Would you like to call her later? I promise not to dig any more until we talk to her." She punctuated her sincerity with a timid smile.

"That won't be necessary. I am sure we can work something out. Let's take another look at the situation." He took off at an easy gait down the porch steps and across the bright green lawn.

Debbie followed slowly and watched as he walked along the boundary line, starting from the street inward. He was tall, though being five-nine Debbie didn't really have far to look up at him. He had a lean, athletic frame without the bulging muscles of a serious jock. She found him as appealing to look at as she had as a teen. He even had a boyish lock of rich chocolate brown hair that flopped across his broad brow. Debbie suppressed the urge to grin.

"That azalea bush by the sidewalk is really the only thing that marks the property line," he said as he marched across the middle of her tilled plot. "Our grandparents never worried about the details of property boundaries. It is no wonder that you got into my yard, but Maxie should have realized that there was not enough room for this size of garden here. It should have gone alongside the shed."

Debbie sighed and swallowed a sarcastic laugh. "She was quite specific about how the garden should be dug. I'm truly sorry for the mistake."

"I usually don't let anyone mess in my yard. It is kind of my stress-relieving hobby that I have taken to the level of obsession. But since you're Maxie's granddaughter. . ."

Debbie was back to feeling like a kid under the scrutiny of his dark brown eyes. She nervously smoothed her curls away from her rounded face. *He obviously still sees me as that silly teenage girl.*

"Ah, there's the old girl now," Scott whispered with a sparkle in the depth of his eyes.

❧

After iced tea, several cookies, and pleasant conversation about the weather, Maxine Julian still avoided discussing the issue of the garden.

"Dandy, did Scott tell you that he recently bought his grandparents' house?" Grandma asked. She patted Scott's large hand and shoved a paper napkin under his glass.

Debbie nodded as she chewed the cookie that seemed to stick in her throat. *Though you failed to mention that detail.* Debbie tried to resist the tug to feel irritated at her grandmother. It was really the easy comradery between Scott and Grandma that was gnawing at her sensibilities.

Scott leaned back in the kitchen chair. "It seemed to take forever for the estate to be settled after the back-to-back funerals. Everything had to be equally divided. . . but I'm glad I was able to buy the house and keep it in the family," Scott shared with them, then downed another cookie in large bites.

Gran nodded in agreement. "I told you that is what Dandy is doing for me. There won't be much to settle when I'm gone."

Debbie didn't like the direction of the conversation and her grandmother's matter-of-fact tone. Sure, these things were inevitable, but they didn't have to be discussed in casual conversation with a. . .non-family member.

Scott suddenly raised his head from contemplation of the cookie plate that was out of his reach. "Do you remember that neighborhood bonfire we had in these backyards? That's back when they allowed that sort of thing inside town."

"Oh, yes," Debbie recalled with renewed interest. "There must have been nearly a hundred people coming and going from that party."

"You were there?" Scott asked, and for the first time his gaze really met hers.

Debbie was confused and could feel her cheeks flushing. *Surely you remember the girl who followed you so closely that I can still repeat every move you made that summer.*

"Dandy was here most of the summer that you and the twins stayed," Gran declared and, reaching behind Debbie, she deftly clasped Debbie's hair back into a ponytail. "You probably would remember her best in pigtails and braces."

Debbie gasped and pulled away from her grandmother's hands.

Scott chuckled. "Sorry, all I can remember of that summer was the stupid way I followed my cousins, Mike and Matt, all around. The twins had just finished their second year of college. They were here to help Grandpa with the closing of his store, and I begged my folks to come too because I idolized those guys at the time."

Debbie couldn't believe what she was hearing. How could he not remember her? Why, she had played a movie theme song over and over when she heard him say he liked it. She played it from her bedroom window when he was in the yard; she hummed it when they were in the same room. She was desperate to show him they had something in common. She even went as far as to join the neighborhood gang in a game of flag football. How could he not remember her—and her crush?

"It's funny," Scott said. "I've never been big on sports, but I played every imaginable game that summer just so I could keep up with those guys." Scott shook his dark head.

Debbie barely heard his words. She should still feel embarrassed, but now she was offended by his lack of ability to even recall her presence. Everyone knew she had been starry-eyed for Scott. Her grandfather had teased her mercilessly. Her best friend Penny had listened to hours of woes when Scott failed to give Debbie the attention she craved.

Of course, she had moved on from her adolescent behavior to more mature ways of looking at relationships—hadn't she? Certainly. Then why were the memories still so raw for her?

Grandma was speaking as she refilled Scott's glass of tea. The subject had obviously changed. "Now, Scott, I wasn't able to be out there this morning when Dandy started her digging, and I have left all the planning to her. She is a good, hard worker, but also very good with . . .why, she's a good homemaker." Grandma smiled and nodded in Debbie's direction.

Debbie's mouth dropped open. What was Grandma saying? She sounded like a sales pitch. *First, I'm the hormone-crazy teen, and now he'll know me as the desperate woman who has to rely on Gran's matchmaking.* Debbie picked up the plate that had just been passed. "Cookie anyone?"

Her offer was ignored as Scott continued to follow Grandma's conversation with no sign of emotion. Debbie's gaze glued to his left hand. She hated it when married men didn't wear wedding bands, but then, Scott was probably very much single. That was an unfortunate state for her jumbled emotions to deal with.

"I had no idea that Dandy would go into your yard." Grandma shrugged and petted Debbie's hand like she was a child. Debbie pulled her hands into her lap. "I can certainly pay for new grass seed."

"I don't blame anyone," Scott said, smiling at Debbie as she took a large bite from an oatmeal cookie. "I'm sure I can get another good patch of grass started by summer, but I'm more interested in a compromise."

He couldn't help feeling like this wasn't all a simple mistake, but he was willing to play along with these apologetic females and reap some benefit. Leaving the garden on his property should allow for more opportunities to see Maxie's beautiful granddaughter, and even he could sacrifice some landscaping perfection for that prospect. He wasn't in the market for a wife, at the moment. He was just enjoying the beautiful scenery.

"What would you say if I offer my land in exchange for a share of the vegetables you grow?" Scott offered the ladies. "I wouldn't really have time for my own garden anyway."

Maxine appeared to sigh in relief, but Debbie looked to her grandmother nervously. "Gran, are you sure we will have enough to split with Mr. Robillard...uh, Scott? You know that you will want to give vegetables to Mom and Dad as well as Aunt Carol."

"Then we'll pack it full of plants," Maxine decided.

"But you like wide, neat rows, Gran," Debbie quietly reminded.

"If you think the garden should be a bit bigger, we can look at extending it," Scott quickly offered before thinking.

"Ah," Maxine laughed, "first you are ready to lynch us for ruining your new grass and now you propose a bigger garden. Kids..." she chuckled.

"Please," Debbie said and paused for breath, "forget I said anything. We'll make this plot work and have plenty to share with you...Mr. Robillard."

Scott noted the use of formality and the icy waves that Debbie emitted. Was he missing something? Had he overstepped the boundaries of her personal space? He had enjoyed the play of color in her cheeks when they first met, but he didn't understand why her sparkling blue eyes now appeared frosty and her blushed cheeks were now set like stone.

But it was settled, and Debbie went back to work on smoothing the clumps from the garden plot, while Scott finally got to work on his flowerbeds. But, though Scott worked on the opposite side of the house from her, all he could envision were large chestnut curls and round, pink cheeks flushed in embarrassment.

He had the distinct feeling that he should remember her, and he tried to play through his mind the summer of thirteen years ago. But it was useless. All he remembered was sweeping, dusting, and stocking his grandfather's hardware store. Then there were the football and basketball games every evening with Mike and Matt. The only girls he could remember were a group that hung around the park whenever his cousins went there to shoot hoops. His cousins were good-looking college freshmen who drew the girls like magnets. Scott, on the other hand, had still been a gangly teen at age seventeen and didn't give the girls much thought when he had so much to learn from his older cousins.

Scott dug his trowel deep into the soil. He wasn't sure how well he was going to like his new neighbor. She stirred strange, confusing emotions in him. In his profession, he should be used to dealing with all types of personalities of his patients. It could be a long spring...and summer...then fall. He was already thinking that he had better plan a garden on his own next year.

A loud clanking noise came from around the house. Scott tried to ignore it, piling debris higher in the old bushel basket. He knew the noise was coming from the garden, but he was afraid if he rushed to offer his assistance, his growing interest in Debbie would be obvious.

The tiller was shut off and the quiet returned to the peaceful neighborhood. Even the birds soon started twittering again. Scott found himself holding his breath as he waited for any sound that would tell him what Debbie was doing now. His hands moved in slow, fluid motion as he tried not to make a sound.

He couldn't wait any longer. He rose and brushed the knees of his jeans, annoyed with himself for his nagging curiosity. He would make a trip to the garage so that his path would give him a clear view of the adjoining backyards and the tilled plot.

Scott rounded the corner of his house and immediately stopped in his purpose-filled tracks. In the middle of the dark brown rectangle of soil sat Debbie. Her long hair was pulled into a loose ponytail and hung down her back. She sat cross-legged beside the tiller, her elbow on her knee and her head resting in her palm as she stared at the still machine.

Scott glanced up at Maxie's house and caught the movement of curtains at the kitchen window.

He knew he should move on to the garage and keep to himself. Debbie seemed to be quite the independent type, and after all, this garden was her mess and problem. But his feet slowly propelled him to the edge of the turned earth.

"Uh. . ." He ran a hand across the back of his head. "Do you think you threw the chain?" he heard himself ask.

Debbie turned her large blue eyes upward, the sunshine illuminating her face. Scott dropped his gaze, trying not to stare, and shifted nervously.

"You wouldn't know of a repair shop for antique yard equipment, would you?" Debbie asked with little life in her voice.

"No." He slowly exhaled the word, and even though he knew he was treading in dangerous waters, he offered, "Maybe I could take a look at it." He stepped closer to the machine, and Debbie suddenly jumped to her feet and beat at the dirt clinging to her loose denim pants. She twisted to reach her backside and bent to brush her calves.

Scott turned his back to her actions and gulped for air, as he forced his heart rate back to normal. He poked at the chain cover, knowing he would need a screwdriver to loosen it. He deliberately looked the tiller over from top to bottom before turning back to Debbie.

She was gone. He was surprised to see her disappearing through the back door of her house. Scott turned back to the machine in dazed confusion. *So, fix the machine, Robillard. Isn't that what you came to do?*

Chapter 3

D ebbie changed her clothes, then grabbing a file of work papers, she sat down in the window seat of her cozy bedroom. Two dormer windows gave her nice views of both the front and back yards. The window seat gave Debbie a clear, bird's-eye view of the garden plot. She watched as Scott returned from a trip to his garage and bent over the rusty tiller.

You ran from the scene, she scolded herself. *But to stay would have shown interest in the situation and to leave was a display of indifference. Wasn't it?*

Debbie had a feeling that, even though she considered herself an adult who happened to be in a job that placed her in authority over teens, she was allowing herself to be pulled back into adolescent games. She flipped open the file folder and took out the first sheet. She tried to study the print, but her gaze returned to the window. Scott made several trips to the garage as twenty minutes lapsed.

Watching him, she could picture Scott as a teenager bending over an old bike. That summer he stayed with his grandparents she had witnessed his kind acts to many people in the neighborhood. Though a busy kid, he always found time to lend a hand where needed.

Grandma called from the bottom of the stairs as Scott was placing the chain cover back in place. "Dandy, come and carry this glass of pop out to Scott for me, please. The day has sure warmed up and he has been working so hard."

Debbie rolled her eyes toward the slanting ceiling. To refuse would be very rude. She pulled herself up from her comfortable cushions, descended the stairs sluggishly, and took the cold glass of soda pop from her grandmother without a word. She had a feeling Grandma was reading her every action with great clarity.

Her leisurely pace brought her to the garden in what seemed to her to be record time. She held the glass out at a stiff arm's length. "Gran thought you could use a cool drink."

She let her gaze drift to the trees as he straightened and dusted his dirty hands.

"I'm very grateful." He took the glass and his fingers brushed hers.

She pulled her arm back. *Oh, would you stop reacting like a kid!* she screamed at the tingling sensation in her hand.

"Let's see if this thing will crank now," Scott said, and she noticed that he set the empty glass in the grass.

With two cranks the old tiller was noisily running again. The chain worked properly and the rotors were once again greedily searching for dirt to devour. Scott motioned her to take the handles. She nodded her thanks, stepped behind the machine, and followed it to the edge of the rectangle.

As she turned to chop a new row of dirt clogs, she saw a car entering Scott's drive and Scott making a beeline to his back door. It was getting to be late afternoon. Maybe he had a dinner date. The thought relieved and distressed her in the same wave of emotion. She pushed the tiller harder and deeper into the soil.

It had been a long day, and after nearly an hour of working on the garden dirt, Debbie was on the last round at Scott's edge of the garden. Her pace was slow, but she pushed on. She brushed stray hairs back behind her ear and felt a splash of water.

Looking up Debbie's face was doused. Scott's sprinkling system had suddenly come on, and she was positioned between two sprinkler heads. Water ran down her forehead, cheeks, and chin. She no longer paid attention to the path of the tiller as she swiped at the rivulets of water tracing her lips. She huffed at the water and gave the tiller a disgusted shove.

All of a sudden the water was coming from every direction. Streams flowed over her shoes and sprayed the tiller from under the blades.

"Oh no," she screeched.

The tiller had gone out of the straight edge of the garden and cut deep into the sprinkler pipe. Debbie killed the motor of the offending dirt digger and scurried across the yard, dodging sprinkler heads that still spouted showers of water.

She searched alongside the back door for a shut-off valve. Finding none, she moved on to the side of the garage and even peeked inside the door. No luck. She looked back at the mess of water pooling in the soaked garden and running through the thin, new grass toward the stand of pines.

Debbie wanted to scream in frustration and cry in despair. She wrung out her drenched T-hirt and trudged to the back door. Her knock was not answered. Sure that Scott was home, she moved to the side of the house where French doors opened from the dining room. She could hear loud music blaring, and she knocked hard.

When Scott finally came to the windowed door his eyes widened. She must look frightfully bad.

"What happened to you? Is it raining?"

Debbie was fearful that she detected a smile around his handsome lips.

"I have a bit of a problem and could use a hand," she forced herself to admit. Two problems in one day were really going to look like a play for his attentions. She sighed and resigned herself to continue. "Do you think you can shut off your sprinkling system?"

Scott's brow creased in confusion. "Sure. I'll have to go down to the basement."

"When you are done, I have something I need to show you."

Debbie stepped away from the door and waited for Scott's return. She noticed that the music was lowered to a more moderate level.

When Scott returned he was not alone. At least six teenage bodies followed in his wake, eyes wide with curiosity. Debbie picked at her wet clothes and wanted to shrink away from embarrassment.

"So what do I need to see?" Scott asked, calm and controlled.

Debbie glanced at the heads behind his shoulders. "Uh. . .the garden. . .backyard. . ." was all she could manage to say with her tongue tied in a fool's knot.

"Give me a minute, guys. I'll be right back," Scott said, pulling the door closed behind him. "Sorry about that. I'm a youth volunteer at my church and this week it was my turn to hold the youth outing at my house." He shrugged and glanced at her.

Scott couldn't stop shaking with silent laughter. She looked like a sodden feline, indignant toward the bathing. Ruffled and brittle around the edges, but helpless to change the circumstances.

He followed her around the side of the house to the garden area. Then he noticed abnormally large pools of water. His head swung back around toward Debbie for an explanation. She simply pointed to the tiller that sat at an angle on the edge of the garden plot.

Looking closer at the rotors, Scott saw a piece of broken white PVC pipe. Realization dawned. The pipe he had had laid a month ago was cut and in desperate need of repair. The end of her garden had come right up along the pipeline. Six inches off course and she had hit the buried line.

"How?" He gestured at the mess.

"Well, I didn't know you had a sprinkler system," she rushed, stopped, and started again. "The sprinklers came on. I was getting drenched and frustrated, and I guess that is when I got out of my row, hitting the pipe." Her shoulders sagged. "I'll have it repaired right away."

Scott breathed deep. How could he be mad when she looked so distraught? He reached out and cupped her shoulder. The heat of her skin through the wet cotton shirt seared his hand. He reconsidered the action and pulled away, wiggling his fingers in surprise.

"Why don't we just wait to discuss the problem tomorrow afternoon? If you don't dig any more and the sprinkler stays off, there won't be any further damage."

She arched a questioning brow at him and he spun away on a direct path back to the house. "I have company," he threw over his shoulder.

Debbie sat on the back porch swing Sunday afternoon. She had chosen to wear a light blue flowery skirt with a lightweight sweater top for a day of church and relaxation. She sat with her eyes closed, one leg tucked up under her, drifting with the sway of the swing.

Grandma was on the front porch visiting with Myrna Yoder and talking to other neighbors who strolled by. It was a beautiful, warm spring day that begged a body to be outdoors. The small new leaves on the trees were bright green and the tulips were opened to catch every ray of sunshine. Debbie loved the clean air and the clear blue sky that was dotted by an occasional puffy white cloud.

After the workout the tiller had given her, her body protested the slightest of moves. She opened her eyes slowly to find herself under inspection. From the foot of the porch steps a small black squirrel gazed back at her. Having grown up outside town, Debbie still found the black squirrels a novelty. They had their origins in Canada, but had drifted south after being released on the Kent State University campus. Their numbers were now quite thick in Dover.

And they could be greedy little snoops. This one tilted his head from side to side, obviously searching for a dropping or handout. Debbie laughed at it, then stomped her foot to shoo it away. The squirrel stayed still a moment and glared at her, then bounded into the shrubbery.

Scott approached the Julian house with a little sense of dread. He knew he would do himself a favor to stay away from Miss Debbie Julian. She confused him, and his reactions to her mere presence were clear signs that this woman could quickly and easily get under his skin— into his soul. But he wasn't looking for a complicated relationship with an equally complicated individual. He was looking for comfortable friendship, mutual love and respect, a mother of his children, and a partner in Christ. He was willing to wait as long as it took for that woman to come around. He was really in no hurry.

But the vision Debbie created in the white wicker swing with her skirt flowing around her bare ankle and her hair softly framing her relaxed face was enough to stir his desire to know her much better.

He approached the porch quietly. Her eyes were closed and she may have been napping. The only seat available was next to her on the swing. The only other chair held a tablecloth that Maxine was airing. He chose the top step to rest his frame on.

Debbie opened her eyes and didn't show surprise at seeing him. She watched as he took his seat on the step. He observed that she braided a small section of her long, free-flowing hair in a natural—almost involuntary—motion. Perhaps it was a nervous habit. Did he make her nervous?

"How was your church service?" she asked suddenly.

"Uh. . .great," Scott stammered. "Pastor Jim had a wonderful lesson on witnessing. How about yours?"

"Oh, the sermon was something broad about world peace. I didn't follow it very well," Debbie confessed, still twining her hair. "Gran's pastor is a friendly older gentleman, but his tone of voice can really drag on and on."

"Are there other programs you are involved in like young adults' or children's work?" Scott leaned into the conversation. He liked to talk about churches and the work of God's people.

"No. . .it is rather small." She stopped swinging. "I guess. . .really. . .if I had the time to look, I would like to find a little larger church with more life. . .well, you know, activities and excited people." Debbie leaned forward to rest her elbows on her knees, a completed braid brushing her left cheek.

"You're welcomed to visit my church." *Thata way to keep your distance, Robillard.* "It's not huge, but we have lots of young families and programs. I work with the men's group, the youth, and the Sunday school. I even volunteer with visitation every other Wednesday on my day off." Scott wasn't bragging. He really enjoyed his church work.

"Oh, I'd never have time for all that." Debbie leaned back in the swing with a stunned look on her face.

Scott didn't want it to sound like he was comparing himself to her. "Now is the best time for me to be active. I don't have a family, my career is rather predictable, and I still have the energy of youth." Scott patted his knee. "The joints only creak a bit."

Debbie smiled. "Sounds easy for you, but I have found working with the school system can be pretty draining on the body and emotions. I don't need to add that to my free time."

Scott had seen it before—Christians who gave so much to other things that they didn't have enough left over for the Lord. He wouldn't make a case of it. Maybe it was just a sign that her goals weren't the same as his.

"I want to be involved in Christian work, just maybe not every week," Debbie said. "I think I am more of a behind-the-scenes kind of person, like with bookkeeping or cooking. And, I'd like to work on praying more."

Okay, maybe our goals aren't so different. "Well, anytime you want to visit, the church sits on Glen Street, right where the hill peaks. Maxie had talked about visiting my church, too, but she is worried about leaving her church after so many years of dedication to it."

"Leave the church? She never told me that," Debbie said quietly with a sigh.

They sat in silence for several minutes. Debbie had set the swing in motion again. Scott shifted on the hard wooden porch step. He could picture himself introducing Debbie to his church friends. There were a couple of gals he thought she would really fit in with.

"After I pay for the broken pipe, can we call the garden quits?" she asked in a hushed tone.

"No," he said too loud and too fast. "I mean, why give up on the garden before we even plant the first seed?" *Rouillard, this is not the way to give each other space. Why has this garden become so important?*

"Because," she drew out the word, "you should realize that it has already caused more trouble than it's worth." Scott smiled at her flushed face that so appealed to him, and she looked away. "Besides, planting seeds is like making a commitment to seeing them through to harvest. We are both busy people. Do we really have time to nurse a garden?"

Commitment is an interesting word choice, Scott thought.

Chapter 4

Scott mulled over Debbie's words as he leaned back against the porch post. "I have been thinking that it is really unfair of me to expect you to do all the work while I benefit from the produce. What do you say to me purchasing some tomato plants and other things for the garden? I'll even help you set them." *I'm willing to commit myself to seeing where this goes.*

Debbie frowned. "You really don't have to. I can explain to Gran that a garden isn't a good idea this year."

"No way. The ground is broken and we are already *committed*." Scott rose to leave. "By the way, I'll be paying for my own piping."

Debbie couldn't find her voice. She watched his every move as he crossed her backyard to his own back door. Before entering, he shot her a brief wave. She knew she had been caught watching him.

He was full of surprises and she couldn't figure him out. *Lord, I need serious counseling here. I am sorry I don't seem to consult with You until I am in a hard spot, but You know this man's mind and You know I don't have time to play games. Each time I try to remove myself from him, circumstances bring us back together. Please take away this giddy girlish feeling I get every time I see him and help me make it through the growing season like an adult.*

Debbie shoved the swing harder as her thoughts were in turmoil, and she talked to her Lord. *Really, his concern for the garden, and me, must be for Gran's benefit, seeing how they seem to share so much. And now, he has turned the tables so that the garden sounds like his project.*

It was time to prepare for a carried-in dinner at Gran's church. *You know, Lord, he would be a lot easier to ignore if he weren't a single, Christian man.* Debbie trudged to the kitchen to pull out her baking pans.

❧

Two weeks later, after the fear of frost had passed, Debbie spent her Saturday morning planting two rows of green beans, two hills of cucumbers, a hill of zucchini, and a row of leaf lettuce. It didn't take long, and soon she was sitting in the grass planning her next row. She would buy some beet seeds. There would still be plenty of room for six rows of sweet corn. She would put the tall growing vegetable on Scott's end of the garden—probably on purpose.

"Going to have room in there for some tomatoes?"

Debbie jumped. "Oh, hi, Scott. I didn't know you were out here." *If I still had that crush, I would be attuned to his every move.* She was feeling that she had made emotional progress after only seeing glimpses of him for the past two weeks. He did look good, though, standing there holding a tray of young plants.

She hurried to her feet and stepped into the dirt. "Why don't I put them along here?" She pointed out a couple rows in the middle of the plot.

"Good. I'll get a bucket of water and be right back to help." He set down the tray and was off to his garage before she could voice an objection.

She counted out twelve plants. The help would sure make the job go faster. She hoed a hole to set each plant in. Scott returned and started pouring water in each hole.

"Let me put some bone meal around those plants before we pull the dirt up to them," Debbie said, retrieving her box of fertilizer.

In no time they were packing dirt around the last little plant. Debbie swiped the hair away from her face with the back of her hand and leaned back on her heels.

"Uh. . ." Scott tilted his head and pointed to her face. "You have a dirt smudge on your cheek."

Debbie brushed her right cheek.

"No, the other cheek."

She tried again.

Scott gave a deep chuckle. "It's worse now. Here. . ." He gently dusted her cheek with his lean fingers.

Debbie froze, enjoying the contact. Her eyes met his dark gaze. The sun seemed to glow warmer and radiated from his hair. The moment between them felt so natural. . .so right.

Scott's fingers traced down her jaw line. Her gaze was drawn to the thin line of his lips. The air between them was heavy when the screen door on the Julian house slammed, and they both jumped apart at the sudden sound. Debbie found herself unexpectedly sitting in the dirt.

"I think I just rubbed the dirt in." Scott gave a nervous laugh, then he rose and offered her a hand up.

She hesitated, but allowed his long fingers to wrap around her own. He tugged her to her feet. She quickly pulled away and turned to meet her grandma, her complexion warmed by more than the bright sun.

Maxine Julian called, "Come to dinner tonight, Scott. It has been such a long time since I had you over. I'll make your favorite."

"Which would be. . .?" Debbie asked.

"Why Scott just loves my fried chicken with mashed potatoes and gravy. Add a side of green beans and top it off with apple pie," Grandma said, rubbing her bony fingers together.

The meal was also one of Debbie's favorites. Did Grandma remember? Debbie avoided it, though, in fear of increasing her waistline, but it would be a great treat.

"I can't wait until we have fresh beans from the garden," Grandma was saying. "There is nothing that compares to fresh vegetables."

Debbie cocked an eyebrow toward the tall man. "So will you be joining us?"

"How could I possibly refuse?"

⬧

Scott had helped her plant corn that afternoon. They worked well together, and he had let her make decisions regarding the garden. Debbie was starting to allow feelings that this was the kind of relationship that could turn into something permanent. It scared her. Was she letting her desires get the best of her, or was she looking at things rationally? Was Scott really the type of man she wanted to spend the rest of her life with?

Debbie was quiet during dinner that evening. She had placed walls around her emotions again. She felt better that way. There really was no reasonable hope for a future with her neighbor, and she couldn't afford to be hurt.

She watched Scott devour six pieces of the succulent chicken, observed his easy comradery with Grandma, and felt out of place. She couldn't blame Grandma for enjoying Scott's warm charm. Debbie figured that Grandma missed her own son, Debbie's father, who was still out in Arizona.

She pushed her pie around her plate. It had lost its temptation.

By the end of the meal, Debbie was confident that an intimate future with Scott was a stretch of her imagination. He was Gran's friend, a neighbor, and not someone Debbie should set her hopes and dreams on. If the Lord were her shepherd, she could trust Him to lead her to the right man, though a better man might be hard to find.

⬧

Debbie sorted the pile of college applications and student records on her desk. She had been helping several senior students all Wednesday morning with last minute decisions about continued education. She stretched, feeling her stomach rumble in anticipation of lunch.

Her phone rang and she picked it up using her practiced greeting.

"Hey, Debbie, this is Scott." His voice sounded rushed.

"Scott?" Her eyes widened and her hand flew to her hair, twisting nervously.

"You know, your neighbor."

She laughed. "I know. This is just. . .a surprise."

"Well. . .this is my day off and I noticed some trouble in the garden." He slowed his voice and sounded more thoughtful.

"Trouble? What kind?"

"Just some dogs. They were attracted to your bone meal and, between the two, dug up all of the tomato plants."

"Oh dear." Her mind spun. She could hurry home on her lunch break and replant them before the sun scorched their roots, but she really didn't have time to leave the office and risk getting dirty. A movement at her door caught her attention.

"I really don't know why I'm calling. I already righted the plants." Scott sighed.

The PE coach, Jesse Conner, had stopped at Debbie's door. He held his lunch bag and a can of pop. He pointed toward the teacher's lounge and motioned for Debbie to hang up. His antics were comical.

"I guess I wanted to tell you in case I forgot to call you tonight." Scott's tone sounded dejected. Debbie shooed the coach away and gave Scott her full attention.

"Thanks. Really, I'd much rather be working in the garden today than in this mound of paperwork." Debbie wanted to say more, but didn't know what it should be.

"You know I recently had a memory come back to me. When I was fixing the chain on Maxie's tiller I was remembering the summer I stayed here with my grandparents," Scott said. "I remember now that I worked on a bicycle chain that summer on a girl's bike."

Debbie's breath caught in her throat.

"That was your bike. Wasn't it?"

"Yes," she breathed. *He remembered!* Her most precious memory of that summer and he remembered it. He may not recall her silly plays for his attention, but he did remember the ten short minutes that he made her feel like she and her broken bike chain were the most important use of his time.

A delightful chill tickled her arms. "You have a way of rescuing me from my troubles."

He chuckled. "Well, it's all in a day's work. Now I should let you get back to those paper mounds. Good-bye."

"Good-bye, and thanks again."

Now just where went my determination not to get carried away by this man? He has never given me any indication that he is any more than a friend.

Coach Conner was back in Debbie's doorway. He had probably never left the hallway. "Sounded like a boyfriend."

"That? Oh, not at all." Debbie laughed, though inside she wished things could have been different.

"Then there would be no problem with your accepting a dinner date with me," he insisted.

"Well, I. . .perhaps." Debbie was reluctant to promise. He really wasn't her type. He seemed very nice, though, and had been petitioning her since her first day on the job. He had no reservations about showing his interest in her.

"We'll set something up as soon as baseball season is over," the coach beamed.

Debbie forced a smile. It was time she moved on from fantasies.

Chapter 5

Another Saturday had dawned and promised a gorgeous spring day. Scott stirred a dash of milk into his cup of coffee. He didn't have any office hours this Saturday, so he had prepared a list of things that needed to be done around the old house—a leaky faucet to replace, a crack to plaster, and hardwood floor to polish. None of the activities excited him, and he dallied by the kitchen window with his cooling cup of coffee.

Movement in the backyard claimed his attention. Debbie stood near the rear of her lot looking like a spring flower. Scott hadn't talked to her since Wednesday, when he had made his lame call to her office. He still couldn't believe he had used the excuse of the dogs' mischief to hear her voice.

Scott noticed that Debbie was watching two men set up a tripod. If the thought hadn't been a ridiculous one, he would have guessed they were surveyors. Scott watched the men study a large sheet of paper, then move their tripod closer to his house.

He set his cup down in the sink and hurried out his back door. "Howdy, neighbor; what's up?" he called cheerfully.

Debbie crossed her arms in front of her. "Just a little preparation work."

Scott waited for her to continue. The yard separating them seemed to stretch like a large plain.

Finally she said, "I'm putting up a fence."

"A fence?" His words fell like breaking glass.

"Next fall, after the garden is done, of course."

Scott didn't like calling to her across the lawn in front of strangers. "Debbie, can I talk to you?"

She nodded but stayed rooted to her spot, making Scott go to her. He thought they had been making good progress in their friendship, but this wasn't a good sign.

"What is this all about?" Scott asked. He reached out to touch her arm, but she gently pulled away.

Debbie steeled herself from his touch and his soft, probing gaze. "I need to know how big the fence will be so I can budget it into my finances."

"But why?" Scott looked wounded. "Your house has been here fifty years without a fence."

She shrugged. "It's a corner lot that gets a lot of traffic, and a nice fence will raise property values."

218

He appeared unconvinced.

"Nothing against any of our neighbors," she said. "It will be a low fence—probably a white picket."

The sound of a shovel hitting stone caused both to turn to the workers. They had uncovered a stone marker in Scott's yard.

"What are they doing?" Scott asked, clearly frustrated.

Debbie shook her head.

"Miss Julian," the older surveyor spoke up, "this would be the property line." He stood barely six feet from the side of Scott's house. "The line should run straight into that pine grove, but we'll double-check it."

"That's impossible," Scott said under his breath.

Debbie's eyes widened as she followed the surveyor's line to the garden. It appeared that the whole garden was actually on her property and, in fact, Scott's sprinkler line was also in her yard. Scott saw the lay of the line also.

"Didn't you have this place surveyed when you bought it?" Debbie asked, finding it hard to keep the smug tone from her voice.

Scott glared at her. "I didn't feel it necessary when my neighbors were so friendly and helpful. I made the mistake of not planning for future neighbors."

His words had bite and smarted as they made contact. This hadn't turned out like she had wanted. She had planned the fence to keep her messes from ruining his landscaping perfection. She supposed she could admit to herself that it was also a display of independence. They could be neighbors but she would keep the fence between them to remind herself that it couldn't be anything more.

Debbie turned her back to him and walked toward the surveyors. Scott seized her arm and spun her back around. He quickly dropped her arm, but his mouth remained open with no sound coming out. She waited.

"I. . .okay. . .I thought we had made some progress," he stammered.

She stared at him. "Progress at what—a garden?"

"No, because that is clearly on your property now." Scott was obviously fighting the urge to get angry. "I thought we were becoming friends."

"Nothing has changed," she insisted. "We are still neighbors."

"Neighbors?"

"Sure."

"If that is how you want it, then I won't bother you about the garden again. You'll have plenty of goods to share with your relatives." He backed away as if repulsed by the sight of her.

"Scott. . .!" She couldn't believe his cold attitude.

He spun away from her and rounded his garage out of sight. Soon she heard his car start up and leave the drive.

Debbie stayed in the yard until the surveyors had finished. Then she entered the house, glad that Grandma was closeted in her sewing room. She pulled herself upstairs, stewing over each of Scott's words.

Lord, I don't want Scott to be the dream forever out of my reach, and I don't want him to be my enemy. What's wrong with wanting to be civilized neighbors? Lord, I give this situation into Your hands. Show me my failures and help me mend this new mess I have created.

She waited for a peace to come, but it didn't. She sat in her window seat and gazed across the backyard. Scott didn't return home until early afternoon. Then she never saw him in the yard.

❧

Scott drove around town, made an unnecessary stop at a super store just to walk around, then ended up at the house of his associate pastor. The two men were very close in age and had quickly become friends when Scott had started attending the church last fall.

Over the noisy play of two toddlers, Scott brought up the subject of Debbie to Pastor Jim.

"You're asking me about women?" Jim laughed, then lowered his voice to a whisper. "Don't tell my wife or she'll gloat, but I don't understand women at all."

Scott sighed. "You're no help, man."

"How long have you known her?"

"We first met about thirteen or fourteen years ago, but I couldn't even tell you what she looked like back then." Scott shrugged. "We really only met at the beginning of this month."

"Well, now, it seems to me that it could be like deer hunting. . .no, more like fishing."

Scott laughed at his friend's quest for an illustration.

"You see," Jim said, gaining confidence in his words, "your Debbie is like the fish that nibbles on the bait. She is tempted but she is afraid of being caught. She will put distance between herself and the bait, but as long as you keep some play on the line, she will be tempted back."

Scott tried to picture Debbie as a fish.

"My friend, you have to keep the bait out there," Jim declared, "until she's not afraid of the hook. Woo her, man. Woo her until she is clay in your hands."

Scott gulped.

"But pray. Ask the Lord if she is the one, and if you get the green light, go for it," Jim stated confidently.

"Jim!" a female voice called from the kitchen.

Jim jumped.

"Wash the kids up for lunch, please."

"Yes, dear," Jim promptly answered and smiled at Scott. "Then you can have this kind of wedded bliss to look forward to." He scooped a child up under each arm and trotted off to the bathroom.

Scott stayed for lunch with Jim's illustration running through his mind. Could he afford to do some more fishing? Was Debbie just scared or bad tempered? She had already ruined his lawn and shrunk his property down in size. What next, his house?

❧

Scott prayed all evening, petitioning God for the direction he should take with Miss

Debbie Julian. He needed to know if he should be content to live as her congenial neighbor or if the Lord was sanctioning a relationship for them.

Sunday morning his answer suddenly arrived in the middle of the worship service. Scott had been prepared to wait, as God usually took His time revealing His plan to His child. But a peace about his future with Debbie completely surrounded him. It was as if a family member had given him a hug and pointed out the path he should travel.

Sunday afternoon, Scott visited with Maxie from the front walk. He was careful to stay off the Julian property even though he didn't see Debbie in sight. He had determined to test the waters slowly and see if he could coax a nibble. If it were meant to be the way he was envisioning, she would eventually let him get close. And when the timing was right, he would hook a ring on her finger and never let her go.

Chapter 6

Wallpapering was the last way Debbie had planned to spend her Memorial Day vacation, but Grandma pleaded that they redecorate the tiny sewing room. Debbie knew that Grandma had given her an extremely fair price on the house, and she felt obligated to work on the projects that her grandmother had been avoiding for the last ten years.

The grueling task of picking out the paper was accomplished on Saturday evening. Debbie compromised with Grandma's passion for big flowers, and they purchased a tasteful floral vine design instead of Debbie's preference for a small stripe. Debbie started some of her measurements on Sunday afternoon. Monday morning she allowed herself to sleep an hour longer than usual, just because it was a holiday, then she dug out the water pan, sponges, a knife, scissors, rulers, and all the tools that might make the papering go smoothly.

The tiny room was right beside the master bedroom on the first level of the house. Debbie set up a card table in the bedroom for her cutting work. She shoved the sewing desk, boxes of crafts and material, a bookshelf, lamps, an ironing board, and a chair all to one side of the room. She quickly primed the old paint job, and just before noon she was ready to hang the first piece.

The piece was nine feet long and needed to curve around a corner and match the straight line with the doorframe. Debbie's two-foot step stool barely allowed her to reach high enough and didn't fit flush against the wall. She wet the paper and stepped up to the top of her stool. The first reach didn't get the paper flush to the ceiling and caused a cramp in her side. She had to relax her arms and lower the paper.

Her second try at fitting the paper left a huge bubble in the top corner and the bottom was hanging three quarters of an inch off. Debbie pounded her fist on the offending bubble.

"How's it coming?" Grandma asked from the doorway, where the furniture allowed a very narrow passage.

"I'm going to have to take this down and readjust it. Hopefully I can still salvage the paper," Debbie grumbled. "It is not a good start. This stool is too short, and I don't have the reach."

"Hold just a minute," Grandma said. "I may have the solution."

Grandma disappeared and Debbie pulled the chair into the corner. She placed one foot on the top of the stool and the other on the back of the chair. She started pulling the wet paper away from the wall. The top third crumpled down on her head, but she kept pulling gently so as not to rip the paper.

When the paper felt loose, she reached up to find the top end. Blinded by paper covering her face, she felt along both sides and down toward her back. Her hand came in contact with something large and warm.

"You look like you could use an extra hand."

Debbie let out a high-pitched scream and teetered on her perch. She had been so absorbed in her project that she hadn't heard anyone enter the room, but she would recognize Scott's voice anywhere. Her balance was failing, but suddenly strong hands grasped both of her sides and steadied her.

"Hold still," he quietly commanded.

Debbie barely breathed as she felt Scott's weight on the stool and the heat from his body against her back. He took the paper from her, and reaching over her, he smoothed the top edge up against the ceiling. Debbie couldn't move. She was trapped between the wall and his blanketing presence.

His arm gently brushed hers as he stepped down from the stool. His hand came to her lower back as she searched for a solid footing. She almost forgot her next task, then hurriedly smoothed the paper the rest of the way down the wall with a large sponge. It was a perfect fit and the bubbles smoothed out with ease.

Debbie turned to thank Scott, but the room was empty. She squeezed out the narrow passageway, and her feet rushed along the short hallway to the kitchen, where Scott and Grandma were chatting. Scott grinned as Debbie braked to an abrupt stop.

She flung a hand pointing back toward the sewing room. "Uh. . .thanks. The first piece is always the hardest." Her movements were awkward and she felt tongue-tied.

"But what she is trying to say is that it would go a lot easier with two sets of hands," Grandma interpreted smoothly.

"Gran. . .!" Debbie screeched, turning beet red. Her old anguish had returned.

"You're right," Scott answered Grandma, "and I'll stay if I'm needed, but I'll go if Debbie tells me everything is under control."

Debbie opened her mouth to reply, but the words didn't come out as she had planned. "I guess I could use some help. . .only if you have time."

Scott's face lit up with a smile. "Certainly."

"Well. . ." Debbie shrugged, speechless. She spun on her heel and darted back to the close walls of the tiny sewing room. *He sure smells great today.* His scent still lingered along with the pungent smell of wallpaper paste.

Soon he was standing in the doorway. "Just tell me what you need done."

Debbie stared at the rolls of cut paper, the pan of water, and everything that littered the small area. She had no response. She couldn't possibly tell him how she wished he would put his arms around her again and let her enjoy being so close to him.

"Is the next piece cut? Perhaps I can get it started along the ceiling."

Debbie nodded mutely and riffled through her pile for the precise piece. Finally finding the right one, she rolled it and submerged it in the water for a short time. Slowly pulling it out, she quickly reached the limit of her arms' extension while still having a good two feet of paper still submerged.

Scott reached around her and took the top of the paper while she pulled the rest out of the water. They worked in companionable silence, hanging three sheets of paper with barely five words between them. The paper was going on with little problem because the area they worked on was smooth and had no obstacles.

Soon they reached the window. There was a sharp turn to make around a corner, then a short distance to where they would need to trim around an outlet and the window frame. Scott started the long piece at the ceiling, smoothing the paper until Debbie could reach it with her sponge. Halfway down Debbie was confronted by a crease that refused to budge. She tried smoothing it into the corner, then out toward the seam. It refused to disappear.

"We are going to need to pull the paper loose and work out this crease," Debbie resigned.

"Okay." Scott started loosening the top half.

The loose paper allowed Debbie to maneuver the crease, but when the paper was tight again, she still had a long oval-shaped bubble to wrestle with. She smoothed it with the straight edge of her ruler and was left with several small bubbles. Taking her sponge over the area brought her back to the original predicament of one big bubble.

Scott had stood patiently in the background as she worked, but now he stepped forward. "May I try?"

Debbie was getting tired and the frustration was wearing at her patience. She tossed him the sponge and moved away.

Scott tried a couple of passes with the sponge, then he moved to her pile of tools. "Do you have a straight pin?"

"Sure. It's a sewing room," was her offhanded answer. She pulled out a narrow drawer in the sewing desk and gently placed a tiny pin in the palm of Scott's large hand.

He worked the bubble into one area, then stuck the pin into the center. Cupping his hands around the perimeter of the bubble, he forced the air toward the pinhole. Instead of air, though, a stream of pasty water shot from the hole and spit directly into Scott's face. He jumped back in surprise, pressing Debbie against the desk in the tight space.

Debbie's breath was briefly knocked from her, but as Scott flailed for his footing, the comedy of the situation hit her. She shook with giggles. It felt good to laugh after the silence and frustrating work of the past hour. Soon she was laughing out loud.

Scott placed a light hand on her shoulder. "Are you okay. I didn't mean to plow you over."

She tried to contain the fit of laughter, but when she looked at his face, a drop of paste dripped from his regal nose and she lost control again. She sank to a sitting position on the floor and held her sides as waves of laughter shook her.

"Are you laughing at me?" Scott knelt beside her.

She took a gulp of air and nodded.

He wiped his face with the tail of his shirt. "I should sue you for poor working conditions." He sighed dramatically.

Laughter gushed from her again, punctuated by hiccups, and soon Scott's deep chuckle joined her as he rested himself on the floor beside Debbie.

"What's so funny?" Grandma asked from the door.

Scott shrugged and smiled. Debbie shook her head, unable to speak through the hiccups.

"Whatever it is," Grandma declared, "I hope it isn't catching." She retreated to a new chorus of laughter, and it was a long time before another piece of wallpaper was hung.

That afternoon when Debbie and Scott finally fitted the last piece of paper near the door of the room, they stepped back in great satisfaction.

"This little room is quite pretty," Debbie said in awe of their work.

Scott nodded. "You could use it as a nursery some day. . .well, since it's near the big bedroom."

They both fell silent. The topic was an awkward one for Debbie to reply to. She bent to gather her tools. Scott started collecting bits and pieces of leftover paper.

"I need to apologize," he said suddenly.

Debbie jerked her head up, confused by his train of thought.

"I shouldn't have gotten upset about the surveying and fencing."

Debbie sighed as she began to realize where the conversation was going.

"You were right," he continued. "We are neighbors and a fence doesn't mean we still can't be friends. Does it?"

Her eyes widened. "Of course not!"

"Good." He visibly relaxed. "Friends." He stuck out his hand.

She tentatively placed her smaller hand within his grasp and watched his fingers engulf her own. His hand felt warm and safe.

"A good job done deserves good food. I've got a German chocolate cake ready," Grandma said from behind them. "Oh, I'm sorry!" Grandma smiled, turning away.

Scott pulled away slowly while his gaze stayed on Debbie's face. "I would welcome some of that cake, Maxie." He took large steps to catch up with the older woman and embraced her in a bear hug.

"Thank you for helping with the papering job," Grandma said, patting the man's face.

"Anything for my gal."

Debbie looked on and once again felt left out of their circle. The old nagging returned to warn her that Scott had no real reason to be friendly and helpful to her if it wasn't for her grandmother. The warmth that had so recently encompassed her now turned to a chill of self-doubt.

Chapter 7

First thing Tuesday morning, Coach Conner caught up to Debbie in an empty hallway.

"Well, the season's over," he said with a distinct note of sadness. "Sure didn't end like I would have liked, but we played good ball."

Debbie smiled and nodded. She hated to admit that she hadn't kept up with the baseball team's record.

"So, how about Friday?"

"Friday?" Debbie asked.

"Yea, our date. We can get some eats and see a movie," he said, bumping her shoulder with his beefy one. "Not much else going on in our little town this time of year."

Debbie reminded herself that she had basically made a promise last week and nodded her consent. "What time?"

"Better make it six," Jeff Conner said and strutted off toward the gym.

Friday came quickly after a week of heavy workload. She had a new wave of SAT and ACT test scores to consult with students about. She counseled with a frantic senior girl who was fearful of not getting into college that fall due to a poor test standing. Then Friday led to some tearful good-byes as the seniors completed their last day of classes. The week had drained Debbie's energy and she longed to close herself up at home for an evening of relaxation.

But Coach Conner was at her door promptly at 6:00 with his 4x4 running along the curb. He treated her to a heavy meal of steak and potatoes at the Texas-style steakhouse. Jeff, as he asked to be called, was warm and friendly, but his favorite line of conversation centered on sports of any variety. Debbie had very little to contribute on the subject.

It was raining after dinner as Jeff kindly helped Debbie up into his large 4x4, then he ran through the list of their movie options.

"Can I request that the movie not be rated R?" Debbie asked.

They agreed upon a comedy with a military setting. It spawned some laughs from Debbie, but she was disappointed in the use of foul language. Glad to see the movie end and aching from the tired strain, Debbie declined Jeff's offer for a nightcap of coffee and doughnuts.

She had him pull up along the side of the house since her key only fit the back door. Jeff hurried around to help her out. She would have preferred ending the evening at the truck, but Jeff took her arm and slowly strolled her through the wet grass up to the porch steps.

"I had a great time," Jeff said. "We should do this again."

Debbie searched for the right words that would let him down gently. She didn't see any point in repeating a date with him. He was a sweet guy, but he didn't show any clear signs of being a Christian, they had little in common, and it just plain didn't feel right. Her gaze drifted to the glow from Scott's front window.

Jeff leaned closer, and Debbie turned in time to offer her cheek for a quick peck.

"Howdy all!" came a loud intrusion.

Debbie was shocked to hear Scott's voice coming from her darkened porch. "Gran, are you there?" she asked.

"No," Scott answered, "Maxie has already gone to bed. It's getting late." He stepped out to where the glow of the street lamp illumined his rigid posture; the porch swing swayed in the shadows.

"Is this your brother, Deb?" Jeff asked congenially.

Scott smirked.

Debbie seethed at Scott's smug attitude. He stood with arms crossed as if he were her personal bodyguard. "Jeff, this happens to be my neighbor, Mr. Robillard. He was only here to check on my grandmother and was on his way home."

Scott stood planted on the top porch step.

Jeff looked back and forth between Scott and Debbie. Debbie shifted nervously under the scrutiny of the two men.

"Listen..." Jeff stammered as he backed away, "I didn't know...I'll see you on Monday, Deb. Have a great weekend." He hurried to his truck and drove away.

Debbie stood in the grass, the dampness seeping through her flat suede shoes.

"Seems like a friendly guy," Scott said.

"Do you often spy on your neighbors' comings and goings?" Debbie retorted. She really didn't mind that Jeff's display of affection had been cut short, but she resented the fact that Scott was prying into her business. He blocked the way up the porch steps, so she remained in the yard.

"I didn't mean. . ." Scott stopped. He was forced to admit to himself that he had purposefully lingered on the porch after coffee with Maxie, knowing that Debbie was out and expected home soon. He had been interested in learning what kind of man appealed to Debbie and whether this relationship had depth that would threaten the future he had hoped he might someday have with her.

"You're right," he finally continued, "I shouldn't have dallied on your porch, and I should have revealed myself sooner. Please accept my apologies and convey them to your friend." Now would have been a good time for him to head home, but he couldn't find the will to move.

He looked down at Debbie where she shifted in discomfort. He watched as her gaze swung around the darkened yard, where long shadows had transformed the inviting backyard into a place of mysterious qualities.

"I hope you had a nice evening," he said on impulse.

She stared up at him in silence.

"You deserve to be shown. . ." he paused, then rambled on, "the love of a good man."

Her eyes widened.

Scott stepped carefully down the steps and passed Debbie. "Good night." The word came out like a whisper.

She didn't change her rigid posture until he was a safe distance across the black expanse of soggy lawn. Then she went directly inside. Scott plodded home under dripping tree limbs; his shoulders dropped in defeat. One step of progress with Debbie always seemed to be met by a step back in the wrong direction. He was getting nowhere moving cautiously. Perhaps he should follow his pounding heart, rush in, and expose his true feelings.

Or, perhaps it was time to get back on his knees and talk with the Instructor.

Debbie stepped into the quiet house and felt her breathing start to settle back to a steady pace. She put the lock in place and peeked out the curtained window in the door. She couldn't explain why she felt so angry with Scott or why his words of kindness moved her to speechlessness. Nothing was making sense anymore, and something had to change.

She turned into the darkened kitchen and for the first time realized Grandma was sitting at the empty table.

"Gran, I didn't know you were still up."

"Why can't you see it, Dandy girl?"

"See what?"

"Are you afraid of him?"

"Afraid of Scott? Of course not," Debbie quickly retorted.

"Why won't you let Scott show you how much he loves you?" Gran asked another question without directly addressing Debbie.

Debbie couldn't believe what she was hearing. She pulled a chair out from the table and sank onto it. "Gran, Scott is your friend. He has often been kind to me, but he is not interested. . .in romance," she choked out.

"Dandy, I always considered you to be one of my brightest grandchildren."

Debbie frowned at her.

"That man's face plainly displays his fondness for you."

Debbie shook her head. "You may want it to be that way. Has he said something about it?"

"Well, no, but he hasn't had to. I know you both well and can see things that you are not willing to," Grandma stated. "And, I know you care for him, too."

Debbie shifted uncomfortably. "Gran," she framed her words gently, "you care for us both, and I think you have let your desire to see something happen between Scott and me cloud your judgment. There is nothing between us and there is no reason why there should ever be."

"God," Grandma said quietly.

"What?"

"God is in both of your lives and He knows each of your needs."

"Yes, Gran, but it doesn't mean He wants us together." Debbie toyed with her fingers nervously. "I don't even know if we have anything in common."

"Your faith is the best thing to have in common," Grandma insisted.

"Have you talked with Scott about this?"

"No," Grandma spoke honestly.

"Have you encouraged him in anyway toward a relationship with me?"

Grandma fidgeted on the hard seat. "Well, I might have contrived the garden mishap. I mean," she paused and smiled, "I encouraged you to place the garden where I was sure you would get into Scott's yard. I knew you would have to meet and solve the problem together. It worked until you had to go and clearly point out the proper boundaries that haven't been considered for at least forty years." Grandma sounded like she was getting herself worked up. "Then I admit to trying to place you two together for meals and projects whenever feasible, but I have never uttered a word to sway either of you until now." Grandma leaned back in the chair having had her say.

❧

Debbie went directly to her window retreat after leaving the kitchen. *What am I missing?* A guy who had his life in perfect order like Scott couldn't be interested in her. She couldn't even juggle her tumbling emotions. *It is like I haven't learned from the mistakes of childhood. I have let myself get stuck on one guy and have placed all my expectations on him. I just know he is going to disappoint me.*

Sure he will.

Only the Lord is constantly there for me.

She talked back and forth to a small voice within her. Her conscience or the Holy Spirit, she wasn't ready to say. She was only assured that the answer would be found in prayer. She reached onto her desk for the Bible she had regrettably not touched all week.

She read and prayed in the glow of an antique-styled lamp until well after midnight. She fell into bed with a certainty that she was loved. Her heavenly Father loved her more than anyone else could. He had her best interests in consideration. She would wait on His lead.

It would not be easy, but first thing in the morning, Debbie knew she had to apologize to Scott. She had let her own insecurities and fears have authority over her actions. If there really was something to Scott's affection, as Grandma had said, then maybe Debbie was too afraid to acknowledge it. No matter what the future held, she had a past to right.

Chapter 8

Debbie fixed another cup of tea and dressed it up with sugar and cream. She kept her vigil at the kitchen window, looking out at the backyard. The evening's rain had given this Saturday morning a clean, polished shine. The day promised many wonders, but Debbie was only intent on one thing, one person.

Watching her neighbor's back door reminded her of when she had been just eight years old and spending the fall weekend with her grandparents. She had joined a group of mischievous children who thought they could prove themselves as grown up as the teenagers if they successfully toilet papered a tree. The Robillards' tree was chosen only for the fact that it was in a side yard that was quickly obscured by evening shadows. The children accomplished their task before bedtime and parted feeling proud.

But Grandma had been wise to Debbie's whereabouts. She dropped casual questions and soon Debbie was crying out her story, no longer the brave little vandal.

The next morning Grandma marched Debbie to the Robillards' back door and Debbie had apologized to Mrs. Robillard. She spent over an hour gathering all the paper she could reach and had plenty of time to think.

None of the other children involved had been reprimanded, even though Debbie had willingly given up the names of her partners. Grandma and Mrs. Robillard had chosen not to pursue the issue and none of the other children came forward on their own. Debbie had cleaned the yard alone, and Mr. Robillard had kindly finished what she could not.

It was a lesson that she would long remember. The labor involved in cleaning the yard was nothing compared to the disappointment Debbie had witnessed in the eyes of the adults she cared greatly for. She valued her relationships and now she had unwillingly driven a wedge between herself and her new neighbor. She never meant to hurt Scott, but her defense mechanism kept throwing darts.

Her gaze was drawn to movement at Scott's garage. He ambled into the backyard carrying a hoe. She watched as he checked over his rhododendron bush, cleaning off the fading blossoms. With slow, deliberate steps, he made his way to the garden plot and gradually circled the perimeter. He stopped at the young tomato plants and gently cut around the base of each with his hoe.

His fluid movements mesmerized Debbie. She watched until the tomatoes were finished, and Scott moved on to tiny heads of green weeds between the rows of newly sprouting lettuce and beets. She collected her composure and left the house.

Scott looked up at Debbie's approach but continued his work down the row. Debbie stopped at the grape arbor and examined the tiny leaves sprouting from the mature vines. Was it painful when those buds burst open?

Scott zipped through the remainder of the row and was soon only a couple of steps from Debbie's side. He leaned back and stretched with exaggerated movements. "Beautiful day," he bellowed.

Debbie watched him carefully. . .shyly.

Suddenly Scott was actively cleaning his shoes and hoe of dirt and talking at a rapid pace. "What are you doing this afternoon? Wouldn't this be a great day for a picnic? There are still trees in bloom over at Tuscora Park. We should take some time to enjoy it."

Where was Debbie's voice? Was this a display of Scott's affection or an attempt to apologize for his spying behavior of the night before? She couldn't interpret the signs. *Now what do I do, Lord?*

"I have some paperwork I should get done, but perhaps Gran would enjoy some time out," Debbie offered.

"Ah, leave Maxie out of this. Saturday is her day to go and play with the old girls. They'll either be shopping, playing dominoes, or pigging out at a buffet," Scott refuted. "Call it a time-out or call it a date, but I'd like to treat you to a playful afternoon."

Debbie was shocked. Scott was talking so fast that she didn't have time to react. He sounded like he had had a caffeine overload. Silently she searched for a proper response.

"Okay," he said after pausing a moment. "You can do your paperwork this morning, then I'll pick you up around four. We'll have an early picnic dinner by the pond and enjoy the evening there. It is predicted to be quite pleasant this evening." His broad smile left no room for arguments.

Debbie nodded mutely, no longer trying to speak. Saying something now might spoil the moment, and she didn't trust her voice.

"Don't worry about the garden," Scott instructed. "I'll pulverize these weeds in no time while you take care of your personal business." He stepped back into the garden soil and attacked a new row. Though his movements were energetic, he was careful to avoid the area where seeds of green beans were still sprouting.

When Scott said no more and she still had no thought to voice, she drifted back to the house. She avoided going directly in and walked around the side yard to the front porch. There were some families out working in yards. A father and son were washing their minivan across the street.

The sun thoroughly warmed Debbie and her mind pictured Scott in the backyard. She still couldn't figure out what had overcome Scott to behave so radically, but perhaps this was a sign from God that she should give a relationship with Scott a chance.

It wasn't quite how she had desired to be approached by her knight in shining armor. Her knight would have wooed her with sweet words and romantic gifts. Scott was riding in on a charger and expecting her to canter alongside. But out of the two, she knew that Scott was the one she could be friends with, and friendship was the best place to start a romance.

By four Scott had pulled his Buick around to the front of Debbie's house. She watched from the window as his feet danced up the walk.

Grandma had stayed curiously in the background all day, and Debbie was able to accomplish a surprising amount of bills, laundry, and cleaning. Grandma left around two with a group of five friends and Debbie had the whole house to herself. She had taken care to pick a comfortable, but attractive casual outfit for the evening. Her navy twill slacks were creased and slimming while her lightweight cardigan covered a wide-necked T-shirt of baby blue.

Scott appeared to have a little better rein on his enthusiasm and met her with a playful grin. Completely the gentleman, he helped her into her side of the car before taking his place behind the wheel. He filled the ten-minute drive to the park with mostly one-sided conversation about the weather and the community.

"Are you hungry?" he asked as he parked his car near the community hall and snack bars.

"Not really."

"Good, then we'll leave the picnic supplies here, and I challenge you to a round of putt-putt."

"Oh, I'm not very good."

"You're in luck; I'm pathetic," he said, leaving the car. He opened her door and helped her out. "Thankfully I have a great drive and can hold my own on a regular course."

Debbie struggled to keep up with his long strides as he led them across the park to the ticket booth. He secured two clubs, balls, and a score pad for them and insisted that Debbie be the first to putt.

They relaxed and kept their conversation focused on the game. Debbie managed to do quite well, keeping her score just below his. Then they came to the loop. Golfers were expected to putt their balls onto a metal track with enough force to send the ball around the loop and out the opposite side. Debbie's first try came right back to her at the starting point. So did her second and third tries.

Scott rooted her on. "Put more force into it."

Debbie whacked the ball with double the energy. The ball winged to the top of the looped track then popped out and disappeared into the bushes at the left side of the green.

Debbie groaned while Scott laughed. He got down on his knees and felt under the scrubby little bushes for her ball. "It went in here, didn't it?"

"I think so."

Scott stood and looked all around the bushes. A line of golfers was forming behind Debbie. Scott gave up. "Here, use mine." He placed a neon green ball in her palm.

This time Debbie's shot was perfect. The ball made the loop and stopped within a foot of the cup. She had an easy, one-stroke putt from there. Handing the ball back to Scott she said, "The ball made all the difference."

But the golf ball didn't have the same effect for Scott. His first attempt missed the track, his second was too weak and rolled back, then his third shot was strong and zipped through the loop. It sailed over the hole, smacked into the wooded edging, bounced back, and dropped into the cup.

"Wow! Did you see that?" Scott leaped over to Debbie and hugged her in his excitement.

Debbie's breathing was choked by his overwhelming closeness. He held her a moment longer than necessary, then pulled back in slow motion, his gaze locking on her eyes. She felt suddenly shy as she recognized a tender warmth in his eyes. She dropped her lashes.

"Clear the course," yelled a teen with a bad attitude.

Scott retrieved his ball and led Debbie up the path. Debbie finished the eighteenth hole with her only hole-in-one, giving her a score that was just three under Scott's. He pouted playfully as they turned in their equipment.

"Okay, now what can I beat *you* at?" he said while surveying the area. The park was beginning to fill up with families. Young children loved the small Ferris wheel, the swings, a mini train, and, of course, the carousel. "How about the batting cages?"

Debbie moaned, "Do I have to?"

"No," Scott smiled. "I'll call a truce if you promise to ride the carousel after our picnic."

Debbie brightened. "I haven't done that kind of thing in years. I'd love to."

Scott grasped Debbie's hand where it hung at her side and pulled her back toward the car. They unloaded their picnic paraphernalia and took it to the edge of the pond. Scott picked out a spot that hadn't been littered by the resident ducks and spread out an old quilt. It was worn and frayed, but the double wedding ring pattern was clearly visible in a variety of colors.

"Is this something your grandmother made?" she asked as Scott set out plates and plastic food containers.

"I really don't remember. My only recollection of the quilt is that my grandparents carried it around in their car during winter in case they ever got snowbound."

"Well, it is charming."

"Yes." Scott was looking at her again, and Debbie felt a warmth not attributed to the setting sun spread through her limbs. "Do you mind. . ." he hesitated, "if I tell you that for weeks I have found you to be quite charming?"

Debbie felt like a corralled group of wild horses had just been released in her stomach.

"I don't want to play games with you, Debbie, but neither do I want to scare you," he said as he reached out to smooth a strand of curls behind her ear. His hand stroked her cheek. "I want you to know that I want to be your friend and to know you much better."

The adoring look in his eyes chased away her fears and defenses. Grandma had read him right, and Debbie knew she trusted his words. Her face spread with a serene smile. She was deliriously happy.

Silently, Scott drew her face toward his own. Across the quilt pattern that represented the bonding of two souls, he kissed her tenderly once, then twice.

❧

For the first time, Scott and Debbie really talked. They discussed family and friends. They exchanged ideas about their mutual faith and goals for the future. Debbie even had a confession to make. Scott was being so open with her that she decided that she needed to get past the roadblock that had been discouraging her from a relationship with him.

"Scott, can I tell you something?" Debbie timidly asked. "You may find it rather silly."

"You can tell me anything." His gaze was tender, and he adjusted his position on the quilt so that he was just a bit closer to her.

"You may not remember that I was around my grandparents' house thirteen years ago when you spent the whole summer with your grandparents, but I was and I remember a lot about you." Debbie shifted nervously, playing with the patches on the quilt. "I had quite a crush on you. You were the focus of my entire summer, and I longed for your attention."

"Ah, I'm sorry, Debbie. I do remember fixing your bike, though. It was an ancient thing."

"My grandmother's."

"But you really were better off not to have me chasing you in return. I was pretty self-absorbed back then, and I wouldn't have appreciated how special you are."

Debbie laughed in spite of herself. "When we met a few weeks ago, I was still so embarrassed by my behavior as a teen. I couldn't believe you didn't remember that. I was sure that my ridiculous plays for your attention would have had a lasting impression."

Scott reached out to cup her chin. "Maybe it is better that I don't remember, because it doesn't really matter about the teen you were. I want to get to know who you are now." His hand traced the features of her face, recording each detail. Debbie leaned into his caresses.

The shadows of approaching night were deep before they packed up the remains of submarine sandwiches, macaroni salad, potato chips, and brownies. Scott had confessed to buying most of it at a deli, but he had assembled the sandwiches and baked the brownies from a boxed mix.

They set their sights on the carousel now, and once again, Scott claimed her hand in his warm clasp. There was a long line of parents and children waiting for the spinning carousel to stop and let them on. Debbie pointed out the gray and red horse she wanted to ride.

When the carousel was ready for a new load, Scott was quick to secure Debbie's horse. He helped her step up and swing her long leg over the little horse. Then Scott climbed on the white horse beside hers. Debbie smiled at his proud posture on the white steed, but didn't voice her thoughts about a knight riding a white stallion. It was a silly thought. Mythical knights didn't exist, but a few lovable, God-fearing men still did. Scott was among that kind, and as long as he kept his focus on Christ, she knew she could be secure in her love for him.

The carousel slowly began to spin. Scott chuckled and hummed an old cowboy tune.

Debbie studied him with an endearing smile. *Love?* Did she really feel that strong emotion? There was no physical fire about to consume her but a warm glow that assured her what they had started today was the development of a lasting bond, a comfortable companionship, and, yes, a mature love.

Debbie leaned her head back as the carousel turned faster and faster. This childish entertainment was liberating. Scott held his palm out to her and she placed her hand in his. It was a natural fit.

They rode the carousel twice, then conceded that it was time to go home.

⁂

The house was dark and quiet as Debbie preceded Scott into her kitchen. Debbie called for her grandmother. When there was no answer, Debbie said, "She must be getting ready for bed; it *is* getting late."

"Why don't you check your messages while I put on some coffee?" Scott said, indicating the blinking red light on the answering machine. "There are still some brownies left." He moved comfortably around the kitchen, finding what he needed.

"Where are your coffee filters?" Scott asked, and Debbie showed him while she waited on the tape to rewind.

Then a professional sounding voice spoke clearly through the machine. "This message is for Debra Julian. Please call this number at Union Hospital concerning your grandmother."

Debbie thought her heart would stop and she reached for Scott. He folded his arms around her quaking shoulders. "It will be all right. Call them back and get an explanation."

"I assumed she was here." Debbie moved to check Grandma's bedroom just to be sure. Then she made the dreaded call. She clutched Scott's hand as she listened intently.

"The nurse who made the call is no longer on duty," Debbie reported to Scott, "but this nurse said Gran is there and stabilized. She has been admitted for at least overnight. The nurse couldn't tell me what was wrong."

Scott pointed to the answering machine. "There is another message that you didn't listen to."

Debbie pressed the play button. "Hi, Debbie, this is Myrna Yoder. I'm at the hospital. Maxine is having stomach trouble and it sounds like food poisoning. Now, the girls and I ate from the same Chinese buffet, and so far we are fine. Well, anyway, you'll want to get down here and bring Maxine some toiletries for an overnight stay. See you soon."

Debbie breathed a little easier as she rushed to collect the things Grandma would be needing. Scott drove Debbie to the hospital without her having to ask him. She wanted him near while she faced the unknown. She prayed the whole way on the short drive. This was much too early to lose the vibrant matriarch.

Grandma had already been placed in a room. Debbie flew down the hall to find her dozing in a hospital bed. The other bed in the sterile room was empty.

"Gran," Debbie spoke quietly and felt Scott come to her side, placing his hand on her shoulder. "What happened, Gran?"

"Dandy?" Maxine Julian opened her eyes that were dulled with pain and medication. "Ah, and Scotty, too." She smiled.

"What has the doctor said?" Scott probed.

"Bad food." Grandma grimaced. "Probably the shrimp, since I'm the only one who likes it."

Scott pulled up a chair for Debbie and she sank gratefully into it.

It was a long wait until the doctor made his last round of the night and assured them that Grandma could easily be released by seven the next morning. Grandma appeared to nod off after midnight while Scott and Debbie talked quietly.

"So, you've heard about my exciting evening; are you going to tell me how your evening was?" Grandma suddenly spoke with her eyes still shut.

"Uh. . ." Debbie didn't know how to tell Grandma that she was right about Scott's regard for her.

"I think your Dandy likes me," Scott answered.

Grandma chuckled. "And you like her. I know."

"So, I would have permission to uh. . .say, court your granddaughter?" Scott asked.

"Wouldn't think of stopping you," Grandma said in a tired voice.

Debbie leaned over and kissed her grandmother's cheek. She and Scott watched in silence as Grandma drifted into a relaxed sleep. Then in the glow of a small lamp in the stark hospital room, Scott leaned down to whisper in Debbie's ear.

"I think I love you."

Debbie gasped. "I think I love you, too!"

"Praise God," Scott whispered.

Epilogue

Debbie filled a bucket with what would be the last of the summer's tomatoes. The early September sun was not as direct as August's had been, and the garden's remaining plants were withering in the chilled nights.

It had been a wonderful summer. Debbie had enjoyed having long days to work alongside Grandma and long evenings to spend with Scott. Grandma had seen to it that he had eaten dinner with them almost every night, even though Debbie teased that he was being spoiled. The garden had flourished under the joint efforts of Scott and Debbie, and they had had plenty to share with Debbie's parents, who came home for several weeks before loading their motor home and setting off toward Maine for a fall foliage trip.

Debbie and her grandmother had started attending Scott's church, and already they both had found places to become involved. Debbie enjoyed the singles' group and had made new friends. She survived an energized week of vacation Bible school and even signed up to assist with the children's puppetry program.

Things were falling into place in her life, and one of the most important of those things was walking across the yard toward her at that moment.

"Did you leave school early?" Scott asked as he leaned down to gather some small red tomatoes.

"No, you must have had long office hours today."

"It has been a long week," he admitted. "You and Maxie going to can these?"

"Certainly! Gran makes wonderful soups from her tomato juice."

They filled Debbie's bucket and still had tomatoes to pile in the grass.

"Can we plan a date for tomorrow evening?" Scott said.

"I can't. Tomorrow is the women's retreat up in Canton, and it won't be over until late."

"Oh." He sounded truly disappointed as he cleaned a bush of all its tomatoes. "I'll be right back." Scott scrambled up from a hunched position and hurried through his back door.

Debbie was ready to haul tomatoes to the house when he returned. Scott reached awkwardly for her hand, and she failed to see that he had something serious on his mind. She joked with him. "Do you want to help me get the dirt out from under my nails?"

Scott gave her an exasperated, lopsided grin. Then taking a deep breath, he spoke. "I had more romantic places in mind, but I started thinking that since this garden is where we met and how our relationship got started, I should do this here."

Debbie frowned at him. "What are you talking about? Are you okay?" His fingers quivered around her left hand.

Scott made a frustrated shake of his head and plugged on. "I asked the Lord back in May—very soon after I met you—to show me if you could be the one I have been waiting for. It didn't take long to feel that God had given me permission to love you." Scott looked lovingly at Debbie's confused expression. "In fact, I was almost giddy about it on the morning I asked you to Tuscora Park, because I already knew I loved you and couldn't wait for you to know it, too."

Debbie sighed. She was so blessed to have him care for her. His hair was tousled and she smoothed it with her free hand.

"Debbie?" His tone caused her to meet his gaze. "We have managed to become good friends by sharing this garden plot. Do you think we could consider sharing all of our future gardens?"

Her eyes widened. His words held deep meaning.

"Debbie. . .dear Dandy, would you marry me?" he asked. Slowly he pulled a golden ring from his pocket. The diamond stone was simple in cut but dazzling in beauty.

Once again he had made her speechless, but she didn't need words. She smiled and leaned into him. Their lips met and she promised to love him through thick and thin for as long as God should grant them life.

❧

Let us not become weary in doing good,
for at the proper time we will reap a harvest
if we do not give up.

GALATIANS 6:9

REBECCA GERMANY

Rebecca Germany works full-time as a fiction editor and has written and compiled several novellas and gift books. She lives in Ohio, where she enjoys country life.

Mix and Match

by Bev Huston

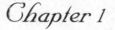

Chapter 1

I t's for your own good."

Melissa stared blankly at her mother. This was not the first time, and probably wouldn't be the last, that they would lock horns over an issue. "I'm not interested in dating. Every one of them has been a disaster."

"Because you set out to make them that way." Katherine Stoddard's anger reflected in her hazel eyes and her flushed cheeks. "Please do this for Gram. It's too late to back out now. She only wants to see you happy, darling." Melissa could hear the concern in her mother's voice.

"I'm happy the way I am. All those goofy guys wanted to change me." Melissa got up from the kitchen stool. She'd never had much success with dating, and tonight wouldn't be any different. It wasn't for lack of trying, either. But it hurt too much when she wasn't accepted for the way she was. "Honestly, Mom, I don't want someone in my life whose mission is to transform and reform me."

"Gram knows that. I'm sure this guy will be different. Now go put on a pretty dress and fix your hair."

Melissa tossed the mail she'd been holding onto the kitchen counter and fought the urge to scream. "That's what I'm saying. You know I don't wear dresses. Why can't I just be me?"

"Please. Gram doesn't ask for much, now does she? She's concerned since. . .since. . ."

"I know. And I'm doing okay." Melissa bit her lip, not daring to look at her mother. She hated how she had to struggle to keep her emotions in check. Still. After all this time. "I'll go get ready." She turned and thumped down the hall to her bedroom, slamming the door for effect. Leaning against it, arms crossed, she tried to think this through. A long-suffering sigh escaped before she seated herself in front of the vanity mirror. She raked a brush forcefully through her curls as she stared at a photograph on her wall. Though she loved this final remembrance of her dad, she hated how it showed all of her flaws.

Defeat weighed heavily on her as she scowled at the picture. She looked like a boy, with flaming red hair, too many freckles, and a pixie nose. She felt shortchanged in every department, not just in height. Plus she lacked backbone, at least when it came to family.

Well, she would go out on this date, but that didn't mean she had to like it. And then an idea began to brew. "I guess I'll just have to be my charming self," she said, unable to hold back a grin. Gram wouldn't try to fix her up again after tonight, despite her prior success with Melissa's cousins Chelsea and Callie.

Jumping up, she yanked open the closet and began searching through her wardrobe. She threw a simple green cotton dress onto the bed then dove onto the floor to seek out footwear. "Ah, these will do nicely!"

Moving back to the vanity, she plopped herself down and began to do her hair. When she finished, she dug through the drawers and pulled out an assortment of makeup. After applying a thick layer of foundation, blush, lipstick, eyeshadow, and eyeliner, she decided to wash it off. "This date calls for the natural look." She giggled to herself.

A tap on her bedroom door diverted her amusement. "Yes?"

"Lissa, honey," her mother said, "I have to run to the store. Are you almost ready?"

"Yes, Mom," she answered sweetly, feeling a little giddy about what she had planned.

"Good. I should be back before your date arrives, but listen for the doorbell just in case."

"Will do."

She heard her mother's footsteps fade down the hallway. A small pang of regret rose in her stomach, but she quickly banished it. Melissa knew she had to do this or forever deal with her family's meddling.

Using a cleansing pad, she rubbed off the makeup and stared into the mirror, lost in thought. Yes, she understood their concern. At twenty-two she still lived at home, wondering what she wanted to do with her life. But ever since that day ten months ago, she'd buried her heart. Melissa knew somewhere, deep inside her, a longing for someone to love existed, but she couldn't get past her grief. God had already taken the most important man in her life—her father—and there were no guarantees it wouldn't happen again. She knew, without a doubt, her heart couldn't bear another such hurt.

The door chime brought her back to the present day. After a last quick glance at her reflection, Melissa headed to meet her date. "Please forgive me, Gram," she whispered.

Bounding down the hall to the front entrance, her pigtails flopped like the large ears she'd worn when she had a part in the school play *Lady and the Tramp*. The capricious feeling somehow gave her courage. She flung open the door.

"Hi. I'm so glad you dropped by," she said brightly.

"You are?" He appeared surprised by her comment. Obviously he didn't think too much about this blind date, either.

"I'm Melissa. What's your name?" She twirled some of her hair around her finger as she spoke.

"Ah, my name's Greg, and I—"

"Nice to meet you!" She reached out and cranked his hand. Inwardly she cringed for making such a fool of herself, but it had to be done. Anyway, it was kind of fun.

"I wanted to invite you—"

"How sweet of you. But I have a better idea."

"I'm afraid there's been some sort of mix-up—"

"No. You're right on time." Her smile faded. Apparently the getup had worked even quicker than she'd thought. Men. They were so predictable. "Oh, I see. You're no longer interested now that you've seen me—is that right?" She hiked her chin and gave an indignant sniff. "You men are all alike. I don't fit your idea of the perfect date." She put on an exaggerated pout. "And now you've had a change of heart." She hoped he'd bought the act.

"No. I haven't had a change of heart. It's just that—"

Rats. He might be harder to lose than she'd thought. She forced her lips into a smile. "Good. Let's get going then." She closed the door and linked her arm with his. "So. I thought we could go rollerblading."

She watched as Greg did a quick visual intake of her looks. If he thought the black, five-buckle-storm-commando boots didn't quite match her feminine dress, he never said a word.

"I've never done—"

"There's always a first time for everything," she interrupted him again. "Where's your car?"

"At home."

"You walked here? No problem. We can take mine."

"Actually I live in the neighborhood—"

"Oh, did you move into the old Hanson house down the block?" She refused to let the poor man finish a sentence.

"Yes. But how did—?"

"It's been up for sale forever." She opened the car door for him and waited until he was seated before she slammed it. She walked around to the driver's side, took a deep breath, yanked open the door, and dropped onto the bucket seat. Before starting the ignition, she fiddled with the air-conditioning dials and, when Greg wasn't looking, turned up the radio volume. When the engine turned over, the music blazed. She laughed inwardly as Greg's hands flew to his ears.

"You like your music loud?" he asked.

"Doesn't everybody?"

"What?"

She put the transmission in reverse and peeled out of the driveway. Greg gripped the armrest and closed his eyes. She repeated herself loudly, "Doesn't everybody?" He nodded then visibly stiffened as she cornered on two wheels. Melissa's heart pounded in her chest. She hoped she knew what she was doing.

The brief drive to the park felt like it took forever since neither could talk over the music. Still, the radio provided a nice barrier while Melissa thought up ideas to make her date hate her. It seemed a shame, too, because he had such caring eyes. His dark hair with its natural wave and a winning smile could cause a girl to swoon. She needed to stop thinking this way, or she'd lose her nerve. Besides, on closer inspection, it appeared to be more like a grimace. No thanks to her driving.

"I've never rollerbladed before," he said quietly when she turned off the engine.

Her ears rang. "You'll love it!" She hoped she hadn't just shouted at him.

They nattered about the Wildcats and their last game as Melissa pulled her brightly colored skating equipment from the trunk of the car, where she always kept it. When they reached the rental shop, Greg pointed to a simple black pair of rollerblades.

Melissa placed her hand over the skates the clerk held and shook her head. "He'll have the neon green and yellow ones, with the matching helmet." Turning to Greg she continued, "This is a fun sport, so you gotta look the part."

Greg smiled at her then took the wild skates now being offered. Together they proceeded to sit on a nearby bench. Melissa dropped beside him and pulled out a package of gum. "Want some?"

"No, thanks."

"I find it helps me keep my rhythm and balance." She popped a piece into her mouth and pocketed the wrapper. In silence they removed their shoes and put on their skates. Melissa fought the urge to giggle when she glanced at Greg.

"I'm not sure I can even stand up in these," he said with a shaky voice as he pushed up and attempted to balance.

She stood, blew a bubble with her gum until it popped, then gathered it all back into her mouth. "You'll do fine," she said as she slapped him on the back.

The force sent him forward down a slight incline, while he waved his arms as he tried to stay upright. He headed straight for a nearby tree. Melissa raised her hand to her mouth and coughed, hoping to hide the smile spreading across her lips. "Hey, you forgot your helmet and knee pads. Wait for me!" Scooping up the accessories, she effortlessly glided to Greg's side.

"I–I wasn't trying to leave you behind."

"Oh, you were just in a mad rush to hug this pine?"

"Very funny." He pulled back from the bark. "I don't know if I can do this, Melissa."

The way he said her name caused a yearning in her heart and made her knees feel like marshmallows. But there wasn't time for that now. "Nonsense," she replied, handing him his helmet and knee pads. "It's fun and safe and anyone can do it."

"So there's no reason I need this equipment?"

"None."

"I'd watch out for a big bolt of lightning if I were you." He gave her a silly grin. Again Melissa felt shame at her deception. But she couldn't back out now.

"Well, it's like walking. You know. Everyone can do it once they learn how."

"Thought so. Did I tell you I didn't walk until I was almost three?"

"Maybe you should have taken up hockey. My dad always said I could skate before I could walk." Pain seared through her at the mention of her father. She looked away from Greg before he could see the hurt in her eyes.

"Maybe it's too late for me." He wobbled again.

"It's never too late," she said, her light tone masking her anguish. "Try leaning on me." What was she doing? She didn't want any contact with this man. She wanted him to dislike her. But as she held him close, for balance, she inhaled his woodsy aftershave. Their cheeks brushed as his muscular arm clung to her waist. "Take a step and glide."

"Okay." His voice seemed as unstable as his equilibrium.

Melissa watched as he jerked ahead. Somehow his presence was almost comforting. Maybe Greg wasn't so bad.

"Hey, I'm still standing!" he yelled back to her.

Melissa floated to his side, trying to ignore her unexpected attraction to this handsome man. "You're doing grea—" She started to respond, but he twisted and plowed into her. "Ow!"

"Sorry. I knew I wouldn't be very good at this. Are you all right?"

Rubbing her ribs and nodding her head, Melissa eyed him for a moment. "Anyone ever tell you you're a pessimist?"

"Is that so bad?" His gaze met hers as he flashed a disarming smile.

"Well, they say opposites attract," she replied softly before she realized what she had said.

❧

Greg fought the urge to limp as they walked from the car to the coffee shop. The last two hours had been rough trying to keep up with Melissa, but he had enjoyed it. He hoped he could stay awake while they relaxed over espressos.

Normally he wouldn't have been this weary. But as the new youth pastor of his church he'd spent most of the day canvassing the neighborhood teens, inviting them to attend a fun night. The hours had felt incredibly long in the scorching Arizona sun. He'd been heading home when he felt led to Melissa's door and trusted God's direction. Maybe a troubled teenager needed to know someone cared.

Her house, no different from any of the others on the block with the red tile roof and beige stucco, drew him. He believed the Holy Spirit had directed his path.

When she opened the door, he felt a thud in his gut as if he'd been punched. He knew instantly she had been the reason God had nudged him to her home. She reminded him of Amy. With eyes that held a depth of sadness that made his heart ache. He wanted to run but couldn't. He should have tried harder to tell her she had mistaken him for someone else, but he couldn't do that, either. He wondered if some poor guy still waited on her door stoop.

And now they were sipping their drinks, enjoying a pause in conversation since he'd told her he was a pastor. She hadn't run. "So do you come here often?"

Melissa put her cup down. "I used to."

He noted the hesitation in her answer and tried to ignore the sorrow in her emerald green eyes. "I guess it's been a little too warm for coffee these days—even if it is only March."

She kept her gaze focused on the table as she rubbed her mug between her palms. "This is where my dad and I would come after a day of hiking or some other adventure."

Nope. He couldn't ignore anything she might be feeling, no matter how much it pulled at his own anguish. Greg reached out and brushed the back of her hand with his fingertips. "Grief takes awhile, Melissa."

She released her cup as if it were on fire, raised her head, and sent him a penetrating gaze that seemed to ask, "What do you know about it?"

"It's a road I'm familiar with," he told her softly in answer to her unspoken question. "It will get easier, but you need to talk about your feelings."

"I'm not so sure."

"You think people are afraid to be around you. Afraid you might start to cry or something, right?"

She nodded.

Greg continued to hold her gaze until she looked away. "If you ever want to talk, Melissa, as a friend or as a pastor, I promise I'll listen."

She visibly stiffened then rose. "We should head home. You're going to be sore tomorrow, and it's Sunday. It wouldn't be good if you missed church." A slight smile softened her.

"I'm not sure I can stand."

Melissa stepped forward to help him as he attempted to rise, and their heads collided.

Pain shot through his temple, but he worried she was hurt. "Oh, Mel, I'm so sorry!" He reached to steady her.

"I have to leave," she whispered with trembling lips.

He sensed a deep struggle within her and felt the need to back off. "Will you be okay?"

She nodded.

"Want me to come?" he asked, already knowing the answer.

She shook her head and quietly slipped away. Greg took a few steps after her then stopped. He stood helpless as he watched her leave the parking lot at a dangerous speed.

"Father, keep her safe," Greg prayed. Then he turned, picked up the sunglasses from the table, and began walking the few blocks home.

The night was beautiful, as usual. He'd only lived in Heaven a few weeks, but already he felt like he belonged. The streets were clean, the people friendly, and he looked forward to learning all about the local history. Of course, he missed the Seattle rain. And he missed Amy.

"Just what are You doing, God?" Greg asked. "Am I to be Melissa's friend or something more?"

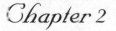

Chapter 2

As tears streamed down Melissa's cheeks, she carefully steered the car into the driveway then cut the ignition. Leaning back against the headrest, she closed her swollen, sore eyes.

"How could he do that? How dare he call me Mel?" she spoke aloud and slammed her fist on the steering wheel, ignoring the discomfort. Melissa took a deep breath. After all, how would Greg know that no one but her dad called her Mel? He'd always wanted a son, and she'd tried so hard to be one for him. She had learned to love hiking, fishing, baseball, and anything else he wanted to do. And now he was gone.

Melissa jumped at the sound of tapping on the glass then rolled down the window to speak to the man in uniform.

"Hi, Melissa, everything all right?"

"Yes, Charlie. Just fine. Were you following me?"

He removed his sunglasses and nodded. "You were speeding. Again."

"I don't think so." She avoided his gaze. She needed another ticket like she needed another blind date. And she didn't want Officer O'Neil to see she'd been crying.

"Must be them heavy boots."

She smiled.

"Still making those flies?" Charlie asked as he leaned down and rested his arm on the car.

"Not as much," she said, remembering the last time she'd made them. Chelsea had needed to learn, or she never would have done it. "I've been kind of busy taking care of the Marshall twins until they can find someone."

"Are you gonna put your dad's web page back online? Carry on the business?" Charlie cleared his throat. "We miss your dad."

When would this hurt go away? She wanted to lash out at Charlie but knew better. His concern helped. "Me, too." Her words were barely audible.

Charlie stood up. "I'm sorry, Melissa. I shouldn't have said anything."

"It's okay. I need to be over this."

"You've got to let it run its course. You can't just decide you should be through grieving and wake up totally different." He put his sunglasses back on. "You and your daddy were close—more so than most. Give yourself a break, Melissa."

Charlie's radio squawked, giving her a reprieve. He meant well, but she couldn't bear to hear what he had to say. All the gang down at the tackle shop wanted her to stop by, listen to their reminiscing, but it would never happen. She had a stack of flies she could give Bill to sell, but she didn't want to part with them. As for the Web page, after she'd read the messages in the guest book following her dad's death, she wondered if she'd ever go back to the site again.

"I've got to run, Melissa. You watch your speed like a good girl. Remember—a day of fishing can sure help a person sort out stuff. Take care now."

" 'Bye," she managed to choke out. After a few minutes she rolled up the window, gathered her stuff, and went inside the house.

"Hi, Mom—it's me!" Melissa hollered as she closed the front door, relieved to be indoors with the air conditioner.

Her mother appeared in the foyer, her sandals clicking on the peach-colored santillo tiles. "Where have you been?" she asked, her gaze lingering on Melissa's outfit. She frowned.

"On that silly old blind date Gram fixed for me," Melissa answered, annoyed that her mother had already forgotten the torture she'd had to endure.

"I beg your pardon? Your blind date has been here, waiting for you for over an hour."

Melissa leaned against the door. A wave of unease washed over her, and she steadied herself. If he's here, who had she been out with for the last three hours? And why had this guy only been waiting an hour? She stumbled forward.

Her mother moved to assist her.

"Is he in the house or out in the back?" Melissa whispered.

She pointed beyond the large potted plants to the living room, and Melissa groaned.

"Let me help you, dear," her mother said loudly for her blind date's ears.

"I guess I have some explaining to do," she raised her voice as well.

The young man stood when Melissa and her mother approached.

"Melissa, this is Jeff."

She mumbled a greeting then reached out and shook his hand, resisting the urge to stare at him. This was what Gram thought she should date? Despite his height and broad shoulders, the guy looked like an IBM computer salesman. Intellectuals were certainly not her type.

"So," her mother began as Melissa sat down on the corner of the coffee table close to where her date had been sitting, "Jeff was delayed with a very serious computer problem at work."

"Ah, yes, I was," he agreed, pushing his thick-framed glasses up the bridge of his nose and lowering himself back into his seat. He seemed nervous or perhaps excited. "We had a bug in an accounting formula that could have been disastrous."

"I gather you were able to fix it?" she asked, relaxing a little when her mother slipped from the room. While her efforts with Greg hadn't worked out as planned, Melissa had the distinct feeling she'd be much more successful with Jeff. And this time she didn't feel the least bit remorseful.

"Eventually." He seemed to be studying her, and she wondered how bad she looked.

"Well, I'm going to play war games tomorrow. Would you like to join me?" She managed to keep a straight face as Jeff's smile faltered.

"Oh, I never play on Sunday."

What a choirboy. "We could go bungee jumping next weekend?" Melissa offered. Getting him to dislike her seemed like a done deal. Why, he was already eyeing his escape route.

Jeff adjusted his glasses again. "I'm not too interested in the outdoors. Perhaps we could catch a movie?"

"Oh, that would be great. We could go see that one about the serial killer. They say it's gruesome." She hoped he wouldn't agree. Gory shows did not appeal to her at all.

"To be honest, M–M–Melissa, I have a weak stomach for violence." He leaned forward, causing his glasses to slip once more. "Wouldn't you like to see something milder? Perhaps a romance?"

"Don't you want to live dangerously? Sitting at a computer all day must be tiresome." Melissa worried her last comment might have been too mean. Jeff seemed like a nice guy, but she needed to put him off. For good.

"I find computer work rather interesting and rejuvenating," he said in a mellow voice, then smiled.

Yikes. How dare he be charming? "I know! What about skydiving?"

Jeff jumped up, startling Melissa. She struggled to keep from falling off the coffee table. "Is everything all right?"

Inching away, Jeff's voice sounded compassionate yet firm. "I don't mean to be rude, but I think it would be best if I just left."

"Now? But I haven't even apologized for not being here."

"Under the circumstances I think it may have been best."

"But I—"

"I'll make my apologies to your grandmother."

Now she felt like a heel. He'd seen through her and taken it like a man. She followed him toward the door. "By the way, Jeff, do you rollerblade?"

With a boyish grin he replied, "Oh, no, that's far too risky. If I were to ruin my hands, my career would be over."

She was speechless, and then Jeff laughed. A deep roar that caught her by surprise, and she joined him.

"Nice meeting you," she said and sincerely meant it. In another place or time Jeff might have been worth pursuing.

He took her hand. "Thanks for not being too hard on me for my tardiness. You're a delight."

Again she found she couldn't speak as she watched him walk away and step into a beat-up old car.

Melissa dropped to the top step and began to laugh. Could anything else go wrong?

She stopped short when she turned and saw her mother in the doorway behind her.

"I'm sorry, Mom."

"I don't know what went on just now, but I'm so glad to see you laughing."

"Oh, this is not good. I was just awful to that poor man. And the other guy!" Melissa put her head in her hands.

"Want to tell me about it?" her mother asked as she seated herself beside Melissa.

What could she say? That she'd just run off someone who reminded her of Clark Kent? If she'd been honest with herself, she felt certain that had she taken those doofy glasses off Jeff, Superman would have emerged. And then she remembered Greg. She sighed. How could things have turned out so poorly? She wanted to crawl into a hole and die.

"Okay, if you won't tell me about Jeff, can you at least tell me where you've been? And what on earth you're wearing?"

Melissa started at the beginning, choking back a sob when she finished.

"Honey, I know you. You have a good heart, and you'd never hurt anyone intentionally."

"Not unless I'm being forced on a blind date, at least," Melissa teased.

They laughed in unison.

"And two in one night is plenty, I gather?"

Melissa felt a smile spread across her lips. "After what I put Greg through, you'd think he'd have left. Yet he stayed with me."

"Can I assume your skates probably went better with your dress than those?" She pointed to Melissa's storm boots.

"I'm making a fashion statement," she said with a chuckle. "I never want to see a dress again. And I've done my duty to Gram. That's my last blind date. I don't care if I never marry."

Her mother leaned close to Melissa and whispered, "And who's the handsome man heading this way?"

Melissa swallowed and fought the excitement she felt at seeing Greg crossing the street toward her. She reminded herself she was finished with men, dating, and finding love. But her heartbeat drowned out her thoughts. Leaving her mother behind on the step, she rushed to meet Greg at the edge of the lawn.

"You left your sunglasses in the coffee shop, and I thought you might need them," Greg said as she approached.

Their hands touched as Melissa took the frames from him and slipped them into her pocket. An instant feeling of warmth flooded her. She felt drawn to him, like being pulled into a whirlpool. "Thank you," was all she could mutter.

"You're welcome."

"Hey, why didn't you tell me who you were?" Melissa asked when she found her voice a few seconds later.

Greg blinked. "Well, I don't—"

Melissa placed her hands on her hips. "It wasn't very nice letting me think you were my blind date. Was it so difficult to tell me who you were?"

"As a matter of fact, it was."

Melissa opened her mouth then slammed it shut. They stared at each other until he started to laugh. She followed suit, amazed at how good it felt. How right everything seemed simply standing there, together.

"Look, Melissa—I should have insisted you let me tell you I wasn't your date. And I'm sorry for that. But I'm not sorry about the evening." He paused. "Are you?"

"I–I—" She sighed. Why fight it? "I had a nice time. I wish I hadn't been so terrible to you." She felt self-conscious and glanced back to see if her mother had gone indoors. She remained on the stoop. *Rats.*

"I'd like to see you again." He paused. "On one condition, that is."

Melissa lowered her gaze to the ground. She knew he was going to be like all the others. He wanted to change something about her, and then all the wonderful things she was feeling would vanish. "And that contingency would be?" she asked in a steady voice belying her trepidation.

With a light touch he brushed his knuckles down her cheek.

She held her breath.

"I pick the radio station we listen to in the car." Then he turned and sauntered away.

❧

Melissa dropped to the couch, exhausted. The Marshall twins were still asleep, and she'd managed to do the dishes and tidy her house. Maybe she could relax for a bit before the next feeding. She closed her eyes, enjoying the silence.

Ding-dong.

Bonnie awoke howling, thanks to the loud chime. Melissa picked up the crying baby and went to answer the door. When she looked in the peephole and saw Greg, her heartbeat quickened.

"Hello," she said, stepping back, allowing him to enter. He looked like a GQ man in his blue suit with a deep burgundy-colored silk tie. He raised an eyebrow when he glanced at the now-quiet bundle in her arms.

"Hello, back."

"Come on in. I'll make us some iced tea."

"I can't stay. I have a meeting. I just wanted to see how you were and ask you a favor."

Before she could reply, Bobbie began to cry. "Could you hold this one while I get the other one?"

"I don't know—"

"Here—just hold her like this," Melissa said as she placed Bonnie in Greg's arms. "Don't look so scared. She won't bite."

"She's so small. I'm afraid I might crush her or something."

Melissa raced to grab Bobbie. Too late. Now both were exercising their lungs.

"How good are you at changing diapers?" Melissa asked as Greg followed her into the kitchen.

"Better at changing tires."

"Okay, how about if you warm the formula and I'll do diaper duty?"

"Ah, sure. I think."

She grabbed the bottles from the fridge and explained how to use the warmer. "I'll take Bobbie and change him then come back for Bonnie."

"Okay." Greg sounded as sure of himself as he did trying to balance on rollerblades. She left him and took Bobbie to the bathroom where she had set up a changing station. A short time later as Melissa headed back toward the kitchen, she became aware that not only had Bobbie stopped crying, but so had Bonnie. She stepped quietly into the room and watched. Greg, seated on a stool, cradled the babe tenderly in his arms as he sang. Bonnie gripped his index finger and cooed in response to Greg's soft baritone.

Melissa's heart warmed at the sight. "Well, for someone who doesn't know a thing about babies, you seem to be doing fine."

Greg didn't take his eyes off Bonnie. "Is she yours? I mean, are they yours?"

"Would it matter?" she asked, wondering why she felt so defensive.

"I could get used to them," he said, looking up with a grin.

Melissa expelled the air trapped in her lungs, not realizing she'd held her breath. "I'm the babysitter. They go back to their parents in a few hours."

"Must be a lot of work. I could hardly get the bottles in the warmer and hold her at the same time."

"I know who to call when I need help."

"I just don't know if you can afford me."

"Excuse me?" Melissa asked, aware he was teasing her.

"I wouldn't want any monetary return for my services."

She gave him one of her stern looks. "You wouldn't?"

Greg shifted on the stool. "I'd want a date."

"Oh, no," she said as she raised her hand, palm out. "I'm finished with dating. They're always disasters."

"Okay, then. I'd want a disaster."

Melissa checked the temperature of the bottles. "These are ready, I think."

"Don't go changing the subject," Greg said as he moved to her side. "I think you owe me two disasters."

"Two? You're only helping with one baby."

"You agreed to another one on Saturday night—remember, on the front lawn? And now one for services rendered today."

"Don't you have a meeting you need to attend?"

"I did. I called my boss and told him a friend needed some help. We're meeting later."

"Your boss?" she asked. "Isn't God your boss?"

Greg laughed. "Still changing the subject, aren't you?"

"How late can you be?" She handed one bottle to Greg and took the other. "Let's sit in the family room where it's comfortable."

"Pastor Jamison has another appointment this morning," Greg said, following her. "I'll meet with him this afternoon."

"Well, I'll tell you what. Once Bonnie and Bobbie are fed, I'll make some lunch.

Since I'm not much better in the kitchen than I am on a date, that should count for another disaster."

"See—that's what I like about you. No pretense. A guy knows what he's getting right from the start."

"I have no idea what you're getting. I may be able to find some peanut butter, but that's about the extent of my repertoire."

"You knew what I meant." He winked, and Melissa felt weak all the way down to her toes.

"I'll get you a cloth," Melissa said as she stood, still feeding Bobbie.

Greg looked confused.

"Bonnie's leaking some formula."

"Oh."

"You don't want to smell like sour milk when you get back to work—and you use it when you burp her."

"A dainty little thing like this?"

"Just you wait. She's louder than Bobbie. She makes me proud to be a woman." Melissa giggled and hoped Greg knew her words were in jest.

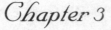

Chapter 3

Greg's favor wasn't really a big deal. The church youth were having a volleyball game that evening, and he wanted her to come. She'd said yes without even thinking. Usually she thought things through first. Of course, nothing was usual about Greg.

After the long day with the twins, Melissa decided to rest for half an hour before getting ready to go out. She stretched across the bed, ignoring the smell of baby spit-up on her shoulder, and closed her eyes.

A tapping noise awoke her. "Melissa, Honey. You have company."

She rubbed her eyes and glanced at the clock. "Oh, no!" She raced to the mirror then groaned.

Her mother slipped into the tidy bedroom and patted Melissa's shoulder. "It's okay. It's the nice blind date."

"I'm late. I need a shower and don't have time. And I smell like baby formula." She felt miserable. This time she wanted to look nice for him. After last night's fiasco it seemed the least she could do. But not puffy-eyed and rumpled, with a messy ponytail. "I look horrible!"

"You're beautiful."

"This is not the time for flattery, Mom. What am I going to do?"

"I'll keep him busy. You wash up and change."

Melissa raced into the bathroom, throwing off her clothes as she went. She jumped into the shower and within a few minutes felt better—and clean. Whipping a towel from the linen shelf, she flung it around her back, knocking the bottle of baby powder over. White talc flew everywhere, covering her from the waist down. Once again she smelled like a newborn.

Leaving the mess in the bathroom—or, in this case, the powder room—Melissa rushed back to her bedroom and dressed in jeans and a T-shirt.

Greg's eyes noticeably brightened when she stepped into the living room.

"Sorry to keep you waiting."

"No problem. With the way you drive, we still have an hour before we have to leave."

"Very funny," she said as they headed for the door.

He placed his hand in the middle of her back and ushered her past him. His touch sent a tingle down her spine. As she went by, he leaned forward, inhaling. "Mmm, love your perfume. It reminds me of something."

"It's very expensive. From France. Eau des Enfants."

He laughed and gave her ponytail a gentle tug.

Melissa pulled her sunglasses from her purse and put them on while walking with Greg to his car. She tipped the frames back down to look over the sporty red convertible.

"This is yours? On a pastor's salary?"

Greg nodded. "It was a gift." He didn't seem overly impressed with the vehicle. In fact, he sounded almost sad.

"Some friend," she replied.

"She's more than a friend." He opened the door for Melissa.

His words caused a sharp pain in Melissa's heart. She? Did Greg have an ex-fiancée? Or an ex-wife?

"I'm not as good a driver as you," he said, getting in the car and starting the engine. "So buckle up."

She grabbed the seatbelt, still pondering his earlier comment. Then she remembered. He'd spoken of grief and had said it was a familiar road. Whether he'd lost a wife or girlfriend didn't matter since it was someone he'd cared deeply about. Someone she could never compete with. Someone very feminine, no doubt. Someone unlike Melissa.

"Do you play volleyball as well as you rollerblade?" Greg's question interrupted her thoughts.

"Best on the team in school."

"No surprise there," he said with a smile.

Yeah, no surprise. She was a tomboy. She needed to stop thinking like this, or the evening would be ruined. After all, hadn't he dropped by this morning to see her? Wasn't she having a date with him on a Saturday night? *Get with the program, girl!*

"How 'bout you?"

"Me? Would you believe captain of the men's team in seminary and MVP?"

She chuckled. "Are you familiar with the story *Pinocchio?*"

"What?" He took his eyes off the road and glanced at her. "I could have been, if we'd had a team."

"Well, I hope you play better than you drive. I don't think we can go any slower."

"I'm just prolonging our time together. Got a problem with that?"

Trouble was, she didn't. No problem at all. "Rats," she muttered.

"Star."

"Where? It isn't dark enough to see the stars, or were you talking about a celebrity?" She knew she verged on rambling.

"It's this annoying habit I have."

Melissa brushed a few stray strands of hair back from her face. "I don't get it."

"I like playing with words. Sometimes when you spell something backward, it forms a new word. Like rats is star."

"Oh. So pot is top."

"Right. It drives my family nuts."

"Stun."

"Hey, you catch on fast." He seemed pleased. "Do you like palindromes, anagrams, or auto-antonyms?"

"Auto what?"

"Antonyms. Like the word *rock*. It means solid, firm, immovable; yet it can also mean to move back and forth, sway."

"I've never heard of that," she said as she tried to think of another auto-antonym. "Left."

Greg put on his turn signal and slowed. "You know a short-cut to the church?"

"No," she replied with a giggle. "I wasn't giving you directions. I thought of another word."

He responded with a chuckle, turned off the blinker, and resumed his speed. "That's a good one. Either you left a place or you were left behind. You're pretty smart for a girl."

And you're pretty handsome for a man, she thought, thankful he had noticed she was indeed female.

❧

What are you, ten?

Greg chided himself as he sought out Melissa on the sidelines before he served. He wanted to make sure she was watching. After looking so bad at rollerblading, he needed to do something to redeem his poor image.

"Grass is gonna grow on you, Greg. Serve," one of the teens on the other team hollered to him.

He pulled his arm back then swung forward, punching the ball over the net. The other side scrambled to volley it back but was unsuccessful. They returned the ball, and he repeated his performance. After his third serve he turned away, seeking out Melissa. He turned back to the play at hand, and the ball bounced off his head. Another player swiped it back over the net. *So much for redeeming my image.*

He caught a glimpse of Melissa on the sidelines laughing. She looked lovely.

"Keep your eyes on the ball," another teen ordered.

With his serve over, Greg took a seat near Melissa, and the next player bounded out to the floor.

"What a great turnout," Melissa said.

"Yeah. I'm surprised."

"Rotating is a good idea. Everyone gets a chance."

"And this old man gets a break."

"Good thing. You had me worried you'd get hurt out there with that head move. Is that an old trick?"

"Ha, ha," he said, pretending to be annoyed. "I'm actually a pretty good player. I think it's in the genes."

"You know what they say about that." She smiled, and he felt a tug at his heart.

"The problem with the gene pool is that there's no lifeguard." She slapped him on the shoulder. "So sit back and watch a pro." She left and took her position on the court.

Yep, he was more than prepared to watch her. But he caught sight of a young girl sitting off by herself, near the door. She seemed timid, almost afraid to come all the way into the gym. He sauntered over.

"I'm Greg, the youth pastor."

"Selina," she replied, still looking at the floor.

"Which team do you want to play on?"

She twisted her foot, causing her shoe to squeak. "I'm not very good."

"It's just for fun. We'd love to have you join us."

"Really?"

"Really!" he said. "You can take my place. I need to get some refreshments ready."

"I could help."

"Wouldn't you rather play?"

She didn't respond.

"You're up next. I'll stick around to make sure you're not competition for me. How's that?"

A little pip of a giggle escaped Selina's mouth. He took that as a yes and ushered the girl over to her place on the court.

Sitting back at the sidelines, he struck up a conversation with two other teenagers. The kids were bright and funny. This had been a great idea. He sure liked being the pastor here.

With Selina settled into the game, Greg headed off to the kitchen for the goodies. A couple of youths followed to help. They set up the food in the small fireside room then went back to the gym.

"Once you left, Greg, our team really got on a roll," Willy said as they walked off the court.

"Thanks," Greg replied.

Willy blushed. "I didn't mean it that way."

Greg tousled the kid's hair. "Okay, gang. Let's head into the other room for refreshments and a time of fellowship."

❦

Melissa felt like an outsider. It had been a long time since she'd talked to God; besides, she wasn't a teen. She didn't have much in common with most of the kids, and they kept Greg busy. In fact, except for a brief exchange on the sidelines, he'd practically ignored her. When he hadn't picked her to be on his team, she'd been hurt. Then his attention hadn't appeared to be on the game. He always seemed to be looking around the gym. As if he were looking for someone. Who was he expecting? Had he forgotten they had come together?

Now, after talking with the kids in the fireside room, they surrounded him. Laughing and joking. Why couldn't she join in? Being on the sidelines distressed her, but fear held her back. Gazing about the room, she noticed Greg motioning to her to come over.

She stood near him, but he didn't speak to her. He continued to talk with the teens, and eventually Melissa drifted away.

She was being silly, she knew, but she felt as if she'd been in Greg's way. He had a job to do, and she needed to learn to take second place to that. But could she? Was she being selfish to want time alone with Greg? Time to get to know him? With his being a youth pastor, would she ever get that chance? It seemed as if everyone wanted a piece of him.

What troubled her more than her unwanted feelings for Greg were her feelings about God. She felt He'd let her down. Where had He been when her father took ill? She couldn't think about that right now. Nor could she think about her overwhelming desire to have Greg comfort her.

Melissa grabbed her purse and asked Willy to let Greg know she had left. Stars twinkled in the clear sky as she walked home. She needed to sort out all the feelings and emotions that were assaulting her. Was she being a spoiled brat, wanting Greg all to herself? Just like with her dad? Her heart ached at the thought.

How could she go from not needing someone to regretting that things weren't working out with Greg? She didn't want to be like her mom. Her dad had done everything for her mom. When he died she didn't even know how to reconcile the checkbook. He had always made everything right. Yet he'd taught Melissa to stand on her own two feet. No, she didn't need a man to fix everything in her life.

But maybe she needed a man to share everything that was right. Now where did that thought come from? If that were true, she knew Greg Kelly wouldn't be that man. For two brief days, though, Melissa had felt like her old self—only to discover there'd be no time to enjoy anything with Greg. The thought made her sad.

She kicked a few stones and muttered to herself then wished she could talk to her dad about her feelings. They'd never really talked about boys. Guess maybe he'd never realized Mel was a girl. That had been fine with her. She loved the same things he did. They fished, hiked, and golfed. And she sat with him for every sports game on TV. Melissa loved being the son her dad always wanted.

"What would you tell me to do, Dad?" she asked aloud.

A gentle breeze came out of nowhere, and the sway of the bougainvillea lining the street sounded like words. As if her dad had whispered the answer to her. *Seize the day.*

It had been one of his favorite songs. She loved it, too. With a slight Celtic flair, both the words and music had spoken to them. Melissa could hear his smooth voice as clear as if he were beside her. But the beauty of the words were simply a memory now.

Melissa pulled a few strands of hair between her lips, an annoying trait she thought she'd broken. Yet, whenever she felt unsure, the hair ended up in her mouth, reminding her she hadn't grown up. She tucked the red wisps behind her ear. Well, she was all grown up, and she didn't need anyone. If that were true, why wasn't she convinced? And why did she suddenly ache for someone to understand her?

Angry with herself, she unlocked the iron grate door and jerked it open. Unshed tears blurred her vision as she struggled with the key in the lock of the front door. Once it unlocked, she marched inside and slammed it shut. The bang hurt her ears, and she cringed at being so childish.

She waited for her mother to appear, but the house remained quiet. Melissa dropped her bag on the bench in the foyer, kicked off her sneakers, and headed to the kitchen. A note on the fridge advised her she had gone to visit Gram.

"Just great. They'll probably set up another blind date for me to look like a loser," she muttered as she got a glass of water and took a few sips. "What's wrong with me?" she said as she padded down the hall to her bedroom. The mess in the bathroom from earlier caught her attention.

Setting her glass down on the counter, she went to grab the vacuum from the closet. She'd have no time to clean in the morning before the twins arrived.

When she finished, she prepared for bed. Though tired, she couldn't sleep. Turning on the lamp, she glanced at her Bible on the nightstand. Exactly where she'd left it the day of the funeral. She picked up the book and flipped through a few pages then set it back down. She knew the answers she needed were not there.

Melissa turned off the light and squeezed her eyes closed, ordering herself to sleep. In the stillness of the house she thought she could still hear the song "Seize the Day" playing softly. She covered her head with a pillow. But the music echoed in her ears. *Seize the day.*

Chapter 4

You're an idiot, Kelly!

Greg hadn't noticed when Melissa left. He wanted to find her, but the equipment had to be put away and the kitchen tidied first; then he had to lock up the church. He drove straight to Melissa's when he finished, but no one answered. He felt a tightness in his stomach. Where could she be?

He dropped down on the front step to wait. He'd stay all night if he had to. With his hands braced on his knees, he rested his head in his palms. An occasional breeze helped in the warm night. Crickets chirped, oblivious to him, while some sort of whirring noise, like an air conditioner, emanated from the house.

Moments later he noticed the sound had stopped. He knocked again. Still no answer. Greg settled back into position, wondering if he should drive back toward the church in search of Melissa.

Soon a car pulled into the driveway, and Mrs. Stoddard greeted him. "You're the wrong blind date guy. Greg, isn't it?"

"That'd be me." He stood and reached out to shake hands.

"Are you coming or going?"

"I sort of lost your daughter this evening. I'm hoping she's home."

Mrs. Stoddard raised an eyebrow and stepped forward to unlock the iron grate door.

Greg felt like a student caught in school for cheating and wanted to explain. "I got kind of tied up with the kids, and I guess Mel grew tired of waiting."

Mrs. Stoddard turned back to him quickly. "What did you say?"

"I got tied up—"

"No. What did you call Melissa?"

Greg shrugged, not sure what he'd just said. "Mel, I guess."

"Oh, dear. That's not good."

He waited while she bit her lip as if trying to think.

"I see her purse and shoes, so she's home. I'll tell her you stopped by."

"I'd like to talk with her."

"It might be best if you wait until the morning." He couldn't help but notice Mrs. Stoddard's pleasantness had slipped to something almost verging on irritation.

"Is something wrong?"

She sighed. "Only Martin, my husband, called her Mel. She's still easily upset since his passing. I'm sure she'll be fine in the morning. Good night."

"Yeah, good night."

Greg stood on the step and stared at the night sky. He wouldn't hurt Melissa for anything, yet that appeared to be just what he'd done. How could he have been such a jerk?

He reminded himself that she'd made it home safe and decided he'd better leave before Mrs. Stoddard called the police. That wouldn't look good. Though he and his boss got along well, the church had already been through a scandal, thanks to some untrue gossip. As a result, Pastor Jamison had become image conscious. Though he'd never said anything, Greg felt certain his boss would have preferred he drive a more sedate car and be married. Yes, staying on Melissa's doorstep would cause a problem.

Since it would be several hours before he could see Melissa, he decided to go home and pray. What did the Lord want him to do about the pretty redhead who'd invaded his life so easily? He knew the importance of staying in God's will. He hoped that will included Melissa.

⮾

"Lissa," her mother called as she rapped on the bedroom door.

"I'm awake." She yawned and stretched.

"No need to get up. Mrs. Marshall called. The twins kept her up most of the night so she is staying home from work. She won't be dropping them off this morning."

Yes! "Thanks, Mom."

"Did you want some breakfast?"

Melissa climbed out of bed and opened the door. "I'm not hungry. I think I'll shower and head to the park."

"You're missing the most important meal of the day, sweetie."

"It's not the first time."

Her mother reached out and touched Melissa's forehead. "You look tired. Why don't you go back to bed?"

"I just need a shower."

"By the way, Greg came by last night. Why didn't you answer the door?"

She swallowed. "I didn't hear anything."

"Seemed as if he'd been here a long time when I came home."

"I went straight to bed after I cleaned up the bathroom. I must have been asleep."

Her mother nodded. "I'll make some banana hotcakes."

She laughed. Her mother always made her favorite pancakes whenever she believed Melissa needed some TLC. Maybe she'd feel more like eating after her shower.

An hour later, feeling like the fatted calf, Melissa headed to the park. Her body needed a lengthy workout, thanks to the pile of food she'd managed to down. She also found this to be the best place to think. Greg had laughed when she told him that.

The park appeared almost empty. Melissa donned her skates and headed off along the rollerblade route. She'd picked up quite a bit of speed when she glanced up, nearly colliding with a rather awkward skater.

"Oops. Sorry," she said as she spun around the man. Coming to an abrupt stop, she leaned down to catch her breath. "You should stay to the right."

"It seems I'm always in the wrong these days," a familiar voice replied.

Melissa's head shot up. "What are you doing here?"

Greg wobbled, and she steadied him. "Do you want the truth?"

"Will I be disappointed?" she asked, wanting to remain angry with him but unable to do so.

"I'm not sure." He pointed to a bench. "Can we sit for a minute?" Once they were seated, Greg continued. "I wanted to surprise you. I figured I'd try to get the hang of this, and then maybe we could start over."

She looked away from his earnest gaze and stared out at the small lagoon. What could she say? *Sorry, Greg—I'm too afraid of losing you?* What a dumb thing to think. And here he was learning to skate—for her. She wrestled with her thoughts.

"You don't have to give me an answer right now," he said, taking her hand. "I want you to know I'm sorry about last night. Your mom explained everything to me. Forgive me?"

Melissa couldn't hear a word Greg said. All she could focus on was that he held her hand. Little electrical shocks of excitement worked their way up her arm to her heart. If she wasn't careful, the ice wall she'd carefully built would start to melt, and then where would she be?

Greg reached up and with a gentle tug turned her face toward him. "Is this the silent treatment, or are you considering my request?"

"I'm not sure," she replied, unable to formulate a coherent thought.

"Okay." He eased up off the bench and turned cautiously to leave. "See you."

"Huh? Are you just giving up? Whatever happened to that old saying, 'If at first you don't succeed, try, try again'?"

He looked back at her and grinned. "That may be the way things are here in Heaven, Arizona. But not where I come from. My grandpappy always said, 'If at first you don't succeed, hide the evidence you even tried.' " He nodded his head. "Good thing I didn't buy these skates."

Melissa stood up, hands on her hips, and watched him struggle to maintain his balance. A light breeze rustled the trees.

Seize the day.

"I think I liked you better when I hated you."

He tossed back his head and laughed then landed on the ground.

Melissa skated to his side. "Are you okay?"

"It takes more than a fall to bruise my ego."

She stared into his eyes and felt her thoughts swimming in circles. She reached out and helped him up. "I'll race you to the rental shop. Loser buys the coffee."

"What I wouldn't give for a miracle right about now."

Melissa took off then hollered over her shoulder. "It'll take more than a miracle to beat me." She wobbled on her skates; then to her astonishment her feet separated, and she sprawled on the ground. A throb from her wrist quickly built to huge proportions, and she fought a wave of dizziness. She'd never fainted in her life, and she wasn't about to start now.

"You don't have to let me win," Greg said when he caught up to her.

His words sounded like an echo in a tunnel. "I feel like the hare," she replied then slumped forward, only vaguely aware that he'd caught her in his arms.

❧

"If you two don't stop hovering over me like a couple of mother hens I'm going to scream!" Melissa said as she narrowed her eyes and glared at Greg and her mother.

Greg looked at Melissa's mother and nudged her with his elbow. "Hmm. Grumpy. Either that means the painkillers have worn off or she's really mad that she has to pay for coffee."

"Technically you didn't win. And I'm not grumpy."

"Of course not, dear," her mother said as she sat in the lawn chair next to Melissa.

"You're right." Greg nodded in agreement. "You're too tall to be Grumpy."

"And you're no Doc," she replied, understanding the reference to Snow White. But she wasn't in a joking mood. She felt stupid that she'd fallen, broken her wrist, and even fainted. How could she possibly care for the twins in this condition?

"Do you need anything?"

"No, thanks, Mom."

"I'm going to head home." Greg stood. "I have to finish planning our fundraiser for next weekend for our upcoming missions trip. Here's my number if you need anything." He handed Melissa's mother a slip of paper.

Melissa forced a smile and nodded cautiously. A rush of warmth flooded her cheeks when she gazed into Greg's dark cinnamon eyes. And the whirlpool feeling she'd experienced once before returned.

"Thanks for taking care of Lissa."

"It's the least I could do since it was my fault." His smile faded, and she detected a note of sorrow in his voice.

Melissa sensed something deeper than just remorse for her accident. She knew her fall wasn't the reason for the pained look on his face. "Don't be silly, Greg. It was my own fault. Now get going. I need some rest." She leaned back on the chaise lounge and closed her eyes. Her mother walked Greg to the back gate.

"Lissa, Charlie's here. He had your car towed home," her mother said when she returned.

Charlie stepped closer to Melissa and looked her over like a concerned parent. "I heard you fell for someone."

Her mother stifled an obvious chuckle.

"Despite my mother's and grandmother's attempts at matchmaking, I'm still single and available. Slightly damaged now." She raised her right arm and winced.

"Well, at least you still have your humor."

"And apparently my car. Thanks, Charlie. How much do I owe you?"

"Nothing. Rob from the department did me a favor." He took a step back. "I'll let you get some rest. And remember—even damaged, you're pretty special."

Melissa didn't dare speak. Her emotions were raw, and Charlie's kindness caused a lump in her throat.

She nodded and watched him leave.

I'm blessed to have such caring friends.

The thought surprised her. But would she go so far as to think God still cared for her, after all? She drifted off to sleep wondering.

Guilt was a heavy burden, and Greg knew where to place that load. Yet he had difficulty with it some days. Every time he gave it over to God, he'd snatch it back. Sometimes he wondered if he should even be a pastor with all his failings. Then he'd be gently reminded of the people in the Bible who weren't so perfect either, but God had used them.

Today, however, his guilt seemed doubled. Melissa. He felt responsible for her injury and something more. He forced the niggling thought from the back of his mind. Amy. Were the two different or somehow the same? He recognized the loss that sometimes dulled Melissa's green eyes. Everything about her drew him closer to her. Did he think he could rescue her? Did he think he could protect her when he hadn't been able to do either for Amy?

He stood and stretched his back, staring out the window at the shiny red car in the driveway. He hated that vehicle for its constant reminder of his failure, of his loss.

Help me, Lord.

Chapter 5

I'm learning the Internet!" Gram slapped her jean-clad knees in delight. "Jeff is teaching us at the community."

Melissa stiffened in her chair. Suddenly her comfortable kitchen seemed anything but. *You haven't been here for ten minutes, and already you're talking about Jeff.* She knew Gram meant well, but today wasn't a good day to be discussing her most recent disaster.

"I warned Jeff you were a free spirit. Apparently you were freer than usual."

She opened her mouth to reply then caught Gram's grin and clamped her lips together.

"Lord knows that boy could use some loosening up." She shook her head. "He's very nice, you know."

"I'm sure he is. And I'm sorry I went a little overboard. But I'm like you. From the stories Dad told me, I know you weren't a cookie-cutter mother. Then there're my own experiences with you as a grandmother."

"Don't try to butter me up."

"I'm not. Just look at you. Seventy-something and you're wearing sneakers, jeans, and a T-shirt that says, 'Old Age Ain't for the Weak.'"

"I wouldn't throw stones if I were you. I seem to recall that while my other granddaughters dressed up their Barbies in glamour gowns, you had yours doing search and rescue and examining crime scenes. Most of the time I think she even wore Ken's clothes."

Melissa feigned innocence. "I did that?"

The doorbell interrupted their conversation.

Gram stood. "I'll get it."

Melissa heard the front door open and Gram's voice registering surprise. She put down her glass and went to see what the commotion was about.

"Lissa, I mistook your young man for a delivery boy," Gram said as she pointed to the flowers in Greg's hand.

"Hi." He handed her a bouquet of pink carnations. He looked handsome in black dress pants and a crisp white button shirt. She figured he'd come straight from work to see her. The thought pleased her. Unless it was a pastoral call.

"Thanks." She reached out to take them, but Gram intervened.

"I'll put these in water. You two sit out in the back where it's quiet. Would you like something to drink, Greg?"

"Iced tea if you have it."

"Coming right up." Gram seemed to disappear. Melissa knew that wouldn't last long. All too soon she'd be out there pushing her and Greg together.

"Thank you for the flowers. That's very sweet of you," Melissa said as they walked out of the house. She took a seat on the lounge, and Greg sat on the chair beside her.

"How's your arm?"

"Not bad," she lied. It appeared as if he felt responsible for her fall, so she didn't tell him the pain had kept her awake most of the night.

He pulled a black marker from his shirt pocket and motioned to her cast. "May I?"

She nodded.

As he drew on the plaster he continued. "I think this is very appropriate."

A small lightning bolt and his signature were now prominently on display. "What's that for?"

"Don't you remember? When you said I didn't need protective wear to skate?"

She felt herself coloring from the warm feeling infusing her heart. Even if her words did sort of come back to haunt her, it delighted her that he'd remembered their conversation.

"I thought if you weren't up to it, we'd just stay here on Saturday."

"Saturday?" she asked.

"Our real date," he said with a half grin. "I'll bring over some videos and pizza."

"Should I dress for the occasion?"

Greg's smile broadened.

"I'll fix her up pretty," Gram offered as she brought out a tray with iced tea, chocolate brownies, and a crystal vase filled with the pink carnations. "Though I did hear she needed new shoes."

Melissa groaned at the reference to her boots.

"I rather liked her footwear," Greg said to Gram as amusement filled his features. "Of course, I'm still trying to decide about the hair style."

Melissa swatted Greg's arm. "C'mon—give me a break."

"I think I already did."

They laughed in unison.

❧

When Melissa's alarm buzzed, she felt as if she'd never slept. She'd tossed and turned all night trying to get comfortable with the heavy cast on her arm. In the early morning hours she finally took a painkiller, but it didn't last long. Why she resisted the medication, she didn't know. But if she didn't start getting some rest soon, she'd have to give in and take them as prescribed.

She slipped out of bed and padded to the shower. Placing a plastic bag carefully around her arm, she turned the water on full force and stood under the spray for what seemed like forever. She had difficulty motivating herself this morning. And she knew why.

Last night, as Greg left, he had asked her to go to church with him. She should have said no. But it had been a wonderful night. They'd watched two movies, eaten pizza, and talked. Melissa had never felt so relaxed in someone's company. She didn't have to pretend to be something she wasn't. And, despite his affliction with word puzzles, she found Greg funny and witty.

She giggled remembering some of the games they had played. It took her awhile, but eventually she caught on. Puns, palindromes, and more auto-antonyms.

But it wouldn't be fun this morning. She felt like a fake going to church when God had drifted so far from her. She wondered if He'd even recognize her.

Melissa did her best with her hair and clothes, rushing to be ready by the time Greg arrived. Her stomach did some kind of little flip when she opened the door and saw him. He looked amazingly good in his blue suit. Not a hair out of place, and a hint of aftershave still lingered.

"Morning, gorgeous."

She ignored his comment even though it made her heart race. "It's too early to be cheery."

"I guess I should have left earlier last night so you could have had more sleep," he said as they walked to the car. His hand touched her back lightly, guiding the way.

Melissa held her breath and resisted her feelings. She mentally argued with herself. What if she came to care for Greg and then lost him? Or maybe he only wanted a friend, since it was clear he still had feelings for someone else. Besides, Greg would probably tire of her tomboy ways. He'd look better with a feminine woman on his arm. Someone like Mattie. What could she possibly offer him? It all added up to the fact that she couldn't risk her heart right now. She felt too vulnerable.

They chatted briefly on the way, and when they reached the parking lot Greg took her hands in his. "I know this is hard for you. Thank you for coming." She thought he might kiss her, but he pulled back. "Wait, and I'll get the door for you."

He placed his warm hand under her elbow, and together they walked into the church. Music played, and she recognized the tune. People greeted one another with joyfulness, and Melissa found herself feeling like a foreigner, no longer a part of God's family.

Throughout the service she observed more than she joined in. Greg had such a pleasing voice that she found herself listening to him sing. Pastor Jamison's sermon didn't bore her, and she was thankful the time passed quickly. A sense of relief flooded her when they left the sanctuary.

As they gathered in the front foyer, many youth and young adults surrounded Greg. He greeted each of them with enthusiasm and listened to their jokes and teasing. Feelings of jealousy threatened Melissa once again.

When Greg took her arm, they moved outside and stood beside the car as another teenager hollered at him. Greg walked to meet the young man halfway across the lawn, and Melissa watched from a distance as they talked. Others stopped and chatted briefly with Greg.

A well-dressed, pretty, young woman came up to Melissa. "Hi. I'm Ursula Jamison."

"Melissa."

"Are you new to Heaven?"

"I've been here all my life. And you?"

"Almost as long." She giggled and glanced over toward Greg. Her smile faded. "Greg's just moved here, and I've been given the job of looking out for him. Since I'm a PK, Daddy thinks I'd make an excellent pastor's wife. So does Greg."

"Well, you know how Greg can pick up strays and drag them in. That's all I am to him. Just another lost sheep." She fought to keep the quiver out of her voice.

Ursula laughed and waved her hand in the air. "I didn't mean to imply that he wouldn't be interested in you. But you're definitely not his type."

Before Melissa could answer, Ursula rushed off to meet Greg, who had started toward them. Melissa couldn't hear Ursula, but Greg's face lit up as they talked. He threw his head back, with dark waves of hair bouncing like in a slow-motion commercial, and placed his hands on Ursula's shoulders. She leaned into his face, sharing more than a friendly greeting. Melissa tried to tell herself it didn't matter since she didn't know what her feelings for Greg were. But if the searing pain in her stomach indicated anything, she needed to sort things out.

"Several of the group are going for lunch and want us to join them," he said when he returned to her. "I hope you don't mind, but I declined."

She didn't reply. Did he not want to be seen with her? Or maybe Ursula had been right about her and Greg having an understanding. She bit her lip and turned to stare out the window as they left the parking lot.

"Did you want to go?"

"Nope."

"I thought maybe you and I could go someplace. . . ."

Something akin to joy fluttered through her until he continued.

"But I figured you'd need to rest, and I have things to do."

How could she even try to compete with Ursula or Amy or whomever? Her heart sank. It would be a whole lot easier on her if she could find something wrong with Greg. Or something she didn't like. Currently he had no faults, or her eyes were covered in scales.

"Is your arm bothering you?" he asked, interrupting her thoughts.

"It's okay."

"You seem rather quiet. I'll bet it hurts more than you let on. I'll take you home, and we can have lunch another time. How does that sound?"

"Sure."

"I've heard about a place called Ming's Chinese restaurant. We'll go there sometime. I don't know where it is, so when we go, it will be up to you to lead."

"Deal," she replied then waited a moment. "You didn't get that one." Suddenly their relationship seemed to be taking a downward spiral. Was it her fears? Her jealousy? Or was Greg just being a friend and she'd read too much into everything?

He slapped his forehead and groaned. "I can't believe I missed that. I think I've met my match."

I hope so, she thought before she could stop herself.

❧

A week had passed since he first met Melissa, and in every way but one she differed from Amy. He felt relieved. Today, however, the pain in her eyes seemed more pronounced than ever before.

"Melissa, we've practically spent the week together. I feel as if I know everything about you, yet nothing at all." *How corny is that?*

"My life is an open book."

"So what's on page 56?"

"That's just yesterday's stuff."

They were seated side by side on the living room sofa. With Mrs. Stoddard in the kitchen, Greg resisted the urge to reach out and take Melissa's hand or brush a strand of hair behind her ear. He wanted to touch her to make some sort of connection. Her warmth filled so many pockets of his life already. He knew he should run the other way, but Melissa's pull was greater. And then he thought about Amy.

"Are you in there, Greg?" Melissa asked, waving a hand in front of his face.

"Sorry."

"I just said how boring my life was, and you proved it." She gave him a slight smile.

"Well, maybe I can help liven it up. After all, I bet you've never had a broken wrist until now."

"You're right about that."

"And we can't forget about the blind date mix-up."

"Yes, that's right up there at the top."

"Pot."

She giggled. "Oh, stop."

"Pots." He leaned back on the sofa, placing his hands behind his head.

"Want a pillow?" she asked.

He closed his eyes. "Better not. I think I could fall asleep in this nice cool room."

"Moor."

"Yes. I'll say it again. I've met my match." He opened one eye and looked at her. "Melissa, tell me why you and God don't talk anymore?"

He watched her stiffen and the smile slip from her pink lips. "You listen to people's problems all week. You don't want to hear mine."

"I wouldn't have asked if I didn't want to know."

She picked up her glass of iced tea and took a sip. "I guess we stopped talking when He stopped listening."

His heart ached when he studied the pained look in her glistening eyes, but he remained quiet, waiting for her to continue.

"I don't think I've ever asked God for much. Just that He would heal Daddy. At first it seemed He had answered my prayers when we found out about the remission. But it didn't last long."

"And because God didn't answer your prayers the way you wanted Him to, you think He deserted you?" Though his words were harsh, he spoke them as softly as he could, understanding more than she could know. He prayed silently while she spoke.

"Didn't He?" she whispered, her bottom lip quivering slightly.

"Melissa, God is like your shadow. He's always there even if you can't see Him. He's never left you. Wherever you go. Even if you don't want Him there." He paused and sat up, leaning closer to her. "We don't know why things happen. But we have to trust that God knows what He's doing. We can't see the master plan, and sometimes the here and now seems painfully overwhelming, but you just have to trust Him."

She nodded, and he could tell she struggled to keep from crying.

"He's been with you through all of your struggles and pain. He yearns to hold you and comfort you. Won't you let Him?"

"I can't."

He couldn't stand it any longer and reached out to pull her gently toward him. He stroked her hair and brushed the single tear that escaped down her cheek. "He won't ever leave. You just call when you need Him. Okay?"

She tipped her head and sighed.

"Humans will let you down, Melissa. Me included. We don't want to, but we're not perfect. The only one you can count on is God." He probably sounded more like a preacher than a friend, but these were truths he'd had to relearn after Amy's accident. He shared from his own heartache, not from a seminary textbook, and he prayed that God would use his words to reach Melissa.

She pulled back from his embrace but remained silent.

" 'Trust in the Lord with all your heart and lean not on your own understanding,' " he quoted from Proverbs. "We don't know why God called your father home, but we're not told to try to understand it. We're told to trust Him."

With his final words Melissa broke down and sobbed in his arms while he struggled with his own emotions. He held her until she grew quiet and then kissed the top of her head.

"You need some rest. Let me help you up."

They walked to the front door in silence. Once outside on the step he turned to her. "You're the best mistake that's ever happened to me. I don't know what God has planned for our relationship, but I'm trying to trust Him to show me. Will you at least think about what I said?"

She nodded, still looking sad and doe-eyed.

He found it difficult leaving her like that, but he knew he couldn't stay. "Take care." He walked away, fighting the urge to run back, gather her in his arms, and make everything better. But only God could do that, no matter how much he wanted to.

Chapter 6

Y ou're in love!"

Melissa laughed. "Nowhere near it." *But maybe a little serious,* she admitted to herself. "I'm not ready for a relationship. I'm still trying to figure out who I am."

Gram gave her a warm hug as she entered the house. She moved to the living room and sat down on the sofa, patting the couch for Melissa to join her. "Tell me more about him." She kicked off her sneakers and settled in. Her jeans had tiny flecks of glitter, and her red T-shirt said, "If things improve with age, I must be near magnificent."

Once comfortably seated, Melissa started to tell Gram all about the last four weeks. "He visits almost every day, even went with me when I had the cast removed. When we came home, he cooked dinner and then later massaged my hand and wrist with moisturizer." She held up her pale arm and looked at it. A ripple of excitement shuddered through her as she remembered his caring touch.

"Is that all you've done so far—hold hands?" Gram asked, impatience resonating in her voice.

Melissa could feel the warmth rising in her cheeks. "There's nothing between us."

Gram smiled. "He's the one."

A tingle zapped through her. How she wished this were true. "It's not that simple. He's a pastor with a great many demands on his time. And I think—I think he has or had a wife already." There. She'd said it. She'd voiced her fears.

"Oh."

Melissa wanted to laugh. It seemed Gram was finally speechless. "It's been a long time since I cared for someone." A moment of trepidation threatened so Melissa blurted out her concern. "And I'm afraid I'll get hurt."

"Lissa, you can't trust anyone but God."

"You sound like Greg."

Gram smiled and patted Melissa's hand. "He seems very wise. Maybe you should listen to him."

She'd been doing just that. "I think I need more time." Though her relationship with God still felt somewhat precarious, she now enjoyed reading her Bible and attending church and home groups. Yet, if she were honest with herself, she knew God still waited with open arms for her full surrender. When would she have the courage to step into His embrace?

"Honey, the pain of your loss will eventually fade. You may never know why, but it doesn't matter."

"I think I know that, but it just hasn't reached my heart yet. How do you deal with it? After all, he was your son."

"It wasn't easy at first. And I still have my days. A mother never expects to outlive her children. But I see our lives as though we are on a large chessboard. I'm a small piece, and my vision is restricted to the square I'm on. But there are other players and other squares. God is the only one who can see the whole board and all the moves."

Melissa liked the analogy.

"I also see how you're starting to blossom now that you are out of the shadow of your dad."

Ouch. "What do you mean?"

"I'm not trying to hurt you, but I know the Bible says all things work for good. Yes, it was difficult to lose Martin, but I think you lived for him. If any good came out of his being called home, it's that you're searching to find yourself. It may be that you still love all the things you did together, or it may be that you did most of them because he loved them. I don't know what you'll find. But I know God will be with you when you do."

Melissa fought the desire to fall into Gram's arms and weep. "Do you think that's why Dad died?"

"I would never suggest such a thing. And don't you hold yourself responsible, young lady." Gram stroked her hair and sighed.

"I took the last batch of flies I'd made down to the shop. The guys seemed really glad to see me, but I felt as if I didn't belong anymore. Charlie and I talked for awhile, but it's not the same without Dad."

"And that's what I'm saying, sweetie. It's time to find out who you are and what you want to do with your life. It's scary, but your mother and I support you totally. So do your cousins, and I'm sure your new young man does as well. But, more important, God is with you all the way."

"Greg said God was like my shadow. Even on days I couldn't see or feel Him, He's still with me."

"If you don't snap up that man, I just might!" Then Gram jumped off the sofa and began to sing "Me and My Shadow."

Melissa watched with misty eyes, blinking often to keep the tears in check. She felt blessed. So very blessed. *Thank You, Lord!*

⁂

They arrived at Heaven Stables on time. Greg, Melissa, and the teens poured out of three vehicles and walked to the stalls.

Melissa couldn't help but notice how great Greg looked in his jeans, T-shirt, and cowboy boots. She watched as he interacted with the kids. Her heart swelled with affection. She'd fought her feelings long enough and finally found herself willing to see where

God would take this relationship. If the opportunity presented itself for her to discuss her growing attraction for Greg, she'd seize the day.

Unless of course her nerves got the better of her. Horseback riding was not a new experience for her, but it had been awhile. She hoped they'd give her a docile pony.

"Wow! Look at the size of that horse," one of the teens said as he pointed to a massive white stallion. "That's the one I want."

Greg chuckled. "It would figure. The smallest kid wants the biggest horse."

"And he can have him," Melissa replied. "I want this little mare here." She moved to a small brown horse with a thick, cream-colored mane.

"Need a hand up?" Greg offered with a twinkle in his eye.

"Maybe I'll let the instructor help me."

"Okay." He stepped closer to her. "Did I tell you how beautiful you look this morning?"

"A few times," she answered, not daring to meet his gaze. Her heartbeat raged, and she wished he'd move back in case he could hear it thumping wildly.

Greg caressed her cheek and then tipped her chin upward. He gazed into her eyes, and she felt the world fade away. She couldn't stop the undertow. He had pulled her in, and now her feelings were spiraling out of control. "You grow more beautiful to me with each passing day," he whispered.

"Oww, yuk!" Willy said. "No PDA, or I'm going home."

Melissa turned to the lad. "PDA?"

Greg laughed and pulled back from her. "He means public displays of affection."

"Yeah, and you two are here to keep an eye on us. We don't want to be your chaperones," Willy quipped.

Melissa and Greg laughed.

Soon everyone mounted a horse and prepared to head out on the trail. Melissa loved the early morning smells and inhaled deeply the pungent odor of the creosote bush.

They traveled in silence at first, becoming familiar with their horses. Greg was up ahead, just behind the instructor. Melissa brought up the rear. She'd grown to care for the youth group and enjoyed helping Greg whenever she could. As their relationship grew stronger, it seemed easier for her to share him. The thought brought a smile to her lips.

They rode to the abandoned mining town and dismounted for lunch. The sun beat down on the dusty old place as they seated themselves in the shade of a dilapidated building.

"I think I'll belly up to the bar," Willy said as he pointed to the saloon sign dangling precariously.

Greg nodded at the boy. "The drinks in there might give new meaning to the word *dry*."

"We have some cold pop over here, Willy." Melissa held out a can of cola for the teen.

In no time the food was eaten. With the many jokes and digs the kids had given Greg, she wondered when they'd had time to fill their mouths. She'd laughed so hard her stomach ached.

Everyone helped with the cleanup then climbed back on their horses. Melissa had been pleased that her pick, Dolly, turned out to be the quietest one of the bunch. Dolly obviously knew the route, allowing Melissa the opportunity to sit back and enjoy the journey.

They stopped when they were about halfway back to the stables. Everyone pulled out water bottles and guzzled down large gulps.

As they started to move out, the instructor's horse pranced off the trail, and she struggled to get the pinto back on course. She hollered back to the group, "Keep a tight hold! It might be a snake or something."

Melissa gripped the leather reins and prayed she wouldn't fall. She couldn't take being in a cast again. Her arm was finally starting to look normal. She glanced up ahead. None of the other horses seemed to be upset. Whatever it was had probably been as scared as they were and left. She relaxed a little.

Before she'd finished her thoughts, Dolly spooked and roared to life like a mechanical bull. Melissa held tight, her fingers white from the pressure. The horse raced past a few in the group then veered off the trail. She bounced hard in the saddle and forced herself to try to gain control of the horse. Cacti whipped against her legs, and everything blurred. She could hear a loud thundering in her ears, and then Greg appeared at her side. With muscular arms she'd never noticed before, he pulled Dolly to a stop then lowered Melissa to the ground. In one quick motion he dismounted and held her.

"Are you okay?"

She nodded and stared into his fear-filled eyes.

"I–I—" He couldn't finish his sentence and simply clutched her to him. When their gazes met again, the fear had been replaced. She knew that look. Love. He loved her. She began to tremble.

"You're shaking. Are you sure you're okay?"

"Fine," she whispered.

And then he lowered his mouth to hers. It seemed as if she'd been waiting for this forever. Her stomach did a loop-de-loop as if she were on a roller coaster. When their lips touched, she forgot her queasiness and responded. His kiss was gentle but full of emotion, and she felt light-headed. She didn't want it to end.

Someone cleared his throat.

"How many times do I have to tell you?" Willy asked.

"No PDA," everyone said then burst into laughter.

Melissa knew her face had flushed worse than a ripe tomato. But she didn't care. In fact, she didn't care if Dolly never came back and she had to walk home. She felt as if she had sprouted wings and nothing could shake her light feeling. Not even an embarrassing comment from a teenager.

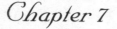

Chapter 7

"I love this place, don't you?" Melissa asked as she walked through the fairgrounds, holding Greg's hand. Cotton candy and caramel apple smells tickled her senses. Bells and laughter rang out around them.

Two weeks had passed since the horseback-riding incident. Or, more important to Melissa, since *the kiss*. Others had followed, but none like that first one that had sent shooting stars throughout her. Yet, despite her joy, she was still uncertain. Ursula always seemed to be hovering nearby, and Greg accepted numerous dinner invitations at Pastor Jamison's house.

"I always wanted to run away with this sort of traveling amusement company." Greg's words brought her back to the present. "I knew I wasn't good enough for the circus."

"Good enough?"

He looked embarrassed. "Yes. I have some talent."

"Am I supposed to guess what it is, or are you going to tell me?" They stopped walking, and she turned to face him.

"If you ever tell anyone, I'll have to kill you."

"Scout's honor. My lips are sealed."

"Maybe I should check?"

She laughed and shook her head. "Don't try to get around this can of worms you've opened."

Greg sighed. "I used to place three hula hoops on the floor in our playroom, grab a pair of rolled up socks, and emcee an entire three-ring show. Then I'd pick up a chair, and I'd become The Great Kelly, the world's best lion tamer."

Melissa struggled not to laugh. "And the lions?"

"The neighbor's cats. And, trust me, they could be vicious. I still have scars." He pulled up his sleeve and showed her a faint, white line on his wrist.

"Ahh, you poor thing. Let me kiss it all better," she said with a pout as she pulled his arm up to her lips.

For a moment the world stood still or simply vanished for Melissa. She was only aware of Greg. His dark eyes held her gaze. She slipped her fingers through his hair and basked in the contentment that seemed to fill her life these days.

She became aware of someone else's presence only when Greg pulled away quickly. "Hey, are you guys still at it?" the boy asked.

"Give it a few more years, Willy, and you'll understand."

"I bumped into Marcus, and he told me you were cleaning up the place. Winning everything." Willy pointed to the stuffed animals Melissa carried.

"You know how rumors go," she answered, worried that Greg might be upset with her skill.

"Don't listen to her modesty. She's incredible."

Willy's eyes lit up. "Wanna help me win something for my mom?"

"Sure."

A short time later Willy left, a large panda bear tucked under his arm.

"That was nice of you."

"I enjoyed it." She laid her head on his shoulder as they wandered through the fairgrounds. They'd been working their way toward the food area when Melissa asked if they could sit down somewhere.

"I thought you'd never ask."

"We could go, if you like."

"I'm waiting until it gets a little darker, and then I'm taking my favorite girl on the Ferris wheel. No one will catch me kissing her there."

"Do I know this woman?"

He chucked her chin. "Oh, yes."

The loop-de-loop feeling had returned. Were her feet still on the ground?

Greg left to buy food while Melissa waited. When Ursula sat down beside her, she wanted to get up and leave.

"Hey. Did Greg win all those for you?"

Melissa hesitated. "Ah, no."

"Where is he anyway? I want him to take me on the Ferris wheel."

"He's over there getting some food."

Ursula stood and headed toward him. Melissa watched as fear boiled in her stomach. Why did it feel as if their perfect evening had been ruined? No matter how much she cared for Greg, there would always be something—or someone—coming between them. *Why, Lord? What am I to learn?*

Greg spoke briefly with Ursula then carried hot dogs and cherry lemonade to their table. They ate in companionable silence, watching the crowd.

"Is my girl ready for the ride of her life?"

"I don't know. Where did Ursula go?"

"Is that what's been bothering you?"

Melissa couldn't answer.

"It's just a little crush. Give her time, and she'll get over it." He pulled her closer. "Now are you ready for the ride of your life?"

"A little sure of yourself, eh?" she teased, knowing that being with him was already the ride of her life. He accepted everything about her and didn't ask for more than he willingly gave. He respected her and appreciated her talents, never trying to compete. She'd never known a man like him, and just thinking about him gave her goose bumps.

"I'll give you your money back if it isn't," he said with a wide grin.

"Deal."

He replied in an instant, "Lead."

"You got it this time."

"Emit."

Even this silly game between them somehow caused her to feel warm and tender toward him. "If this is the experience you claim it will be, what's your reward?"

"Drawer."

"You're a nut."

"Takes one to know one." He pulled her into his embrace while they waited for their turn on the ride. "Besides, I have all the reward I need right here in my arms."

On the wheel Greg held her hand as they went around and around. She loved the view, with a crimson sunset off in the distance. When they were stopped at the top, he turned to her. "You've brought so much joy into my life, Mel." He kissed her forehead, nuzzled her neck then found her lips with his.

Melissa realized that for the first time since her dad's death it didn't hurt being called Mel. In fact, it felt right hearing Greg say it. Everything felt right, and she thanked God that she'd finally trusted Him. It seemed as if her life was now on track. And she'd finally had a date that didn't constitute a disaster.

When she looked down on the ground, she could see Ursula watching, and a feeling of foreboding surrounded her. She shivered.

❧

Melissa checked her watch. Not quite noon. Maybe she'd wait inside the church for Greg. Perhaps he could even leave early for their lunch date.

She entered the building and made her way to the office. The church secretary waved as she left her desk.

"Your timing is perfect. I have to get more paper, and we store it in the basement. Can you answer the phone if it rings? Greg's in with Pastor Jamison."

"Sure." She sat down at the desk and waited.

Daniel Jamison raised his voice. "I'm telling you, Greg—Melissa Stoddard is not pastor's wife material."

"You're right. She's not pastor's wife—"

The phone rang, and Melissa attempted a pleasant greeting, while her stomach churned and she felt like dying. Why hadn't Greg defended her? How could he have agreed? Maybe she embarrassed him.

A panicked voice drew her back to the phone conversation. "Please—I need to speak to Greg Kelly right away. Tell him it's about Amy."

"Yes," she replied, her world spinning out of control. As she turned to knock on the study door, it flew open. Greg stopped.

Melissa stammered. "Phone. It's for you. It's Amy." She turned and fled. He called after her, but she couldn't stop. What could he say? Nothing would take away this hurt, this pain. Nothing. Amy had returned, and she wasn't pastor's wife material. Anguish, like a sharp razor, twisted in her stomach.

Oh, God, why? Did You bring me this far only to abandon me? Help me. Don't let me fall apart.

Once safely in the car she put her fingertips to her lips. The memory of his first kiss, *the kiss,* burned. She'd been a fool.

She peeled out of the parking lot. A horn blared. She didn't care. She wove between the cars, attempting to put as much distance between her and Greg as she could. She checked the rearview mirror for the flashy red car. It was nowhere to be seen. She fought the disappointment. If only he'd come after her. Tell her some lie, anything.

She kept driving. A few blocks later she glanced in the mirror again and then drove onto the shoulder. A car pulled in behind her. She waited for the driver.

"Afternoon, Melissa." He tipped his hat. "Are you wearing them big boots again or something?"

"Just give me a ticket, Charlie," she snapped, wishing she'd never noticed his flashing lights. Wishing she'd never stayed in Heaven. Wishing she'd never gone out with the wrong guy, who turned out to be the right guy. What a mess.

Charlie leaned his large frame in the window toward her. "I get off in five. You look like you could use a friend, rather than a ticket."

"I've had enough of my friends. Give me the ticket."

He pulled out his book and started writing. She stared ahead. Surely Greg would have had time to catch her by now. Why hadn't he followed her and made everything right? Amy. It always came back to her. He loved Amy, not her. Amy was probably pastor's wife material. While Melissa would only ruin his reputation. His perfect pastor image with his perfect pastor wardrobe.

Charlie handed her a slip of paper. "Melissa, go see your grandmother."

She slipped the car in gear and tore away from the side of the road. At a stoplight she looked at the ticket. Bless his heart—he'd only given her a warning. She headed toward Heavenly Village Retirement Community. Charlie had been right. She needed her Gram.

"Daniel, I have to leave town. It's an urgent family matter," Greg said to his boss after taking the phone call Melissa had given him.

Pastor Jamison stood up behind his desk, compassion etched in his fatherly features. "Can I help in any way, son?"

"Pray for Amy."

"I do, and I will." He stepped around the desk and laid a hand on Greg's shoulder. "And I'll be praying for you as well."

Greg felt a lump in his throat. He thanked God for the great relationship he and Daniel had established right from the start. "I'll make sure I'm back in time for the youth mission trip."

"You take whatever time you need. I'll go on the trip, if I have to. Besides, now might be a good time to get away for awhile."

He knew Daniel was referring to Melissa, but he ignored his pastor's concern. "If you see Melissa, tell her I had to leave unexpectedly."

"Let me pray for you before you go."

A short time later Greg headed to the airport. He tried to call Melissa but reached only the answering machine. He hung up without leaving a message. Something was wrong. He hadn't missed the distressed look on her face when he'd opened the door. Was it worry about the phone call? Or had she heard what Daniel had said about her?

With slow and heavy steps he wandered the airport until his flight back to Seattle. Sweat beaded on his brow, and he raked his hand through his hair in frustration. Back and forth he paced, wondering where Melissa had gone. He needed to talk to her. He needed to see her smile. And kiss her good-bye in case he didn't come back.

He called her again, and this time he left a message. "Melissa, I'm going to be out of town. I'll call you as soon as I can." It probably wasn't what she wanted to hear, but in the crowded airport he didn't want to tell her how he felt.

They announced his flight, and he picked up his bags. He marched to the gate like a solider off to war. Where were his loved ones seeing him off, praying for his safe return? Only one person here in Heaven loved him. And now he worried that might no longer be the case.

If he didn't return, would it matter anyway? Yes, it would. No matter what happened, or where he went, Melissa would always have a piece of his heart. But Amy needed him. May need him for the rest of her life.

That meant he had nothing to offer Melissa. He wished he hadn't left the phone message. Unless he was coming back to Heaven, he'd never call her again. It would only hurt her—and him. He'd rather have her hate him than to think he'd made a choice—when he'd had no choice at all.

❧

"You must be mistaken, honey. No one would ever question your character." Gram still held her close, and Melissa didn't reply. "You sit down, and I'll get us some tea." She filled the kettle and set it on the stove.

Melissa sat in Gram's kitchen nook and pulled a tissue from her purse. She dabbed at her red, swollen eyes then sighed. "I think Greg has a wife or fiancée."

Gram sat next to Melissa. Her hair, neatly styled, belied her age, as did the jeans and top she had donned. "There's no place like Heaven" was emblazoned on the front of the bright yellow T-shirt. "Why do you believe there's someone else?"

"Her name's Amy."

"I don't think you're giving Greg enough credit. I'm certain he would have told you if he were taken."

"He gets a faraway look on his face when her name is mentioned. And then he appears to be in pain." Melissa stared out the window.

Gram poured the tea and busied herself with the sugar and cream. "You love him, don't you?"

She shook her head no, then nodded. She couldn't fool her Gram. She loved Greg. She'd loved him the moment he'd hugged that silly old pine tree the first night they'd met.

"Are you going to walk away from him?"

"I have no choice, Gram. First of all, he's gone. And, second, Pastor Jamison is telling him whom he can and cannot see. And it's not me."

"I think you may be jumping to conclusions here, sweetie."

Melissa turned and eyed her Gram. "I was there."

"I'm sure it's not what you're thinking." Gram patted Melissa's hand. "You need to talk to him."

She'd had enough pain. Did she have to face Greg and have him spell it out, too? No, this time Gram didn't understand, and Melissa couldn't take her advice. She couldn't let her heart be ripped any further. She never wanted to see Greg again. Even if it meant she had to leave Heaven and everything she loved—including him.

Chapter 8

G reg, good to have you back," Daniel Jamison greeted him when he entered the church office.

He reached out and shook his boss's hand. "It's great to be here. I thought I missed the Seattle rain. Guess I didn't." The dreary weather didn't help with the gloom that had settled over him and his family, either.

"You're cutting it awful close, I'd say. What time does the mission trip leave tomorrow?"

He perched on the edge of the secretary's desk. "We'll be meeting here at four thirty a.m."

"You'll forgive me if I'm not here to see you off?"

"No problem. We have a bon voyage crew. Many of our senior citizens in the church have each prayed daily for one of our youth. They'll be here tomorrow morning to pray for them and see us off. Just before I left, some strong friendships were beginning to form. I hope it's continued."

"That's great," Daniel said as he strolled toward his office. "I think this would look good in the denominational newsletter."

Greg shook his head. Some things never change. He slid off the desk and went into his own office, closing the door behind him. He picked up the phone and dialed Melissa's number. The line was busy.

He shuffled some papers then tried the number again. This time he got through, but the answering machine picked up. He left a message asking her to call him.

At the end of the day when he hadn't heard from her, he headed home to do some laundry and finish packing. He prayed she would call, but by eleven p.m. his phone had remained silent. Maybe he should go over there. He knew he should get some sleep since four a.m. came early, but he needed to talk to Melissa. He'd thought of her continually in Seattle. He had no doubts about how he felt. God had granted him a peace about it too.

He jumped into his car and drove over to her place. All the lights were out. Should he wake her up? It would be another week before he saw her if he didn't. He knocked on the door but received no answer. He assumed she must be out and went home, feeling as if he'd lost his best friend.

He had a message on his answering machine when he returned. He hit the play button and listened.

"Greg, it's Melissa."

She didn't sound right. Like maybe she'd been crying. He turned up the volume.

"I'm sorry I'm not telling you this in person." She paused. "I think it would be best if we don't see each other anymore. It's hard for me to say this, but I think God brought you into my life when I needed someone, but it's time I stopped depending on you and moved on. Thanks for everything, *friend*."

She'd made it very clear he had only been a temporary thing. She considered him a friend by the way she'd pointedly said the word.

He slammed his fist on the bookcase, and the picture frames rattled. Not only did his hand hurt, but so did his heart.

But he would not give up. He'd pray and think of something by the time he arrived back in town. He believed God had indeed brought them together as Melissa had said, and he felt certain God didn't want them apart. He loved Melissa, and he'd prove it to her.

Melissa hung up the phone and bowed her head. *Forgive me, Lord, for not telling the truth. And for trusting Greg, rather than You.*

It wouldn't be easy trying to forget him, but she appreciated what they'd shared.

"Lissa, what's the catalog for?" her mother called out from the kitchen.

She walked into the room and sat at the table. "It's for Heaven Community College."

Her mother stared wide-eyed at her.

"What? You never heard of college?"

"Okay, what's going on?"

"Since I'm no longer babysitting the twins and I've decided to give up my lucrative fly-fish business, I decided it was time to figure out what I want to be when I grow up."

"And?" Her mother sat down and waited for her to continue.

"I'm still thinking."

"Are you going to tell me what happened between you and Greg? Or are you going to run away?"

"Going to college is not running away."

Her mother shook her head. "I'm not saying that at all. I know you're hurting. I want to help."

"Let's just say I'm not pastor's wife material and leave it at that."

"Oh, honey." Her mother stood and embraced her. "Anyone would be a fool if they thought that."

"Thanks, Mom." She pulled away from the hug. "I think I'll be okay. I'm trusting God, and I won't analyze this to death. I don't know why He brought Greg into my life, but I'm thankful He did."

"My little girl's grown up."

"Don't go getting sentimental on me now!" They laughed, and Melissa padded off to bed.

She flipped through her Bible and stopped at Proverbs 3. It was the verse Greg had shared with her. "I'm trusting You, God. Help me get past this. Help me to move on with my life."

But as she spoke the words aloud, she had the distinct feeling they merely bounced off the walls and shattered when they landed on the floor. Broken into a million pieces, like her heart. But she couldn't hold Greg back from his job, and she didn't want to take him from Amy. Why did doing the right thing have to hurt so much?

❧

"Lissa, what perfect timing. Jeff just finished our Internet class, and we're going to take some refreshments in the dining room."

Melissa felt herself freeze on the spot. She didn't want to spend time with Jeff. Especially now with Greg gone. Gram always believed in getting back in the saddle once you've been thrown. Dating, in her eyes, would be the same. Falling off a horse seemed less painful to Melissa.

Gram made certain Jeff sat beside her once they reached the busy dining hall. He seemed nervous and pushed up his glasses several times before he finally spoke. "It's nice to see you again, Melissa."

"Thanks. I hear you're doing a great job teaching."

"I enjoy it."

"Melissa loves technology," Gram said, leaning between them. "She has one of those little music players that sounds like the band is in the room when she plays it."

"MP3?" Jeff asked.

Melissa shook her head. "Minidisc."

"And don't forget your little electronic black thingy. Jeff has one, too."

"Visor?"

"Palm IIIc," Melissa said.

"See—you two even talk the same language. Look at how well you're communicating. I knew what I was doing. . . ." Gram's voice trailed off, and a smile played across her lips. Melissa couldn't miss the gleam in her eyes. Then she read Gram's new T-shirt: *Matchmaker*.

Dread filled her. Stopping Gram would be like trying to calm a tornado.

"Jeff, why don't you show Lissa your web page?"

He cleared his throat and stood. "Ah. Yeah. Sure."

Melissa looked around the room. No way out. She followed him to the library in silence, his shiny shoes squeaking with every step.

"Your Gram is such a great lady." He sat down at the computer and reached for the mouse. After a few clicks a video bounced onto the screen.

"Yeah, we love her." Melissa moved closer to get a better view. As the screen flashed before her, Jeff provided a brief narration.

"This is like a public service announcement site. It provides awareness for the dangers of drunk drivers. Several major medical facilities, police agencies, and fire halls help support the site."

"I like the colors you've used. The flash looks good, but can you slow down the image montage?"

Jeff clicked a few keys faster than Melissa could say Internet, and the flash ran again. Pictures of tragic crash scenes transitioned onto the monitor one after the other. Some of them were horrific.

"Wait. Can you stop that graphic?"

"I can do better than that," he replied. More fast *tick-tick-tick* as he typed in commands. The image popped up, and Melissa scrutinized it carefully.

"Someone you know?"

She blinked back tears and squeaked out, "Yes."

"Doesn't look like anyone could have survived. My stuff is at home, but if I'm not mistaken this accident was in Portland or maybe Seattle. The driver walked away while the passenger sustained massive burns."

Melissa gazed at the screen. Greg's tortured face leaned over someone—a woman—on the stretcher. She figured it was Amy. Had Greg been driving?

"...check my notes and find the story."

"I'm sorry. I missed what you said."

"I can probably find the article since I had to get permission for the photographs."

Did she want to know? No, she didn't. These last two weeks God had constantly reminded her to trust Him, and she had. Greg would stay devoted to Amy, even if she had been badly burned. Thus, she would never try to force Greg to choose. The time had come to let him go for good. "No. Thanks for the offer, though."

"If you change your mind, let me know."

"Your site's impressive. Is that what you do for a living?"

"No. This is just fun stuff. Like your fly-fish web page."

"Well, don't hold that against me. I'm still learning."

"Your HTML code looked good. Use scripts much?"

"Nah. I don't have time to learn the difficult stuff. The mouse rollover is my masterpiece."

Jeff laughed, and Melissa realized he was actually a nice guy. Too bad things had worked out the way they had. She wondered what would have happened had Greg not shown up. She shook her head, hoping to rid herself of such thoughts.

"I have to get going. Thanks, Jeff."

"Yeah, it's been fun. If you ever need help with your web page, give me a call."

"You'll be the first one I turn to if I need someone." And she meant it.

After saying good-bye to Jeff and then Gram, Melissa left the community residence. She could tell it would be only a matter of time before Gram hatched another scheme. Maybe Melissa could be in Timbuktu by then. She had to find a way to stop the blind-date disasters.

Chapter 9

Melissa gave up. She couldn't fight Gram. She missed Greg, but she knew she needed to get over him. Whether he had a wife or girlfriend or whatever didn't matter. What mattered was that he would not be hers. He'd warned her that people would let her down. She figured everyone else might, but not him. She'd figured wrong.

She figured she'd never go out on another blind date, either. Again, she'd figured wrong. But this time she held her ground. This time she had terms. She'd agree to this folly, but then no more. No matter what happened, she'd never have to be set up again. What troubled her right now was how easily Gram had accepted her conditions. Perhaps her worries were for nothing. Or maybe she'd be forced to spend her evening with Jeff. Maybe she'd get a headache—fast.

"Honey, you'd better get ready. Your date's due soon."

"Can't I go like this?"

Her mother sighed.

"Fine. I'll change."

"And, Lissa?"

"I know. No storm commando boots," she said as she stood up from the table and placed her dirty dishes in the sink.

"I wasn't going to say that."

"Sorry, Mom. But you know how I hate this matchmaking stuff."

"We want to see you happy. Like you were with—" She stopped. "I mean—"

"I know what you mean." Melissa gave her mother a hug and headed off to her room to get ready for her date. Or, as Greg had called it, her disaster.

If she ever did find the man God had planned for her, she'd have lots of silly stories to share. At this point, though, it was difficult for Melissa to laugh about any of them.

She'd realized that what she'd had with Greg had not been about being dependent or having someone to fix everything. It had been about sharing. About carrying one another's burdens. It had been about loving someone and being loved in return.

Stop it. Don't think about that now.

She showered and put on a nice pair of white slacks with an emerald green shell.

Pulling out the set of pearls her Gram had given her, she slipped them around her neck. Gram had told her they were for her wedding. Maybe she should take them off.

Her mother knocked. "I'm going next door to check on Mrs. Wilson. Listen for the doorbell, will you?"

It felt a little like *déjà vu* for Melissa as she opened the door and stepped out of her bedroom. Hadn't her mother conveniently left the house on her last blind date? "Okay, Mom."

"You look lovely, darling."

"Thanks. Should I take the pearls off?"

"Gram gave them to you to wear, not keep in a box. You know how she feels about that."

Melissa knew. Gram didn't save things for special occasions; every day was a special occasion for her. "Okay."

Melissa paced the kitchen waiting for her date. She felt nervous.

The door chime brought her out of her thoughts. Her heart quickened, and she tried to calm herself. As she approached the front door, she resisted peering through the peephole and simply opened it wide.

Her mouth dropped in surprise.

"Hi," he said with a smile that threatened to stop her heart.

Melissa seemed paralyzed.

"I hope I'm not late. I wouldn't want someone else to whisk you away."

"You're my date?"

"Your real date." He held up jazzy rollerblades. "And you're not dressed right."

She snatched a lock of hair and clamped it between her lips.

"I've been practicing. I'll beat you this time for sure."

Finally she found her tongue. "Greg, I can't go out with you. We've been through this. I'm sorry."

"Mel, please. I need to explain about Amy."

She winced. He called her Mel, and it still felt so right. But it was all wrong. She needed to close the door and leave Greg behind. She couldn't bear to be hurt again.

"Please."

She let him in the house and prayed she wouldn't regret it. Once they were seated in the kitchen, she poured two glasses of iced tea and sat as far away from him as she could.

"I don't know what you heard that day at the church, but I can assure you, it's not what you think."

He was reopening her wounds. Would she be able to stand it?

"I don't know where to start."

Melissa gave him a hint. "Amy." She watched as his eyes clouded and pain etched his features.

"Amy. One of my greatest failures in life," he said with a sigh. "I should have been there for her. Protected her. Kept her safe."

"Greg, only God could do all those things. Sometimes we only see what we should have done later, after the catastrophe."

"I knew. I just didn't do anything." He raked a hand through his wavy hair.

"Why don't you start at the beginning? Were you married already?"

"Married?" He looked up, his eyes wide open. "No," he said, shaking his head. "Is that what you think? She's my little sister."

Melissa struggled with her feelings. She felt relieved that Greg wasn't married, but it pained her to think of all Amy had gone through.

"She was engaged to a guy I couldn't stand. I did everything to try to break them up. When it finally happened—after I'd stopped trying—Amy was devastated. Though I had not been responsible for the parting, I still felt like a heel. So I kept to myself. We didn't talk about what had happened, and Amy slipped away from us, becoming despondent."

Melissa moved to Greg's side and took his hand. It was simply an act of friendship, she told herself.

"She began going out drinking and trying drugs, but I never noticed. I didn't want to notice. One night she nearly died in a terrible accident."

She'd seen the pictures, and it wrenched her heart.

"Her date had been drinking, and they crashed into a guard rail. The car caught fire. Burns covered most of her body, and she's been in and out of a coma ever since."

"I'm so sorry, Greg."

"It's all my fault. I didn't want her to marry a jerk. Who was I to determine what was best for her?"

"You did it because you loved her."

"Obviously not enough. I never saw her problems. I'm the reason she spends her days in a hospital. She took a turn for the worse and nearly died. That's why I went back. She's stable again. But what type of life does she have in a bed connected to tubes?" Melissa recognized the bitterness in his voice.

"Greg, you could no more save your sister than I could my father. And, in the words of a dear friend of mine, we have to trust God and lean not on our own understanding. Forgive yourself."

"I drive her car as a constant reminder of what I did to her."

"Maybe she gave it to you as a constant reminder of the love she has for her big brother."

For the first time since they'd started talking, he smiled at her. "I told Pastor Jamison he was wrong about you."

She inhaled deeply, remembering the painful words he'd spoken. "That's not what I heard."

"Did you hear everything?"

"Just the part about your agreeing with him that I'm not suitable for you."

"Oh." He looked into her eyes with longing. "I should tell you that Ursula had a hand in her father's distrust of you. Us. Guess she wanted to pay us back for the night we went to the fair."

"That doesn't surprise me." She felt a pang of sorrow for the girl and prayed God would bless Ursula.

"And, yes, I said you were not pastor's wife material—on the outside. But that on the inside there was no one better for the job."

Had he said what she hoped he'd said?

"I know God is still doing a great work in us. We have lots of things to sort out. But that's the best part of growing old together. Sharing the joys as well as the pains. If we were perfect, what type of life would that be?"

Melissa's eyes pooled with unshed tears. "No, we're not perfect—"

"But I think we're perfect for each other," he interrupted her and looked into her eyes.

"A tomboy like me? With Mr. Immaculately Dressed and Pressed?"

"A beautiful woman, inside and out, with a heart bigger than the state of Arizona. A heart I love. In fact, I love everything about you, Mel. Can you forgive me? Can you love me?"

She flung her arms around his neck. "Yes. Yes."

"Want to be married at the park on rollerblades?"

"No. I think I actually want to wear the white dress." She giggled and pulled back to seek out his eyes. Their gazes locked, and she forced herself to breathe.

"Okay, but there's one thing."

She stiffened. As she felt the panic rise in her, she closed her eyes and forced herself to listen.

Trust Me.

She relaxed. "I know—you get to pick the radio station."

"That too," he said with a grin then dropped his hands from her shoulders to her waist, encircling her. He raised an eyebrow as if he were about to lecture her. "Don't ever change. I love you just the way you are."

Joy burst forth along with a multitude of tears. "And I love you."

A sweet sensation of belonging enveloped her as they kissed. Then he leaned forward and whispered in her ear, "So will you be wearing boots under the dress?"

BEV HUSTON

Bev Huston lives in British Columbia (where residents don't tan, they rust) with her husband, two children, sister and two cats who give new meaning to the word aloof. Bev began her writing career in 1994 when, out of frustration, she wrote a humorous column about call waiting service, which sold right away. She is a contributing editor for The Christian Communicator and spent four years as the inspirational reviewer for Romantic Times Bookclub.

Name That Tune

by Yvonne Lehman

Dedication

To Elizabeth and Adam
for their invaluable music information

Sing joyfully to the LORD, you righteous;
it is fitting for the upright to praise him.
Praise the LORD with the harp;
make music to him on the ten-stringed lyre.
PSALM 33:1–2

Chapter 1

On Friday morning, Eva Alono acknowledged Tristan with a "Hi," mingled with the other quartet members greeting him as he walked through the doorway of the practice room with the morning mail. Even when he said, "This one's from Vizcaya," Eva felt a sense of regret rather than hope. She remained seated and kept rubbing her horsehair bow across the rosin, preparing it for the practice session. Next, she'd make sure her violin strings were in tune.

Tristan walked closer. "Addressed to you, Eva."

"Me?" She quickly laid her bow aside and took the letter. Normally, since she'd contacted Vizcaya, they'd sent seasonal programs addressed to the Classical Strings Quartet, not her personally. One of her major goals was for the quartet to become recognized in their hometown of Miami. If their résumé could include having played at Vizcaya, they'd have made their mark locally.

She'd sent their press kit to the museum over two years ago and was left wondering if they'd trashed it. Excitement mounted as she held the envelope up to the light from the window, trying to see inside. "Is it an invitation? Or just more of their promotional material? Oh, I can't look."

Tristan laughed. "You'll never find out that way."

Rissa reached out her hand. "Here, let me."

"No." Eva lowered her arm and held the letter close to her chest.

Amid the sighs and head shakes, Tyrone drew out a low, plaintive moan from his cello.

Rissa turned away. "She's not going to open it. Let's get on with our practice. I have a date with my mate."

"Okay," Eva retorted. "I'll do it. Where's a letter opener?"

"On the end of your hand," Tristan said.

Eva shook her head. She couldn't open it with her finger and chance leaving a ragged edge. If this was an invitation or even a belated personal response, it belonged in the quartet's scrapbook and a copy in her personal one.

Rissa produced a fingernail file.

Eva read the letter, occasionally glancing up at the expectant faces. She tried to keep her own face straight. Finally she could stand it no longer. "Yippee! We've hit the jackpot. Who says a prophet's not respected in his own hometown?"

The group's excitement matched Eva's until Rissa asked the question, "What's the date we're to play?"

"During the Renaissance Festival."

"That lasts four days," Tyrone said.

"No." Eva shook her head. "They want us for only one day. They must have had a cancellation and chose us. You know they plan their programs long in advance."

"You're right," Tristan said. "The festival is only a few weeks from now. Cynthia and I are planning to set a wedding date, and we both have agreed it should be as soon as possible. We've wasted too many years apart already."

Rissa said what was on Eva's mind. "We've waited for two years just to get a response from Vizcaya. The date's not going to be negotiable."

Tyrone sighed. "You know, I have to check with my better half now before making any decisions."

Rissa cast a longing look at Eva. "We'll try our best, Eva." She glanced around at the others. "Won't we, guys?"

"Sure," both men replied and set to tuning their instruments.

The practice seemed like a waste of time to Eva. However, she inwardly praised herself for playing the required notes even if her heart wasn't in it. The entire group sounded dull and lifeless. Not long ago they would be literally jumping up and down at this opportunity. One day at Vizcaya could have lifelong career implications.

Now, it didn't seem to matter to her friends. She felt they were so caught up in their personal lives that they no longer cared about the quartet and its future.

By the time the practice ended, she felt like the letter had given her the emotion of a sugar high that had now plunged her into a deep low. The others said they'd get back to her about their schedules as soon as possible.

It began to look like one of her major goals might bite the dust. This was no longer a goal of the quartet, just hers alone.

"Let's go to lunch," Rissa suggested.

Both Tristan and Tyrone had other plans.

"How about you, Eva?" Rissa asked.

Eva shook her head. "Thanks, but I'm playing at the restaurant tonight. Mine and Grandpa's dirty laundry is piled up and so is my bedroom. Some other time, okay?"

"Sure." A light sparked in Rissa's eyes. "I can always run by SilkWood and see if Jason's free."

Eva was happy that Rissa and Jason had found each other, but she missed that closeness and time she used to spend with Rissa.

Rissa must have sensed her melancholy. "Oh, Eva. I know things aren't turning out the way we've planned for years. The quartet still means the world to each of us. It's just that right now we're caught up in having found our life's mate. You understand?"

"Sure," Eva said. "I'm okay." She forced a small laugh. "I just miss my friends."

Rissa hugged her. "We'll always be friends."

Eva nodded. "I know."

After the others left, Eva walked around in the workshop part of the basement, hardly aware of the familiar odor of wood, glue, and varnish. Her gaze swept across the repair section where some violins needed major repair while others needed only a new string.

In another section violins lay in varied stages of being made. Most of her work consisted of making the beginner violins. Some fit the hands of a small child, while others were for adults. Grandpa made most of the violins that would be played by the experts. But she was learning.

That idea didn't excite her today. She thought about how everything in her life was being turned upside down. Often, she thought about her three major goals in life that she'd planned out four years ago. One was to serve the Lord with her life and music, another was for the quartet to become known as professional in her hometown, and the last was to someday make a violin comparable to the Stradivarius.

"At least I still have the goal of serving the Lord," Eva said aloud to herself, feeling rather guilty that her tone of voice sounded resentful instead of joyful.

She walked over to the CD player where Mozart was ready and waiting since this morning, when Grandpa had listened to it. She agreed with her grandpa and former music instructors, who had said people who love Mozart's music regard it as the closest thing to heaven on earth. She pushed the PLAY button and welcomed the melodic tones of the great master.

As she listened, a nagging thought found its way to the forefront. Was she destined to be an old maid? She'd heard older people say they wanted to grow old gracefully. She was only twenty-six, but many people that age were married and had children. She hoped, if she must face life without a mate, she might do it gracefully.

A deep sigh escaped her throat. For a moment longer, she listened to the heavenly music while a sense of earthly loneliness wafted over her.

Later that evening, the front door of the restaurant closed behind the silhouette of a man, blocking out the bright sun that had caused Eva to blink against the evening's slanting rays.

"Welcome to Alono's, sir. Do you have a reservation?"

"No, but I would like a table for one, please."

"I'm sorry, but tonight is reservations only. The house is filled."

He looked around. "Unless they're invisible, I would say the house is not filled and there are many available tables, miss."

Eva took in a deep breath, steeling herself for whatever reaction might come from informing him that the dinner hour was almost upon them and all tables were reserved. However, his head turned toward her again with a rather indignant lift of his chin. Her eyes had readjusted to the dimness of the restaurant, and her breath came out in a rush. The most telling sign was the realization that he held in his hand—a violin case.

"You're. . . ?"

Her gaze played over the dark hair that curled about his ears and down the back of his neck. Something about the curved shape of his nose and heavy eyebrows over piercing dark eyes was exactly like the newspaper picture she'd pored over not two hours ago—even to the dark suit and bow tie.

"If that means I may have a table, then yes, I am," he said.

His piercing gaze bore into hers as his chin lowered, as if he were a little boy pleading for a piece of candy. Was he flirting with her? Well, she'd encountered all sorts of guises patrons often used to get a table when none were available. She would say to him what she'd heard her parents say when some of their friends dropped in at the last moment.

"I will find you a table if I have to build it myself, Mr. Baldovino."

"You. . .own the restaurant?" he asked.

"My parents do," she said. "I'm Eva Alono."

That slight movement of his eyebrows up, then down in rhythm to his nod gave her the impression of a conductor giving his nod to the orchestra at the beginning of a concert.

Strangely, she could almost hear the music.

"Thank you," he said. "I'm Georgio to such a lovely young lady who appears to know me."

"Thank you," she said, not accustomed to such a compliment from a famous violinist, or anyone for that matter, except maybe her grandpa. In fact, she'd never been face-to-face with such a famous violinist before. The newspaper articles and advertisements said he had been a child prodigy, the son of famous opera stars and musicians. He'd been the child actor in many productions of *Madame Butterfly*, accustomed to audiences and orchestras. In his teen years, he'd played the violin in the orchestra while his parents performed. Now, at only thirty years of age, he had become one of the most widely acclaimed violinists in the world and in a matter of weeks would be performing at the concert hall.

"I only know you from some of your publicity," she said. "I have already made arrangements for one of the best seats at your concert."

She thought he looked surprised, but he said, "I'm honored."

She smiled. "So, what can I do but offer you the best seat in our restaurant?" She picked up a printed program and stepped out from behind the partition. "We don't use menus on Fridays, we use a program."

He paused. "Is this a private party?"

"No," she said. "It's just that Friday nights are so popular, we insist upon reservations. Would you prefer a table up front?"

He followed her into the large dining area and looked around at tables where waiters and waitresses were ensuring their stations were properly set up. "Perhaps near the stage," he said, "at the side."

Eva felt like she was walking on air and at the same time was afraid she'd trip over her own feet or bump into a table. She felt sure he'd wanted to sit at the side so he wouldn't be in the light from the stage when the entertainment began.

The thought of that caused her heart to drop into her socks—except she wasn't wearing socks. How could she possibly play the violin with Georgio Baldovino listening?

Poorly, probably!

At least she was dressed elegantly in a Spanish-style red dress with a vee neckline and a multilayered gold necklace. She wore large hoop earrings, and her dark hair was pulled back into a twist, adorned with a gold clasp. On Friday nights, when her schedule allowed, she donned Spanish-style clothes and became part of the restaurant's entertainment. Tonight, the maître d' was delayed, so Eva was elected by her parents to seat any patrons with reservations who might come earlier than the dinner hour.

Georgio approved of the small table for two at the side, where he would have a perfect view of the stage. "Very nice." He stood holding on to the back of the chair. "Would you join me for a moment, or are you too busy making tables for your invisible guests?"

She hoped the dim lighting covered her blush. She did not respond to his request, being sure her imagination had conjured up the thought that he asked her to join him. Such a thing could happen only in one's dreams.

"I'll. . .I'll get your water." She laid the program on the table.

He nodded and pulled out his chair, sat, and placed his violin under the table.

Eva hurried into the kitchen. Marco, the waiter for the section she'd just left, followed her in and picked up a gold-rimmed crystal goblet.

"I'll take his water," she told him.

Marco looked dumbfounded, and the chef glanced up from where he was artistically decorating dessert dishes with strings of liquid chocolate.

Lest they think Marco had done something wrong, she quickly told them about Georgio Baldovino.

The chef seemed to think his chocolate was more important, and Marco shrugged a shoulder.

"Never mind," she said. "Just don't come near his table until I give the word."

Marco filled the goblet with water. Looking unhappy, he handed it to her.

Eva took a deep breath, left the kitchen, and walked toward the table, where Georgio was looking at the program. She was placing the goblet on the table when someone walked up beside her. Perhaps the maître d' had arrived. Just as she started to let go of the glass, the person in that deep baritone voice she'd never forgotten said, "Hello, Beautiful."

More startled than when she'd recognized Georgio Baldovino, Eva whirled around, despite telling herself to remain calm upon looking at that tall, blond man with the dreamy sea green eyes. Her emotions didn't obey, and her fingers loosened from around the glass. She felt it tip. Her head jerked toward it and she tried to reach it, just as Georgio tried. Their hands collided and the goblet toppled over. The fragile glass clinked against the table and shattered as if a soprano had sung her high C note. Water poured across the table.

Eva gasped as Georgio jumped up, jerked his violin from under the table, and stepped back, causing the chair to overturn and crash to the floor.

In horror, she stared at Georgio, who held out his violin case and gazed at it as if someone had attacked his baby. He managed to mumble in a relieved tone, "It's not wet."

"Are. . .are you?" Eva stammered.

"No." He nodded toward the table with an expression of disdain. "However, you have a completely doused table and a huge puddle forming on the floor."

Jack Darren stepped closer and reached for the centerpiece on the table. "Eva, maybe you can find a sponge or something to clean this up." He moved the centerpiece to another table. "Speaking of sponges," he said in the manner of one telling a story, "have you ever wondered how much deeper the ocean would be without sponges?"

It took a moment, then a small chuckle sounded from Georgio. Eva felt relieved that he would laugh rather than storm out of the restaurant in disgust. Eva smiled after a fleeting glance at Jack, then at Georgio, who returned her smile, then laid his violin on a nearby chair.

Jack always had a way of putting people—except her—at ease. He could turn a sticky situation into a bearable one and make you see the humor in things instead of getting bent out of shape.

The water incident began to seem trivial. Come to think of it, although proving herself to be a total klutz, she felt rather good about being called "lovely" and "beautiful" by two different men in less than five minutes.

One was a man she wanted to know better. The other was one she had tried to forget.

Chapter 2

While Eva summoned a waiter, Jack introduced himself to the man with the violin and recognized the name of Georgio Baldovino. He quickly deduced that Eva hadn't met the violinist before and they weren't here together, otherwise she wouldn't have been bringing water to his table when there were numerous waiters and waitresses about.

It held to reason she was trying to meet this fellow. Spilling his water was one way to do it, but it was also taking a chance. Had the water seeped into his violin case, this restaurant could well be in for a lawsuit.

But he didn't think she did it purposely. He'd startled her. Had he been anyone but Jack Darren, he felt sure she would have remained as calm as a cucumber. He understood her reaction. He'd hoped she'd grown out of the resentment she'd had for him and the hurt she'd felt over the entire incident with him and her grandpa. Apparently, she hadn't. Perhaps she'd never expected, and never wanted, to see him again.

Eva returned, followed by Marco, who greeted Jack exuberantly, then set about seeing that a younger waiter, obviously being trained by Marco, returned the table and floor to its previous condition.

"Again, I'm sorry," Eva said, moving closer to Baldovino. "Please excuse me now. I play the violin at the beginning of the meal."

"How delightful," Baldovino said with exuberance.

"No," Eva contradicted. "Compared with you, I'm very much the amateur."

"Ah," he returned. "And compared with you, I am the rain and you are the rainbow. And you will return to me, no?"

"Thank you. Yes."

Jack realized Eva had a confidence now that she hadn't four years ago. He stepped over to Eva, feeling daunted by her indifference to him, and this. . .exchange. . .going on between her and Baldovino. Neither suggested that he join them. "Are your parents here?" he asked.

"Yes, and I just saw Grandpa go to the family table. Go on back."

After knocking on the Alonos' office door, Jack received the kind of "welcome home" greeting from Eva's parents that he'd desired. As he expected, they told him to sit at the family table. He got a cup of coffee and seated himself with Grandpa Al, across the room from where Baldovino now sat and where Marco was putting two place settings. As if sensing someone looking at him, Baldovino's gaze seemed to meet Jack's from across the room, which was beginning to fill with expectant patrons.

Jack quickly returned his attention to his coffee cup.

"So, you found yourself, huh?" Al asked in that blunt way of his.

Jack laughed lightly. "That is why I left, isn't it?" He looked at the wise old man. "I discovered I took myself with me. Couldn't escape him. And, too," he added on a wistful note, "I discovered I left a part of myself right here in my own hometown."

Al was nodding as he eyed the waiters taking gold-rimmed crystal goblets of water to the tables.

"And you're not surprised at that," Jack said, rather than ask.

"No." Al returned his attention to Jack. "You were sort of a lost soul after your parents decided to take their production tours abroad. Left you without a base."

Jack was nodding. "Thanks to you, I found that base. And I have it now no matter where I alight. Now I'd like to give others the kind of lifeline you gave to me."

Al reached over and grasped Jack's arm. "Good to have you home, Jack."

"Like the saying goes, home is where the heart is."

Al gave him that knowing stare, then focused on the stage when Roberto Alono announced, "Welcome." After a brief greeting and informing the patrons about their choice of two entrées, Roberto announced the protocol for the evening, although it was printed on the programs.

Jack knew the reason for the programs. Many patrons came to Alono's precisely for the opportunity to see Roberto and Beverly Alono and would seek autographs from the once-famous pair.

After adding his own words about the artists who would entertain between courses, Roberto introduced Eva. He said she was one of a string quartet of growing popularity and working with her grandpa in his business of violin making and repair.

"My lovely daughter, Eva Alono, will now play our invocation on the violin." A serious look crossed his face as he looked out at the guests and said, "Blessed be the name of the Lord."

Strange, how nothing seemed to change in four years, then again everything seemed to change. The routine was basically the same. Sometimes the Alono family had groups come in and perform. Jack himself had played the piano and sung many times.

Jack remembered his parents singing there one evening. His dad played the piano while his mom stood with her arm resting on it, looking at his dad while they sang, "So in Love."

Jack had glanced at Eva and saw a special light in her eyes as she gazed at him. He had looked away and dismissed it. He hadn't been ready to consider love on a serious plane.

Now, Eva coolly disregarded him.

The restaurant patrons became courteously silent as Eva stepped into the spotlight. She smiled briefly, lifted the violin to her shoulder, placed the side of her face on the chin rest, raised the bow, and with a professional expertise began playing the beautiful melody of "Let Us Break Bread Together."

Jack closed his eyes to concentrate, not on the woman, but on the words that included breaking bread together, drinking the cup together, praising God together, on one's knees. He knew the words and the meaning of the song, which was a traditional spiritual.

He felt the joy of the song about one facing the rising sun, imploring the Lord to have mercy on him. Jack had experienced it. He had even sung it here in this place, words that had been beautiful words, but not the priority of his life. The memory of it, and the Alonos, had drawn him back. . .back to his roots.

When Eva finished, Jack, along with the patrons, applauded as she made an appreciative bow, then left the stage to share a table, not with her family, but with someone who could possibly present the opportunity for her to have a much larger audience than she could ever have at Alono's.

After the salad course, Roberto Alono and his English wife, Beverly, who looked as Spanish as any other flamenco dancer with her russet-colored hair and dark eyes, wowed the crowd with their bright costumes and fancy footwork and the flirtatious glances between the pair.

They had been professional artists of the dance before retiring. They had canceled tours and settled down to raise Eva and help Al with the care of his ailing wife. They opened Alono's Restaurant. Now they danced only for each other and to the Lord.

After the dance, Beverly and Roberto changed into evening clothes and joined Jack and Al. Waiters brought out huge round trays balanced on their hands and shoulders, then served the chosen entrées to the happy guests conversing in lively tones.

Having read the program, Jack felt they, too, would look forward to the break between the entrées and dessert when the folksinging with guitar would be performed by several of the waiters and waitresses who were students of music.

"Well," Beverly commented, "looks like Eva is occupied this evening."

Jack explained the status of Baldovino.

Of course they had heard of him, and Al filled in the rest from what he'd known and read in the paper.

"Ohh," Beverly said with lifted eyebrows, while Roberto stared across the room. "Did you know about this, Al?"

His "no" was as drawn out as Beverly's exclamation. "She would have mentioned it or perhaps have shouted it from the rooftops."

A delighted little laugh escaped Beverly's exquisite throat. "Then perhaps this is rather like a director who drops in at a community theater and discovers a star."

They all laughed lightly while Jack pasted a smile on his face.

Later, after the performances ended and guests lingered over coffee while a pianist played, Jack noticed that Baldovino was showing his violin to Eva. Likely, it was a Stradivarius. Knowing how she felt about the violin, Jack knew that would impress her more than anything he could do.

From Eva's point of view, Jack had taken from her what she had considered a most valuable and desired asset—something he could not return to her.

And judging from her reticence tonight, she had not forgiven him.

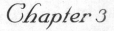

Chapter 3

Eva couldn't wait to get Rissa on the phone.

"Oh, Rissa. Sorry if I woke you. But this couldn't wait. You'll never guess whose table I shared last night at the restaurant."

Rissa laughed. "Sure I can. This will pay you back for calling before I've had my morning coffee. It's Jack. He called yesterday to let me know he's back in town and said he would surprise you at the restaurant. Ha. Gotcha!"

Eva moaned. Her emotional balloon was momentarily deflated. "No, Rissa. I mean, Jack was there, but that's not who I'm excited about."

"Well, it sure used to be," Rissa reminded her.

Eva closed her eyes against that statement and the memories it elicited. She didn't want to think about Jack. She didn't want to talk about Jack. He was history. "That was years ago."

"Okay, without caffeine I couldn't possibly imagine who would make you chance waking me early on Saturday morning if it's not Jack."

Eva wished the name Jack was not in Rissa's vocabulary! She said with the best Italian accent she could muster, "I met Georgio."

"Georgio? What is that?"

"A person," Eva wailed.

"Well, Georgio who?"

"Rissa. There's only one Georgio."

Eva could almost hear Rissa thinking. "Not. . .not the one in the newspaper article that you cut out and danced around with!"

"The one and only. Not only did I spend the evening with him. He's coming here at ten o'clock this morning."

Now, Eva could visualize Rissa sitting up in bed with her mouth wide open in disbelief. Eva laughed. "We ate together. We talked and he asked me to call him Georgio. Annnnd. . ." She stretched out the word. "He even said I was a lovely lady."

Eva forced away the word "beautiful" that Jack had said. But that was only a phrase. She'd often said, "Come on, baby," to her cat named Scat. But Scat was still a cat.

"Eva! That's terrific."

"Woke you up quicker than caffeine, didn't it?" Eva laughed.

"I'll say," Rissa replied. "See how things can change? Lately, you've been concerned about being an old maid. Now, you're telling me you've got two gorgeous guys at your beck and call."

"Rissa, stop that. Jack has never been at my beck and call. He wouldn't help me start a band and he left. Stayed away four years, doing who knows what." She took a deep breath, trying to stifle her resentment of having a keen idea of "what" he had been doing.

"Well, I think Jack came to his senses and that's why he came home. And you said you're going to see Georgio this morning?"

Eva sighed. "I guess I'd better be honest with you, Rissa. Georgio came to the restaurant with a purpose. He had a problem with his violin. At the music store, he was told that Al Alono was a noted violin maker and repairman. The manager told Georgio if Grandpa wasn't home, he'd likely be at Alono's since it was Friday evening. After dinner, I took Georgio to Grandpa, and the appointment was made for ten o'clock this morning. And you can believe I'll be downstairs when he comes. That is, if I ever get off this phone."

"You go, girl, and make yourself irresistible."

"I was that last night," Eva said in an exaggerated tone. "Today, I become plain ol' Eva again."

"Honey, you could never be plain. You know the Lord works in mysterious ways. I have a feeling this is going to lead somewhere special."

Eva inhaled deeply. "Oh, Rissa. I wasn't too realistic last night in that fanciful setting of candlelight and soft music. But in the light of this beautiful clear spring day outside my window, I have to face the fact he's just coming to get his violin repaired."

"Just be there," Rissa said. "Remember, not long ago I had no idea Jason existed. Now look!"

"Oh, why are we talking like this?" Eva wailed. "A famous violinist is coming to get his violin repaired and we're talking moonlight and roses. Last night I was just a distraction for him. Who knows; he's probably even married."

"Make sure you're down there to find out."

"Okay, gotta go. I'll let you know what happens."

Eva showered, then put in a CD and listened to violin music while she dressed. Applying makeup wasn't the easiest thing to do while envisioning fragile little fairies flitting around on gossamer wings in rhythm to the airy tones of a violinist.

Unless an emergency occurred, the basement shop wasn't open on weekends and Eva often slept in on Saturdays unless the quartet was away for a performance. Was it only coincidence—or divine providence—that she had nothing pressing for today?

Although they'd had many noted violinists come to Grandpa, and he'd been a noted one himself in earlier years, no one of Georgio's stature had come to their shop.

Food wasn't on her top-priority list at the moment, but a growling stomach in front of Georgio would surely be a discordant note. She toasted a bagel, slathered it with cream cheese, and downed a cup of coffee with it.

At 9:45 she switched off the music and descended the stairs to the basement shop. She floated down as if it were every day that she dressed in a silk blouse and dress slacks and took extra care with her makeup and hair. Although she'd switched off the CD, her senses could still hear the mellow strands of Vivaldi.

That is, until she walked into the basement and saw Jack tuning the object of her frustration.

Jack smiled and said, "Good morning, Eva," just as Al said, "You going somewhere this morning, hon?"

Eva hardly glanced at Jack when she responded blandly, "Good morning." She avoided looking at his violin and bow, which he laid on the partition near the front where customers entered the basement shop. Like last night, there was no hug for Jack, no special welcome. She gave her full attention to Al.

She laughed lightly. "I always go *somewhere* on Saturdays, Grandpa."

"Mmhmm." Grandpa gave her a sideways glance over the top of his reading glasses, which sat midway on his nose. "Beautiful day for going *somewhere.*"

"Right," Jack said. "Just look out there." He waved his hand toward the wide windows and French door. "A day without sunshine is like. . ."

He waited until Eva finally looked around at Al, and at him, before he finished. Her gaze questioned him.

"Well, like. . .night," he said.

At least that got a groan from her, accompanied by a thin smile. He'd already determined to pretend he didn't notice her reserve toward him and find a way to have her dispense with it. "Al and I are going to look at a shop I'm considering opening up as a music store. Come with us, Eva. I'd like to know what you think."

Her obvious reluctance to answer gave him a good indication of what she thought. She focused her attention on the child's violin on which Al, never idle, was affixing the chin rest that had slipped off. Al finished with the chin rest and moved away to place it with items that were ready for customers to pick up. Just as she looked over at Jack and opened her mouth to respond, a movement drew her attention to the entrance.

Jack knew, without looking toward the entry, what put the light in her eyes and the heightened color in her cheeks. It wasn't the sunshine—but the one and only Georgio Baldovino, with violin case in hand. The door music chimed as he came in looking almost like a regular guy in slacks and a short-sleeved shirt.

Last night at the restaurant, Al had offered to take the violin home with him and assess the damage so that Baldovino could get his Stradivarius back as soon as possible. Baldovino wasn't willing to let the Stradivarius out of his sight. Al understood that, and they'd arranged for the violinist to come this morning at ten o'clock. That's when Jack decided to come and reassure Baldovino that Al wasn't a mediocre repairman but as expert at making and repairing violins as Baldovino was at playing them.

After his warm and gracious greeting to a most-receptive Eva, Baldovino gave Jack a curious look, then a serious one as Al walked up to the partition.

Baldovino lay the case on the partition and opened it. "This is a Stradivarius. I'm sure you're competent, but I do need to know your qualifications."

"Absolutely," Al said, gently touching the violin as if it were a newborn babe. Eva looked at it just as longingly as Jack felt.

"How long have you been repairing violins?"

Al laughed lightly. "Oh, I started about the time God gave Moses the Ten Commandments."

Jack and Eva smiled, having heard that statement many times. Baldovino nodded, but they all knew that wasn't enough.

"Seems that long, anyway," Al said. "I studied violin making in LA, the oldest and most famous of such schools. I've been repairing them for about fifty years. I began making my own about forty years ago and now they bear my own name. A mentor and friend of mine worked with Mertzanoff."

"Mertzanoff?" Baldovino's eyes widened. "The research scientist who unveiled the secret of the Strad tone?"

Al nodded.

"The Alono." Baldovino gazed at Al with an expression of awe. "I didn't make that kind of connection last night. Forgive me."

Al raised both hands. "No. No. I need no praise."

"If it's true what I've heard, you deserve great acclaim. Is it true that a group of two hundred leading musicians met in New York to select the violin they preferred and yours was chosen?"

Al nodded as Baldovino added, "And a Strad was included in the competition."

That's why Jack determined to be here this morning. To confirm to the famous Baldovino he had no reason for concern about Al repairing his violin. Jack picked up his instrument and placed it beneath his chin, lifted his bow, and played chords that Mozart had written.

Baldovino sucked in his breath, then exhaled when Jack finished. "That's a Strad."

Jack shook his head. "It's the Alono."

Baldovino's laugh was one of disbelief. "May I?"

While Baldovino played the same chords that Jack had played, Jack's immediate reaction was envy. Jack had the gift of perfect pitch and knew when an instrument was off the slightest amount. Baldovino had the magic touch—an artist with a gift that went beyond any amount of training or practice.

"That was beautiful," Eva whispered when Baldovino stopped playing.

"I've had many great artists try out various violins in here," Al said. "But never with such beauty. I am honored."

"Could I take a picture of you and Grandpa to hang on the wall with the others?" Eva asked.

"Now I am honored," Baldovino said graciously, then he resumed playing until she returned from her office with the camera.

Jack watched as Eva positioned Al and Baldovino facing the sunlight with the workshop background of musical instruments lying on tables and hanging from hooks and displayed on the walls. Baldovino lifted the Alono in a playing position.

"I don't suppose you would allow me to use any of these in publicity?" Eva asked tentatively.

Jack could do nothing but watch silently as Baldovino's dark gaze surveyed the beautiful Eva standing in front of the door. The backdrop of sunlight made a golden halo around her dark brown hair as it lay softly against her shoulders. The blue silk blouse caressed her mature figure with a soft glow.

A smile graced Baldovino's aristocratic face as he said what Jack thought. "How could I refuse the request of such a lovely young woman? Of course, I would want to approve any project, but for my personal pleasure, I would like a picture of the three of us, then. . ." He lowered his head and narrowed his eyes in what Jack supposed was a flirtatious gesture. His voice held a baritone quality. "I would like a picture of you and me." He took the camera from her willing hands and turned. "Jack?"

Jack didn't like this at all. He didn't mind snapping the three of them. But he didn't care for the duo in which Baldovino held the Alono while Baldovino looked into her eyes and Eva stared at him with open admiration. Her gaze reminded Jack of how he felt about Baldovino's short but masterful playing of a Mozart aria. However, he suspected Eva did not separate the man from the violin playing.

The picture-taking session ended and Al, who had examined the violin said, "This is your problem. There's a slight separation here at the edge. That gives your violin an inferior tonal quality."

Baldovino nodded as if that were no surprise. "That has happened before. You think it's the glue?"

"No, I don't think so," Al said. "If the glue were stronger than the wood, that would result in mechanical stress leading to splintered wood and separated joints. Then repair would be very difficult." He shrugged a shoulder. "This is what you can expect from having a very old instrument." He laughed lightly. "Even if it is a Stradivarius."

"Yes," Baldovino said with complete confidence. "I'm convinced you know your business." He took a deep breath. "I will leave my Strad with you." He looked longingly at it like a mother might do when leaving her baby for the first time. Then he looked at Al. "Could I take the Alono while my Strad is being repaired?"

"It belongs to Jack," Al said.

The clatter of plastic against the hardwood floor turned their attention to Eva, who stooped to retrieve a CD case she'd dropped. Her quick glance toward Jack and the slight flaring of her nostrils as if she'd taken in a deep breath were the only indications of what Jack knew was resentment seething inside her. Al grimaced slightly as he turned again toward the Strad, closed the lid, and zipped the case.

Glancing at Baldovino, who looked from one to the other, Jack suspected the man guessed more than Jack cared to reveal. A sly look appeared in the violinist's eyes. "May I borrow your violin?"

"If you need to practice while the Strad is being repaired, you may do it here." He said something similar to what Baldovino had said the night before. "I won't part with my Alono."

Baldovino nodded. "I would like to play it for awhile. And if it has the quality it displayed today, then I would like to buy it."

For the first time since Baldovino walked into the shop, or even since he'd seen him at the restaurant with Eva, Jack felt in control. "It's not for sale."

Baldovino lowered his head slightly, and his brow furrowed. "I know the cost of great violins. I'm willing to pay the price."

Jack knew the cost, too. He knew that if Baldovino played the Alono for several days, he would sell his soul for it. He was almost willing to do that now. But he could only repeat, "It's not for sale."

"Do you play this violin before audiences?"

"No way," Jack said "I guess you'd say I just fiddle around. Jack-of-all-trades, you might say." He laughed lightly. Georgio acknowledged the comment with a nod, yet his gaze held curiosity.

Seeing Al's smile and Eva's stiff expression, Jack figured he might as well admit openly what he'd learned about his own limitations. "I don't have the concert violin touch, if that's what you mean. I could play it, yes. But not with the feeling you put into it with the first movement of the bow across the string. I'm sure that was recognized at an early age."

Georgio accepted that. It wasn't a compliment, just a fact. He gazed longingly at the Alono. "I've heard everything has its price. Think about it."

Jack didn't have to think about it. He was aware that the sale of that Alono could set him up for life without his having to start at the bottom and work his way up. It was best not to think about it. He picked up the Alono and moved it to its case. "I'll leave it here, and you're welcome to play it if I or Al or Eva are here."

Eva turned not only her head, but her entire body away from Jack at that remark.

"Thank you." Baldovino gazed a moment longer at the Alono, then the case of his Strad. Jack knew he didn't want to leave either. Then his gaze moved to Eva. "I would feel better with some kind of security. If I can't have the violin, I would like to take the girl."

Eva looked over at him, then flashed a gorgeous smile when he added as if he were modest, "That is, with her permission." While their gazes locked, Baldovino walked closer to her. "If you are willing to go with me, I would love to see some of those places we talked about last evening."

Eva nodded, without a trace of uncertainty. Her confidence had grown along with her maturity, as well it should. She had every reason for confidence. She was beautiful, intelligent, successful—what more could a man want in a woman?

"I would like that," she said.

Walking toward Jack, who stood at the end of the partition, she darted him a resentful glance and her silence spoke louder than words. It reminded him of a mild version of the way she'd looked at him four years ago when she'd stormed, "That violin should be mine, not yours!"

He wondered what she was thinking now. She no longer cared for the jack-of-all-trades with the Alono. She had shifted her affections to a master concert violinist with a Strad.

As she walked around him and toward Baldovino, Jack realized the violinist had watched every move, every nuance. Baldovino's parting glance held Jack's for a lengthy moment with something akin to challenge in his gaze. He opened the door, allowing Eva to pass in front of him. With a nod, as if he had finished a performance, Baldovino walked away from the shop with Eva.

Jack knew, without a doubt, this was a man thing.

As plain as the sunshine streaming through the glass panes, Jack knew what Baldovino's gaze had meant. He might as well have said, "It's your call, Jack. You want the girl. I want the violin. How about a trade? If you won't let me have the violin, then I'll take the girl."

The idea that Eva would have something to say about that did nothing to assuage the uneasiness Jack felt. He had asked Eva to accompany him to his prospective shop. Her response had been to walk out and get into a black European convertible with Baldovino.

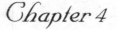

Chapter 4

Eva assumed Georgio was unattached since no female was with him, nor had one been mentioned. She didn't protest when Georgio said he would like to drive, if she didn't mind. Driving was both a challenge and a pleasure for him since he was accustomed to being chauffeured so much of the time.

She felt cocooned in a world of luxury after she and Georgio were ensconced in the luxury car's deep maroon interior. Likely she would soon awaken to find this was all a dream—like an admiring fan suddenly riding around with a famous movie star. She had found Georgio easy to talk to last evening, but suddenly felt—

"Eva?"

She quickly turned her head to face him, noting that he was turned toward her with one arm draped over the steering wheel. A faint scent of musky male cologne mingled with the car's aroma of leather warmed by the midmorning sun. "Oh, I'm sorry."

"You are deep in thought," Georgio said.

She might as well be honest. "I was thinking that I feel very much the amateur in your presence."

His glance and smile were reassuring. "That is very good for my self-esteem. It gives me the opportunity to try to impress you."

"Your playing does that. I have a recording of your playing with the Vienna Philharmonic."

"Were my feet not so big, that might never have happened."

Eva looked down. "Your feet?"

Georgio laughed lightly. "You know the saying about an artist's difficulty of getting his foot in the door. It helps to have accomplished parents and relatives who have a musical history. The doors were open before I was born."

"There's something to be said about your talent."

"The genes, I think that's called." Georgio shook his head. "I doubt that any of my relatives have genes that aren't musical."

Eva laughed as he smiled. "I shudder to think what practice would have been like without the genes. Being a Baldovino, I had to become a success."

"You sound American," Eva said.

He shrugged slightly and looked over at her with a smile. "My mother is American, my father, Italian. I speak with an Italian accent when there. You know the saying, 'When in Rome, do as the Romans do.'"

"That sounds biblical, like something the apostle Paul said. Are you. . .a Christian?"

"I didn't realize that was a biblical quote." He straightened in his seat and turned the key in the ignition. "I have visited some of the finest churches in the world, but generally I have time for nothing but the violin. That is why this time of relaxation before the upcoming concert is so important to me. That is why I am enjoying your company so much. You are a breath of fresh air."

Eva loved the compliment, but she felt that was a charming way of his avoiding the subject of religion. He backed the car out of the parking space and headed down the long driveway.

"Have you been to Miami before?" she asked.

"Yes, but not to sightsee. I'm staying at our family's beach house, which is used by various relatives. My visit to Miami has been primarily as a beachcomber. Of course, I do know a little about the city, the main roads, et cetera." He stopped at the end of the driveway. "Now, what sights would you like to show me?"

Eva mentioned several places including Vizcaya, hoping to get into the conversation about the quartet's invitation to play there. However, as he pulled out onto the road, he broached the subject she'd rather leave behind.

"If I'm not being too personal, what is this between you and Jack? What does that fellow do? Is he a relative? A friend?"

Eva hardly knew how to respond. "He's been a friend of the family for years. His parents are part of a professional touring choral group. Jack has a wonderful voice and has sung at the restaurant in the past. As a teenager, he stayed behind in school while his parents traveled much of the time. He and Grandpa hit it off from the first time Jack performed at Alono's. After that, Jack came often to Grandpa's shop. Jack has perfect pitch and was a great help with tone. In return, Grandpa taught Jack a lot about violin making."

Georgio nodded, with a sympathetic look, as if he were familiar with that lifestyle.

"He began to hang out at the restaurant, even worked there in the summers, and also became attached to Grandpa. Grandpa was a mentor and like a father or grandfather to Jack."

"I hope I'm not being too personal and of course you don't have to answer. But, were you in love with Jack?"

She wished he hadn't asked. "Well," she hedged, "as much as a silly teenager, and later a college girl, could be."

"You're not now?"

"Oh, please. I was a young girl. I always looked up to him because he was a few years older and all my friends swooned over him, thinking he was so magnificent. You see, when he wasn't at the shop or the restaurant, he was a knight with a Renaissance group. He wore armor and rode a white horse. I suppose, for a while, I saw him as a real knight and I as some sort of princess to be rescued from the humdrum of life. That was. . .fantasy. I'm. . .not a teenager anymore."

She really didn't want to reveal how she'd felt rejected by Jack. However, the words spilled forth despite her preference to change the subject. "After Grandpa gave him the Alono, he left to make his mark in the world. And stayed away for four years."

Georgio seemed to be concentrating on the traffic for a long moment. Then he spoke in a low tone. "You don't like Jack's having that Alono violin."

Eva's heavy sigh preceded her honesty. "No."

"Neither do I," Georgio said. "You and I have that in common."

❧

Eva was eager to return to her tour-guide role and switched the conversation to Vizcaya. She explained what a wonderful opportunity it was for the quartet to play at the famous museum, that it was a long-awaited goal of the group and now seemed only her goal.

Georgio raised his hand from the wheel, lifting it into the air. "Then why not give Vizcaya an affirmative answer? You would be taking nothing from the quartet. Surely they would be as receptive to a trio, duet, or even solo."

Now why hadn't she thought of that? She might even mention it to Vizcaya.

She gave Georgio a brief description as the house and grounds came into view. "Miami's famous Vizcaya Museum and Gardens is a Renaissance masterpiece," she said, "on Biscayne Bay."

He took on an appreciative look as he gestured toward the scene before him. "Ah, this resembles a lavish Italianate villa."

"It's one of South Florida's leading attractions. It portrays the history of Miami and four hundred years of European history. The architecture represents the Italian Renaissance."

"Impressive," Georgio said as he turned the wheel and the sports car crept along through the immaculate grounds.

"Around two hundred thousand people visit the museum each year," Eva said. "There have been such dignitaries as presidents, queens, kings. Also the Summit of the Americas was held here with the president and thirty-four leaders of the Western Hemisphere. Oh," she added, facing him and smiling, "and perhaps will be visited by a renown violinist."

Georgio's dark gaze and smile held warmth. "I would love to have you lead me on a tour if my schedule permits. Today, however, I would like to get my bearings here in Miami and go by the concert hall and look at the stage, if you don't mind."

"You're driving," Eva said.

He nodded and his foot pressed the accelerator.

After driving past the concert hall, Georgio said he would like to take her to his beach house for lunch. After Eva agreed, he used a cell phone to make a call.

"Elena," he said. "I'm bringing a guest for lunch. Great. See you soon."

He didn't explain who Elena was. Obviously, he had a wife or someone staying with him. When the house came into view, Eva was mildly surprised it was an older style, then recalled Georgio said it had been in the family for a long time.

"The spectacular part of the house," Georgio said of the structure situated on an incline, "is the glass walls and windows that reveal an incredible view of the ocean."

Georgio parked alongside a rental car and a late-model economy car.

They walked up onto the open porch. At the side was a glass-enclosed piazza.

The beach house looked as comfortable and cozy inside as the middle-aged man and woman that Georgio introduced as an invaluable married couple, Elena and Victor. "They take care of the house when it's unoccupied and take care of us when we vacation here."

Eva shook their hands and got a strong impression by the pleasant way they responded to Georgio's remarks that they were not just hired hands, but they liked each other. They both excused themselves from the room.

Her eyes were drawn to a doorway across which a man, talking on a phone, paced back and forth.

"That's Hastings," Georgio said. "He is agent and public relations executive for the upcoming concert and anything that might come up as a result of the promotion." He lowered his voice and leaned near when Hastings again appeared and glanced their way. "I think all this could be done from New York via the phone and computer, but Hastings insists upon the personal touch. Frankly," he said, "I think he just likes the beach and a few days away from his wife and kids."

Eva laughed with him. "This is a beautiful place."

Hastings appeared at the doorway, covered the mouthpiece, and lowered the phone. "Sir, are you available to speak with the concert manager?"

He nodded. "Eva, would you mind waiting for me on the piazza? We can eat out there."

Soon, Elena joined her with salad, delicate sandwiches, a platter of fresh fruit, and a plate of pastries.

"Mr. Baldovino's favorite drink is coffee. But we have—"

Eva lifted her hand. "Coffee's fine with me." The two of them engaged in conversation about the lovely weather and the wonderful view.

Georgio soon joined Eva at the small white wrought iron table. He apologized for the phone call and explained a few appointments he had coming up. She wondered how he found time to relax.

Eva spread her napkin on her lap and Georgio did the same. She wondered if she should just say an open-eyed, silent blessing. Her glance across the table, however, revealed him smiling.

"Do you always play an invocation," he asked, "or do you use words?"

Eva laughed. "Since I didn't bring my violin, I think words would be appropriate."

He gestured with his hand toward her and a slight nod. Eva bowed her head and said a few words of thanks for the food.

Eva really wanted to know Georgio's personal status—wife, former wife, fiancée—but didn't want to chance giving the impression she expected something personal to develop between the two of them.

She needn't have worried. Georgio asked about her studies at the university, where she had majored in music and had started the quartet during her senior year in college. "Grandpa said he taught me to play the violin as soon as I could hold a bow."

Georgio nodded understanding. "I doubt I've ever had a day without some form of music. I consider myself fortunate for that. Speaking of music," he said as they munched on pastry and drank coffee, "why does Jack want to hold on to his violin when he claims no particular interest in playing it? Yet, he had it out this morning and offered to allow me to play it with supervision. Was he trying to impress me?"

Eva shook her head on that one. "No. Jack doesn't think like that. He would want you to appreciate it."

Georgio looked at his coffee cup for a long moment. Then his gaze met Eva's. "Do you think," he asked, "that your grandpa could make me an Alono like Jack's?"

"If he really wanted to," Eva said, "I think he could. He studied tone scientifically to discover why the violin does what it does. But—"

"Uh-oh," Georgio said. "Now comes the negative side of this."

Eva nodded. "Grandpa considers that Alono his crowning accomplishment. He's not trying to compete with other violin makers or the Strad."

She looked at Georgio's thoughtful expression as he gazed out over the ocean. She remembered that Grandpa had said he could teach her to make a violin like the Alono. After Jack left with the Alono, she wanted to show them both that she could make her own. She tried for awhile, then gave it up. Grandpa had said one must put love into the making of a violin for it to be great. She realized that if Grandpa was right, and she continued, her masterpiece would emulate a heartbreak.

That dormant ambition of hers began to stir. "Perhaps," she said and waited as the word brought Georgio's attention back to her. She lifted her chin slightly. "Perhaps I will make you an Alono."

Chapter 5

Jack sat on the front row in the sanctuary of the church, waiting to make his announcement. He wondered what he would see when he stood before the congregation on Sunday morning. Would he have to look out at Eva and Baldovino?

A part of him would be glad if Baldovino was a Christian and going to be serious about Eva and she about him. However, another part of him wanted to let Eva know how the four years away from home had changed him and had made him realize there was no other woman who touched his heart like she did. He had returned with the intention of finding out if there might be a future for them together.

Perhaps he already had his answer.

Then the pastor was introducing him, saying that most of the congregation would remember when Jack played the piano and sang solos as well as sang in the choir. "He's been in France for several years studying bow making and has returned," the pastor said, then mentioned that Jack had talked over an idea with him and the choir director. They were delighted to endorse the plans Jack had for his life and for the church.

"Jack Darren," the pastor said.

Jack walked up onto the dais. "First," he said, holding on to each side of the wooden structure in front of him, "let me say how good it is to be back. I feel like I've come home. Not only to the city, but to the Lord. I've had my training and opportunities. Now I want to give something back to this area and this church."

He glanced toward the pastor and Jim, the choir director, and mentioned that they had endorsed his idea. "We would like to form an orchestra for the church." He knew there were several in the congregation who played instruments.

"If you're interested, meet with me and Jim in the choir room after the service. The players need to have a certain level of experience. Also, in our talking about a music ministry, some of us want to teach those who would like to learn to play an instrument or learn more about singing. Just like you have your children's choirs, you can also develop a children's orchestra. This does what we are supposed to do. Train up our children in church and encourage them to use their talents and abilities for the Lord."

Jack had tried not to look directly at Eva, or anyone for that matter, but he'd felt drawn to her gaze before he returned to his seat on the front pew.

Would Eva join the orchestra? Her participation would almost ensure success. He could play the piano, she and Al the violin. Her quartet might join them. He knew a couple others in the church who played instruments, and there were surely high school band students who could learn to play church music as easily as they learned marches and tunes for their school concerts.

But, would Eva join? Four years ago she had asked him to help her start a string band, but he had left to go to New York, then Paris. . .with the Alono to which she felt entitled.

Jack could barely keep his mind on the congregational singing, the choir's special anthem, and the pastor's message. As soon as it all ended, he hurried to the choir room. When Al came in without Eva, Jack's heart sank. When Eva walked in, his heart sang.

He felt as if the music of his heart were audible and as if a visible warm glow had spread over him. She must surely detect his pleasure at her appearance. "Eva. You'll be—"

He didn't finish saying what an asset she would be to the orchestra. She was shaking her head. "I'll hurry and get out of your way. I just wanted to ask if it will be okay if I take the Alono to Georgio's beach house for him to practice this evening."

Jack felt a rebuke form in his throat and tried not to verbalize it. After all, he had been magnanimous enough to tell Baldovino he could play it in the presence of Al or Eva. He hadn't expected it to be at the man's beach house. "This evening, you say?" managed to escape from his fractured voice box.

Eva nodded. "All afternoon he will be at the home of the concert hall's administrator, meeting Miami's important people."

"No need to explain." Jack didn't want to hear that after Baldovino associated with those "important people," he and Eva would be alone at night, at a secluded beach house by the ocean.

"Do you want the Alono to stay at Grandpa's?"

"No, no. That. . .that's fine. Of course you may take it. I made the offer, remember?"

"Thanks." She turned and walked out of the choir room, leaving him feeling like a song that wouldn't be sung.

He remembered the Eva of four years ago. The light in her eyes each time she had looked at him indicated a young girl who wanted to be the special person in his life. He'd pretended not to notice.

Now she looked at him with mere tolerance, when she looked at all.

What were her dreams now?

To be a concert violinist?

To be the special person in the life of one?

Eva parked near the cars that had been there the day before. Georgio came off the porch when she opened the trunk to take out the violins.

"The Alono," she said, handing it to him. "And Grandpa said the Strad is dry. He doesn't like to do business on Sunday, so you can pay him at your convenience if it's repaired to your satisfaction."

He thanked her for bringing the violins. Inside, she again saw Hastings pacing past a doorway. Georgio laughed. "I think he cannot live without a telephone at his ear."

He led her into a small music room in which a baby grand piano was most dominant. They set down the violins. "You did come prepared to join me for dinner, as I asked?"

"Even if I hadn't," Eva said loudly enough for the ears of Elena, who she could see in the nearby kitchen and walked toward it, "that aroma of food would be too enticing to refuse."

A smiling Elena served them a wonderful dinner at a long, narrow table in a dining area adjacent to the kitchen, separated only by an island.

After dinner Georgio asked if she'd like to walk on the beach. "Elena and Victor often leave after dinner," he said, "but they will stay until after we return from our walk. Although it's secluded here, I will not leave the Alono unattended." Eva appreciated that kind of thoughtfulness.

Eva enjoyed the cool breeze, the quietness of the scene except for the sound of the ocean's rhythm beneath a tranquil sky.

How different from a couple of days ago when she fretted about not having a mate. Now she walked along the beach with an extraordinarily talented man. She decided to let him lead if there were to be a conversation. After all, he had come here to relax.

"Eva," he said, after they'd walked for awhile. "Do you have a special boyfriend?"

"I haven't had time for that." Eva laughed, thinking of her full schedules for years. "After high school, there was Grandma's long illness. I moved in with Grandpa and tried to help, but Grandpa wanted to do as much as he could for Grandma and wouldn't leave her side for long. Jack and I helped keep the shop going. After she died, I had college, the quartet, and the restaurant. In the past couple of years, the quartet has had several local performances and even a cruise."

"Sounds like you have a full life," Georgio said.

Eva sighed. "Now, it looks like the quartet may break up. They're all getting married."

She felt like this might be a time to ask a pertinent question. "Are you married or anything?"

"I haven't had time for that," he said, mimicking what she had said. "I've been on a world tour for the past three years. That is how one becomes world famous. Once I have achieved a certain amount of fame, then I can refuse bookings. However—" He spread his hands. "Am I not then obligated to the public? All is not as perfect as it might seem. Once you have reached the top, you're expected to be perfect. I must practice every day."

Eva was well aware that if she missed a day's practice, she could tell a difference in the ease of playing. And yet her requirements were nothing like Georgio's. "Is that a burden?"

He smiled. "No. I love it. It's a vital part of me. I care for my violin like a father would care for his baby. Perhaps better. But lately, I have had visions of grandeur, like finding a wife and raising a family. It would be such a change. But I am ready to think about those things."

"You have found someone you want to settle down with?"

"There should be love, no?" He spread his hands in what she was becoming accustomed to his doing often. "Oh, I know about finding women attractive and spending time with them. But, how do you know if you're in love?"

Eva thought it was love when someone was always present in your mind. When your heart leapt at the sight of him. But, even children claimed to be in love with young boys. Married people divorced who had claimed to be in love. "I'm. . .not sure," Eva said.

"Neither am I," Georgio said. "That is one reason I decided on a vacation here. To get away from the disturbance and to clear my mind."

"Is it working?" Eva asked.

He stopped and turned to face her. "I think it's beginning to. And a big part of that can be credited to you. Thank you."

Eva looked up at him and met his thoughtful, questioning gaze. Was Georgio trying to forget someone?

Could Georgio make her forget what she had felt for Jack—both the love of the past and the resentment of the present? She didn't protest when Georgio lifted his hand, placed a finger beneath her chin, and bent to gently press his lips against hers.

The sweetness of the kiss was like a thank-you.

He straightened and said, "You are so kind to spend time with me. I am grateful. You are teaching me many things."

"I? Teach you? What would that be?"

"About your city, you, those around you, your everyday life, confiding in me about some of your hopes and dreams and disappointments. I was never allowed to express any doubts or fears or apprehensions about myself or life. You do not. . .um. . .take relationships lightly. What I mean is, you are a Christian. You do not just. . .enjoy life and have fun."

Eva wasn't exactly sure what he was asking. "I do enjoy life and have fun, but I don't consider fun being anything that can harm my body or emotional well-being. You're right; I don't take relationships lightly."

He was nodding, saying, "Umhmm. You have that morality faith as was expressed at your parents' restaurant."

"I'm a Christian," she said. "And morality is part of it. Are you?"

"No. I believe in God, but I think there are many roads that lead to Him. Why do you not believe that?"

Eva wondered if she were adequate for this debate. "Anything I might say doesn't really matter. It only matters what God says. And the Bible, which I believe is His book to us, says that Jesus is the only way to God. I'm not saying it. God said it."

"Really?" He looked rather surprised.

Eva felt so inadequate. "Well, I don't know how else to say it."

"You did fine," he said. "Just fine."

Eva watched him as he looked out at the ocean with a rather amused look on his face and that mysterious twist of his lips resembling a smile. He did not look disturbed or intrigued. Apparently he wasn't and didn't take her words to heart as he gazed out toward a horizon that had disappeared into the sky.

Suddenly he stopped. "Shall we return to the beach house? I suspect you and I could make beautiful music together."

If she'd been chewing any, she would have swallowed her gum. Since she wasn't, she swallowed a gulp of air and had to struggle not to cough.

Did he mean they might make music together. . .personally?

She looked over at him, and he gave her a sideways glance. A small light sparked his dark eyes, and he smiled as they walked back toward the beach house.

He led her into the music room. "Would you like to play the Alono?" he asked.

She stared at it. She would not be able to play it with ease, not with those old feelings rising up inside her. "No, I really wouldn't."

He played briefly on the Strad. "The tone sounds as good as ever to me," he said. "Would you like to play this one?"

She gladly took it.

From the instant she placed the violin on her shoulder and lay the side of her chin against it, Eva felt what Georgio had said about this being one's baby. Her own violin was a huge part of who she was and what she did. Hers was a fine violin; however, Georgio's was the world's best. She was afraid her hand would tremble and she'd be the world's first to screech a bow across the strings of a Stradivarius.

Willing herself to relax, she drew the bow across the G, D, A, and E as a warmup. The tone was so easy, smooth, and clear. They played together some classical fun tunes she knew by memory that the quartet often played.

Georgio placed Johann Sebastian Bach's *Concerto for Two Violins in D Minor* on the stand. She played, looking at the music, while Georgio played from memory on the Alono.

Yes, they made beautiful music together.

Afterward, Georgio played solo while she became the captivated audience.

When he finished, he bowed to her applause. He returned the Alono to its case and handed it to her.

"The Strad is my baby," he said. "But I wouldn't mind having a second child. I would need to play more on the Alono to make sure it is all I believe it to be."

Eva understood. "And I wouldn't mind playing more on the Strad."

"Deal," he said. "I don't want to take you from your daily activities, and I have appointments tomorrow. All right if I call you?"

"Sure. If I'm not in, leave word with Grandpa or on the answering machine."

He smiled as he walked her to her car. "We did indeed make beautiful music together, no?"

She returned his smile. "Yes."

⁂

After returning home, Eva took the Alono to her room and opened the case. She looked at it a long time. Then she reached out to touch it. She hadn't wanted to play it.

She had loved Jack with all the love a young girl could have. Now, she could understand his going away to music school, then Paris to learn bow making. She couldn't blame him for taking the violin since Grandpa had wanted him to have it.

Why couldn't she put the past behind her? Why, as she looked at the Alono, couldn't she see the face of Georgio Baldovino instead of the smiling, handsome face of that blond, green-eyed man that she'd be better off to forget?

Needing to get things settled in her mind once and for all, Eva went into the kitchen, where Grandpa was having a snack, like he always did before going to bed.

She sat across from him at the table and told him about her evening at the beach and how much Georgio admired the Alono.

Grandpa nodded and smiled. "I knew the moment he heard it, he was impressed with the tone."

"He really wants it," Eva said.

"If Jack were going to sell it, that would have been done while he was trying to find out where he fit in with the music field. I don't believe he will ever sell it now."

Eva decided to ask what she wanted to know for four years. "Grandpa. Why did you give the Alono to Jack?"

He looked over at her for a long time. She thought he wasn't going to answer. Finally, he took a deep breath, then exhaled. "I know you didn't understand that, Eva. And I felt bad about it. But I have to do what I think is right. You remember what I told you, when I said I was going to give it to Jack?"

Eva nodded. "You said I should make my own."

He nodded. "You didn't take that the way I meant it. You wanted to be a violin maker. Then your goal should not be to have the Alono, but to make a comparable one."

"I. . .tried for a while," she said.

"Yes, I know. But a violin that plays beautiful music must be made with love, not resentment. That's why I couldn't make Alonos every day of the week. I reached my goal. I had nothing more to prove. Afterward, I just wanted to make wonderful instruments for musicians to play, not those only for the rich and famous. You understand?"

"Yes, and I could understand if you wanted to keep it or have it put in some museum or music center or rented it out to classical violinists. But. . .give it to Jack?"

Grandpa nodded. "I did that for two reasons."

She waited.

That incredible look, full of love, crossed his face. . .the look of love and of teacher, older, wiser, and she felt she was in for a lecture.

"Because he needed it, child. The same principle as when Jesus was asked why He ate with sinners. He said that the well don't need a physician but the sick do. Jack was at a turning point in his life. A young man with dreams, uncertainties, opportunities, beginning to get off the straight and narrow. You had me and your family. Jack had a piece of wood."

Finally, he said, "If you had that Alono, you wouldn't need to make your own. But if you wanted to be a great violin maker, you don't need my Alono. You make the best violin you can, using the mathematical equations with all the ingredients. Then you listen for the tone and with your heart. When it stirs your emotions, you have made a great violin."

She waited. He didn't speak further.

"Grandpa, you said you gave it to Jack for two reasons. What's the other one?"

"That," he said, in a kind but firm tone, "is not for me to say. Both the Alono and the explanation now belong to Jack."

Chapter 6

On Monday, Eva and Tristan went to Vizcaya to finalize plans for their playing instead of chancing their response being lost in the mail. That done, they set up a practice session for the next morning.

When she returned home, Grandpa said Georgio had come and paid his bill. He also said the sound of the Strad was perfect and thanked him profusely. He asked Grandpa to give her the message that he was expecting a call from California and would not be able to practice on the Alono that evening, but he hoped they could get together soon. He wanted to test the sound of the Alono further.

Eva wondered if Georgio would call for her to bring the Alono to his beach house again on Tuesday.

Ironic, she thought, that it was the Alono that played a part in her facing facts that Jack hadn't cared for her in a special way. Now the Alono was one of the reasons she and Georgio spent time together and had enjoyed a wonderful evening the night before.

That night, before falling asleep, she prayed that she might stop thinking of Jack and how she used to feel about him and resenting him for not returning her affection.

As she thought of Jack and Georgio, she admitted to herself that one could not force oneself to think of another in a romantic way. She drifted off to sleep with the memory of the music that she and Georgio had elicited from the Strad and the Alono the night before.

On Tuesday morning, Eva went downstairs shortly before nine o'clock. Tristan was talking with Grandpa, who was replacing a broken string on a child's violin.

Tristan greeted Eva, and the two of them headed for the music room, where Rissa's voice became audible. Eva stopped short at the doorway for an instant when her gaze met Jack's. For an instant when their eyes met, she seemed transported back to four years ago when that green gaze had melted her heart.

Immediately she shook that thought away and hoped the others would simply take her moment's hesitation as surprise at seeing Jack there, holding the cello.

"Tyrone can't come this morning," Tristan said. "I asked Jack, since we need to get things finalized about what we'll play at Vizcaya."

Jack hadn't been concerned four years ago, so she preferred he not be involved now. She quickly reprimanded herself for that attitude.

"Before we get into that," Rissa said. "Eva, Jack and I were just talking about his orchestra. I'm planning to participate when I can. How about you?"

Eva didn't want to do anything to infer that she still had feelings for Jack. She preferred to keep her distance. Opening up her violin case, she said, "All I have on my mind right now is Vizcaya."

"One good thing," Tristan said. "If any one of us can't make it, Jack could fill in."

Not wanting Jack to think she still cared about him, Eva said flippantly, "Oh, that's good to hear. Who knows where I might be? Perhaps touring the world with none other than the great Georgio Baldovino."

"Yeah, yeah," Tristan said. "Rissa's been telling wild tales about things like that. When you dream, you dream big."

"Really. I told him we practice mornings whenever we can. He said he would like to come some morning when he's free."

"Sure," Tristan said and laughed.

"It's true," Rissa said. "She's been to his beach house and everything."

"Everything?" Tristan said ominously.

"Not. . .everything!" Eva said. "You guys are embarrassing me." She had a sudden urge to make sure Jack knew she didn't care if he had that Alono. "But. . .who could resist a man with a Stradivarius?"

The others were grinning like crazy while she did a little shimmy with her shoulder and lifted her chin in a mock "better-than-you" playfulness.

They didn't laugh. Jack lifted his eyebrows and looked beyond her with a bland gaze. Tristan looked as if he'd choke on a laugh. Rissa drew her eyebrows together and was making funny motions with her eyes.

Eva was trying to figure out what was wrong with them when she heard a familiar voice say, "My lucky day or what? I just happen to know a man who has a Stradivarius."

Eva gritted her teeth, squeezed her eyes shut, and grimaced.

Georgio laughed and the others joined in.

Eva turned to face him. "I. . .was just being. . .silly."

"Good," he said immediately. "I could use a little silliness in my life. I'm beginning to realize I've been much too stodgy for too long."

"Well, you've come to the right place to loosen up," Tristan said.

Georgio walked over to Jack. "You're part of this group now?"

"Only as a friend," Jack said. "And a fill-in when needed. The cellist couldn't come this morning. "I'm number one jack-of-all-trades. I play many instruments but none too well. I'd better warm up before we get into the practice."

"Maybe you can give us some ideas," Tristan said to Georgio.

"I'm sure you know what you're doing. Let me hear what you have in mind."

He listened as they played.

"Very good," Georgio said when they finished. "You have played this before, right?"

"Oh, yes, many times," Eva said.

"Locally?"

"Yes," Eva said, "but we want this to be absolutely perfect for Vizcaya."

Georgio nodded. "I suggest you vary the program somewhat. Likely, the music lovers of the area have already heard you. They would like the old favorites and to be introduced to something new."

"Or something old," Jack said.

They all looked at him. He shrugged a shoulder. "It's not my call, but you're playing during the Renaissance Festival. Shouldn't you go with that theme?"

"I wasn't aware of the festival," Georgio said. He looked at Jack. "I think you're exactly right about keeping with the theme. Consider the Baroque composers."

Jack and Georgio entered into an animated conversation about early music as they mentioned Corelli and Bach.

Jack made an offer. "I hadn't ordered any early music for my shop, but I'm sure we can find some around."

Georgio lifted a shoulder and an eyebrow. "Anything can be faxed, can it not?"

Jack laughed. "Perfect answer."

Rissa was skeptical. "Will we have time to learn the new music?"

"We don't have to memorize it. Even the best—"Jack stopped speaking suddenly and glanced at Georgio. "Well, maybe not the best." He laughed lightly. "But even symphony orchestras have their music in front of them."

The rest of the practice session was a fun excursion of their playing classical music. Georgio played the Alono. At Jack's suggestion, they turned to contemporary Christian music.

Eva couldn't help smiling. If Georgio Baldovino wasn't too good to use sheet music, then certainly the quartet could use it at Vizcaya.

❦

For the rest of the week, Eva settled into the routine of practice in the mornings, working in the shop in the afternoons, and spending evenings at Georgio's beach house. They'd have dinner, walk on the beach briefly, then play music.

Georgio had the Baroque music that had been faxed to him. With his instruction, Eva found the Renaissance music much easier than if she'd had to tackle the violin part alone.

"You'll do fine," Georgio complimented after a particularly good session on Friday evening.

"Thanks," Eva said. "But it won't sound nearly as good on my violin as on the Strad."

He held out the Alono. "Play this one."

Eva's breath caught in her throat for a moment. She felt her face grow warm under the scrutiny of Georgio's questioning gaze.

"I'd. . .rather not. I've gotten over my resentment of Grandpa's giving it to Jack, but I wouldn't feel right asking to play it. I don't want Jack to think I care about it."

"I see." Georgio took on that mysterious playful look she'd noticed several times. She hoped he didn't detect the uneasiness she felt when he talked about Jack or when she was around Jack.

"You're not playing in Jack's church orchestra?"

"I. . .have my other practices and recently I took up playing the Strad."

He laughed. "Ah," he said. "Priorities." He smiled so sweetly at her. "You were able to do a fine rendition of Bach and the early composers with little practice. I daresay you could whip out a hymn or two with no problem."

Eva felt torn. She could justify not being in the orchestra by what she just said. Those were excuses though, not reasons. She would love to play in the church orchestra and was rather envious that she hadn't started it herself. But as long as being around Jack made her so. . .uncomfortable, she couldn't possibly be a part of it.

Georgio put the Alono in its case and zipped it up. "Have you asked Jack to sell the Alono to you?"

Eva laughed at that. "I could never afford it."

He grinned. "A reduced price, perhaps. Or finance it." He shrugged. "Even I could buy it and you could make payments to me. If Jack would sell it."

She shook her head. "Jack won't sell it. But even if he would, I don't want it. I mean, if Grandpa had given it to me as an heirloom, then I'd treasure it. It's the principle that disturbs me."

"The principle," Georgio repeated. "You don't want the Alono. Jack doesn't want to play it. Your grandpa gave it away." A short laugh escaped his throat. "Then why ever can't I have it?"

Eva laughed, too. It wasn't funny, but ironic. "I honestly don't know."

"Tomorrow," he said. "Let us go to his shop and face your Jack once again."

"He's not my Jack," Eva said more sharply than she intended.

Georgio nodded. "I should have said, 'the Alono's Jack.'"

Eva turned from him to put the Strad in its case.

"I have used the Alono long enough to know its quality," he said. "I would like to return it to Jack and thank him. Will you accompany me to his shop in the morning? I don't know where it is."

Eva faced him and nodded. "I need to take some of my violins over there anyway."

Georgio walked her out to her car as usual. He closed the door, then leaned down at the open window. "Thank you, Eva. I sincerely enjoy the time we spend together."

"So do I," Eva said.

She returned his smile. Driving away from the house, she turned on the Bach concerto. While it played in the background, she thought of how she never would have thought she'd be comfortable spending time with a famous concert violinist like Georgio Baldovino.

And yet, she felt so uncomfortable just hearing the name of Jack.

❧

Jack wasn't surprised to see Baldovino and Eva together. He'd learned from Al that the two of them spent each evening together at the beach house and that Eva had begun work on her own Alono.

He was surprised, however, that Eva came into his shop. She seemed to go out of her way to avoid him. Maybe she wanted to impress upon him that she no longer cared for him the way she had years ago.

Jack helped them bring in some of Eva's violins. Then Baldovino set the Alono on the glass cabinet top.

"This entire wall," Jack said, motioning behind himself as he stood behind the glass partition, "is for the display violins. I will keep beginner ones in a back room since those will be most of the sells."

Eva nodded. "This is quite impressive, Jack."

"Thank you," he said, realizing that was the closest she'd come to being more than tolerant of him since he'd returned. She quickly walked away and looked around at the walls on which hung some guitars, fiddles, and banjos. She touched some of the same kind of instruments leaned against the walls and on stands.

Baldovino drew his attention again as he began to talk about his gratitude to Jack for allowing him to play the Alono. "I suspect you knew I would find the Alono irresistible and you'd raise the price. If so, you were right. I will pay what you ask."

"Sorry," Jack said. "It's still not for sale."

"Then why did you have me play it?"

Jack's glance met Eva's after Baldovino asked the question, as if she, too, wanted to know the answer to that question. She quickly turned toward the racks that contained music books of many levels of expertise and CDs of country, bluegrass, contemporary, and classical music.

Jack glanced back at Baldovino. "I offered it because your Strad was being repaired. And also because I wanted someone of your stature to play it."

With a lift of an eyebrow, Baldovino seemed to accept that. "My offer will stand," he said. He glanced around. "Nice shop. Could I see some of your bows?"

Jack slid aside the glass door and handed him one. He knew it was strong, evenly balanced and weighted, stiff but light.

Baldovino checked it out. "Appears to be excellent. Where do you get your hair?"

"Usually from horses," Jack said.

Even Eva could not help laughing at that. Bows were strung with horsehair.

Jack unzipped the case, and Baldovino took the Alono and tried the bow on the strings. "Yes, this is symphony quality. Very smooth tone. And I see you have not bleached the horsehair. Although some violinists disagree with me, I think the darker hair grabs better; it produces more volume. And of course the stick is made from Pernambuco wood from Brazil."

"Of course," Jack agreed. "Fiberglass is adequate for beginners, also for their parents' pocketbooks."

Baldovino returned the Alono to the case and zipped it. "You mentioned once that you were a jack-of-all trades. I rather think you are a master of many."

Jack wasn't sure what he meant by "many." "I studied with the best in France. And most of my horsehair comes from the Moroccan horses of China."

"The more I see of you, the more I feel you and I have a lot in common."

As far as Jack could see, they had nothing in common. "What's that?"

"A knowledge of music, a love for it. We both have..." He looked up toward the banjos hanging on the wall. "How shall I say it? Ah—an appreciation for the finer things in life."

Baldovino's fingers grazed over the Alono case as he glanced toward Eva, who was examining some shakers in the form of fruit and vegetables. His head dipped slightly, but he looked up at Jack beneath raised eyebrows.

Like before, Jack got the clear impression Baldovino wasn't referring to the Alono just then. However, he spoke of it again. 'Will you keep the Alono in your shop?"

"No," Jack said. "It's not for sale, and I don't want to chance its being stolen. I will keep it at my house."

Baldovino nodded. "On display there, like a valuable piece of art."

Jack shook his head. "It's more valuable to me than that."

The violinist looked thoughtful for a moment. "I sense there's a story here."

Jack nodded. "Oh, yes. Perhaps there will be opportunity to share it with you."

Baldovino didn't invite Jack to do that. He obviously wasn't intrigued enough to carry the conversation further. He walked around the shop. Every once in awhile, Baldovino touched Eva's shoulder or leaned near her and gestured toward an instrument or a CD or a music book. They both said a casual good-bye to Jack and walked out together.

Jack looked after them long after they'd vanished from sight.

A sense of loneliness invaded him. The words of a song ran through his mind. *Tic Toc. Tic Toc. The clock stopped when the old man died.*

His glance swept over his shop. So many musical instruments and items of music. Yet not a note of music sounded in the shop.

He looked at his valuable, expensive stringed instrument.

He had a violin he said he wouldn't sell.

He had an Alono he rarely played.

He even had a story nobody cared to hear.

Chapter 7

Jack generally didn't consider himself a bow tie sort of person, but this occasion called for it. Any other time he would have welcomed the opportunity to sit in seats reserved for special guests of performers. Tonight, however, he found the idea miserable. He, Al, and Eva were Baldovino's guests for the evening.

If Baldovino's Strad had not needed to be repaired, then perhaps Jack would be escorting Eva to the concert instead of being her and Al's chauffeur for the evening, only to leave her to be Georgio's dinner guest after it ended.

And tonight, when Eva would be Baldovino's guest at dinner, all the "important" people in music would know her and that would increase her opportunities considerably. Yes, Baldovino could give Eva the kind of life that Jack couldn't imagine anyone not wanting. He had wanted it once. Then he discovered that was not so important. He hadn't been willing to concentrate on one area of music and become an expert. He didn't have the desire to be top in any particular musical field.

After his studies in music, he'd worked in various clubs as a pianist, a soloist, and later a backup fiddle player for a well-known country music singer. Then he remembered that Al had taught him how to make bows and had said the finest bow makers came from France. He checked it out and decided he needed something more substantial as a career than clubs and backup for a fading star.

He'd let the years go by without letting the people he loved know that he loved them. He'd been too young and foolish for his mind to listen to his heart. Years passed. Then he discovered what he was looking for deep inside was not center stage at all. It was a filling of the empty spot in his heart that only the Creator could fill upon his complete commitment to the Lord.

Now, Jack felt like he was coming apart at the seams and there was no glue to put him together again.

He knew why Baldovino invited Al. He was grateful for Al's having repaired his Strad. Jack figured he invited him, perhaps to soften him up, hoping he'd change his mind about selling the Alono.

There was a certain playfulness about Baldovino, like some kind of smug knowing in his expression and thin smile. Or was it a twist of sardonic humor knowing Jack cared about Eva and yet she was spending time with the great violinist?

Jack leaned over closer to Eva. "Is Baldovino a Christian?"

"No," she said, and her voice sounded sad. "He believes in God and right living, but doesn't believe Jesus is the only way to God." She paused, glanced away, then back again. "But our mission as Christians is to enlighten unbelievers, isn't it?"

"Exactly," Jack said, but he wondered if Eva was thinking about the Bible's warning against relationships with unbelievers.

He straightened in his seat for two reasons. One, this wasn't the time or place to discuss the matter of faith since the orchestra was coming onto the stage and the audience began to applaud. Two, the fragrance of Eva's delicate perfume had an unsettling effect upon his senses. Or, maybe it was just the nearness of Eva herself.

She looked particularly beautiful in a form-fitting black dress with rhinestones along the vee-cut neckline and her hair back in a chic French chignon.

But he must control his thoughts, dispense with his hopes about Eva. Perhaps she and Baldovino were meant for each other. Saying "God's will be done" was one thing. Feeling good about it was another.

Jack joined the applause. The first violinist played his tuning note. The conductor strode out on the stage and shook hands with the first violinist. He bowed to the audience, stepped up on his box, lifted his baton, and the orchestra began transporting listeners into a sublime world of music, playing Franz Liszt's *Les Prelude, Symphonic Poem no. 3*.

When the soprano came onstage, Eva leaned near Jack and with a delighted smile and eyes dancing with pleasure, she pointed to the program that listed the musical poems in French with the English translation beside them. "You understand all this," she said.

"So can you, if you can read English," he said.

She looked at him with dancing eyes and a warm, uninhibited smile. For awhile Jack thought she liked him, but when Georgio Baldovino appeared, striding out like he owned the world, Eva looked at the violinist as if he really did. The expression on her face glowed with awe and anticipation as she turned her attention away from Jack and joined the thunderous applause for Baldovino, who took center stage and bowed magnificently.

The concert was to be a special treat, combining themes of great composers. Usually an orchestra chose one theme for a concert. Tonight, they combined Liszt and Bach.

To make matters worse, Jack liked Baldovino. He liked the fact that such a gifted, famous man saw the worth in Eva.

From the moment Baldovino's bow touched the Strad, he drew out the most heavenly music Jack had ever heard as he played Johann Sebastian Bach's *Violin Concerto no. 1 in A Minor*. Jack found himself smiling broadly after the initial exposition, then Baldovino entered into what seemed to be a musical dialogue with the orchestra as if the two clashed, reminding Jack of dueling banjos. In the final gigue of two extended solos, Baldovino used a bowing technique that resulted in a curious croaking effect, delighting the audience.

In Bach's *Violin Concerto no. 2 in E Major*, Baldovino opened with an impassioned melody, followed by serenity, and ending with a dancelike finale.

The audience rose in another standing ovation.

The concert concluded with Tchaikovsky's *Symphony no. 4 in F Minor*.

Not being able to come up with a more apt example, Jack felt himself much like a Cinderella at the stroke of midnight, who turned away from the magical evening and faced the reality of returning to his place among the cinders.

For an instant, he jealously told himself that perhaps he should have excelled in something more glamorous than bow making.

Jack gazed at Eva going against the flow of the crowd as she made her way backstage after the concert. Jack felt bereft, as if he had lost her without ever having really found her. Her being in love with him had been an ego trip for him years ago. When he settled down to seriousness, he began to realize what a wonderful person Eva was.

He'd returned with the determination that if she were not already taken, he wanted to pursue a serious relationship with her. Perhaps that would have worked except for the appearance of Georgio Baldovino.

Eva was beautiful and would easily make Baldovino shine even brighter by being his dinner guest with the orchestra.

Baldovino had. . ."everything."

Even Al recognized that. On the way home, he said, "Looks like our Eva hit the jackpot."

"Not a 'Jack pot,'" he replied. "Looks more like a 'Baldovino pot. . .of gold!'"

He glanced at Al, who stared at him with that "what are you gonna do about it?" look. Jack never had been able to hide anything from Al. It had been Al who had cautioned him about Eva's fragile feelings when they were younger. Jack had flippantly replied that Eva was but one in a long line of admiring females.

"Sometimes I'm tempted to give her the Alono," Jack said.

Al harrumphed. "If she doesn't like you now, would she like you if you gave her a violin?"

"No," Jack said. "She would just like the violin. She's angry with me."

A light laugh escaped Al's throat. "Reminds me of how I got mad at Ruth for dying and leaving me."

"At least she's not indifferent to me."

"That's something," Al said. "What you do with your violin is up to you. But you remember what I told you about it."

"That's what changed my life." Jack took a deep breath and let out a long sigh. He admitted to himself what had been nagging at the back of his mind for quite some time. Almost as if an audible voice had spoken, he knew there were two things he had to do.

One, despite any rejection he would likely receive, he had to let Eva know he loved her.

Chapter 8

Jack became more nervous by the moment about what he intended to. All day he vacillated between telling himself how foolish such an action would be and telling himself he must follow through.

What would he do if Baldovino were there? Was today the time to do it? Was it too late? Was Vizcaya the place? Was he just setting himself up for humiliation for the rest of his life?

Determined, he decided on dressy/casual attire and not to wear a suit as Baldovino likely would. The quartet had talked of wearing their matching outfits of navy and white since they were not out-front performers, but would provide background music to the guests touring the museum.

He arrived after noon, knowing the quartet was to play for a couple of hours inside the museum in the morning, afternoon, and evening between the outdoor Medieval activities. Deciding afternoon was not the time to carry out his mission, he watched a little of the Medieval jousting and remembered when he was a knight and when many young women, including Eva, admired him much the way Eva was now admiring the famous violinist.

One big difference. She'd been a young college girl then. She was a woman now.

If Baldovino were there at Vizcaya, then Jack saw no way he could get Eva alone and talk with her. He didn't see him.

He listened to the quartet playing their Renaissance music in the evening. Most guests took the music for granted. A few took time to lightly applaud. The sound was good enough to merit enthusiastic ovation.

"Eva, could I talk with you privately?" he asked when the quartet was putting their instruments into their cases.

She laid her violin in its case, then straightened and looked at him curiously.

He must have looked as ill as he felt. This was the turning point of his entire life. He had to know if there was a chance for him, although he felt he already knew. He was bold in most areas and never self-conscious. This weak-kneed, butterfly stomach sort of thing was entirely new to him.

He kept telling himself that he and Eva had known each other for years. They were like family in many ways. He could say anything to her. She was not an unkind person. However, his ego and pride played a part in this, too. But, he mustn't let pride stand in the way of at least facing what he felt for her and letting her know, regardless of the consequence. He felt like a coward, but not telling her would be even worse cowardice.

If the truth were out, and he received her rejection, then he wouldn't have to wonder and could move on, as difficult as that might be. But he didn't want to live out his life having been a coward.

"Is Baldovino here?" he asked.

"I haven't seen him," she replied. "His tour manager was to fly in this morning. Georgio said he'd come tonight if he could.

"Is something wrong?" she asked quickly, likely seeing some horrible expression on his face. "Have you seen him?"

"No. Nothing like that. I was just asking."

"Is Grandpa all right?"

"He's all right. It's. . .me."

"You? Jack?" Her stare filled with concern. "Are. . .are you ill?"

"Ill?" He expelled a deep breath. "Not in the way you're implying. I feel rather like I've got the flu, but—"

"Oh, Jack. Well, go home and take something and get in bed."

Tristan, Tyrone, and Rissa were looking at him now. "Do you need to leave with them?"

"No. I drove," she said.

"Could we. . .talk in private?"

"Sure," she said.

The others said their good-byes, and Eva left her violin with an attendant.

Jack led her out into the fan-shaped garden of Italian-clipped topiary, water displays, and French parterres. A beautiful setting for having one's heart broken. Perhaps he could stick his head in a water fountain and drown.

"Orange juice and aspirin and rest won't help what ails me," Jack said. "I don't have the flu. I just. . .feel like it. . .sort of. I have a problem."

"A problem?"

He followed her lead now as she passed through a double grotto and entered the high-walled secret garden.

"Eva," he said, lest she continue toward the maze garden in which he'd likely end up at a dead end, which was the way he felt already. A scent of jasmine wafted on the light evening breeze as the sky deepened to a deep blue hue.

She stopped and looked up at him with concern in her expression.

He couldn't stand it any longer. *Say it. . .get it over with.* This was not some romantic interlude in which he should get on his knees. This was a confession to a woman who resented him. Was he crazy? Probably. But he'd decided to do it and do it he would.

He'd even rehearsed but couldn't remember how to say it. He supposed there was no way but to blurt it out.

He grasped her upper arms, lest she slap him and run away before he finished.

"I love you," he said.

She stared. She seemed like one of the statues in the garden. She didn't blink. She didn't open her mouth. Had she ceased to breathe? Had he shocked the life out of her?

He'd said it. Maybe he should explain it.

"I always cared for you. But I saw you as one of many girls who seemed to think I was that knight in shining armor on a white horse. I reveled in it, but in those days I took no girl seriously. I knew you cared for me, but so did others. After I went away, I realized what you really meant to me. More than any other woman. I've related to others, but my heart always returned to you. I found myself, so to speak. I found the Lord in a more committed way. I needed a career and had an opportunity to learn a trade. I realized my heart was here in my own hometown. I longed to see the Alonos again. And you. I wondered if your presence in my heart was only because I missed each of you so much. I had to return and find out. The moment I saw you that first night at Alono's, I knew. I love you."

He wondered if he'd spoken in French or English. She didn't seem to comprehend. But she hadn't moved away.

When you've come this far. . .why not. . .?

He drew her to himself, enfolded her in his arms, lowered his face to her uplifted one, and his lips met hers. No sweeter music ever played than the tune so eloquently stirring in his heart, mind, and body.

Reluctantly, he moved away. She stood staring at him with her lips parted, her face stark, and her eyes wide with astonishment. Her shoulder seemed to move slightly upward as if there were a shrug in it, and her head seemed to shake slightly. He could not read that body language. Did her shoulder shrug mean that his declaration meant nothing? Did the shake of her head mean she could not accept his love? She looked like he had said the most asinine thing one could say.

He felt heat begin to rise into his face, and he felt a weakness throughout his body. "I'm sorry if I offended you. I just thought you should know. Forgive me if I was out of line."

Maybe her heart already belonged to Baldovino.

Did she let him kiss her?

She seemed to have melted into his arms. Her lips seemed welcoming. Or had she just been too shocked to resist?

He was so caught up in the emotion of it, he couldn't even be sure if she had responded or simply tolerated his embrace and his kiss.

She continued to stare.

"I had to let you know how I feel. You don't have to say anything."

She didn't.

He turned and walked away, hardly knowing what direction he was taking, but hoping he wouldn't end up in the maze garden, where he'd never find his way out.

❦

Eva didn't know how long she stood there, oblivious to anything around her. Not until she heard Georgio's voice did she return to some semblance of normalcy and realized her fingers lay gently on her lips that Jack had so thoroughly kissed.

She lowered her hand and faced Georgio.

"I tried to get here sooner," he said. "But that was impossible. Fortunately, I have already heard you perform your Renaissance music."

Eva could only nod. Making a sudden switch from the happenings with Jack to the presence of Georgio proved to be a difficult transition.

"I'm dry," Georgio said. "Could I get you something to drink?"

Eva nodded and felt she'd just begun to learn to talk. "Wa—water, please."

She still stood in the same spot when Georgio returned with two glasses of water with a slice of lemon on the edges. He looked around and spoke of the lovely evening.

After a few sips in silence, Georgio spoke. "Could we stroll through the gardens? I've never seen them."

When they came to a secluded spot, he turned to her. "To my regret, my agent tells me my vacation must end soon and I must return to my obligations elsewhere. I have so enjoyed our times together."

"Oh, I have, too," Eva said with exuberance. "I will never forget it."

"Neither will I," he said. "Could you join me tomorrow night at the beach house? There is something very important I'd like to discuss with you."

"Yes," Eva said.

He looked at her for a long moment, but she could find no words to say. He smiled then, reached out his hand, and touched her arm. "Are you ready to leave?"

"Not just yet," she said. "I. . .I will see you tomorrow."

"Very good," he said and smiled. "Good night."

Eva found a bench beneath a tree and lowered herself to a sitting position.

Why wasn't her pulse racing because Georgio said he had something "very important" to discuss with her? She would be ecstatically anticipatory if things had remained as they had been with Jack.

But. . .Jack kissed her. He said he loved her.

A few weeks ago she had no one special.

And now. . .would she have to decide between two men. . . one who had come into her life so recently. . .and the other one whom she had loved so ardently for years?

With her hands clasped on her lap, Eva took several deep, needed breaths, as if she were Miss Muffet on a tuffet, expecting a spider to come and sit down beside her.

Chapter 9

Now that Jack had done one of the two things he'd intended to do, the time had come for the second task, which might prove to be as unacceptable as when he told Eva he loved her.

He got the phone number that Al had while repairing the Strad and called Baldovino. Soon he was on his way to the beach house.

A man led Jack into a front room that had a spectacular view of the ocean. Baldovino laid aside a magazine and stood when Jack came into the room. He offered Jack refreshments, which Jack refused, and the man who'd led him in left the room. Jack accepted the offer to sit in a chair across from Baldovino.

Jack laid his violin case across his knees. Baldovino simply glanced at it, then gazed blandly at Jack.

Jack plunged in. "This is the Alono." He laid his hand on the case. "It can be yours."

Baldovino lifted an eyebrow and looked as if he'd expected that all along. "How much?"

"It's a gift," Jack said. "On one condition."

Baldovino leaned farther back against his chair. "Ah, this sounds like a business transaction. I get the Alono and I return the girl to you."

"No," Jack said. "I love Eva. I would not attempt to do something like this underhandedly. I can't buy her. You can't give her to me." He paused a moment. "Frankly, I'm more inclined to give you the violin because you have the girl. She deserves the best, and a man trying to live without the Lord is not the best."

Baldovino looked amused. "I seem to be doing all right." He lifted both eyebrows and gave Jack a quick once-over as if he might be the one who needed help.

Jack nodded. "You seem to be. But if it hasn't happened already, the time will come when you feel there's an empty spot in your heart and life that even fame and money can't fill. I've been there. Only God's spirit can bring that kind of filling."

Baldovino gestured with his hand as if that subject didn't matter. "Getting back to the Alono. You say I can't give you Eva. You don't want money." He shrugged. "What's your condition?"

"My condition is that you listen to the reason I'm giving it."

"Proceed." Baldovino crossed his arms over his chest.

Jack took a shaky breath. "This violin should be played by a master. I'm not that. I'll say to you what Al said to me that I couldn't escape. I hope you won't be able to escape it, either. It's a free gift demonstrating the gift of eternal life with God. You can't buy it. You can't accomplish enough to earn or deserve it. It's a free gift. You only have to believe Jesus is the Son of God. He died as forgiveness for our sins and He rose from the dead. You accept that in your heart and turn to a life of serving Him, and that's called salvation from eternal separation from God."

They sat in silence for a long moment.

Georgio didn't speak or move, reminding him of Eva's reaction the night before.

Jack knew his condition had been met. Georgio had listened.

There was only one thing to do.

Jack stood. He picked up the violin case by the handle and held it out to Georgio.

Georgio's dark eyes searched Jack's. "You're taking a chance on losing the Alono and Eva, too."

Jack nodded. "I know. And that is even more reason to want you to find salvation, to be the kind of man she deserves. You can't be that without the Holy Spirit in your life. You can't have the Holy Spirit without believing and following Jesus Christ." Jack blinked as if the bright midmorning sunlight against the windows were accosting his eyes.

"You know what this violin is worth?"

"Yes, of course," Jack replied. "But not as much as my eternal soul. Jesus paid with His life. He gave Himself up to die for me. Anything I have to give is small in comparison."

"And if I don't believe or accept what you've said, I must return the violin?"

"No. I will be pleased if one of your ability plays this violin and brings pleasure to others. But I would hope this gesture will do what Al hoped it would do for me. I couldn't forget that, and you won't, either. Al said the violin was mine to keep, to hide, to throw away, to give away, to play. When a gift is given, you shouldn't tell the recipient what to do with it. But never forget why it was given. I hope it will have the same effect on you."

Jack took a small tract out of his shirt pocket. "This briefly tells of the plan of salvation much better than I did."

Georgio stared at it, while awkwardly his hands lay on top of the violin case lying on his knees.

It occurred to Jack that Georgio might not believe the Alono was in the case. He took it, laid the case on the couch, and unzipped the lid. He took it out and showed Georgio Al's mark on the back.

"I'm willing to pay you for it," Baldovino said.

"No," Jack said. "This is not about money. It's about your eternal soul. Your salvation."

Baldovino spoke thoughtfully. "I impress women with my violin playing. You could win Eva's favor, if not her love, by giving her the Alono." He shrugged. "Yet, you will not."

"No. Al said someday I would know what to do with this violin. I know. . .this is what I want to do."

Baldovino still looked skeptical. He spoke slowly. "So. You will give up your prized possession because of your faith."

"Yes."

Baldovino shook his head and a scoff escaped his throat. "Amazing."

⁂

"I want to talk to you about love," Georgio said.

Eva stopped short on the sandy beach where the two of them had been strolling after a lovely dinner prepared by Elena. She put her hand to her chest. "Oh. . ." She thought the world of Georgio. But she couldn't consider making any kind of commitment at this time. Not since—

Georgio raised both hands. He laughed lightly. "No. No. Don't worry. I know you are in love with Jack."

"What?"

"Whether you want to admit it or not, you're in love with Jack."

Eva scoffed. "How can you say that?"

"For one thing," he said. "Last night I arrived at Vizcaya earlier than I let on. One of your friends said you had gone into the garden. I walked out there, then saw you and Jack. I made a hasty retreat back into the building."

"Oh, I'm sorry. I didn't expect that to happen."

"No. No. I'm not asking for an explanation. That is your business. I suspected you loved Jack that first night I met you two at the Alono Restaurant."

"I didn't give Jack the time of day that night."

Georgio lifted a finger and looked mischievous. "That was the first clue. But that night, you did not miss a note in your violin playing although you were obviously impressed with my being a successful violinist." He smiled. "You spilled the water at the sound of the voice of the one who touches your heart. I have kept that in mind."

Eva relaxed somewhat, now that Georgio wasn't asking her for a commitment nor expressing undying love for her.

She said coyly, "Then why did you kiss me that night, right here on the beach?"

He spread his hands and looked askance. "That was a kiss? Ah." He scoffed then. "That was more like the tuning note before the violinist plays. I can do much better."

He leaned forward and Eva jumped back. They both laughed.

"Actually, though," he said, "let me count the reasons. You are a beautiful woman and I am a man. I like you. Beyond my own selfish reasons, I wanted to confirm to myself and to you that you are in love with someone else, whether or not you choose to admit it."

"I. . .tried not to."

"Now, a kiss is more like what you and Jack did in that garden."

"He kissed me. I. . .I don't think I kissed him."

"Oh, ho!" Georgio exclaimed. "If that was not a kiss, then God didn't make little green apples."

Eva ducked her head and looked down at the sand. "I really don't know what happened. I was surprised. Then shocked."

Georgio lifted her chin with his fingers. "Let me shock you further."

⁂

Shocked she was, when Georgio told her what Jack had done in giving him the Alono.

As he continued the story, Eva realized, however, that she should not be shocked. It sounded so much like Grandpa, and now she realized how Jack demonstrated his commitment to the Lord in his settling down to a business, being faithful to the church, and using his musical ability for the Lord.

But this was a much bigger issue than what she thought of either Georgio or Jack as men. "Did his gift have an impact on you?"

Georgio sighed. "I suppose I'm reluctant to be too serious about all this. But Jack was right. I left that Alono on the couch all day. I wouldn't touch it. I'd pass through the room or in the hallway and look in its direction. I no longer see it as just a wonderful violin. I see it as possibly the only way to a relationship with God." He looked up toward the darkening sky. "Jack was right. I cannot face the Alono without knowing there is a decision for me to make."

Before she could even ask if he wanted to talk about such a decision, he stopped walking and faced her again. "How does this make you feel that Jack gave away the Alono?"

The seagull that spread its wings, lifted off from the beach, and soared out over the ocean simulated the burden that left her heart.

Tears welled up in her eyes. "I realize I was never really so much upset about Grandpa giving the Alono to Jack. My resentment of Jack was because I felt rejected by him. I loved him."

"You love him now."

Eva nodded.

"I will give you the Alono. It belongs to you and Jack."

"No." Eva was adamant about that. "I understand Grandpa now. The Alono is a witness to his faith in Jesus Christ. Now it has been that to Jack. Whatever it might become to you, it is something that should be played by a person of your ability. And. . .Jack's having given it to you makes me love him even more."

Georgio sighed. "You could not love him if he gave you the violin you wanted. And yet you love him for giving away the violin you wanted. Women! Who can understand them?"

He laughed and put his arm around her shoulders. "I do love you in a special way, Eva."

She looked up at him and nodded. "And I love you, Georgio. For the person you are. Not just because you're a great violinist."

He smiled. "Let us seal this mutual admiration society with a temporary farewell dinner Friday night at the Alono Restaurant. Okay?"

Chapter 10

Jack didn't know what it was about. Baldovino had called his shop and invited him to dinner at the Alono Restaurant on Friday night. He was led to the table where the violinist and Eva sat.

She looked particularly beautiful in a colorful Spanish-style dress and her hair back in a French chignon. The glow of the candle danced with light and shadow on her face, which wore a soft expression, and her eyes seemed to glow with warmth. Was that the look of love—for Baldovino?

Was this a thank-you dinner for the Alono and for Eva? Maybe Baldovino wanted to gloat that he had won the girl.

Baldovino had a silly grin on his face. Eva spoke to Jack but avoided looking into his eyes. She and Baldovino seemed to be speaking an indecipherable eye language. Jack felt like knocking his water glass over and making a dash for the back door.

As if there were no issues, and perhaps there were none, Baldovino began to talk about bows. "Before I leave Miami," he said, "I would like to buy one of your bows."

Jack met his gaze. "Are you trying to repay me for the Alono?"

Baldovino laughed. "I daresay a bow wouldn't come close to what the Alono is worth."

Jack acknowledged that with a nod. "True. But the best ones are expensive."

"I'm aware of that," Georgio said. "My bows are made by French masters—likely your teachers."

Jack was aware that the sale of one of his best bows meant he would have no business worries for quite awhile. It meant his business could grow slowly without his worrying about it. Any other time Jack would be overjoyed at what this man just said.

At the moment, however, another thought burdened his mind. Baldovino would buy his bow. Baldovino would be Eva's beau.

He didn't know if he could get through this dinner gracefully.

"My cue," Eva said. She pushed away from the table and walked up onto the stage. She reached for the violin lying atop the piano, then began to play, "There's a Sweet, Sweet Spirit in This Place."

Jack stared at Eva. She was not playing her violin. The tone had to be either the Alono. . .or the Strad. Feeling as she had about his having the Alono, he felt this had to be Baldovino's Strad.

His spirit was anything but sweet at the moment. He took a deep breath and told himself to accept the inevitable and prepare for the worst.

Baldovino kept glancing at him with what appeared to be a twinkle in his eyes. Maybe it was just the candlelight. Maybe it was a gloat that the best man won. Perhaps Baldovino was the best man. . .for Eva.

When Eva returned to the table, Jack didn't ask if she'd played the Strad. Over salad, Baldovino asked how Jack's business was going. After some idle chitchat, Al came over. After greeting them, he spoke primarily to Baldovino. "I heard you'll be leaving soon. Just wanted to say how much I've enjoyed meeting you. Your concert was fabulous. And I appreciate how happy you've made my granddaughter these past weeks."

Georgio stood and shook hands with Al, expressing his gratitude for all he'd done, including having such an adorable granddaughter. Al returned to the Alono family table. Eva seemed to concentrate on her salad, making only a few remarks here and there. Jack suspected her being unusually quiet meant she was embarrassed for his having declared his undying love for her.

Roberto Alono then took the microphone and after a few words, he and Bev began their flamenco dance while waiters removed salad plates.

During the main course, Baldovino took the subject where Jack hadn't expected, but had hoped and prayed about.

"I want to thank you both for the time and attention you've given me. And you, Jack, for the Alono. If you would take money for it, I would gladly pay it."

Jack shook his head.

Baldovino nodded and smiled. "I do want you both to know that I'm not some infidel. I have attended church. I have read much of the Bible. I am familiar with the great hymns and spiritual music."

He gestured with his hands, including his fork.

"Almost everyone knows of Handel's *Messiah*. I have played those great religious songs. Have heard them sung. I know the words. I think they're wonderful. How can anyone listen to beautiful music and say there is no God? It is beyond man. My playing is a result of many factors, and yet it is still beyond me. I am as amazed as my fans at the beauty of music and the ability of a person to be a part of it."

Jack didn't take another bite while Baldovino was expressing his belief in God. This had turned out to be much bigger than his own personal wants. An eternal soul lay in the balance. When Baldovino paused to take another bite, Jack said, "Almost everyone believes there is a God. That's not the main point."

Baldovino lifted a finger while chewing, then swallowed. Then he nodded. "I understand that now. I never doubted that Jesus maybe was the Son of God. Who else does so much for humanity than those who believe that? I thought that was one way to God—not the only way." He sighed and shook his head. "I didn't know one needed to take a stand on it."

He tackled his food again, so Jack decided to do the same. If Baldovino understood it, then what more was there to say? The matter now lay between him and God.

Eva excused herself from the table without having eaten much of her food.

As soon as she was a few steps away, Baldovino leaned toward Jack. "I know you love her."

How quickly a subject could change from the spiritual to the personal. What could he say? He wasn't sorry. He didn't have to explain his actions to Baldovino. Or did he? He could try. "If I had known—"

"No. No." Baldovino lifted his hand. "That was just an observation. I wonder. . .do you think you and I could be friends?"

Was this guy rubbing it in? "I don't know," Jack said. "How involved were you with the woman I love?"

"Ah!" Baldovino said. "I do not kiss and tell."

Jack felt like punching the guy in the face. However, maybe Baldovino felt like doing the same to him.

"I will say," Baldovino began, "Eva is a masterpiece. What does one do with a masterpiece? Perhaps you were inclined not to play a fine musical instrument. But I. . .hey, am a master of performance."

He raised his right hand with his index finger like one making a very fine point. "Wait! Wait!"

Jack wasn't sure what to make of the egotistical, triumphant attitude of Baldovino that turned playful. The violinist shook his head and gave Jack a look of one reprimanding another.

Baldovino laughed then, and Jack knew it likely was at his own reddening face. "You have nothing to worry about. I happened upon the garden at Vizcaya and witnessed you and Eva making emotional music together. That kind of melody has not existed between her and me. Besides, one of the reasons I took these few weeks away from people and activity in which I am normally involved was to ponder the relationship with a woman who has been special to me for some time. A serious commitment would involve changes in careers of one or the other of us. She is an acclaimed soprano with a touring philharmonic. I have studied the relationship of you and your Eva."

"Studied?"

Baldovino nodded. "You see, I came here to get away from Maria and her morality faith. I prayed to God that if there was something to the Jesus thing, then let me know. Then He smacked me in the face with it at every turn, beginning with the first night when Eva played an invocation, then her parents expressed their faith, and on it went. Then your giving me the Alono and a sermon."

The two of them laughed lightly. Jack loved the way God could work in lives when humans felt so helpless. "I think you've played a few games there."

"Well," Baldovino said with a lift of his aristocratic chin. "The relationship between you two fascinated me. It reminded me of my own with Maria. But I will say I enjoyed spending time with Eva. She helped me understand Maria. I believe Eva and I have become friends."

Jack was having trouble processing what was taking place. Then his attention turned to the stage, where Eva had again taken the microphone.

She announced to the quieting patrons that there was a special surprise tonight. She introduced Baldovino, who rose to the rousing applause and made his way to the stage. He reached for the violin and bow that lay on top of the piano while Eva returned to the table. Jack watched her expression as she gazed at Baldovino with unabashed appreciation. Or was it. . .something else?

Baldovino said he and Eva hadn't fallen in love. But. . . could he speak for Eva?

Baldovino began to speak over the microphone. "I will be playing on an Alono violin, one of the finest in the world. Also, I would like to play in tribute to the maker of the violin, the one who gave me this priceless instrument, and the one who gave me weeks of pleasure when I was a stranger in your city. Most of all, this is an answer to the Maker of my soul."

Jack knew by the second note that Baldovino was playing "Amazing Grace." Eva faced him then and looked straight into his eyes. He couldn't read the expression, however. The tears, from her eyes, or his own, perhaps both, obscured visibility.

He closed his eyes and thanked God that a soul had been saved from eternal separation from his Maker. One in a position to tell a wide audience of their need for Jesus Christ. The amazing sound of music that enveloped the room from a master violinist expressed with indescribable beauty the grace of God.

Eva looked up at Georgio as he stood at the table, violin case in hand. "I will not stay for dessert," he said. "I will say good-bye, but I hope we keep in touch."

Eva stood, and so did Jack, who shook Georgio's hand. Eva hugged him, and he kissed her cheek.

"Thank you both," he said. "If you will excuse me now, I have an important call to make to someone else who has been concerned about my soul. If things go as I hope, then perhaps we can be friends as couples."

Eva looked after Georgio until he was out of sight. He had filled her life in so many ways. She could see now that God had a purpose in it, too. That was a lesson she must remember—that people who come into our lives may not be for our sake only, but for their eternal souls. She was grateful for that special man who had touched her life in such a beautiful way.

"Eva," Jack said. "You're ignoring me."

With a sideways glance, she shrugged. "How long did you ignore me?"

"Oh, no." He groaned. "You're going to make me wait four years before you tell me if there's a chance for us?"

"Four years?" She huffed. "You ignored me even before that. So. . .just give me time. I'm. . .thinking."

"Okay," he said. "I can sit here for four, six, eight years. However long it takes."

Eva picked at the dessert that was set before her, knowing that Jack had begun to eat his. She had wondered how to tell Jack that she loved him, too. Somehow she couldn't just blurt it out. That simply wasn't romantic enough.

She'd returned to trying to make a great Alono. After all, that was her name as well as Grandpa's. She'd looked at the plaque Grandpa kept over one of his workbenches. She'd read the verse hundreds of times—

Now finish the work, so that your eager willingness to do it may be matched by your completion of it, according to your means.

For if the willingness is there, the gift is acceptable according to what one has, not according to what he does not have.

2 Corinthians 8:11–12

Maybe she could make the best violin she could and give it to Jack to replace the Alono and to show him she no longer resented his having had it but was grateful to Grandpa's wisdom in making it an object of one's witness to one's faith.

Suddenly, Jack rose from his seat, tossed his napkin on his plate, and strode away from the table. Eva drew in a quick breath. Had he given up? So soon? Had she behaved like a silly schoolgirl, when he would expect a woman to return his love? Should she run after him?

The next thing she knew, he'd hopped up onto the stage and grabbed the microphone. "This is unconventional and not part of the program," he said. "So feel free to leave if you wish. I can't perform like the great Georgio Baldovino, but I want to express my love with my music to the one who can turn my life's song into one of beauty or one of despair. The last time I heard this song, I was not ready to accept true love nor was I capable of giving it. This is for the love of my life. I want this to be. . .our song."

Eva stared as he sat down on the piano stool, stretched out his arms, placed his hands on the keys, and began not only to play but to sing "So in Love."

Eva laid her fork down and put her hands on her lap. When Marco came near, she gave him her car keys and instruction. He nodded and grinned.

When Jack finished, he came to the table. With his hands on the edge, he said, "I can't wait four years. I can't even wait four minutes. Do I stand a chance that you could love me?"

Eva tried to look demure. "Could you meet me on the back veranda? I will then give you my answer in about four seconds."

"I hope it will be accompanied by three words," he said.

She smiled demurely. "Follow me."

Outside, she picked up the violin she'd had Marco put on a table and walked over to a shadowed spot, lighted only by the moonlight and twinkling stars.

She began to play "So in Love," and Jack joined in with the lyrics of being "close to you beneath the stars." He came nearer, singing, "So in love with you am I."

He took the violin from her and laid it aside and then took her in his arms.

"I love you, Jack," she said. "Since the first time I saw you. Oh, I think it was a crush at first, but it grew. Even when I tried not to love you, I did."

He held her. "I've always loved you, too, Eva. As a young girl, as a friend. And now I love you as a woman. I want us to build a life together. To marry, have children, love each other." He took a deep breath and took on a troubled look. "I couldn't give you the Alono. I can only offer my heart, my lifetime commitment, my love."

"That's all I want," Eva said.

This time, she knew she responded to his kiss, perhaps even initiated it.

Georgio could play the Alono. Jack played the strings of her heart.

And she could name that tune. It was love.

YVONNE LEHMAN

Yvonne Lehman, bestselling author of more than 3,000,000 books in print, founded and directed the Blue Ridge Mountains Christian Writers Conference for twenty-five years and is now director of the Blue Ridge "Autumn in the Mountains" Novelist Retreat. She has joined Lighthouse Publishing of the Carolinas as Acquisitions and Managing Editor of Candlelight Romance and Guiding Light Women's Fiction. She earned a master's degree in English from Western Carolina University and has taught English and creative writing on the college level. Her recent releases include a three-book series set in Savannah, Georgia, (Harlequin Heartsong) and Hearts of Carolina series of eight novels (four in North Carolina, four in South Carolina). In April 2014, her 50th novel Hearts That Survive—A Novel of the TITANIC (Abingdon) released, and she signs periodically at the Titanic Museum in Pigeon Forge, Tennessee. Her first non-fiction book is Divine Moments (Grace Publishing), a compilation of 50 articles written by various authors. She blogs at www.christiansread.com and Novel Rocket Blog.

SUDDEN SHOWERS

by Gail Sattler

Chapter 1

Sharmane Winters leaned back on the park bench. Today was the first day of her summer vacation. Originally she had planned to drive up-country and explore the scenery, stopping for the night wherever she happened to be at suppertime. Unfortunately, her car now sat in her mechanic's lot awaiting a very expensive part which, upon its arrival, was going to eat up most of her vacation money and all of her one-week vacation.

Instead of sitting at home feeling sorry for herself, Sharmane intended to make the best of it. While she tried thinking of something to do that didn't involve her car, she grabbed a book and headed to the city park.

With birds chirping in the branches overhead and children screaming in the playground in the distance, Sharmane settled in and submerged herself in the lives of the characters. Totally engrossed as the plot thickened, she purposely ignored the darkening sky until a peal of thunder sounded in the distance, forcing her to pay attention.

Raindrops rustled the leaves as Sharmane raised her head to the thick clouds. A louder boom of thunder sounded as the patter of the rain increased to a steady drone and a flash of lightning lit the sky. Sharmane counted the seconds before the boom, trying to gauge how close the storm actually was.

The drizzle changed to a torrent. Sharmane abandoned the bench and huddled next to the trunk of the large oak in an attempt to keep dry until it passed. Since the sun had been shining brightly when she left, she had ignored the forecast and left her umbrella behind, a decision she now regretted.

Since she could no longer read, she fished through her purse for a scrap of paper to use as a bookmark but accidentally dropped the book. She picked it up and began to page through to find where she left off as more lightning flashed, followed by an immediate peal of thunder.

A large hand wrapped around her arm. "Come on!"

Sharmane screeched and yanked her arm away. A tall, wet man stood in front of her.

She hugged her purse to her chest, mentally preparing herself to hit him with it. "What are you doing?" she squeaked in a vain effort to sound calm, positive the stranger could hear the rapid hammering of her heart above the drone of the rain.

"Trying to get you out of here."

Sharmane backed up squarely against the tree, prepared to kick him if she had to, even though she doubted her soft sneakers would do much damage. Another bolt of lightning flashed, accompanied by a boom of thunder directly overhead. The stranger extended his hand, but she didn't take it.

He stood about ten inches taller than she did, and his wet clothing molded to his body emphasizing his height and the width of his broad shoulders, making the idea of opposing him almost laughable. If he wanted to, Sharmane had no doubt he could pick her up and throw her over his shoulder and carry her wherever he wanted, caveman style, with very little effort.

She concentrated on his face, hoping the unwavering eye contact would make him back off. That was a mistake. His eyes were a soft shade of sable brown, almost the same color as his hair, which lay stuck to his forehead. She wondered if when it was dry, his hair and eyes would be the same unique color. His lips were tightly drawn, making his lower lip protrude slightly, like a little boy pouting, except he was far too large and handsome for that.

"Don't you know that the most dangerous place in a lightning storm is under a tree? Do you want to become another statistic? We'll be safe inside one of the stores across the street."

As the force of the rain increased, Sharmane peeked out from under the protective cover of the tree. Lightning snaked directly overhead, lighting up the entire sky. As much as she hated to admit it, the man was right.

A shiver ran up her spine at the thought of getting soaked to the skin, but being wet in no way compared to being fried alive. Another bolt of lightning immediately followed by a peal of thunder helped Sharmane make up her mind in a hurry. "All right. Let's go."

This time, when he grabbed her hand, she didn't fight. She held on tight and ran with him across the soggy field, waited for two cars to go by before crossing the street, then dashed under the narrow awning of the row of stores. Sharmane gasped for breath and fiddled with her purse to bide some time while she recovered, hoping to avoid the embarrassment of being so winded after such a short run.

A shudder wracked her body from the top of her wet head to her freezing feet. Her socks were so wet that cold water squished between her toes, and a dribble of water snaked down her back. The only thing still dry was her book, safely zippered inside her leather purse.

The downpour splattered harshly on the pavement not sheltered by the narrow awning, falling so hard that the raindrops bounced before joining the growing stream in the gutter. Shivering again, she wrapped her arms around herself in an attempt to warm up.

***

Alex swiped a lock of dripping hair off his forehead as he studied the woman he had literally dragged out from under a tree. Her hair lay plastered to the top of her head, and her clothes were so wet everything stuck to her body in a way that appeared most uncomfortable.

He still could barely believe he was doing this, when he should have been at work.

Less than an hour ago, he'd stormed out of his office, much to the shock of his secretary, only meaning to go for a long walk. When he stepped outside, it briefly registered that the sky had darkened, because it had been sunny when he left for work, but he didn't care. He was so angry from yet another major corporate foul-up that he didn't feel the cold; at least he hadn't then.

In order to clear his mind and work the frustration out of his system, he meant to walk around the promenade at the perimeter of the park. Once didn't do it, and he was halfway through his second time around when it started to rain, which he found very fitting, considering his mood. And it wasn't just a little rain. In the blink of an eye the skies opened to a torrential downpour, sending everyone fleeing for cover. He had started to jog through the center of the park to get back to his dry, safe office. Then he saw the woman, who had been sitting on the bench on his first trip around the park, huddled under the tree still reading her book while lightning flashed directly overhead.

He couldn't, in good conscience, leave her there. Even if the lightning didn't hit that particular tree today, which being realistic, it probably wouldn't, he had only done the responsible thing. But he certainly hadn't meant to frighten her.

He looked at her again. The wet woman was pretty. She could probably stand to lose a few pounds, but so could he. He straightened his posture, his hand unconsciously resting on his stomach, and turned to face her.

Her blond hair hung in clumps at the moment, but when he first saw her it was fluffy and slightly curly at the ends and framed her face quite attractively. She had a pointy little chin, big blue eyes, and a pouty little mouth, which, when not fixed in a stubborn line, suited her pixie-like features.

A gust of wind caused them both to shiver at the same time.

Forcing a smile, he turned to the as yet unnamed woman and cleared his throat in an attempt to compose himself.

"My name's Alex. I have an idea." Alex jerked his head to one side at the same time as he hitched his thumb over his shoulder. "Let's go in there and warm up with a hot cup of coffee. My treat."

For a moment, he thought she was going to refuse, but just as she opened her mouth someone opened the door, and the alluring aroma of fresh brewing coffee wafted out.

She glanced from side to side, eyed the crowd, and turned back to him. "Thank you," she mumbled, then smiled weakly. "I'd appreciate that."

He smiled back and ushered the wet woman inside.

The hot coffee helped to ward off the chill somewhat. He sipped the coffee slowly, enjoying the liquid heat, knowing he should have been back at the office long ago, but he couldn't make himself move.

"So, do you often sit outside in the rain, Miss. . . ?" He let the word hang in the air as a smile tipped up the corners of his mouth and one eyebrow raised slightly.

Her cheeks flushed. "My name is Sharmane."

Alex's smile widened, and he nodded at the strange introduction.

"It was warm and sunny when I got there."

A rumble of thunder sounded in the distance, indicating the storm was passing as quickly as it had begun. "Yes, it sure came up fast."

"Not really. They predicted it on the forecast; I just ignored it."

They sipped the coffee in unison, then both stared into their cups. It was almost like looking in a mirror. Alex couldn't think of a thing to say. He'd never lacked for conversation with a pretty woman before, and it didn't exactly do wonders for his ego.

"Feeling warmer now?" he finally asked.

"I guess so, except my feet are freezing because my socks are wet. And when my feet are cold, I'm cold all over."

Alex forced himself to smile when he really wanted to bury his face in his hands. He studied the bottom of his empty cup. "So take your socks off," he mumbled to no one in particular.

Her eyes opened wide as she stared at him. "What a great idea!"

Alex's ears heated up. He hadn't meant for her to hear that, nor could he believe she took him seriously.

With one quick gulp, she finished her coffee and thunked the cup down on the table. "Let's go outside, the rain stopped."

He followed her in silence. The second they got outside, she leaned against the building, pulled off one sneaker, then the sock, stuffed the sock into an outside pocket on her purse, slipped her bare foot back into the wet sneaker, and repeated the process. When both bare feet were again covered, she stood straight, beaming a smile from ear to ear. "That feels so much better. How about you? I'd imagine your socks are wet, too. Don't be shy."

The last thing he'd ever been called was shy, but he wasn't going to take off his socks, especially in front of a stranger or anyone else who happened to be walking by. He should have been at work, straightening out the mess with the quarterly budgets.

"Well, Alex, thanks for the coffee and for statistically saving my life today. I guess I should be going home now."

And he should have been back at work a long time ago. Being drenched by the sudden downpour then warming up by sharing a coffee with a pretty woman went a long way toward softening his foul mood. However, the words that came out of his mouth surprised him more than he surprised her.

"I've got nothing better to do. If you don't mind, I'd like to walk you home."

While she stood staring at him, he crooked his elbow and patted his arm to encourage her.

Hesitantly, she did tuck her hand inside, so he covered it with his other hand, patted it, and started to walk.

"I normally would have brought my car, but it's in the shop. I'm supposed to be on vacation this week. How about you?"

Visions of the mountains of papers and reports on his desk flashed through his mind. He couldn't remember it being any other way, from the time he started the company to present. He also couldn't remember the last time he'd had a vacation.

The stress was getting to him, and he knew it. What he'd done this morning was nothing short of certifiable. When the same budget report came back to him the third time with more errors, he'd lost it. Rather than say something he'd surely regret, he tossed off his suit jacket and left. His secretary tried to stop him, and the best he could do was shout on his way out the door that he'd be back some time that afternoon and to cancel his appointments. He'd never done anything so irresponsible in his life.

Instead of rushing back to do damage control, here he was walking in the opposite direction with a woman he'd just met.

He should have felt guilty, but he didn't. The work would still be there when he returned, whether it was in an hour, a day, or a week. He had competent staff, except for the latest fiasco. Terry knew how to run things in his absence. The company wouldn't fold just because he wasn't there.

Alex smiled as the weight of the world lifted from his shoulders. "I'm on vacation, too."

She sighed. "Well, it looks like you don't have any plans either. I mean, I did have plans, but without my car, everything kind of went out the window."

"Plans?"

She sighed again. "I'm stuck here in the city, but I'm not going to waste my time off. Instead of heading over to the island, I'm going to visit all the tourist spots I've never bothered to see because I live here, and do a bunch of stuff I've never done before, right in my own hometown. For the entire week, I'm going to do nothing but goof off."

Goof off? The idea held a certain appeal. Alex had traveled all over the world on business, but he'd never seen the attractions in his own backyard that people came from all over the world to see. Vancouver was one of the most beautiful places in the world, and he ignored it because he lived here.

"I don't have any plans either. I think I'm going to do the same."

She smiled, and his heart melted. "Well, maybe I'll see you some other time this week. Since my car is going to be really expensive to fix, I was planning on doing mostly stuff that's free or at least really cheap."

The thought of simple activities appealed to him. For a week, he could forget about being Alexander Brunnel the corporate executive and just be a regular guy, no stress, no worries.

"That sounds like a great idea. How about if I joined you? My car isn't in the shop; I wouldn't mind picking you up. We could go farther than walking, and it would be better than taking the bus."

"I don't know," she drawled. "We just met. I don't even know you."

"I could show you my driver's license and three major credit cards, and if that's not enough, I can supply references." He tried to give her his most engaging smile. "We'll be going to public places; you'll be safe."

She stopped in front of a small, older bungalow with neatly mown grass and a small flower bed beneath the front window. The house itself needed at least a coat of paint, and a few of the shingles were warped. "This is my house."

He tried not to cringe. It was nothing like what he was used to. The best he could come up with to describe it was the word "modest."

Alex escorted her to the door and waited for her to unlock it. "It's more fun to sightsee when you're not alone." He'd seen a lot of the world alone. At the time he hadn't thought about it, but perhaps that was why he didn't enjoy it as much as he thought he would.

"I suppose."

He grasped her hands then did his best to give Sharmane his most charming smile. "I would really love to goof off with you, and then when it's over, we can part as friends, no obligations, no hassles. How's that sound?"

She narrowed one eye and cocked her head. "I guess so. . . ."

"Great. I'll see you tomorrow morning."

Alex turned away and headed back to the office. He wasn't going to tie up any loose ends. He would simply pick up his suit jacket, tell Terry to look after things for the week, and leave.

He'd never goofed off in his life, and he couldn't remember ever looking forward to something more.

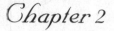

Chapter 2

Sharmane zipped her backpack shut at the exact second the doorbell rang.

A very different Alex stood in her doorway. Gone were the dress slacks, shirt, tie, and leather shoes, replaced by comfortably worn jeans, a T-shirt, and sneakers that had seen better days. Yesterday, she had thought it odd that he looked like he'd just stepped out of the office. Today, he looked like a man on vacation.

Last night, when she should have been sleeping, she'd lain awake staring at the ceiling and thinking about Alex. She had prayed long and hard, asking God if she was doing the right thing.

Again, she compared his appearance to yesterday. She wouldn't ask, but she wondered if he wasn't really on vacation after all. Perhaps he had been dressed so nicely because he was looking for work and had just finished an interview for a potential job. Being unemployed would explain why the idea of accompanying her on her cheap activities appealed to him so much and why he could do it with no advance preparation.

"Good morning, Sharmane. And what plans do we have for the day?"

"It looks like today will be sunny, so I thought we'd start by going to the Capilano Suspension Bridge. After that, I didn't want to make all the decisions, so I thought we could talk about what else we're going to do."

He smiled warmly. "That sounds great."

She followed him to his car, which was an older model economy car very similar to her own, except hers was newer and in much better shape. The condition of his car was almost questionable, but not wanting to be rude, she got in anyway and tucked her pack behind the seat. The interior was in worse shape than the exterior, but it was clean.

To her surprise, it started instantly and the motor purred like a finely tuned sports car.

He rested one hand on the stick shift and turned to her. "Believe it or not, I've never been to the suspension bridge. You might have to give me directions."

Sharmane pulled a map out of her backpack. "Me neither. But my neighbor went recently and she said it was packed with Japanese tourists, so I figured it would be a good place to start."

She watched as he fastened his seat belt. Even in profile, Alex was a very handsome man. And she had been right yesterday. When dry, his hair was exactly the same color as his eyes.

Rather than stare, she fixed her attention to the map. "It's funny, I've lived in Vancouver all my adult life, but I've never been to most of the popular tourist spots. I guess since I figure I can go anytime, that's why I haven't. So this week, that's what I want to do."

He nodded as he entered the traffic flow. "Same here."

Sharmane raised her head from the map. "I don't know anything about you."

When he turned to smile, her breath caught. It was almost like he practiced being distracting. His wide smile created the most attractive crinkles at the corners of his warm brown eyes, and his whole face shone. The man was movie-star handsome, and he likely knew it.

"There's not much about me to tell. I was raised in the suburbs of Vancouver, I came from a family of two boys and one girl, and we went to church every Sunday. I graduated from high school back in 1987, which makes me thirty-one years old. I've never been married, and my favorite color is blue."

Sharmane tried not to let her mouth gape open. "Church every Sunday?"

Briefly, he glanced at her then turned his attention back to his driving. "Yes. And I still do. Do you have a problem with that?"

"No. Not at all. I go to church every Sunday, too. Are you a Christian?" Her heart pounded, waiting for his reply.

"Yes, I am. I was born and raised in a Christian home and made my decision to follow Christ when I was in my teens. What about you?"

"I became a Christian as an adult."

"That's great. Praise the Lord." He glanced at her again and smiled, making her insides quiver, and turned his head forward as he drove. "So now you know all about me. Tell me about yourself, Sharmane."

She really didn't know much more about him than before, but she supposed she would find out more later. "I grew up in Kelowna then moved to Vancouver with my family in my teens. I'm twenty-nine, I've never been married either, and my favorite color is green."

He didn't volunteer any more personal information but instead changed the subject to the weather forecast, which was a determining factor for their choice of activities. Somehow they ended up discussing the news as they made their way through the city.

"I turn right after the bridge, right?"

She quickly paged through the map. "Yes. Right on Marine Drive, then north on Capilano Road." Sharmane looked up just in time to see the stone lions resting on their perches at the entrance to the Lions Gate Bridge.

"I hear they're talking again about budgeting to fix the existing bridge versus a new crossing."

The buzz of the tires humming on the metal grate set Sharmane's nerves on edge, and she forced herself to unclench her teeth. She didn't cross the Lions Gate Bridge often, because the sensation of almost slipping while driving on the grated bridge deck so high above the water always made her feel like she was going to throw up. She preferred to know there was good, solid concrete below her. The few times she ever crossed the Burrard Inlet, she tried to use the Second Narrows Bridge.

The green-lighted arrow above the lane they were in changed to an amber X. The middle lane of the three-lane bridge was now switching direction to accommodate the traffic flow, and they were in that lane. Her guts wrenched. "Alex! They're closing the lane! Hurry!"

He had the nerve to chuckle. "Don't worry, we've got lots of time. Besides, it's monitored. They won't switch the other side to green until they've done a visual check that the lane is clear."

She tried to keep her voice from wavering, especially since Alex was unaffected. He changed lanes on the horrible metal surface without a hint of unease, and then they were back on cement roads and solid land. "I hate the Lions Gate Bridge," she grumbled.

The rest of the trip went without incident, and they soon arrived at the Capilano Canyon.

Sharmane slung the backpack over her shoulders, and they headed for the rope suspension bridge hanging over the ravine. The river churned and beat upon the rocks far, far below.

"This brochure says that it's 450 feet long, which is the world's longest suspension bridge, and that it's 230 feet above ground."

Alex simply nodded and they both looked down the length of the bridge, which seemed much longer when looking at it from the new perspective. The bridge swayed slightly with the movement and shifting weights. They stood back to watch the people venturing across.

Some people inched along cautiously, holding onto both sides of the rope railings at the same time as they walked in the exact center of the narrow bridge. A few hung onto the same side with both hands, but most walked relatively normally, using one hand to steady themselves as they walked slowly across. One rambunctious teenager stood in the center of the bridge halfway across and lifted both hands in the air while his friend snapped his picture.

When a lull in the flow of people crossing finally occurred, Alex's voice came from directly behind her, so close he was almost speaking in her ear. She didn't know he had been standing that close. "Well, are we going to do it, or not?"

Sharmane nodded. She grasped the rope railing tightly and took her first shaky step. The bridge shifted as she put her weight forward, and the unreasonable fear that the bridge would tip sent a surge of adrenaline coursing through her veins. Frantically, she grabbed the other side's railing as well and began to walk across slowly, guiding herself by hanging onto both sides at the same time, as countless others had done before her. She refused to think of the river below, and she kept her gaze fixed straight ahead, not down, not to the side. She didn't want to see the rushing water far below them as she crossed. At least on the Lions Gate Bridge, bad as it was, she was in a car.

Working her way forward slowly, guiding herself across by continuing to grasp both sides as she moved along, she gradually became used to the movement of the bridge as she walked and managed to loosen her grip as she progressed. Her heart pounded, and she still didn't look down.

Without letting go, she turned her head to speak over her shoulder at Alex. "This is fun!"

In a moment of bravery, she looked all the way behind herself to see that Alex was only holding onto one side.

He raised his chin slightly. "Don't look now, but someone is coming."

Sharmane froze in one place, still gripping both sides as she waited to see what would happen next.

"You've got to keep walking, Sharmane. You can do it."

She managed to let go long enough to let the other person past and then continued across once again using the rope railing on either side to guide her.

Finally, she was once more on solid ground.

"I fail to see why you wanted to come here if walking across the bridge was going to terrify you."

Sharmane laughed as a slight breeze rippled through her hair. She filled her lungs with the fresh, cool mountain air, tilted her head back, and shook it so her hair cascaded behind her as she reveled in her achievement. "It's the adventure. The accomplishment of overcoming fear. Doing something you've never done before. Wasn't that fun?"

He shrugged his shoulders. "If you say so."

"It was kind of like going on a roller coaster. Kind of scary but exhilarating at the same time."

"I suppose."

"Let's keep going. I want to go down the trail and find some animals to take pictures of. Did you bring a camera?"

"No, I didn't."

"I can make double prints for you, if you want. Think of it as paying you back for the coffee yesterday."

"Thank you, I'd appreciate it."

"You know, I was going to do this alone, but this is so much more fun."

Alex nodded in response as they walked to the fenced observation area overlooking the canyon. He watched Sharmane shuck off her backpack, withdraw a small camera from one of the outside pouches, and start snapping a few pictures of the scenery. Like her house, the camera was modest and functional, just like the car he'd already heard so much about. He suspected everything she owned would fit into the same category.

"Okay, I've got a few pictures. Let's go do the trail."

The trail consisted of a mulched path wide enough for two people to walk side by side and lasted only a short fifteen to twenty minutes. They didn't see any wildlife except for birds and squirrels, but they stopped often to read the signs describing some of the plants and points of interest along the way. Very little was said, and being surrounded by trees, not people, had a profound effect on Alex.

The only noise was their footsteps in the mulch and the gurgling of the river in the distance. There was no need to rush, no need to keep an eye on the time, no need to hustle to his next appointment, and no need to worry that his messages were stacking up.

Sharmane was walking beside him, and unlike his business associates, his staff, the people at his church, even his friends, she didn't want anything from him. All she wanted was to walk beside him in the quiet and enjoy the scenery.

This was exactly what he needed, and for the first time in years, he was at peace. He didn't care if people wondered why he was walking around smiling for no apparent reason. He owed no one an explanation.

Too soon, they re-entered the clearing, and along with it, a crowd of people. For once, he didn't need his watch to tell him what time it was. His stomach told him it was lunchtime.

Small concession stands dotted the area, as well as a large number of tables, many of them still empty. He reached into his back pocket. "Can I get you something?"

Her hand on his arm stopped him. "You don't need to buy lunch. This is my treat; I brought enough for both of us. I thought it would be cheaper for you than buying something. Come on."

She led him to one of the tables on the edge of the grouping, plunked her backpack into the center of the table, and began unpacking an assortment of containers, as well as two juice boxes, onto the table.

Her words finally brought him out of his stupor. "If you'd like to give thanks for this, we can eat."

Alex couldn't believe it. She'd brought him lunch to save him money. Quickly, he bowed his head and folded his hands in his lap. "Dear Lord, thank You for this wonderful day and this getaway vacation to enjoy the beauty of Your creation. Thank You also for this food before us, Your continued blessings, and this day together. Amen."

"Amen." She slid a container of sandwiches toward him. "Dig in. I hope you like mustard."

Ignoring the crowd around them, he listened to Sharmane recapping some of the things they'd seen and done, at the same time enjoying the sound of her cheery voice and watching her animated expressions. But his mind was racing too much to respond.

All night long he'd tried to figure out what made him want to spend a week with this woman, and he hadn't come up with any answers. Now, he knew.

No one saw him as Alex Brunnel, the man. Instead, people only saw him as A. R. Brunnel, founder and owner of Arby Enterprises, Inc. People perceived him as one of the rich and famous set. He was rich, but he certainly wasn't famous, nor did he particularly like the lifestyle that went with it or the people who did. Because of it, though, people treated him differently than their other friends, and that included members of his church, where people should have known better.

Outside of his business he tried to lead an ordinary life, but people didn't share their ordinary daily happenings with him. If they weren't asking him to fund a project, they were asking if he could give someone they knew a job, or else they tried to impress him. He didn't want to be someone to be impressed. He wanted to be simply one of the guys.

Most of the single women he knew constantly flirted with him as a marriage prospect, compounded by their mothers frequently inviting him for a "casual" lunch or dinner, which was never casual when he got there. His own family was no better in their matchmaking attempts. And because of this, many of the other single men treated him with a cold respect to his face, but he could tell they were jealous. They didn't know what it was like to be pursued for only the wrong reasons.

He tried to be generous with his tithes and offerings and did his best to help those who needed it. Over time, though, the never-ending flow of people asking him for money or favors or trying to match him with their single daughters simply wore him down.

All he wanted was a simple friendship that had nothing to do with anything he owned or had achieved or what he could do for the other person.

And then he met Sharmane. After this week, she would never see him again, which was apparently fine with her. She had made him lunch, without expecting anything in return. It was such an ordinary thing for most people, but not for him.

It made him realize he needed more than a vacation from his work, he needed a vacation from his life. After the week was over he would be strengthened and refreshed, and he could go back to the rat race a new man. Until then, being with Sharmane was exactly what he needed. However, the only way to do this would be to not let her know who he really was. He couldn't take the chance that once she knew, she would become just like everyone else.

With Sharmane, he intended to be just Alex Brunnel, ordinary guy, and not A. R. Brunnel, walking wallet.

"Well, I guess that's about it for the Capilano Canyon. What do you want to do this afternoon?"

Alex blinked and concentrated on Sharmane's question. "I don't know. How about Stanley Park?"

"Sure, since we're so close. Let's go."

He helped gather the empty containers, and Sharmane again lifted her backpack to her shoulders. Now that he knew what had been in it, he felt guilty knowing she'd carried that weight all the time, just so they could have a cheap lunch. It made him appreciate her all the more.

She handed him her camera. "I want you to take a couple of pictures of me just so I can prove I did this. You wait here, and I'm going to stand by the entrance to the bridge. Take my picture so you get lots of scenery around me, and then I'm going to do the same as that kid did earlier. When I get to the middle, I'm going to wave. Then take my picture again. See you on the other side." That said, she jogged off in the direction of the bridge.

Alex found it strangely humbling to have someone give him orders. He suspected the time spent this week with Sharmane would provide many opportunities to experience things he wasn't used to.

He lifted Sharmane's camera to his eye to scan the area before she got there.

"Mr. Brunnel? Is that you?"

Alex didn't move, nor did he lower the camera in the hope that the speaker would think he was mistaken. He didn't look, but by the sound of the voice the next time, the speaker was closer. "Mr. Brunnel? What are you doing here?"

Alex tightened his grip on the camera then brought it down to his side. Everyone he knew should have been at work, and if not, this crowded tourist attraction should have been a safe hiding place. However, he hadn't calculated teenagers into the equation. Since it was summer holidays, they weren't in school.

One of his nephew's friends from the youth group approached him, his girlfriend clinging to his arm.

Quickly, he scanned the area for Sharmane. Fortunately she was still heading toward the bridge, having been distracted by something along the way.

Alex nodded a greeting. "Kyle, Allyson. Hello."

"Where's Jason? I saw his car. But I didn't see yours."

There was a good reason for that. Yesterday, Sharmane had told him about her eight-year-old compact with some kind of transmission problem. If the expense of one repair was such a financial strain that it canceled her vacation, he didn't want to intimidate her by picking her up in his new car. Therefore, for the week, he'd traded his brand-new luxury car for his nephew's fifteen-year-old import.

Jason was thrilled with the trade, but Jason's father was not. However, Alex couldn't think of anyone else he could swap cars with on short notice and not need to explain why. His mechanic had agreed to do a tune-up and quick check, and then had ended up doing an all-nighter fixing every little thing wrong with Jason's car, which was quite an extensive list. Jason wouldn't recognize his own car when he got it back.

"Jason's not here. He had to work today, and he's got my car."

Kyle's blank expression told him that Kyle didn't understand what was going on, but fortunately he didn't ask for details. "Oh. Well. See you 'round, I guess."

They took their leave, giving Alex the chance to once again watch Sharmane.

He snapped a few pictures just as she arrived at the entrance to the bridge and then positioned himself to get a good shot of her once she made it to the center. She waved bravely, and once he had a few more pictures, he pocketed the camera and joined her on the other side. Sharmane wanted to bypass the gift shop, but Alex insisted that he had to have one tacky souvenir of every place they went. He bought a small souvenir for Sharmane and she tried to protest, but he gave it to her anyway.

Alex didn't say much as he drove back across the Lions Gate Bridge and into Stanley Park.

"I know!" Sharmane chirped. "How about if we go around the Seawall? I've been to the Aquarium recently, but I've never actually been on the Seawall."

"Uh, me neither."

"It's five and a half miles around. Maybe we can rent in-line skates."

Alex knotted his brows. He'd never been on in-line skates in his life and doubted he could go five blocks without falling, never mind five miles. "I'd think I'd rather walk."

Chapter 3

Sharmane slipped her camera into her pocket. Alex hadn't said no, but he hadn't exactly been enthusiastic. Walking around the Seawall might not exactly be a "touristy" thing to do, but it was something she'd never done.

They started their walk at Brockton Point. First she took a picture of Alex standing at the railing overlooking the inlet, and then he took her picture as she ran to the water's edge to pick up a seashell. Then they began their journey around the perimeter of Stanley Park.

If she had been alone she wouldn't have gone on the Seawall because parts of it tended to be secluded. Being with a man who towered over her by nearly a foot made her feel safe. However, walking with Alex was as quiet as if she had been alone.

She wished she knew what was going on in his mind. At times he slowed his pace, looked out toward the water, inhaled deeply, and smiled as he exhaled. After awhile she couldn't stand the silence and found herself starting to babble. Alex didn't seem to mind. He agreed or disagreed with her comments and, to her surprise, encouraged her to keep yakking.

The tide was at midpoint when they arrived at the statue of the lady in the wetsuit. Sharmane snapped a picture of it. "Lots of people think she's a mermaid, but she's not, you know."

"I once read a little history blurb on her, but I can't remember the story."

"Me neither. I'll have to look it up when I get home."

As they continued on, Alex joined her in some small talk and a few jokes, as well as tossing suggestions for the rest of the week back and forth without coming to a firm decision.

The next point of interest was the dreaded Lions Gate Bridge. Despite Sharmane's apprehension of driving over it, being underneath the massive structure fascinated her. The thumps and clanks of the traffic on the metal surface increased in volume as they approached. Once directly beneath it they stopped to better see the magnitude of the construction from that viewpoint.

"I never expected it to be this noisy underneath. Aren't you going to take a picture of it?"

Sharmane pretended to shudder. "No way. I hate that bridge."

Alex laughed. It was a wonderful sound, deep and rich, and it warmed her heart. Sharmane found herself taking a picture of the stupid bridge not because she wanted to remember the bridge, but because the picture would remind her of Alex's laugh.

"There. I hope you're happy," she grumbled.

To her surprise, he stepped in front of her, grasping her hands over the top of the small camera. A smile lit his face, and he spoke so softly she barely heard him. "You know, I am happy. This is exactly what I needed. I want to thank you for including me in your plans."

She stared up at his face, mesmerized. She didn't know why, but Sharmane knew he wasn't joking. She had no idea why goofing off around town would mean so much to him, but she had to take his words at face value.

Small crinkles still highlighted the corners of his eyes. "Come on," he said. "Let's keep going."

To her surprise, he didn't completely drop her hands. He let go the hand holding her camera but kept her other hand still clasped within his. He smiled and began to walk as if it were natural for them to be holding hands.

Even though it shouldn't have, it felt right. He was easy to talk to. Before she realized what she was saying, she'd told him all about her job as office gofer and accounts payable clerk. They shared their favorite Bible verses, as well as discussed their respective churches. Sharmane found herself almost envying him his years growing up in an atmosphere where his family all attended the same church and worshiped together, since her family were not Christians.

As they passed Prospect Point and began their journey on the ocean side of the park, the air became cooler. By the time they reached Siwash Rock, the constant breeze off the ocean became downright cold, making her regret her choice of shorts instead of cotton pants.

When she could no longer suppress the chill, she shivered. Alex stopped dead in his tracks, checked the goose bumps running up her bare arms and legs, and frowned. He began to rub her arms with his large and very warm hands, the friction warming her marginally.

"Why didn't you say you were cold? Let's change sides. Maybe I can block the wind."

She expected him to simply move to her other side, but he took his time to pick the camera out of her fingers and slip it into his pocket before he stepped to shelter her from the cold. Without hesitation, he grasped her other hand and continued walking at a slightly faster pace.

"Look over there." Alex pointed out to the ocean. "Can you see it? There's a seal."

"I think technically that's a sea lion, although I can't say I know what the difference is. I think I'll look it up when I get home, when I check out the story of the lady in the wetsuit."

He smiled again, and Sharmane felt something inside her stomach quiver. "Will you really?"

Sharmane swallowed past the frog in her throat. "Uh, yeah." Part of her wanted to take a picture of the animal, but a bigger part didn't want to let go of his hand. She tried to convince herself the only reason was that his hand was so warm.

Only a few brave souls were in the water when they reached the Third Beach, in comparison to the offshore beach near their starting point at the east side of the park, which had been crowded.

They kept walking and soon turned to a southeasterly direction with the wind at their backs. Away from the ocean the temperature continued to warm as they made their way inland and walked toward the Lost Lagoon.

Countless ducks, Canada geese, and majestic swans floated leisurely in the calm water. Along the shore of the small lake many swans sat atop nests surrounded on three sides by wire fences with the open side toward the water. Signs cautioned people not to bother the swans.

Sharmane pointed to a mother swan as they passed a nest. "It looks like soon there's going to be little swanlings swimming around."

He smiled that adorable smile again. "Swanlings?"

"You know. Baby swans. I don't know what they're called."

"Let me guess. Something else for you to look up, right?"

She returned his smile and nodded. "Right."

"I had no idea going on vacation would be so educational."

"I'm not going to comment."

Before she had to ask, Alex reached into his pocket and returned her camera. Unfortunately, in order to take any pictures, he had to release her hand and Sharmane missed the contact. Despite the beauty of the lagoon, she limited herself to three shots, and they continued on.

They followed the path to walk underneath West Georgia Street and approached the marina.

Sharmane sighed. "Look at all those yachts. You know, just one of them costs more than I make in a year. Also, I think you have to pay a huge membership fee to join these things. Have you ever wondered what it would be like to be so rich?"

Alex stiffened. This was the last thing he wanted to talk about with Sharmane. "It's not all it's cracked up to be," he mumbled. He knew exactly how much the membership here cost, because he knew people who moored their boats here.

"You know, the only time I've ever been on a boat is the ferry to Vancouver Island. That's where I was going to go, you know. I was going to drive all over Vancouver Island all week." She breathed a defeated little sigh that nearly broke his heart.

Alex could count the times he'd taken the ferry on one hand, even though he'd lived here his entire life. Every time he had to go to the island on business, he flew because the ferry took too long. "Why don't we do that tomorrow? We can take an early ferry out of Tswwassen, and I'll bet you'd like to see the flowers at the Butchart Gardens. We can spend the morning there, spend a little time in Victoria, drive to Nanaimo for dinner, then come home on the late ferry to Horseshoe Bay."

Her eyes widened, and her smile made his heart quicken. "That sounds great!"

While she was still lost in thought, Alex picked up her hand and led her onward. They were almost finished at the Seawall, and after all that walking he was starving and more than a little tired.

"I hope you don't mind if I take lots of pictures."

He grinned. He was beginning to wonder if that camera was permanently attached to her. "I think I expected that."

Her tiny hand squeezed his. "Thanks, Alex. That's going to be such fun."

Alex tightened his grip, not allowing her to let go as they headed for his nephew's car. He couldn't remember the last time he'd been able to enjoy the simplicity of holding a woman's hand without fear of complications. He couldn't help but like Sharmane, and surely she could see that. Yet, she didn't cling to him as other women did as soon as he let his guard down.

She insisted on stopping for a quick burger, and Alex didn't argue. Conversation flowed, and he'd never enjoyed a greasy burger and limp fries more.

Much too soon, they were standing at her front door. Sharmane reached inside her backpack and removed her wallet.

"How much do I owe you? Remember, you paid for my admission. And I want to pay for half the gas."

"Don't worry about it."

"And tomorrow there will be the cost of the ferry and even more gas. I want to give you the money now, in case it bruises your male ego for me to pay in front of you."

"Forget it."

She crossed her arms, still holding her wallet in one hand. "We agreed to each pay our own expenses, and I intend to do exactly that. And I'm going to pay for at least half of the gas since we're using your car. I know you weren't planning on doing this. I don't want to burden you with all the expense."

He bit his bottom lip to hold back his smile. The money she was talking about was pocket change to him. "It's no burden; don't worry about it. I'm having a wonderful time."

Sharmane rested her hand on his forearm. Alex stared down at the point of contact. Her touch was gentle, and he was sure she only meant to emphasize her words, but his pulse jumped at her simple gesture.

"I mean it, Alex. I know you hadn't planned all this driving and stuff. I don't want it to be a big expense for you. I'm serious. Let me pay."

Alex didn't doubt that she meant it, and he was no longer smiling. "I don't want your money. All I want is your company."

She shook her head. "I know exactly how much gas your car takes, so don't try and fool me. I'm also paying for my own admissions and for half the ferry cost. If I don't pay for my share of this vacation, it ends today."

Alex felt like he'd just been punched in the gut. He couldn't believe this was happening to him, of all people. His words almost choked him, but he forced himself to say it. "All right. I'll let you know how much you owe me for the gas."

"Not just the gas. Everything."

He sucked in a deep breath and let it go. He didn't want her to pay a thing. Suddenly, he needed more than just an escape for himself; he wanted this to be the best vacation Sharmane ever had.

"Alex. . ."

He gritted his teeth. "Okay. I'll keep track of what everything costs, and you can pay me at the end of the week."

Her frown changed into a wide smile, and Alex never thought that losing a battle could feel so good.

"Okay, then I'll see you tomorrow. Good night." And the door closed.

For a few moments Alex remained standing, facing the closed door. He didn't think it would ever happen, but he thought he just might be falling in love.

Chapter 4

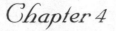

Alex checked the time as he rang Sharmane's doorbell. He still couldn't believe he was here. The sun had only just started to rise a few minutes ago. He should still have been in bed at this hour, yet he'd already been driving for an hour.

By taking an extra hot shower he'd managed to erase most of the stiffness from his legs, but he still regretted his suggestion of another day filled with more walking. If nothing else, this was a reminder to get some regular exercise rather than sit behind his desk all week long.

The door opened. "Cygnets!" Sharmane exclaimed.

Alex blinked. The words he expected to hear were "good morning," or even better would have been "good to see you." He glanced behind himself for something out of the ordinary, and seeing nothing, turned back to Sharmane.

She laughed at his blank expression. "Baby swans are called cygnets."

"That's nice. Are you ready to go?"

She nodded. "Yes. I have been waiting for you. I will only be a minute."

Today she was dressed in jeans and a baggy pink T-shirt. Her blond hair was tied in a loose ponytail, and she looked fresh and alert, unlike how he felt. Rather than dwell on his own misery, he followed her inside.

Her house was small and functional yet had a homey and friendly atmosphere. Once in the kitchen, she picked up her backpack, giving him a bad feeling.

"I hope you haven't packed a lunch this time."

"But—"

He held up one hand. "Please, don't argue, I want to buy you lunch. Consider it my treat."

She opened her mouth, but before she could speak, Alex stiffened, crossed his arms, narrowed his eyes, and glared down at her. Sharmane's eyes widened, her mouth closed, and without a word, she laid the backpack on the table then returned a number of containers to the fridge.

"Thank you," he muttered.

She reached inside the backpack one more time. "Have you had breakfast?"

Alex pressed one hand into his stomach. Just the mention of food caused it to grumble. He'd given his housekeeper the week off, so he didn't have to face her questions every day, and he hadn't had time to fix himself something, so he'd left without eating. "No."

She pulled out a bag containing three muffins. "Me neither. We can eat these in the car while we're waiting in the ferry lineup."

He would give her that one, but only as a technicality.

She ignored his lack of response. "I made coffee, and I've got a spare travel mug you can borrow. Want some?"

"Yes, please," he mumbled.

She poured the coffee, transferred her wallet and camera from the backpack into her purse, and nearly shoved him out the door.

Sharmane tried to wipe the smile off her face as she made herself comfortable in Alex's car. For years she had wanted to tour Vancouver Island. Finally, she had saved up enough money to spend a week in motels and cover all the expenses comfortably. When her transmission blew, her dream crumbled, and she didn't know if she would ever get another opportunity. Alex's suggestion to catch the first ferry and do it in a day might have been pushing it, but this was exactly what she wanted to do. She'd miss the whale watching tour she wanted to attend, but this was the next best thing.

She gazed out the window and sighed. "Look, the sky is still a little pink from the sunrise."

He mumbled something she couldn't quite hear.

"Smile! It's going to be a gorgeous day!" She turned to face him, but he wasn't wearing anything close to a smile. "You're not a morning person, are you?"

"I'm not used to getting up before dawn," he mumbled again.

Sharmane patted herself on the back for the coffee she'd thought to make this morning, because he certainly could use it. After a few sips his mood improved, and soon he was behaving human again.

Since it was so early, they managed to avoid most of the rush hour traffic. They arrived at the ferry dock in plenty of time to catch the first sailing and ate the muffins before they were directed onto the ferry.

Today they were both prepared for the cold. They donned their jackets and climbed the stairs to the upper deck to enjoy the morning ocean air. Conversation flowed easily as they walked through all areas of the ferry, and Alex even apologized for being such a grump. They refilled their coffee mugs at the cafeteria just before all passengers descended to the lower levels to prepare for docking at Victoria.

By the time they arrived at the Butchart Gardens, Sharmane was ready to burst at the seams. She couldn't wipe the smile off her face as they stood in the short lineup to enter, and she was in such a great mood she couldn't bring herself to protest as Alex paid her admission.

The beauty of the well laid out grounds and the myriad of color and fragrance was like nothing she had imagined. None of the tourist brochures served justice to the magnificence of the acres and acres of flowers from around the globe.

The wonder of God's creation was everywhere, from every delicate blossom to the selectively arranged boulders, from the carefully laid out rose garden to the area quarried out for the tall arching fountain, from the quaintly styled tea house and restaurant to the serenity of the fishes and turtles in the quiet pond surrounded by the large weeping trees.

Her favorite of all was the sunken Japanese Garden, and she shot an entire roll of film in that area alone.

Even though plants and flowers weren't exactly a "guy" thing, Alex very politely expressed his appreciation of the various sections. She appreciated the way he humored her by frequently offering to take a picture of her amongst the flowers, especially the roses, which were her favorites. Sharmane found herself laughing when he struck up a few silly poses standing among the pretty blossoms so she could take his picture.

Despite wanting to stay longer, Sharmane didn't want to push her luck. Only because he made her promise, she bit her tongue when he treated her to lunch at the tearoom. Following that, they walked one last time through the Japanese Gardens and headed for the exit. However, instead of going to the gate, Alex went to the gift shop.

"Alex, I—"

He wagged one finger in the air. "I told you, I want to buy a tacky souvenir of every place we go, and you agreed."

She nodded and sighed. She would have three rolls of pictures to remind her of this very special day, but a small souvenir probably wouldn't hurt.

The vast selection of things to buy astounded her. The gift shop held everything from seed packets to posters to jewelry and china to clothing. They browsed through every item the store held, and Sharmane enjoyed every minute of it. For the longest time, she adored a thin gold watch with a picture of a rose on the face and rhinestones all around instead of numbers. Since she already had a perfectly good watch, Sharmane selected a T-shirt with a rose on it instead, and Alex bought a key chain and a pot holder he claimed was for his mother.

Before they left, Sharmane made a short detour to the ladies room, and they left for their next destination, Victoria's famed Inner Harbor area. Because he had humored her at the Butchart Gardens, she pretended to enjoy the antique car museum in downtown Victoria, but they both enjoyed the wax museum. They walked into the Empress Hotel to check out the grand old building, and she couldn't help but be impressed by the harpist in one of the elegant dining rooms.

By midafternoon, they were back in the car and on the highway headed for Nanaimo. The countryside was beautiful and mostly undisturbed, and taking into account all the sights of the day, Sharmane couldn't remember ever having enjoyed herself more. The sky started to cloud over, which made the long drive ahead of them more comfortable without the sun blaring down on them.

"That was wonderful, especially the gardens. Thank you so much for doing this."

"Don't mention it. It was nice."

"Nice? What kind of lame word is 'nice'?"

He laughed, making Sharmane's insides turned to jelly.

"The flowers were *nice,* but I liked the frogs best."

Sharmane couldn't hold back her smile, so she swatted him in the arm. "Since we got lots of pictures of you, I'll have doubles made up. Don't you have a camera?"

His smile disappeared in the blink of an eye, and his attention turned completely to the road in front of them. "Yes, I have a camera, it's just—I think you'd probably take better pictures than me."

"You just lack confidence. It's not hard to take good pictures, but it is an art. You have to have a critical eye and a little imagination. I took a course once. You know, the kind for serious hobbyists. It was a lot of fun, and I learned a lot."

Apparently, he also had an interest in photography as a hobby, because he was able to share some good tips on lighting and perspective, making her wonder how he possibly could have thought she would take better pictures.

Throughout the three-hour drive, she was both surprised and delighted to share all their common interests and then amiably agree to disagree on others.

She couldn't help but like him, but she tempered her thoughts with the knowledge that despite all the time they'd spent together in the last three days, she really didn't know much about him.

Every time she talked to him he divulged many personal details about his likes and dislikes, his preferences, and his interests. However, she didn't know anything about his life. Every time the conversation drifted to his job, his family, his friends, or anything else that would have told her specific information he became evasive; and he did it in such a way that the conversation was over by the time she realized he hadn't told her what she wanted to know.

She still didn't know what he did for a living or if he even had a job, nor did she know where he lived or which church he went to, even though she'd been more than open in telling him those same details about herself.

At first she had tried not to think about it, but the more he sidestepped her hints, then her direct questions, she began to suspect he was doing it on purpose, and she wished she knew why. If he was embarrassed because he was unemployed, she thought she'd been more than clear that it didn't matter to her. Last night, she'd wanted to call him and discuss their plans for the day, but she'd lost the cell phone number he had given her. When she tried to look his number up in the phone book, the only A. Brunnel listed was an address in an area where only the very wealthy lived.

By the time they arrived at Nanaimo they were starving, so they picked the first restaurant they saw, which was a Chinese buffet. As was becoming common, they talked until they lost track of time, then ran laughing to the car, because neither of them could remember when the last ferry sailed.

Fortunately, they caught it, and Sharmane considered it one more adventure to make the trip across the Strait of Georgia in the dark.

The night had turned cold, and Alex was glad he'd remembered to bring a jacket, because that allowed them to stand on the upper deck to enjoy the quiet of the water in the silence of the dark night. Unfortunately the sky was black, the heavy cloud cover completely obliterating the moon and stars. The glory of God's universe above them would have been the perfect end to a perfect day.

Despite countless marathon sessions with his business, he couldn't ever remember being so tired, but this was a good tired. For two days they'd done nothing but walk and sightsee, and despite knowing how stiff he was going to be tomorrow, he knew he'd never regret it. He closed his eyes and inhaled a deep breath of the cool ocean air. A particularly cold gust caused them both to shiver, but he didn't want to go inside. Without speaking, he gently rested his hands on Sharmane's shoulders and guided her to stand with her back nestled into him so they could stand together for warmth. He kept one hand on her shoulder and covered her hand holding the railing with his.

She was so short he could comfortably rest his chin on the top of her head. She didn't protest, and except for the odd strand of hair blowing up to tickle his face, nothing moved except the air around them and the gentle vibration and slight rocking of the moving ferry.

If he could make time stand still, this would be the moment. Already, he had to acknowledge how much he would miss her when their time together was up.

He had never been the sentimental type, but he was accumulating a host of souvenirs so that he would never forget this short week.

Deep down inside, he had to know that Sharmane would not easily forget him. He had more or less tagged along on her dream, but she had created his. He knew she had plenty of photos with him in them, but he wanted to be more than a fond reminder relegated to an old box of vacation memories. He wanted her to think of him often, because he knew he would think of her every day.

During the few minutes they had not been together at the gift shop at the Butchart Gardens, he'd bought the watch she'd been so enamored with.

The woman had elegant taste. When he paid for the watch, he confirmed what he suspected when she first looked at it. What she assumed were rhinestones adorning the watch were really diamonds. No doubt when she saw it out of the display case she would realize that, and knowing Sharmane, she would also question his ability to pay for it. As much as he battled with it, he knew that when their vacation was over his conscience would not let them separate without telling her who he really was. Once she knew, she wouldn't question the expense. Also, once she knew, he doubted she would ever want to see him again because of his deceit.

Alex squeezed his eyes shut and pressed himself closer to Sharmane. He couldn't lie to himself; he was deceiving her. He prayed God would forgive him, but he didn't want to take the chance that when he told her the truth, everything would change. Sunday he would confess, but until then, as difficult as it was, he would continue to keep his secrets.

He knew she was starting to wonder what it was he was hiding, and so far he'd been able to circumvent her questions, but he didn't know how long he would be able to keep it up and still remain credible.

He bowed his head and nuzzled his face into her hair, wondering if this would be the only time he'd be able to hold her like this, using the cold for an excuse. In not being completely honest with her, he was forfeiting his right to do what he most wanted, and that was to court her properly.

"Did you feel that? It's starting to rain."

Alex raised his head, and a drop of rain landed on his forehead. "It's just a drop or two. It might stop." He prayed for it to stop. He didn't want the moment to be broken.

The drizzle increased. She moved, forcing him to release her. "It's not. We'd better go inside."

The mood inside was nothing like the early morning trip. Most people were sitting quietly, the outer decks on all levels were all but deserted, and with the exception of the noise of the ferry's engine, all was quiet.

Sharmane sat in one of the padded seats beside the window, so Alex lowered himself beside her. It was good to get his weight off his feet, but he would have preferred to be outside in the cool air to stay alert.

"So where do you think we should go tomorrow?"

Alex fought to hold back a yawn. "Is there anything we can do that we won't have to walk all day? I'm positive we walked twice as much today as we did yesterday."

Her eyebrows scrunched, and she squeezed her lips together in such a way that her mouth tilted. "I don't know. I doubt it. Let me think." Her blond hair hung in a straggly mess around her face, and she swiped one hand through it to push it back.

He forced himself to look away. The urge to kiss her was almost overwhelming. Instead, he pressed himself into the soft seat, stretched his weary legs out in front of him, and draped one arm behind her along the back of the chair.

Outside, the rain increased to a steady drone. Every once in awhile, the wind splattered a gust of rain against the window. Inside the ferry's sitting area, all was warm and dry.

"It's probably going to rain all day, so we'll have to pick something indoors."

"Sounds like a good idea."

"You're probably all flowered out, so I guess you don't want to go to Queen Elizabeth Park to see the conservatory where all the flowers are."

"You got that right."

If he couldn't kiss her, then he had to touch her. Alex brushed his fingers along her shoulder, and when she didn't seem to mind he pulled her just a little closer. She took him up on his hint and rested her head on his shoulder.

"What about the art gallery?"

There weren't many places that attracted tourists where he would see some of the upper crust people he knew, but the art gallery would surely be one of them, and therefore, he refused to go there. "Nope. Too boring."

"I guess going up the gondola and taking a hike on Grouse Mountain is out. You wouldn't count the long drive as being inside, would you?"

He rested his head against the side of hers, smiling to himself at the softness of her hair. "Nope."

"I have a coupon for skydiving at that place in Matsqui. You don't have to walk, you just kind of fall."

He let his eyes drift shut. "You're joking, right?" he mumbled.

Sharmane chuckled. She had been joking, but she knew someone who had tried skydiving once. An instructor went down with the person to make sure the parachute opened properly and all went well. She didn't really want to do such a dangerous thing, but she had to ask, just to see his reaction—which was exactly as she expected.

"Yes, I'm joking. Besides, I don't think they do parachuting in the rain. We could go to the Vancouver Aquarium at Stanley Park. That's indoors. But it means walking."

"Uh-uh."

Sharmane felt his head press into the top of hers a little more. She could see that he was tired, after all, for two days they had done nothing but walk, but she really couldn't think of anything touristy that involved sitting. For a few minutes, she tried to think of something to do that didn't involve too much walking.

"How about the Pacific Space Center? They have lots of features to sit for. I hear the laser show is great."

She waited, but there was no response. Sharmane was about to lift her head when she heard Alex's soft snore.

Chapter 5

Alex pocketed the tickets, led Sharmane to one of the rear cars, and stood behind her as she climbed the two stairs.

She turned her head back over her shoulder and smiled so sweetly he nearly stumbled. "I've never been on a real train. Taking the Royal Hudson was such a great idea!"

"It came to me in a moment of genius."

She rolled her eyes and harrumphed, and they stepped into the car to select their seats. Alex motioned Sharmane to take the window seat, and they waited for all the passengers to board.

She was being so polite about it, but he still felt stupid about last night. The last thing he remembered was discussing suggestions for the remainder of their vacation, and the next thing he knew Sharmane was shaking him, saying that they were about to dock.

The hour-long drive between her house and his was taking its toll. In addition to the late hours, all the driving, the lack of sleep, and two days of solid walking, the motion of the ferry had finished him off. He couldn't remember the last time he'd been so embarrassed. But, Sharmane had been so gracious about it he felt another piece of his heart melting away in her grasp, and she didn't even know it. He wished he could explain that because of the distance between her house and his, he'd only had four hours sleep that night, but he couldn't without admitting that he lived in the exclusive British Properties area of West Vancouver.

He stared out the window as he spoke. "I'm really sorry about last night." The words having been said, he returned his attention to her face.

"Don't worry about it. I guess I'm used to more activity than you are. I do a lot of running around at work; it's a very busy office, and I'm constantly doing errands and running back and forth to the stockroom all day."

She looked him straight in the eye and he knew what she expected him to say. He cleared his throat. "I'm used to sitting a lot."

She sighed, and her disappointment pierced his soul. Evading her questions was taking its toll; the guilt was getting to him, but there wasn't any other way. When he did come clean, she would hate him for it. He couldn't allow that to happen until he had spent all the time with her he could. After their excursion today, there were only three days left of their time together, but that was only if they counted Sunday, which he wasn't sure she did.

The porter, dressed in a classic uniform, walked down the aisle checking tickets, and the train pulled out of the station at the reasonable time of ten a.m. Today, the sun had been up before he was. And also today, the only walking they would do would be for an hour in Squamish. After that, they would climb aboard the *MV Britannia* for a cruise returning to Vancouver's Harbor Cruises Marina, where they would be bused back to the train station to collect the car and go home, unless they made other plans for the evening.

Sharmane patted her purse. "Did you bring your camera today? I brought extra film."

He smiled, not wanting to think of how many rolls she'd already taken. "I'm going to leave all the photography up to you."

Her return smile did strange things to his stomach, things that had nothing to do with the swaying of the train as it lumbered down the track.

"I've never been to Squamish before. I'll bet they have a section of town specially made up for the tourists to have lunch. That will be so much fun. And I'm so excited about taking the cruise back. I don't even care if it's still raining." She patted her purse again. "This time I brought my fold-up umbrella. I don't want to get caught in the rain again." She proceeded to dig a pile of brochures out of her purse and began to flip through them. "I got these while you were paying for the tickets. It says that King George rode the Royal Hudson number 2860 in 1939. It was restored in 1974, and now it's the only antique steam engine in main line service in North America today."

He looked down at her purse. He could never figure out the hidden depths of a woman's purse, and he didn't figure this was the time to find out. "This is a vacation, not a fact-finding mission. Can't you just enjoy the ride?"

"But I am enjoying the ride."

Alex couldn't stop himself. He reached for her hand and gave it a gentle squeeze. "Me, too." Without letting go, he switched his attention to the mountain scenery on one side, and the Queen Charlotte Channel on the other as they rode toward the town of Squamish. The contrast between the mountain on one side and the water on the other would have made a marvelous picture. He let his mind wander to one day renting a helicopter with Sharmane and flying over the channel to get a picture of the old black train on the track on the mountainside in what was probably a breathtaking scenic shot.

Sharmane looked down at their joined hands and felt the heat creeping up her cheeks. He'd been more than clear that he didn't want to let go, and she didn't protest. She was enjoying more than just the ride.

Her original plans of driving around alone could in no way compare to what she was now experiencing. She'd never before felt so close to another person, most especially not a man. More than the simple pleasure of not being alone, it even went beyond sharing a good time with a friend. Sharmane in no way believed in love at first sight, but even knowing how short a time it had been since they met, she wondered if she could possibly be falling for a man she really didn't know.

He was kind and gentle, generous to a fault; they shared many common interests, but other than basic personality traits, what she knew about him could fit in a thimble.

Considering the questionable condition of his car in comparison to the way it ran, she thought he could be a mechanic, but he admitted to sitting most of the time, and a mechanic wouldn't do that. She suspected he wasn't unemployed as she originally assumed, but still, she couldn't be sure because every time she brought up anything even remotely hinting at what he did for a living, he very efficiently skirted the issue. Likewise, details of his home, including the location and if it was a small apartment or a castle fit for a king were also vague.

Another thing that confused her was that so far everything they had done was relatively inexpensive, as far as tourist spots went. However, she had sneaked a peek at the prices for the different packages for today's excursion, and he had chosen the most expensive options, and then insisted that it was his treat, telling her in no uncertain terms that for once, she was not to argue.

The change in his demeanor had caught her off guard. She had seen a brief glimpse of it when he insisted she not pack a lunch before their excursion to Vancouver Island. But today at the train station, when she had actually started to argue with him, the change had shocked her. Instead of the carefree and gentle Alex she was used to, in an instant he became a man she didn't want to cross, a man whose authority was not to be questioned. She wasn't the only one to notice. Even the clerk at the ticket counter treated him differently than the other people buying tickets. But when he tucked his wallet into the pocket of his jeans and turned around, all was the same again, as if nothing had happened.

She didn't understand it, and she didn't know what to think. All she knew was that she'd never enjoyed herself so much.

"I think you wanted to discuss what we were going to do tomorrow and Saturday."

Sharmane blinked, shaken out of her musings. "Uh, yes. The forecast is bright and sunny for both days."

He smiled, and Sharmane's foolish heart fluttered.

"How about something that's supposed to be the ultimate in relaxing. Ever been fishing?"

"Fishing?"

He nodded. "You know. You sit in a boat in the middle of a lake, put a worm on a hook, toss it into the water, and pull out a fish."

"I've never been fishing before. I don't know what to do, and I don't have a fishing rod or anything."

"Me neither. But my brother and his son go fishing all the time. It sounds pretty easy, and they seem to have a good time. I can find out their favorite spot, and I'll bet I could even borrow all their fishing equipment and their boat. It's one of those six-seater types."

Sharmane's breath caught and her whole body stiffened. "Really? You can borrow a boat? A real boat? They wouldn't mind?"

"Stan's been telling me for years I should give it a try, so I think he'd welcome the opportunity to give it to me."

"Wow. . .a boat. . ."

"It's not a big deal. We're going on a boat today for the return trip."

She waved her free hand in the air, which also served to remind her that he was still holding onto her left hand. "That's different. That's a big cruise ship with a restaurant and hundreds of people on it, a whole crew and a captain and everything. I think it would be fun to go on a little boat, just the two of us."

He patted her hand. "Then it's settled. Today, we'll be pampered, and tomorrow, we'll be lazy."

And they were pampered. They had a lovely brunch in the train's parlor car and then returned to their seats to chat while they enjoyed the beauty of the scenery on their trip through the mountains.

By the time the arrived at the Squamish station, the rain had stopped.

As soon as they left the passenger car, they walked alongside the train so Sharmane could take a few pictures of the grand old engine. Even though it wasn't moving, steam still puffed out the smokestack. She made sure to take a picture of the front of the glossy black engine, highlighting the big shiny numbers.

During their leisurely stroll in Squamish, even though neither of them was hungry, they stopped at the cutest little bistro for coffee and dessert. As usual, they got lost in conversation, and again had to run all the way to where the *MV Britannia* was docked.

Once aboard, Sharmane imagined what it must have been like aboard the *Titanic* as they sailed along, the wind in her hair and the ocean breeze in her face, only she could always see the shore, and this boat wasn't going to sink. Midafternoon, they had a meal of baked salmon unlike any Sharmane had ever experienced and then spent the rest of the trip on the outside deck.

As they neared Lion's Bay, they passed the ferry coming out of the Horseshoe Bay terminal on its way to Nanaimo, and the people on both boats waved at each other in passing. While exploring the cruise ship, Sharmane discovered that while nowhere near the size of an ocean liner, the *MV Britannia's* capacity was five hundred people, which she considered absolutely huge.

An air-conditioned tour bus returned them to the rail station, but rather than drive through rush hour traffic, Alex insisted on stopping for dinner. She was surprised that she could eat anything, considering all she'd eaten in the course of their day, but told herself that such a vacation could only happen once in a lifetime.

Too soon, they were standing on her doorstep. After Alex made sure there were no intruders inside, he stepped close to her and rested his fingers on her cheek, making Sharmane's heartbeat quicken.

"I'd really like to invite myself in, but I have to be at my brother's house before it gets too late, so I can get all that fishing stuff and make sure everything is okay with the boat."

His fingers moved slightly, and his thumb drifted to her chin. Sharmane struggled to breathe. Holding hands, which should have been merely an affectionate gesture, had set her insides aflutter, but now his simple touch turned her knees to jelly. She forced herself to clear her throat so she could speak. "Do you want to phone him first?"

He stepped closer. Her heart started to pound. "No, I'll call him on my cell; I don't want to get to his house too late, they all have to get up for work in the morning. I'll be back to pick you up at nine o'clock."

She could feel a slight pressure as he tipped up her chin. Part of her had been waiting for this moment, but part of her didn't want it. As much as she liked him, she didn't know anything about him.

Her eyes drifted shut anyway. His lips brushed hers briefly instead of the longer kiss she'd expected and had come to realize she wanted. He stepped back leaving her feeling strangely disappointed.

"See you tomorrow, Sharmane."

Chapter 6

Sharmane gasped as Alex pulled up in front of her house. There sat a white pickup which emphasized the perfection of the sleek candy-apple red speedboat behind it. She dashed out of the house leaving the door wide open and was standing beside the boat before Alex fully exited the truck.

She ran her fingers on the smooth finish. She'd never seen a boat like this up close, much less ridden in one. "Your brother let you *borrow* this?"

He grinned in response. "Pretty nice, huh?"

"This isn't for fishing. This is a speedboat."

"He fishes from it. But I think they water-ski mostly."

"Water-ski?" She pulled her hand back as quickly as if the boat were red-hot.

He grinned. "Don't worry, I didn't bring the skis. I didn't think it would be a good idea to try something like that without having someone experienced along. I only brought the fishing stuff."

Sharmane let her hand drop to her side. "Oh. Okay."

He opened the passenger door, where she could see a small tackle box, a net, and two broken-down fishing rods stuffed behind the seat. "Get your stuff, and let's get going."

"I packed a lunch, and this time I hope you're not going to argue with me."

He laughed again, spreading warmth from Sharmane's heart to the tips of her toes. "I knew you would. Thank you."

She dashed into the house and returned with her backpack and camera, and they were on their way.

Sharmane carefully read his brother's handwritten directions to the Pitt River, where after much tribulation, Alex managed to back the trailer into the water and set the boat afloat. Soon everything they needed was stowed, and they were gliding north on their way to Pitt Lake, which was only accessible by boat.

The wind pushed Sharmane's hair back as she leaned slightly over the side, where her face wasn't sheltered by the small windshield. "This is so different than the ocean. It's so fresh and clean."

"Stan says this is a tidal lake. Except for it being fresh water, it's almost like the ocean. Except it's inland."

Sharmane laughed. "Those things make it not like the ocean at all."

The waterway widened, and Alex steered the boat into the center. The sparkling glossy red speedboat seemed drastically out of place in the pristine natural setting. The water was glassy smooth, so still that Sharmane could see perfect reflections of the blue sky and fluffy clouds above. Trees and boulders lined the shore, the varying shades of green also reflected in the water so perfectly it was like looking in a mirror, except for a slight ripple of the lake's surface. She snapped a couple pictures, knowing she could never completely capture the undefiled beauty on film.

Sharmane inhaled deeply, fully enjoying the scent of the water mingled with the pure woodsy scent of the trees.

The boat slowed, gradually drifting to a stop. "This seems like as good a spot as any."

She almost didn't feel right about being here, it was so perfect, but she could see other boats floating around closer to the shore. Another motorboat appeared briefly in the distance, turned around, and sped away, fading into the distance of the long lake. "How do you tell which spots are best for fishing?"

He shrugged his shoulders. "I don't know."

"Are we supposed to just let the boat float, or are we supposed to be driving slowly? Or is there an anchor or something?"

"I don't know that either."

"Much good you are. And when we catch our fish, do you have any idea what to do with it?"

He raised one finger in the air. "Yes. Stan says it's catch and release-only here. You have to let it go."

Her smile dropped. "Let it go? What's the point of fishing then?"

Again, he shrugged his shoulders. "It's a sport. The challenge of human versus fish. I have no intention of cutting open a fish and scooping out its innards, do you?"

Sharmane shuddered at the thought. "Catch and release will be fine."

Alex patted his shirt pocket. "Stan said we catch it, scoop it into the net, take the hook out of its mouth, pat it, and let it go. I've got the fishing licenses right here. Let's get started."

He pulled two white beat-up hats out from under the seat and plunked one on her head then the other on his. "These are Stan and Jason's fishing hats. Necessary equipment, they say."

Before she could think of a reply, he slotted the two fishing rods together, opened the tackle box, then pulled out a folded up piece of paper. "They told me that we can use either lures or flies to fish, depending on what kind of fish we want to catch."

"You mean we get a choice?"

He held up a shiny metal thing with a multi-edged hook dangling from it. "According to Stan, this kind of thing," he shook it for emphasis, "is a type of lure called a Wobbler."

Sharmane examined it. "What kind of fish does it catch?"

"I don't know. But I think he said you catch salmon and trout with flies." He opened the second slot and picked up a long skinny thing made with pink and white feathers fastened to a single hook. "This is a fly. There's a bunch of different kinds here. There's a

Hootchie, a Rolled Muddler, a Doc Spratley, and that one is called a Woolly-something-or-other. He told me a few more, but I didn't write them all down."

"Oh, those are too cute to get all wet and let a fish put one in its mouth. What about those?" She pointed to the third drawer.

"These are called spinners." He held one up. "If I remember correctly, this one is called a Dragonfly, but Stan spoke so fast, I don't remember the other names. It was hard enough to write down the names of the flies."

"What's the difference?"

He opened his mouth at the same time as he shrugged his shoulders.

Sharmane lifted her palms toward him to silence him. "Let me guess, you don't know."

"You guessed right." He started to fasten the pretty pink fly to one of the lines. "I think you should use the pink one. It looks like something a woman should use. I'll use this green one."

"If your brother does so much fishing and even has a boat how come you don't go with him?"

"No time. It's not something I did as a boy, either. My family went to church on Sunday, not fishing. Stan and Jason tend to go Saturdays, but they don't go as often as they used to, now that Jason's seventeen."

Sharmane did a little mental calculating on the age of Alex's brother. "You must be the youngest, and Stan is the oldest right?"

"Uh-huh," he mumbled, sticking his tongue out the corner of his mouth as he threaded the line through the hole to fasten the pretty green feathered thing to the other line. He waved one hand in the air and grinned. "Ladies first."

"I don't know what to do."

"Put your thumb on the reel, release the catch, hold the rod over your shoulder, and cast. I'll wait for you to do it first."

"Thanks a lot," she muttered.

Doing exactly as instructed, Sharmane rested the rod on her shoulder then moved it slightly with every count, readying herself to cast it out. "One. . Two. . . Thr—"

"Wait! Stop! You've hooked me!"

Sharmane dropped the rod to the boat floor with a clatter. The sight of Alex holding the hook on his shoulder made her feel faint at what she'd done. "Alex! I'm sorry! Where's the first aid kit!"

He shook his head. "You just got my shirt, not me. Can you pull it out so it doesn't rip?"

She couldn't stop her fingers from trembling, but she did manage to work the hook out of the fabric without leaving a hole. "I'm so sorry."

"Don't worry about it. Try again. This time, I'll stand farther away."

"I don't think this was such a good idea."

"Nonsense. No damage was done."

This time she stood at the back of the boat, while Alex stood in the front. She swung the rod with all her might and let the line go.

Alex peered down over the side of the boat. "I think you're supposed to cast the flies as far as you can over the surface of the water and drag it in, not send it straight down."

"I told you I'd never done this before." She reeled it in then laid her rod down. "Your turn."

Alex made a great show of patting his hat, sitting straight and tall, and squaring his shoulders. Sharmane didn't know why he was trying so hard to look superior, when the silly hat totally negated his efforts.

He cleared his throat and cast. Sharmane watched it go almost straight up and then fall straight down about eight feet off the side of the boat. "You didn't do any better than I did."

He reeled it in. "We'll get the hang of this. This is supposed to be relaxing."

After a number of attempts, their casting improved and soon they were able to cast out a fair distance. They tried casting out at the same time off opposite sides of the boat but kept clashing rods, so they decided to take turns casting from the same side. Besides, Sharmane was in no rush to get a fish. They would only be letting it go.

Alex took his turn to cast. "I cast mine farther than you did."

"Did not."

"Did too."

"Says who?"

"Bet I catch the first fish."

"Bet you don't."

"Even if I don't, mine will be bigger."

"No way." Sharmane laid her rod on the bottom of the boat and leaned over the side. She slapped the water, splashing a few drops on him. "Take that!"

"Hey! No fair!" He finished reeling in his empty fly and then turned with a grin that Sharmane didn't want to interpret. "Your turn," he said, a little too sweetly.

"I think it's time we had lunch, don't you think?"

"Coward."

She held out a container and smiled back sweetly. "With or without mustard?"

He accepted it but didn't open it. He dipped one hand over the side, scooped out a palm full of water, and threw it at her.

"Hey!" Sharmane grabbed the net, dipped it in the water, then wiggled it over his head so droplets splashed all over him.

Alex dipped his hat over the side of the boat and then tossed the water at her, but Sharmane saw it coming and ducked, only getting hit by a few stray drops.

"Stop it, Alex; you're rocking the boat too much!"

"I can swim."

She opened her mouth to retort, but the words left her. Alex had plopped the limp, wet hat back on his head. A few drops of water trickled down his cheek, and he sat completely still, grinning like an idiot, waiting.

Sharmane had never seen him like this, but from the brilliance of his smile and the simple joy in his face, it struck her that he needed to goof around more often.

All week long, since she couldn't figure out what he wasn't telling her, she tried to understand why. Up until now, he'd been reserved, almost formal, despite the casual activities they'd chosen.

Now, she finally put her finger on it. Alex was that one person who was lonely in a crowd, although she didn't know why. Perhaps she would never know the reason for his secrets, but they no longer mattered. If by goofing around together she had helped him find whatever he was looking for, she thanked God she could help her Christian brother.

When they first agreed to spend the week together, it had been Alex's suggestion that at the end of the week, they part as friends, along with the unspoken statement that they would never see each other again. If he needed this week to sort out his private dilemmas, then that was the way it would be. It was a week she would never forget, and she had to be thankful for the company. This vacation had turned into more fun than she ever could have realized.

"Never mind. I surrender. Now let's eat lunch and catch a fish."

She wasn't surprised when Alex reached for her hands as they prayed over their sandwiches. What did surprise her was that she realized when their vacation was over, she would miss him.

After their lunch was finished, Alex cast his fly while Sharmane stuffed the empty containers into her backpack.

Alex went stiff. "I caught something!"

Sharmane dropped the backpack. His line was tight and the fishing rod curved with tension as he struggled to reel in a fighting fish. Up until now, she'd considered fishing boring, but now her heart was pounding and she had to restrain herself from shouting to cheer him on as he pitted his limited skill against the fish.

She grabbed the net and leaned to the side of the boat, ready to scoop it up.

To her shock, he braced his feet wide apart and stood. The boat rocked perilously.

"What are you doing! Sit down!"

"I can't! I have to pull it in!" He pulled the rod over his shoulder, winding furiously, making the boat rock even worse.

Sharmane frantically grabbed onto the side of the boat, leaning to the side in an attempt to counterbalance Alex as he leaned his weight backward against the pull of the fish. "You don't have to do anything!" she yelled. "We're only going to let it go anyway."

He leaned forward and yanked again. "It's the principle of the thing."

"I refuse to drown because of a principle!"

One final yank and the fish cleared the water. The thing was well over a foot long and thrashed so hard she didn't know how she was going to fit it in the net. Alex staggered back, then landed on his behind on the seat, making the boat rock even worse. Sharmane fumbled for the net and tried to capture the wriggling fish, but because of the fish's struggles and the motion of the boat, she couldn't get it in the net. Finally, Alex let the fish drop to the floor, so she dropped the net and clambered to subdue it with her hands.

"Yuck! It's slimy!"

Alex dropped his rod and also attempted to still the fish. "Of course it's slimy. It's a fish."

Together they pinned the squirming fish to the floor.

"I don't think it's good for it to be out of the water," Sharmane ground out between her teeth.

Alex nodded so fast the soggy hat fell off. "You hold it still, and I'll get the hook out if its mouth. Ready?"

Sharmane did her best to wrap both hands around it while Alex used the pliers from his brother's tackle box to pry the hook out of the fish's mouth as best as he could.

"Don't hurt it! Look, it's got a hole in its chin." She couldn't believe the burn of tears starting in the back of her eyes in sympathy for a dumb fish as she rose to her knees to start the process of putting the poor injured thing back in the water.

"Wait. I haven't patted it yet."

She lifted her head, about to tell him her thoughts on that, but the second she made eye contact, she saw Alex holding her camera with a napkin.

"Smile!"

"Now just a—"

The click of the camera silenced her. He touched the wiggling fish's head. "There. I patted it. Now put it back."

As gently as she could manage the thrashing fish, she bent over the side and nearly had the fish into the water when she heard another click.

"You didn't just take a picture of my rear—"

He grinned defiantly. "I want this one for my collection. I'll call it, 'Returning To the Wild.' Maybe I should enter it in a photography contest. I'd probably win."

The fish landed in the water with a splash. Rather than watch it swim away, Sharmane turned toward Alex about to tell him what she thought of his photography skills, but he took one look at her and burst out laughing.

Sharmane pressed her lips together and lunged for him, making the boat shift with the sudden movement. Sharmane felt herself about to fall, so she grabbed the front of his shirt to steady herself before she fell overboard. The combination of the rocking boat and abrupt motion caused both of them to drop to their knees.

The strong scent of the fish from her hands, which were entangled in his shirt, wafted between them. She stared at the way she was holding his shirt, unable to believe what she had done. He looked down too, but all he did was laugh.

She gave him a gentle shake. "What's gotten into you?"

Alex opened his mouth to speak, but no words came out. He didn't have an answer. All he could think of was how they were, how he only had to move a couple of inches, and he was in the perfect position to kiss her.

He didn't want to touch her with his slimy hands, and he couldn't drop her camera, so he relaxed his body, and her firm grip naturally drew them closer, although he was sure that was not her intent.

Before she could realize what he was doing, he tilted his head and claimed her mouth with his own, kissing her the way he had wanted to for days. And with his kiss, he gave her the last piece of his heart.

Gradually, they separated. He tried to analyze her dazed expression, hoping and praying what was happening to her was even a fraction of what was happening to him. If there had been any doubt before, he now knew for sure that he had fallen in love.

Her voice came out in a raspy whisper. "I think that's enough fishing. We should go home."

Chapter 7

Alex knocked on Sharmane's door and waited. Today felt different than yesterday. It was Saturday, but it wasn't simply that there hadn't been the usual rush hour traffic to contend with. The week was over and the weekend had begun, a reminder that Monday loomed closer.

He still hadn't pieced together what happened yesterday. After they'd both collected their wits they'd given up on fishing and instead had taken the boat around the lake a few times, taking turns driving. Since they both stunk like fish, rather than going out to a restaurant Sharmane had invited him to her house for dinner. It wasn't the same as the countless times he'd been invited to the home of a single woman. The good china had not been set out, no one had taken pains to dress up. The meal was ordinary and dessert was not rich or fancy—only store-bought cookies. Best of all, after dinner they'd both put their feet up on the coffee table and watched television with no hidden agendas.

It had felt relaxed and domestic. And he'd liked it. Unfortunately, he was forced to leave earlier than he wanted because he had to return the boat.

The door opened.

Alex cleared his throat and stiffened. "So what are our plans for today?"

"I have to go to the mall."

"The mall? You can go to the mall any day."

She patted her purse. "I have to drop off all my film at the one-hour photo place, because this is the last day of our vacation and I promised I'd give you copies. Tomorrow is back to normal with church and stuff, and Monday is back to work."

Alex felt like he'd just been punched in the gut. He knew it was coming, but now that the last day had come, he wasn't ready. Just in case, he'd brought along the watch to give to her, but hearing her say it only proved how much he didn't want it to happen.

He forced himself to smile. "If we must go shopping, let's do tourist shopping. Let's go to Robson Street."

Her eyes lit up, and he felt somewhat better. "That sounds like a great idea!"

"And you can leave your camera at home today, right?"

She grinned. "Only if you insist."

The Robson Street shopping area of downtown Vancouver was everything their fishing trip wasn't. It was crowded, noisy, busy with sights and sounds, and smelled with everything from scented soap to exotic foods to mingled perfumes from the crowd to car exhaust. People talked and laughed, babies cried, traffic rumbled, music drifted from a few open doors, and nothing was still.

She wanted to go into every store, and Alex didn't mind. He held onto her hand from the moment they left the car and wouldn't let go, claiming he didn't want to get separated in the crowd. Together they checked out the wide variety of the specialty shops and checked everything the trendy area had to offer—every imaginable souvenir, holograms, naturally scented soaps, jade carvings and jewelry, and countless handmade crafts.

At the photo store, Alex couldn't believe his eyes at the number of rolls of film she emptied out of her purse, and she wasn't the least bit embarrassed about it.

They stopped for lunch at a sidewalk café and treated themselves to frozen yogurt with waffle cones so fresh they were still slightly warm.

Alex made sure to buy a few souvenirs, but every purchase was bittersweet, because he knew everything would remind him of today, their last day together, and how it would end. Very soon, he would have to tell her who he was. And she would hate him for it.

She wanted to stop for an early dinner, and Alex didn't want to do or say anything to spoil the day. Once seated inside the restaurant, she pulled out all the photos and divided them evenly, since she'd gotten doubles of everything. They laughed at many of them, and others made him feel reminiscent, even though it had only been a few days.

Too soon, she gathered all her purchases and photos and checked her watch. "They said my car would be ready at six, so we'd better go. If you don't mind, can you drop me off at the auto shop? Then you don't have to worry about driving me home."

Alex opened his mouth but no words came out. This was it. It was over.

"We'd better hurry. I don't want them to close before we get there."

He had no choice but to follow.

Sharmane wondered if she'd said or done something wrong, because Alex was silent most of the trip. In a way, even though it was strange, she preferred the silence. For their last few minutes together, it seemed right. The finality of their vacation being over left her with such an overwhelming sadness she didn't know if she could talk without breaking into tears.

She didn't know if it was good or bad when they pulled into the parking lot at the repair shop. Rather than draw out a long good-bye, Sharmane opened the car door before he turned off the ignition and held out the envelope that she had prepared last night.

"This is for you."

His eyebrows knotted as he accepted it.

"Promise me you won't open it until you get home."

"But—"

"Promise me. Please."

"Uh, okay, I promise."

"And thanks for everything, Alex. It's been a great week. Bye!" With that, Sharmane turned and dashed toward the building before she did or said something she would regret.

"Wait! Sharmane!"

She didn't stop. It was painful enough to say good-bye; she couldn't allow it to drag out.

She barely managed to compose herself to face the mechanic. While he searched for the work order, Sharmane watched Alex's car meld into the traffic and disappear. He didn't know it, but he'd taken a piece of her heart with him. No matter what he was hiding, even if it was that he was a convicted felon, she couldn't deny it. The final parting stab in her heart told her what she hadn't wanted to admit. She was more than halfway in love with him, and now, he was gone without ever knowing it.

Having her car back was a hollow victory. Once Sharmane arrived home, she felt restless when she should have felt good with her life back to normal. Where once she had anticipated browsing at leisure through the scores of photographs, she couldn't look at them. Instead, she sat on the couch holding a scented soap she had bought today and thought of how Alex had teased her about why she wanted to smell like a watermelon.

She'd lived by herself for years, but because Alex was never coming back, she'd never felt so lonely.

The unexpected rap of a knock on her door made her suddenly grateful for whoever was stopping by for an unscheduled visit.

Her heart nearly stopped when she opened the door. It was Alex.

"I have something for you." He reached into his pocket.

Sharmane should have felt it coming. She had kept track of the amount of gas and expenses they'd incurred and tucked the cash into an envelope, then given it to him at the last minute on purpose. In a way, it was cowardly, but she had thought it would work, except here he was about to try to return it.

"Please, Alex. Don't do this. Don't spoil what was a wonderful vacation by having it end on an argument."

"We can talk about that later." He fumbled in his pocket and pulled out a small bag. "I was saving this for our last day together, but you ran off before I could give it to you."

Her heart pounded. She recognized the Butchart Gardens logo. At the same time that she didn't want a gift from him, she was thrilled that he had. Her hands shook when she pulled out the watch she'd been drooling over. For one of the few times in her life, she was almost speechless. Tears burned the backs of her eyes. "Oh, Alex," she mumbled, trying to speak past the tightness in her throat. "I don't know what to say. Thank you."

"Then don't say anything. I'm glad you like it."

He stepped closer to take off her old watch and fasten the new one onto her wrist. The rose pictured was beautiful, and the stones shone even more than they did in the artificial light of the store. Rather than give the neighbors a show of what was happening on her doorstep, she was about to invite him in, but the sparkle of the watch stopped her.

She tilted it to catch the sunlight. The light played into a rainbow of brilliant colors with the cut of the stones, and the beauty of it stopped all other thoughts. Suddenly, a sinking feeling settled into the pit of her stomach. The rhinestones shone too much, meaning they weren't rhinestones; they were diamonds, and therefore, the watch was worth far more than she originally thought.

The second she looked up, he cringed, confirming her suspicion. She opened her mouth to speak, but his words cut her off.

"I know what you're going to say." He rested his fingers on her arm. "I want you to have it."

"But—"

He reached into his back pocket and pulled out the envelope she'd given him. "And I'm giving this back. Sharmane, I can't accept this."

Her head started to spin. She couldn't allow this sudden show of male ego to override common sense. She pointed to the street, toward his car. The money they were talking about had to be at least three car payments on his. . .

Her arm drifted back down to her side and Sharmane blinked, but the sight before her didn't change. The car parked in front of her house, the only car in the vicinity, was a very new, shiny foreign luxury car. She didn't know what it was, only that it was well beyond her lifestyle. "Where's your car?"

"That was my nephew's car. We traded cars for the week. I have mine back now."

She stared at the car then back at him. "That car costs more money than I make in a year."

"If I can afford the car, I can certainly afford the watch."

"And here I've been insisting on paying for my half of the gas and stuff. Is there anything else I should know that's going to make me feel even more stupid?"

"Sharmane, I—"

The phone rang inside the house, but Sharmane ignored it. "How dare you lie to me."

"I didn't lie. I just didn't tell you the truth."

She rested her fists on her hips. "And there's a difference?"

"Well, technically. . ."

The phone continued to ring.

"Aren't you going to answer that?"

"The answering machine will get it. Talk."

"I might have misled you a little."

She looked at the car again. "A little? I think you have some explaining to do."

He dragged one palm down his face. "You know the Arby Building, where we met?"

Sharmane blinked. She remembered it well. It was the high-rise office tower next to the park. "Of course. I was worried that you didn't have a job, but you work for Arby, don't you? And it must be a pretty good job, too."

He squeezed his eyes shut. "It's a little more complicated than that. I actually—"

The phone stopped ringing. Her recorded voice delivered a cheery message, followed by Barry's. "Hey, Sharmane! Where are you? I'm calling to remind you that Frank and Darlene's party is tonight, and it's not too late to change your mind. You can wear that little red number I got you last week. And that perfume in the green bottle. Call me before seven if you can make it. Bye."

Sharmane opened her mouth to continue, but Alex stepped forward, forcing her to step back into the house. He shut the door abruptly and crossed his arms. "Who was that?

Apparently I'm not the only one to be keeping secrets here."

"Secrets? You want to talk about secrets? Look who's talking! What do you do that you can afford a car like that?"

He crossed his arms over his chest. "I don't just work for Arby Enterprises. I own it."

"Own it? You told me your name is Alex Brunnel. Or is it?"

"I haven't lied to you, although I have been guilty of omission. My full name is Alexander R. Brunnel. I was going to register the name for the business license as ARB Enterprises, but Jason started calling it Arby to tease me, and it kind of stuck."

She stared at him while his words sank in. The owner of Arby Enterprises would be wealthy beyond her wildest imagination. A millionaire.

Sharmane shook her head and backed up another step. "No. This can't be happening."

"Who was that on the phone? How is your boyfriend going to feel about you being out with another man all week? Talk about breaking trust. You led me to believe you were single."

"Boyfriend? That was Barry, my brother, with another matchmaking attempt! And what gives you the right to talk about trust? You led me to believe you were unemployed, but nothing could be further from the truth. How could I ever believe a thing you say? Get out."

Before her eyes, his face turned to stone. In an instant, he turned and stomped out. The slam of the door echoed in the silent house.

Sharmane buried her face in her hands and pressed her forehead into the back of the closed door. "Dear Lord," she mumbled, "please help me. Was I right to be so angry? Is it possible to fall in love with someone you barely know, and then find you don't know them at all? Why do I feel so empty inside? I don't know what to pray for, but I trust You and whatever You choose to show me."

A knock sounded on the door. She wasn't going to answer it, but whoever it was knocked again then rang the doorbell.

Sharmane rubbed her eyes to make herself presentable then opened the door.

Alex stood in the doorway, water dripping down his face, his wet hair plastered to his head, his clothes drenched.

"It's raining. May I come in?"

Sure enough, the rain pelted down behind him. Just like the day they'd met, a sudden shower had come out of nowhere.

She nodded.

"Can we talk?"

She nodded again and led him to the couch.

As they sat, he cleared his throat and reached for her hands, holding them gently while he spoke.

"I couldn't let it end like this," he said, his voice low and quiet. "I have to explain. I can only say I was being selfish. When we first met, running away for a week was exactly what I thought I needed, but I worried that when you found out about me, everything would change. I justified trading the car so you wouldn't feel intimidated. I wanted you to think of me just as an ordinary man, so I started to lead you to believe things that were not true. As the week progressed, I wanted to tell you the truth, but by then, everything had spiraled out of control. And then I didn't want to take the chance that something like this would happen. That you'd hate me, and it would be over."

She couldn't comment. She couldn't speak. She could barely think. A gentle squeeze of her hands made her throat tighten, further inhibiting her from speaking.

"I was starting to fall in love with you, Sharmane. And I was hoping that you could feel even a little of the same toward me."

All she could do was stare at their joined hands. Everything he did and said indicated sincerity, but she really didn't know, because she didn't know who Alex really was.

"I'm dying here. Please say something."

"I don't know what to say. I thought I was starting to get to know you, but I really don't know you at all."

"But you do. For the first time since I can remember, I could relax and not care about who was watching or that anyone wanted anything from me. I didn't have to worry about people pretending to like me or that I wouldn't like them. When you threw me out, I stood there beside the car, kicking myself for what I'd done. And when the rain started, it seemed so fitting. I just laid my head on the roof of the car and prayed for God to give me the strength to talk to you again."

She nodded, but didn't speak. She, too, had prayed for strength.

"What I'd really like is for us to get to know each other better. Let me show you who Alex Brunnel really is. I didn't believe in love at first sight but it's happened, and I'm hoping the same has happened to you. I hope it won't be all that long, that with God's blessings, we'll soon be married. I love you, Sharmane."

She wanted to protest, but she couldn't. Even though she couldn't justify his deception, she could understand why he'd done what he had.

"I think I love you, too, but this has all happened so fast. I need more time."

His eyes closed for a few seconds, and she could both see and feel him relax at the same time.

"Can we start by attending church together tomorrow morning?"

Sharmane smiled. "I don't know if I'm ready to meet your family, but I'd like it if you could come to church with me, and after that, I was going to meet my brother. Do you want to tell him he doesn't need to play matchmaker any more?"

Sharmane ran her fingers through Alex's wet hair, and his large hands cupped her face. "Yes, I'll show him you've found Mr. Right." And his kiss ended his reply.

GAIL SATTLER

Gail Sattler lives in Vancouver, BC, where you don't have to shovel rain, with her husband, three sons, two dogs, and a lizard who is quite cuddly for a reptile. When she's not writing, Gail is making music, playing electric bass for a local jazz band, and acoustic bass for a community orchestra. When she's not writing or making music, Gail likes to sit back with a hot coffee and a good book.

TEST OF TIME

by Pamela Kaye Tracy

Dedication

To the faculty, staff, and students of York
Christian College during the '79–'81 school years.
Friendships made in the presence of
Christ are everlasting.

*"Do not judge, and you will not be judged.
Do not condemn, and you will not be condemned.
Forgive, and you will be forgiven."*
LUKE 6:37

Chapter 1

Peach. And mint green. She'd chosen the colors because they made her think of sherbet, cool and summery. The peach-colored wall did feel cool to Rebecca Payne's cheek, but there was nothing summery about the empty room now. Her bottom lip trembled, but she bit down to stop that foolish impulse. It was just a room, an empty room, nothing more. Reba forced herself to step away. Inanimate walls offered no comfort. Still, for the last three years, this room had been the hub of Reba's home. Hers and Ray's.

"Mommy, don't cry. You said Daddy's in heaven."

Yes, Reba had told Ray's five-year-old daughter that. Believe it? She wasn't sure, but no way was Reba going to allow Hannah to be hurt by any of this. It had been six months since Ray's death. Reba was mourning a home; Hannah was mourning her father. There were two Rays, and Reba didn't know which one to mourn. She loved the one who had sat in the peach-colored room, with his feet on the coffee table stroking his daughter's hair while Hannah told him about sticking her face in the grass, pretending it was water, and seeing how long she could hold her breath. The other Ray was the man who had put a lien on the house—had it ever really been a home to him?—without her knowledge. That Ray had also borrowed against a life insurance policy before it matured. He'd owned three credit cards she wasn't aware of, although her name was on the plastic, and now she owed money she never knew had been spent.

What kind of wife was she? Her husband had a gambling problem, and she hadn't a clue.

"Mommy, are we leaving yet? Bark wants to go." Hannah stood, forlorn, in the empty hallway with her shirt half tucked in, and the dog's leash clutched tightly in her fist.

Reba took one last look around. "I'm just making sure we didn't leave anything."

"Like what? All the rooms are empty. We sold everything." Hannah's bottom lip trembled, but she didn't have the maturity to use her top teeth as a clasp. "Even my bed."

I'd lament a princess bed, too, if I were five. Sometimes Reba wondered if she'd ever been five. At that age, she'd already been in second grade, her father calling her profoundly gifted. At home, she'd shared a room with her sisters who all wanted a private room. None of them wanted to share with a little girl who still wet the bed. Reba gathered Hannah into her arms and walked out the front door for the last time.

Hannah wiggled to the ground. "Let's go."

The station wagon started on the second try. Bark, the chihuahua with nerves of steel, yapped angrily at the house disappearing from his view. Was he telling it not to follow or barking his disappointment at its failure to remain a home?

"Where are we going again?" Hannah's long blond hair needed washing. Her stubby fingers left a streak of dirt that smudged the map of New Mexico, the state they were leaving.

Reba gripped the steering wheel. As soon as they arrived at their new home and got a few paychecks behind them, she'd work on Hannah: Shine her daughter up; take her for a haircut; buy her new clothes—clothes that would do a future kindergartner proud. Hannah glared fiercely at the map, trying to mimic her father. Since the child couldn't read, the map was nothing but a prop for a little girl who needed to feel important, loved.

"We're going to Iowa. Creed, Iowa. Say it," Reba urged.

"Creed, Iwa."

"Close enough." Pulling out on the interstate, Reba set the cruise control and pointed the car in the direction of a place she'd planned never to return to. Her undergraduate days were memories best forgotten. This was not a full circle she'd ever imagined completing. She was going back to help a dear friend in a bind. The regular English teacher at Shiloh Christian College left on emergency leave just one week before classes began. Reba had an advanced degree in English and needed a job. Most of all, she needed to get away from Albuquerque, New Mexico, and the pall of a life that hadn't really been hers.

When Hannah wasn't looking, Reba slipped off the wedding ring Ray had placed on her finger and dropped it in her purse. She'd worn it through the funeral, through the burial, and during the meal she'd shared with Ray's parents last night. They, and Hannah, needed to see the ring; Reba didn't.

A college freshman sat opposite Mason Clark. Mason squinted. Was this really his college roommate's brother? Mason could see no resemblance between this pierced, wacky-haired teenager and Mason's one-time valedictorian suite-mate.

"So, like, what I want to do is transfer from the morning class into a different afternoon class."

Mason fought the urge to tell the young man about proper campus attire. School didn't officially start until Monday. James—who insisted he be called Jag—was checking in early and calling on his big brother's best friend.

"Why?"

"Well, like, I hear this Mrs. Robards is, like, really strict and hard. I want a different English teacher. I, um, well, English is not my favorite subject."

Jag leaned forward. That's when Mason saw the tattoo peek out from under the T-shirt sleeve. Praying hands? Was that covered in the student handbook?

A tattoo? Unbelievable. Mason had met Barry's parents. They were conservative types from Blair, Nebraska. They'd frowned at Barry wearing his baseball cap backward.

"You sure you're Barry's brother?" Mason asked.

"Yep, I got a picture to prove it."

The smile did it. Mason could see a hint of his old roommate's smirk in that slight uplift of the lips. Mason wanted to bury his head in his hands. His superiors thought he could relate to this generation; he was only twenty-seven, and at one time he thought maybe he'd be able to. But he'd never been as daring as them. The closest he'd come to rebellion was one night—best forgotten —just two weeks before his college graduation, and that had been an accident.

Jag's record didn't read like the felony report Mason expected. According to the references, James Aaron Gilroy was an "A" student who worked summers at a camp for the mentally challenged and nights at a video store. His COMPASS and SAT scores showed he was more than ready for college. English should be no problem for this kid. Under the heading "high school activities" Jag had included both football and chess club.

"So, the only reason you want to transfer is because you're afraid of having Mrs. Robards as a teacher?"

"I'm not afraid!"

"Okay, you hope to avoid having Mrs. Robards as a teacher?"

"That's better."

"Mrs. Robards no longer teaches here. I'm not sure who is taking her place. You'll have a different teacher."

"That's cool." Jag visibly relaxed. Sitting back in the stiff, wooden chair, he studied Mason's office with interest.

"Ah, Mr. Clark. I couldn't help but overhear." Cindy, the history department's work-study student paused at the door. She sent Jag a look that was clearly an invitation to chat later. "The new lady is moving into her office. I think her name is Mrs. Payne."

"Wow," said Jag. "Maybe I should check her out. See if she looks easy."

The word choice was not the best, but Mason knew what the kid meant. What Jag wanted was to transfer into Mr. Hillman's English class, and not because Jag had problems with his mother tongue. Jack Hillman was in charge of the school newspaper and often dismissed class early in order to get back to putting out the latest edition of the *Shiloh Reporter*. He was also a notoriously easy grader, which was why that particular English class was full. Jag's transfer couldn't happen.

Jag was out of his seat and down the hall, following Cindy, in seconds. Mason frowned as he walked behind the girl. There was only one empty office down this hall. It had been Mrs. Robards's. After she left, it had been allotted to him. Two days ago, he'd rolled fresh, white paint on those office walls. If not for the paint fumes, *he* would have moved in this morning.

Cindy stood at the door to that office. Jag balanced on tiptoes and stared in. The look on the kid's face said he'd found the English teacher of his dreams!

Great, thought Mason. *The English teacher of Jag's dreams has taken residence in my new office*. Well, even if it made him an ogre, he'd let the new woman know her mistake before she had too much moved in.

"Excuse me." Mason sidestepped Jag's feet and got his first look at. . .

"Rebecca Harper," he whispered, loud.

"It's Payne now," she said, turning around. Reddish-brown hair caught the sunlight. Her head tilted in the inquisitive angle he remembered so well. The pug nose—he'd once dreamed about kissing that nose—was as cute as ever.

Reba still had the ability to make him tongue-tied with simply a look. *Yep,* thought Mason, relinquishing his new office and any hope of having a coherent conversation.

She'd come close to ruining his life—well, maybe he was exaggerating a little—just two weeks before he graduated from college. Worse, he could tell by the look in her eyes, she didn't remember him.

Chapter 2

Jag immediately entered the small office and took the hammer out of Reba's hand.

"I'm Jag. I'll hang the curtain for you, ma'am."

"I'll help," Cindy offered.

Reba surrendered the hammer but didn't move. "This office isn't big enough for four people."

"I'm in your nine a.m. English class." Jag pushed aside the chair Reba had been about to stand on. Sticking two nails in his mouth, he held up the white curtain rod and aligned the end with the pencil lines Reba had marked.

Cindy shrugged and scooted out into the hall to watch.

"What are you doing here?" Mason asked. Not that he wanted to have a conversation in front of Jag, but waiting was impossible.

"I'm going to teach English. I didn't catch your name."

My name; she wants to know my name. "Mason." He meant to sound annoyed, but did he intend to sound angry? "Mason Clark. I know you're going to teach English, but why here?"

"This is where I received the job offer, Ma—" Recognition dawned in her eyes.

Mason watched as her fingers went together, a tight resemblance of praying hands, then fidgeting hands, finally nervous hands. She didn't really remember him, did she? What she remembered was his name.

"You two know each other?" Jag had the rod attached and was reaching for the curtain.

"Yes," said Reba.

"Not really," said Mason.

"Not really," echoed Reba.

"Yes," said Mason.

Jag looked at them both and summed it up. "Cool." He stuffed the curtain in Reba's hand, gave a two-fingered salute, and exited.

"I didn't know you taught here." Reba sat the curtain down on her desk.

"Would that have stopped you from coming?"

"No."

"But people might find out—"

"Mason, that night was over six years ago. I don't think it's currently a hot topic for dinner conversation."

"I remember."

She stepped around her desk and looked in his eyes. "I'll bet you do remember. You always worried about the wrong things, Mason. Let it go."

"But what if—"

"If you worry about it, people will notice, and then it will come up. If you let go, no one will think about it."

"My job is to offer guidance. I'd hate for the students to find out that I've been advising them against doing things I, myself, have done."

Picking up the curtain, she jabbed the first hook in the fold. "Mason, the only one who ever believed you were perfect was you."

The elementary school was catty-corner from Clark Hall, and Hannah had found the playground. From the second-story window, Reba watched the five-year-old swing as high as she could. Opening the window, Reba called an unnecessary, "Be careful."

Hannah waved while Bark jumped at her feet. His red leash, which should have been in Hannah's hand, trailed behind him like the tail of an erratic kite. The boy from earlier, Jag, looked up from the bench he was sitting on. Iowa cottonwoods shaded the small playground. The few freshmen who had shown up early for orientation milled around the grounds. This boy, the tall one who could put up a curtain without standing on tiptoe, pointed at Hannah and then at Reba, his nonverbal communication asking the question, "Does she belong to you?" Reba nodded, momentarily worrying about Stranger Danger, and then berating herself for suspecting everyone. Surely, a scant thirty-six hours out of New Mexico, she could move about freely.

"I'll watch her," the boy called.

Reba hesitated.

"I'm in your nine a.m. English class." He shouted the words as if they were the magic combination for permission. And, they were. This was Creed, Iowa, after all. Reba smiled, waved, and turned around to face her office. Her very empty office.

She didn't own any outdated English textbooks to make the office look academic and her shelves impressive. She hadn't taught before, so no one had given her the crafty wooden apples or brightly colored certificates scripted with "Teachers Have Class" or "To Teach Is to Touch a Mind." She didn't even own an electric pencil sharpener.

The only things Reba could add to the office were a handful of diplomas and a picture of Hannah.

"Rebecca, do you have a moment?"

He was back. Mason Clark. Funny how she'd almost failed to recognize him from all those years ago. He had changed. Gone was the skinny, too-tall-for-his-feet nerd. There were muscles where skin and bone used to be. Short, wavy, brown hair complemented chocolate eyes. Reba suspected his dirty blue backpack had been replaced by a leather briefcase. Two years ahead of her in school, he'd been so devoted to the straight and narrow that he never looked right or left.

"Come in, Mason."

He glanced at the reams of computer paper stacked on the one student chair, then stepped to the window and leaned back against the radiator. Taking note of the empty bookcase and unadorned walls, he remarked, "Kinda bare in here."

"My contract is only for a year. Dean Steward thinks Mrs. Robards will come back. I'd best not get my hopes up."

He crossed his arms and frowned. Now that was a look she remembered. Almost everything else had changed. A perfect crease ran down each leg of his tan Dockers. He'd been a button-down cambric shirt kind of guy as a student, now he was a golf shirt kind of guy. Mason had always tried to project success. Now it looked as if he'd refined that talent. Reba refused to be impressed. She reached for her soda and tried to look nonchalant.

"I didn't know you'd kept in touch with Roger Howard." Mason didn't move.

She'd forgotten how direct he could be. "He's my husband's. . .my late. . . He was Ray's uncle."

"Ray?"

"My husband. He died. Six months ago." Reba mentally added, *three hours, two minutes;* it had been straight up noon.

"I'm sorry." Mason's face lost its defensive look. He'd always been perfect for leading the devotionals. Sincerity became an art form when attached to Mason Clark. "It must have been sudden."

Yes, bullets were sudden. That was true. "Mason, you're not in here to talk about the last few years of my life. What do you want?"

"You always were to the point."

"And you were always trying to make sure the point was safe before you sharpened it."

"Reba, you didn't know me that well."

"I wrote for the school paper, Mr. Class President. Remember? I had to make your successes interesting." Reba went to the window and watched Hannah and Jag for a few moments, but the determined look on Mason's face distracted her. She'd seen that look often, from him. Back during their school days, he'd always made time for her interviews but acted busy. Like she was interrupting his valuable schedule. He didn't look busy now.

"I know you think the past is swept under the carpet, but I'm not so sure. Some of our students are precariously balanced between two worlds. I have to deal with them every day. It's in their best interest to have a role model they can rely on."

One thing for sure, Mason Clark was still a headache.

"Tell you what," Reba reached down, picked up her purse, and slung it over her shoulder, "you don't need to worry about the past. I won't even tell anyone that I know you. It will be like we're meeting for the first time."

"That's not quite honest."

"What do you want?"

"I want to keep it low-key."

"You got it."

"Reba, I don't think you understand."

"No, I do understand. I just don't care."

Mason left, shaking his head and muttering tersely. Reba stared at the barren bookcase shelves. Maybe she could pretend Mason wasn't around to chip away at a past that was already set in cement.

He'd always had luck on his side. The very building was named after his family. Clark Hall. It sounded like a name for a television weatherman. She remembered Shiloh's Family Days and the masses of Clarks who flocked to the campus to support Mason, picnic, get their picture taken for the school paper, and laugh. Oh, they'd donated plenty of money, too. She'd written their story two years in a row. The Clarks who needed multiple pews in the Shiloh Chapel.

Reba had usually sat with about four others who did not have family attending. She'd tried not to mind that only she and the foreign exchange students were alone.

She locked the office door behind her. The sun shone through the windows of Clark Hall's second story and accented dust particles that swirled toward the high ceiling's track lighting. All the offices had closed doors, except the one at the end. Mason's, no doubt. He probably put as much time into his job as he had school.

Shaking her head, she chuckled at a distant memory. Every senior class president had a goal. They all wanted to contribute something from their graduating class, something that would be remembered by future crops of students. Mason wanted to update the college's front sign. Instead of the ancient, imposing looking, wooden-roofed board, Mason wanted a glossy, plexiglass sign. He'd gotten it, too.

She'd had to write three articles about that sign. Mason had dedicated almost half a year to raising the money. The sign had fallen over during a tornado watch not even a year later. The remaining pieces—those that hadn't blown away—were too numerous to reconstruct.

Reba wondered if Mason knew what real worries were. Did he have to worry about anything serious? Did he understand what it felt like to budget for his next meal? Had he ever coasted down a busy street concerned about his car's brakes? Could he imagine the trials a single parent faced—especially a single parent who didn't know who had killed her husband, because they hadn't been caught?

Chapter 3

The first Monday of school was always disorganized. Mason directed two lost freshman out of his History 101 class and into the Spanish room next door.

The yellowing window shade at the back of the room had a jagged tear. The sun managed to shine through in just a way to blind him. He left the security of the podium and started walking between the aisles. "Read the syllabus. It is law. Notice how tardies affect your final grade."

The door opened. Jag walked in. Mason felt sure that some of the students were mentally deducting a point from Jag's final grade. Those students would probably even verify the points with Jag at the end of the semester. Most students didn't look as if they cared. They probably didn't believe Mason. A few did exactly what he wanted them to, which was read the syllabus.

"I want you to especially note the attendance policy. Three absences and you're dropped."

Jag hadn't even taken a seat. His hand shot in the air, and he asked, "What about sports-excused absences?"

"Coach Martin will give me the names and dates. If you read the syllabus you'll notice I wrote that. Also, your homework is due the next time you attend class."

"All of it?" Jag asked.

"All of it."

Mason walked around while the students read his syllabus. His first-hour class rubbed sleep from their eyes while they mused over homework and six upcoming tests. His text for this class started with Christopher Columbus.

After more than half the class penned their names on the syllabus's signature sheet, Mason had them open their textbooks to page seven and called on Jag to read the chapter's introduction. Picking up the roll, Mason tried to put names to faces. There were three names he couldn't pronounce, and four people hadn't bothered to show up. It was an unfounded rumor that instructors did nothing on the first day, as those students who hadn't bothered to purchase the textbook were finding out.

Jag read until the end of the section. Mason chose two more students, then assigned six questions before dismissal. Two more classes went exactly the same.

Mason ate lunch in the cafeteria, then headed over to his office. Unless he missed his guess, there'd be some students waiting. Since there wasn't an opening for a full-time counselor, Mason taught but was allotted a few students to guide. His degree was in Social Sciences, and his minor in History had not been obtained with teaching in mind. He wanted to be a full-time counselor. He wanted to help students figure out they weren't alone; Christ walked with them, and they all could shape their own destinies. His dream was tarnishing. What they hadn't told him in college was that youth had its own language, and there was no way to decipher the code. Worse, he suspected he'd missed out on his own generation's jargon.

The waiting room was full. A few students started to stand when he entered, but Linda Simms, the secretary, shooed them back. "Give him a moment."

"All for me?" He raised an eyebrow. Mason worked with the students whose last names began with G–M. Most of them had registered over the summer. Their schedules should be fairly accurate. Usually the changes didn't come until day three.

He helped the first student with a job-related transfer, then helped a second student who felt overburdened and wanted to change his schedule. When a third student asked about changing English teachers, Mason caught on. Mrs. Robards transition from sixty-ish lady with beehive, to twentyish lady with sparkling eyes had not gone unnoticed by the male population of Shiloh Christian College.

Taking a breath, he stuffed the transfer cards back into his desk and opened his office door to announce, "If you're hoping to transfer into Mrs. Payne's English classes, they're full."

The waiting room emptied. Linda shook her head. "Now why didn't I think of that?"

"Have you met Rebecca Ha—Payne?"

"No, but I hear she'll be coaching the softball team, so I expect I'll get to know her real soon."

The powers-that-be had all kinds of things planned for Rebecca Payne. Mason wondered if Reba was ready to coach softball, sponsor a sorority, and help with the yearbook. Somehow, he doubted it. There was an air of sadness about her that hadn't been there before. Oh sure, she was mourning a husband, but something else had gone missing from her personality. Just what, Mason couldn't put his finger on. "I'm going to step out for a moment." Mason left Linda alphabetizing freshman files and restocking drop/add slips.

Fall in Iowa was a beautiful collage of oranges, browns, reds, and greens. The wind whipped through Mason's hair as he strolled down the curving sidewalk toward Clark Hall. His office, and Reba's, occupied the second floor. The first floor was devoted to classes. The hallway smelled like chalk, perfume, and dust. Reba's class was at the end. Peering in, he saw her standing by the chalkboard. She'd written her name in neat curls of letters.

The students were reading a piece of paper, probably her syllabus. A few of the guys alternated their attention between the paper and the woman.

Mason watched as Reba walked to the board and wrote, "No Payne, No Gain." Next to that, she wrote, "Know Payne, Know Gain."

Now this was the Reba he remembered. Her blue jean skirt brushed against perfectly shaped knees. Her white shirt, covered with a crocheted vest, accented a slender form that looked too young to be in front of a classroom. He'd thought that this morning when they'd introduced her in chapel. Her hair was shorter than before, barely touching her shoulders, but with a natural curl that bounced when she spoke. She was still animated. He'd loved those interviews when she worked on the paper. She'd balanced a notebook on her lap and kept her pencil stuck above her ear. She never took a single note. Reba couldn't, because she talked with her hands. Every word came with a gesture, yet she never misquoted him or left out an important detail.

Mason needed to get back to the office. He had plenty of things to do. Transferring more students into her classes was not one of them, though with every fiber of his being, Mason knew had he needed an English credit, he'd be first in line trying to enroll.

Chapter 4

The day-care center was two blocks north of SCC. Reba parked her car and hurried in, surprised at how much she had missed spending the day with Hannah. Hannah had been two when Reba and Ray got married. From that time on, Reba had embraced motherhood and relished seeing the world through Hannah's eyes.

The letter A was at the top of the color page. Hannah haphazardly crayoned blue and orange onto what was supposed to be an apple. Reba signed the time card and braced herself to receive forty-five pounds of happy child.

"Do I start kindergarten tomorrow?"

"No, Monday, but we're headed there now."

"Good. Marky's going to be in my class."

"Marky?" Reba looked around.

"His mother already picked him up. He has a cat, too."

"We're not getting a cat."

"Okay, but if we had a cat, we wouldn't ever have mice. That's what Marky said."

Shiloh Christian Academy was on the same plot of land as the college—a plus in Reba's mind. It had day-care, too, although Reba was hoping not to have to use it. Air-conditioning escaped out the doors as they went in. A secretary greeted them with a smile and a sheaf of papers to fill out. Reba handed over copies of Hannah's birth certificate and medical records.

The kindergarten teacher met them in her room. The Christian school tested all incoming students, but Reba wasn't worried. Hannah was bright, already knew her letters, most of the single sounds, and how to write her name. While Hannah pointed out colors on a chart, Reba explored the school. Ray would have loved this place with its hallway self-esteem posters and trophy case of spelling bee ribbons and Bible Bowl awards.

"Mrs. Payne?" The kindergarten teacher called down the hall. *What was the woman's name again?* Reba wondered. Luckily the sign outside the class proclaimed, Welcome to Mrs. Henry's Kindergarten Class.

Hannah stood at the chalkboard drawing circles while Mrs. Henry handed Reba a supply list and said, "She did fine."

Reba skimmed the inventory and realized from now until the next paycheck, McDonalds was out. "Hannah, the bathroom is right down the hall. I want you to go there and wash your hands after."

Skipping between the desks, Hannah paused at one and said, "I'll sit here. Marky is way across the room." That important announcement accomplished, Hannah bounced out of the room.

"You have some questions?" Mrs. Henry sat on Marky's desk.

"No, not really. I wanted to let you know that Hannah's father died a few months ago. I'm not sure she understands he isn't coming back. She's usually happy, but every once in a while. . . Well, every once in a while." Reba stopped. How could she put into words something she sensed as a mother. "She's wet her pants a few times, and that's unusual. Um, she stares into space a lot more now. I made sure the office had my home phone, my office, and my cellphone. Don't hesitate to call if you notice anything unusual or if she needs me for anything."

Mrs. Henry nodded, her face somber. "How did he die?"

How did he die? It made sense that someone would ask that question. Reba had known it would happen, expected it, but she didn't want to answer.

The words came out a croak. "He was in an accident."

"Ready, Mama?" Hannah stood at the doorway, already alert to the fact that Reba was talking about Ray. Hannah's head tilted to the side inquisitively. Ray had that habit, too, always looking like there was something more to be said.

Taking Hannah's hand, Reba left the kindergarten room as fast as dignity would allow and before the teacher could ask any more questions. Grief was such a tangible sorrow and not one Reba was willing to touch with a stranger.

"Are we going to the store? I want a pink shirt."

"This school has a dress code, honey. Looks like you'll be wearing lots of blue and white."

"Dress code?"

"It means all the students wear the same outfit."

"No cartoons?"

"No cartoons, but we'll get you a special headband. Okay?"

A few minutes later, Reba realized she'd be washing clothes every night. She picked out one navy blue jumper and white collared shirt. They'd also be eating lots of peanut butter. The school supply aisle was not the bargain it advertised. Hannah didn't want plain yellow pencils; she wanted cartoon character ones. They cost a dollar more. The smallest bottle of glue looked pitiful traveling down the conveyor belt towards checkout. And, although Reba hadn't touched a single designer folder or school box, there they were, traveling merrily toward her checkbook.

"Hannah Lynn Payne!" Reba plucked mouse-eared erasers out of the cashier's hand. "We don't need these."

When the amount glowed from the register, Reba knew even if she turned her purse upside down and unloaded every spare chunk of change from the black hole, she'd not have enough. It was only a matter of cents, but sales tax obviously differed from New Mexico to Iowa. Reba had no clue what to put back. She'd been as frugal as possible. Not the uniform. She could use pencils from her office, but. . .

"Everything okay?"

At first, Reba thought the checkout lady was asking the question, but the male voice didn't jive with the blond perm or red lipstick.

Mason Clark stood behind her. He held an electric pencil sharpener box in one hand and an open wallet in the other. "Do you need some money?"

"No."

The cashier repeated the amount.

"Reba, let me help."

"We bought too much," Reba insisted, grabbing the pack of eraser tops. The deduction didn't change the decimal, nor did it effect the ten's place.

Who turned off the air-conditioning? Reba wondered, wiping perspiration from her brow. If she'd been wearing a sweater, she'd have shed it by now.

When the plastic ruler and watercolors left the conveyor belt, Hannah's mouth opened. "Mama!"

"This is stupid." Mason handed the cashier a fifty and growled, "If you don't charge me for all her belongings, I'll talk to your manager."

The cashier hit the sale key.

"Maybe I'll go to the manager," Reba sputtered. "I told you we didn't need any money."

"The manager is my cousin, Phil. He's a senior at Shiloh. You won't have him in class." Mason took the bag containing his pencil sharpener and guided Reba out of the way so the next customer could be taken care of.

Hannah had the plastic bag with their purchases. It was bigger than she was. The child had given up so much. Reba didn't want to take anything else away.

"Fine. Thank you. On payday I'll return the money."

"Payday? That's going to be more than three weeks for you. Do you need a loan?"

Reba rolled her eyes. "No, everything is fine."

"Didn't your husband provide for you before. . . ?" Mason's gaze traveled downward. "Who is this?"

"My daughter, Hannah."

"Daughter?"

"I'm in school. Want to see my new blue dress?" Hannah started to rip the bag, but Reba took it.

"Mason, it's going to be hard acting like we barely know each other if you insist on paying for school supplies. Thanks for helping. I do appreciate it. I don't like it, but I do appreciate it. We need to go now. I haven't fed Hannah yet."

"McDonald's," Hannah suggested.

"Spaghetti from our stove top," Reba amended.

"But you said—" Hannah began.

"I said we'd see. That doesn't mean yes." Taking Hannah firmly by the hand, Reba started for the door.

"I like spaghetti," Mason said.

"Come over," Hannah invited "I'll show you the neat doghouse we built in our backyard. Bark likes it."

The exit was just a few feet away, so close. Hannah always warmed up to strangers. So had Ray. The invitation had more to do with snazzy pencils than common sense, but what five-year-old had sense? Reba looked at the exit longingly before arguing, "Mason, this is ten-minute spaghetti, nothing special."

"I was going home to a microwave dinner. Spaghetti sounds plenty special. Besides, you can call it payback for the school supplies."

"Fine." Reba sent Mason a tight smile and exited the store. She didn't want anyone to know she was broke. Now Mason would know when he saw her house. . .and what was not in it.

Stupid, stupid, Mason told himself as he headed for his Cherokee. He needed to avoid Reba, not dine with her. And she had a kid! This Ray character, who didn't think to provide for his wife, must have been been dishwater blond, because Hannah didn't look much like Reba. The kid was cute. Mason's nieces and nephews were cute, too, and they especially looked cute once he peeled their sticky hands off his jeep's door handles, or should they come to his house, away from his books. The kids all loved him.

Barely a week went by when a niece or nephew didn't call to see if they could spend the night with him. At Christmas, Mason was the only adult to receive coloring books and yo-yos in his stocking. He was the only Clark over twenty-one to have every action figure from the latest space movies. Half of it, he knew, was his brothers and sisters letting him know that it was his turn to produce grandchildren. The other half was some invisible force that drew kids to him.

Reba turned into the driveway of the house straight across from Clark Hall. That made sense. The Webbs were missionaries in India. It was the perfect house for Reba to rent.

Hannah jumped out of the passenger side and ran to the end of the driveway to point to where he should park, which was right behind Reba, the only place to park. Hannah obviously took after her mother: bossy.

Reba went into the house without a backward glance. Clearly, she didn't want him here. The sensible thing to do would be to suddenly remember a conflict of schedule. Instead, he opened the door, stepped outside, and let Hannah grab his hand and drag him around to the back.

"This is Bark. He's a chiwowwow."

What the dog was, was a poofed-up sausage of a canine with twigs for legs. Bark took an immediate dislike to Mason. Growling, the beast bared his teeth and made attacking bull movements.

"Bark!" Reba called from the kitchen window.

Bark shut his mouth, gave Mason a dirty look, and strutted to his doghouse.

"What is that?" To Mason's eye it looked like the dog lived in a short, wooden teepee with many doors.

"That's his doghouse. Isn't it beyoooootiful? Me and Mommy made it this morning. And we didn't use a hammer."

No kidding. Before he had time to format a comment about the doghouse that badly needed to be condemned or the pink ribbon stuck on the dog's head and inching its way toward the dog's chin, Hannah was dragging Mason over to a tree. "I'm going to build a treehouse." Next, she sat on the awkward swing. The seat was so off balance that Hannah had to hold herself in place. "We hung this up, too. Mama's afraid of hives so she hurried. I like climbing to the top of trees; I'm not afraid of hives. I wanted to help. Mama says I'm too little, but I like hammers. They are my favorite thing, except when they smash my finger instead of the nail. Once I smashed Mama's finger instead of the nail, but we got the bookcase together, except it leans. Do you think the books will fall out?"

He opened his mouth to answer.

Hannah lowered her voice and confided, "Mama comes out here and swings when I'm not looking."

Mason looked back at the house and through the kitchen window where he could see Reba preparing the spaghetti.

"And this is where we go if there's a torndo." Hannah pointed to the cellar. "I've never been in a torndo. Mama says it's when the wind blows hard. I saw *The Wizard of Oz*, so I hope one happens. Have you ever been in a torndo?" This time she waited for an answer.

"When I was in college, a tornado came through this area. It didn't really strike here, but it blew a lot of things down."

"Houses?" Hannah said hopefully.

"No."

"People in rocking chairs?"

"No."

"Dogs?" Hannah glanced at Bark and looked indecisive.

"Signs," Mason told her. "Cheap signs."

Chapter 5

The serious softball players were angry that this was their first practice. A few didn't care. Five of the players complained about having to practice at all. While observing and encouraging their warm-up exercises, Reba tried to tie names to the histories she'd studied over the weekend.

Reba had gone over all their stats and knew both she and they were at a serious disadvantage. Even though this was only intramurals, the first game was Saturday. Plus, these girls would be hers when softball season started. Many of them were already hers, on the volleyball team. Shiloh wasn't known for its women's athletics Reba wasn't known for losing.

Cindy, the English department's student aide, smiled encouragingly. Too bad Cindy could catch but not throw. Reba started putting the girls to positions.

"Tiffany." The first name came out strong, but Reba choked on the last name. Her third baseman's last name was...but surely, Clark was a popular name. They couldn't all be related to Mason.

Redheaded, a gum chewer, and sassy, Tiffany Clark wore tight shorts and makeup that begged comment. Reba would guess the girl majored in complaining and had a bright future.

Reba snapped her own gum and crooked a finger. "My notes say that you only played half season last year. Want to tell me why?"

Reba's notes also said why.

"The coach and I had a difference of opinion."

"Yes?"

Tiffany had the grace to shift her glance downward, but the gumption to state, "She said she was the coach, and I said she wasn't."

The girls were waiting for the next move.

"Are we gonna have that problem this year?" Reba asked.

"I don't know. I guess that depends on whether you coach or just sit there and tell us what to do."

"Just so you know," Reba said, "it will not take me half a season to bench you."

"Just so you know," Tiffany responded, this time look-ing Reba in the eye, "I'm good."

Reba smiled. "Let's see how good." Putting the girls into places, Reba stepped up to

bat. Cindy was fighting tears over being placed in right field. Tiffany snapped gum and—
"Hi, Uncle Mason!"

The ball Reba meant to line to third limped to the pitcher.

Except for passing Mason in the hall and noticing him at chapel every morning, Reba had managed to avoid the man.

He had charmed Hannah, and almost every night for the last two weeks she'd asked when he was coming back over. Reba and Bark weren't won that easily.

Mason had turned the spaghetti dinner into a big deal. He taught Hannah to coil the noodles around her fork. He made a happy face with the meatballs. He took up too much space in the kitchen, and he wore the wrong aftershave.

He wore jeans today. A light blue T-shirt accented how much his shoulders had spread in comparison to his lean body.

Tiffany snapped a bubble. Reba turned just in time to witness an exaggerated rolling of the eyes. This time, Reba's bat sent the ball screaming to third, where Tiffany didn't even have time to move to catch it.

Before the girl could comment, the catcher tossed Reba another ball, and she spun one between Tiffany's legs.

Two complainers shut up. They turned the bills of their baseball caps around, squatted, and yelled, "Aaa, batter, batter."

Two hours later, the only one who left practice unhappy was Cindy. Mason had opened his briefcase, graded papers, talked on his cell phone, and watched Reba the whole time. When practice ended, he walked with Tiffany to his car, and they drove off. *Yeah, right, like he was here for his niece.* Reba knew better. Still, it was much too soon to enjoy the attention of a single man—especially a single man who made bumping into her a hobby while claiming that they needed to avoid each other and the past.

She had enough to worry about without Mason adding to it. There were times when she still turned in the night, expecting to hear Ray snoring. Occasionally, she caught the scent of his aftershave at the grocery store. Hannah still ran through the front door yelling, "Mom, Da—"

Reba was putting the last bat away when she glanced at her watch. Six fifteen.

Six fifteen!

Day-care at Hannah's school ended at six. Every fifteen minutes tardy was an additional five dollars. Racing across the baseball field, she managed a record two-minute sprint.

"I was the only one, Mommy." Hannah's scolding surpassed the day-care teacher's disapproving look.

"I'm sorry, honey. I was helping the softball players and time got away from me."

The uniform Reba had put on Hannah this morning looked like it had seen combat. There was a tear in the sleeve. A ketchup drip made a path from collar to hem. One sock stretched toward Hannah's knee; the other hid in her shoe. Dirt had found a magnet. "Marky never goes to day-care. His mother picks him up right at three. I want to be picked up at three."

"I will pick you up at three on Mondays and Wednesdays."

Hannah's sigh said, *not good enough*. Reba rubbed between her daughter's shoulder blades and took a breath. It was truly a beautiful day. She'd finally mastered all her students' names; softball practice turned out better than she'd hoped possible; Hannah missed being with her mommy, and Mason had come to practice.

No! Reba stopped in her tracks so suddenly that Hannah stumbled.

"What, Mommy?"

"Nothing, baby; I was just thinking."

Thinking things best left alone, Reba told herself. From every angle, Mason Clark looked to be a nice guy, but Reba had been fooled before. This time, she had Hannah to think about.

Over a hundred college students attended Shiloh Church. Mason figured another hundred trekked across town to Community Church, just to be different, and he knew at least another hundred didn't bother to attend on Wednesday nights. Of course, he figured that same hundred didn't come on Sundays either.

Mason taught a class on faith and works. Most of his students were the kind who were willing to get their hands dirty in order to make society a better place. He had future social workers, counselors, and lawyers, plus a few soon-to-be ministers. He also had a handful of females who'd placed him on their wish list. Dating a student was not something Mason intended to do.

Mason struggled to vary what his group did. School had been in session for a month. Their first service project had been sewing dolls for the small hospital that Creed shared with neighboring Trinity, Iowa. The tiny cloth dolls were used to demonstrate to children just where the surgery would take place. A doll used to explain a tonsillectomy would have an X drawn on its throat. The students gathered in the hospital's small cafeteria, pushed tables together, and stitched for two hours. Cindy and two other girls managed five dolls each. Mason had struggled through two. The rest of the young men had produced snowmanlike monstrosities that were sure to cause soon-to-be young owners to either howl with laughter or scream with fright.

Mason tried to organize at least one outing a month. He'd been wondering what to do next. Seeing Reba's house spearheaded an idea, though he knew she'd hate it. That's why he'd proposed doing it this Saturday. The girls' volleyball team had an away game. As assistant coach, Reba needed to attend. Mason's class would have at least a three-hour window in which to work. The Webbs had been gone four years. The first renter had not been kind to the old house.

There were sixteen in his class. Half of those nodded that they could be there.

Jag grumbled, "I have to take pictures of the volleyball match for the paper."

"You could miss it once," Cindy said. "Someone else could take pictures."

"No, I'm working, too. Mrs. Payne is taking Hannah along and hired me to watch her."

Mason looked from Cindy to Jag. They were dating, already—too soon, in Mason's opinion. Cindy's blond hair was swept into a ponytail, and she wore a dress. Jag's jeans were torn. His T-shirt advertised a rock group, a Christian rock group, but still not a

T-shirt to wear to church.

What was Reba thinking, hiring Jag to babysit? Hannah was much too impressionable. It had to be money. Cindy probably charged more an hour than Jag. That had to be it.

The class agreed on the time; Mason dismissed them, erased the dry erase board, and stepped out into the hallway. He hadn't seen Reba in church. Maybe she attended Community. Of course, back in college, she'd been one of the hundred that hadn't attended services regularly. Had that changed? Most of his friends got even more serious about church once they had children. His older brother, Richard, had.

Mason chuckled as he entered the foyer. Groups of people milled around, talking, planning, hugging. He didn't see Tiffany, and he'd promised to drive her to the store. Tiffany was a handful, and so much like Richard that Mason sometimes wanted to throttle her. The whole family had prayed. Tiffany hated church, refused to attend after she turned sixteen, and seemed to be drifting into the wrong crowd. Always one to be on the go, as a senior in high school, Tiffany had attended Encounter in Abilene, Texas, only because it got her out of town. The weekend rally among Christian youth was a turning point. Mason could only imagine what words, songs, prayers, got through to the girl, but she came back with a new perspective.

Had that happened to Reba? Had she found peace with God after being expelled from Shiloh? There had to be some difference for Roger Howard, a noted Bible professor, to recommend her for employment. The man had pull, but the fact that she was a relative wouldn't earn her even a last-minute position. Her IQ would be in her favor, but her age would not. Mason wondered when Roger, who was on a mission trip in Africa, would return. Reba needed family.

She'd been a sophomore, just like Tiffany was now, when she got kicked out of Shiloh. That was six years ago. Hannah was in kindergarten. The little girl had mentioned that fact no less than ten times during supper. Kindergarten meant at least five years old. Reba became a mother about a year after leaving Shiloh. How had she wound up with Professor Howard's nephew? Mason had to admire her, though. She'd still managed to finish school and get an advanced degree. She was a smart one. That's how he'd first met her. He was a junior, and she a lowly freshman. Only seven students had signed up for Latin: five religion majors, Mason, and Rebecca Harper.

His first thought when she walked into the classroom, pushing the envelope on the dress code—much like his niece and Jag—was that she might be all of twelve years old. Then, she'd proceeded to rearrange the grading curve so that five prospective pastors and Mason had to form a killer study group and make the library a second home. He hadn't taken Latin second semester. He'd next met up with her the following year as class president. She worked on the school paper. She no longer looked twelve, yet she still appeared fragile to him. Mason Clark, youngest son of Wayne and Betty Clark, suddenly didn't think the world centered on him. He knew the world centered on her, and that he wanted to be in that sunshine.

"Hey, Uncle Mason, you coming?" Tiffany yanked on his arm. "You feeling okay?"

One of the deacons was locking the doors. "Yep; I'm thinking about our service project this Saturday."

"I think it's cool that you're going to work on Mrs. Payne's house. It's a dump and could be so pretty. I like her dog."

"You like Bark?"

If Mason knew one thing about Tiffany, it was that she never stood still. So, when she stopped, grinned, and got a funny look in her eye, he knew he was in for something. "What?"

"How do you know her dog's name is Bark?"

"She has the office down from mine."

"Really—what's my dog's name?"

"You have a dog?"

"Only for the past ten years."

"Tiffany, so what if I know her dog's name?"

"Oh, Uncle Mason, this is cool. She's good. We have the best workouts. You know, I did wonder why you came to my softball practice. I mean, you never did before."

"I was giving you a ride to the movies."

"Yeah, but you got there two hours early. One of the girls said she saw you and Mrs. Payne at Wal-Mart together. I can't believe you didn't tell me!"

"Tiffany, there's nothing to tell." Mason forced himself not to predict, *yet.*

Chapter 6

The volleyball team lost, but Reba had high hopes. They were only a month into their season. Both Cindy and Tiffany had acted distracted. The referee had been less than consistent. Volleyball was not Reba's game. She'd been a so-so player. At five foot three, she'd never managed the maneuvers necessary to do more than set the ball.

Reba ushered her group of students into the station wagon. Hannah sat in the middle, between Reba and Tiffany. Cindy and Jag were in the backseat.

"Pizza?" Tiffany suggested.

"Ice cream," Cindy countered.

"I need to get back to the dorm," Jag said.

Reba wondered if the young man was savvy enough to realize that neither pizza nor ice cream were in her budget yet.

The wind blew leaves across the neighborhood as she pulled onto her street. The rev of an overexuberant lawn mower warred with the noise of a friendly football game across the way. Reba thought that was one of the great things about her house. There was always something to see. She and Hannah often sat on the porch swing for hours and watched the college students play, study, and court.

As she pulled into the driveway, Reba noticed full bags stacked by the huge cottonwood in her front yard. The ankle-deep leaves were all gone. Closer scrutiny revealed there was no longer a hole in her screen door, and the porch swing looked suspiciously cleaner? Darker? Painted!

Tiffany's grin spoke volumes. Jag and Cindy had Cheshire smiles. From the backyard came a young man Reba didn't know. What looked to be pieces from Bark's doghouse were in his arms.

Count to ten, Reba told herself. After the wagon stopped, somehow Hannah managed to get from the middle to outside before Tiffany. Bark came around the corner. First he jumped on the strange young man's leg to be petted. Then, he ran to Hannah and jumped on her. He quickly circled to sniff Reba's shoe, and once assuring himself that his family was all right, he raced to the backyard and barked his Number Three Special Killer Guard Dog impersonation.

"It's Mason," Reba muttered.

"Yep," Tiffany agreed.

Unlocking the front door, Reba was greeted by the mess she'd left this morning. At least Mason hadn't had the audacity to enter her house. She quickly went to the back door.

The porch rails had been fixed. Hannah's swing now hung equally balanced. Bark's new doghouse had one door. Everything looked great, including the man pushing the lawn mower. This was quite possibly the first time she'd seen Mason in shorts.

"Mason Clark, come here!"

He kept pushing the mower and pointed to his ears to let her know he couldn't hear.

Cindy helped Hannah into her swing. Laughter joined mower until Reba put her hands over her ears.

Jag was in the kitchen. "Mason ordered pizza. Do you have paper plates or can I borrow your wagon to go to the store?"

"We have napkins. That will work." Looking out the side window, Reba saw the rest of Mason's crew. They were cutting down the bush that had melded with the fence in a great tangle of limbs and chain links before dying. No way could she gripe at Mason in front of all these students who had given up part of their Saturday for her.

One of the students looked up and waved. "Hi, Mrs. Payne. You have a great dog."

Reba nodded. So far the only person Bark hadn't welcomed into his domain was Mason.

What did Bark know that Reba didn't?

❧

It was all Mason could do to keep his eyes closed while Jag said grace. Mason wanted to watch Reba. The students' easy laughter helped somewhat, but it took Reba until the second piece of pizza before she relaxed. Although Mason knew she was irritated at him, it was worth it to see her laugh and joke with his Bible school class.

After the final piece of pizza disappeared, most of the students headed for the dorms. Reba did the few dishes and watched out the kitchen window as Cindy and Jag took Hannah to the swing. Mason stuffed the pizza boxes into the trash.

"I'll do that later." Reba folded the dish towel over the faucet and sat at the table, one leg curled under the other, and sipped her soda while watching Hannah in the backyard. "You probably have other things to do."

Mason honestly couldn't think of anyplace he'd rather be. "No, let me. This is easy."

"I can't believe you did all this. The kids from your Bible class are great."

"I had most of them last year, too. There are only two new ones. Jag, and a girl who's on your softball team."

"Mason, this is too much. Please don't surprise me again."

"Why not?"

"Didn't you tell me, that first day in my office, that you didn't want people to tie us together?"

"I've rethought that. You surprised me. I expected to find a Mrs. Robards impersonator, and instead I found a piece of my past who can still leave me speechless."

"Speechless! You? Never."

"You mean to tell me you didn't know?"

"Know what?"

"I always felt tongue-tied around you. When we went to school here, all I wanted to do was take you out."

She'd been swirling her soda glass, clinking the ice first on one side then the other. The glass stilled; Reba let go and folded her hands. "I didn't know. Why didn't you tell—no, I can figure that out. I was so confused all those years ago. Do you know how old I am, Mason?"

"I know you're a lot younger than I. That's one of the reasons I never asked you out. Class presidents manage to be privy to lots of interesting tidbits. You had the highest IQ in the school, yet you never joined the Honor Society or represented Shiloh at any of the conferences."

Reba looked out the window, that faraway look back on her face. "This place was my first taste of freedom. I started sight-reading at three. I don't even remember how I learned. Freaked my parents out. I had a sister in second grade who needed remedial tutoring. It used to annoy her when I tried to tell her the right answers.

"When they took me to kindergarten, the school arranged for testing. Suddenly I was in a program for gifted children, not just a program but a whole different school. A van came and picked me up every morning and brought me back in the late afternoon.

"My whole elementary experience was put under a microscope. They kept bar graphs of everything. I can still hear the questions: How much sleep did I need? Was my milk allergy related to my intelligence? How many ear infections did I have? And how high was my tolerance to pain?

"As for academics, I learned a lot, but was always the youngest in my class. I never felt like I belonged. Yet, as my parents kept telling me, 'What an opportunity.' You know, all I ever wanted was to change places with my sisters. Believe me, my elementary school experience was all the Honor Society I wanted. A high IQ doesn't mean friendship and fun."

"And I always wanted things to come easy," Mason admitted. He tied the top of the trash bag and took it to the back door. He helped himself to another soda and sat at the table. "My two older brothers were straight A students. So were my three sisters. The first time I brought home my report card and my family found out I was average, they thought it was because I was the baby. They blamed themselves and by second grade I had a tutor. I think, at that time, I was the only Clark who didn't touch things and have them turn to gold. I had to work twice as hard at everything."

"Mason, why aren't you married?"

A cool breeze swayed the curtains of the window above the sink. Reba had lined the ledge with flowers. An embroidered sampler exclaimed, "Kiss the Cook." Mason knew somewhere there was probably a similar stitching urging, "Hug the Chef." His mother had the same decorations in her kitchen. "After I left Shiloh, I went to the University of Lincoln for my postgraduate work. I dated, even got engaged, but never found exactly what or whom I was looking for. Tell me about . . .Ray?"

"I met Ray because of Roger Howard. Mr. Howard was my Bible teacher when I was here. He liked me. Said my answers to his Bible tests weren't rote. He stuck up for me, you know."

Mason knew. Roger had quoted Scripture about forgiveness and cited examples of other students who had made similar mistakes and yet not been expelled. Not that Mason had been in attendance at the impromptu school board meeting that late Saturday night. He'd just had family on the school board, family who was sure there'd been a mistake about Mason's involvement.

Mason had stuck up for her, too, but he'd bet she didn't know that. He'd demanded that he be expelled, along with her. He'd threatened to call the Shiloh newspaper and report discrimination. Sunday morning, instead of going to church, he'd headed to Reba's dorm, determined to sit down with her and mastermind a plan—a plan to what, he hadn't known—but it hadn't mattered. She wasn't there. By Monday, she hadn't just left the school, she'd left Iowa. And Mason had always felt slightly guilty that he'd graduated two weeks later when she'd lost all her credits.

"I knew that." Mason wanted to take her hand, tell her he was sorry, but now was not the time. "Mr. Howard's quite a man. I had him for Bible, too. I've always respected him."

"I went to live with his sister."

"What about your family?"

Reba choked back a laugh. "They were so mad. Here I was, with opportunities beyond belief. As Mom said on the phone that night, 'We've spent so much time on you.' I was the first Harper to go to college. I'll bet you didn't know that. When Mr. Howard offered to get me into another school, they were thrilled. Guess how old I was when all that happened, Mason?"

He shook his head.

"Sixteen."

And she'd looked twelve, he remembered.

"My parents thought by sending me to a Christian college, I'd be safe. Me, I no longer cared, but when I got here I loved it. It was the first time I didn't have to fit in some predetermined mold. Even better, my sisters weren't telling their boyfriends that I was weird. I could take whatever class I wanted, sorta, and make friends, but everyone was. . ." She didn't meet his eyes, instead staring at her glass.

"Was?"

"So different. Mature. They knew things I didn't. Things you couldn't read about in books."

"How old was Ray?"

"Nine years older than I. Thirty when he died. He was the son of the family I was staying with. Mr. Howard's nephew."

"You married pretty fast."

She started twirling the soda again. "No, I didn't."

"Well, Hannah's five. It's only been six years since I last saw you."

"Oh." The glass slid toward the edge of the table. Reba stopped it and took a breath. "Ray already had Hannah when we married, but in all the ways that count, she is my daughter."

Chapter 7

Reba wrote PLEASE DOUBLE-SPACE across the top of a freshman English com-
position. Five down, forty to go. Gray, heavy clouds hung low in the sky. They
hovered, close, seeming to eavesdrop on the music Reba's radio played. October
already, and there'd be snow soon. Hannah could hardly wait. Reba checked her watch.
She had fifteen minutes before day-care ended.

Footsteps sounded outside, hesitating at the door. Reba waited, trying not to anticipate.
She and Mason had formed a tentative friendship. He hadn't pressed for more information
after the night he'd helped fix up her house, and Reba hadn't finished analyzing exactly
why she'd opened up to him. Had she felt free to discuss her past because Mason Clark
had participated in one of its turning points? He might well be the only person who could
understand what she'd gone through. Had the wall gone tumbling because he genuinely
seemed to want to know about her?

Truthfully, she was amazed he'd stuck around long enough for a friendship to form.
What a riot to find out he'd had a crush on her. He'd seemed so removed from everything
she'd been doing back then.

"You need anything else, Mrs. Fayne?" Cindy stepped into the office.

"No, I'm fine. You go."

"Jag's babysitting for you tonight. Can I come over?"

"Not tonight." Reba wanted to say yes. She had to respect that Cindy bothered to ask.
That spoke volumes about what kind of girl she was. And Jag was a find. Not only could he
make Reba laugh, but he knew exactly when to interrupt conversations. He'd picked exactly
the right time to barge into the kitchen for a soda that Saturday—before she'd told Mason
too much.

Never in her wildest imagination had Reba thought to hire a male babysitter. Linda
Simms, the department secretary, recommended a handful of girls, but Jag came with Cindy.
Within a few minutes, Reba knew who Hannah felt more comfortable with. His references were impeccable. He had three younger sisters to prove experience, and his school
records were carbon copies of Reba's own. No wonder his hair stuck straight up and his arm
was tattooed; he was making a statement, telling the world not to assume.

Maybe if she'd had more of his self-assurance, she'd have had an easier time. Jag's
parents had allowed him to go to a regular school after elementary, plus they'd kept him

in an age-appropriate grade.

She put the rest of the essays into a folder, locked the office, and walked to Hannah's school.

"Hey, Mama, guess what?" Hannah left the kindergarten line and skipped toward Reba. The safety patrol student hurried to keep up. Hannah shoved a handful of papers in Reba's hands and hugged a bunny-shaped backpack. "Next Thursday is Open House, and Mrs. Henry wants you to send brownies."

"Are you sure?"

"Yup; she said that it would be nice for mommies to bring brownies and be on time. Didn't I give you that note last week?"

"Thursday? Oh, Hannah, I've got a volleyball game."

The backpack hit the ground, and Hannah dragged it for a few feet before saying, "But you'll come here first?"

Searching the papers in her hand, Reba found the notice. Seven. The game started at four thirty, and she was in charge because the head coach had a doctor's appointment. Reba bit her lip. At the earliest, it would end at seven. . .but it was a half-hour drive away. "I'll see what I can do, Hannah. I promise."

Times like this, she really missed Ray. With two parents, at least one could surely schedule important events such as Open House.

"We're working on 'G' today. I colored Gary the Great Dane who eats grapefruit. I really wanted to color Gloria the gorilla who eats gumdrops, but Marky grabbed that one first."

Hannah skipped ahead. She looked both ways and waited for Reba to catch up before they crossed the street. Heading for the backyard, she kept her promise to feed Bark each afternoon. For some reason, Hannah had the idea that taking good care of Bark was a habit that would earn her a cat.

Reba opened the door, turned the television on for noise, and went into the kitchen. Two hours until Wednesday night services. Reba had been slow finding a place to worship. The church on campus was convenient, but going there with her own students left her open for attending church as a teacher more than as a fellow Christian. When worshipping, Reba wanted to make friends, deepen her walk, and be a part of a family. Mason spent a lot of time rehashing homework assignments after the closing prayer. Maybe if she didn't have Hannah, she'd be more open to that kind of accessibility, but she wanted Hannah to understand that you went to church for worship, not to interface about school schedules.

Still, Mason and Tiffany acted like her attendance at their congregation was like a gift. Reba found it hard not to look forward to such a welcome. Hannah had switched allegiance from Mason to Tiffany and liked the college girls who taught the kindergarten class.

Opening the kitchen window, already knowing the answer, Reba hollered, "What church do you want to go to tonight? Community?"

"No," Hannah shot back, "our church, across the street. I like that one. I can hear Bark barking when we stand outside."

Well, that was certainly an important consideration when deciding on a church home. Shiloh didn't have volleyball practice on Wednesday, and the Christian elementary school didn't assign homework, so Wednesday was actually a pretty easy day. Reba stirred macaroni and cheese into a dinner, kept one eye on the backyard, and read her curriculum book for tomorrow's lesson. Mason said teaching got easier. She believed that. Right now she had to do every assignment the students did, trying to predict where questions would arrive. Already she'd discovered textbooks weren't perfect. She'd had to go back and change grades after her first test because of comma splices.

She was deep in the world of "commas of address" when the phone rang.

"Hi, Thelma." Reba settled down on a kitchen chair. Ray's mom was a talker. During their half-hour conversation, Reba agreed to return to Albuquerque for Thanksgiving. Hannah needed to spend time with her grandparents, and Reba missed them, too.

Ray's parents were the best thing that had happened to Reba. What an amazing awakening to suddenly live in a home where the family sat down to dinner together, discussed daily events, thanked the Father for all His blessings, and enjoyed board games more than television.

Living with the Paynes had also been eye-opening about how carefully some families had to budget money. Reba's family made and spent money in the same breath. Darrel Payne, a minister, had budgeted God first and everything else after. That first year living with the Paynes had done more to prepare Reba for life than all the fancy preparatory schools.

After agreeing to let Thelma and Darrel pay for half the plane fare, Reba put Hannah on the phone for a quick Granny hello.

By the time Hannah hung up the phone, Reba had set supper on the table, but her appetite was gone. They were going back to Albuquerque. November would have been Ray's birthday. It made sense that Thelma and Darrel Payne wanted family close. What would it be like to sit across from Thelma and Darrel and face Ray's empty chair? Also, Reba never felt comfortable knowing that the men who shot and killed Ray hadn't been caught.

⟳

The service project for October was going door-to-door in the neighborhood and passing out fliers inviting people to church. Mason didn't canvas. Instead, he paced the sidewalk, trying to keep all the students in sight. His older brother Richard remembered taking sodas and munchies from strangers. Mason didn't trust that much. He put two males and one female per group. They handed out a handwritten invitation to attend services, a business card with the address and phone number of the church, and a one-page Bible study. If anyone expressed interest in the Bible study, the students were to offer to sit outside, whip out their Bibles, and help explain the paper. They'd spent four weeks going over the Bible study in class, role-playing the questions people who'd never been to church might ask. Mason loved it because it gave opportunity for the students to ask questions they, themselves, might have but were too self-conscious to ask.

The good news was, about every fifth house already belonged to a church family. The bad news was, not even every fifth house was willing to give time to the students. It wasn't by accident that Mason ended the excursion in Reba's neighborhood. He knew she and Hannah spent lots of time on the front porch. Any excuse to be in the neighborhood got him a little closer to gaining her trust. Actually, he figured Bark would be harder to win than Reba, but that was more a physical battle than an emotional one.

Cindy and Jag already cuddled on her porch swing. Tiffany danced across the front yard with Hannah riding on her feet.

"We already ordered pizza," Jag said.

Reba smiled weakly.

The sweet sound of a campus devotional drifted across the lawn.

"Mommy, can I?"

After getting permission, Hannah dragged Tiffany across the street. They were followed by a troop of students. Hannah started young on her college experience.

"She already knows more songs than I do." Reba scooted over so Mason could sit on the porch swing.

He sat down, purposely not hugging the edge and purposely sitting close enough so his hand could accidentally brush against her hair after he rested it across the back. "I have two nephews who can speak Spanish simply because their next-door neighbors speak Spanish. Children are amazing."

"How did your service project go?"

"We managed to hand out twenty information packs. As for how it went, well, we won't know that until we see visitors at services."

"I don't remember anyone ever knocking on our door," Reba remarked.

"Where did you grow up?"

"Arizona."

"Ah, not exactly the Bible Belt. I know you said your parents sent you to a Christian college because they thought it would be safe, but how did they decide on Iowa?"

"Pure happenstance. I was in a program for advanced kids called Vanguard. I'd completed their curriculum. Only a few colleges were open to the idea of letting a sixteen-year-old live in the dorm. One of the Vanguard counselors recommended Shiloh. She'd attended here and loved it. She made a few phone calls. I wound up being part of a study charting how starting college early bodes for younger students. They especially were interested in the differences between small versus large campuses. Needless to say, I'm not part of a success ratio."

"You were straight A."

"I was also racking up demerits at the speed of light."

She stopped, and Mason wondered if her next thought was, *Before I got kicked out.* Someday they needed to broach that subject, get it out of the way, and at least for him, start forgiving.

"Enough of that," Reba said. "Let's talk about you."

"Me? I'm not nearly as interesting as you."

"Just how big is your family?"

"Big enough to still be front-page news. You were the only reporter to poke fun at how many pews my family took up on Visitor's Day in chapel."

"I was amazed."

"You should see us at Christmas. Speaking of which, my mother said you could come to our place for Thanksgiving. It's about a two-hour drive. There are tons of children Hannah's age."

"Thanks, but Hannah and I are flying to New Mexico. Ray's parents really want us to be home for the holiday."

It was unreasonable to be jealous of a dead man, but it seemed no matter what topic Mason and Reba settled on, Ray was a part. Mason preferred Bark as competition.

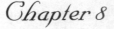

Chapter 8

I t was amazing how quickly Creed, Iowa, had become home. Reba's shoes crunched through snow as she made her way to the front door.

"Mommy, let's call now so Bark can come home! Hurry."

Mason "dog-sat" while Reba and Hannah had enjoyed Thanksgiving in New Mexico. "Let's just get the suitcases unpacked."

Mason had been true to his word. Reba had been afraid he'd forget to come over and turn on the thermostat, but heat greeted their arrival.

Hannah raced up the stairs, her suitcase bumping behind her.

Two seconds later she was back. "Can I call now?"

"Let's go check your room first?"

"Oh," said Hannah, "did I have to put the clean clothes in my dresser and the dirty clothes in the bathroom?"

"That was the idea."

Hannah raced back upstairs. Reba went around turning on all the lights. That was another habit she'd developed after Ray was killed. The dark seemed too frightening.

Taking her suitcases to her room, she turned on the light and blinked at the sudden glare. The room was small, the closet smaller yet. In some ways, selling all their furniture had been a blessing. There was no way it would have fit in this house. A crocheted blanket covered the bed. Reba had made it after graduating college. She'd married Ray and set about being a wife.

Funny, she'd thought Ray had been more like his parents. He'd acted like them when he'd moved back home. When they'd gotten their own house, he'd been different. Good, still kind, but not as focused. He'd hated that she was smarter than he, not that he'd admit to it. He'd insisted she stay home and raise Hannah. She'd loved that part; raising Hannah had been a dream. They'd played in the park, watched movies, and learned to roller-skate. It was like getting a piece of her own childhood back, and Reba learned that the greatest thing in life was not getting more letters after her name, but getting chocolate-laced hugs from a little girl who called her Mommy. A little girl who now stood in the doorway.

"Can we call now? Hey, why are you just standing there? Are you sad? I know, you miss Bark. We better hurry."

Mason answered on the second ring, as if he'd been by the phone waiting. He immediately came, bringing Bark and leftover turkey. He left when the ten o'clock news came on, and Hannah gleefully remarked that she was staying up so late that maybe she wouldn't need to go to school tomorrow.

The freshmen came back to classes in much better moods. Most had gotten a fix of family and were glad to be back in a place where parental reins were a distant memory. Still, there were a few who openly admitted they did not intend to return a second semester. Others were quiet, already knowing grades would be a problem when it came to who was footing the bill.

Reba stood by the podium at the front of the classroom. She pulled her sweater tighter around her. Usually the heater made the room unbearable, but today the cold seemed to seep through the planks in the floor. She looked around the room. It was hers now. She'd put cheerful posters over the dents in the walls. She'd had the students make bright-colored collages along with their essays. "Okay, Cindy, why don't you give the class an opinion about gas prices?"

"Fredrick's Gas Station downtown has the highest prices I've ever seen."

Reba nodded. "Jag, give us a factual statement."

"Fredrick's charges $1.52 a gallon for unleaded."

Cindy glowed. Jag could have given any kind of a response, but the fact that he chose to add to hers showed their togetherness.

Later, walking to her office, Reba tried to remember feeling any interest in the college boys while at Shiloh. No, she'd spent most of her time dating a townie. She'd never forget him. Glenn Fields was the reason she'd gotten kicked out of Shiloh.

Opening her office door, she stepped inside, laid her book bag on the floor, and crossed to the window. Cindy and Jag were making snow angels. Winter break was in three short weeks, and the two would be separated for almost a month.

Reba checked her calendar. Volleyball season was over, and preparations for the yearbook were in full swing. Jag and about five others diligently took pictures. Cindy helped.

"What are you doing tonight?" Mason stood at the door. His brown-and-white sweater had snowflakes clinging to it.

"Where's your coat?" Reba moved toward him, then paused. Ever since he'd dog-sat Bark, she'd fought the urge to touch his hair, straighten his tie, kiss his check. It was all Bark's fault. Reba and Hannah hadn't even been gone a week, and in that short time, Bark had decided Mason was master.

Now when Mason stopped by, Bark wiggled all over and begged to be picked up. Since Mason lived a mere two blocks away, Hannah loved to walk down to the end of the street—as far as she was allowed to go. If she saw Mason, she'd holler for him to come over. If that didn't work, she let go of Bark's leash, and the dog was off. Reba took to making sure she always cooked for three, just in case.

"Reba? You okay?" Mason hadn't moved.

"Oh, snow days do this to me. I tend to drift. What am I doing tonight? Why?"

"Well, if you were willing to get Jag to watch Hannah, I thought we'd go out. Just the two of us."

He was asking her out on a real date—not just an I'm-a-nice-guy-who-keeps-coming-around-for-no-reason-and-let's-do-something. Reba suddenly wanted to say "yes" although that would mess everything up. The minute she agreed, there'd be more intimate talks. He'd want to know more about her marriage with Ray. Luckily, tonight's dilemma was easy. "It's the Winter Program at Hannah's school. I can't miss it. She still reminds me about missing Open House."

"Okay. I'll go to the Winter Program with you, but how about this weekend? Saturday? Just you and me."

So much for putting off the decision. "Mason, things are good between us. Why chance ruining it?"

"Because we might not ruin it, as you say, but improve it. I'm willing to be honest. I was half in love with you when you were sixteen. I figure the other half arrived the day I saw you in my office and you didn't know who I was."

"I remembered quick enough!"

He stepped into the office, closing the door behind him. Reba's mouth went dry. She sat on the top of the radiator, although she was no longer cold. Mason put his hands on either side of her. She'd noticed his eyes were the color of chocolate, but she hadn't known how deep the swirls of toffee and caramel went. She somehow had missed the invitation there. Oh, she'd known he was interested, but—

"Reba," he said, his voice next to her ear, "I'm going to make sure you never forget me again."

Then, he kissed her.

❧

Families filled the auditorium. Mason looked around, surprised by how many people he recognized. There were a few scattered singles, and Mason was humbled by the fact that had he not joined Reba, she'd be sitting alone at Hannah's Winter Program. He'd taken his three-pew family for granted.

The head of the school board said an opening prayer, the principal gave a short greeting, and the lights dimmed. Children dressed as trees decorated the stage. Who knew trees could sing so well? Reba leaned forward, mesmerized. By following her gaze, he figured out which tree was Hannah. The kindergartners stole the show. If they weren't falling, then they were singing the song a beat after the rest or five decibels louder.

Afterwards the families went to the cafeteria for hot chocolate and dessert.

Hannah, the tree, ran off but quickly returned, leading another tree by a limb. She pushed that tree toward Mason. "This is Marky. He's my best friend. He has a dog *and* a cat."

Mason shook the limb.

"Are you Hannah's daddy?"

Reba froze beside him, a brownie halfway to her mouth. Hannah lost her smile also.

"No," Mason said. "I'm just a friend."

Marky ran off. Hannah gave Mason a confused look, then followed her friend.

"I'm sorry," Mason said, taking Reba's hand. "I was not expecting that question."

"Neither was I."

"What does Hannah know? I mean, you haven't even told me how Ray died."

"Hannah's too young to know. It would just scare her."

"Death is part of living. Surely, she needs to know that."

"Ray didn't die because he was sick. He was murdered."

She started wringing her hands. Mason took one and stroked her fingers. She started to jerk away, but he applied gentle pressure and didn't ask any more questions.

"You don't have to tell me."

"So much for keeping secrets. That is why we came to Creed. I wanted Hannah away from the papers. I didn't want to chance her hearing anything about Ray. I want her to remember the man who played catch with her in the yard. I don't want her knowing that Ray borrowed money from the wrong people, and when he didn't pay it back on time, they killed him."

Mason's apartment looked out over a convenience store and a parking lot. A week had passed since Reba confided in him, and she had avoided him ever since. He hadn't a clue how to approach her. That she avoided him proved she didn't want to talk about it. He honestly didn't think they could leave the incident alone, though. It was out there; they needed to get past it. If Mason was honest with himself, Ray's death wasn't the only issue they needed to face and resolve.

He walked to work. It was easier than driving on ice. Opening the door to Clark Hall, Mason switched on the light, took off his overshoes, and stuck them in a closet, then hurried up the stairs.

"Mr. Clark."

Jag sat in the waiting room. The secretary hadn't arrived.

"How did you get in, Jag?"

"Do you really want to know?"

"Yes."

"I picked the lock. You have a ridiculously easy lock to pick. It didn't even take me a minute."

"Where did you learn to pick locks?"

"Television."

"I'd rather you not do it again, okay?"

Jag hadn't taken his tennis shoes off. Snow clung to them, and a wet circle was spreading on the floor.

Mason hung up his coat and walked to his office. Jag didn't move. His legs were straight out, crossed, and for the first time he avoided Mason's eyes. *Oh, no,* thought Mason, *Cindy.*

"Come in, Jag. Let's get it over with."

Jag picked up a folder from the seat next to him. His jean jacket was unbuttoned, and if Mason wasn't mistaken, he was wearing the same shirt as yesterday. Mason sat at his desk. Jag took the same seat he'd occupied back in August when he'd wanted to transfer into a different English class. That had been the day Jag met Cindy. That had been the day Mason met Reba, again.

"You know I'm taking pictures for the school newspaper?" Jag spoke to his hands. They writhed as much as Reba's usually did.

"I think that's great. I've seen your work. You're good."

"Yesterday, the editor assigned me to take a picture of you. He wants one of Mrs. Payne, too."

Mason could understand the newspaper wanting Reba's, although if he remembered right, they'd already done the "Meet the New Teacher" article.

Jag put a folder on Mason's desk. "I took this from the editor's desk. I've had it since five yesterday. I could not decide what to do."

Mason took the folder. Opening it, he saw two double-spaced typed pages. This wasn't about Cindy. It was the headline that jumped out at him. ALCOHOL, RESPONSIBILITY, AND FRIENDSHIP: HOW DO THEY MIX?

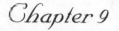

Chapter 9

The elementary school called at noon. Hannah's temperature was almost one hundred. Reba raced over, signed Hannah out, and came back to Clark Hall. She had two classes and no time to get a substitute.

Cindy ran to Reba's house and brought back some medicine and blankets. Reba put Hannah next to the radiator on the floor. Linda Simms agreed to keep an eye on her, and Reba decided to get her lectures done quickly and assign library time. Anything to keep close to her baby. Her first class went fine. Her two o'clock was a little different. Jag arrived ten minutes late. Instead of taking his usual chair in the front, he headed for the back and then avoided her gaze. When she called on him, he answered the questions but initiated no discussion. By the time she'd hurried through her notes, her own head was pounding.

She barely managed to get her office door open before she heard Hannah's words. "Mommy, I threw up."

Linda Simms mouthed, *It was spit*.

Hannah was getting too big to carry. The sidewalks were slippery, and any other day Mason would be there to offer his help. After getting some broth inside Hannah and turning out the bedroom light, Reba sat at her new, used couch and hit the button on her answering machine. Dean Steward's voice was curt, "Mrs. Fayne, could you attend a meeting in my office at three?"

It was stand-up three now. Reba got her directory and called the dean's office to beg off. Five minutes later, she hurried around the living room picking up Hannah's toys and the mass of ungraded papers on the coffee table. Whatever Dean Steward wanted to talk about was so vital that he was coming over.

Peeking out the window, Reba felt her stomach hit the ground. Not only was the dean making his way to her house, but Jack Hillman, the sponsor of Shiloh's school paper, and Mason Clark were trudging along.

Mason brought in kitchen chairs so there'd be enough seats in the living room. Reba poured coffee and waited.

Dean Steward cleared his throat. "This is the first time we've faced a situation like this."

"Like this?" Reba asked.

Mason opened his briefcase, pulled out a folder, then handed her a piece of paper.

Reba read the headline, skimmed the rest, then closed her eyes. Mason had worried about this since her first day. Their names were near the end of the article. "When will this hit the stands?"

"Next Friday," Jack Hillman grunted.

"We would rather the piece not run—" Dean Steward began.

"But most of my journalism students already know. Furthermore, that's what the paper is for: to print information. Sometimes that information is. . ." Jack frowned and gave Reba a compassionate look. "I thought I'd pull the article, but it's not negative. It's mostly informative. I think we can turn this into a good thing. Look at you now, Reba."

Reba decided not to tell him about her doubts or Ray's death. She looked at Mason. Funny, now that the past was about to hit the present, he looked calm.

"Is my job in danger?" Reba asked.

"No," Dean Steward said. "We knew about your past before we hired you, and we also knew about your present. As far as we're concerned, you've presented a wonderful Christian example to our students. We're pleased with your performance. When Roger Howard told us about your work in Albuquerque, the board was unanimous about hiring you. This meeting is mainly to try to formulate a response. Students will have questions."

"Mommy, I threw up!" Hannah called from the top of the stairs.

Before Reba could stand, Mason did. "Gentlemen, Mrs. Payne has a daughter who needs her attention. The last time she and I faced a dean about this matter, she paid the consequences. This time, it's my turn."

❦

Glenn Fields had relocated to Omaha, Nebraska. A few phone calls and Mason had an address. It had been a sleepless night, a prayerful night, a night when Mason desperately wanted to call his own father but decided that this time, it was all up to him.

During the long drive, he tried to rehearse what he wanted to say. Nothing sounded right, but closure seemed to dictate that without meeting with Glenn, there would still be this area of open wound.

Mason was often guilty of presupposing. He'd expected Glenn to live in a run-down apartment in a part of town best avoided. Instead, Glenn's house was near a golf course where the snow hid the favorite pastime of the neighboring residents.

Children played in the yard. Their snowsuits hid age and weight. The front door opened before Mason could stop the car.

Glenn Fields had been Reba's friend. Mason knew the guy. It was hard not to. Mason had kept up with Reba's activities, and Glenn was one of Reba's activities. Still, if Glenn had passed Mason on the street, Mason wouldn't have recognized him.

The first thing Mason noticed was the absence of a wheelchair, or at least crutches. Glenn held the door open invitingly.

The living room was bigger than Mason's apartment.

After a handshake, Glenn introduced, "This is my wife, Bunny."

Bunny had obviously just gotten off the exercise bike Mason could see in the family room. She looked a lot like Cindy with her swept-back hair and winning smile. "We're glad you stopped by. It will do the two of you good to talk."

Bunny had coffee waiting in the kitchen. Glenn limped slightly as they walked. If Mason hadn't been looking, he wouldn't have noticed it.

"Thanks," Mason said, accepting a steaming mug. "I appreciate your meeting with me."

"I'm curious. Why are you here?"

Mason took a folded piece of paper out of his pocket. "I thought I'd let you look at this."

Glenn read it, then passed it back. "So."

"I owe you an apology," Mason said. "When you—we—were in the accident, I didn't even feel sorry when you lost your leg. I figured you'd asked for it by drinking and driving."

"Tell me something I don't know." Glenn's words could have been harsh, but they weren't. They were curious.

"Did you know Reba is now teaching at Shiloh?"

"Yes."

Mason blinked. "Really."

"She's been here twice. Brought her little girl. The kids play just fine. You see, Reba did feel sorry about my leg. She's kept in touch with me. But, if it will soothe your conscience, that accident wasn't your fault. I harbor no grudges. It was my own stupidity."

"Am I here to soothe my conscience?" Mason took a sip of coffee. It burned, but he forced himself not to flinch. "I guess I am. Look, I've felt guilty since that night. I managed to stay in school; Reba didn't. I walked away from that accident; you didn't. Now, Reba's little girl might find out about this incident because maybe there was something I could have done that night six years ago that I didn't."

"Reba's a lot tougher than you think. She always has been."

Mason nodded. "Well, I've got an idea. It's not perfect. It might not even make things better, but I think it's worthwhile. I wondered if you were interested in helping out."

Shiloh's chapel period began at eight in the morning. As a student, Reba had paid over eighty dollars in tardy and absence fines her first year. Her second year, she'd doubled that. As a teacher, she hadn't missed or been late even once.

She sensed the looks from some of the students. The paper had been issued that morning. Readership had probably doubled thanks to the story about her and Mason.

Reba looked around, not down. She had been baptized two months before she married Ray. She'd made mistakes, but so had Paul, so had the disciple Peter, so had Dean Steward—she just couldn't name his.

Jag fell into step next to her. "You okay?"

"Fine; quit worrying."

"They made Harry Raymond take your picture when I refused."

"Well, Harry in no way did me the justice you would have."

To Reba's surprise, Linda Simms was sitting with the teachers. Was she here for support? Good; Reba welcomed it. Slipping in next to Linda, Reba reached for a song-book and waited. Dean Steward led the opening prayer. After the amen, he paused. His posture and facial expression encouraged—no, demanded—that the room quiet down. "We're having a special program this morning."

Mason stepped to the podium. "My name is Mason Clark. Many of you know me as your history teacher. Others know me as a guidance counselor. If you've missed meeting me, maybe you ought to check out the Faith/Works class at Shiloh Church.

"Six years ago, I graduated from Shiloh Christian College. I cannot tell you how many times, I, like you, sat in the audience and listened to speakers. I looked forward to being a speaker myself. And, in my visions, the best thing about being a teacher and counselor at Shiloh, was that I could do it better because *I* was a grand example."

Reba looked about the auditorium. She'd watched Mason stand at that podium many times, but never had he made her shiver.

Mason continued, "This week I've spent a good deal of time in Proverbs. Chapter 11, verse 2 especially hit home. 'When pride comes, then comes disgrace, but with humility comes wisdom.'"

Reba looked about the auditorium. No one was asleep. If the eyes strayed from Mason, they went to her. . .or they watched the man stepping up the center aisle.

Glenn Fields!

For the next half hour, Mason alternated between quoting Scripture and admitting a mistake from his past. A mistake that really hadn't been his. The students listened, because in reality, the world was all around them, and drinking was a national pastime they couldn't ignore.

Before Glenn took over the microphone, he rolled up his pant leg. The artificial limb looked real from a distance, pink up close. Reba closed her eyes. While Glenn spoke, she remembered.

It had been a Friday. Her roommate had gone home for the weekend, and Reba was ready to rock. Glenn Fields was not like anybody she'd met. He'd dropped out of high school. He had a place of his own. He used words she wouldn't say, and he never ran out of things to do.

They'd gone bowling. Reba remembered how scared she had been when he started drinking—though to her shame, it wasn't because of the drinking, but because there were other Shiloh students at the bowling alley who were watching. Even the fear was accom-panied by a thrill of daring.

Why did Mason face the students this morning as if he owed them an explanation? He'd been at the bowling alley. He'd watched Glenn drink. When the lights of the bowling alley dimmed and Shiloh's curfew neared, Mason had offered her a ride home.

Reba had no clue whether accepting that ride would have made the outcome differ-ent. Mason, ever the good scout, had followed them to Glenn's car and tried to take the car keys.

Glenn answered with his fists. To Reba's surprise, Mason didn't turn his cheek.

She'd been in the passenger seat already. Mason left Glenn and ran to her side of the car. Reba could still see his hands reaching for her as Glenn, furious, slammed himself behind the wheel, jabbed the keys into the ignition, and began to move the car.

Mason ran to his car and started to follow.

Traffic didn't notice the spectacle edging into its midst. Glenn looked in the rearview mirror, saw Mason, and stepped on the gas. He didn't look as he pulled out into the street. Metal met metal and—

"Reba, are you all right?" Linda whispered.

Just as Reba still didn't know how to answer the questions about Ray's death, being asked "Are you all right?" at this moment wasn't one easily addressed.

❦

Her ten o'clock class didn't have an empty seat. Every student made it on time. Reba opened her teacher's manual and started on adjectives. The students didn't whisper or pass notes. When the class ended, instead of filing out the door, every student made his or her way to the front. Cindy was the first to offer a hug.

Reba remembered her very first day at Shiloh. She'd gotten out of her mother's car and had been hugged by many people she didn't know. It had been a shock. Her family was not one to show physical demonstrations.

When did I stop hugging? Reba wondered. Sure, she hugged Hannah, and she hugged. . . Who else did she hug?

No one since Ray.

By the time the last young man shook her hand, Reba was ready to sit down. Mason stood at the door of her classroom. With flowers. Glenn Fields was behind him, smiling.

"Don't tell me you two became friends?" Reba's voice croaked as she fought the tears.

"Glenn says we have to."

Shaking her head, Reba took the flowers and asked, "Why?"

"Well," said Mason, "Glenn expects you to visit often now that you're this close. If we should happen, to say, get married, then I'll be around a lot more."

"I'm not ready to talk marriage."

"I know. That's why I brought flowers instead of a ring."

Epilogue

The last day of school dawned with the sunshine of promise. Reba scanned the church's flower-decked auditorium as she walked down the aisle on her father's arm. She felt a little faint. Instead of a typical chapel program, today Shiloh Christian College hosted a wedding.

Hannah held the flower basket tightly, her knuckles white. Thelma and Darrel Payne sniffled from the front row. Reba's father joined her mother and sisters on the bride's side; as for Mason's side of the church, seven rows of Clarks beamed approval.

Reba felt Mason take her hand. His fingers tightened. Never, in her whole life, had Reba felt so secure, so loved, so safe. Hannah didn't leave; she took Reba's other hand.

God had even taken her fear of Ray's murderers away. Instead of facing the world alone, Reba and Hannah had Mason and at least seven pews full of backup bodyguards. And, there was the Greatest Bodyguard of all overseeing the whole shebang.

The minister started, "We gather in God's presence to unite Rebecca Suzanne and Mason Dean in holy matrimony. . . ."

Pamela Tracy

Pamela Tracy started writing at a very young age (a series of romances, all with David Cassidy as the hero. Sometimes Bobby Sherman would interfere). Then, while earning a BA in Journalism at Texas Tech University in Lubbock, Texas, she picked up the pen again (only this time, it was an electric typewriter on which she wrote a very bad fiction novel). First published in 1999 by Barbour Publishing, she has since published more than twenty-five books in multiple genres. She's a Carol Award winner (from American Christian Fictions Writers) as well as both a Carol and Rita finalist (from Romance Writers of America).

Sweet Surprise

Romance Collection

Contemporary romances served
with delightful desserts!

8 WEDDINGS
and a Miracle
Romance Collection

Weather the storms of life alongside nine modern couples
who hope to make it to the altar,
though they may need a miracle to intervene.

THE
Most Eligible
BACHELOR
ROMANCE COLLECTION

Nine historical romances celebrate
marrying for all the right reasons!